I0669988

THE GARDEN
of ALLAH

THE GARDEN
of ALLAH

By ROBERT HICHENS

AUTHOR OF "THE WOMAN WITH THE FAN,"
"FELIX," "TONGUES OF CONSCIENCE," ETC.

Fredonia Books
Amsterdam, The Netherlands

The Garden of Allah

by
Robert Hichens

ISBN: 1-58963-632-5

Reprinted from the 1904 edition

Fredonia Books
Amsterdam, The Netherlands
http://www.fredoniabooks.com

CONTENTS

CONTENTS

THE GARDEN OF ALLAH

BOOK I

PRELUDE

CHAPTER I

THE fatigue caused by a rough sea journey, and, perhaps, the consciousness that she would have to be dressed before dawn to catch the train for Beni-Mora, prevented Domini Enfilden from sleeping. There was deep silence in the Hôtel de la Mer at Robertville. The French officers who took their pension there had long since ascended the hill of Addouna to the barracks. The *cafés* had closed their doors to the drinkers and domino players. The lounging Arab boys had deserted the sandy Place de la Marine. In their small and dusky bazaars the Israelites had reckoned up the takings of the day, and curled themselves up in gaudy quilts on their low divans to rest. Only two or three *gendarmes* were still about, and a few French and Spaniards at the Port, where, moored against the wharf, lay the steamer *Le Général Bertrand,* in which Domini had arrived that evening from Marseilles.

In the hotel the fair and plump Italian waiter, who had drifted to North Africa from Pisa, had swept up the crumbs from the two long tables in the *salle-à-manger,* smoked a thin, dark cigar over a copy of the *Dépêche Algérienne,* put the paper down, scratched his blonde head, on which the hair stood up in bristles, stared for a while at nothing in the firm manner of weary men who are at the same time thoughtless and depressed, and thrown himself on his narrow bed in the dusty corner of the little room on the stairs near the front door. Madame, the landlady, had laid aside her front and said her prayer to the Virgin. Monsieur, the landlord, had muttered his last curse against the Jews and drunk his last glass of rum. They snored like honest people recruiting their strength for the mor-

row. In number two Suzanne Charpot, Domini's maid, was
dreaming of the Rue de Rivoli.

But Domini, with wide-open eyes, was staring from her big,
square pillow at the red brick floor of her bedroom, on which
stood various trunks marked by the officials of the Douane.
There were two windows in the room looking out towards the
Place de la Marine, below which lay the station. Closed *persiennes* of brownish-green, blistered wood protected them. One
of these windows was open. Yet the candle at Domini's bed-
side burnt steadily. The night was warm and quiet, without
wind.

As she lay there, Domini still felt the movement of the sea.
The passage had been a bad one. The ship, crammed with
French recruits for the African regiments, had pitched and
rolled almost incessantly for thirty-one hours, and Domini and
most of the recruits had been ill. Domini had had an inner
cabin, with a skylight opening on to the lower deck, and had
heard above the sound of the waves and winds their groans and
exclamations, rough laughter, and half-timid, half-defiant con-
versations as she shook in her berth. At Marseilles she had seen
them come on board, one by one, dressed in every variety of
poor costume, each one looking anxiously around to see what
the others were like, each one carrying a mean yellow or black
bag or a carefully-tied bundle. On the wharf stood a Zouave, in
tremendous red trousers and a fez, among great heaps of dull
brown woollen rugs. And as the recruits came hesitatingly
along he stopped them with a sharp word, examined the tickets
they held out, gave each one a rug, and pointed to the gangway
that led from the wharf to the vessel. Domini, then leaning
over the rail of the upper deck, had noticed the different expressions with which the recruits looked at the Zouave. To all
of them he was a phenomenon, a mystery of Africa and of the
new life for which they were embarking. He stood there im-
pudently and indifferently among the woollen rugs, his red fez
pushed well back on his short, black hair cut *en brosse,* his
bronzed face twisted into a grimace of fiery contempt, throwing,
with his big and muscular arms, rug after rug to the anxious
young peasants who filed before him. They all gazed at his
legs in the billowing red trousers; some like children regarding
a Jack-in-the-box which had just sprung up into view, others
like ignorant, but superstitious, people who had unexpectedly
come upon a shrine by the wayside. One or two seemed disposed to laugh nervously, as the very stupid laugh at anything

they see for the first time. But fear seized them. They refrained convulsively and shambled on to the gangway, looking sideways, like fowls, and holding their rugs awkwardly to their breasts with their dirty, red hands.

To Domini there was something pitiful in the sight of all these lads, uprooted from their homes in France, stumbling helplessly on board this ship that was to convey them to Africa. They crowded together. Their poor bundles and bags jostled one against the other. With their clumsy boots they trod on each other's feet. And yet all were lonely strangers. No two in the mob seemed to be acquaintances. And every lad, each in his different way, was furtively on the defensive, uneasily wondering whether some misfortune might not presently come to him from one of these unknown neighbours.

A few of the recruits, as they came on board, looked up at Domini as she leant over the rail; and in all the different coloured and shaped eyes she thought she read a similar dread and nervous hope that things might turn out pretty well for them in the new existence that had to be faced. The Zouave, wholly careless or unconscious of the fact that he was an incarnation of Africa to these raw peasants, who had never before stirred beyond the provinces where they were born, went on taking the tickets, and tossing the woollen rugs to the passing figures, and pointing ferociously to the gangway. He got very tired of his task towards the end, and showed his fatigue to the latest comers, shoving their rugs into their arms with brusque violence. And when at length the wharf was bare he spat on it, rubbed his short-fingered, sunburnt hands down the sides of his blue jacket, and swaggered on board with the air of a dutiful but injured man who longed to do harm in the world. By this time the ship was about to cast off, and the recruits, ranged in line along the bulwarks of the lower deck, were looking in silence towards Marseilles, which, with its tangle of tall houses, its forest of masts, its long, ugly factories and workshops, now represented to them the whole of France. The bronchial hoot of the siren rose up menacingly. Suddenly two Arabs, in dirty white burnouses and turbans bound with cords of camel's hair, came running along the wharf. The siren hooted again. The Arabs bounded over the gangway with grave faces. All the recruits turned to examine them with a mixture of superiority and deference, such as a schoolboy might display when observing the agilities of a tiger. The ropes fell heavily from the posts of the quay into the water, and were drawn up dripping by the sailors, and *Le Général Bertrand* began to move out slowly among the motionless ships.

Domini, looking towards the land with the vague and yet inquiring glance of those who are going out to sea, noticed the church of Notre dame de la Garde, perched on its high hill, and dominating the noisy city, the harbour, the cold, grey squadrons of the rocks and Monte Cristo's dungeon. At the time she hardly knew it, but now, as she lay in bed in the silent inn, she remembered that, keeping her eyes upon the church, she had murmured a confused prayer to the Blessed Virgin for the recruits. What was the prayer? She could scarcely recall it. A woman's petition, perhaps, against the temptations that beset men shifting for themselves in far-off and dangerous countries; a woman's cry to a woman to watch over all those who wander.

When the land faded, and the white sea rose, less romantic considerations took possession of her. She wished to sleep, and drank a dose of a drug. It did not act completely, but only numbed her senses. Through the long hours she lay in the dark cabin, looking at the faint radiance that penetrated through the glass shutters of the skylight. The recruits, humanised and drawn together by misery, were becoming acquainted. The incessant murmur of their voices dropped down to her, with the sound of the waves, and of the mysterious cries and creaking shudders that go through labouring ships. And all these noises seemed to her hoarse and pathetic, suggestive, too, of danger.

When they reached the African shore, and saw the lights of houses twinkling upon the hills, the pale recruits were marshalled on the white road by Zouaves, who met them from the barracks of Robertville. Already they looked older than they had looked when they embarked. Domini saw them march away up the hill. They still clung to their bags and bundles. Some of them, lifting shaky voices, tried to sing in chorus. One of the Zouaves angrily shouted to them to be quiet. They obeyed, and disappeared heavily into the shadows, staring about them anxiously at the feathery palms that clustered in this new and dark country, and at the shrouded figures of Arabs who met them on the way.

The red brick floor was heaving gently, Domini thought. She found herself wondering how the cane chair by the small wardrobe kept its footing, and why the cracked china basin in the iron washstand, painted bright yellow, did not stir and rattle. Her dressing-bag was open. She could see the silver backs and tops of the brushes and bottles in it gleaming. They made her think suddenly of England. She had no idea why. But it was too warm for England. There, in the autumn time, an open window would let in a cold air, probably a biting blast. The wooden shutter would be shaking. There would be, perhaps, a sound of rain. And Domini found herself vaguely pitying England and the people mewed up in it for the winter. Yet how many winters she had spent there, dreaming of liberty and doing dreary things—things without savour, without meaning, without salvation for brain or soul. Her mind was still dulled to a certain extent by the narcotic she had taken. She was a strong and active woman, with long limbs and well-knit muscles, a clever fencer, a tireless swimmer, a fine horse-woman. But to-night she felt almost neurotic, like one of the weak or dissipated sisterhood for whom " rest cures " are invented, and by whom bland doctors live. That heaving red floor continually emphasised for her her present feebleness. She hated feebleness. So she blew out the candle and, with misplaced energy, strove resolutely to sleep. Possibly her resolution defeated its object. She continued in a condition of dull and heavy wakefulness till the darkness became intolerable to her. In it she saw perpetually the long procession of the pale recruits winding up the hill of Addouna with their bags and bundles, like spectres on a way of dreams. Finally she resolved to accept a sleepless night. She lit her candle again and saw that the brick floor was no longer heaving. Two of the books that she called her " bed-books " lay within easy reach of her hand. One was Newman's *Dream of Gerontius,* the other a volume of the Badminton Library. She chose the former and began to read.

Towards two o'clock she heard a long-continued rustling. At first she supposed that her tired brain was still playing her tricks. But the rustling continued and grew louder. It sounded like a noise coming from something very wide, and spread out as a veil over an immense surface. She got up, walked across the floor to the open window and unfastened the *persiennes.* Heavy rain was falling. The night was very black, and smelt rich and damp, as if it held in its arms strange offerings—a merchandise altogether foreign, tropical and alluring. As she stood there, face to face with a wonder that she could not see, Domini forgot Newman. She felt the brave companionship of mystery. In it she divined the beating pulses, the hot, surging blood of freedom.

She wanted freedom, a wide horizon, the great winds, the

great sun, the terrible spaces, the glowing, shimmering radiance, the hot, entrancing noons and bloomy, purple nights of Africa. She wanted the nomad's fires and the acid voices of the Kabyle dogs. She wanted the roar of the tom-toms, the clash of the cymbals, the rattle of the negroes' castanets, the fluttering, painted figures of the dancers. She wanted—more than she could express, more than she knew. It was there, want, aching in her heart, as she drew into her nostrils this strange and wealthy atmosphere.

When Domini returned to her bed she found it impossible to read any more Newman. The rain and the scents coming up out of the hidden earth of Africa had carried her mind away, as if on a magic carpet. She was content now to lie awake in the dark.

Domini was thirty-two, unmarried, and in a singularly independent—some might have thought a singularly lonely—situation. Her father, Lord Rens, had recently died, leaving Domini, who was his only child, a large fortune. His life had been a curious and a tragic one. Lady Rens, Domini's mother, had been a great beauty of the gipsy type, the daughter of a Hungarian mother and of Sir Henry Arlworth, one of the most prominent and ardent English Catholics of his day. A son of his became a priest, and a famous preacher and writer on religious subjects. Another child, a daughter, took the veil. Lady Rens, who was not clever, although she was at one time almost universally considered to have the face of a muse, shared in the family ardour for the Church, but was far too fond of the world to leave it. While she was very young she met Lord Rens, a Lifeguardsman of twenty-six, who called himself a Protestant, but who was really quite happy without any faith. He fell madly in love with her and, in order to marry her, became a Catholic, and even a very devout one, aiding his wife's Church by every means in his power, giving large sums to Catholic charities, and working, with almost fiery zeal, for the spread of Catholicism in England.

Unfortunately, his new faith was founded only on love for a human being, and when Lady Rens, who was intensely passionate and impulsive, suddenly threw all her principles to the winds, and ran away with a Hungarian musician, who had made a furore one season in London by his magnificent violin-playing, her husband, stricken in his soul, and also wounded almost to the death in his pride, abandoned abruptly the religion of the woman who had converted and betrayed him.

Domini was nineteen, and had recently been presented at Court when the scandal of her mother's escapade shook the town, and changed her father in a day from one of the happiest to one of the most cynical, embittered and despairing of men. She, who had been brought up by both her parents as a Catholic, who had from her earliest years been earnestly educated in the beauties of religion, was now exposed to the almost frantic persuasions of a father who, hating all that he had formerly loved, abandoning all that, influenced by his faithless wife, he had formerly clung to, wished to carry his daughter with him into his new and most miserable way of life. But Domini, who, with much of her mother's dark beauty, had inherited much of her quick vehemence and passion, was also gifted with brains, and with a certain largeness of temperament and clearness of insight which Lady Rens lacked. Even when she was still quivering under the shock and shame of her mother's guilt and her own solitude, Domini was unable to share her father's intensely egoistic view of the religion of the culprit. She could not be persuaded that the faith in which she had been brought up was proved to be a sham because one of its professors, whom she had above all others loved and trusted, had broken away from its teachings and defied her own belief. She would not secede with her father, but remained in the Church of the mother she was never to see again, and this in spite of extraordinary and dogged efforts on the part of Lord Rens to pervert her to his own Atheism. His mind had been so warped by the agony of his heart that he had come to feel as if by tearing his only child from the religion he had been led to by the greatest sinner he had known, he would be, in some degree at least, purifying his life tarnished by his wife's conduct, raising again a little way the pride she had trampled in the dust.

Her uncle, Father Arlworth, helped Domini by his support and counsel in this critical period of her life, and Lord Rens in time ceased from the endeavour to carry his child with him as companion in his tragic journey from love and belief to hatred and denial. He turned to the violent occupations of despair, and the last years of his life were hideous enough, as the world knew and Domini sometimes suspected. But though Domini had resisted him she was not unmoved or wholly uninfluenced by her mother's desertion and its effect upon her father. She remained a Catholic, but she gradually ceased from being a devout one. Although she had seemed to stand firm she had in truth been shaken, if not in her belief.

in a more precious thing—her love. She complied with the ordinances, but felt little of the inner beauty of her faith. The effort she had made in withstanding her father's assault upon it had exhausted her. Though she had had the strength to triumph at the moment, a partial and secret collapse was the price she had afterwards to pay. Father Arlworth, who had a subtle understanding of human nature, noticed that Domini was changed and slightly hardened by the tragedy she had known, and was not surprised or shocked. Nor did he attempt to force her character back into its former way of beauty. He knew that to do so would be dangerous, that Domini's nature required peace in which to become absolutely normal once again after the shock it had sustained.

When Domini was twenty-one he died, and her safest guide, the one who understood her best, went from her. The years passed. She lived with her embittered father, and drifted into the unthinking worldliness of the life of her order. Her home was far from ideal. Yet she would not marry. The wreck of her parents' domestic life had rendered her mistrustful of human relations. She had seen something of the terror of love, and could not, like other women, regard it as safety and as sweetness. So she put it from her, and strove to fill her life with all those lesser things which men and women grasp, as the Chinese grasp the opium pipe, those things which lull our comprehension of realities to sleep.

When Lord Rens died, still blaspheming, and without any of the consolations of religion, Domini felt the imperious need of change. She did not grieve actively for the dead man. In his last years they had been very far apart, and his death relieved her from the perpetual contemplation of a tragedy. Lord Rens had grown to regard his daughter almost with enmity in his enmity against her mother's religion, which was hers. She had come to think of him rather with pity than with love. Yet his death was a shock to her. When he could speak no more, but only lie still, she remembered suddenly just what he had been before her mother's flight. The succeeding period, long though it had been and ugly, was blotted out. She wept for the poor, broken life now ended, and was afraid for his future in the other world. His departure into the unknown roused her abruptly to a clear conception of how his action and her mother's had affected her own character. As she stood by his bed she wondered what she might have been if her mother had been true, her father happy, to the end. Then she felt afraid of herself, recognising partially, and for the first time, how all these years had seen her long indifference. She felt self-conscious too, ignorant of the real meaning of life, and as if she had always been, and still remained, rather a complicated piece of mechanism than a woman. A desolate enervation of spirit descended upon her, a sort of bitter, and yet dull, perplexity. She began to wonder what she was, capable of what, of how much good or evil, and to feel sure that she did not know, had never known or tried to find out. Once, in this state of mind, she went to confession. She came away feeling that she had just joined with the priest in a farce. How can a woman who knows nothing about herself make anything but a worthless confession? she thought. To say what you have done is not always to say what you are. And only what you are matters eternally.

Presently, still in this perplexity of spirit, she left England with only her maid as companion. After a short tour in the south of Europe, with which she was too familiar, she crossed the sea to Africa, which she had never seen. Her destination was Beni-Mora. She had chosen it because she liked its name, because she saw on the map that it was an oasis in the Sahara Desert, because she knew it was small, quiet, yet face to face with an immensity of which she had often dreamed. Idly she fancied that perhaps in the sunny solitude of Beni-Mora, far from all the friends and reminiscences of her old life, she might learn to understand herself. How? She did not know. She did not seek to know. Here was a vague pilgrimage, as many pilgrimages are in this world—the journey of the searcher who knew not what she sought. And so now she lay in the dark, and heard the rustle of the warm African rain, and smelt the perfumes rising from the ground, and felt that the unknown was very near her—the unknown with all its blessed possibilities of change.

CHAPTER II

Long before dawn the Italian waiter rolled off his little bed, put a cap on his head, and knocked at Domini's and at Suzanne Charpot's doors.

It was still dark, and still raining, when the two women came out to get into the carriage that was to take them to the station. The Place de la Marine was a sea of mud, brown and sticky as nougat. Wet palms dripped by the railing near a desolate kiosk painted green and blue. The sky was grey and low. Curtains of tarpaulin were let down on each side of the carriage, and the coachman, who looked like a Maltese, and wore a round cap edged with pale yellow fur, was muffled up to the ears. Suzanne's round, white face was puffy with fatigue, and her dark eyes, generally good-natured and hopeful, were dreary, and squinted slightly, as she tipped the Italian waiter, and handed her mistress's dressing-bag and rug into the carriage. The waiter stood on the discoloured step, yawning from ear to ear. Even the tip could not excite him. Before the carriage started he had gone into the hotel and banged the door. The horses trotted quickly through the mud, descending the hill. One of the tarpaulin curtains had been left unbuttoned by the coachman. It flapped to and fro, and when its movement was outward Domini could catch short glimpses of mud, of glistening palm-leaves with yellow stems, of gas-lamps, and of something that was like an extended grey nothingness. This was the sea. Twice she saw Arabs trudging along, holding their skirts up in a bunch sideways, and showing legs bare beyond the knees. Hoods hid their faces. They appeared to be agitated by the weather, and to be continually trying to plant their naked feet in dry places. Suzanne, who sat opposite to Domini, had her eyes shut. If she had not from time to time passed her tongue quickly over her full, pale lips she would have looked like a dead thing. The coquettish angle at which her little black hat was set on her head seemed absurdly inappropriate to the occasion and her mood. It suggested a hat being worn at some festival. Her black, gloved hands were tightly twisted together in her lap, and she allowed her plump body to wag quite loosely with the motion of the carriage, making no attempt at resistance. She had really the appearance of a corpse sitting up. The tarpaulin flapped monotonously. The coachman cried out in the dimness to his horses like a bird, prolonging his call drearily, and then violently cracking his whip. Domini kept her eyes fixed on the loose tarpaulin, so that she might not miss one of the wet visions it discovered by its reiterated movement. She had not slept at all, and felt as if there was a gritty dryness close behind her eyes. She also felt very alert and enduring, but not in the least natural. Had some extraordinary event occurred; had the carriage, for instance, rolled over the edge of the road into the sea, she was convinced that she could not have managed to be either surprised or alarmed. If anyone had asked her whether she was tired she would certainly have answered " No."

Like her mother, Domini was of a gipsy type. She stood five feet ten, had thick, almost coarse and wavy black hair that was parted in the middle of her small head, dark, almond-shaped, heavy-lidded eyes, and a clear, warmly-white skin, unflecked with colour. She never flushed under the influence of excitement or emotion. Her forehead was broad and low. Her eyebrows were long and level, thicker than most women's. The shape of her face was oval, with a straight, short nose, a short, but rather prominent and round chin, and a very expressive mouth, not very small, slightly depressed at the corners, with perfect teeth, and red lips that were unusually flexible. Her figure was remarkably athletic, with shoulders that were broad in a woman, and a naturally small waist. Her hands and feet were also small. She walked splendidly, like a Syrian, but without his defiant insolence. In her face, when it was in repose, there was usually an expression of still indifference, some thought of opposition. She looked her age, and had never used a powder-puff in her life. She could smile easily and easily become animated, and in her animation there was often fire, as in her calmness there was sometimes cloud. Timid people were generally disconcerted by her appearance, and her manner did not always reassure them. Her obvious physical strength had something surprising in it, and woke wonder as to how it had been, or might be, used. Even when her eyes were shut she looked singularly wakeful.

Domini and Suzanne got to the station of Robertville much too early. The large hall in which they had to wait was miserably lit, blank and decidedly cold. The ticket-office was on the left, and the room was divided into two parts by a broad, low counter, on which the heavy luggage was placed before being weighed by two unshaven and hulking men in blue smocks. Three or four Arab touts, in excessively shabby European clothes and turbans, surrounded Domini with offers of assistance. One, the dirtiest of the group, with a gaping eye-socket, in which there was no eye, succeeded by his passionate volubility and impudence in attaching himself to her in a sort of official capacity. He spoke fluent, but faulty, French, which attracted Suzanne, and, being abnormally muscular and active, in an amazingly short time got hold of all their boxes and bags and ranged them on the counter. He then indulged in a dramatic performance, which he apparently considered likely to rouse into life and attention the two unshaven men in smocks, who were smoking cigarettes, and staring vaguely at the metal sheet on which the luggage was placed to be weighed Suzanne remained expectantly in attendance, and Domini, having nothing to do, and seeing no bench to rest on, walked slowly up and down the hall near the entrance.

It was now half-past four in the morning, and in the air Domini fancied that she felt the cold breath of the coming dawn. Beyond the opening of the station, as she passed and repassed in her slow and aimless walk, she saw the soaking tarpaulin curtains of the carriage she had just left glistening in the faint lamp-light. After a few minutes the Arabs she had noticed on the road entered. Their brown, slipperless feet were caked with sticky mud, and directly they found themselves under shelter in a dry place they dropped the robes they had been holding up, and, bending down, began to flick it off on to the floor with their delicate fingers. They did this with extraordinary care and precision, rubbed the soles of their feet repeatedly against the boards, and then put on their yellow slippers and threw back the hoods which had been drawn over their heads.

A few French passengers straggled in, yawning and looking irritable. The touts surrounded them, with noisy offers of assistance. The men in smocks still continued to smoke and to stare at the metal sheet on the floor. Although the luggage now extended in quite a long line upon the counter they paid no attention to it, or to the violent and reiterated cries of the Arabs who stood behind it, anxious to earn a tip by getting it weighed and registered quickly. Apparently they were wrapped in savage dreams. At length a light shone through the small opening of the ticket-office, the men in smocks stirred and threw down their cigarette stumps, and the few travellers pressed forward against the counter, and pointed to their boxes with their sticks and hands. Suzanne Charpot assumed an expression of attentive suspicion, and Domini ceased from walking up and down. Several of the recruits came in hastily, accompanied by two Zouaves. They were wet, and looked dazed and tired out. Grasping their bags and bundles they went towards the platform. A train glided slowly in, gleaming faintly with lights. Domini's trunks were slammed down on the weighing machine, and Suzanne, drawing out her purse, took her stand before the shining hole of the ticket-office.

In the wet darkness there rose up a sound like a child

calling out an insulting remark. This was followed immediately by the piping of a horn. With a jerk the train started,
passed one by one the station lamps, and, with a steady jangling
and rattling, drew out into the shrouded country. Domini
was in a wretchedly-lit carriage with three Frenchmen, facing
the door which opened on to the platform. The man opposite
to her was enormously fat, with a coal-black beard growing up
to his eyes. He wore black gloves and trousers, a huge black
cloth hat, and a thick black cloak with a black buckle near the
throat. His eyes were shut, and his large, heavy head drooped
forward. Domini wondered if he was travelling to the funeral
of some relative. The two other men, one of whom looked like
a commercial traveller, kept shifting their feet upon the hot-
water tins that lay on the floor, clearing their throats and sigh-
ing loudly. One of them coughed, let down the window, spat,
drew the window up, sat sideways, put his legs suddenly up on
the seat and groaned. The train rattled more harshly, and
shook from side to side as it got up speed. Rain streamed
down the window-panes, through which it was impossible to
see anything.

Domini still felt alert, but an overpowering sensation of
dreariness had come to her. She did not attribute this sensation to fatigue. She did not try to analyse it. She only felt as
if she had never seen or heard anything that was not cheerless,
as if she had never known anything that was not either sad, or
odd, or inexplicable. What did she remember? A train of
trifles that seemed to have been enough to fill all her life; the
arrival of the nervous and badly-dressed recruits at the wharf,
their embarkation, their last staring and pathetic look at France,
the stormy voyage, the sordid illness of almost everyone on
board, the approach long after sundown to the small and unknown town, of which it was impossible to see anything clearly,
the marshalling of the recruits pale with sickness, their pitiful
attempt at cheerful singing, angrily checked by the Zouaves in
charge of them, their departure up the hill carrying their poor
belongings, the sleepless night, the sound of the rain falling,
the scents rising from the unseen earth. The tap of the Italian
waiter at the door, the damp drive to the station, the long wait
there, the sneering signal, followed by the piping horn, the
jerking and rattling of the carriage, the dim light within it
falling upon the stout Frenchman in his mourning, the streaming water upon the window-panes. These few sights, sounds,
sensations were like the story of a life to Domini just then,

were more, were like the whole of life; always dull noise, strange, flitting, pale faces, and an unknown region that remained perpetually invisible, and that must surely be ugly or terrible.

The train stopped frequently at lonely little stations. Domini looked out, letting down the window for a moment. At each station she saw a tiny house with a peaked roof, a wooden railing dividing the platform from the country road, mud, grass bending beneath the weight of water-drops, and tall, dripping, shaggy eucalyptus trees. Sometimes the station-master's children peered at the train with curious eyes, and depressed-looking Arabs, carefully wrapped up, their mouths and chins covered by folds of linen, got in and out slowly.

Once Domini saw two women, in thin, floating white dresses and spangled veils, hurrying by like ghosts in the dark. Heavy silver ornaments jangled on their ankles, above their black slippers splashed with mud. Their sombre eyes stared out from circles of Kohl, and, with stained, claret-coloured hands, whose nails were bright red, they clasped their light and bridal raiment to their prominent breasts. They were escorted by a gigantic man, almost black, with a zigzag scar across the left side of his face, who wore a shining brown burnous over a grey woollen jacket. He pushed the two women into the train as if he were pushing bales, and got in after them, showing enormous bare legs, with calves that stuck out like lumps of iron.

The darkness began to fade, and presently, as the grey light grew slowly stronger, the rain ceased, and it was possible to see through the glass of the carriage window.

The country began to discover itself, as if timidly, to Domini's eyes. She had recently noticed that the train was going very slowly, and she could now see why. They were mounting a steep incline. The rich, damp earth of the plains beyond Robertville, with its rank grass, its moist ploughland and groves of eucalyptus, was already left behind. The train was crawling in a cup of the hills, grey, sterile and abandoned, without roads or houses, without a single tree. Small, grey-green bushes flourished here and there on tiny humps of earth, but they seemed rather to emphasise than to diminish the aspect of poverty presented by the soil, over which the dawn, rising from the wet arms of night, shed a cold and reticent illumination. By a gash in the rounded hills, where the earth was brownish yellow, a flock of goats with flapping ears tripped slowly, followed by two Arab boys in rags. One of the boys was playing upon a pipe covered with red arabesques. Domini heard two or three bars of the melody. They were ineffably wild and bird-like, very clear and sweet. They seemed to her to match exactly the pure and ascetic light cast by the dawn over these bare, grey hills, and they stirred her abruptly from the depressed lassitude in which the dreary chances of recent travel had drowned her. She began, with a certain faint excitement, to realise that these low, round-backed hills were African, that she was leaving behind the sea, so many of whose waves wept along European shores, that somewhere, beyond the broken and near horizon line toward which the train was creeping, lay the great desert, her destination, with its pale sands and desolate cities, its sunburnt tribes of workers, its robbers, war-riors and priests, its ethereal mysteries of mirage, its tragic splendours of colour, of tempest and of heat. A sense of a wider world than the compressed world into which physical fatigue had decoyed her woke in her brain and heart. The little Arab, playing carelessly upon his pipe with the red arabesques, was soon invisible among his goats beside the dry water-course that was probably the limit of his journeying, but Domini felt that like a musician at the head of a proces-sion he had played her bravely forward into the dawn and Africa.

At Ah-Souf Domini changed into another train and had the carriage to herself. The recruits had reached their destination. Hers was a longer pilgrimage and still towards the sun. She could not afterwards remember what she thought about during this part of her journey. Subsequent events so coloured all her memories of Africa that every fold of its sun-dried soil was endowed in her mind with the significance of a living thing. Every palm beside a well, every stunted vine and clambering flower upon an *auberge* wall, every form of hill and silhouette of shadow, became in her heart intense with the beauty and the pathos she used, as a child, to think must lie beyond the sunset. And so she forgot.

A strange sense of leaving all things behind had stolen over her. She was really fatigued by travel and by want of sleep, but she did not know it. Lying back in her seat, with her head against the dirty white covering of the shaking carriage, she watched the great change that was coming over the land.

It seemed as if God were putting forth His hand to with-draw gradually all things of His creation, all the furniture He had put into the great Palace of the world; as if He meant to leave it empty and utterly naked.

So Domini thought.

First He took the rich and shaggy grass, and all the little flowers that bloomed modestly in it. Then He drew away the orange groves, the oleander and the apricot trees, the faithful eucalyptus with its pale stems and tressy foliage, the sweet waters that fertilised the soil, making it soft and brown where the plough seamed it into furrows, the tufted plants and giant reeds that crowd where water is. And still, as the train ran on, His gifts were fewer. At last even the palms were gone, and the Barbary fig displayed no longer among the crumbling boulders its tortured strength, and the pale and fantastic evolutions of its unnatural foliage. Stones lay everywhere upon the pale yellow or grey-brown earth. Crystals glittered in the sun like shallow jewels, and far away, under clouds that were dark and feathery, appeared hard and relentless mountains, which looked as if they were made of iron carved into horrible and jagged shapes. Where they fell into ravines they became black. Their swelling bosses and flanks, sharp sometimes as the spines of animals, were steel coloured. Their summits were purple, deepening where the clouds came down to ebony.

Journeying towards these terrible fastnesses were caravans on which Domini looked with a heavy and lethargic interest. Many Kabyles, fairer than she was, moved slowly on foot towards their rock villages.

Over the withered earth they went towards the distant mountains and the clouds. The sun was hidden. The wind continued to rise. Sand found its way in through the carriage windows. The mountains, as Domini saw them more clearly, looked more gloomy, more unearthly. There was something unnatural in their hard outlines, in the rigid mystery of their innumerable clefts. That all these people should be journeying towards them was pathetic, and grieved the imagination.

The wind seemed so cold, now the sun was hidden, that she had drawn both the windows up and thrown a rug over her. She put her feet up on the opposite seat, and half closed her eyes. But she still turned them towards the glass on her left, and watched. It seemed to her quite impossible that this shaking and slowly moving train had any destination. The desolation of the country had become so absolute that she could not conceive of anything but still greater desolation lying beyond. She had no feeling that she was merely traversing a tract of sterility. Her sensation was that she had passed the boundary of the world God had created, and come into some other place, upon which He had never looked and of which He had no knowledge.

Abruptly she felt as if her father had entered into some such region when he forced his way out of his religion. And in this region he had died. She had stood on the verge of it by his deathbed. Now she was in it.

There were no Arabs journeying now. No tents huddled among the low bushes. The last sign of vegetation was obliterated. The earth rose and fell in a series of humps and depressions, interspersed with piles of rock. Every shade of yellow and of brown mingled and flowed away towards the foot of the mountains. Here and there dry water-courses showed their teeth. Their crumbling banks were like the rind of an orange. Little birds, the hue of the earth, with tufted crests, tripped jauntily among the stones, fluttered for a few yards and alighted, with an air of strained alertness, as if their minute bodies were full of trembling wires. They were the only living things Domini could see.

She thought again of her father. In some such region as this his soul must surely be wandering, far away from God.

She let down the glass.

The wind was really cold and blowing gustily. She drank it in as if she were tasting a new wine, and she was conscious at once that she had never before breathed such air. There was a wonderful, a startling flavour in it, the flavour of gigantic spaces and of rolling leagues of emptiness. Neither among mountains nor upon the sea had she ever found an atmosphere so fiercely pure, clean and lively with unutterable freedom. She leaned out to it, shutting her eyes. And now that she saw nothing her palate savoured it more intensely. The thought of her father fled from her. All detailed thoughts, all the minutiæ of the mind were swept away. She was bracing herself to an encounter with something gigantic, something unshackled, the being from whose lips this wonderful breath flowed.

When two lovers kiss their breath mingles, and, if they really love, each is conscious that in the breath of the loved one is the loved one's soul, coming forth from the temple of the body through the temple door. As Domini leaned out, seeing nothing, she was conscious that in this breath she drank there was a soul, and it seemed to her that it was the soul which flames in the centre of things, and beyond. She could not think any longer of her father as an outcast because he had abandoned a religion. For all religions were surely here, marching side by side, and behind them, background to them, there was something far greater than any religion. Was it snow or fire? Was it the lawlessness of that which has made laws, or the calm of that which has brought passion into being? Greater love than is in any creed, or greater freedom than is in any human liberty? Domini only felt that if she had ever been a slave at this moment she would have died of joy, realising the boundless freedom that circles this little earth.

"Thank God for it!" she murmured aloud.

Her own words woke her to a consciousness of ordinary things—or made her sleep to the eternal.

She closed the window and sat down.

A little later the sun came out again, and the various shades of yellow and of orange that played over the wrinkled earth deepened and glowed. Domini had sunk into a lethargy so complete that, though not asleep, she was scarcely aware of the sun. She was dreaming of liberty.

Presently the train slackened and stopped. She heard a loud chattering of many voices and looked out. The sun was now shining brilliantly, and she saw a station crowded with Arabs in white burnouses, who were vociferously greeting friends in the train, were offering enormous oranges for sale to the passengers, or were walking up and down gazing curiously into the carriages, with the unblinking determination and indifference to a return of scrutiny which she had already noticed and thought animal. A guard came up, told her the place was El-Akbara, and that the train would stay there ten minutes to wait for the train from Beni-Mora. She decided to get out and stretch her cramped limbs. On the platform she found Suzanne, looking like a person who had just been slapped. One side of the maid's face was flushed and covered with a faint tracery of tiny lines. The other was greyish white. Sleep hung in her eyes, over which the lids drooped as if they were partially paralysed. Her fingers were yellow from peeling an orange, and her smart little hat was cocked on one side. There were grains of sand on her black gown, and when she saw her mistress she at once began to compress her lips, and to assume the expression of obstinate patience characteristic of properly-brought-up servants who find themselves travelling far from home in outlandish places.

"Have you been asleep, Suzanne?"

" No, Mam'zelle."

" You've had an orange? "

" I couldn't get it down, Mam'zelle."

" Would you like to see if you can get a cup of coffee here? "

" No, thank you, Mam'zelle. I couldn't touch this Arab stuff."

" We shall soon be there now."

Suzanne made all her naturally small features look much smaller, glanced down at her skirt, and suddenly began to shake the grains of sand from it in an outraged manner, at the same time extending her left foot. Two or three young Arabs came up and stood, staring, round her. Their eyes were magnificent, and gravely observant. Suzanne went on shaking and patting her skirt, and Domini walked away down the platform, wondering what a French maid's mind was like. Suzanne's certainly had its limitations. It was evident that she was horrified by the sight of bare legs. Why?

As Domini walked along the platform among the fruit-sellers, the guides, the turbaned porters with their badges, the staring children and the ragged wanderers who thronged about the train, she thought of the desert to which she was now so near. It lay, she knew, beyond the terrific wall of rock that faced her. But she could see no opening. The towering summits of the cliffs, jagged as the teeth of a wolf, broke crudely upon the serene purity of the sky. Somewhere, concealed in the darkness of the gorge at their feet, was the mouth from which had poured forth that wonderful breath, quivering with freedom and with unearthly things. The sun was already declining, and the light it cast becoming softened and romantic. Soon there would be evening in the desert. Then there would be night. And she would be there in the night with all things that the desert holds.

A train of camels was passing on the white road that descended into the shadow of the gorge. Some savage-looking men accompanied them, crying continually, " Oosh! Oosh! " They disappeared, desert-men with their desert-beasts, bound no doubt on some tremendous journey through the regions of the sun. Where would they at last unlade the groaning camels? Domini saw them in the midst of dunes red with the dying fires of the west. And their shadows lay along the sands like weary things reposing.

She started when a low voice spoke to her in French, and, turning round, saw a tall Arab boy, magnificently dressed in pale blue cloth trousers, a Zouave jacket braided with gold, and a fez, standing near her. She was struck by the colour of his skin, which was faint as the colour of *café au lait,* and by the contrast between his huge bulk and his languid, almost effeminate, demeanour. As she turned he smiled at her calmly, and lifted one hand toward the wall of rock.

" Madame has seen the desert? " he asked.

" Never," answered Domini.

" It is the garden of oblivion," he said, still in a low voice and speaking with a delicate refinement that was almost mincing. " In the desert one forgets everything; even the little heart one loves, and the desire of one's own soul."

" How can that be? " asked Domini.

" Shal-làh. It is the will of God. One remembers nothing any more."

His eyes were fixed upon the gigantic pinnacles of the rocks. There was something fanatical and highly imaginative in their gaze.

" What is your name? " Domini asked.

" Batouch, Madame. You are going to Beni-Mora? "

" Yes, Batouch."

" I too. To-night, under the mimosa trees, I shall compose a poem. It will be addressed to Irena, the dancing-girl. She is like the little moon when it first comes up above the palm trees."

Just then the train from Beni-Mora ran into the station, and Domini turned to seek her carriage. As she was coming to it she noticed, with the pang of the selfish traveller who wishes to be undisturbed, that a tall man, attended by an Arab porter holding a green bag, was at the door of it and was evidently about to get in. He glanced round as Domini came up, half drew back rather awkwardly as if to allow her to precede him, then suddenly sprang in before her. The Arab lifted in the bag, and the man, endeavouring hastily to thrust some money into his hand, dropped the coin, which fell down between the step of the carriage and the platform. The Arab immediately made a greedy dive after it, interposing his body between Domini and the train; and she was obliged to stand waiting while he looked for it, grubbing frantically in the earth with his brown fingers, and uttering muffled exclamations, apparently of rage. Meanwhile, the tall man had put the green bag up on the rack, gone quickly to the far side of the carriage, and sat down looking out of the window.

Domini was struck by the mixture of indecision and blundering haste which he had shown, and by his impoliteness. Evidently he was not a gentleman, she thought, or he would surely have obeyed his first impulse and allowed her to get into the train before him. It seemed, too, as if he were determined to be discourteous, for he sat with his shoulder deliberately turned towards the door, and made no attempt to get his Arab out of the way, although the train was just about to start. Domini was very tired, and she began to feel angry with him, contemptuous too. The Arab could not find the money, and the little horn now piped its warning of departure. It was absolutely necessary for her to get in at once if she did not mean to stay at El-Akbara. She tried to pass the grovelling Arab, but as she did so he suddenly sprang up, jumped on to the step of the carriage, and, thrusting his body half through the doorway, began to address a torrent of Arabic to the passenger within. The horn sounded again, and the carriage jerked backwards preparatory to starting on its way to Beni-Mora.

Domini caught hold of the short European jacket the Arab was wearing, and said in French:

"You must let me get in at once. The train is going."

The man, however, intent on replacing the coin he had lost, took no notice of her, but went on vociferating and gesticulating. The traveller said something in Arabic. Domini was now very angry. She gripped the jacket, exerted all her force, and pulled the Arab violently from the door. He alighted on the platform beside her and nearly fell. Before he had recovered himself she sprang up into the train, which began to move at that very moment. As she got in, the man who had caused all the bother was leaning forward with a bit of silver in his hand, looking as if he were about to leave his seat. Domini cast a glance of contempt at him, and he turned quickly to the window again and stared out, at the same time putting the coin back into his pocket. A dull flush rose on his cheek, but he attempted no apology, and did not even offer to fasten the lower handle of the door.

"What a boor!" Domini thought as she bent out of the window to do it.

When she turned from the door, after securing the handle, she found the carriage full of a pale twilight. The train was stealing into the gorge, following the caravan of camels which she had seen disappearing. She paid no more attention to her companion, and her feeling of acute irritation against him died away for the moment. The towering cliffs cast mighty shadows, the darkness deepened, the train, quickening its speed, seemed straining forward into the arms of night. There was a chill in the air. Domini drank it into her lungs again, and again was startled, stirred, by the life and the mentality of it. She was conscious of receiving it with passion, as if, indeed, she held her lips to a mouth and drank some being's very nature into hers. She forgot her recent vexation and the man who had caused it. She forgot everything in mere sensation. She had no time to ask, "Whither am I going?" She felt like one borne upon a wave, seaward, to the wonder, to the danger, perhaps, of a murmuring unknown. The rocks leaned forward; their teeth were fastened in the sky; they enclosed the train, banishing the sun and the world from all the lives within it. She caught a fleeting glimpse of rushing waters far beneath her; of crumbling banks, covered with *débris* like the banks of a disused quarry; of shattered boulders, grouped in a wild disorder, as if they had been vomited forth from some underworld or cast headlong from the sky; of the flying shapes of fruit trees, mulberries and apricot trees, oleanders and palms; of dull yellow walls guarding pools the colour of absinthe, imperturbable and still. A strong impression of increasing cold and darkness grew in her, and the noises of the train became hollow, and seemed to be expanding, as if they were striving to press through the impending rocks and find an outlet into space; failing, they rose angrily, violently, in Domini's ears, protesting, wrangling, shouting, declaiming. The darkness became like the darkness of a nightmare. All the trees vanished, as if they fled in fear. The rocks closed in as if to crush the train. There was a moment in which Domini shut her eyes, like one expectant of a tremendous blow that cannot be avoided.

She opened them to a flood of gold, out of which the face of a man looked, like a face looking out of the heart of the sun.

CHAPTER III

It flashed upon her with the desert, with the burning heaps of carnation and orange-coloured rocks, with the first sand wilderness, the first brown villages glowing in the late radiance of the afternoon like carven things of bronze, the first oasis of palms, deep green as a wave of the sea and moving like a wave, the first wonder of Sahara warmth and Sahara distance. She passed through the golden door into the blue country, and saw this face, and, for a moment, moved by the exalted sensation of a

magical change in all her world, she looked at it simply as a new
sight presented, with the sun, the mighty rocks, the hard, blind
villages, and the dense trees, to her eyes, and connected it with
nothing. It was part of this strange and glorious desert region
to her. That was all, for a moment.

In the play of untempered golden light the face seemed pale
It was narrow, rather long, with marked and prominent features,
a nose with a high bridge, a mouth with straight, red lips, and a
powerful chin. The eyes were hazel, almost yellow, with curious
markings of a darker shade in the yellow, dark centres that
looked black, and dark outer circles. The eyelashes were very
long, the eyebrows thick and strongly curved. The forehead
was high, and swelled out slightly above the temples. There
was no hair on the face, which was closely shaved. Near the
mouth were two faint lines that made Domini think of physical
suffering, and also of mediæval knights. Despite the glory of
the sunshine there seemed to be a shadow falling across the
face.

This was all that Domini noticed before the spell of change
and the abrupt glory was broken, and she knew that she was
staring into the face of the man who had behaved so rudely at
the station of El-Akbara. The knowledge gave her a definite
shock, and she thought that her expression must have changed
abruptly, for a dull flush rose on the stranger's thin cheeks and
mounted to his rugged forehead. He glanced out of the window
and moved his hands uneasily. Domini noticed that they
scarcely tallied with his face. Though scrupulously clean, they
looked like the hands of a labourer, hard, broad, and brown.
Even his wrists, and a small section of his left forearm, which
showed as he lifted his left hand from one knee to the other,
were heavily tinted by the sun. The spaces between the fingers
were wide, as they usually are in hands accustomed to grasping
implements, but the fingers themselves were rather delicate and
artistic.

Domini observed this swiftly. Then she saw that her neigh
bour was unpleasantly conscious of her observation. This vexed
her vaguely, perhaps because even so trifling a circumstance was
like a thin link between them. She snapped it by ceasing to
look at or think of him. The window was down. A delicate
and warm breeze drifted in, coming from the thickets of the
palms. In flashing out of the darkness of the gorge Domini
had had the sensation of passing into a new world and a new
atmosphere. The sensation stayed with her now that she was

no longer dreaming or giving the reins to her imagination, but was calmly herself. Against the terrible rampart of rock the winds beat across the land of the Tell. But they die there frustrated. And the rains journey thither and fail, sinking into the absinthe-coloured pools of the gorge. And the snows and even the clouds stop, exhausted in their pilgrimage. The gorge is not their goal, but it is their grave, and the desert never sees their burial. So Domini's first sense of casting away the known remained, and even grew, but now strongly and quietly. It was well founded, she thought. For she looked out of the carriage window towards the barrier she was leaving, and saw that on this side, guarding the desert from the world that is not desert, it was pink in the evening light, deepening here and there to rose colour, whereas on the far side it had a rainy hue as of rocks in England. And there was a lustre of gold in the hills, tints of glowing bronze slashed with a red line as the heart of a wound, but recalling the heart of a flower. The folds of the earth glistened. There was flame down there in the river bed. The wreckage of the land, the broken fragments, gleamed as if braided with precious things. Everywhere the salt crystals sparkled with the violence of diamonds. Everywhere there was a strength of colour that hurled itself to the gaze, unabashed and almost savage, the colour of summer that never ceases, of heat that seldom dies, in a land where there is no autumn and seldom a flitting cold.

Down on the road near the village there were people; old men playing the " lady's game " with stones set in squares of sand, women peeping from flat roofs and doorways, children driving goats. A man, like a fair and beautiful Christ, with long hair and a curling beard, beat on the ground with a staff and howled some tuneless notes. He was dressed in red and green. No one heeded him. A distant sound of the beating of drums rose in the air, mingled with piercing cries uttered by a nasal voice. And as if below it, like the orchestral accompaniment of a dramatic solo, hummed many blending noises; faint calls of labourers in the palm-gardens and of women at the wells; chatter of children in dusky courts sheltered with reeds and pale-stemmed grasses; dim pipings of homeward-coming shepherds drowned, with their pattering charges, in the golden vapours of the west; soft twitterings of birds beyond brown walls in green seclusions; dull barking of guard dogs; mutter of camel drivers to their velvet-footed beasts.

The caravan which Domini had seen descending into the

gorge reappeared, moving deliberately along the desert road towards the south. A watch-tower peeped above the palms. Doves were circling round it. Many of them were white. They flew like ivory things above this tower of glowing bronze, which slept at the foot of the pink rocks. On the left rose a mass of blood-red earth and stone. Slanting rays of the sun struck it, and it glowed mysteriously like a mighty jewel.

As Domini leaned out of the window, and the salt crystals sparkled to her eyes, and the palms swayed languidly above the waters, and the rose and mauve of the hills, the red and orange of the earth, streamed by in the flames of the sun before the passing train like a barbaric procession, to the sound of the hidden drums, the cry of the hidden priest, and all the whispering melodies of these strange and unknown lives, tears started into her eyes. The entrance into this land of flame and colour, through its narrow and terrific portal, stirred her almost beyond her present strength. The glory of this world mounted to her heart, oppressing it. The embrace of Nature was so violent that it crushed her. She felt like a little fly that had sought to wing its way to the sun and, at a million miles' distance from it, was being shrivelled by its heat. When all the voices of the village fainted away she was glad, although she strained her ears to hear their fading echoes. Suddenly she knew that she was very tired, so tired that emotions acted upon her as physical exertion acts upon an exhausted man. She sat down and shut her eyes. For a long time she stayed with her eyes shut, but she knew that on the windows strange lights were glittering, that the carriage was slowly filling with the ineffable splendours of the west. Long afterwards she often wondered whether she endowed the sunset of that day with supernatural glories because she was so tired. Perhaps the salt mountain of El-Alia did not really sparkle like the celestial mountains in the visions of the saints. Perhaps the long chain of the Aures did not really look as if all its narrow clefts had been powdered with the soft and bloomy leaves of unearthly violets, and the desert was not cloudy in the distance towards the Zibans with the magical blue she thought she saw there, a blue neither of sky nor sea, but like the hue at the edge of a flame in the heart of a wood fire. She often wondered, but she never knew.

The sound of a movement made her look up. Her companion was changing his place and going to the other side of the compartment. He walked softly, no doubt with the desire not to disturb Domini. His back was towards her for an instant, and she noticed that he was a powerful man, though very thin, and that his gait was heavy. It made her think again of his labourer's hands, and she began to wonder idly what was his rank and what he did. He sat down in the far corner on the same side as herself and stared out of his window, crossing his legs. He wore large boots with square toes, clumsy and unfashionable, but comfortable and good for walking in. His clothes had obviously been made by a French tailor. The stuff of them was grey and woolly, and they were cut tighter to the figure than English clothes generally are. He had on a black silk necktie, and a soft brown travelling hat dented in the middle. By the way in which he looked out of the window, Domini judged that he, too, was seeing the desert for the first time. There was something almost passionately attentive in his attitude, something of strained eagerness in that part of his face which she could see from where she was sitting. His cheek was not pale, as she had thought at first, but brown, obviously burnt by the sun of Africa. But she felt that underneath the sunburn there was pallor. She fancied he might be a painter, and was noting all the extraordinary colour effects with the definiteness of a man who meant, perhaps, to reproduce them on canvas.

The light, which had now the peculiar, almost supernatural softness and limpidity of light falling at evening from a declining sun in a hot country, came full upon him, and brightened his hair. Domini saw that it was brown with some chestnut in it, thick, and cut extremely short, as if his head had recently been shaved. She felt convinced that he was not French. He might be an Austrian, perhaps, or a Russian from the south of Russia. He remained motionless in that attitude of profound observation. It suggested great force not merely of body, but also of mind, an almost abnormal concentration upon the thing observed. This was a man who could surely shut out the whole world to look at a grain of sand, if he thought it beautiful or interesting.

They were near Beni-Mora now. Its palms appeared far off, and in the midst of them a snow-white tower. The Sahara lay beyond and around it, rolling away from the foot of low, brown hills, that looked as if they had been covered with a soft powder of bronze. A long spur of rose-coloured mountains stretched away towards the south. The sun was very near his setting. Small, red clouds floated in the western quarter of the sky, and the far desert was becoming mysteriously dim and blue like a remote sea. Here and there thin wreaths of smoke ascended from it, and lights glittered in it, like earth-bound stars.

Domini had never before understood how strangely, how strenuously, colour can at moments appeal to the imagination. In this pageant of the East she saw arise the naked soul of Africa; no faded, gentle thing, fearful of being seen, fearful of being known and understood; but a phenomenon vital, bold and gorgeous, like the sound of a trumpet pealing a great *réveille*. As she looked on this flaming land laid fearlessly bare before her, disdaining the clothing of grass, plant and flower, of stream and tree, displaying itself with an almost brazen *insouciance*, confident in its spacious power, and in its golden pride, her heart leaped up as if in answer to a deliberate appeal. The fatigue in her died. She responded to this *réveille* like a young warrior who, so soon as he is wakened, stretches out his hand for his sword. The sunset flamed on her clear, white cheeks, giving them its hue of life. And her nature flamed to meet it. In the huge spaces of the Sahara her soul seemed to hear the footsteps of Freedom treading towards the south. And all her dull perplexities, all her bitterness of *ennui,* all her questionings and doubts, were swept away on the keen desert wind into the endless plains. She had come from her last confession asking herself, " What am I ? " She had felt infinitely small confronted with the pettiness of modern, civilised life in a narrow, crowded world. Now she did not torture herself with any questions, for she knew that something large, something capable, something perhaps even noble, rose up within her to greet all this nobility, all this mighty frankness and fierce, undressed sincerity of nature. This desert and this sun would be her comrades, and she was not afraid of them.

Without being aware of it she breathed out a great sigh, feeling the necessity of liberating her joy of spirit, of letting the body, however inadequately and absurdly, make some demonstration in response to the secret stirring of the soul. The man in the far corner of the carriage turned and looked at her. When she heard this movement Domini remembered her irritation against him at El-Akbara. In this splendid moment the feeling seemed to her so paltry and contemptible that she had a lively impulse to make amends for the angry look she had cast at him. Possibly, had she been quite normal, she would have checked such an impulse. The voice of conventionality would have made itself heard. But Domini could act vigorously, and quite carelessly, when she was moved. And she was deeply moved now, and longed to lavish the humanity, the sympathy and ardour that were quick in her. In answer to the stranger's movement she turned towards him, opening her lips to speak to him. Afterwards she never knew what she meant to say, whether, if she had spoken, the words would have been French or English. For she did not speak.

The man's face was illuminated by the setting sun as he sat half round on his seat, leaning with his right hand palm downwards on the cushions. The light glittered on his short hair. He had pushed back his soft hat, and exposed his high, rugged forehead to the air, and his brown left hand gripped the top of the carriage door. The large, knotted veins on it, the stretched sinews, were very perceptible. The hand looked violent. Domini's eyes fell on it as she turned. The impulse to speak began to fail, and when she glanced up at the man's face she no longer felt it at all. For, despite the glory of the sunset on him, there seemed to be a cold shadow in his eyes. The faint lines near his mouth looked deeper than before, and now suggested most powerfully the dreariness, the harshness of long-continued suffering. The mouth itself was compressed and grim, and the man's whole expression was fierce and startling as the expression of a criminal bracing himself to endure inevitable detection. So crude and piercing indeed was this mask confronting her that Domini started and was inclined to shudder. For a minute the man's eyes held hers, and she thought she saw in them unfathomable depths of misery or of wickedness. She hardly knew which. Sorrow was like crime, and crime like the sheer desolation of grief to her just then. And she thought of the outer darkness spoken of in the Bible. It came before her in the sunset. Her father was in it, and this stranger stood by him. The thing was as vital, and fled as swiftly as a hallucination in a madman's brain.

Domini looked down. All the triumph died out in her, all the exquisite consciousness of the freedom, the colour, the bigness of life. For there was a black spot on the sun—humanity, God's mistake in the great plan of Creation. And the shadow cast by humanity tempered, even surely conquered, the light. She wondered whether she would always feel the cold of the sunless places in the golden dominion of the sun.

The man had dropped his eyes too. His hand fell from

the door to his knee. He did not move till the train ran into
Beni-Mora, and the eager faces of countless Arabs stared in
upon them from the scorched field of manœuvres where Spahis
were exercising in the gathering twilight.

CHAPTER IV

HAVING given her luggage ticket to a porter, Domini passed
out of the station followed by Suzanne, who looked and walked
like an exhausted marionette. Batouch, who had emerged from
a third-class compartment before the train stopped, followed
them closely, and as they reached the jostling crowd of Arabs
which swarmed on the roadway he joined them with the air of
a proprietor.

" Which is Madame's hotel? "

Domini looked round.

" Ah, Batouch! "

Suzanne jumped as if her string had been sharply pulled, and
cast a glance of dreary suspicion upon the poet. She looked at
his legs, then upwards.

He wore white socks which almost met his pantaloons.
Scarcely more than an inch of pale brown skin was visible. The
gold buttons of his jacket glittered brightly. His blue robe
floated majestically from his broad shoulders, and the large
tassel of his fez fell coquettishly towards his left ear, above
which was set a pale blue flower with a woolly green leaf.

Suzanne was slightly reassured by the flower and the bright
buttons. She felt that they needed a protector in this mob of
shouting brown and black men, who clamoured about them like
savages, exposing bare legs and arms, even bare chests, in a
most barbarous manner.

" We are going to the Hotel du Désert," Domini continued. " Is it far? "

" Only a few minutes, Madame."

" I shall like to walk there."

Suzanne collapsed. Her bones became as wax with apprehension. She saw herself toiling over leagues of sand towards
some nameless hovel.

" Suzanne, you can get into the omnibus and take the hand-
bags."

At the sweet word omnibus a ray of hope stole into the
maid's heart, and when a nicely-dressed man, in a long blue

coat and indubitable trousers, assisted her politely into a vehicle
which was unmistakable she almost wept for joy.

Meanwhile Domini, escorted serenely by the poet, walked
towards the long gardens of Beni-Mora. She passed over a
wooden bridge. White dust was flying from the road, along
which many of the Arab aristocracy were indolently strolling,
carrying lightly in their hands small red roses or sprigs of pink
geranium. In their white robes they looked, she thought, like
monks, though the cigarettes many of them were smoking fought
against the illusion. Some of them were dressed like Batouch
in pale-coloured cloth. They held each other's hands loosely as
they sauntered along, chattering in soft contralto voices. Two
or three were attended by servants, who walked a pace or two
behind them on the left. These were members of great families,
rulers of tribes, men who had influence over the Sahara people.
One, a shortish man with a coal-black beard, moved so majestically that he seemed almost a giant. His face was very pale.
On one of his small, almost white, hands glittered a diamond
ring. A boy with a long, hooked nose strolled gravely near
him, wearing brown kid gloves and a turban spangled with
gold.

"That is the Kaïd of Tonga, Madame," whispered Batouch,
looking at the pale man reverently. "He is here *en permission.*"

"How white he is."

"They tried to poison him. Ever since he is ill inside.
That is his brother. The brown gloves are very *chic.*"

A light carriage rolled rapidly by them in a white mist of
dust. It was drawn by a pair of white mules, who whisked
their long tails as they trotted briskly, urged on by a cracking
whip. A big boy with heavy brown eyes was the coachman.
By his side sat a very tall young negro with a humorous pointed
nose, dressed in primrose yellow. He grinned at Batouch out
of the mist, which accentuated the coal-black hue of his whimsical, happy face.

"That is the Agha's son with Mabrouk."

They turned aside from the road and came into a long
tunnel formed by mimosa trees that met above a broad path.
To right and left were other little paths branching among the
trunks of fruit trees and the narrow twigs of many bushes that
grew luxuriantly. Between sandy brown banks, carefully
flattened and beaten hard by the spades of Arab gardeners,
glided streams of opaque water that were guided from the

desert by a system of dams. The Kaid's mill watched over them and the great wall of the fort. In the tunnel the light was very delicate and tinged with green. The noise of the water flowing was just audible. A few Arabs were sitting on benches in dreamy attitudes, with their heelless slippers hanging from the toes of their bare feet. Beyond the entrance of the tunnel Domini could see two horsemen galloping at a tremendous pace into the desert. Their red cloaks streamed out over the sloping quarters of their horses, which devoured the earth as if in a frenzy of emulation. They disappeared into the last glories of the sun, which still lingered on the plain and blazed among the summits of the red mountains.

All the contrasts of this land were exquisite to Domini and, in some mysterious way, suggested eternal things; whispering through colour, gleam, and shadow, through the pattern of leaf and rock, through the air, now fresh, now tenderly warm and perfumed, through the silence that hung like a filmy cloud in the golden heaven.

She and Batouch entered the tunnel, passing at once into definite evening. The quiet of these gardens was delicious, and was only interrupted now and then by the sound of wheels upon the road as a carriage rolled by to some house which was hidden in the distance of the oasis. The seated Arabs scarcely disturbed it by their murmured talk. Many of them indeed said nothing, but rested like lotus-eaters in graceful attitudes, with hanging hands, and eyes, soft as the eyes of gazelles, that regarded the shadowy paths and creeping waters with a grave serenity born of the inmost spirit of idleness.

But Batouch loved to talk, and soon began a languid monologue.

He told Domini that he had been in Paris, where he had been the guest of a French poet who adored the East; that he himself was "instructed," and not like other Arabs; that he smoked the hashish and could sing the love songs of the Sahara; that he had travelled far in the desert, to Souf and to Ouargla beyond the ramparts of the Dunes; that he composed verses in the night when the uninstructed, the brawlers, the drinkers of absinthe and the domino players were sleeping or wasting their time in the darkness over the pastimes of the lewd, when the sybarites were sweating under the smoky arches of the Moorish baths, and the *maréchale* of the dancing-girls sat in her flat-roofed house guarding the jewels and the amulets of her gay confederation. These verses were written both in Arabic and in French, and the poet of Paris and his friends had found them beautiful as the dawn, and as the palm trees of Ourlana by the Artesian wells. All the girls of the Ouled Naïls were celebrated in these poems—Aishoush and Irena, Fatma and Baalï. In them also were enshrined legends of the venerable marabouts who slept in the Paradise of Allah, and tales of the great warriors who had fought above the rocky precipices of Constantine and far off among the sands of the South. They told the stories of the Koulouglis, whose mothers were Moorish slaves, and romances in which figured the dark-skinned Beni M'Zab and the freed negroes who had fled away from the lands in the very heart of the sun.

All this information, not wholly devoid of a naive egoism, Batouch poured forth gently and melodiously as they walked through the twilight in the tunnel. And Domini was quite content to listen. The strange names the poet mentioned, his liquid pronunciation of them, his allusions to wild events that had happened long ago in desert places, and to the lives of priests of his old religion, of fanatics, and girls who rode on camels caparisoned in red to the dancing-houses of Sahara cities—all these things cradled her humour at this moment and seemed to plant her, like a mimosa tree, deep down in this sand garden of the sun.

She had forgotten her bitter sensation in the railway carriage when it was recalled to her mind by an incident that clashed with her present mood.

Steps sounded on the path behind them, going faster than they were, and presently Domini saw her fellow-traveller striding along, accompanied by a young Arab who was carrying the green bag. The stranger was looking straight before him down the tunnel, and he went by swiftly. But his guide had something to say to Batouch, and altered his pace to keep beside them for a moment. He was a very thin, lithe, skittish-looking youth, apparently about twenty-three years old, with a chocolate-brown skin, high cheek bones, long, almond-shaped eyes twinkling with dissipated humour, and a large mouth that smiled showing pointed white teeth. A straggling black moustache sprouted on his upper lip, and long coarse strands of jet-black hair escaped from under the front of a fez that was pushed back on his small head. His neck was thin and long, and his hands were wonderfully delicate and expressive, with rosy and quite perfect nails. When he laughed he had a habit of throwing his head forward and tucking in his chin, letting the tassel of his fez fall over his temple to left or right. He was dressed in white with a burnous, and had a many-coloured piece of silk with frayed edges wound about his waist, which was as slim as a young girl's.

He spoke to Batouch with intense vivacity in Arabic, at the same time shooting glances half-obsequious, half-impudent, wholly and even preternaturally keen and intelligent at Domini. Batouch replied with the dignified languor that seemed peculiar to him. The colloquy continued for two or three minutes Domini thought it sounded like a quarrel, but she was not accustomed to Arabs' talk. Meanwhile, the stranger in front had slackened his pace, and was obviously lingering for his neglectful guide. Once or twice he nearly stopped, and made a movement as if to turn round. But he checked it and went on slowly. His guide spoke more and more vehemently, and suddenly, tucking in his chin and displaying his rows of big and dazzling teeth, burst into a gay and boyish laugh, at the same time shaking his head rapidly. Then he shot one last sly look at Domini and hurried on, airily swinging the green bag to and fro. His arms had tiny bones, but they were evidently strong, and he walked with the light ease of a young animal. After he had gone he turned his head once and stared full at Domini. She could not help laughing at the vanity and consciousness of his expression. It was childish. Yet there was something ruthless and wicked in it too. As he came up to the stranger the latter looked round, said something to him, and then hastened forward. Domini was struck by the difference between their gaits. For the stranger, although he was so strongly built and muscular, walked rather heavily and awkwardly, with a peculiar shuffling motion of his feet. She began to wonder how old he was. About thirty-five or thirty-seven, she thought.

"That is Hadj," said Batouch in his soft, rich voice.

"Hadj?"

"Yes. He is my cousin. He lives in Beni-Mora, but he, too, has been in Paris. He has been in prison too."

"What for?"

"Stabbing."

Batouch gave this piece of information with quiet indifference, and continued:

"He likes to laugh. He is lazy. He has earned a great deal of money, and now he has none. To-night he is very gay, because he has a client."

"I see. Then he is a guide?"

"Many people in Beni-Mora are guides. But Hadj is always lucky in getting the English."

"That man with him isn't English!" Domini exclaimed.

She had wondered what the traveller's nationality was, but it had never occurred to her that it might be the same as her own.

"Yes, he is. And he is going to the Hotel du Désert. You and he are the only English here, and almost the only travellers. It is too early for many travellers yet. They fear the heat. And besides, few English come here now. What a pity! They spend money, and like to see everything. Hadj is very anxious to buy a costume at Tunis for the great *fête* at the end of Ramadan. It will cost fifty or sixty francs. He hopes the Englishman is rich. But all the English are rich and generous."

Here Batouch looked steadily at Domini with his large, unconcerned eyes.

"This one speaks Arabic a little."

Domini made no reply. She was surprised by this piece of information. There was something, she thought, essentially un-English about the stranger. He was certainly not dressed by an English tailor. But it was not only that which had caused her mistake. His whole air and look, his manner of holding himself, of sitting, of walking—yes, especially of walking—were surely foreign. Yet, when she came to think about it, she could not say that they were characteristic of any other country. Idly she had said to herself that the stranger might be an Austrian or a Russian. But she had been thinking of his colouring. It happened that two *attachés* of those two nations, whom she had met frequently in London, had hair of that shade of rather warm brown.

"He does not look like an Englishman," she said presently.

"He can talk in French and in Arabic, but Hadj says he is English."

"How should Hadj know?"

"Because he has the eyes of the jackal, and has been with many English. We are getting near to the Catholic church, Madame. You will see it through the trees. And there is Monsieur the Curé coming towards us. He is coming from his house, which is near the hotel."

At some distance in the twilight of the tunnel Domini saw a black figure in a soutane walking very slowly towards them

The stranger, who had been covering the ground rapidly with his curious, shuffling stride, was much nearer to it than they were, and, if he kept on at his present pace, would soon pass it. But suddenly Domini saw him pause and hesitate. He bent down and seemed to be doing something to his boot. Hadj dropped the green bag, and was evidently about to kneel down and assist him when he lifted himself up abruptly, looked before him as if at the priest who was approaching, then turned sharply to the right into a path which led out of the garden to the arcades of the Rue Berthe. Hadj followed, gesticulating frantically, and volubly explaining that the hotel was in the opposite direction. But the stranger did not stop. He only glanced swiftly back over his shoulder once, and then continued on his way.

"What a funny man that is!" said Batouch. "What does he want to do?"

Domini did not answer him, for the priest was just passing them, and she saw the church to the left among the trees. It was a plain, unpretending building, with a white wooden door set in an arch. Above the arch were a small cross, two windows with rounded tops, a clock, and a white tower with a pink roof. She looked at it, and at the priest, whose face was dark and meditative, with lustrous, but sad, brown eyes. Yet she thought of the stranger.

Her attention was beginning to be strongly fixed upon this unknown man. His appearance and manner were so unusual that it was impossible not to notice him.

"There is the hotel, Madame!" said Batouch.

Domini saw it standing at right angles to the church, facing the gardens. A little way back from the church was the priest's house, a white building shaded by date palms and pepper trees. As they drew near the stranger reappeared under the arcade, above which was the terrace of the hotel. He vanished through the big doorway, followed by Hadj.

While Suzanne was unpacking Domini came out on to the broad terrace which ran along the whole length of the Hotel du Désert. Her bedroom opened on to it in front, and at the back communicated with a small *salon*. This *salon* opened on to a second and smaller terrace, from which the desert could be seen beyond the palms. There seemed to be no guests in the hotel. The verandah was deserted, and the peace of the soft evening was profound. Against the white parapet a small, round table and a cane arm-chair had been placed. A sub-

dued patter of feet in slippers came up the stairway, and an
Arab servant appeared with a tea-tray. He put it down on
the table with the precise deftness which Domini had already
observed in the Arabs at Robertville, and swiftly vanished.
She sat down in the chair and poured out the tea, leaning her
left arm on the parapet.

Her head was very tired and her temples felt compressed.
She was thankful for the quiet round her. Any harsh voice
would have been intolerable to her just then. There were many
sounds in the village, but they were vague, and mingled, flowing
together and composing one sound that was soothing, the
restrained and level voice of Life. It hummed in Domini's ears
as she sipped her tea, and gave an under-side of romance to the
peace. The light that floated in under the round arches of the
terrace was subdued. The sun had just gone down, and the
bright colours bloomed no more upon the mountains, which
looked like silent monsters that had lost the hue of youth and
had suddenly become mysteriously old. The evening star shone
in a sky that still held on its Western border some last pale
glimmerings of day, and, at its signal, many dusky wanderers
folded their loose garments round them, slung their long guns
across their shoulders, and prepared to start on their journey,
helped by the cool night wind that blows in the desert when the
sun departs.

Domini did not know of them, but she felt the near presence
of the desert, and the feeling quieted her nerves. She was
thankful at this moment that she was travelling without any
woman friend and was not persecuted by any sense of obliga-
tion. In her fatigue, to rest passive in the midst of quiet, and
soft light, calm in the belief, almost the certainty, that this
desert village contained no acquaintance to disturb her, was to
know all the joy she needed for the moment. She drank it in
dreamily. Liberty had always been her fetish. What woman
had more liberty than she had, here on this lonely verandah,
with the shadowy trees below?

The bell of the church near by chimed softly, and the
familiar sound fell strangely upon Domini's ears out here in
Africa, reminding her of many sorrows. Her religion was
linked with terrible memories, with cruel struggles, with hateful
scenes of violence. Lord Rens had been a man of passionate
temperament. Strong in goodness when he had been led by
love, he had been equally strong in evil when hate had led him.
Domini had been forced to contemplate at close quarters the

raw character of a warped man, from whom circumstance had stripped all tenderness, nearly all reticence. The terror of truth was known to her. She had shuddered before it, but she had been obliged to watch it during many years. In coming to Beni-Mora she had had a sort of vague, and almost childish, feeling that she was putting the broad sea between herself and it. Yet before she had started it had been buried in the grave. She never wished to behold such truth again. She wanted to look upon some other truth of life—the truth of beauty, of calm, of freedom. Lord Rens had always been a slave, the slave of love, most of all when he was filled with hatred, and Domini, influenced by his example, instinctively connected love with a chain. Only the love a human being has for God seemed to her sometimes the finest freedom; the movement of the soul upward into the infinite obedient to the call of the great Liberator. The love of man for woman, of woman for man, she thought of as imprisonment, bondage. Was not her mother a slave to the man who had wrecked her life and carried her spirit beyond the chance of heaven? Was not her father a slave to her mother? She shrank definitely from the contemplation of herself loving, with all the strength she suspected in her heart, a human being. In her religion only she had felt in rare moments something of love. And now here, in this tremendous and conquering land, she felt a divine stirring in her love for Nature. For that afternoon Nature, so often calm and meditative, or gently indifferent, as one too complete to be aware of those who lack completeness, had impetuously summoned her to worship, had ardently appealed to her for something more than a temperate watchfulness or a sober admiration. There had been a most definite demand made upon her. Even in her fatigue and in this dreamy twilight she was conscious of a latent excitement that was not lulled to sleep.

And as she sat there, while the darkness grew in the sky and spread secretly along the sandy rills among the trees, she wondered how much she held within her to give in answer to this cry to her of self-confident Nature. Was it only a little? She did not know. Perhaps she was too tired to know. But however much it was it must seem meagre. What is even a woman's heart given to the desert or a woman's soul to the sea? What is the worship of anyone to the sunset among the hills, or to the wind that lifts all the clouds from before the face of the moon?

A chill stole over Domini. She felt like a very poor woman, who can never know the joy of giving, because she does not possess even a mite.

The church bell chimed again among the palms. Domini heard voices quite clearly below her under the arcade. A French *café* was installed there, and two or three soldiers were taking their *apéritif* before dinner out in the air. They were talking of France, as people in exile talk of their country, with the deliberateness that would conceal regret and the child's instinctive affection for the mother. Their voices made Domini think again of the recruits, and then, because of them, of Notre Dame de la Garde, the mother of God, looking towards Africa. She remembered the tragedy of her last confession. Would she be able to confess here to the Father whom she had seen strolling in the tunnel? Would she learn to know here what she really was?

How warm it was in the night, and how warmth, as it develops the fecundity of the earth, develops also the possibilities in many men and women. Despite her lassitude of body, which kept her motionless as an idol in her chair, with her arm lying along the parapet of the verandah, Domini felt as if a confused crowd of things indefinable, but violent, was already stirring within her nature, as if this new climate was calling armed men into being. Could she not hear the murmur of their voices, the distant clashing of their weapons?

Without being aware of it she was dropping into sleep. The sound of a footstep on the wooden floor of the verandah recalled her. It was at some distance behind her. It crossed the verandah and stopped. She felt quite certain that it was the step of her fellow-traveller, not because she knew he was staying in the hotel, but rather because of the curious, uneven heaviness of the tread.

What was he doing? Looking over the parapet into the fruit gardens, where the white figures of the Arabs were flitting through the trees?

He was perfectly silent. Domini was now wide awake. The feeling of calm serenity had left her. She was nervously troubled by this presence near her, and swiftly recalled the few trifling incidents of the day which had begun to delineate a character for her. They were, she found, all unpleasant, all, at least, faintly disagreeable. Yet, in sum, what was their meaning? The sketch they traced was so slight, so confused, that it told little. The last incident was the strangest. And again she saw the long and luminous pathway of the tunnel, flickering with light and shade, carpeted with the pale reflections of the leaves and narrow branches of the trees, the black figure of the priest far down it, and the tall form of the stranger in an attitude of painful hesitation. Each time she had seen him, apparently desirous of doing something definite, hesitation had overtaken him. In his indecision there was something horrible to her, something alarming.

She wished he was not standing behind her, and her discomfort increased. She could still hear the voices of the soldiers in the *café*. Perhaps he was listening to them. They sounded louder.

The speakers were getting up from their seats. There was a jingling of spurs, a tramp of feet, and the voices died away. The church bell chimed again. As it did so Domini heard heavy and uneven steps cross the verandah hurriedly. An instant later she heard a window shut sharply.

"Suzanne!" she called.

Her maid appeared, yawning, with various parcels in her hands.

"Yes, Mademoiselle."

"I sha'n't go down to the *salle-à-manger* to-night. Tell them to give me some dinner in my *salon*."

"Yes, Mademoiselle."

"You did not see who was on the verandah just now?"

The maid looked surprised.

"I was in Mademoiselle's room."

"Yes. How near the church is."

"Mademoiselle will have no difficulty in getting to Mass. She will not be obliged to go among all the Arabs."

Domini smiled.

"I have come here to be among the Arabs, Suzanne."

"The porter of the omnibus tells me they are dirty and very dangerous. They carry knives, and their clothes are full of fleas."

"You will feel quite differently about them in the morning. Don't forget about dinner."

"I will speak about it at once, Mademoiselle."

Suzanne disappeared, walking as one who suspects an ambush.

After dinner Domini went again to the verandah. She found Batouch there. He had now folded a snow-white turban round his head, and looked like a young high priest of some ornate religion. He suggested that Domini should come out with him to visit the Rue des Ouled Naïls and see the strange dances of the Sahara. But she declined.

"Not to-night, Batouch. I must go to bed. I haven't slept for two nights."

"But I do not sleep, Madame. In the night I compose verses. My brain is alive. My heart is on fire."

"Yes, but I am not a poet. Besides, I may be here for a long time. I shall have many evenings to see the dances."

The poet looked displeased.

"The gentleman is going," he said. "Hadj is at the door waiting for him now. But Hadj is afraid when he enters the street of the dancers."

"Why?"

"There is a girl there who wishes to kill him. Her name is Aishoush. She was sent away from Beni-Mora for six months, but she has come back, and after all this time she still wishes to kill Hadj."

"What has he done to her?"

"He has not loved her. Yes, Hadj is afraid, but he will go with the gentleman because he must earn money to buy a costume for the *fête* of Ramadan. I also wish to buy a new costume."

He looked at Domini with a dignified plaintiveness. His pose against the pillar of the verandah was superb. Over his blue cloth jacket he had thrown a thin white burnous, which hung round him in classic folds. Domini could scarcely believe that so magnificent a creature was touting for a franc. The idea certainly did occur to her, but she banished it. For she was a novice in Africa.

"I am too tired to go out to-night," she said decisively.

"Good-night, Madame. I shall be here to-morrow morning at seven o'clock. The dawn in the garden of the gazelles is like the flames of Paradise, and you can see the Spahis galloping upon horses that are beautiful as——"

"I shall not get up early to-morrow."

Batouch assumed an expression that was tragically submissive and turned to go. Just then Suzanne appeared at the French window of her bedroom. She started as she perceived the poet, who walked slowly past her to the staircase, throwing his burnous back from his big shoulders, and stood looking after him. Her eyes fixed themselves upon the section of bare leg that was visible above his stockings white as the driven snow, and a faintly sentimental expression mingled with their defiance and alarm.

Domini got up from her chair and leaned over the parapet. A streak of yellow light from the doorway of the hotel lay upon the white road below, and in a moment she saw two figures come out from beneath the verandah and pause there. Hadj was one, the stranger was the other. The stranger struck a match and tried to light a cigar, but failed. He struck another match, and then another, but still the cigar would not draw. Hadj looked at him with mischievous astonishment.

"If Monsieur will permit me——" he began.

But the stranger took the cigar hastily from his mouth and flung it away.

"I don't want to smoke," Domini heard him say in French. Then he walked away with Hadj into the darkness.

As they disappeared Domini heard a faint shrieking in the distance. It was the music of the African hautboy.

The night was marvellously dry and warm. The thickly growing trees in the garden scarcely moved. It was very still and very dark. Suzanne, standing at her window, looked like a shadow in her black dress. Her attitude was romantic. Perhaps the subtle influence of this Sahara village was beginning to steal even over her obdurate spirit.

The hautboy went on crying. Its notes, though faint, were sharp and piercing. Once more the church bell chimed among the date palms, and the two musics, with their violently differing associations, clashing together smote upon Domini's heart with a sense of trouble, almost of tragedy. The pulses in her temples throbbed, and she clasped her hands tightly together. That brief moment, in which she heard the duet of those two voices, was one of the most interesting, yet also one of the most painful she had ever known. The church bell was silent now, but the hautboy did not cease. It was barbarous and provocative, shrill with a persistent triumph.

Domini went to bed early, but she could not sleep. Just before midnight she heard someone walking up and down on the verandah. The step was heavy and shuffling. It came and went, came and went, without pause till she was in a fever of uneasiness. Only when two chimed from the church did it cease at last.

She whispered a prayer to Notre Dame de la Garde, The Blessed Virgin, looking towards Africa. For the first time she felt the loneliness of her situation and that she was far away.

CHAPTER V

TOWARDS morning Domini slept. It was nearly eight o'clock when she awoke. The room was full of soft light which told of the sun outside, and she got up at once, put on a pair of slippers and opened the French window on to the verandah. Already Beni-Mora was bathed in golden beams and full of gentle activities. A flock of goats pattered by towards the edge of the oasis. The Arab gardeners were lazily sweeping small leaves from the narrow paths under the mimosa and pepper trees. Soldiers in loose white suits, dark blue sashes and the fez, were hastening from the Fort towards the market. A distant bugle rang out and the snarl of camels was audible from the village. Domini stood on the verandah for a moment, drinking in the desert air. It made her feel very pure and clean, as if she had just bathed in clear water. She looked up at the limpid sky, which seemed full of hope and of the power to grant blessings, and she was glad that she had come to Beni-Mora. Her lonely sensation of the previous night had gone. As she stood in the sun she was conscious that she needed re-creation and that here she might find it. The radiant sky, the warm sun and the freedom of the coming day and of many coming desert days, filled her heart with an almost childish sensation. She felt younger than she had felt for years, and even foolishly innocent, like a puppy dog or a kitten. Her thick black hair, unbound, fell in a veil round her strong, active body, and she had the rare consciousness that behind that other more mysterious veil her soul was to-day a less unfit companion for its mate than it had been since her mother's sin.

Cleanliness—what a blessed condition that was, a condition to breed bravery. In this early morning hour Beni-Mora looked magically clean. Domini thought of the desperate dirt of London mornings, of the sooty air brooding above black trees and greasy pavements. Surely it was difficult to be clean of soul there. Here it would be easy. One would tune one's lyre in accord with Nature and be as a singing palm tree beside a water-spring. She took up a little vellum-bound book which she had laid at night upon her dressing-table. It was *Of the Imitation of Christ,* and she opened it at haphazard and glanced down on a sunlit page. Her eyes fell on these words:

"Love watcheth, and sleeping, slumbereth not. When

weary it is not tired; when straitened it is not constrained; when frightened it is not disturbed; but like a vivid flame and a burning torch it mounteth upwards and securely passeth through all. Whosoever loveth knoweth the cry of this voice."

The sunlight on the page of the little book was like the vivid flame and the burning torch spoken of in it. Heat, light, a fierce vitality. Domini had been weary so long, weary of soul, that she was almost startled to find herself responding quickly to the sacred passion on the page, to the bright beam that kissed it as twin kisses twin. She knelt down to say her morning prayer, but all she could whisper was:

"O, God, renew me. O, God, renew me. Give me power to feel, keenly, fiercely, even though I suffer. Let me wake. Let me feel. Let me be a living thing once more. O, God, renew me, renew me!"

While she prayed she pressed her face so hard against her hands that patches of red came upon her cheeks. And afterwards it seemed to her as if her first real, passionate prayer in Beni-Mora had been almost like a command to God. Was not such a fierce prayer perhaps a blasphemy?

She rose from that prayer to the first of her new days.

After breakfast she looked over the edge of the verandah and saw Batouch and Hadj squatting together in the shadow of the trees below. They were smoking cigarettes and talking eagerly. Their conversation, which was in Arabic, sounded violent. The accented words were like blows. Domini had not looked over the parapet for more than a minute before the two guides saw her and rose smiling to their feet.

"I am waiting to show the village to Madame," said Batouch, coming out softly into the road, while Hadj remained under the trees, exposing his teeth in a sarcastic grin, which plainly enough conveyed to Domini his pity for her sad mistake in not engaging him as her attendant.

Domini nodded, went back into her room and put on a shady hat. Suzanne handed her a large parasol lined with green, and she descended the stairs rather slowly. She was not sure whether she wanted a companion in her first walk about Beni-Mora. There would be more savour of freedom in solitude. Yet she had hardly the heart to dismiss Batouch, with all his dignity and determination. She resolved to take him for a little while and then to get rid of him on some pretext.

Perhaps she would make some purchases in the bazaars and send him to the hotel with them.

"Madame has slept well?" asked the poet as she emerged into the sun.

"Pretty well," she answered, nodding again to Hadj, whose grin became more mischievous, and opening her parasol. "Where are we going?"

"Wherever Madame wishes. There is the market, the negro village, the mosque, the casino, the statue of the Cardinal, the bazaars, the garden of the Count Ferdinand Anteoni."

"A garden," said Domini. "Is it a beautiful one?"

Batouch was about to burst into a lyric ecstasy, but he checked himself and said:

"Madame shall see for herself and tell me afterwards if in all Europe there is one such garden."

"Oh, the English gardens are wonderful," she said, smiling at his patriotic conceit.

"No doubt. Madame shall tell me, Madame shall tell me," he repeated with imperturbable confidence.

"But first I wish to go for a moment into the church," she said. "Wait for me here, Batouch."

She crossed the road, passed the modest, one-storied house of the priest, and came to the church, which looked out on to the quiet gardens. Before going up the steps and in at the door she paused for a moment. There was something touching to her, as a Catholic, in this symbol of her faith set thus far out in the midst of Islamism. The cross was surely rather lonely here, raised above the white-robed men to whom it meant nothing. She was conscious that since she had come to this land of another creed, and of another creed held with fanaticism, her sentiment for her own religion, which in England for many years had been but lukewarm, had suddenly gained in strength. She had an odd, almost manly, sensation that it was her duty in Africa to stand up for her faith, not blatantly in words to impress others, but perseveringly in heart to satisfy herself. Sometimes she felt very protective. She felt protective to-day as she looked at this humble building, which she likened to one of the poor saints of the Thebaïd, who dwelt afar in desert places, and whose devotions were broken by the night-cries of jackals and by the roar of ravenous beasts. With this feeling strong upon her she pushed open the door and went in.

The interior was plain, even ugly. The walls were painted a

hideous drab. The stone floor was covered witn small, hard, straw-bottomed chairs and narrow wooden forms for the patient knees of worshippers. In the front were two rows of private chairs, with velvet cushions of various brilliant hues and velvet-covered rails. On the left was a high stone pulpit. The altar, beyond its mean black and gold railing, was dingy and forlorn. On it there was a tiny gold cross with a gold statuette of Christ hanging, surmounted by a canopy with four pillars, which looked as if made of some unwholesome sweetmeat. Long candles of blue and gold and bouquets of dusty artificial flowers flanked it. Behind it, in a round niche, stood a painted figure of Christ holding a book. The two adjacent side chapels had domed roofs representing the firmament. Beneath the pulpit stood a small harmonium. At the opposite end of the church was a high gallery holding more chairs. The mean, featureless windows were filled with glass half white, half staring red dotted with yellow crosses. Round the walls were reliefs of the fourteen stations of the Cross in white plaster on a gilt ground framed in grey marble. From the roof hung vulgar glass chandeliers with ropes tied with faded pink ribands. Several frightful plaster statues daubed with scarlet and chocolate brown stood under the windows, which were protected with brown woollen curtains. Close to the entrance were a receptacle for holy water in the form of a shell, and a confessional of stone flanked by boxes, one of which bore the words, " Grâces obtenues," the other, " Demandes," and a card on which was printed, " Litanies en honneur de Saint Antoine de Padoue."

There was nothing to please the eye, nothing to appeal to the senses. There was not even the mystery which shrouds and softens, for the sunshine streamed in through the white glass of the windows, revealing, even emphasising, as if with deliberate cruelty, the cheap finery, the tarnished velvet, the crude colours the meretricious gestures and poses of the plaster saints. Yet as Domini touched her forehead and breast with holy water, and knelt for a moment on the stone floor, she was conscious that this rather pitiful house of God moved her to an emotion she had not felt in the great and beautiful churches to which she was accustomed in England and on the Continent. Through the windows she saw the outlines of palm leaves vibrating in the breeze; African fingers, feeling, with a sort of fluttering suspicion, if not enmity, round the heart of this intruding religion, which had wandered hither from some distant place, and

stayed, confronting the burning glance of the desert. Bold,
little, humble church! Domini knew that she would love it.
But she did not know then how much.

She wandered round slowly with a grave face. Yet now and
then, as she stood by one of the plaster saints, she smiled. They
were indeed strange offerings at the shrine of Him who held
this Africa in the hollow of His hand, of Him who had ordered
the pageant of the sun which she had seen last night among the
mountains. And presently she and this little church in which
she stood alone became pathetic in her thoughts, and even the
religion which the one came to profess in the other pathetic
too. For here, in Africa, she began to realise the wideness of
the world, and that many things must surely seem to the Creator
what these plaster saints seemed just then to her.

"Oh, how little, how little!" she whispered to herself. "Let
me be bigger! Oh, let me grow, and here, not only hereafter!"

The church door creaked. She turned her head and saw the
priest whom she had met in the tunnel entering. He came up
to her at once, saluted her, and said:

"I saw you from my window, Madame, and thought I
would offer to show you our little church here. We are very
proud of it."

Domini liked his voice and his naïve remark. His face, too,
though undistinguished, looked honest, kind, and pathetic, but
with a pathos that was unaffected and quite unconscious. The
lower part of it was hidden by a moustache and beard.

"Thank you," she answered. "I have been looking round
already."

"You are a Catholic, Madame?"

"Yes."

The priest looked pleased. There was something childlike
in the mobility of his face.

"I am glad," he said simply. "We are not a rich community in Beni-Mora, but we have been fortunate in bygone
years. Our great Cardinal, the Father of Africa, loved this
place and cherished his children here."

"Cardinal Lavigerie?"

"Yes, Madame. His house is now a native hospital. His
statue faces the beginning of the great desert road. But we
remember him and his spirit is still among us."

The priest's eyes lit up as he spoke. The almost tragic
expression of his face changed to one of enthusiasm.

"He loved Africa, I believe." Domini said.

" His heart was here. And what he did! I was to have been one of his *frères armés,* but my health prevented, and afterwards the association was dissolved."

The sad expression returned to his face.

" There are many temptations in such a land and climate as this," he said. " And men are weak. But there are still the White Fathers whom he founded. Glorious men. They carry the Cross into the wildest places of the world. The most fanatical Arabs respect the White Marabouts."

" You wish you were with them? "

" Yes, Madame. But my health only permits me to be a humble parish priest here. Not all who desire to enter the most severe life can do so. If it were otherwise I should long since have been a monk. The Cardinal himself showed me that my duty lay in other paths."

He pointed out to Domini one or two things in the church which he admired and thought worthy; the carving of the altar rail into grapes, ears of corn, crosses, anchors; the white embroidered muslin that draped the tabernacle; the statue of a bishop in a red and gold mitre holding a staff and Bible, and another statue representing a saint with a languid and consumptive expression stretching out a Bible, on the leaves of which a tiny, smiling child was walking.

As they were about to leave the church he made Domini pause in front of a painting of Saint Bruno dressed in a white monkish robe, beneath which was written in gilt letters:

> " Saint Bruno ordonne à ses disciples
> De renoncer aux biens terrestres
> Pour acquérir les biens celestes."

The disciples stood around the saint in grotesque attitudes of pious attention.

" That, I think, is very beautiful," he said. " Who could look at it without feeling that the greatest act of man is renunciation? "

His dark eyes flamed. Just then a faint soprano bark came to them from outside the church door, a very discreet and even humble, but at the same time anxious, bark. The priest's face changed. The almost passionate asceticism of it was replaced by a soft and gentle look.

" Bous-Bous wants me," he said, and he opened the door for Domini to pass out.

A small white and yellow dog, very clean and well brushed,

was sitting on the step in an attentive attitude. Directly the priest appeared it began to wag its short tail violently and to run round his feet, curving its body into semi-circles. He bent down and patted it.

"My little companion, Madame," he said. "He was not with me yesterday, as he was being washed."

Then he took off his hat and walked towards his house, accompanied by Bous-Bous, who had suddenly assumed an air of conscious majesty, as of one born to preside over the fate of an important personage.

Domini stood for a moment under the palm trees looking after them. There was a steady shining in her eyes.

"Madame is a Catholic too?" asked Batouch, staring steadily at her.

Domini nodded. She did not want to discuss religion with an Arab minor poet just then.

"Take me to the market," she said, mindful of her secret resolve to get rid of her companion as soon as possible.

They set out across the gardens.

It was a celestial day. All the clear, untempered light of the world seemed to have made its home in Beni-Mora. Yet the heat was not excessive, for the glorious strength of the sun was robbed of its terror, its possible brutality, by the bright and feathery dryness and coolness of the airs. She stepped out briskly. Her body seemed suddenly to become years younger, full of elasticity and radiant strength.

"Madame is very strong. Madame walks like a Bedouin."

Batouch's voice sounded seriously astonished, and Domini burst out laughing.

"In England there are many strong women. But I shall grow stronger here. I shall become a real Arab. This air gives me life."

They were just reaching the road when there was a clatter of hoofs, and a Spahi, mounted on a slim white horse, galloped past at a tremendous pace, holding his reins high above the red peak of his saddle and staring up at the sun. Domini looked after him with critical admiration.

"You've got some good horses here," she said when the Spahi had disappeared.

"Madame knows how to ride?"

She laughed again.

"I've ridden ever since I was a child."

"You can buy a fine horse here for sixteen pounds," remarked

Batouch, using the pronoun "tu," as is the custom of the Arabs.

"Find me a good horse, a horse with spirit, and I'll buy him," Domini said. "I want to go far out in the desert, far away from everything."

"You must not go alone."

"Why not?"

"There are bandits in the desert."

"I'll take my revolver," Domini said carelessly. "But I will go alone."

They were in sight of the market now, and the hum of voices came to them, with nasal cries, the whine of praying beggars, and the fierce braying of donkeys. At the end of the small street in which they were Domini saw a wide open space, in the centre of which stood a quantity of pillars supporting a peaked roof. Round the sides of the square were arcades swarming with Arabs, and under the central roof a mob of figures came and went, as flies go and come on a piece of meat flung out into a sunny place.

"What a quantity of people! Do they all live in Beni-Mora?" she asked.

"No, they come from all parts of the desert to sell and to buy. But most of those who sell are Mozabites."

Little children in bright-coloured rags came dancing round Domini, holding out their copper-coloured hands, and crying shrilly, "'Msee, M'dame! 'Msee, M'dame!" A deformed man, who looked like a distorted beetle, crept round her feet, gazing up at her with eyes that squinted horribly, and roaring in an imperative voice some Arab formula in which the words "Allah-el-Akbar" continually recurred. A tall negro, with a long tuft of hair hanging from his shaven head, followed hard upon her heels, rolling his bulging eyes, in which two yellow flames were caught, and trying to engage her attention, though with what object she could not imagine. From all directions tall men with naked arms and legs, and fluttering white garments, came slowly towards her, staring intently at her with lustrous eyes, whose expression seemed to denote rather a calm and dignified appraisement than any vulgar curiosity. Boys, with the whitest teeth she had ever beheld, and flowers above their well-shaped, delicate ears, smiled up at her with engaging impudence. Her nostrils were filled with a strange crowd of odours, which came from humanity dressed in woollen garments, from fruits exposed for sale in rush panniers, from round close bouquets of roses ringed with tight borders of green leaves, from burning incense twigs, from raw meat, from amber ornaments and strong perfumes in glass phials figured with gold —attar of rose, orange blossom, geranium and white lilac. In the shining heat of the sun sounds, scents and movements mingled, and were almost painfully vivid and full of meaning and animation. Never had a London mob on some great *fête* day seemed so significant and personal to Domini as this little mob of desert people, come together for the bartering of beasts, the buying of burnouses, weapons, skins and jewels, grain for their camels, charms for their women, ripe glistening dates for the little children at home in the brown earth houses.

As she made her way slowly through the press, pioneered by Batouch, who forced a path with great play of his huge shoulders and mighty arms, she was surprised to find how much at home she felt in the midst of these fierce and uncivilised-looking people. She had no sense of shrinking from their contact, no feeling of personal disgust at their touch. When her eyes chanced to meet any of the bold, inquiring eyes around her she was inclined to smile as if in recognition of these children of the sun, who did not seem to her like strangers, despite the unknown language that struggled fiercely in their throats. Nevertheless, she did not wish to stay very long among them now. She was resolved to get a full and delicately complete first impression of Beni-Mora, and to do that she knew that she must detach herself from close human contact. She desired the mind's bird's-eye view—a height, a watch-tower and a little solitude. So, when the eager Mozabite merchants called to her she did not heed them, and even the busy patter of the informing Batouch fell upon rather listless ears.

"I sha'n't stay here," she said to him. "But I'll buy some perfumes. Where can I get them?"

A thin youth, brooding above a wooden tray close by, held up in his delicate fingers a long bottle, sealed and furnished with a tiny label, but Batouch shook his head.

"For perfumes you must go to Ahmeda, under the arcade."

They crossed a sunlit space and stood before a dark room, sunk lightly below the level of the pathway in a deserted corner. Shadows congregated here, and in the gloom Domini saw a bent white figure hunched against the blackened wall, and heard an old voice murmuring like a drowsy bee. The perfume-seller was immersed in the Koran, his back to the buying world. Batouch was about to call upon him, when Domini checked the exclamation with a quick gesture. For the first time the mystery that coils like a great black serpent in the shining heart of the East startled and fascinated her, a mystery in which indifference and devotion mingle. The white figure swayed slowly to and fro, carrying the dull, humming voice with it, and now she seemed to hear a far-away fanaticism, the bourdon of a fatalism which she longed to understand.

" Ahmeda ! "

Batouch shouted. His voice came like a stone from a catapult. The merchant turned calmly and without haste, showing an aquiline face covered with wrinkles, tufted with white hairs, lit by eyes that shone with the cruel expressiveness of a falcon's. After a short colloquy in Arabic he raised himself from his haunches, and came to the front of the room, where there was a small wooden counter. He was smiling now with a grace that was almost feminine.

" What perfume does Madame desire ? " he said in French.

Domini gazed at him as at a deep mystery, but with the searching directness characteristic of her, a fearlessness so absolute that it embarrassed many people.

" Please give me something that is of the East—not violets, not lilac."

" Amber," said Batouch.

The merchant, still smiling, reached up to a shelf, showing an arm like a brown twig, and took down a glass bottle covered with red and green lines. He removed the stopper, made Domini take off her glove, touched her bare hand with the stopper, then with his forefinger gently rubbed the drop of perfume which had settled on her skin till it was slightly red.

" Now, smell it," he commanded.

Domini obeyed. The perfume was faintly medicinal, but it filled her brain with exotic visions. She shut her eyes. Yes, that was a voice of Africa too. Oh ! how far away she was from her old life and hollow days. The magic carpet had been spread indeed, and she had been wafted into a strange land where she had all to learn.

" Please give me some of that," she said.

The merchant poured the amber into a phial, where it lay like a thread in the glass, weighed it in a scales and demanded a price. Batouch began at once to argue with vehemence, but Domini stopped him.

" Pay him," she said, giving Batouch her purse.

The perfume-seller took the money with dignity, turned

away, squatted upon his haunches against the blackened wall, and picked up the broad-leaved volume which lay upon the floor. He swayed gently and rhythmically to and fro. Then once more the voice of the drowsy bee hummed in the shadows. The worshipper and the Prophet stood before the feet of Allah.

And the woman—she was set afar off, as woman is by white-robed men in Africa.

"Now, Batouch, you can carry the perfume to the hotel and I will go to that garden."

"Alone? Madame will never find it."

"I can ask the way."

"Impossible! I will escort Madame to the gate. There I will wait for her. Monsieur the Count does not permit the Arabs to enter with strangers."

"Very well," Domini said.

The seller of perfumes had led her towards a dream. She was not combative, and she would be alone in the garden. As they walked towards it in the sun, through narrow ways where idle Arabs lounged with happy aimlessness, Batouch talked of Count Anteoni, the owner of the garden.

Evidently the Count was the great personage of Beni-Mora. Batouch spoke of him with a convinced respect, describing him as fabulously rich, fabulously generous to the Arabs.

"He never gives to the French, Madame, but when he is here each Friday, upon our Sabbath, he comes to the gate with a bag of money in his hand, and he gives five franc pieces to every Arab who is there."

"And what is he? French?"

"He is Italian; but he is always travelling, and he has made gardens everywhere. He has three in Africa alone, and in one he keeps many lions. When he travels he takes six Arabs with him. He loves only the Arabs."

Domini began to feel interested in this wandering maker of gardens, who was a pilgrim over the world like Monte Cristo.

"Is he young?" she asked.

"No."

"Married?"

"Oh, no! He is always alone. Sometimes he comes here and stays for three months, and is never once seen outside the garden. And sometimes for a year he never comes to Beni-Mora. But he is here now. Twenty Arabs are always working in the garden, and at night ten Arabs with guns are always awake, some in a tent inside the door and some among the trees."

" Then there is danger at night? "

" The garden touches the desert, and those who are in the desert' without arms are as birds in the air without wings."

They had come out from among the houses now into a broad, straight road, bordered on the left by land that was under cultivation, by fruit trees, and farther away by giant palms, between whose trunks could be seen the stony reaches of the desert and spurs of grey-blue and faint rose-coloured mountains. On the right was a shady garden with fountains and stone benches, and beyond stood a huge white palace built in the Moorish style, and terraced roofs and a high tower ornamented with green and peacock-blue tiles. In the distance, among more palms, appeared a number of low, flat huts of brown earth. The road, as far as the eyes could see, stretched straight forward through enormous groves of palms, whose feathery tops swayed gently in the light wind that blew from the desert. Upon all things rained a flood of blue and gold. A blinding radiance made all things glad.

" How glorious light is! " Domini exclaimed, as she looked down the road to the point where its whiteness was lost in the moving ocean of the trees.

Batouch assented without enthusiasm, having always lived in the light.

" As we return from the garden we will visit the tower," he said, pointing to the Moorish palace. "It is a hotel, and is not yet open, but I know the guardian. From the tower Madame will see the whole of Beni-Mora. Here is the negro village."

They traversed its dusty alleys slowly. On the side where the low brown dwellings threw shadows some of the inhabitants were dreaming or chattering, wrapped in garments of gaudy cotton. Little girls in the fiercest orange colour, with tattooed foreheads and leathern amulets, darted to and fro, chasing each other and shrieking with laughter. Naked babies, whose shaven heads made a warm resting-place for flies, stared at Domini with a lustrous vacancy of expression. At the corners of the alleys unveiled women squatted, grinding corn in primitive hand-mills, or winding wool on wooden sticks. Their heads were covered with plaits of imitation hair made of wool, in which barbaric silver ornaments were fastened, and their black necks and arms jingled with chains and bangles set with squares of red coral and large dull blue and green stones. Some of them called boldly to Batouch, and he answered them with careless impudence. The palm-wood door of one of the houses stood wide open, and Domini looked in. She saw a dark space with floor and walls of earth, a ceiling of palm and brushwood, a low divan of earth without mat or covering of any kind.

"They have no furniture?" she asked Batouch.

"No. What do they want with it? They live out here in the sun and go in to sleep."

Life simplified to this extent made her smile. Yet she looked at the squatting figures in the gaudy cotton rags with a stirring of envy. The memory of her long and complicated London years, filled with a multitude of so-called pleasures which had never stifled the dull pain set up in her heart by the rude shock of her mother's sin and its result, made this naked, sunny, barbarous existence seem desirable. She stood for a moment to watch two women sorting grain for cous-cous. Their guttural laughter, their noisy talk, the quick and energetic movements of their busy black hands, reminded her of children's gaiety. And Nature rose before her in the sunshine, confronting artifice and the heavy languors of modern life in cities. How had she been able to endure the yoke so long?

"Will Madame take me to London with her when she returns?" said Batouch, slyly.

"I am not going back to London for a very long time," she replied with energy.

"You will stay here many weeks?"

"Months, perhaps. And perhaps I shall travel on into the desert. Yes, I must do that."

"If we followed the white road into the desert, and went on and on for many days, we should come at last to Tombouctou," said Batouch. "But very likely we should be killed by the Touaregs. They are fierce and they hate strangers."

"Would you be afraid to go?" Domini asked him, curiously

"Why afraid?"

"Of being killed?"

He looked calmly surprised.

"Why should I be afraid to die? All must pass through that door. It does not matter whether it is to-day or to-morrow."

"You have no fear of death, then?"

"Of course not. Have you, Madame?"

He gazed at Domini with genuine astonishment.

"I don't know," she answered.

And she wondered and could not tell.

"There is the Villa Anteoni."

Batouch lifted his hand and pointed. They had turned aside from the way to Tombouctou, left the village behind them, and come into a narrow track which ran parallel to the desert. The palm trees rustled on their right, the green corn waved, the narrow cuttings in the earth gleamed with shallow water. But on their other side was limitless sterility; the wide, stony expanse of the great river bed, the Oued-Beni-Mora, then a low earth cliff, and then the immense airy flats stretching away into the shining regions of the sun. At some distance, raised on a dazzling white wall above the desert in an unshaded place, Domini saw a narrow, two-sided white house, with a flat roof and a few tiny loopholes instead of windows. One side looked full upon the waterless river bed, the other, at right angles to it, ran back towards a thicket of palms and ended in an arcade of six open Moorish arches, through which the fierce blue of the cloudless sky stared, making an almost theatrical effect. Beyond, masses of trees were visible, looking almost black against the intense, blinding pallor of wall, villa and arcade, the intense blue above.

"What a strange house!" Domini said. "There are no windows."

"They are all on the other side, looking into the garden."

The villa fascinated Domini at once. The white Moorish arcade framing bare, quivering blue, blue from the inmost heart of heaven, intense as a great vehement cry, was beautiful as the arcade of a Geni's home in Fairyland. Mystery hung about this dwelling, a mystery of light, not darkness, secrets of flame and hidden things of golden meaning. She felt almost like a child who is about to penetrate into the red land of the winter fire, and she hastened her steps till she reached a tall white gate set in an arch of wood, and surmounted with a white coat of arms and two lions. Batouch struck on it with a white knocker and then began to roll a cigarette.

"I will wait here for Madame."

Domini nodded. A leaf of wood was pulled back softly in the gate, and she stepped into the garden and confronted a graceful young Arab dressed in pale green, who saluted her respectfully and gently closed the door.

"May I walk about the garden a little?" she asked.

She did not look round her yet, for the Arab's face interested and even charmed her. It was aristocratic, enchantingly indolent, like the face of a happy lotus-eater. The great, lustrous eyes were tender as a gazelle's and thoughtless as the eyes of a sleepy child. His perfectly-shaped feet were bare on the shining sand. In one hand he held a large red rose and in the other a half-smoked cigarette.

Domini could not help smiling at him as she put her question, and he smiled contentedly back at her as he answered, in a low, level voice:

"You can go where you will. Shall I show you the paths?"

He lifted his hand and calmly smelt his red rose, keeping his great eyes fixed upon her. Domini's wish to be alone had left her. This was surely the geni of the garden, and his company would add to its mystery and fragrance.

"You need not stay by the door?" she asked.

"No one will come. There is no one in Beni-Mora. And Hassan will stay."

He pointed with his rose to a little tent that was pitched closed to the gate beneath a pepper tree. In it Domini saw a brown boy curled up like a dog and fast asleep. She began to feel as if she had eaten hashish. The world seemed made for dreaming.

"Thank you, then."

And now for the first time she looked round to see whether Batouch had implied the truth. Must the European gardens give way to this Eastern garden, take a lower place with all their roses?

She stood on a great expanse of newly-raked smooth sand, rising in a very gentle slope to a gigantic hedge of carefully trimmed evergreens, which projected at the top, forming a roof and casting a pleasant shade upon the sand. At intervals white benches were placed under this hedge. To the right was the villa. She saw now that it was quite small. There were two lines of windows—on the ground floor and the upper story. The lower windows opened on to the sand, those above on to a verandah with a white railing, which was gained by a white staircase outside the house built beneath the arches of the arcade. The villa was most delicately simple, but in this riot of blue and gold its ivory cleanliness, set there upon the shining sand which was warm to the foot, made it look magical to Domini. She thought she had never known before what spotless purity was like.

"Those are the bedrooms," murmured the Arab at her side.

"There are only bedrooms?" she asked in surprise.

"The other rooms, the drawing-room of Monsieur the

Count, the dining-room, the smoking-room, the Moorish bath, the room of the little dog, the kitchen and the rooms for the servants are in different parts of the garden. There is the dining-room."

He pointed with his rose to a large white building, whose dazzling walls showed here and there through the masses of trees to the left, where a little raised sand-path with flattened, sloping sides wound away into a maze of shadows diapered with gold.

"Let us go down that path," Domini said almost in a whisper.

The spell of the place was descending upon her. This was surely a home of dreams, a haven where the sun came to lie down beneath the trees and sleep.

"What is your name?" she added.

"Smaïn," replied the Arab. "I was born in this garden. My father, Mohammed, was with Monsieur the Count."

He led the way over the sand, moving silently on his long, brown feet, straight as a reed in a windless place. Domini followed, holding her breath. Only sometimes she let her strong imagination play utterly at its will. She let it go now as she and Smaïn turned into the golden diapered shadows of the little path and came into the swaying mystery of the trees. The longing for secrecy, for remoteness, for the beauty of far away had sometimes haunted her, especially in the troubled moments of her life. Her heart, oppressed, had overleaped the horizon line in answer to a calling from hidden things beyond. Her emotions had wandered, seeking the great distances in which the dim purple twilight holds surely comfort for those who suffer. But she had never thought to find any garden of peace that realised her dreams. Nevertheress, she was already conscious that Smaïn with his rose was showing her the way to her ideal, that her feet were set upon its pathway, that its legendary trees were closing round her.

Behind the evergreen hedge she heard the liquid bubbling of a hidden waterfall, and when they had left the untempered sunlight behind them this murmur grew louder. It seemed as if the green gloom in which they walked acted as a sounding-board to the delicious voice. The little path wound on and on between two running rills of water, which slipped incessantly away under the broad and yellow-tipped leaves of dwarf palms, making a music so faint that it was more like a remembered sound in the mind than one which slid upon the ear. On either hand towered a jungle of trees brought to this home in the desert from all parts of the world.

There were many unknown to Domini, but she recognised several varieties of palms, acacias, gums, fig trees, chestnuts, poplars, false pepper trees, the huge olive trees called Jamelons, white laurels, indiarubber and cocoanut trees, bananas, bamboos, yuccas, many mimosas and quantities of tall eucalyptus trees. Thickets of scarlet geranium flamed in the twilight. The hibiscus lifted languidly its frail and rosy cup, and the red gold oranges gleamed amid leaves that looked as if they had been polished by an attentive fairy.

As she went with Smaïn farther into the recesses of the garden the voice of the waterfall died away. No birds were singing. Domini thought that perhaps they dared not sing lest they might wake the sun from its golden reveries, but afterwards, when she knew the garden better, she often heard them twittering with a subdued, yet happy, languor, as if joining in a nocturn upon the edge of sleep. Under the trees the sand was yellow, of a shade so voluptuously beautiful that she longed to touch it with her bare feet like Smaïn. Here and there it rose in symmetrical little pyramids, which hinted at absent gardeners, perhaps enjoying a siesta.

Never before had she fully understood the enchantment of green, quite realised how happy a choice was made on that day of Creation when it was showered prodigally over the world. But now, as she walked secretly over the yellow sand between the rills, following the floating green robe of Smaïn, she rested her eyes, and her soul, on countless mingling shades of the delicious colour; rough, furry green of geranium leaves, silver green of olives, black greer of distant palms from which the sun held aloof, faded green of the eucalyptus, rich, emerald green of fan-shaped, sunlit palms, hot, sultry green of bamboos, dull, drowsy green of mulberry trees and brooding chestnuts. It was a choir of colours in one colour, like a choir of boys all with treble voices singing to the sun.

Gold flickered everywhere, weaving patterns of enchantment, quivering, vital patterns of burning beauty. Down the narrow, branching paths that led to inner mysteries the light ran in and out, peeping between the divided leaves of plants, gliding over the slippery edges of the palm branches, trembling airily where the papyrus bent its antique head, dancing among the big blades of sturdy grass that sprouted in tufts here and there, resting languidly upon the glistening magnolias that were besieged by somnolent bees. All the greens and all the golds of Creation were surely met together in this profound retreat to prove the perfect harmony of earth with sun.

And now, growing accustomed to the pervading silence, Domini began to hear the tiny sounds that broke it. They came from the trees and plants. The airs were always astir, helping the soft designs of Nature, loosening a leaf from its stem and bearing it to the sand, striking a berry from its place and causing it to drop at Domini's feet, giving a faded geranium petal the courage to leave its more vivid companions and resign itself to the loss of the place it could no longer fill with beauty. Very delicate was the touch of the dying upon the yellow sand. It increased the sense of pervading mystery and made Domini more deeply conscious of the pulsing life of the garden.

"There is the room of the little dog," said Smaïn.

They had come out into a small open space, over which an immense cocoanut tree presided. Low box hedges ran round two squares of grass which were shadowed by date palms heavy with yellow fruit, and beneath some leaning mulberry trees Domini saw a tiny white room with two glass windows down to the ground. She went up to it and peeped in, smiling.

There, in a formal *salon*, with gilt chairs, oval, polished tables, faded rugs and shining mirrors, sat a purple china dog with his tail curled over his back sternly staring into vacancy. His expression and his attitude were autocratic and determined, betokening a tyrannical nature, and Domini peeped at him with precaution, holding herself very still lest he should become aware of her presence and resent it.

"Monsieur the Count paid much money for the dog," murmured Smaïn. "He is very valuable."

"How long has he been there?"

"For many years. He was there when I was born, and I have been married twice and divorced twice."

Domini turned from the window and looked at Smaïn with astonishment. He was smelling his rose like a dreamy child.

"You have been divorced twice?"

"Yes. Now I will show Madame the smoking-room."

They followed another of the innumerable alleys of the garden. This one was very narrow and less densely roofed with trees than those they had already traversed. Tall shrubs bent forward on either side of it, and their small leaves almost meeting were transformed by the radiant sunbeams into tongues of

pale fire, quivering, well nigh transparent. As she approached
them Domini could not resist the fancy that they would burn
her. A brown butterfly flitted forward between them and
vanished into the golden dream beyond.

"Oh, Smaïn, how you must love this garden!" she said.

A sort of ecstasy was waking within her. The pure air, the
caressing warmth, the enchanted stillness and privacy of this
domain touched her soul and body like the hands of a saint with
power to bless her.

"I could live here for ever," she added, "without once wishing to out into the world."

Smaïn looked drowsily pleased.

"We are coming to the centre of the garden," he said, as
they passed over a palm-wood bridge beneath which a stream
glided under the red petals of geraniums.

The tongues of flame were left behind. Green darkness
closed in upon them and the sand beneath their feet looked
blanched. The sense of mystery increased, for the trees were
enormous and grew densely here. Pine needles lay upon the
ground, and there was a stirring of sudden wind far up above
their heads in the tree-tops.

"This is the part of the garden that Monsieur the Count
loves," said Smaïn. "He comes here every day."

"What is that?" said Domini, suddenly stopping on the
pale sand.

A thin and remote sound stole to them down the alley, clear
and frail as the note of a night bird.

"It is Larbi playing upon the flute. He is in love. That is
why he plays when he ought to be watering the flowers and
raking out the sand."

The distant love-song of the flute seemed to Domini the last
touch of enchantment making this indeed a wonderland. She
could not move, and held up her hands to stay the feet of Smaïn,
who was quite content to wait. Never before had she heard
any music that seemed to mean and suggest so much to her as
this African tune played by an enamoured gardener. Queer
and uncouth as it was, distorted with ornaments and tricked
out with abrupt runs, exquisitely unnecessary grace notes, and
sudden twitterings prolonged till a strange and frivolous Eternity tripped in to banish Time, it grasped Domini's fancy and
laid a spell upon her imagination. For it sounded as naïvely
sincere as the song of a bird, and as if the heart from which it
flowed were like the heart of a child, a place of revelation, not of

concealment. The sun made men careless here. They opened their windows to it, and one could see into the warm and glowing rooms. Domini looked at the gentle Arab youth beside her, already twice married and twice divorced. She listened to Larbi's unending song of love. And she said to herself, " These people, uncivilised or not, at least live, and I have been dead all my life, dead in life." That was horribly possible. She knew it as she felt the enormously powerful spell of Africa descending upon her, enveloping her quietly but irresistibly. The dream of this garden was quick with a vague and yet fierce stirring of realities. There was a murmuring of many small and distant voices, like the voices of innumerable tiny things following restless activities in a deep forest. As she stood there the last grain of European dust was lifted from Domini's soul. How deeply it had been buried, and for how many years.

" The greatest act of man is the act of renunciation." She had just heard those words. The eyes of the priest had flamed as he spoke them, and she had caught the spark of his enthusiasm. But now another fire seemed lit within her, and she found herself marvelling at such austerity. Was it not a fanatical defiance flung into the face of the sun? She shrank from her own thought, like one startled, and walked on softly in the green darkness.

Larbi's flute became more distant. Again and again it repeated the same queer little melody, changing the ornamentation at the fantasy of the player. She looked for him among the trees but saw no one. He must be in some very secret place. Smaïn touched her.

" Look ! " he said, and his voice was very low.

He parted the branches of some palms with his delicate hands, and Domini, peering between them, saw in a place of deep shadows an isolated square room, whose white walls were almost entirely concealed by masses of purple bougainvillea. It had a flat roof. In three of its sides were large arched window-spaces without windows. In the fourth was a narrow doorway without a door. Immense fig trees and palms and thickets of bamboo towered around it and leaned above it. And it was circled by a narrow riband of finely-raked sand.

" That is the smoking-room of Monsieur the Count," said Smaïn. " He spends many hours there. Come and I will show the inside to Madame."

They turned to the left and went towards the room. The flute was close to them now.

"Larbi must be in there," Domini whispered to Smaïn, as a person whispers in a church.

"No, he is among the trees beyond."

"But someone is there."

She pointed to the arched window-space nearest to them. A thin spiral of blue-grey smoke curled through it and evaporated into the shadows of the trees. After a moment it was followed gently and deliberately by another.

"It is not Larbi. He would not go in there. It must be——"

He paused. A tall, middle-aged man had come to the doorway of the little room and looked out into the garden with bright eyes.

CHAPTER VI

DOMINI drew back and glanced at Smaïn. She was not accustomed to feeling intrusive, and the sudden sensation rendered her uneasy.

"It is Monsieur the Count," Smaïn said calmly and quite aloud.

The man in the doorway took off his soft hat, as if the words effected an introduction between Domini and him.

"You were coming to see my little room, Madame?" he said in French. "If I may show it to you I shall feel honoured."

The timbre of his voice was harsh and grating, yet it was a very interesting, even a seductive, voice, and, Domini thought, peculiarly full of vivid life, though not of energy. His manner at once banished her momentary discomfort. There is a freemasonry between people born in the same social world. By the way in which Count Anteoni took off his hat and spoke she knew at once that all was right.

"Thank you, Monsieur," she answered. "I was told at the gate you gave permission to travellers to visit your garden."

"Certainly."

He spoke a few words in fluent Arabic to Smaïn, who turned away and disappeared among the trees.

"I hope you will allow me to accompany you through the rest of the garden," he said, turning again to Domini. "It will give me great pleasure."

"It is very kind of you."

The way in which the change of companion had been effected

made it seem a pleasant, inevitable courtesy, which neither implied nor demanded anything."

" This is my little retreat," Count Anteoni continued, standing aside from the doorway that Domini might enter.

She drew a long breath when she was within.

The floor was of fine sand, beaten flat and hard, and strewn with Eastern rugs of faint and delicate hues, dim greens and faded rose colours, grey-blues and misty topaz yellows. Round the white walls ran broad divans, also white, covered with prayer rugs from Bagdad, and large cushions, elaborately worked in dull gold and silver thread, with patterns of ibises and flamingoes in flight. In the four angles of the room stood four tiny smoking-tables of rough palm wood, holding hammered ash-trays of bronze, green bronze torches for the lighting of cigarettes, and vases of Chinese dragon china filled with velvety red roses, gardenias and sprigs of orange blossom. Leather footstools, covered with Tunisian thread-work, lay beside them. From the arches of the window-spaces hung old Moorish lamps of copper, fitted with small panes of dull jewelled glass, such as may be seen in venerable church windows. In a round copper brazier, set on one of the window-seats, incense twigs were drowsily burning and giving out thin, dwarf columns of scented smoke. Through the archways and the narrow doorway the dense walls of leafage were visible standing on guard about this airy hermitage, and the hot purple blossoms of the bougainvillea shed a cloud of colour through the bosky dimness.

And still the flute of Larbi showered soft, clear, whimsical music from some hidden place close by.

Domini looked at her host, who was standing by the doorway, leaning one arm against the ivory-white wall.

" This is my first day in Africa," she said simply. " You may imagine what I think of your garden, what I feel in it. I needn't tell you. Indeed, I am sure the travellers you so kindly let in must often have worried you with their raptures."

" No," he answered, with a still gravity which yet suggested kindness, " for I leave nearly always before the travellers come. That sounds a little rude? But you would not be in Beni-Mora at this season, Madame, if it could include you."

" I have come here for peace," Domini replied simply.

She said it because she felt as if it was already understood by her companion.

Count Anteoni took down his arm from the white wall and

pulled a branch of the purple flowers slowly towards him through the doorway.

"There is peace—what is generally called so, at least—in Beni-Mora," he answered rather slowly and meditatively. "That is to say, there is similarity of day with day, night with night. The sun shines untiringly over the desert, and the desert always hints at peace."

He let the flowers go, and they sprang softly back, and hung quivering in the space beyond his thin figure. Then he added:

"Perhaps one should not say more than that."

"No."

Domini sat down for a moment. She looked up at him with her direct eyes and at the shaking flowers. The sound of Larbi's flute was always in her ears.

"But may not one think, feel a little more?" she asked.

"Oh, why not? If one can, if one must? But how? Africa is as fierce and full of meaning as a furnace, you know."

"Yes, I know—already," she replied.

His words expressed what she had already felt here in Beni-Mora, surreptitiously and yet powerfully. He said it, and last night the African hautboy had said it. Peace and a flame. Could they exist together, blended, married?

"Africa seems to me to agree through contradiction," she added, smiling a little, and touching the snowy wall with her right hand. "But then, this is my first day."

"Mine was when I was a boy of sixteen."

"This garden wasn't here then?"

"No. I had it made. I came here with my mother. She spoilt me. She let me have my whim."

"This garden is your boy's whim?"

"It was. Now it is a man's——"

He seemed to hesitate.

"Paradise," suggested Domini.

"I think I was going to say hiding-place."

There was no bitterness in his odd, ugly voice, yet surely the words implied bitterness. The wounded, the fearful, the disappointed, the condemned hide. Perhaps he remembered this, for he added rather quickly:

"I come here to be foolish, Madame, for I come here to think. This is my special thinking place."

"How strange!" Domini exclaimed impulsively, and leaning forward on the divan.

" Is it? "

" I only mean that already Beni-Mora has seemed to me the ideal place for that."

" For thought? "

" For finding out interior truth."

Count Anteoni looked at her rather swiftly and searchingly. His eyes were not large, but they were bright, and held none of the languor so often seen in the eyes of his countrymen. His face was expressive through its mobility rather than through its contours. The features were small and refined, not noble, but unmistakably aristocratic. The nose was sensitive, with wide nostrils. A long and straight moustache, turning slightly grey, did not hide the mouth, which had unusually pale lips. The ears were set very flat against the head, and were finely shaped. The chin was pointed. The general look of the whole face was tense, critical, conscious, but in the defiant rather than in the timid sense. Such an expression belongs to men who would always be aware of the thoughts and feelings of others concerning them, but who would throw those thoughts and feelings off as decisively and energetically as a dog shakes the water-drops from its coat on emerging from a swim.

" And sending it forth, like Ishmael, to shift for itself in the desert," he said.

The odd remark sounded like neither statement nor question, merely like the sudden exclamation of a mind at work.

" Will you allow me to take you through the rest of the garden, Madame? " he added in a more formal voice.

" Thank you," said Domini, who had already got up, moved by the examining look cast at her.

There was nothing in it to resent, and she had not resented it, but it had recalled her to the consciousness that they were utter strangers to each other.

As they came out on the pale riband of sand which circled the little room Domini said :

" How wild and extraordinary that tune is! "

" Larbi's. I suppose it is, but no African music seems strange to me. I was born on my father's estate, near Tunis. He was a Sicilian, but came to North Africa each winter. I have always heard the tom-toms and the pipes, and I know nearly all the desert songs of the nomads."

" This is a love-song, isn't it? "

" Yes. Larbi is always in love, they tell me. Each new dancer catches him in her net. Happy Larbi! "

" Because he can love so easily? "

" Or unlove so easily. Look at him, Madame."

At a little distance, under a big banana tree, and half hidden by clumps of scarlet geraniums, Domini saw a huge and very ugly Arab, with an almost black skin, squatting on his heels, with a long yellow and red flute between his thick lips. His eyes were bent down, and he did not see them, but went on busily playing, drawing from his flute coquettish phrases with his big and bony fingers.

" And I pay him so much a week all the year round for doing that," the Count said.

His grating voice sounded kind and amused. They walked on, and Larbi's tune died gradually away.

" Somehow I can't be angry with the follies and vices of the Arabs," the Count continued. " I love them as they are; idle, absurdly amorous, quick to shed blood, gay as children, whimsical as—well, Madame, were I talking to a man I might dare to say pretty women."

" Why not? "

" I will, then. I glory in their ingrained contempt of civilisation. But I like them to say their prayers five times in the day as it is commanded, and no Arab who touches alcohol in defiance of the Prophet's law sets foot in my garden."

There was a touch of harshness in his voice as he said the last words, the sound of the autocrat. Somehow Domini liked it. This man had convictions, and strong ones. That was certain. There was something oddly unconventional in him which something in her responded to. He was perfectly polite, and yet, she was quite sure, absolutely careless of opinion. Certainly he was very much a man.

" It is pleasant, too," he resumed, after a slight pause, " to be surrounded by absolutely thoughtless people with thoughtful faces and mysterious eyes—wells without truth at the bottom of them."

She laughed.

" No one must think here but you! "

" I prefer to keep all the folly to myself. Is not that a grand cocoanut? "

He pointed to a tree so tall that it seemed soaring to heaven.

" Yes, indeed. Like the one that presides over the purple dog."

" You have seen my fetish? "

" Smain showed him to me, with reverence."

"Oh, he is king here. The Arabs declare that on moonlight nights they have heard him joining in the chorus of the Kabyle dogs."

"You speak almost as if you believed it."

"Well, I believe more here than I believe anywhere else. That is partly why I come here."

"I can understand that—I mean believing much here."

"What! Already you feel the spell of Beni-Mora, the desert spell! Yes, there is enchantment here—and so I never stay too long."

"For fear of what?"

Count Anteoni was walking easily beside her. He walked from the hips, like many Sicilians, swaying very slightly, as if he liked to be aware how supple his body still was. As Domini spoke he stopped. They were now at a place where four paths joined, and could see four vistas of green and gold, of magical sunlight and shadow.

"I scarcely know; of being carried who knows where—in mind or heart. Oh, there is danger in Beni-Mora, Madame, there is danger. This startling air is full of influences, of desert spirits."

He looked at her in a way she could not understand—but it made her think of the perfume-seller in his little dark room, and of the sudden sensation she had had that mystery coils, like a black serpent, in the shining heart of the East.

"And now, Madame, which path shall we take? This one leads to my drawing-room, that on the right to the Moorish bath."

"And that?"

"That one goes straight down to the wall that overlooks the Sahara."

"Please let us take it."

"The desert spirits are calling to you? But you are wise. What makes this garden rather remarkable is not its arrangement, the number and variety of its trees, but the fact that it lies flush with the Sahara—like a man's thoughts of truth with Truth, perhaps."

He turned up the tail of the sentence and his harsh voice gave a little grating crack.

"I don't believe they are so different from one another as the garden and the desert."

She looked at him directly.

"It would be too ironical."

"But nothing is," the Count said.

"You have discovered that in this garden?"

"Ah, it is new to you, Madame!"

For the first time there was a sound of faint bitterness in his voice.

"One often discovers the saddest thing in the loveliest place," he added. "There you begin to see the desert."

Far away, at the small orifice of the tunnel of trees down which they were walking, appeared a glaring patch of fierce and quivering sunlight.

"I can only see the sun," Domini said.

"I know so well what it hides that I imagine I actually see the desert. One loves one's kind, assiduous liar. Isn't it so?"

"The imagination? But perhaps I am not disposed to allow that it is a liar."

"Who knows? You may be right."

He looked at her kindly with his bright eyes. It did not seem to strike him that their conversation was curiously intimate, considering that they were strangers to one another, that he did not even know her name. Domini wondered suddenly how old he was. That look made him seem much older than he had seemed before. There was such an expression in his eyes as may sometimes be seen in eyes that look at a child who is kissing a rag doll with deep and determined affection. "Kiss your doll!" they seemed to say. "Put off the years when you must know that dolls can never return a kiss."

"I begin to see the desert now," Domini said after a moment of silent walking. "How wonderful it is!"

"Yes, it is. The most wonderful thing in Nature. You will think it much more wonderful when you fancy you know it well."

"Fancy!"

"I don't think anyone can ever really know the desert. It is the thing that keeps calling, and does not permit one to draw near."

"But then, one might learn to hate it."

"I don't think so. Truth does just the same, you know. And yet men keep on trying to draw near."

"But sometimes they succeed."

"Do they? Not when they live in gardens."

He laughed for the first time since they had been together, and all his face was covered with a network of little moving lines.

" One should never live in a garden, Madame."

" I will try to take your word for it, but the task will be difficult."

" Yes? More difficult, perhaps, when you see what lies beside my thoughts of truth."

As he spoke they came out from the tunnel and were seized by the fierce hands of the sun. It was within half an hour of noon, and the radiance was blinding. Domini put up her parasol sharply, like one startled. She stopped.

" But how tremendous! " she exclaimed.

Count Anteoni laughed again, and drew down the brim of his grey hat over his eyes. The hand with which he did it was almost as burnt as an Arab's.

" You are afraid of it? "

" No, no. But it startled me. We don't know the sun really in Europe."

" No. Not even in Southern Italy, not even in Sicily. It is fierce there in summer, but it seems further away. Here it insists on the most intense intimacy. If you can bear it we might sit down for a moment? "

" Please."

All along the edge of the garden, from the villa to the boundary of Count Anteoni's domain, ran a straight high wall made of earth bricks hardened by the sun and topped by a coping of palm wood painted white. This wall was some eight feet high on the side next to the desert, but the garden was raised in such a way that the inner side was merely a low parapet running along the sand path. In this parapet were cut small seats, like window-seats, in which one could rest and look full upon the desert as from a little cliff. Domini sat down on one of them, and the Count stood by her, resting one foot on the top of the wall and leaning his right arm on his knee.

" There is the world on which I look for my hiding-place," he said. " A vast world, isn't it? "

Domini nodded without speaking.

Immediately beneath them, in the narow shadow of the wall, was a path of earth and stones which turned off at the right at the end of the garden into the oasis. Beyond lay the vast river bed, a chaos of hot boulders bounded by ragged low earth cliffs, interspersed here and there with small pools of gleaming water. These cliffs were yellow. From their edge stretched the desert, as Eternity stretches from the edge of Time. Only to the left was the immeasurable expanse intruded upon by a long spur of mountains, which ran out boldly for some distance and then stopped abruptly, conquered and abashed by the imperious flats. Beneath the mountains were low, tent-like, cinnamon-coloured undulations, which reminded Domini of those made by a shaken-out sheet, one smaller than the other till they melted into the level. The summits of the most distant mountains, which leaned away as if in fear of the desert, were dark and mistily purple. Their flanks were iron grey at this hour, flecked in the hollows with the faint mauve and pink which became carnation colour when the sun set.

Domini scarcely looked at them. Till now she had always thought that she loved mountains. The desert suddenly made them insignificant, almost mean to her. She turned her eyes towards the flat spaces. It was in them that majesty lay, mystery, power, and all deep and significant things. In the midst of the river bed, and quite near, rose a round and squat white tower with a small cupola. Beyond it, on the little cliff, was a tangle of palms where a tiny oasis sheltered a few native huts. At an immense distance, here and there, other oases showed as dark stains show on the sea where there are hidden rocks. And still farther away, on all hands, the desert seemed to curve up slightly like a shallow wine-hued cup to the misty blue horizon line, which resembled a faintly seen and mysterious tropical sea, so distant that its sultry murmur was lost in the embrace of the intervening silence.

An Arab passed on the path below the wall. He did not see them. A white dog with curling lips ran beside him. He was singing to himself in a low, inward voice. He went on and turned towards the oasis, still singing as he walked slowly.

" Do you know what he is singing? " the Count asked.

Domini shook her head. She was straining her ears to hear the melody as long as possible.

" It is a desert song of the freed negroes of Touggourt—' No one but God and I knows what is in my heart.' "

Domini lowered her parasol to conceal her face. In the distance she could still hear the song, but it was dying away.

" Oh! what is going to happen to me here? " she thought.

Count Anteoni was looking away from her now across the desert. A strange impulse rose up in her. She could not resist it. She put down her parasol, exposing herself to the blinding sunlight, knelt down on the hot sand, leaned her arms on the white parapet, put her chin in the upturned palms of her hands and stared into the desert almost fiercely.

"No one but God and I knows what is in my heart," she thought. "But that's not true, that's not true. For I don't know."

The last echo of the Arab's song fainted on the blazing air. Surely it had changed now. Surely, as he turned into the shadows of the palms, he was singing, "No one but God knows what is in my heart." Yes, he was singing that. "No one but God—no one but God."

Count Anteoni looked down at her. She did not notice it, and he kept his eyes on her for a moment. Then he turned to the desert again.

By degrees, as she watched, Domini became aware of many things indicative of life, and of many lives in the tremendous expanse that at first had seemed empty of all save sun and mystery. She saw low, scattered tents, far-off columns of smoke rising. She saw a bird pass across the blue and vanish towards the mountains. Black shapes appeared among the tiny mounds of earth, crowned with dusty grass and dwarf tamarisk bushes. She saw them move, like objects in a dream, slowly through the shimmering gold. They were feeding camels, guarded by nomads whom she could not see.

At first she persistently explored the distances, carried forcibly by an *élan* of her whole nature to the remotest points her eyes could reach. Then she withdrew her gaze gradually, reluctantly, from the hidden summoning lands, whose verges she had with difficulty gained, and looked, at first with apprehension, upon the nearer regions. But her apprehension died when she found that the desert transmutes what is close as well as what is remote, suffuses even that which the hand could almost touch with wonder, beauty, and the deepest, most strange significance.

Quite near in the river bed she saw an Arab riding towards the desert upon a prancing black horse. He mounted a steep bit of path and came out on the flat ground at the cliff top. Then he set his horse at a gallop, raising his bridle hand and striking his heels into the flanks of the beast. And each of his movements, each of the movements of his horse, was profoundly interesting, and held the attention of the onlooker in a vice, as if the fates of worlds depended upon where he was carried and how soon he reached his goal. A string of camels laden with wooden bales met him on the way, and this chance encounter seemed to Domini fraught with almost terrible possibilities. Why? She did not ask herself. Again she sent her

gaze further, to the black shapes moving stealthily among the
little mounds, to the spirals of smoke rising into the glimmering
air. Who guarded those camels? Who fed those distant
fires? Who watched beside them? It seemed of vital consequence to her that she should know.

Count Anteoni took out his watch and glanced at it.

"I am looking to see if it is nearly the hour of prayer," he
said. "When I am in Beni-Mora I usually come here then."

"You turn to the desert as the faithful turn towards
Mecca?"

"Yes. I like to see men praying in the desert."

He spoke indifferently, but Domini felt suddenly sure that
within him there were depths of imagination, of tenderness,
even perhaps of mysticism.

"An atheist in the desert is unimaginable," he added. "In
cathedrals they may exist very likely, and even feel at home. I
have seen cathedrals in which I could believe I was one, but—
how many human beings can you see in the desert at this
moment, Madame?"

Domini, still with her round chin in her hands, searched the
blazing region with her eyes. She saw three running figures
with the train of camels which was now descending into the
river bed. In the shadow of the low white tower two more
were huddled, motionless. She looked away to right and left,
but saw only the shallow pools, the hot and gleaming boulders,
and beyond the yellow cliffs the brown huts peeping through
the palms. The horseman had disappeared.

"I can see five," she answered.

"Ah! you are not accustomed to the desert."

"There are more?"

"I could count up to a dozen. Which are yours?"

"The men with the camels and the men under that tower."

"There are four playing the *jeu des dames* in the shadow
of the cliff opposite to us. There is one asleep under a red rock
where the path ascends into the desert. And there are two
more just at the edge of the little oasis—Filiash, as it is called.
One is standing under a palm, and one is pacing up and down."

"You must have splendid eyes."

"They are trained to the desert. But there are probably a
score of Arabs within sight whom I don't see."

"Oh! now I see the men at the edge of the oasis. How
oddly that one is moving. He goes up and down like a sailor on
the quarter-deck."

"Yes, it is curious.   And he is in the full blaze of the sun.
That can't be an Arab."

He drew a silver whistle from his waistcoat pocket, put it to
his lips and sounded a call.   In a moment Smain same running
lightly over the sand.   Count Anteoni said something to him in
Arabic.   He disappeared, and speedily returned with a pair of
field-glasses.   While he was gone Domini watched the two doll-
like figures on the cliff in silence.   One was standing under a
large isolated palm tree absolutely still, as Arabs often stand.
The other, at a short distance from him and full in the sun,
went to and fro, to and fro, always measuring the same space
of desert, and turning and returning at two given points which
never varied.   He walked like a man hemmed in by walls, yet
around him were the infinite spaces.   The effect was singularly
unpleasant upon Domini.   All things in the desert, as she had
already noticed, became almost terribly significant, and this
peculiar activity seemed full of some extraordinary and even
horrible meaning.   She watched it with straining eyes.

Count Anteoni took the glasses from Smaïn and looked
through them, adjusting them carefully to suit his sight.

"*Ecco!*" he said.   "I was right.   That man is not an
Arab."

He moved the glasses and glanced at Domini.

"You are not the only traveller here, Madame."

He looked through the glasses again.

"I knew that," she said.

"Indeed?"

"There is one at my hotel."

"Possibly this is he.   He makes me think of a caged tiger,
who has been so long in captivity that when you let him out he
still imagines the bars to be all round him.   What was he
like?"

All the time he was speaking he was staring intently through
the glasses.   As Domini did not reply he removed them from
his eyes and glanced at her inquiringly.

"I am trying to think what he looked like," she said slowly.
"But I feel that I don't know.   He was quite unlike any ordinary man."

"Would you care to see if you can recognise him?   These
are really marvellous glasses."

Domini took them from him with some eagerness.

"Twist them about till they suit your eyes."

At first she could see nothing but a fierce yellow glare.   She turned the screw and gradually the desert came to her, startlingly distinct. The boulders of the river bed were enormous. She could see the veins of colour in them, a lizard running over one of them and disappearing into a dark crevice, then the white tower and the Arabs beneath it. One was an old man yawning; the other a boy. He rubbed the tip of his brown nose, and she saw the henna stains upon his nails. She lifted the glasses slowly and with precaution. The tower ran away. She came to the low cliff, to the brown huts and the palms, passed them one by one, and reached the last, which was separated from its companions. Under it stood a tall Arab in a garment like a white night-shirt.

" He looks as if he had only one eye! " she exclaimed.

" The palm-tree man—yes."

She travelled cautiously away from him, keeping the glasses level.

" Ah! " she said on an indrawn breath.

As she spoke the thin, nasal cry of a distant voice broke upon her ears, prolonging a strange call.

" The Mueddin," said Count Anteoni.

And he repeated in a low tone the words of the angel to the prophet: " Oh thou that art covered arise . . . and magnify thy Lord; and purify thy clothes, and depart from uncleanness."

The call died away and was renewed three times. The old man and the boy beneath the tower turned their faces towards Mecca, fell upon their knees and bowed their heads to the hot stones. The tall Arab under the palm sank down swiftly. Domini kept the glasses at her eyes. Through them, as in a sort of exaggerated vision, very far off, yet intensely distinct, she saw the man with whom she had travelled in the train. He went to and fro, to and fro on the burning ground till the fourth call of the Mueddin died away. Then, as he approached the isolated palm tree and saw the Arab beneath it fall to the earth and bow his long body in prayer, he paused and stood still as if in contemplation. The glasses were so powerful that it was possible to see the expressions on faces even at that distance. The expression on the traveller's face was, or seemed to be, at first one of profound attention. But this changed swiftly as he watched the bowing figure, and was succeeded by a look of uneasiness, then of fierce disgust, then—surely— of fear or horror. He turned sharply away like a driven man, and hurried off along the cliff edge in a striding walk, quickening his steps each moment till his departure became a flight. He disappeared behind a projection of earth where the path sank to the river bed.

Domini laid the glasses down on the wall and looked at Count Anteoni.

" You say an atheist in the desert is unimaginable? "

" Isn't it true? "

" Has an atheist a hatred, a horror of prayer? "

" Chi lo sa? The devil shrank away from the lifted Cross."

" Because he knew how much that was true it symbolised."

" No doubt had it been otherwise he would have jeered, not cowered. But why do you ask me this question, Madame? "

" I have just seen a man flee from the sight of prayer."

" Your fellow-traveller? "

" Yes. It was horrible."

She gave him back the glasses.

" They reveal that which should be hidden," she said.

Count Anteoni took the glasses slowly from her hands. As he bent to do it he looked steadily at her, and she could not read the expression in his eyes.

" The desert is full of truth. Is that what you mean? " he asked.

She made no reply. Count Anteoni stretched out his hand to the shining expanse before them.

" The man who is afraid of prayer is unwise to set foot beyond the palm trees," he said.

" Why unwise? "

He answered her very gravely.

" The Arabs have a saying: ' The desert is the garden of Allah.' "

.   .   .   .   .

Domini did not ascend the tower of the hotel that morning. She had seen enough for the moment, and did not wish to disturb her impressions by adding to them. So she walked back to the Hotel du Désert with Batouch.

Count Anteoni had said good-bye to her at the door of the garden, and had begged her to come again whenever she liked, and to spend as many hours there as she pleased.

" I shall take you at your word," she said frankly. " I feel that I may."

As they shook hands she gave him her card. He took out his.

" By the way," he said, " the big hotel you passed in coming here is mine. I built it to prevent a more hideous one being built, and let it to the proprietor. You might like to ascend the tower. The view at sundown is incomparable. At present the hotel is shut, but the guardian will show you everything if you give him my card."

He pencilled some words in Arabic on the back from right to left.

" You write Arabic, too? " Domini said, watching the form-ing of the pretty curves with interest.

" Oh, yes; I am more than half African, though my father was a Sicilian and my mother a Roman."

He gave her the card, took off his hat and bowed. When the tall white door was softly shut by Smaïn, Domini felt rather like a new Eve expelled from Paradise, without an Adam as a companion in exile.

" Well, Madame? " said Batouch. " Have I spoken the truth? "

" Yes. No European garden can be so beautiful as that. Now I am going straight home."

She smiled to herself as she said the last word.

Outside the hotel they found Hadj looking ferocious. He exchanged some words with Batouch, accompanying them with violent gestures. When he had finished speaking he spat upon the ground.

" What is the matter with him? " Domini asked.

" The Monsieur who is staying here would not take him to-day, but went into the desert alone. Hadj wishes that the nomads may cut his throat, and that his flesh may be eaten by jackals. Hadj is sure that he is a bad man and will come to a bad end."

" Because he does not want a guide every day! But neither shall I."

" Madame is quite different. I would give my life for Madame."

" Don't do that, but go this afternoon and find me a horse. I don't want a quiet one, but something with devil, something that a Spahi would like to ride."

The desert spirits were speaking to her body as well as to her mind. A physical audacity was stirring in her, and she longed to give it vent.

" Madame is like the lion. She is afraid of nothing."

" You speak without knowing, Batouch. Don't come for me

this afternoon, but bring round a horse, if you can find one, to-morrow morning."

" This very evening I will——"

" No, Batouch. I said to-morrow morning."

She spoke with a quiet but inflexible decision which silenced him. Then she gave him ten francs and went into the dark house, from which the burning noonday sun was carefully excluded. She intended to rest after *déjeuner,* and towards sunset to go to the big hotel and mount alone to the summit of the tower.

It was half-past twelve, and a faint rattle of knives and forks from the *salle-à-manger* told her that *déjeuner* was ready. She went upstairs, washed her face and hands in cold water, stood still while Suzanne shook the dust from her gown, and then descended to the public room. The keen air had given her an appetite.

The *salle-à-manger* was large and shady, and was filled with small tables, at only three of which were people sitting. Four French officers sat together at one. A small, fat, perspiring man of middle age, probably a commercial traveller, who had eyes like a melancholy toad, was at another, eating olives with anxious rapidity, and wiping his forehead perpetually with a dirty white handkerchief. At the third was the priest with whom Domini had spoken in the church. His napkin was tucked under his beard, and he was drinking soup as he bent well over his plate.

A young Arab waiter, with a thin, dissipated face, stood near the door in bright yellow slippers. When Domini came in he stole forward to show her to her table, making a soft, shuffling sound on the polished wooden floor. The priest glanced up over his napkin, rose and bowed. The French officers stared with an interest they were too chivalrous to attempt to conceal. Only the fat little man was entirely unconcerned. He wiped his forehead, stuck his fork deftly into an olive, and continued to look like a melancholy toad entangled by fate in commercial pursuits.

Domini's table was by a window, across which green Venetian shutters were drawn. It was at a considerable distance from the other guests, who did not live in the house, but came there each day for their meals. Near it she noticed a table laid for one person, and so arranged that if he came to *déjeuner* he would sit exactly opposite to her. She wondered if it was for the man at whom she had just been looking through Count

Anteoni's field-glasses, the man who had fled from prayer in the "Garden of Allah." As she glanced at the empty chair standing before the knives and forks, and the white cloth, she was uncertain whether she wished it to be filled by the traveller or not. She felt his presence in Beni-Mora as a warring element. That she knew. She knew also that she had come there to find peace, a great calm and remoteness in which she could at last grow, develop, loose her true self from cramping bondage, come to an understanding with herself, face her heart and soul, and—as it were—look them in the eyes and know them for what they were, good or evil. In the presence of this total stranger there was something unpleasantly distracting which she could not and did not ignore, something which roused her antagonism and which at the same time compelled her attention. She had been conscious of it in the train, conscious of it in the tunnel at twilight, at night in the hotel, and once again in Count Anteoni's garden. This man intruded himself, no doubt unconsciously, or even against his will, into her sight, her thoughts, each time that she was on the point of giving herself to what Count Anteoni called "the desert spirits." So it had been when the train ran out of the tunnel into the blue country. So it had been again when she leaned on the white wall and gazed out over the shining fastnesses of the sun. He was there like an enemy, like something determined, egoistical, that said to her, "You would look at the greatness of the desert, at immensity, infinity, God!—Look at me." And she could not turn her eyes away. Each time the man had, as if without effort, conquered the great competing power, fastened her thoughts upon himself, set her imagination working about his life, even made her heart beat faster with some thrill of—what? Was it pity? Was it a faint horror? She knew that to call the feeling merely repugnance would not be sincere. The intensity, the vitality of the force shut up in a human being almost angered her at this moment as she looked at the empty chair and realised all that it had suddenly set at work. There was something insolent in humanity as well as something divine, and just then she felt the insolence more than the divinity. Terrifically greater, more overpowering than man, the desert was yet also somehow less than man, feebler, vaguer. Or else how could she have been grasped, moved, turned to curiosity, surmise, almost to a sort of dread— all at the desert's expense—by the distant, moving figure seen through the glasses?

Yes, as she looked at the little white table and thought of all this, Domini began to feel angry. But she was capable of effort, whether mental or physical, and now she resolutely switched her mind off from the antagonistic stranger and devoted her thoughts to the priest, whose narrow back she saw down the room in the distance. As she ate her fish—a mystery of the seas of Robertville—she imagined his quiet existence in this remote place, sunny day succeeding sunny day, each one surely so like its brother that life must become a sort of dream, through which the voice of the church bell called melodiously and the incense rising before the altar shed a drowsy perfume. How strange it must be really to live in Beni-Mora, to have your house, your work here, your friendships here, your duties here, perhaps here too the tiny section of earth which would hold at the last your body. It must be strange and monotonous, and yet surely rather sweet, rather safe.

The officers lifted their heads from their plates, the fat man stared, the priest looked quietly up over his napkin, and the Arab waiter slipped forward with attentive haste. For the swing door of the *salle-à-manger* at this moment was pushed open, and the traveller—so Domini called him in her thoughts—entered and stood looking with hesitation from one table to another.

Domini did not glance up. She knew who it was and kept her eyes resolutely on her plate. She heard the Arab speak, a loud noise of stout boots tramping over the wooden floor, and the creak of a chair receiving a surely tired body. The traveller sat down heavily. She went on slowly eating the large Robert-ville fish, which was like something between a trout and a herring. When she had finished it she gazed straight before her at the cloth, and strove to resume her thoughts of the priest's life in Beni-Mora. But she could not. It seemed to her as if she were back again in Count Anteoni's garden. She looked once more through the glasses, and heard the four cries of the Mueddin, and saw the pacing figure in the burning heat, the Arab bent in prayer, the one who watched him, the flight. And she was indignant with herself for her strange inability to govern her mind. It seemed to her a pitiful thing of which she should be ashamed.

She heard the waiter set down a plate upon the traveller's table, and then the noise of a liquid being poured into a glass. She could not keep her eyes down any more. Besides, why should she? Beni-Mora was breeding in her a self-conscious-ness—or a too acute consciousness of others—that was unnatural in her. She had never been sensitive like this in her former life, but the fierce African sun seemed now to have thawed the ice of her indifference. She felt everything with almost unpleasant acuteness. All her senses seemed to her sharpened. She saw, she heard, as she had never seen and heard till now. Suddenly she remembered her almost violent prayer—" Let me be alive! Let me feel! " and she was aware that such a prayer might have an answer that would be terrible.

Looking up thus with a kind of severe determination, she saw the man again. He was eating and was not looking towards her, and she fancied that his eyes were downcast with as much conscious resolution as hers had been a moment before. He wore the same suit as he had worn in the train, but now it was flecked with desert dust. She could not " place " him at all. He was not of the small, fat man's order. They would have nothing in common. With the French officers? She could not imagine how he would be with them. The only other man in the room—the servant had gone out for the moment—was the priest. He and the priest—they would surely be antagonists. Had he not turned aside to avoid the priest in the tunnel? Probably he was one of those many men who actively hate the priesthood, to whom the soutane is anathema. Could he find pleasant companionship with such a man as Count Anteoni, an original man, no doubt, but also a cultivated and easy man of the world? She smiled internally at the mere thought. Whatever this stranger might be she felt that he was as far from being a man of the world as she was from being a Cockney sempstress or a veiled favourite in a harem. She could not, she found, imagine him easily at home with any type of human being with which she was acquainted. Yet no doubt, like all men, he had somewhere friends, relations, possibly even a wife, children.

No doubt—then why could she not believe it?

The man had finished his fish. He rested his broad, burnt hands on the table on each side of his plate and looked at them steadily. Then he turned his head and glanced sideways at the priest, who was behind him to the right. Then he looked again at his hands. And Domini knew that all the time he was thinking about her, as she was thinking about him. She felt the violence of his thought like the violence of a hand striking her.

The Arab waiter brought her some ragout of mutton and peas, and she looked down again at her plate.

As she left the room after *déjeuner* the priest again got up and bowed. She stopped for a moment to speak to him. All the French officers surveyed her tall, upright figure and broad, athletic shoulders with intent admiration. Domini knew it and was indifferent. If a hundred French soldiers had been staring at her critically she would not have cared at all. She was not a shy woman and was in nowise uncomfortable when many eyes were fixed upon her. So she stood and talked a little to the priest about Count Anteoni and her pleasure in his garden. And as she did so, feeling her present calm self-possession, she wondered secretly at the wholly unnatural turmoil— she called it that, exaggerating her feeling because it was unusual—in which she had been a few minutes before as she sat at her table.

The priest spoke well of Count Anteoni.

" He is very generous," he said.

Then he paused, twisting his napkin, and added:

" But I never have any real intercourse with him, Madame, I believe he comes here in search of solitude. He spends days and even weeks alone shut up in his garden."

" Thinking," she said.

The priest looked slightly surprised.

" It would be difficult not to think, Madame, would it not? "

" Oh, yes. But Count Anteoni thinks rather as a Bashi-Bazouk fights, I fancy."

She heard a chair creak in the distance and glanced over her shoulder. The traveller had turned sideways. At once she bade the priest good-bye and walked away and out through the swing door.

All the afternoon she rested. The silence was profound. Beni-Mora was enjoying a siesta in the heat. Domini revelled in the stillness. The fatigue of travel had quite gone from her now and she began to feel strangely at home. Suzanne had arranged photographs, books, flowers in the little *salon*, had put cushions here and there, and thrown pretty coverings over the sofa and the two low chairs. The room had an air of cosiness, of occupation. It was a room one could sit in without restlessness, and Domini liked its simplicity, its bare wooden floor and white walls. The sun made everything right here. Without the sun—but she could not think of Beni-Mora without the sun.

She read on the verandah and dreamed, and the hours slipped quickly away. No one came to disturb her. She heard no footsteps, no movements of humanity in the house. Now and then the sound of voices floated up to her from the gardens.

mingling with the peculiar dry noise of palm leaves stirring in a breeze. Or she heard the distant gallop of horses' feet. The church bell chimed the hours and made her recall the previous evening. Already it seemed far off in the past. She could scarcely believe that she had not yet spent twenty-four hours in Beni-Mora. A conviction came to her that she would be there for a long while, that she would strike roots into this sunny place of peace. When she heard the church bell now she thought of the interior of the church and of the priest with an odd sort of familiar pleasure, as people in England often think of the village church in which they have always been accustomed to worship, and of the clergyman who ministers in it Sunday after Sunday. Yet at moments she remembered her inward cry in Count Anteoni's garden, " Oh, what is going to happen to me here? " And then she was dimly conscious that Beni-Mora was the home of many things besides peace. It held warring influences. At one moment it lulled her and she was like an infant rocked in a cradle. At another moment it stirred her, and she was a woman on the edge of mysterious possibilities. There must be many individualities among the desert spirits of whom Count Anteoni had spoken. Now one was with her and whispered to her, now another. She fancied the light touch of their hands on hers, pulling gently at her, as a child pulls you to take you to see a treasure. And their treasure was surely far away, hidden in the distance of the desert sands.

As soon as the sun began to decline towards the west she put on her hat, thrust the card Count Anteoni had given her into her glove and set out towards the big hotel alone. She met Hadj as she walked down the arcade. He wished to accompany her, and was evidently filled with treacherous ideas of supplanting his friend Batouch, but she gave him a franc and sent him away. The franc soothed him slightly, yet she could see that his childish vanity was injured. There was a malicious gleam in his long, narrow eyes as he looked after her. Yet there was genuine admiration too. The Arab bows down instinctively before any dominating spirit, and such a spirit in a foreign woman flashes in his eyes like a bright flame. Physical strength, too, appeals to him with peculiar force. Hadj tossed his head upwards, tucked in his chin, and muttered some words in his brown throat as he noted the elastic grace with which the rejecting foreign woman moved till she was out of his sight. And she never looked back at him. That was a keen arrow in her quiver. He fell into a deep reverie under the arcade and his face became suddenly like the face of a sphinx.

Meanwhile Domini had forgotten him. She had turned to the left down a small street in which some Indians and superior Arabs had bazaars. One of the latter came out from the shadow of his hanging rugs and embroideries as she passed, and, addressing her in a strange mixture of incorrect French and English, begged her to come in and examine his wares.

She shook her head, but could not help looking at him with interest.

He was the thinnest man she had ever seen, and moved and stood almost as if he were boneless. The line of his delicate and yet arbitrary features was fierce. His face was pitted with small-pox and marked by an old wound, evidently made by a knife, which stretched from his left cheek to his forehead, ending just over the left eyebrow. The expression of his eyes was almost disgustingly intelligent. While they were fixed upon her Domini felt as if her body were a glass box in which all her thoughts, feelings, and desires were ranged for his inspection. In his demeanour there was much that pleaded, but also something that commanded. His fingers were unnaturally long and held a small bag, and he planted himself right before her in the road.

"Madame, come in, venez avec moi. Venez—venez! I have much—I will show—j'ai des choses extraordinaires! Tenez! Look!"

He untied the mouth of the bag. Domini looked into it, expecting to see something precious—jewels perhaps. She saw only a quantity of sand, laughed, and moved to go on. She thought the Arab was an impudent fellow trying to make fun of her.

"No, no, Madame! Do not laugh! Ce sable est du désert. Il y a des histoires la-dedans. Il y a l'histoire de Madame. Come bazaar! I will read for Madame—what will be—what will become—I will read—I will tell. Tenez!" He stared down into the bag and his face became suddenly stern and fixed. "Déja je vois des choses dans la vie de Madame. Ah! Mon Dieu! Ah! Mon Dieu!"

"No, no," Domini said.

She had hesitated, but was now determined.

"I have no time to-day."

The man cast a quick and sly glance at her, then stared once more into the bag.

"Ah! Mon Dieu! An! Mon Dieu!" he repeated. "The life to come—the life of Madame—I see it in the bag!"

His face looked tortured. Domini walked on hurriedly. When she had got to a little distance she glanced back. The man was standing in the middle of the road and glaring into the bag. His voice came down the street to her.

"Ah! Mon Dieu! Ah! Mon Dieu! I see it—I see—je vois la vie de Madame—Ah! Mon Dieu!"

There was an accent of dreadful suffering in his voice. It made Domini shudder.

She passed the mouth of the dancers' street. At the corner there was a large Café Maure, and here, on rugs laid by the side of the road, numbers of Arabs were stretched, some sipping tea from glasses, some playing dominoes, some conversing, some staring calmly into vacancy, like animals drowned in a lethargic dream. A black boy ran by holding a hammered brass tray on which were some small china cups filled with thick coffee. Halfway up the street he met three unveiled women clad in voluminous white dresses, with scarlet, yellow, and purple handkerchiefs bound over their black hair. He stopped and the women took the cups with their henna-tinted fingers. Two young Arabs joined them. There was a scuffle. White lumps of sugar flew up into the air. Then there was a babel of voices, a torrent of cries full of barbaric gaiety.

Before it had died out of Domini's ears she stood by the statue of Cardinal Lavigerie. Rather militant than priestly, raised high on a marble pedestal, it faced the long road which, melting at last into a faint desert track, stretched away to Tombouctou. The mitre upon the head was worn surely as if it were a helmet, the pastoral staff with its double cross was grasped as if it were a sword. Upon the lower cross was stretched a figure of the Christ in agony. And the Cardinal, gazing with the eyes of an eagle out into the pathless wastes of sand that lay beyond the palm trees, seemed, by his mere attitude, to cry to all the myriad hordes of men the deep-bosomed Sahara mothered in her mystery and silence, " Come unto the Church! Come unto me!"

He called men in from the desert. Domini fancied his voice echoing along the sands till the worshippers of Allah and of his Prophet heard it like a clarion in Tombouctou.

When she reached the great hotel the sun was just beginning to set. She drew Count Anteoni's card from her glove and rang the bell. After a long interval a magnificent man, with the features of an Arab but a skin almost as black as a negro, opened the door.

"Can I go up the tower to see the sunset?" she asked, giving him the card.

The man bowed low, escorted her through a long hall full of furniture shrouded in coverings, up a staircase, along a corridor with numbered rooms, up a second staircase and out upon a flat-terraced roof, from which the tower soared high above the houses and palms of Beni-Mora, a landmark visible half-a-day's journey out in the desert. A narrow spiral stair inside the tower gained the summit.

"I'll go up alone," Domini said. "I shall stay some time and I would rather not keep you."

She put some money into the Arab's hand. He looked pleased, yet doubtful too for a moment. Then he seemed to banish his hesitation and, with a deprecating smile, said something which she could not understand. She nodded intelligently to get rid of him. Already, from the roof, she caught sight of a great visionary panorama glowing with colour and magic. She was impatient to climb still higher into the sky, to look down on the world as an eagle does. So she turned away decisively and mounted the dark, winding stair till she reached a door. She pushed it open with some difficulty, and came out into the air at a dizzy height, shutting the door forcibly behind her with an energetic movement of her strong arms.

The top of the tower was small and square, and guarded by a white parapet breast high. In the centre of it rose the outer walls and the ceiling of the top of the staircase, which prevented a person standing on one side of the tower from seeing anybody who was standing at the opposite side. There was just sufficient space between parapet and staircase wall for two people to pass with difficulty and manœuvring.

But Domini was not concerned with such trivial details, as she would have thought them had she thought of them. Directly she had shut the little door and felt herself alone— alone as an eagle in the sky—she took the step forward that brought her to the parapet, leaned her arms on it, looked out and was lost in a passion of contemplation.

At first she did not discern any of the multitudinous minutiæ in the great evening vision beneath and around her. She only felt conscious of depth, height, space, colour, mystery, calm. She did not measure. She did not differentiate. She simply stood there, leaning lightly on the snowy plaster work, and experienced something that she had never experienced before, that she had never imagined. It was scarcely vivid; for in everything that is vivid there seems to be something small, the point to which wonders converge, the intense spark to which many fires have given themselves as food, the drop which contains the murmuring force of innumerable rivers. It was more than vivid. It was reliantly dim, as is that pulse of life which is heard through and above the crash of generations and centuries falling downwards into the abyss; that persistent, enduring heart-beat, indifferent in its mystical regularity, that ignores and triumphs, and never grows louder nor diminishes, inexorably calm, inexorably steady, undefeated—more—utterly unaffected by unnumbered millions of tragedies and deaths.

Many sounds rose from far down beneath the tower, but at first Domini did not hear them. She was only aware of an immense, living silence, a silence flowing beneath, around and above her in dumb, invisible waves. Circles of rest and peace, cool and serene, widened as circles in a pool towards the unseen limits of the satisfied world, limits lost in the hidden regions beyond the misty, purple magic where sky and desert met. And she felt as if her brain, ceaselessly at work from its birth, her heart, unresting hitherto in a commotion of desires, her soul, an eternal flutter of anxious, passionate wings, folded themselves together gently like the petals of roses when a summer night comes into a garden.

She was not conscious that she breathed while she stood there. She thought her bosom ceased to rise and fall. The very blood dreamed in her veins as the light of evening dreamed in the blue.

She knew the Great Pause that seems to divide some human lives in two, as the Great Gulf divided him who lay in Abraham's bosom from him who was shrouded in the veil of fire.

BOOK II

THE VOICE OF PRAYER

CHAPTER VII

THE music of things from below stole up through the ethereal spaces to Domini without piercing her dream. But suddenly she started with a sense of pain so acute that it shook her body and set the pulses in her temples beating. She lifted her arms swiftly from the parapet and turned her head. She had heard a little grating noise which seemed to be near to her, enclosed with her on this height in the narrow space of the tower. Slight as it was, and short—already she no longer heard it—it had in an instant driven her out of Heaven, as if it had been an angel with a flaming sword. She felt sure that there must be something alive with her at the tower summit, something which by a sudden movement had caused the little noise she had heard. What was it? When she turned her head she could only see the outer wall of the staircase, a section of the narrow white space which surrounded it, an angle of the parapet and blue air.

She listened, holding her breath and closing her two hands on the parapet, which was warm from the sun. Now, caught back to reality, she could hear faintly the sounds from below in Beni-Mora. But they did not concern her, and she wished to shut them out from her ears. What did concern her was to know what was with her up in the sky. Had a bird alighted on the parapet and startled her by scratching at the plaster with its beak? Could a mouse have shuffled in the wall? Or was there a human being up there hidden from her by the masonry?

This last supposition disturbed her almost absurdly for a moment. She was inclined to walk quickly round to the opposite side of the tower, but something stronger than her inclination, an imperious shyness, held her motionless. She had been carried so far away from the world that she felt unable to face the scrutiny of any world-bound creature. Having been in the transparent region of magic it seemed to her as if her secret, the great secret of the absolutely true, the naked personality hidden in every human being, were set blazing in her eyes like some torch borne in a procession, just for that moment. The moment past, she could look anyone fearlessly in the face; but not now, not yet.

While she stood there, half turning round, she heard the sound again and knew what caused it. A foot had shifted on the plaster floor. There was someone else then looking out over the desert. A sudden idea struck her. Probably it was Count Anteoni. He knew she was coming and might have decided to act once more as her cicerone. He had not heard her climbing the stairs, and, having gone to the far side of the tower, was no doubt watching the sunset, lost in a dream as she had been.

She resolved not to disturb him—if it was he. When he had dreamed enough he must inevitably come round to where she was standing in order to gain the staircase. She would let him find her there. Less troubled now, but in an utterly changed mood, she turned, leaned once more on the parapet and looked over, this time observantly, prepared to note the details that, combined and veiled in the evening light of Africa, made the magic which had so instantly entranced her.

She looked down into the village and could see its extent, precisely how it was placed in the Sahara, in what relation exactly it stood to the mountain ranges, to the palm groves and the arid, sunburnt tracts, where its life centred and where it tailed away into suburban edges not unlike the ragged edges of worn garments, where it was idle and frivolous, where busy and sedulous. She realised for the first time that there were two distinct layers of life in Beni-Mora—the life of the streets, courts, gardens and market-place, and above it the life of the roofs. Both were now spread out before her, and the latter, in its domestic intimacy, interested and charmed her. She saw upon the roofs the children playing with little dogs, goats, fowls, mothers in rags of gaudy colours stirring the barley for cous-cous, shredding vegetables, pounding coffee, stewing meat, plucking chickens, bending over bowls from which rose the steam of soup; small girls, seated in dusty corners, solemnly winding wool on sticks, and pausing, now and then, to squeak to distant members of the home circle, or to smell at flowers laid beside them as solace to their industry. An old grandmother rocked and kissed a naked baby with a pot belly. A big grey rat stole from a rubbish heap close by her, flitted across the sunlit space, and disappeared into a cranny. Pigeons circled above the home activities, delicate lovers of the air, wandered among the palm tops, returned and fearlessly alighted on the brown earth para-pets, strutting hither and thither and making their perpetual, characteristic motion of the head, half nod, half genuflection. Veiled girls promenaded to take the evening cool, folding their arms beneath their flowing draperies, and chattering to one another in voices that Domini could not hear. More close at hand certain roofs in the dancers' street revealed luxurious sofas on which painted houris were lolling in sinuous attitudes, or were posed with a stiffness of idols, little tables set with coffee cups, others round which were gathered Zouaves intent on card games, but ever ready to pause for a caress or for some jesting absurdity with the women who squatted beside them. Some men, dressed like girls, went to and fro, serving the dancers with sweetmeats and with cigarettes, their beards flowing down with a grotesque effect over their dresses of embroidered muslin, their hairy arms emerging from hanging sleeves of silk. A negro boy sat holding a tom-tom between his bare knees and beating it with supple hands, and a Jewess performed the stomach dance, waving two handkerchiefs stained red and purple, and singing in a loud and barbarous contralto voice which Domini could hear but very faintly. The card-players stopped their game and watched her, and Domini watched too. For the first time, and from this immense height, she saw this universal dance of the east; the doll-like figure, fantastically dwarfed, waving its tiny hands, wriggling its minute body, turning about like a little top, strutting and bending, while the soldiers—small almost from here as toys taken out of a box— assumed attitudes of deep attention as they leaned upon the card-table, stretching out their legs enveloped in balloon-like trousers.

Domini thought of the recruits, now, no doubt, undergoing elsewhere their initiation. For a moment she seemed to see their coarse peasant faces rigid with surprise, their hanging jaws, their childish, and yet sensual, round eyes. Notre Dame de la Garde must seem very far away from them now.

With that thought she looked quickly away from the Jewess and the soldiers. She felt a sudden need of something more nearly in relation with her inner self. She was almost angry as she realised how deep had been her momentary interest in a scene suggestive of a license which was surely unattractive to her. Yet was it unattractive? She scarcely knew. But she knew that it had kindled in her a sudden and very strong curiosity, even a vague, momentary desire that she had been born in some tent of the Ouled Naïls—no, that was impossible. She had not felt such a desire even for an instant. She looked towards the thickets of the palms, towards the mountains full of changing, exquisite colours, towards the desert. And at once the dream began to return, and she felt as if hands slipped under her heart and uplifted it.

What depths and heights were within her, what deep, dark valleys, and what mountain peaks! And how she travelled within herself, with swiftness of light, with speed of the wind. What terrors of activity she knew. Did every human being know similar terrors?

The colours everywhere deepened as day failed. The desert spirits were at work. She thought of Count Anteoni again, and resolved to go round to the other side of the tower. As she moved to do this she heard once more the shifting of a foot on the plaster floor, then a step. Evidently she had infected him with an intention similar to her own. She went on, still hearing the step, turned the corner and stood face to face in the strong evening light with the traveller. Their bodies almost touched in the narrow space before they both stopped, startled. For a moment they stood still looking at each other, as people might look who have spoken together, who know something of each other's lives, who may like or dislike, wish to avoid or to draw near to each other, but who cannot pretend that they are complete strangers, wholly indifferent to each other. They met in the sky, almost as one bird may meet another on the wing. And, to Domini, at any rate, it seemed as if the depth, height, space, colour, mystery and calm—yes, even the calm—which were above, around and beneath them, had been placed there by hidden hands as a setting for their encounter, even as the abrupt pageant of the previous day, into which the train had emerged from the blackness of the tunnel, had surely been created as a frame for the face which had looked upon her as if out of the heart of the sun. The assumption was absurd, unreasonable, yet vital. She did not combat it because she felt it too powerful for common sense to strive against. And it seemed to her that the stranger felt it too, that she saw her sensation reflected in his eyes as he stood between the parapet and the staircase wall, barring—in despite of himself—her path. The moment seemed long while they stood motionless. Then the man took off his soft hat awkwardly, yet with real politeness, and stood quickly sideways against the parapet to let her pass. She could have passed if she had brushed against him, and made a movement to do so. Then she checked herself and looked at him again as if she expected him to speak to her. His hat was still in his hand, and the light desert wind faintly stirred his short brown hair. He did not speak, but stood there crushing himself against the plaster work with a sort of fierce timidity, as if he dreaded the touch of her skirt against him, and longed to make himself small, to shrivel up and let her go by in freedom.

"Thank you," she said in French.

She passed him, but was unable to do so without touching him. Her left arm was hanging down, and her bare hand knocked against the back of the hand in which he held his hat. She felt as if at that moment she touched a furnace, and she saw him shiver slightly, as over-fatigued men sometimes shiver in daylight. An extraordinary, almost motherly, sensation of pity for him came over her. She did not know why. The intense heat of his hand, the shiver that ran over his body, his attitude as he shrank with a kind of timid, yet ferocious, politeness against the white wall, the expression in his eyes when their hands touched—a look she could not analyse, but which seemed to hold a mingling of wistfulness and repellance, as of a being stretching out arms for succour, and crying at the same time, "Don't draw near to me! Leave me to myself!"—everything about him moved her. She felt that she was face to face with a solitariness of soul such as she had never encountered before, a solitariness that was cruel, that was weighed down with agony. And directly she had passed the man and thanked him formally she stopped with her usual decision of manner. She had abruptly made up her mind to talk to him. He was already moving to turn away. She spoke quickly, and in French.

"Isn't it wonderful here?" she said; and she made her voice rather loud, and almost sharp, to arrest his attention.

He turned round swiftly, yet somehow reluctantly, looked at her anxiously, and seemed doubtful whether he would reply.

After a silence that was short, but that seemed, and in such circumstances was, long, he answered, in French:

"Very wonderful, Madame."

The sound of his own voice seemed to startle him. He stood as if he had heard an unusual noise which had alarmed him, and looked at Domini as if he expected that she would share in his sensation. Very quietly and deliberately she leaned her arms again on the parapet and spoke to him once more.

" We seem to be the only travellers here."

The man's attitude became slightly calmer. He looked less momentary, less as if he were in haste to go, but still shy, fierce and extraordinarily unconventional.

" Yes, Madame; there are not many here."

After a pause, and with an uncertain accent, he added:

" Pardon, Madame—for yesterday."

There was a sudden simplicity, almost like that of a child, in the sound of his voice as he said that. Domini knew at once that he alluded to the incident at the station of El-Akbara, that he was trying to make amends. The way he did it touched her curiously. She felt inclined to stretch out her hand to him and say, " Of course ! Shake hands on it ! " almost as an honest schoolboy might. But she only answered:

" I know it was only an accident. Don't think of it any more."

She did not look at him.

" Where money is concerned the Arabs are very persistent," she continued.

The man laid one of his brown hands on the top of the parapet. She looked at it, and it seemed to her that she had never before seen the back of a hand express so much of character, look so intense, so ardent, and so melancholy as his.

" Yes, Madame."

He still spoke with an odd timidity, with an air of listening to his own speech as if in some strange way it were phenomenal to him. It occurred to her that possibly he had lived much in lonely places, in which his solitude had rarely been broken, and he had been forced to acquire the habit of silence.

" But they are very picturesque. They look almost like some religious order when they wear their hoods. Don't you think so ? "

She saw the brown hand lifted from the parapet, and heard her companion's feet shift on the floor of the tower. But this time he said nothing. As she could not see his hand now she looked out again over the panorama of the evening, which was deepening in intensity with every passing moment, and immediately she was conscious of two feelings that filled her with wonder: a much stronger and sweeter sense of the African magic than she had felt till now, and the certainty that the greater force and sweetness of her feeling were caused by the fact that she had a companion in her contemplation. This was strange. An intense desire for loneliness had driven her out of Europe to this desert place, and a companion, who was an utter stranger, emphasised the significance, gave fibre to the beauty, intensity to the mystery of that which she looked on. It was as if the meaning of the African evening were suddenly doubled. She thought of a dice-thrower who throws one die and turns up six, then throws two and turns up twelve. And she remained silent in her surprise. The man stood silently beside her. Afterwards she felt as if, during this silence in the tower, some powerful and unseen being had arrived mysteriously, introduced them to one another and mysteriously departed.

The evening drew on in their silence and the dream was deeper now. All that Domini had felt when first she approached the parapet she felt more strangely, and she grasped, with physical and mental vision, not only the whole, but the innumerable parts of that which she looked on. She saw, fancifully, the circles widen in the pool of peace, but she saw also the things that had been hidden in the pool. The beauty of dimness, the beauty of clearness, joined hands. The one and the other were, with her, like sisters. She heard the voices from below, and surely also the voices of the stars that were approaching with the night, blending harmoniously and making a music in the air. The glowing sky and the glowing mountains were as comrades, each responsive to the emotions of the other. The lights in the rocky clefts had messages for the shadowy moon, and the palm trees for the thin, fire-tipped clouds about the west. Far off the misty purple of the desert drew surely closer, like a mother coming to fold her children in her arms.

The Jewess still danced upon the roof to the watching Zouaves, but now there was something mystic in her tiny movements, which no longer roused in Domini any furtive desire not really inherent in her nature. There was something beautiful in everything seen from this altitude in this wondrous evening light.

Presently, without turning to her companion, she said:

" Could anything look ugly in Beni-Mora from here at this hour, do you think? "

Again there was the silence that seemed characteristic of this man before he spoke, as if speech were very difficult to him.

" I believe not, Madame."

" Even that woman down there on that roof looks graceful— the one dancing for those soldiers."

He did not answer. She glanced at him and pointed.

" Down there, do you see? "

She noticed that he did not follow her hand and that his face became stern. He kept his eyes fixed on the trees of the garden of the Gazelles near Cardinal Lavigerie's statue and replied:

" Yes, Madame."

His manner made her think that perhaps he had seen the dance at close quarters and that it was outrageous. For a moment she felt slightly uncomfortable, but determined not to let him remain under a false impression, she added carelessly:

" I have never seen the dances of Africa. I daresay I should think them ugly enough if I were near, but from this height everything is transformed."

" That is true, Madame."

There was an odd, muttering sound in his voice, which was deep, and probably strong, but which he kept low. Domini thought it was the most male voice she had ever heard. It seemed to be full of sex, like his hands. Yet there was nothing coarse in either the one or the other. Everything about him was vital to a point that was so remarkable as to be not actually unnatural but very near the unnatural.

She glanced at him again. He was a big man, but very thin. Her experienced eyes of an athletic woman told her that he was capable of great and prolonged muscular exertion. He was big-boned and deep-chested, and had nervous as well as muscular strength. The timidity in him was strange in such a man. What could it spring from? It was not like ordinary shyness, the *gaucherie* of a big, awkward lout unaccustomed to woman's society but able to be at his ease and boisterous in the midst of a crowd of men. Domini thought that he would be timid even of men. Yet it never struck her that he might be a coward, unmanly. Such a quality would have sickened her at once, and she knew she would have at once divined it. He did not hold himself very well, but was inclined to stoop and to keep his head low, as if he were in the habit of looking much on the ground. The idiosyncrasy was rather ugly, and suggested melancholy to her, the melancholy of a man given to over-much meditation and afraid to face the radiant wonder of life.

She caught herself up at this last thought. She—thinking naturally that life was full of radiant wonder! Was she then so utterly transformed already by Beni-Mora? Or had the thought come to her because she stood side by side with someone whose sorrows had been unfathomably deeper than her own, and so who, all unconsciously, gave her a knowledge of her own—till then unsuspected—hopefulness?

She looked at her companion again. He seemed to have relinquished his intention of leaving her, and was standing quietly beside her, staring towards the desert, with his head slightly drooped forward. In one hand he held a thick stick. He had put his hat on again. His attitude was much calmer than it had been. Already he seemed more at ease with her. She was glad of that. She did not ask herself why. But the intense beauty of evening in this land and at this height made her wish enthusiastically that it could produce a happiness such as it created in her in everyone. Such beauty, with its voices, its colours, its lines of tree and leaf, of wall and mountain ridge, its mystery of shapes and movements, stillness and dreaming distance, its atmosphere of the far off come near, chastened by journeying, fine with the unfamiliar, its solemn changes towards the impenetrable night, was too large a thing and fraught with too much tender and lovable invention to be worshipped in any selfishness. It made her feel as if she could gladly be a martyr for unseen human beings, as if sacrifice would be an easy thing if made for those to whom such beauty would appeal. Brotherhood rose up and cried in her, as it surely sang in the sunset, in the mountains, the palm groves and the desert. The flame above the hills, their purple outline, the moving, feathery trees, dark under the rose-coloured glory of the west, and most of all the immeasurably remote horizons, each moment more strange and more eternal, made her long to make this harsh stranger happy.

"One ought to find happiness here," she said to him very simply.

She saw his hand strain itself round the wood of his stick.

"Why?" he said.

He turned right round to her and looked at her with a sort of anger.

"Why should you suppose so?" he added, speaking quite quickly, and without his former uneasiness and consciousness.

"Because it is so beautiful and so calm."

"Calm!" he said. "Here!"

There was a sound of passionate surprise in his voice. Domini was startled. She felt as if she were fighting, and must fight hard if she were not to be beaten to the dust. But when she

looked at him she could find no weapons. She said nothing.
In a moment he spoke again.

"You find calm here," he said slowly. "Yes, I see."

His head dropped lower and his face hardened as he looked
over the edge of the parapet to the village, the blue desert.
Then he lifted his eyes to the mountains and the clear sky and
the shadowy moon. Each element in the evening scene was
examined with a fierce, painful scrutiny, as if he was resolved to
wring from each its secret.

"Why, yes," he added in a low, muttering voice full of a sort
of terrified surprise, "it is so. You are right. Why, yes, it is
calm here."

He spoke like a man who had been suddenly convinced,
beyond power of further unbelief, of something he had never
suspected, never dreamed of. And the conviction seemed to be
bitter to him, even alarming.

"But away out there must be the real home of peace, I
think," Domini said.

"Where?" said the man, quickly.

She pointed towards the south.

"In the depths of the desert," she said. "Far away from
civilisation, far away from modern men and modern women,
and all the noisy trifles we are accustomed to."

He looked towards the south eagerly. In everything he did
there was a flame-like intensity, as if he could not perform an
ordinary action, or turn his eyes upon any object, without
calling up in his mind, or heart, a violence of thought or of
feeling.

"You think it—you think there would be peace out there,
far away in the desert?" he said, and his face relaxed slightly,
as if in obedience to some thought not wholly sad.

"It may be fanciful," she replied. "But I think there must.
Surely Nature has not a lying face."

He was still gazing towards the south, from which the night
was slowly emerging, a traveller through a mist of blue. He
seemed to be held fascinated by the desert which was fading
away gently, like a mystery which had drawn near to the light
of revelation, but which was now slipping back into an underworld of magic. He bent forward as one who watches a departure in which he longs to share, and Domini felt sure that he
had forgotten her. She felt, too, that this man was gripped by
the desert influence more fiercely even than she was, and that he
must have a stronger imagination, a greater force of projection

even than she had.   Where she bore a taper he lifted a blazing
torch.

A roar of drums rose up immediately beneath them. From
the negro village emerged a ragged procession of thick-lipped
men, and singing, capering women tricked out in scarlet and
yellow shawls, headed by a male dancer clad in the skins of
jackals, and decorated with mirrors, camels' skulls and chains
of animals' teeth. He shouted and leaped, rolled his bulging
eyes, and protruded a fluttering tongue. The dust curled up
round his stamping, naked feet.

"Yah-ah-là! Yah-ah-là!"

The howling chorus came up to the tower, with a clash of
enormous castanets, and of poles beaten rhythmically together.

"Yi-yi-yi-yi!" went the shrill voices of the women.

The cloud of dust increased, enveloping the lower part of
the procession, till the black heads and waving arms emerged as
if from a maelstrom. The thunder of the drums was like the
thunder of a cataract in which the singers, disappearing towards
the village, seemed to be swept away.

The man at Domini's side raised himself up with a jerk, and
all the former fierce timidity and consciousness came back to his
face. He turned round, pulled open the door behind him, and
took off his hat.

"Excuse me, Madame," he said. "Bon soir!"

"I am coming too," Domini answered.

He looked uncomfortable and anxious, hesitated, then, as if
driven to do it in spite of himself, plunged downward through
the narrow doorway of the tower into the darkness. Domini
waited for a moment, listening to the heavy sound of his tread
on the wooden stairs. She frowned till her thick eyebrows
nearly met and the corners of her lips turned down. Then she
followed slowly. When she was on the stairs and the footsteps
died away below her she fully realised that for the first time in
her life a man had insulted her. Her face felt suddenly very
hot, and her lips very dry, and she longed to use her physical
strength in a way not wholly feminine. In the hall, among the
shrouded furniture, she met the smiling doorkeeper. She
stopped.

"Did the gentleman who has just gone out give you his
card?" she said abruptly.

The Arab assumed a fawning, servile expression.

"No, Madame, but he is a very good gentleman, and I know
well that Monsieur the Count——"

Domini cut him short.

" Of what nationality is he? "

" Monsieur the Count, Madame? "

" No, no."

" The gentleman? I do not know. But he can speak Arabic Oh, he is a very nice——"

" Bon soir," said Domini, giving him a franc.

When she was out on the road in front of the hotel she saw the stranger striding along in the distance at the tail of the negro procession. The dust stirred up by the dancers whirled about him. Several small negroes skipped round him, doubtless making eager demands upon his generosity. He seemed to take no notice of them, and as she watched him Domini was reminded of his retreat from the praying Arab in the desert that morning.

" Is he afraid of women as he is afraid of prayer? " she thought, and suddenly the sense of humiliation and anger left her, and was succeeded by a powerful curiosity such as she had never felt before about anyone. She realised that this curiosity had dawned in her almost at the first moment when she saw the stranger, and had been growing ever since. One circumstance after another had increased it till now it was definite, concrete. She wondered that she did not feel ashamed of such a feeling so unusual in her, and surely unworthy, like a prying thing. Of all her old indifference that side which confronted people had always been the most sturdy, the most solidly built. Without affectation she had been a profoundly incurious woman as to the lives and the concerns of others, even of those whom she knew best and was supposed to care for most. Her nature had been essentially languid in human intercourse. The excitements, troubles, even the passions of others had generally stirred her no more than a distant puppet-show stirs an absent-minded passer in the street.

In Africa it seemed that her whole nature had been either violently renewed, or even changed. She could not tell which. But this strong stirring of curiosity would, she believed, have been impossible in the woman she had been but a week ago, the woman who travelled to Marseilles dulled, ignorant of herself, longing for change. Perhaps instead of being angry she ought to welcome it as a symptom of the re-creation she longed for.

While she changed her gown for dinner that night she debated within herself how she would treat her fellow-guest when she met him in the *salle-à-manger*. She ought to cut him after what had occurred, she supposed. Then it seemed to her that to do so would be undignified, and would give him the impression that he had the power to offend her. She resolved to bow to him if they met face to face. Just before she went downstairs she realised how vehement her internal debate had been, and was astonished. Suzanne was putting away something in a drawer, bending down and stretching out her plump arms.

"Suzanne!" Domini said.

"Yes, Mam'zelle!"

"How long have you been with me?"

"Three years, Mam'zelle."

The maid shut the drawer and turned round, fixing her shallow, blue-grey eyes on her mistress, and standing as if she were ready to be photographed.

"Would you say that I am the same sort of person to-day as I was three years ago?"

Suzanne looked like a cat that has been startled by a sudden noise.

"The same, Mam'zelle?"

"Yes. Do you think I have altered in that time?"

Suzanne considered the question with her head slightly on one side.

"Only here, Mam'zelle," she replied at length.

"Here!" said Domini, rather eagerly. "Why, I have only been here twenty-six hours."

"That is true. But Mam'zelle looks as if she had a little life here, a little emotion. Mon Dieu! Mam'zelle will pardon me, but what is a woman who feels no emotion? A packet. Is it not so, Mam'zelle?"

"Well, but what is there to be emotional about here?"

Suzanne looked vaguely crafty.

"Who knows, Mam'zelle? Who can say? Mon Dieu! This village is dull, but it is odd. No band plays. There are no shops for a girl to look into. There is nothing *chic* except the costumes of the Zouaves. But one cannot deny that it is odd. When Mam'zelle was away this afternoon in the tower Monsieur Helmuth——"

"Who is that?"

"The Monsieur who accompanies the omnibus to the station. Monsieur Helmuth was polite enough to escort me through the village. Mon Dieu, Mam'zelle, I said to myself, 'Anything might occur here.'"

"Anything! What do you mean?"

But Suzanne did not seem to know. She only made her figure look more tense than ever, tucked in her round little chin, which was dimpled and unmeaning, and said:

"Who knows, Mam'zelle? This village is dull, that is true, but it is odd. One does not find oneself in such places every day."

Domini could not help laughing at these Delphic utterances, but she went downstairs thoughtfully. She knew Suzanne's practical spirit. Till now the maid had never shown any capacity of imagination. Beni-Mora was certainly beginning to mould her nature into a slightly different shape. And Domini seemed to see an Eastern potter at work, squatting in the sun and with long and delicate fingers changing the outline of the statuette of a woman, modifying a curve here, an angle there, till the clay began to show another woman, but with, as it were, the shadow of the former one lurking behind the new personality.

The stranger was not at dinner. His table was laid and Domini sat expecting each moment to hear the shuffling tread of his heavy boots on the wooden floor. When he did not come she thought she was glad. After dinner she spoke for a moment to the priest and then went upstairs to the verandah to take coffee. She found Batouch there. He had renounced his determined air, and his *café-au-lait* countenance and huge body expressed enduring pathos, as of an injured, patient creature laid out for the trampling of Domini's cruel feet.

"Well?" she said, sitting down by the basket table.

"Well, Madame?"

He sighed and looked on the ground, lifted one white-socked foot, removed its yellow slipper, shook out a tiny stone from the slipper and put it on again, slowly, gracefully and very sadly. Then he pulled the white sock up with both hands and glanced at Domini out of the corners of his eyes.

"What's the matter?"

"Madame does not care to see the dances of Beni-Mora, to hear the music, to listen to the story-teller, to enter the *café* of El Hadj where Achmed sings to the keef smokers, or to witness the beautiful religious ecstasies of the dervishes from Oumach. Therefore I come to bid Madame respectfully good-night and to take my departure."

He threw his burnous over his left shoulder with a sudden gesture of despair that was full of exaggeration. Domini smiled.

" You've been very good to-day," she said.

" I am always good, Madame. I am of a serious disposition. Not one keeps Ramadan as I do."

" I am sure of it. Go downstairs and wait for me under the arcade."

Batouch's large face became suddenly a rendezvous of all the gaieties.

" Madame is coming out to-night? "

" Presently. Be in the arcade."

He swept away with the ample magnificence of joyous bearing and movement that was like a loud Te Deum.

" Suzanne! Suzanne! "

Domini had finished her coffee.

" Mam'zelle! " answered Suzanne, appearing.

" Would you like to come out with me to-night? "

" Mam'zelle is going out? "

" Yes, to see the village by night."

Suzanne looked irresolute. Craven fear and curiosity fought a battle within her, as was evident by the expressions that came and went in her face before she answered.

" Shall we not be murdered, Mam'zelle, and are there interesting things to see? "

" There are interesting things to see—dancers, singers, keef smokers. But if you are afraid don't come."

" Dancers, Mam'zelle! But the Arabs carry knives. And is there singing? I—I should not like Mam'zelle to go without me. But——"

" Come and protect me from the knives then. Bring my jacket—any one. I don't suppose I shall put it on."

As she spoke the distant tom-toms began. Suzanne started nervously and looked at Domini with sincere apprehension.

" We had better not go, Mam'zelle. It is not safe out here. Men who make a noise like that would not respect us."

" I like it."

" That sound? But it is always the same and there is not music in it."

" Perhaps there is more in it than music. The jacket? "

Suzanne went gingerly to fetch it. The faint cry of the African hautboy rose up above the tom-toms. The evening *fête* was beginning. To-night Domini felt that she must go to the distant music and learn to understand its meaning, not only for herself, but for those who made it and danced to it night after night. It stirred her imagination, and made her in love with mystery, and anxious at least to steal to the very threshold of the barbarous world. Did it stir those who had had it in their ears ever since they were naked, sunburned babies rolling in the hot sun of the Sahara? Could it seem as ordinary to them as the cold uproar of the piano-organ to the urchins of White-chapel, or the whine of the fiddle to the peasants of Touraine where Suzanne was born? She wanted to know. Suzanne returned with the jacket. She still looked apprehensive, but she had put on her hat and fastened a sprig of red geranium in the front of her black gown. The curiosity was in the ascendant.

"We are not going quite alone, Mam'zelle?"

"No, no. Batouch will protect us."

Suzanne breathed a furtive sigh.

The poet was in the white arcade with Hadj, who looked both wicked and deplorable, and had a shabby air, in marked contrast to Batouch's ostentatious triumph. Domini felt quite sorry for him.

"You come with us too," she said.

Hadj squared his shoulders and instantly looked vivacious and almost smart. But an undecided expression came into his face.

"Where is Madame going?"

"To see the village."

Batouch shot a glance at Hadj and smiled unpleasantly.

"I will come with Madame."

Batouch still smiled.

"We are going to the Ouled Naïls," he said significantly to Hadj.

"I—I will come."

They set out. Suzanne looked gently at the poet's legs and seemed comforted.

"Take great care of Mademoiselle Suzanne," Domini said to the poet. "She is a little nervous in the dark."

"Mademoiselle Suzanne is like the first day after the fast of Ramadan," replied the poet, majestically. "No one would harm her were she to wander alone to Tombouctou."

The prospect drew from Suzanne a startled gulp. Batouch placed himself tenderly at her side and they set out, Domini walking behind with Hadj.

CHAPTER VIII

THE village was full of the wan presage of the coming of the
moon. The night was very still and very warm. As they skirted
the long gardens Domini saw a light in the priest's house. It
made her wonder how he passed his solitary evenings when he
went home from the hotel, and she fancied him sitting in some
plainly-furnished little room with Bous-Bous and a few books,
smoking a pipe and thinking sadly of the White Fathers of
Africa and of his frustrated desire for complete renunciation.
With this last thought blended the still remote sound of the
hautboy. It suggested anything rather than renunciation;
mysterious melancholy—successor to passion—the cry of longing, the wail of the unknown that draws some men and women
to splendid follies and to ardent pilgrimages whose goal is the
mirage.

Hadj was talking in a low voice, but Domini did not listen to
him. She was vaguely aware that he was abusing Batouch, saying that he was a liar, inclined to theft, a keef smoker, and in a
general way steeped to the lips in crime. But the moon was
rising, the distant music was becoming more distinct. She could
not listen to Hadj.

As they turned into the street of the sand-diviner the first ray
of the moon fell on the white road. Far away at the end of the
street Domini could see the black foliage of the trees in the
Gazelles' garden, and beyond, to the left, a dimness of shadowy
palms at the desert edge. The desert itself was not visible. Two
Arabs passed, shrouded in burnouses, with the hoods drawn up
over their heads. Only their black beards could be seen. They
were talking violently and waving their arms. Suzanne shuddered and drew close to the poet. Her plump face worked and
she glanced appealingly at her mistress. But Domini was not
thinking of her, or of violence or danger. The sound of the
tom-toms and hautboys seemed suddenly much louder now that
the moon began to shine, making a whiteness among the white
houses of the village, the white robes of the inhabitants, a greater
whiteness on the white road that lay before them. And she was
thinking that the moon whiteness of Beni-Mora was more
passionate than pure, more like the blanched face of a lover than
the cool, pale cheek of a virgin. There was excitement in it,
suggestion greater even than the suggestion of the tremendous
coloured scenes of the evening that preceded such a night. And

she mused of white heat and of what it means—the white heat of the brain blazing with thoughts that govern, the white heat of the heart blazing with emotions that make such thoughts seem cold. She had never known either. Was she incapable of knowing them? Could she imagine them till there was physical heat in her body if she was incapable of knowing them? Suzanne and the two Arabs were distant shadows to her when that first moon-ray touched their feet. The passion of the night began to burn her, and she thought she would like to take her soul and hold it out to the white flame.

As they passed the sand-diviner's house Domini saw his spectral figure standing under the yellow light of the hanging lantern in the middle of his carpet shop, which was lined from floor to ceiling with dull red embroideries and dim with the fumes of an incense brazier. He was talking to a little boy, but keeping a wary eye on the street, and he came out quickly, beckoning with his long hands, and calling softly, in a half-chuckling and yet authoritative voice:

"Venez, Madame, venez! Come! come!"

Suzanne seized Domini's arm.

"Not to-night!" Domini called out.

"Yes, Madame, to-night. The vie of Madame is there in the sand to-night. Je la vois, je la vois. C'est là dans le sable to-night."

The moonlight showed the wound on his face. Suzanne uttered a cry and hid her eyes with her hands. They went on towards the trees. Hadj walked with hesitation.

"How loud the music is getting," Domini said to him.

"It will deafen Madame's ears if she gets nearer," said Hadj, eagerly. "And the dancers are not for Madame. For the Arabs, yes, but for a great lady of the most respectable England! Madame will be red with disgust, with anger. Madame will have *mal-au-cœur*."

Batouch began to look like an idol on whose large face the artificer had carved an expression of savage ferocity.

"Madame is my client," he said fiercely. "Madame trusts in me."

Hadj laughed with a snarl.

"He who smokes the keef is like a Mehari with a swollen tongue," he rejoined.

The poet looked as if he were going to spring upon his cousin, but he restrained himself and a slow, malignant smile curled about his thick lips like a snake.

"I shall show to Madame a dancer who is modest, who is beautiful, Hadj-ben-Ibrahim," he said softly.

"Fatma is sick," said Hadj, quickly.

"It will not be Fatma."

Hadj began suddenly to gesticulate with his thin, delicate hands and to look fiercely excited.

"Halima is at the Fontaine Chaude," he cried.

"Keltoum will be there."

"She will not. Her foot is sick. She cannot dance. For a week she will not dance. I know it."

"And—Irena? Is she sick? Is she at the Hammam Salahine?"

Hadj's countenance fell. He looked at his cousin sideways, always showing his teeth.

"Do you not know, Hadj-ben-Ibrahim?"

"*Ana ma 'audi ma nek oûl lek!*" * growled Hadj in his throat.

They had reached the end of the little street. The whiteness of the great road which stretched straight through the oasis into the desert lay before them, with the statue of Cardinal Lavigerie staring down it in the night. At right angles was the street of the dancers, narrow, bounded with the low white houses of the ouleds, twinkling with starry lights, humming with voices, throbbing with the clashing music that poured from the rival *cafés maures,* thronged with the white figures of the desert men, strolling slowly, softly as panthers up and down. The moonlight was growing brighter, as if invisible hands began to fan the white flame of passion which lit up Beni-Mora. A patrol of Tirailleurs Indigènes passed by going up the street, in yellow and blue uniforms, turbans and white gaiters, their rifles over their broad shoulders. The faint tramp of their marching feet was just audible on the sandy road.

"Hadj can go home if he is afraid of anything in the dancing street," said Domini, rather maliciously. "Let us follow the soldiers."

Hadj started as if he had been stung, and looked at Domini as if he would like to strangle her.

"I am afraid of nothing," he exclaimed proudly. "Madame does not know Hadj-ben-Ibrahim."

Batouch laughed soundlessly, shaking his great shoulders. It was evident that he had divined his cousin's wish to supplant

---

* "I have nothing to say to you."

him and was busily taking his revenge. Domini was amused, and as they went slowly up the street in the wake of the soldiers she said:

"Do you often come here at night, Hadj-ben-Ibrahim?"

"Oh, yes, Madame, when I am alone. But with ladies——"

"You were here last night, weren't you, with the traveller from the hotel?"

"No, Madame. The Monsieur of the hotel preferred to visit the *café* of the story-teller, which is far more interesting. If Madame will permit me to take her——"

But this last assault was too much for the poet's philosophy. He suddenly threw off all pretence of graceful calm, and poured out upon Hadj a torrent of vehement Arabic, accompanying it with passionate gestures which filled Suzanne with horror and Domini with secret delight. She liked this abrupt unveiling of the raw. There had always lurked in her an audacity, a quick spirit of adventure more boyish than feminine. She had reached the age of thirty-two without ever gratifying it, or even fully realising how much she longed to gratify it. But now she began to understand it and to feel that it was imperious.

"I have a barbarian in me," she thought.

"Batouch!" she said sharply.

The poet turned a distorted face to her.

"Madame!"

"That will do. Take us to the dancing-house."

Batouch shot a last ferocious glance at Hadj and they went on into the crowd of strolling men.

The little street, bright with the lamps of the small houses, from which projected wooden balconies painted in gay colours, and with the glowing radiance of the moon, was mysterious despite its gaiety, its obvious dedication to the cult of pleasure. Alive with the shrieking sounds of music, the movement and the murmur of desert humanity made it almost solemn. This crowd of boys and men, robed in white from head to heel, preserved a serious grace in its vivacity, suggested besides a dignified barbarity a mingling of angel, monk and nocturnal spirit. In the distance of the moonbeams, gliding slowly over the dusty road with slippered feet, there was something soft and radiant in their moving whiteness. Nearer, their pointed hoods made them monastical as a procession stealing from a range of cells to chant a midnight mass. In the shadowy dusk of the tiny side alleys they were like wandering ghosts intent on unholy errands or returning to the graveyard.

On some of the balconies painted girls were leaning and smoking cigarettes. Before each of the lighted doorways from which the shrill noise of music came, small, intent crowds were gathered, watching the performance that was going on inside. The robes of the Arabs brushed against the skirts of Domini and Suzanne, and eyes stared at them from every side with a scrutiny that was less impudent than seriously bold.

" Madame! "

Hadj's thin hand was pulling Domini's sleeve.

" Well, what is it? "

" This is the best dancing-house. The children dance here."

Domini's height enabled her to peer over the shoulders of those gathered before the door, and in the lighted distance of a white-walled room, painted with figures of soldiers and Arab chiefs, she saw a small wriggling figure between two rows of squatting men, two baby hands waving coloured handkerchiefs, two little feet tapping vigorously upon an earthen floor, for background a divan crowded with women and musicians, with inflated cheeks and squinting eyes. She stood for a moment to look, then she turned away. There was an expression of disgust in her eyes.

" No, I don't want to see children," she said. " That's too——"

She glanced at her escort and did not finish.

" I know," said Batouch. " Madame wishes for the real ouleds."

He led them across the street. Hadj followed reluctantly. Before going into this second dancing-house Domini stopped again to see from outside what it was like, but only for an instant. Then a brightness came into her eyes, an eager look.

" Yes, take me in here," she said.

Batouch laughed softly, and Hadj uttered a word below his breath.

" Madame will see Irena here," said Batouch, pushing the watching Arabs unceremoniously away.

Domini did not answer. Her eyes were fixed on a man who was sitting in a corner far up the room, bending forward and staring intently at a woman who was in the act of stepping down from a raised platform decorated with lamps and small bunches of flowers in earthen pots.

" I wish to sit quite near the door," she whispered to Batouch as they went in.

"But it is much better——"

"Do what I tell you," she said. "The left side of the room."

Hadj looked a little happier. Suzanne was clinging to his arm. He smiled at her with something of mischief, but he took care, when a place was cleared on a bench for their party, to sit down at the end next the door, and he cast an anxious glance towards the platform where the dancing-girls attached to the *café* sat in a row, hunched up against the bare wall, waiting their turn to perform. Then suddenly he shook his head, tucked in his chin and laughed. His whole face was transformed from craven fear to vivacious rascality. While he laughed he looked at Batouch, who was ordering four cups of coffee from the negro attendant. The poet took no notice. For the moment he was intent upon his professional duties. But when the coffee was brought, and set upon a round wooden stool between two bunches of roses, he had time to note Hadj's sudden gaiety and to realise its meaning. Instantly he spoke to the negro in a low voice. Hadj stopped laughing. The negro sped away and returned with the proprietor of the *café,* a stout Kabyle with a fair skin and blue eyes.

Batouch lowered his voice to a guttural whisper and spoke in Arabic, while Hadj, shifting uneasily on the end seat, glanced at him sideways out of his almond-shaped eyes. Domini heard the name "Irena," and guessed that Batouch was asking the Kabyle to send for her and make her dance. She could not help being amused for a moment by the comedy of intrigue, complacently malignant on both sides, that was being played by the two cousins, but the moment passed and left her engrossed, absorbed, and not merely by the novelty of the surroundings, by the strangeness of the women, of their costumes, and of their movements. She watched them, but she watched more closely, more eagerly, rather as a spy than as a spectator, one who was watching them with an intentness, a still passion, a fierce curiosity and a sort of almost helpless wonder such as she had never seen before, and could never have found within herself to put at the service of any human marvel.

Close to the top of the room on the right the stranger was sitting in the midst of a mob of Arabs, whose flowing draperies almost concealed his ugly European clothes. On the wall immediately behind him was a brilliantly-coloured drawing of a fat Ouled Naïl leering at a French soldier, which made an unconventional background to his leaning figure and sunburnt face, in which there seemed now to be both asceticism and something so different and so powerful that it was likely, from moment to moment, to drive out the asceticism and to achieve the loneliness of all conquering things. This fighting expression made Domini think of a picture she had once seen representing a pilgrim going through a dark forest attended by his angel and his devil. The angel of the pilgrim was a weak and almost childish figure, frail, bloodless, scarcely even radiant, while the devil was lusty and bold, with a muscular body and a sensual aquiline face, which smiled craftily, looking at the pilgrim. There was surely a devil in the watching traveller which was pushing the angel out of him. Domini had never before seemed to see clearly the legendary battle of the human heart. But it had never before been manifested to her audaciously in the human face.

All around the Arabs sat, motionless and at ease, gazing on the curious dance of which they never tire—a dance which has some ingenuity, much sensuality and provocation, but little beauty and little mystery, unless—as happens now and then— an idol-like woman of the South, with all the enigma of the distant desert in her kohl-tinted eyes, dances it with the sultry gloom of a half-awakened sphinx, and makes of it a barbarous manifestation of the nature that lies hidden in the heart of the sun, a silent cry uttered by a savage body born in a savage land.

In the *café* of Tahar, the Kabyle, there was at present no such woman. His beauties, huddled together on their narrow bench before a table decorated with glasses of water and sprigs of orange blossom in earthen vases, looked dull and cheerless in their gaudy clothes. Their bodies were well formed, but somnolent. Their painted hands hung down like the hands of marionettes. The one who was dancing suggested Duty clad in Eastern garb and laying herself out carefully to be wicked. Her jerks and wrigglings, though violent, were inhuman, like those of a complicated piece of mechanism devised by a morbid engineer. After a glance or two at her Domini felt that she was bored by her own agilities. Domini's wonder increased when she looked again at the traveller.

For it was this dance of the *ennui* of the East which raised up in him this obvious battle, which drove his secret into the illumination of the hanging lamps and gave it to a woman, who felt half confused, half ashamed at possessing it, and yet could not cast it away.

If they both lived on, without speaking or meeting, for another half century, Domini could never know the shape of the devil in this man, the light of the smile upon its face.

The dancing woman had observed him, and presently she began slowly to wriggle towards him between the rows of Arabs, fixing her eyes upon him and parting her scarlet lips in a greedy smile. As she came on the stranger evidently began to realise that he was her bourne. He had been leaning forward, but when she approached, waving her red hands, shaking her prominent breasts, and violently jerking her stomach, he sat straight up, and then, as if instinctively trying to get away from her, pressed back against the wall, hiding the painting of the Ouled Naïl and the French soldier. A dark flush rose on his face and even flooded his forehead to his low-growing hair. His eyes were full of a piteous anxiety and discomfort, and he glanced almost guiltily to right and left of him as if he expected the hooded Arab spectators to condemn his presence there now that the dancer drew their attention to it. The dancer noticed his confusion and seemed pleased by it, and moved to more energetic demonstrations of her art. She lifted her arms above her head, half closed her eyes, assumed an expression of languid ecstasy and slowly shuddered. Then, bending backward, she nearly touched the floor, swung round, still bending, and showed the long curve of her bare throat to the stranger, while the girls, huddled on the bench by the musicians, suddenly roused themselves and joined their voices in a shrill and prolonged twitter. The Arabs did not smile, but the deepness of their attention seemed to increase like a cloud growing darker. All the luminous eyes in the room were steadily fixed upon the man leaning back against the hideous picture on the wall and the gaudy siren curved almost into an arch before him. The musicians blew their hautboys and beat their tom-toms more violently, and all things, Domini thought, were filled with a sense of climax. She felt as if the room, all the inanimate objects, and all the animate figures in it, were instruments of an orchestra, and as if each individual instrument was contributing to a slow, and great, and irresistible crescendo. The stranger took his part with the rest, but against his will, and as if under some terrible compulsion.

His face was scarlet now, and his shining eyes looked down on the dancer's throat and breast with a mingling of eagerness and horror. Slowly she raised herself, turned, bent forwards quivering, and presented her face to him, while the women twittered once more in chorus. He still stared at her without moving. The hautboy players prolonged a wailing note, and the tom-toms gave forth a fierce and dull murmur almost like a death-roll.

"She wants him to give her money," Batouch whispered to Domini. "Why does not he give her money?"

Evidently the stranger did not understand what was expected of him. The music changed again to a shrieking tune, the dancer drew back, did a few more steps, jerked her stomach with fury, stamped her feet on the floor. Then once more she shuddered slowly, half closed her eyes, glided close to the stranger, and falling down deliberately laid her head on his knees, while again the women twittered, and the long note of the hautboys went through the room like a scream of interrogation.

Domini grew hot as she saw the look that came into the stranger's face when the woman touched his knees.

"Go and tell him it's money she wants!" she whispered to Batouch. "Go and tell him!"

Batouch got up, but at this moment a roguish Arab boy, who sat by the stranger, laughingly spoke to him, pointing to the woman. The stranger thrust his hand into his pocket, found a coin and, directed by the roguish youth, stuck it upon the dancer's greasy forehead. At once she sprang to her feet. The women twittered. The music burst into a triumphant melody, and through the room there went a stir. Almost everyone in it moved simultaneously. One man raised his hand to his hood and settled it over his forehead. Another put his cigarette to his lips. Another picked up his coffee-cup. A fourth, who was holding a flower, lifted it to his nose and smelt it. No one remained quite still. With the stranger's action a strain had been removed, a mental tension abruptly loosened, a sense of care let free in the room. Domini felt it acutely. The last few minutes had been painful to her. She sighed with relief at the cessation of another's agony. For the stranger had cer-tainly—from shyness or whatever cause—been in agony while the dancer kept her head upon his knees.

His angel had been in fear, perhaps, while his devil——

But Domini tried resolutely to turn her thoughts from the smiling face.

After pressing the money on the girl's forehead the man made a movement as if he meant to leave the room, but once again the curious indecision which Domini had observed in him before cut his action, as it were, in two, leaving it half finished. As the dancer, turning, wriggled slowly to the platform, he buttoned up his jacket with a sort of hasty resolution, pulled it down with a jerk, glanced swiftly round, and rose to his feet. Domini kept her eyes on him, and perhaps they drew his, for, just as he was about to step into the narrow aisle that led to the door he saw her. Instantly he sat down again, turned so that she could only see part of his face, unbuttoned his jacket, took out some matches and busied himself in lighting a cigarette. She knew he had felt her concentration on him, and was angry with herself. Had she really a spy in her? Was she capable of being vulgarly curious about a man? A sudden movement of Hadj drew her attention. His face was distorted by an expression that seemed half angry, half fearful. Batouch was smiling seraphically as he gazed towards the platform. Suzanne, with a pinched-up mouth, was looking virginally at her lap. Her whole attitude showed her consciousness of the many blazing eyes that were intently staring at her. The stomach dance which she had just been watching had amazed her so much that she felt as if she were the only respectable woman in the world, and as if no one would suppose it unless she hung out banners white as the walls of Beni-Mora's houses. She strove to do so, and, meanwhile, from time to time, cast sideway glances towards the platform to see whether another stomach dance was preparing. She did not see Hadj's excitement or the poet's malignant satisfaction, but she, with Domini, saw a small door behind the platform open, and the stout Kabyle appear followed by a girl who was robed in gold tissue, and decorated with cascades of golden coins.

Domini guessed at once that this was Irena, the returned exile, who wished to kill Hadj, and she was glad that a new incident had occurred to switch off the general attention from the stranger.

Irena was evidently a favourite. There was a grave movement as she came in, a white undulation as all the shrouded forms bent slightly forward in her direction. Only Hadj caught his burnous round him with his thin fingers, dropped his chin, shook his hood down upon his forehead, leaned back against the wall, and, curling his legs under him, seemed to fall asleep. But beneath his brown lids and long black lashes his furtive eyes followed every movement of the girl in the sparkling robe.

She came in slowly and languidly, with a heavy and cross expression upon her face, which was thin to emaciation and painted white, with scarlet lips and darkened eyes and eye-brows. Her features were narrow and pointed. Her bones were tiny, and her body was so slender, her waist so small, that, with her flat breast and meagre shoulders, she looked almost like a stick crowned with a human face and hung with brilliant draperies. Her hair, which was thick and dark brown, was elaborately braided and covered with a yellow silk handker-chief. Domini thought she looked consumptive, and was bit-terly disappointed in her appearance. For some unknown reason she had expected the woman who wished to kill Hadj, and who obviously inspired him with fear, to be a magnificent and glowing desert beauty. This woman might be violent. She looked weary, anæmic, and as if she wished to go to bed, and Domini's contempt for Hadj increased as she looked at her. To be afraid of a thin, tired, sleepy creature such as that was too pitiful. But Hadj did not seem to think so. He had pulled his hood still further forward, and was now merely a bundle concealed in the shade of Suzanne.

Irena stepped on to the platform, pushed the girl who sat at the end of the bench till she moved up higher, sat down in the vacant place, drank some water out of the glass nearest to her, and then remained quite still staring at the floor, utterly indif-ferent to the Arabs who were devouring her with their eyes. No doubt the eyes of men had devoured her ever since she could remember. It was obvious that they meant nothing to her, that they did not even for an instant disturb the current of her dreary thoughts.

Another girl was dancing, a stout, Oriental Jewess with a thick hooked nose, large lips and bulging eyes, that looked as if they had been newly scoured with emery powder. While she danced she sang, or rather shouted roughly, an extraordinary melody that suggested battle, murder and sudden death. Care-less of onlookers, she sometimes scratched her head or rubbed her nose without ceasing her contortions. Domini guessed that this was the girl whom she had seen from the tower dancing upon the roof in the sunset. Distance and light had indeed transformed her. Under the lamps she was the embodiment of all that was coarse and greasy. Even the pitiful slenderness of Irena seemed attractive when compared with her billowing charms, which she kept in a continual commotion that was almost terrifying.

"Hadj is nearly dead with fear," whispered Batouch, com-placently.

Domini's lips curled.

"Does not Madame think Irena beautiful as the moon on the waters of the Oued Beni-Mora?"

"Indeed I don't," she replied bluntly. "And I think a man who can be afraid of such a little thing must be afraid of the children in the street."

"Little! But Irena is tall as a female palm in Ourlana."

"Tall!"

Domini looked at her again more carefully, and saw that Batouch spoke the truth. Irena was unusually tall, but her excessive narrowness, her tiny bones, and the delicate way in which she held herself deceived the eye and gave her a little appearance.

"So she is; but who could be afraid of her? Why, I could pick her up and throw her over that moon of yours."

"Madame is strong. Madame is like the lioness. But Irena is the most terrible girl in all Beni-Mora if she loves or if she is angry, the most terrible in all the Sahara."

Domini laughed.

"Madame does not know her," said Batouch, imperturbably. "But Madame can ask the Arabs. Many of the dancers of Beni-Mora are murdered, each season two or three. But no man would try to murder Irena. No man would dare."

The poet's calm and unimpassioned way of alluding to the most horrible crimes as if they were perfectly natural, and in no way to be condemned or wondered at, amazed Domini even more than his statement about Irena.

"Why do they murder the dancers?" she asked quickly.

"For their jewels. At night, in those little rooms with the balconies which Madame has seen, it is easy. You enter in to sleep there. You close your eyes, you breathe gently and a little loud. The woman hears. She is not afraid. She sleeps. She dreams. Her throat is like that"—he threw back his head, exposing his great neck. "Just before dawn you draw your knife from your burnous. You bend down. You cut the throat without noise. You take the jewels, the money from the box by the bed. You go down quietly with bare feet. No one is on the stair. You unbar the door—and there before you is the great hiding-place."

"The great hiding-place!"

"The desert, Madame."

He sipped his coffee. Domini looked at him, fascinated. Suzanne shivered. She had been listening. The loud contralto cry of the Jewess rose up, with its suggestion of violence and of rough indifference. And Domini repeated softly:

" The great hiding-place."

With every moment in Beni-Mora the desert seemed to become more—more full of meaning, of variety, of mystery, of terror. Was it everything? The garden of God, the great hiding-place of murderers! She had called it, on the tower, the home of peace. In the gorge of El-Akbara, ere he prayed, Batouch had spoken of it as a vast realm of forgetfulness, where the load of memory slips from the weary shoulders and vanishes into the soft gulf of the sands.

But was it everything then? And if it was so much to her already, in a night and a day, what would it be when she knew it, what would it be to her after many nights and many days? She began to feel a sort of terror mingled with the most extraordinary attraction she had ever known.

Hadj crouched right back against the wall. The voice of the Jewess ceased in a shout. The hautboys stopped playing. Only the tom-toms roared.

" Hadj can be happy now," observed Batouch in a voice of almost satisfaction, " for Irena is going to dance. Look! There is the little Miloud bringing her the daggers."

An Arab boy, with a beautiful face and a very dark skin, slipped on to the platform with two long, pointed knives in his hand. He laid them on the table before Irena, between the bouquets of orange blossom, jumped lightly down and disappeared.

Directly the knives touched the table the hautboy players blew a terrific blast, and then, swelling the note, till it seemed as if they must burst both themselves and their instruments, swung into a tremendous and magnificent tune, a tune tingling with barbarity, yet such as a European could have sung or written down. In an instant it gripped Domini and excited her till she could hardly breathe. It poured fire into her veins and set fire about her heart. It was triumphant as a great song after war in a wild land, cruel, vengeful, but so strong and so passionately joyous that it made the eyes shine and the blood leap, and the spirit rise up and clamour within the body, clamour for utter liberty, for action, for wide fields in which to roam, for long days and nights of glory and of love, for intense hours of emotion and of life lived with exultant desperation. It was a melody that seemed to set the soul of Creation dancing before an ark. The tom-toms accompanied it with an irregular but rhythmical roar which Domini thought was like the deep-voiced shouting of squadrons of fighting men.

Irena looked wearily at the knives. Her expression had not changed, and Domini was amazed at her indifference. The eyes of everyone in the room were fixed upon her. Even Suzanne began to be less virginal in appearance under the influence of this desert song of triumph. Domini did not let her eyes stray any more towards the stranger. For the moment indeed she had forgotten him. Her attention was fastened upon the thin, consumptive-looking creature who was staring at the two knives laid upon the table. When the great tune had been played right through once, and a passionate roll of tom-toms announced its repetition, Irena suddenly shot out her tiny arms, brought her hands down on the knives, seized them and sprang to her feet. She had passed from lassitude to vivid energy with an abruptness that was almost demoniacal, and to an energy with which both mind and body seemed to blaze. Then, as the hautboys screamed out the tune once more, she held the knives above her head and danced.

Irena was not an Ouled Naïl. She was a Kabyle woman born in the mountains of Djurdjura, not far from the village of Tamouda. As a child she had lived in one of those chimneyless and windowless mud cottages with red tiled roofs which are so characteristic a feature of La Grande Kabylie. She had climbed barefoot the savage hills, or descended into the gorges yellow with the broom plant and dipped her brown toes in the waters of the Sebaou. How had she drifted so far from the sharp spurs of her native hills and from the ruddy-haired, blue-eyed people of her tribe? Possibly she had sinned, as the Kabyle women often sin, and fled from the wrath that she would understand, and that all her fierce bravery could not hope to conquer. Or perhaps with her Kabyle blood, itself a brew composed of various strains, Greek, Roman, as well as Berber, were mingling some drops drawn from desert sources, which had manifested themselves physically in her dark hair, mentally in a nomadic instinct which had forbidden her to rest among the beauties of Aït Ouaguennoun, whose legendary charm she did not possess. There was the look of an exile in her face, a weariness that dreamed, perhaps, of distant things. But now that she danced that fled, and the gleam of flame-lit steel was in her eyes.

Tangled and vital impressions came to Domini as she watched. Now she saw Jaël and the tent, and the nails driven into the temples of the sleeping warrior. Now she saw Medea in the

moment before she tore to pieces her brother and threw the
bloody fragments in Aetes's path; Clytemnestra's face while
Agamemnon was passing to the bath, Delilah's when Samson
lay sleeping on her knee. But all these imagined faces of named
women fled like sand grains on a desert wind as the dance
went on and the recurrent melody came back and back and
back with a savage and glorious persistence. They were too
small, too individual, and pinned the imagination down too
closely. This dagger dance let in upon her a larger atmosphere,
in which one human being was as nothing, even a goddess or a
siren prodigal of enchantments was a little thing not without a
narrow meanness of physiognomy.

She looked and listened till she saw a grander procession
troop by, garlanded with mystery and triumph: War as a shape
with woman's eyes: Night, without poppies, leading the stars
and moon and all the vigorous dreams that must come true:
Love of woman that cannot be set aside, but will govern the
world from Eden to the abyss into which the nations fall to
the outstretched hands of God: Death as Life's leader, with a
staff from which sprang blossoms red as the western sky: Savage
Fecundity that crushes all barren things into the silent dust:
and then the Desert.

That came in a pale cloud of sand, with a pale crowd of worshippers, those who had received gifts from the Desert's hands
and sought for more: white-robed Marabouts who had found
Allah in his garden and become a guide to the faithful through
all the circling years: murderers who had gained sanctuary
with barbaric jewels in their blood-stained hands: once tortured
men and women who had cast away terrible recollections in
the wastes among the dunes and in the treeless purple distances,
and who had been granted the sweet oases of forgetfulness to
dwell in: ardent beings who had striven vainly to rest content
with the world of hills and valleys, of sea-swept verges and
murmuring rivers, and who had been driven, by the labouring
soul, on and on towards the flat plains where roll for ever the
golden wheels of the chariot of the sun. She saw, too, the winds
that are the Desert's best-loved children: Health with shining
eyes and a skin of bronze: Passion, half faun, half black-browed
Hercules: and Liberty with upraised arms, beating cymbals
like monstrous spheres of fire.

And she saw palm trees waving, immense palm trees in the
south. It seemed to her that she travelled as far away from
Beni-Mora as she had travelled from England in coming to

Beni-Mora. She made her way towards the sun, joining the pale crowd of the Desert's worshippers. And always, as she travelled, she heard the clashing of the cymbals of Liberty. A conviction was born in her that Fate meant her to know the Desert well, strangely well; that the Desert was waiting calmly for her to come to it and receive that which it had to give to her; that in the Desert she would learn more of the meaning of life than she could ever learn elsewhere. It seemed to her suddenly that she understood more clearly than hitherto in what lay the intense, the over-mastering and hypnotic attraction exercised already by the Desert over her nature. In the Desert there must be, there was—she felt it—not only light to warm the body, but light to illuminate the dark places of the soul. An almost fatalistic idea possessed her. She saw a figure—one of the Messengers—standing with her beside the corpse of her father and whispering in her ear " Beni-Mora "; taking her to the map and pointing to the word there, filling her brain and heart with suggestions, till—as she had thought almost without reason, and at haphazard—she chose Beni-Mora as the place to which she would go in search of recovery, of self-knowledge. It had been pre-ordained. The Messenger had been sent. The Messenger had guided her. And he would come again, when the time was ripe, and lead her on into the Desert. She felt it. She knew it.

She looked round at the Arabs. She was as much a fatalist as any one of them. She looked at the stranger. What was he?

Abruptly in her imagination a vision rose. She gazed once more into the crowd that thronged about the Desert having received gifts at the Desert's hands, and in it she saw the stranger.

He was kneeling, his hands were stretched out, his head was bowed, and he was praying. And, while he prayed, Liberty stood by him smiling, and her fiery cymbals were like the aureoles that illumine the beautiful faces of the saints.

For some reason that she could not understand her heart began to beat fast, and she felt a burning sensation behind her eyes.

She thought that this extraordinary music, that this amazing dance, excited her too much.

The white bundle at Suzanne's side stirred. Irena, holding the daggers above her head, had sprung from the little platform and was dancing on the earthen floor in the midst of the Arabs.

Her thin body shook convulsively in time to the music. She marked the accents with her shudders. Excitement had grown in her till she seemed to be in a feverish passion that was half exultant, half despairing. In her expression, in her movements, in the way she held herself, leaning backwards with her face looking up, her breast and neck exposed as if she offered her life, her love and all the mysteries in her, to an imagined being who dominated her savage and ecstatic soul, there was a vivid suggestion of the two elements in Passion—rapture and melancholy. In her dance she incarnated passion whole by conveying the two halves that compose it. Her eyes were nearly closed, as a woman closes them when she has seen the lips of her lover descending upon hers. And her mouth seemed to be receiving the fiery touch of another mouth. In this moment she was a beautiful woman because she looked like womanhood. And Domini understood why the Arabs thought her more beautiful than the other dancers. She had what they had not—genius. And genius, under whatever form, shows to the world at moments the face of Aphrodite.

She came slowly nearer, and those by the platform turned round to follow her with their eyes. Hadj's hood had slipped completely down over his face, and his chin was sunk on his chest. Batouch noticed it and looked angry, but Domini had forgotten both the comedy of the two cousins and the tragedy of Irena's love for Hadj. She was completely under the fascination of this dance and of the music that accompanied it. Now that Irena was near she was able to see that, without her genius, there would have been no beauty in her face. It was painfully thin, painfully long and haggard. Her life had written a fatal inscription across it as their life writes upon the faces of poor street-bred children the one word—Want. As they have too little this dancing woman had had too much. The sparkle of her robe of gold tissue covered with golden coins was strong in the lamplight. Domini looked at it and at the two sharp knives above her head, looked at her violent, shuddering movements, and shuddered too, thinking of Batouch's story of murdered dancers. It was dangerous to have too much in Beni-Mora.

Irena was quite close now. She seemed so wrapped in the ecstasy of the dance that it did not occur to Domini at first that she was imitating the Ouled Naïl who had laid her greasy head upon the stranger's knees. The abandonment of her performance was so great that it was difficult to remember its money value to her and to Tahar, the fair Kabyle. Only when she was actually opposite to them and stayed there, still performing her shuddering dance, still holding the daggers above her head, did Domini realise that those half-closed, passionate eyes had marked the stranger woman, and that she must add one to the stream of golden coins. She took out her purse but did not give the money at once. With the pitiless scrutiny of her sex she noticed all the dancer's disabilities. She was certainly young, but she was very worn. Her mouth drooped. At the corners of her eyes there were tiny lines tending downward. Her forehead had what Domini secretly called a martyred look. Nevertheless, she was savage and triumphant. Her thin body suggested force; the way she held herself consuming passion. Even so near at hand, even while she was pausing for money, and while her eyes were, doubtless, furtively reading Domini, she shed round her a powerful atmosphere, which stirred the blood, and made the heart leap, and created longing for unknown and violent things. As Domini watched her she felt that Irena must have lived at moments magnificently, that despite her almost shattered condition and permanent weariness—only cast aside for the moment of the dance—she must have known intense joys, that so long as she lived she would possess the capacity for knowing them again. There was something burning within her that would burn on so long as she was alive, a spark of nature that was eternally red hot. It was that spark which made her the idol of the Arabs and shed a light of beauty through her haggard frame.

The spirit blazed.

Domini put her hand at last into her purse and took out a piece of gold. She was just going to give it to Irena when the white bundle that was Hadj made a sudden, though slight, movement, as if the thing inside it had shivered. Irena noticed it with her half-closed eyes. Domini leaned forward and held out the money, then drew back startled. Irena had changed her posture abruptly. Instead of keeping her head thrown back and exposing her long throat, she lifted it, shot it forward. Her meagre bosom almost disappeared as she bent over. Her arms fell to her sides. Her eyes opened wide and became full of a sharp, peering intensity. Her vision and dreams dropped out of her. Now she was only fierce and questioning, and horribly alert. She was looking at the white bundle. It shifted again. She sprang upon it, showing her teeth, caught hold of it. With a swift turn of her thin hands she tore back

the hood, and out of the bundle came Hadj's head and face
livid with fear. One of the daggers flashed and came up at
him. He leaped from the seat and screamed. Suzanne echoed
his cry. Then the whole room was a turmoil of white garments
and moving limbs. In an instant everybody seemed to be leaping, calling out, grasping, struggling. Domini tried to get up,
but she was hemmed in, and could not make a movement upward
or free her arms, which were pressed against her sides by the
crowd around her. For a moment she thought she was going
to be severely hurt or suffocated. She did not feel afraid, but
only indignant, like a boy who has been struck in the face and
longs to retaliate. Someone screamed again. It was Hadj.
Suzanne was on her feet, but separated from her mistress.
Batouch's arm was round her. Domini put her hands on the
bench and tried to force herself up, violently setting her broad
shoulders against the Arabs who were towering over her and
covering her head and face with their floating garments as they
strove to see the fight between Hadj and the dancer. The heat
almost stifled her, and she was suddenly aware of a strong
musky smell of perspiring humanity. She was beginning to
pant for breath when she felt two burning, hot, hard hands
come down on hers, fingers like iron catch hold of hers, go
under them, drag up her hands. She could not see who had
seized her, but the life in the hands that were on hers mingled
with the life in her hands like one fluid with another, and seemed
to pass on till she felt it in her body, and had an odd sensation as if her face had been caught in a fierce grip, and her
heart too.

Another moment and she was on her feet and out in the
moonlit alley between the little white houses. She saw the stars,
and the painted balconies crowded with painted women looking
down towards the *café* she had left and chattering in shrill
voices. She saw the patrol of Tirailleurs Indigènes marching
at the double to the doorway in which the Arabs were still
struggling. Then she saw that the traveller was beside her.
She was not surprised.

" Thank you for getting me out," she said rather bluntly.
" Where's my maid? "

" She got away before us with your guide, Madame."

He held up his hands and looked at them hard, eagerly,
questioningly.

" You weren't hurt? "

He dropped his hands quickly.

" Oh, no, it wasn't——"

He broke off the sentence and was silent. Domini stood still, drew a long breath and laughed. She still felt angry and laughed to control herself. Unless she could be amused at this episode she knew that she was capable of going back to the door of the *café* and hitting out right and left at the men who had nearly suffocated her. Any violence done to her body, even an unintentional push against her in the street—if there was real force in it—seemed to let loose a devil in her, such a devil as ought surely only to dwell inside a man.

" What people! " she said. " What wild creatures! "

She laughed again. The patrol pushed its way roughly in at the doorway.

" The Arabs are always like that, Madame."

She looked at him, then she said, abruptly:

" Do you speak English? "

Her companion hesitated. It was perfectly obvious to her that he was considering whether he should answer " Yes " or " No." Such hesitation about such a matter was very strange. At last he said, but still in French:

" Yes."

And directly he had said it she saw by his face that he wished he had said " No."

From the *café* the Arabs began to pour into the street. The patrol was clearing the place. The women leaning over the balconies cried out shrilly to learn the exact history of the tumult, and the men standing underneath, and lifting up their bronzed faces in the moonlight, replied in violent voices, gesticulating vehemently while their hanging sleeves fell back from their hairy arms.

" I am an Englishwoman," Domini said.

But she too felt obliged to speak still in French, as if a sudden reserve told her to do so. He said nothing. They were standing in quite a crowd now. It swayed, parted suddenly, and the soldiers appeared holding Irena. Hadj followed behind, shouting as if in a frenzy of passion. There was some blood on one of his hands and a streak of blood on the front of the loose shirt he wore under his burnous. He kept on shooting out his arms towards Irena as he walked, and frantically appealing to the Arabs round him. When he saw the women on their balconies he stopped for a moment and called out to them like a man beside himself. A Tirailleur pushed him on. The women, who had been quiet to hear him, burst forth again into a paroxysm of chatter. Irena looked utterly indifferent and walked feebly. The little procession disappeared in the moonlight accompanied by the crowd.

"She has stabbed Hadj," Domini said. "Batouch will be glad."

She did not feel as if she were sorry. Indeed, she thought she was glad too. That the dancer should try to do a thing and fail would have seemed contradictory. And the streak of blood she had just seen seemed to relieve her suddenly and to take from her all anger. Her self-control returned.

"Thank you once more," she said to her companion. "Good-night."

She remembered the episode of the tower that afternoon, and resolved to take a definite line this time, and not to run the chance of a second desertion. She started off down the street, but found him walking beside her in silence. She stopped.

"I am very much obliged to you for getting me out," she said, looking straight at him. "And now, good-night."

Almost for the first time he endured her gaze without any uncertainty, and she saw that though he might be hesitating, uneasy, even contemptible—as when he hurried down the road in the wake of the negro procession—he could also be a dogged man.

"I'll go with you, Madame," he said.

"Why?"

"It's night."

"I'm not afraid."

"I'll go with you, Madame."

He said it again harshly and kept his eyes on her, frowning.

"And if I refuse?" she said, wondering whether she was going to refuse or not.

"I'll follow you, Madame."

She knew by the look on his face that he, too, was thinking of what had happened in the afternoon. Why should she wish to deprive him of the reparation he was anxious to make—obviously anxious in an almost piteously determined way? It was poor pride in her, a mean little feeling.

"Come with me," she said.

They went on together.

The Arabs, stirred up by the fracas in Tahar's *café*, were seething with excitement, and several of them, gathered together in a little crowd, were quarrelling and shouting at the end of the street near the statue of the Cardinal. Domini's escort saw them and hesitated.

"I think, Madame, it would be better to take a side street," he said.

"Very well. Let us go to the left here. It is bound to bring us to the hotel as it runs parallel to the house of the sand diviner."

He started.

"The sand diviner?" he said in his low, strong voice.

"Yes."

She walked on into a tiny alley. He followed her.

"You haven't seen the thin man with the bag of sand?"

"No, Madame."

"He reads your past in sand from the desert and tells what your future will be."

The man made no reply.

"Will you pay him a visit?" Domini asked curiously.

"No, Madame. I do not care for such things."

Suddenly she stood still.

"Oh, look!" she said. "How strange! And there are others all down the street."

In the tiny alley the balconies of the houses nearly met. No figures leaned on their railings. No chattering voices broke the furtive silence that prevailed in this quarter of Beni-Mora. The moonlight was fainter here, obscured by the close-set buildings, and at the moment there was not an Arab in sight. The sense of loneliness and peace was profound, and as the rare windows of the houses, minute and protected by heavy gratings, were dark, it had seemed to Domini at first as if all the inhabitants were in bed and asleep. But, in passing on, she had seen a faint and blanched illumination; then another; the vague vision of an aperture; a seated figure making a darkness against whiteness; a second aperture and seated figure. She stopped and stood still. The man stood still beside her.

The alley was an alley of women. In every house on either side of the way a similar picture of attentive patience was revealed: a narrow Moorish archway with a wooden door set back against the wall to show a steep and diminutive staircase winding up into mystery; upon the highest stair a common candlestick with a lit candle guttering in it, and, immediately below, a girl, thickly painted, covered with barbarous jewels and magnificently dressed, her hands, tinted with henna, folded in her lap, her eyes watching under eyebrows heavily dark-

ened, and prolonged until they met just above the bridge of
the nose, to which a number of black dots descended; her
naked, brown ankles decorated with large circlets of gold or
silver. The candle shed upon each watcher a faint light that
half revealed her and left her half concealed upon her white
staircase bounded by white walls. And in her absolute silence,
absolute stillness, each one was wholly mysterious as she gazed
ceaselessly out towards the empty, narrow street.

The woman before whose dwelling Domini had stopped
was an Ouled Naïl, with a square headdress of coloured handkerchiefs and feathers, a pink and silver shawl, a blue skirt
of some thin material powdered with silver flowers, and a
broad silver belt set with squares of red coral. She was sitting upright, and would have looked exactly like an idol set
up for savage worship had not her long eyes gleamed and
moved as she solemnly returned the gaze of Domini and of
the man who stood a little behind looking over her shoulder.

When Domini stopped and exclaimed she did not realise to
what this street was dedicated, why these women sat in
watchful silence, each one alone on her stair waiting in the
night. But as she looked and saw the gaudy finery she began to understand. And had she remained in doubt an
incident now occurred which must have enlightened her.

A great gaunt Arab, one of the true desert men, almost
black, with high cheek bones, hollow cheeks, fierce falcon's
eyes shining as if with fever, long and lean limbs hard as iron,
dressed in a rough, sacklike brown garment, and wearing a
turban bound with cords of camel's hair, strode softly down
the alley, slipped in front of Domini, and went up to the
woman, holding out something in his scaly hand. There was
a brief colloquy. The woman stretched her arm up the staircase, took the candle, held it to the man's open hand, and bent
over counting the money that lay in the palm. She counted
it twice deliberately. Then she nodded. She got up, turned,
holding the candle above her square headdress, and went
slowly up the staircase followed by the Arab, who grasped
his coarse draperies and lifted them, showing his bare legs.
The two disappeared without noise into the darkness, leaving
the stairway deserted, its white steps, its white walls faintly
lit by the moon.

The woman had not once looked at the man, but only at the
money in his scaly hand.

Domini felt hot and rather sick. She wondered why she

had stood there watching. Yet she had not been able to turn away. Now, as she stepped back into the middle of the alley and walked on with the man beside her she wondered what he was thinking of her. She could not talk to him any more. She was too conscious of the lighted stairways, one after one, succeeding each other to right and left of them, of the still figures, of the watching eyes in which the yellow rays of the candles gleamed. Her companion did not speak; but as they walked he glanced furtively from one side to the other, then stared down steadily on the white road. When they turned to the right and came out by the gardens, and Domini saw the great tufted heads of the palms black against the moon, she felt relieved and was able to speak again.

"I should like you to know that I am quite a stranger to all African things and people," she said. "That is why I am liable to fall into mistakes in such a place as this. Ah, there is the hotel, and my maid on the verandah. I want to thank you again for looking after me."

They were at a few steps from the hotel door in the road. The man stopped, and Domini stopped too.

"Madame," he said earnestly, with a sort of hardly controlled excitement, "I—I am glad. I was ashamed—I was ashamed."

"Why?"

"Of my conduct—of my awkwardness. But you will forgive it. I am not accustomed to the society of ladies—like you. Anything I have done I have not done out of rudeness. That is all I can say. I have not done it out of rudeness."

He seemed to be almost trembling with agitation.

"I know, I know," she said. "Besides, it was nothing."

"Oh, no, it was abominable. I understand that. I am not so coarse-fibred as not to understand that."

Domini suddenly felt that to take his view of the matter, exaggerated though it was, would be the kindest course, even the most delicate.

"You were rude to me," she said, "but I shall forget it from this moment."

She held out her hand. He grasped it, and again she felt as if a furnace were pouring its fiery heat upon her.

"Good-night."

"Good-night, Madame. Thank you."

She was going away to the hotel door, but she stopped.

"My name is Domini Enfilden," she said in English.

The man stood in the road looking at her. She waited. She expected him to tell her his name. There was a silence. At last he said hesitatingly, in English with a very slight foreign accent:

"My name is Boris—Boris Androvsky."

"Batouch told me you were English," she said.

"My mother was English, but my father was a Russian from Tiflis. That is my name."

There was a sound in his voice as if he were insisting like a man making an assertion not readily to be believed.

"Good-night," Domini said again.

And she went away slowly, leaving him standing on the moonlit road.

He did not remain there long, nor did he follow her into the hotel. After she had disappeared he stood for a little while gazing up at the deserted verandah upon which the moonrays fell. Then he turned and looked towards the village, hesitated, and finally walked slowly back towards the tiny, shrouded alley in which on the narrow staircases the painted girls sat watching in the night.

CHAPTER IX

ON the following morning Batouch arrived with a handsome grey Arab horse for Domini to try. He had been very penitent the night before, and Domini had forgiven easily enough his pre-occupation with Suzanne, who had evidently made a strong impression upon his susceptible nature. Hadj had been but slightly injured by Irena, but did not appear at the hotel for a very sufficient reason. Both the dancer and he were locked up for the moment, till the Guardians of Justice in Beni-Mora had made up their minds who should be held responsible for the uproar of the previous night. That the real culprit was the smiling poet was not likely to occur to them, and did not seem to trouble him. When Domini inquired after Hadj he showed majestic indifference, and when she hinted at his crafty share in the causing of the tragedy he calmly replied:

"Hadj-ben-Ibrahim will know from henceforth whether the Mehari with the swollen tongue can bite."

Then, leaping upon the horse, whose bridle he was holding, he forced it to rear, caracole and display its spirit and its paces before Domini, sitting it superbly, and shooting many sly glances at Suzanne, who leaned over the parapet of the verandah watching, with a rapt expression on her face.

Domini admired the horse, but wished to mount it herself before coming to any conclusion about it. She had brought her own saddle with her and ordered Batouch to put it on the animal. Meanwhile she went upstairs to change into her habit. When she came out again on to the verandah Boris Androvsky was there, standing bare-headed in the sun and looking down at Batouch and the horse. He turned quickly, greeted Domini with a deep bow, then examined her costume with wondering, startled eyes.

" I'm going to try that horse," she said with deliberate friendliness. " To see if I'll buy him. Are you a judge of a horse? "

" I fear not, Madame."

She had spoken in English and he replied in the same language. She was standing at the head of the stairs holding her whip lightly in her right hand. Her splendid figure was defined by the perfectly-fitting, plain habit, and she saw him look at it with a strange expression in his eyes, an admiration that was almost ferocious, and that was yet respectful and even pure. It was like the glance of a passionate schoolboy verging on young manhood, whose natural instincts were astir but whose temperament was unwarped by vice; a glance that was a burning tribute, and that told a whole story of sex and surely of hot, inquiring ignorance—strange glances of a man no longer even very young. It made something in her leap and quiver. She was startled and almost angered by that, but not by the eyes that caused it.

" *Au revoir,*" she said, turning to go down.

" May I—might I see you get up? " said Androvsky.

" Get up! " she said.

" Up on the horse? "

She could not help smiling at his fashion of expressing the act of mounting. He was not a sportsman evidently, despite his muscular strength.

" Certainly, if you like. Come along."

Without thinking of it she spoke rather as to a schoolboy, not with superiority, but with the sort of bluffness age sometimes uses good-naturedly to youth. He did not seem to resent it and followed her down to the arcade.

The side saddle was on and the poet held the grey by the

bridle. Some Arab boys had assembled under the arcade to
see what was going forward. The Arab waiter lounged at
the door with the tassel of his fez swinging against his pale
cheek. The horse fidgetted and tugged against the rein, lifting his delicate feet uneasily from the ground, flicking his
narrow quarters with his long tail, and glancing sideways with
his dark and brilliant eyes, which were alive with a nervous
intelligence that was almost hectic. Domini went up to him
and caressed him with her hand. He reared up and snorted.
His whole body seemed a-quiver with the desire to gallop
furiously away alone into some far distant place.

Androvsky stood near the waiter, looking at Domini and at
the horse with wonder and alarm in his eyes.

The animal, irritated by inaction, began to plunge violently
and to get out of hand.

"Give me the reins," Domini said to the poet. "That's it.
Now put your hand for me."

Batouch obeyed. Her foot just touched his hand and she
was in the saddle.

Androvsky sprang forward on to the pavement. His
eyes were blazing with anxiety. She saw it and laughed
gaily.

"Oh, he's not vicious," she said. "And vice is the only
thing that's dangerous. His mouth is perfect, but he's nervous and wants handling. I'll just take him up the gardens
and back."

She had been reining him in. Now she let him go, and
galloped up the straight track between the palms towards the
station. The priest had come out into his little garden with
Bous-Bous, and leaned over his brushwood fence to look after
her. Bous-Bous barked in a light soprano. The Arab boys
jumped on their bare toes, and one of them, who was a boot-
black, waved his board over his shaven head. The Arab waiter
smiled as if with satisfaction at beholding perfect competence.
But Androvsky stood quite still looking down the dusty road
at the diminishing forms of horse and rider, and when they
disappeared, leaving behind them a light cloud of sand films
whirling in the sun, he sighed heavily and dropped his chin
on his chest as if fatigued.

"I can get a horse for Monsieur too. Would Monsieur
like to have a horse?"

It was the poet's amply seductive voice. Androvsky started.

"I don't ride," he said curtly.

"I will teach Monsieur. I am the best teacher in Beni-Mora. In three lessons Monsieur will——"

"I don't ride, I tell you."

Androvsky was looking angry. He stepped out into the road. Bous-Bous, who was now observing Nature at the priest's garden gate, emerged with some sprightliness and trotted towards him, evidently with the intention of making his acquaintance. Coming up to him the little dog raised his head and uttered a short bark, at the same time wagging his tail in a kindly, though not effusive manner. Androvsky looked down, bent quickly and patted him, as only a man really fond of animals and accustomed to them knows how to pat. Bous-Bous was openly gratified. He began to wriggle affectionately. The priest in his garden smiled. Androvsky had not seen him and went on playing with the dog, who now made preparations to lie down on his curly back in the road in the hope of being tickled, a process he was an amateur of. Still smiling, and with a friendly look on his face, the priest came out of his garden and approached the playmates.

"Good morning, M'sieur," he said politely, raising his hat. "I see you like dogs."

Androvsky lifted himself up, leaving Bous-Bous in a prayerful attitude, his paws raised devoutly towards the heavens. When he saw that it was the priest who had addressed him his face changed, hardened to grimness, and his lips trembled slightly.

"That's my little dog," the priest continued in a gentle voice. "He has evidently taken a great fancy to you."

Batouch was watching Androvsky under the arcade, and noted the sudden change in his expression and his whole bearing.

"I—I did not know he was your dog, Monsieur, or I should not have interfered with him," said Androvsky.

Bous-Bous jumped up against his leg. He pushed the little dog rather roughly away and stepped back to the arcade. The priest looked puzzled and slightly hurt. At this moment the soft thud of horse's hoofs was audible on the road and Domini came cantering back to the hotel. Her eyes were sparkling, her face was radiant. She bowed to the priest and reined up before the hotel door, where Androvsky was standing.

"I'll buy him," she said to Batouch, who swelled with satisfaction at the thought of his commission. "And I'll go for a long ride now—out into the desert."

"You will not go alone, Madame?"

It was the priest's voice. She smiled down at him gaily.

" Should I be carried off by nomads, Monsieur? "

" It would not be safe for a lady, believe me."

Batouch swept forward to reassure the priest.

" I am Madame's guide. I have a horse ready saddled to accompany Madame. I have sent for it already, M'sieur."

One of the little Arab boys was indeed visible running with all his might towards the Rue Berthe. Domini's face suddenly clouded. The presence of the guide would take all the edge off her pleasure, and in the short gallop she had just had she had savoured its keenness. She was alive with desire to be happy.

" I don't need you, Batouch," she said.

But the poet was inexorable, backed up by the priest.

" It is my duty to accompany Madame. I am responsible for her safety."

" Indeed, you cannot go into the desert alone," said the priest.

Domini glanced at Androvsky, who was standing silently under the arcade, a little withdrawn, looking uncomfortable and self-conscious. She remembered her thought on the tower of the dice-thrower, and of how the presence of the stranger had seemed to double her pleasure then. Up the road from the Rue Berthe came the noise of a galloping horse. The shoeblack was returning furiously, his bare legs sticking out on either side of a fiery light chestnut with a streaming mane and tail.

" Monsieur Androvsky," she said.

He started.

" Madame? "

" Will you come with me for a ride into the desert? "

His face was flooded with scarlet, and he came a step forward, looking up at her.

" I! " he said with an accent of infinite surprise.

" Yes. Will you? "

The chestnut thundered up and was pulled sharply back on its haunches. Androvsky shot a sideways glance at it and hesitated. Domini thought he was going to refuse and wished she had not asked him, wished it passionately.

" Never mind," she said, almost brutally in her vexation at what she had done.

" Batouch! "

The poet was about to spring upon the horse when Androvsky caught him by the arm.

" I will go," he said.

Batouch looked vicious.

" But Monsieur told me he did not——"

He stopped. The hand on his arm had given him a wrench that made him feel as if his flesh were caught between steel pincers. Androvsky came up to the chestnut.

" Oh, it's an Arab saddle," said Domini.

" It does not matter, Madame."

His face was stern.

" Are you accustomed to them ? "

" It makes no difference."

He took hold of the rein and put his foot in the high stirrup, but so awkwardly that he kicked the horse in the side. It plunged.

" Take care ! " said Domini.

Androvsky hung on, and climbed somehow into the saddle, coming down in it heavily, with a thud. The horse, now thoroughly startled, plunged furiously and lashed out with its hind legs. Androvsky was thrown forward against the high red peak of the saddle with his hands on the animal's neck. There was a struggle. He tugged at the rein violently. The horse jumped back, reared, plunged sideways as if about to bolt. Androvsky was shot off and fell on his right shoulder heavily. Batouch caught the horse while Androvsky got up. He was white with dust. There was even dust on his face and in his short hair. He looked passionate.

" You see," Batouch began, speaking to Domini, " that Monsieur cannot——"

" Give me the rein ! " said Androvsky.

There was a sound in his deep voice that was terrible. He was looking not at Domini, but at the priest, who stood a little aside with an expression of concern on his face. Bous-Bous barked with excitement at the conflict. Androvsky took the rein, and, with a sort of furious determination, sprang into the saddle and pressed his legs against the horse's flanks. It reared up. The priest moved back under the palm trees, the Arab boys scattered. Batouch sought the shelter of the arcade, and the horse, with a short, whining neigh that was like a cry of temper, bolted between the trunks of the trees, heading for the desert, and disappeared in a flash.

" He will be killed," said the priest.

Bous-Bous barked frantically.

" It is his own fault," said the poet. " He told me himself just now that he did not know how to ride."

" Why didn't you tell me so ? " Domini exclaimed.

Madame——"

But she was gone, following Androvsky at a slow canter lest she should frighten his horse by coming up behind it. She came out from the shade of the palms into the sun. The desert lay before her. She searched it eagerly with her eyes and saw Androvsky's horse far off in the river bed, still going at a gallop towards the south, towards that region in which she had told him on the tower she thought that peace must dwell. It was as if he had believed her words blindly and was frantically in chase of peace. And she pursued him through the blazing sunlight. She was out in the desert at length, beyond the last belt of verdure, beyond the last line of palms. The desert wind was on her cheek and in her hair. The desert spaces stretched around her. Under her horse's hoofs lay the sparkling crystals on the wrinkled, sun-dried earth. The red rocks, seamed with many shades of colour that all suggested primeval fires and the relentless action of heat, were heaped about her. But her eyes were fixed on the far-off moving speck that was the horse carrying Androvsky madly towards the south. The light and fire, the great airs, the sense of the chase intoxicated her. She struck her horse with the whip. It leaped, as if clearing an immense obstacle, came down lightly and strained forward into the shining mysteries at a furious gallop. The black speck grew larger. She was gaining. The crumbling, cliff-like bank on her left showed a rent in which a faint track rose sharply to the flatness beyond. She put her horse at it and came out among the tiny humps on which grew the halfa grass and the tamarisk bushes. A pale sand flew up here about the horse's feet. Androvsky was still below her in the difficult ground where the water came in the floods. She gained and gained till she was parallel with him and could see his bent figure, his arms clinging to the peak of his red saddle, his legs set forward almost on to his horse's withers by the short stirrups with their metal toe-caps. The animal's temper was nearly spent. She could see that. The terror had gone out of his pace. As she looked she saw Androvsky raise his arms from the saddle peak, catch at the flying rein, draw it up, lean against the saddle back and pull with all his force. The horse stopped dead.

"His strength must be enormous," Domini thought with a startled admiration.

She pulled up too on the bank above him and gave a halloo. He turned his head, saw her, and put his horse at the bank, which was steep here and without any gap.

"You can't do it," she called.

In reply he dug the heels of his heavy boots into the horse's flanks and came on recklessly. She thought the horse would either refuse or try to get up and roll back on its rider. It sprang at the bank and mounted like a wild cat. There was a noise of falling stones, a shower of scattered earth-clods dropping downward, and he was beside her, white with dust, streaming with sweat, panting as if the labouring breath would rip his chest open, with the horse's foam on his forehead, and a savage and yet exultant gleam in his eyes.

They looked at each other in silence, while their horses, standing quietly, lowered their narrow, graceful heads and touched noses with delicate inquiry. Then she said:

"I almost thought——"

She stopped.

"Yes?" he said, on a great gasping breath that was like a sob.

"—that you were off to the centre of the earth, or—I don't know what I thought. You aren't hurt?"

"No."

He could only speak in monosyllables as yet. She looked his horse over.

"He won't give much more trouble just now. Shall we ride back?"

As she spoke she threw a longing glance at the far desert, at the verge of which was a dull green line betokening the distant palms of an oasis.

Androvsky shook his head.

"But you——" She hesitated. "Perhaps you aren't accustomed to horses, and with that saddle——"

He shook his head again, drew a tremendous breath and said:

"I don't care, I'll go on, I won't go back."

He put up one hand, brushed the foam from his streaming forehead, and said again fiercely:

"I won't go back."

His face was extraordinary with its dogged, passionate expression showing through the dust and the sweat; like the face of a man in a fight to the death, she thought, a fight with fists. She was glad at his last words and liked the iron sound in his voice.

"Come on then."

And they began to ride towards the dull green line of the

oasis, slowly on the sandy waste among the little round humps
where the dusty cluster of bushes grew.

" You weren't hurt by the fall? " she said. " It looked a bad
one."

" I don't know whether I was. I don't care whether I was "
He spoke almost roughly.

" You asked me to ride with you," he added. " I'll ride with
you."

She remembered what Batouch had said. There was pluck
in this man, pluck that surged up in the blundering awkwardness, the hesitation, the incompetence and rudeness of him like a
black rock out of the sea. She did not answer. They rode on,
always slowly. His horse, having had its will, and having known
his strength at the end of his incompetence, went quietly, though
always with that feathery, light, tripping action peculiar to pure-
bred Arabs, an action that suggests the treading of a spring
board rather than of the solid earth. And Androvsky seemed
a little more at home on it, although he sat awkwardly on
the chair-like saddle, and grasped the rein too much as the
drowning man seizes the straw. Domini rode without looking
at him, lest he might think she was criticising his performance.
When he had rolled in the dust she had been conscious of a
sharp sensation of contempt. The men she had been accustomed to meet all her life rode, shot, played games as a
matter of course. She was herself an athlete, and, like nearly all
athletic women, inclined to be pitiless towards any man who was
not so strong and so agile as herself. But this man had killed
her contempt at once by his desperate determination not to be
beaten. She knew by the look she had just seen in his eyes that
if to ride with her that day meant death to him he would have
done it nevertheless.

The womanhood in her liked the tribute, almost more than
liked it.

" Your horse goes better now," she said at last to break the
silence.

" Does it? " he said.

" You don't know! "

" Madame, I know nothing of horses or riding. I have not
been on a horse for twenty-three years."

She was amazed.

" We ought to go back then," she exclaimed.

" Why? Other men ride—I will ride. I do it badly.
Forgive me."

" Forgive you! " she said.   " I admire your pluck. But why have you never ridden all these years? "

After a pause he answered:

" I—I did not—I had not the opportunity."

His voice was suddenly constrained. She did not pursue the subject, but stroked her horse's neck and turned her eyes towards the dark green line on the horizon. Now that she was really out in the desert she felt almost bewildered by it, and as if she understood it far less than when she looked at it from Count Anteoni's garden. The thousands upon thousands of sand humps, each crowned with its dusty dwarf bush, each one precisely like the others, agitated her as if she were confronted by a vast multitude of people. She wanted some point which would keep the eyes from travelling but could not find it, and was mentally restless as the swimmer far out at sea who is pursued by wave on wave, and who sees beyond him the unceasing foam of those that are pressing to the horizon. Whither was she riding? Could one have a goal in this immense expanse? She felt an overpowering need to find one, and looked once more at the green line.

" Do you think we could go as far as that? " she asked Androvsky, pointing with her whip.

" Yes, Madame."

" It must be an oasis. Don't you think so? "

" Yes. I can go faster."

" Keep your rein loose. Don't pull his mouth. You don't mind my telling you. I've been with horses all my life."

" Thank you," he answered.

" And keep your heels more out. That's much better. I'm sure you could teach me a thousand things; it will be kind of you to let me teach you this."

He cast a strange look at her. There was gratitude in it, but much more; a fiery bitterness and something childlike and helpless.

" I have nothing to teach," he said.

Their horses broke into a canter, and with the swifter movement Domini felt more calm. There was an odd lightness in her brain, as if her thoughts were being shaken out of it like feathers out of a bag. The power of concentration was leaving her, and a sensation of carelessness—surely gipsy-like—came over her. Her body, dipped in the dry and thin air as in a clear, cool bath, did not suffer from the burning rays of the sun, but felt radiant yet half lazy too. They went on and on in silence as intimate friends might ride together, isolated from the world and content in each other's company, content enough to have no need of talking. Not once did it strike Domini as strange that she should go far out into the desert with a man of whom she knew nothing, but in whom she had noticed disquieting peculiarities. She was naturally fearless, but that had little to do with her conduct. Without saying so to herself she felt she could trust this man.

The dark green line showed clearer through the sunshine across the gleaming flats. It was possible now to see slight irregularities in it, as in a blurred dash of paint flung across a canvas by an uncertain hand, but impossible to distinguish palm trees. The air sparkled as if full of a tiny dust of intensely brilliant jewels, and near the ground there seemed to quiver a maze of dancing specks of light. Everywhere there was solitude, yet everywhere there was surely a ceaseless movement of minute and vital things, scarce visible sun fairies eternally at play.

And Domini's careless feeling grew. She had never before experienced so delicious a recklessness. Head and heart were light, reckless of thought or love. Sad things had no meaning here and grave things no place. For the blood was full of sunbeams dancing to a lilt of Apollo. Nothing mattered here. Even Death wore a robe of gold and went with an airy step. Ah, yes, from this region of quivering light and heat the Arabs drew their easy and lustrous resignation. Out here one was in the hands of a God who surely sang as He created and had not created fear.

Many minutes passed, but Domini was careless of time as of all else. The green line broke into feathery tufts, broadened into a still far-off dimness of palms.

"Water!"

Androvsky's voice spoke as if startled. Domini pulled up. Their horses stood side by side, and at once, with the cessation of motion, the mysticism of the desert came upon them and the marvel of its silence, and they seemed to be set there in a wonderful dream, themselves and their horses dreamlike.

"Water!" he said again.

He pointed, and along the right-hand edge of the oasis Domini saw grey, calm waters. The palms ran out into them and were bathed by them softly. And on their bosom here and there rose small, dim islets. Yes, there was water, and yet——
The mystery of it was a mystery she had never known to brood even over a white northern sea in a twilight hour of winter, was

deeper than the mystery of the Venetian *laguna morta,* when the Angelus bell chimes at sunset, and each distant boat, each bending rower and patient fisherman, becomes a marvel, an eerie thing in the gold.

" Is it mirage? " she said to him almost in a whisper.

And suddenly she shivered.

"Yes, it is, it must be."

He did not answer. His left hand, holding the rein, dropped down on the saddle peak, and he stared across the waste, leaning forward and moving his lips. She looked at him and forgot even the mirage in a sudden longing to understand exactly what he was feeling. His mystery—the mystery of that which is human and is forever stretching out its arms—was as the fluid mystery of the mirage, and seemed to blend at that moment with the mystery she knew lay in herself. The mirage was within them as it was far off before them in the desert, still, grey, full surely of indistinct movement, and even perhaps of sound they could not hear.

At last he turned and looked at her.

" Yes, it must be mirage," he said. " The nothing that seems to be so much. A man comes out into the desert and he finds there mirage. He travels right out and that's what he reaches— or at least he can't reach it, but just sees it far away. And that's all. And is that what a man finds when he comes out into the world? "

It was the first time he had spoken without any trace of reserve to her, for even on the tower, though there had been tumult in his voice and a fierceness of some strange passion in his words, there had been struggle in his manner, as if the pressure of feeling forced him to speak in despite of something which bade him keep silence. Now he spoke as if to someone whom he knew and with whom he had talked of many things.

" But you ought to know better than I do," she answered.

" I! "

" Yes. You are a man, and have been in the world, and must know what it has to give—whether there's only mirage, or something that can be grasped and felt and lived in, and——"

"Yes, I'm a man and I ought to know," he replied. " Well, I don't know, but I mean to know."

There was a savage sound in his voice.

" I should like to know, too," Domini said quietly. " And I feel as if it was the desert that was going to teach me."

" The desert—how? "

" I don't know."

He pointed again to the mirage.

" But that's what there is in the desert."

" That—and what else? "

" Is there anything else? "

" Perhaps everything," she answered. " I am like you. I want to know."

He looked straight into her eyes and there was something dominating in his expression.

" You think it is the desert that could teach you whether the world holds anything but a mirage," he said slowly. " Well, I don't think it would be the desert that could teach me."

She said nothing more, but let her horse go and rode off. He followed, and as he rode awkwardly, yet bravely, pressing his strong legs against his animal's flanks and holding his thin body bent forward, he looked at Domini's upright figure and brilliant, elastic grace—that gave in to her horse as wave gives to wind —with a passion of envy in his eyes.

They did not speak again till the great palm gardens of the oasis they had seen far off were close upon them. From the desert they looked both shabby and superb, as if some millionaire had poured forth money to create a Paradise out here, and, when it was nearly finished, had suddenly repented of his whim and refused to spend another farthing. The thousands upon thousands of mighty trees were bounded by long, irregular walls of hard earth, at the top of which were stuck distraught thorn bushes. These walls gave the rough, penurious aspect which was in such sharp contrast to the exotic mystery they guarded. Yet in the fierce blaze of the sun their meanness was not disagreeable. Domini even liked it. It seemed to her as if the desert had thrown up waves to protect this daring oasis which ventured to fling its green glory like a defiance in the face of the Sahara. A wide track of earth, sprinkled with stones and covered with deep ruts, holes and hummocks, wound in from the desert between the earthen walls and vanished into the heart of the oasis. They followed it.

Domini was filled with a sort of romantic curiosity. This luxury of palms far out in the midst of desolation, untended apparently by human hands—for no figures moved among them, there was no one on the road—suggested some hidden purpose and activity, some concealed personage, perhaps an Eastern Anteoni, whose lair lay surely somewhere beyond them. As she had felt the call of the desert she now felt the call of the oasis.

In this land thrilled eternally a summons to go onward, to seek, to penetrate, to be a passionate pilgrim. She wondered whether her companion's heart could hear it.

" I don't know why it is," she said, " but out here I always feel expectant. I always feel as if some marvellous thing might be going to happen to me."

She did not add " Do you? " but looked at him as if for a reply.

" Yes, Madame," he said.

" I suppose it is because I am new to Africa. This is my first visit here. I am not like you. I can't speak Arabic."

She suddenly wondered whether the desert was new to him as to her. She had assumed that it was. Yet as he spoke Arabic it was almost certain that he had been much in Africa.

" I do not speak it well," he answered.

And he looked away towards the dense thickets of the palms. The track narrowed till the trees on either side cast patterns of moving shade across it and the silent mystery was deepened. As far as the eye could see the feathery, tufted foliage swayed in the little wind. The desert had vanished, but sent in after them the message of its soul, the marvellous breath which Domini had drunk into her lungs so long before she saw it. That breath was like a presence. It dwells in all oases. The high earth walls concealed the gardens. Domini longed to look over and see what they contained, whether there were any dwellings in these dim and silent recesses, any pools of water, flowers or grassy lawns.

Her horse neighed.

" Something is coming," she said.

They turned a corner and were suddenly in a village. A mob of half-naked children scattered from their horses' feet. Rows of seated men in white and earth-coloured robes stared upon them from beneath the shadow of tall, windowless earth houses. White dogs rushed to and fro upon the flat roofs, thrusting forward venomous heads, showing their teeth and barking furiously. Hens fluttered in agitation from one side to the other. A grey mule, tethered to a palm-wood door and loaded with brushwood, lashed out with its hoofs at a negro, who at once began to batter it passionately with a pole, and a long line of sneering camels confronted them, treading stealthily, and turning their serpentine necks from side to side as they came onwards with a soft and weary inflexibility. In the distance there was a vision of a glaring market-place crowded with moving forms and humming with noises.

The change from mysterious peace to this vivid and concentrated life was startling.

With difficulty they avoided the onset of the camels by pulling their horses into the midst of the dreamers against the walls, who rolled and scrambled into places of safety, then stood up and surrounded them, staring with an almost terrible interest upon them, and surveying their horses with the eyes of connoisseurs. The children danced up and began to ask for alms, and an immense man, with a broken nose and brown teeth like tusks, laid a gigantic hand on Domini's bridle and said, in atrocious French:

"I am the guide, I am the guide. Look at my certificates. Take no one else. The people here are robbers. I am the only honest man. I will show Madame everything. I will take Madame to the inn. Look—my certificates! Read them! Read what the English lord says of me. I alone am honest here. I am honest Mustapha! I am honest Mustapha!"

He thrust a packet of discoloured papers and dirty visiting-cards into her hands. She dropped them, laughing, and they floated down over the horse's neck. The man leaped frantically to pick them up, assisted by the robbers round about. A second caravan of camels appeared, preceded by some filthy men in rags, who cried, "Oosh! oosh!" to clear the way. The immense man, brandishing his recovered certificates, plunged forward to encounter them, shouting in Arabic, hustled them back, kicked them, struck at the camels with a stick till those in front receded upon those behind and the street was blocked by struggling beasts and resounded with roaring snarls, the thud of wooden bales clashing together, and the desperate protests of the camel-drivers, one of whom was sent rolling into a noisome dust heap with his turban torn from his head.

"The inn! This is the inn! Madame will descend here. Madame will eat in the garden. Monsieur Alphonse! Monsieur Alphonse! Here are clients for *déjeuner*. I have brought them. Do not believe Mohammed. It is I that—I will assist Madame to descend. I will——"

Domini was standing in a tiny *cabaret* before a row of absinthe bottles, laughing, almost breathless. She scarcely knew how she had come there. Looking back she saw Androvsky still sitting on his horse in the midst of the clamouring mob. She went to the low doorway, but Mustapha barred her exit.

" This is Sidi-Zerzour. Madame will eat in the garden. She is tired, fainting. She will eat and then she will see the great Mosque of Zerzour."

" Sidi-Zerzour! " she exclaimed. " Monsieur Androvsky, do you know where we are? This is the famous Sidi-Zerzour, where the great warrior is buried, and where the Arabs make pilgrimages to worship at his tomb."

" Yes, Madame."

He answered in a low voice.

" As we are here we ought to see. Do you know, I think we must yield to honest Mustapha and have *déjeuner* in the garden. It is twelve o'clock and I am hungry. We might visit the mosque afterwards and ride home in the afternoon."

He sat there hunched up on the horse and looked at her in silent hesitation, while the Arabs stood round staring.

" You'd rather not? "

She spoke quietly. He shook his feet out of the stirrups. A number of brown hands and arms shot forth to help him. Domini turned back into the *cabaret*. She heard a tornado of voices outside, a horse neighing and trampling, a scuffling of feet, but she did not glance round. In about three minutes Androvsky joined her. He was limping slightly and bending forward more than ever. Behind the counter on which stood the absinthe bottle was a tarnished mirror, and she saw him glance quickly, almost guiltily into it, put up his hands and try to brush the dust from his hair, his shoulders.

" Let me do it," she said abruptly. " Turn round."

He obeyed without a word, turning his back to her. With her two hands, which were covered with soft, loose suede gloves, she beat and brushed the dust from his coat. He stood quite still while she did it. When she had finished she said :

" There, that's better."

Her voice was practical. He did not move, but stood there.

" I've done what I can, Monsieur Androvsky."

Then he turned slowly, and she saw, with amazement, that there were tears in his eyes. He did not thank her or say a word.

A small and scrubby-looking Frenchman, with red eyelids and moustaches that drooped over a pendulous underlip, now begged Madame to follow him through a small doorway beyond which could be seen three just shot gazelles lying in a patch of sunlight by a wired-in fowl-run. Domini went after him, and Androvsky and honest Mustapha——still vigorously proclaiming his own virtues—brought up the rear. They came into the most curious garden she had ever seen.

It was long and narrow and dishevelled, without grass or flowers. The uneven ground of it was bare, sun-baked earth, hard as parquet, rising here into a hump, falling there into a depression. Immediately behind the *cabaret*, where the dead gazelles with their large glazed eyes lay by the fowl-run, was a rough wooden trellis with vines trained over it, making an arbour. Beyond was a rummage of orange trees, palms, gums and fig trees growing at their own sweet will, and casting patterns of deep shade upon the earth in sharp contrast with the intense yellow sunlight which fringed them where the leafage ceased. An attempt had been made to create formal garden paths and garden beds by sticking rushes into little holes drilled in the ground, but the paths were zig-zag as a drunkard's walk, and the round and oblong beds contained no trace of plants. On either hand rose steep walls of earth, higher than a man, and crowned with prickly thorn bushes. Over them looked palm trees. At the end of the garden ran a slow stream of muddy water in a channel with crumbling banks trodden by many naked feet. Beyond it was yet another lower wall of earth, yet another maze of palms. Heat and silence brooded here like reptiles on the warm mud of a tropic river in a jungle. Lizards ran in and out of the innumerable holes in the walls, and flies buzzed beneath the ragged leaves of the fig trees and crawled in the hot cracks of the earth.

The landlord wished to put a table under the vine close to the *cabaret* wall, but Domini begged him to bring it to the end of the garden near the stream. With the furious assistance of honest Mustapha he carried it there and quickly laid it in the shadow of a fig tree, while Domini and Androvsky waited in silence on two straw-bottomed chairs.

The atmosphere of the garden was hostile to conversation. The sluggish muddy stream, the almost motionless trees, the imprisoned heat between the surrounding walls, the faint buzz of the flies caused drowsiness to creep upon the spirit. The long ride, too, and the ardent desert air, made this repose a luxury. Androvsky's face lost its emotional expression as he gazed almost vacantly at the brown water shifting slowly by between the brown banks and the brown walls above which the palm trees peered. His aching limbs relaxed. His hands hung loose between his knees. And Domini half closed her eyes. A curious peace descended upon her. Lapped in the heat and silence for the moment she wanted nothing. The faint buzz of the flies sounded in her ears and seemed more silent than even the silence to which it drew attention. Never before, not in Count Anteoni's garden, had she felt more utterly withdrawn from the world. The feathery tops of the palms were like the heads of sentinels guarding her from contact with all that she had known. And beyond them lay the desert, the empty, sun-lit waste. She shut her eyes, and murmured to herself, " I am in far away. I am in far away." And the flies said it in her ears monotonously. And the lizards whispered it as they slipped in and out of the little dark holes in the walls. She heard Androvsky stir, and she moved her lips slowly. And the flies and the lizards continued the refrain. But she said now, " We are in far away."

Honest Mustapha strode forward. He had a Bashi-Bazouk tread to wake up a world. *Déjeuner* was ready. Domini sighed. They took their places under the fig tree on either side of the deal table covered with a rough white cloth, and Mustapha, with tremendous gestures, and gigantic postures sug-gesting the untamed descendant of legions of freeborn, sun-suckled men, served them with red fish, omelette, gazelle steaks, cheese, oranges and dates, with white wine and Vals water.

Androvsky scarcely spoke. Now that he was sitting at a meal with Domini he was obviously embarrassed. All his move-ments were self-conscious. He seemed afraid to eat and refused the gazelle. Mustapha broke out into turbulent surprise and prolonged explanations of the delicious flavour of this desert food. But Androvsky still refused, looking desperately discon-certed.

" It really is delicious," said Domini, who was eating it. " But perhaps you don't care about meat."

She spoke quite carelessly and was surprised to see him look at her as if with sudden suspicion and immediately help himself to the gazelle.

This man was perpetually giving a touch of the whip to her curiosity to keep it alert. Yet she felt oddly at ease with him. He seemed somehow part of her impression of the desert, and now, as they sat under the fig tree between the high earth walls, and at their *al fresco* meal in unbroken silence—for since her last remark Androvsky had kept his eyes down and had not uttered a word—she tried to imagine the desert without him.

She thought of the gorge of El-Akbara, the cold, the dark-ness, and then the sun and the blue country. They had framed

his face.   She thought of the silent night when the voice of the
African hautboy had died away.   His step had broken its
silence.   She thought of the garden of Count Anteoni, and of
herself kneeling on the hot sand with her arms on the white
parapet and gazing out over the regions of the sun, of her dream
upon the tower, of her vision when Irena danced.   He was there,
part of the noon, part of the twilight, chief surely of the worshippers who swept on in the pale procession that received gifts
from the desert's hands.   She could no longer imagine the desert
without him.   The almost painful feeling that had come to her
in the garden—of the human power to distract her attention
from the desert power—was dying, perhaps had completely
died away.   Another feeling was surely coming to replace it;
that Androvsky belonged to the desert more even than the
Arabs did, that the desert spirits were close about him, clasping
his hands, whispering in his ears, and laying their unseen hands
about his heart.   But——

They had finished their meal.   Domini set her chair once
more in front of the sluggish stream, while honest Mustapha
bounded, with motions suggestive of an ostentatious panther, to
get the coffee.   Androvsky followed her after an instant of
hesitation.

" Do smoke," she said.

He lit a small cigar with difficulty.   She did not wish to
watch him, but she could not help glancing at him once or twice,
and the conviction came to her that he was unaccustomed to
smoking.   She lit a cigarette, and saw him look at her with a
sort of horrified surprise which changed to staring interest.
There was more boy, more child in this man than in any man
she had ever known.   Yet at moments she felt as if he had penetrated more profoundly into the dark and winding valleys of
experience than all the men of her acquaintance.

" Monsieur Androvsky," she said, looking at the slow waters
of the stream slipping by towards the hidden gardens, " is the
desert new to you? "

She longed to know.

" Yes, Madame."

" I thought perhaps—I wondered a little whether you had
travelled in it already."

" No, Madame.   I saw it for the first time the day before
yesterday."

" When I did."

" Yes."

So they had entered it for the first time together. She was silent, watching the pale smoke curl up through the shade and out into the glare of the sun, the lizards creeping over the hot earth, the flies circling beneath the lofty walls, the palm trees looking over into this garden from the gardens all around, gardens belonging to Eastern people, born here, and who would probably die here, and go to dust among the roots of the palms.

On the earthen bank on the far side of the stream there appeared, while she gazed, a brilliant figure. It came soundlessly on bare feet from a hidden garden; a tall, unveiled girl, dressed in draperies of vivid magenta, who carried in her exquisitely-shaped brown hands a number of handkerchiefs—scarlet, orange, yellow green and flesh colour. She did not glance into the *auberge* garden, but caught up her draperies into a bunch with one hand, exposing her slim legs far above the knees, waded into the stream, and bending, dipped the handkerchiefs in the water.

The current took them. They streamed out on the muddy surface of the stream, and tugged as if, suddenly endowed with life, they were striving to escape from the hand that held them.

The girl's face was beautiful, with small regular features and lustrous, tender eyes. Her figure, not yet fully developed, was perfect in shape, and seemed to thrill softly with the spirit of youth. Her tint of bronze suggested statuary, and every fresh pose into which she fell, while the water eddied about her, strengthened the suggestion. With the golden sunlight streaming upon her, the brown banks, the brown waters, the brown walls throwing up the crude magenta of her bunched-up draperies, the vivid colours of the handkerchiefs that floated from her hand, with the feathery palms beside her, the cloudless blue sky above her, she looked so strangely African and so completely lovely that Domini watched her with an almost breathless attention.

She withdrew the handkerchiefs from the stream, waded out, and spread them one by one upon the low earth wall to dry, letting her draperies fall. When she had finished disposing them she turned round, and, no longer preoccupied with her task, looked under her level brows into the garden opposite and saw Domini and her companion. She did not start, but stood quite still for a moment, then slipped away in the direction whence she had come. Only the brilliant patches of colour on.

the wall remained to hint that she had been there and would
come again. Domini sighed.

"What a lovely creature!" she said, more to herself than to
Androvsky.

He did not speak, and his silence made her consciously
demand his acquiescence in her admiration.

"Did you ever see anything more beautiful and more characteristic of Africa?" she asked.

"Madame," he said in a slow, stern voice, "I did not look at
her."

Domini felt piqued.

"Why not?" she retorted.

Androvsky's face was cloudy and almost cruel.

"These native women do not interest me," he said. "I see
nothing attractive in them."

Domini knew that he was telling her a lie. Had she not
seen him watching the dancing girls in Tahar's *café?* Anger
rose in her. She said to herself then that it was anger at man's
hypocrisy. Afterwards she knew that it was anger at Androvsky's telling a lie to her.

"I can scarcely believe that," she answered bluntly.

They looked at each other.

"Why not, Madame?" he said. "If I say it is so?"

She hesitated. At that moment she realised, with hot astonishment, that there was something in this man that could make
her almost afraid, that could prevent her even, perhaps, from
doing the thing she had resolved to do. Immediately she felt
hostile to him, and she knew that, at that moment, he was feeling hostile to her.

"If you say it is so naturally I am bound to take your word
for it," she said coldly.

He flushed and looked down. The rigid defiance that had
confronted her died out of his face.

Honest Mustapha broke joyously upon them with the coffee.
Domini helped Androvsky to it. She had to make a great
effort to perform this simple act with quiet, and apparently
indifferent, composure.

"Thank you, Madame."

His voice sounded humble, but she felt hard and as if ice
were in all her veins. She sipped her coffee, looking straight
before her at the stream. The magenta robe appeared once
more coming out from the brown wall. A yellow robe succeeded it, a scarlet, a deep purple. The girl, with three curious

young companions, stood in the sun examining the foreigners with steady, unflinching eyes. Domini smiled grimly. Fate gave her an opportunity. She beckoned to the girls. They looked at each other but did not move. She held up a bit of silver so that the sun was on it, and beckoned them again. The magenta robe was lifted above the pretty knees it had covered. The yellow, the scarlet, the deep purple robes rose too, making their separate revelations. And the four girls, all staring at the silver coin, waded through the muddy water and stood before Domini and Androvsky, blotting out the glaring sunshine with their young figures. Their smiling faces were now eager and confident, and they stretched out their delicate hands hopefully to the silver. Domini signified that they must wait a moment.

She felt full of malice.

The girls wore many ornaments. She began slowly and deliberately to examine them; the huge gold earrings that were as large as the little ears that sustained them, the bracelets and anklets, the triangular silver skewers that fastened the draperies across the gentle swelling breasts, the narrow girdles, worked with gold thread, and hung with lumps of coral, that circled the small, elastic waists. Her inventory was an adagio, and while it lasted Androvsky sat on his low straw chair with this wall of young womanhood before him, of young womanhood no longer self-conscious and timid, but eager, hardy, natural, warm with the sun and damp with the trickling drops of the water. The vivid draperies touched him, and presently a little hand stole out to his breast, caught at the silver chain that lay across it, and jerked out of its hiding-place—a wooden cross.

Domini saw the light on it for a second, heard a low, fierce exclamation, saw Androvsky's arm push the pretty hand roughly away, and then a thing that was strange.

He got up violently from his chair with the cross hanging loose on his breast. Then he seized hold of it, snapped the chain in two, threw the cross passionately into the stream and walked away down the garden. The four girls, with a twittering cry of excitement, rushed into the water, heedless of draperies, bent down, knelt down, and began to feel frantically in the mud for the vanished ornament. Domini stood up and watched them. Androvsky did not come back. Some minutes passed. Then there was an exclamation of triumph from the stream. The girl in magenta held up the dripping cross with the bit of silver chain in her dripping fingers. Domini cast a swift glance

behind her. Androvsky had disappeared. Quickly she went to
the edge of the water. As she was in riding-dress she wore no
ornaments except two earrings made of large and beautiful
turquoises. She took them hastily out of her ears and held
them out to the girl, signifying by gestures that she bartered
them for the little cross and chain. The girl hesitated, but the
clear blue tint of the turquoise pleased her eyes. She yielded,
snatched the earrings with an eager, gave up the cross and chain
with a reluctant, hand. Domini's fingers closed round the wet
gold. She threw some coins across the stream on to the bank,
and turned away, thrusting the cross into her bosom.

And she felt at that moment as if she had saved a sacred
thing from outrage.

At the *cabaret* door she found Androvsky, once more surrounded by Arabs, whom honest Mustapha was trying to beat
off. He turned when he heard her. His eyes were still full of
a light that revealed an intensity of mental agitation, and she
saw his left hand, which hung down, quivering against his side.
But he succeeded in schooling his voice as he asked:

" Do you wish to visit the village, Madame? "

" Yes. But don't let me bother you if you would rather——"

" I will come. I wish to come."

She did not believe it. She felt that he was in great pain,
both of body and mind. His fall had hurt him. She knew that
by the way he moved his right arm. The unaccustomed exercise
had made him stiff. Probably the physical discomfort he was
silently enduring had acted as an irritant to the mind. She remembered that it was caused by his determination to be her companion, and the ice in her melted away. She longed to make
him calmer, happier. Secretly she touched the little cross that
lay under her habit. He had thrown it away in a passion.
Well, some day perhaps she would have the pleasure of giving
it back to him. Since he had worn it he must surely care for it,
and even perhaps for that which it recalled.

" We ought to visit the mosque, I think," she said.

" Yes, Madame."

The assent sounded determined yet reluctant. She knew
this was all against his will. Mustapha took charge of them,
and they set out down the narrow street, accompanied by a little
crowd. They crossed the glaring market-place, with its booths
of red meat made black by flies, its heaps of refuse, its rows of
small and squalid hutches, in which sat serious men surrounded
by their goods. The noise here was terrific. Everyone seemed

shouting, and the uproar of the various trades, the clamour of hammers on sheets of iron, the dry tap of the shoemaker's wooden wand on the soles of countless slippers, the thud of the coffee-beater's blunt club on the beans, and the groaning grunt with which he accompanied each downward stroke mingled with the incessant roar of camels, and seemed to be made more deafening and intolerable by the fierce heat of the sun, and by the innumerable smells which seethed forth upon the air. Domini felt her nerves set on edge, and was thankful when they came once more into the narrow alleys that ran everywhere between the brown, blind houses. In them there was shade and silence and mystery. Mustapha strode before to show the way, Domini and Androvsky followed, and behind glided the little mob of barefoot inquisitors in long shirts, speechless and intent, and always hopeful of some chance scattering of money by the wealthy travellers.

The tumult of the market-place at length died away, and Domini was conscious of a curious, far-off murmur. At first it was so faint that she was scarcely aware of it, and merely felt the soothing influence of its level monotony. But as they walked on it grew deeper, stronger. It was like the sound of countless multitudes of bees buzzing in the noon among flowers, drowsily, ceaselessly. She stopped under a low mud arch to listen. And when she listened, standing still, a feeling of awe came upon her, and she knew that she had never heard such a strangely impressive, strangely suggestive sound before.

" What is that? " she said.

She looked at Androvsky.

" I don't know, Madame. It must be people."

" But what can they be doing? "

" They are praying in the mosque where Sidi-Zerzour is buried," said Mustapha.

Domini remembered the perfume-seller. This was the sound she had heard in his sunken chamber, infinitely multiplied. They went on again slowly. Mustapha had lost something of his flaring manner, and his gait was subdued. He walked with a sort of soft caution, like a man approaching holy ground. And Domini was moved by his sudden reverence. It was impressive in such a fierce and greedy scoundrel. The level murmur deepened, strengthened. All the empty and dim alleys surrounding the unseen mosque were alive with it, as if the earth of the houses, the palm-wood beams, the iron bars of the tiny, shuttered windows, the very thorns of the brushwood roofs were

praying ceaselessly and intently in secret under voices. This
was a world intense with prayer as a flame is intense with heat,
with prayer penetrating and compelling, urgent in its persistence, powerful in its deep and sultry concentration, yet almost
oppressive, almost terrible in its monotony.

"Allah-Akbar! Allah-Akbar!" It was the murmur of the
desert and the murmur of the sun. It was the whisper of the
mirage and of the airs that stole among the palm leaves. It was
the perpetual heart-beat of this world that was engulfing her,
taking her to its warm and glowing bosom with soft and
tyrannical intention.

"Allah! Allah! Allah!" Surely God must be very near,
bending to such an everlasting cry. Never before, not even
when the bell sounded and the Host was raised, had Domini felt
the nearness of God to His world, the absolute certainty of
a Creator listening to His creatures, watching them, wanting
them, meaning them some day to be one with Him, as she felt
it now while she threaded the dingy alleys towards these countless men who prayed.

Androvsky was walking slowly as if in pain.

"Your shoulder isn't hurting you?" she whispered.

This long sound of prayer moved her to the soul, made her
feel very full of compassion for everybody and everything, and
as if prayer were a cord binding the world together. He shook
his head silently. She looked at him, and felt that he was moved
also, but whether as she was she could not tell. His face was
like that of a man stricken with awe. Mustapha turned round
to them. The everlasting murmur was now so near that it
seemed to be within them, as if they, too, prayed at the tomb
of Zerzour.

"Follow me into the court, Madame," Mustapha said, "and
remain at the door while I fetch the slippers."

They turned a corner, and came to an open space before an
archway, which led into the first of the courts surrounding the
mosque. Under the archway Arabs were sitting silently, as if
immersed in profound reveries. They did not move, but stared
upon the strangers, and Domini fancied that there was enmity in
their eyes. Beyond them, upon an uneven pavement surrounded
with lofty walls, more Arabs were gathered, kneeling, bowing
their heads to the ground, and muttering ceaseless words in deep,
almost growling, voices. Their fingers slipped over the beads of
the chaplets they wore round their necks, and Domini thought
of her rosary. Some prayed alone, removed in shady corners

with faces turned to the wall. Others were gathered into knots. But each one pursued his own devotions, immersed in a strange, interior solitude to which surely penetrated an unseen ray of sacred light. There were young boys praying, and old, wrinkled men, eagles of the desert, with fierce eyes that did not soften as they cried the greatness of Allah, the greatness of his Prophet, but gleamed as if their belief were a thing of flame and bronze. The boys sometimes glanced at each other while they prayed, and after each glance they swayed with greater violence, and bowed down with more passionate abasement. The vision of prayer had stirred them to a young longing for excess. The spirit of emulation flickered through them and turned their worship into war.

In a second and smaller court before the portal of the mosque men were learning the Koran. Dressed in white they sat in circles, holding squares of some material that looked like cardboard covered with minute Arab characters, pretty, symmetrical curves and lines, dots and dashes. The teachers squatted in the midst, expounding the sacred text in nasal voices with a swiftness and vivacity that seemed pugnacious. There was violence within these courts. Domini could imagine the worshippers springing up from their knees to tear to pieces an intruding dog of an unbeliever, their sinking to their knees again while the blood trickled over the sun-dried pavement and the lifeless body lay there to rot and draw the flies.

" Allah! Allah! Allah! "

There was something imperious in such ardent, such concentrated and untiring worship, a demand which surely could not be overlooked or set aside. The tameness, the half-heartedness of Western prayer and Western praise had no place here. This prayer was hot as the sunlight, this praise was a mounting fire. The breath of this human incense was as the breath of a furnace pouring forth to the gates of the Paradise of Allah. It gave to Domini a quite new conception of religion, of the relation between Creator and created. The personal pride which, like blood in a body, runs through all the veins of the mind of Mohammedanism, that measureless hauteur which sets the soul of a Sultan in the twisted frame of a beggar at a street corner, and makes impressive, even almost majestical, the filthy marabout, quivering with palsy and devoured by disease, who squats beneath a holy bush thick with the discoloured rags of the faithful, was not abased at the shrine of the warrior Zerzour, was not cast off in the act of adoration. These Arabs humbled themselves in the body. Their foreheads touched the stones. By their attitudes they seemed as if they wished to make themselves even with the ground, to shrink into the space occupied by a grain of sand. Yet they were proud in the presence of Allah, as if the firmness of their belief in him and his right dealing, the fury of their contempt and hatred for those who looked not towards Mecca nor regarded Ramadan, gave them a patent of nobility. Despite their genuflections they were all as men who knew, and never forgot, that on them was conferred the right to keep on their head-covering in the presence of their King. With their closed eyes they looked God full in the face. Their dull and growling murmur had the majesty of thunder rolling through the sky.

Mustapha had disappeared within the mosque, leaving Domini and Androvsky for the moment alone in the midst of the worshippers. From the shadowy interior came forth a ceaseless sound of prayer to join the prayer without. There was a narrow stone seat by the mosque door and she sat down upon it. She felt suddenly weary, as one being hypnotised feels weary when the body and spirit begin to yield to the spell of the operator. Androvsky remained standing. His eyes were fixed on the ground, and she thought his face looked almost phantom-like, as if the blood had sunk away from it, leaving it white beneath the brown tint set there by the sun. He stayed quite still. The dark shadow cast by the towering mosque fell upon him, and his immobile figure suggested to her ranges of infinite melancholy. She sighed as one oppressed. There was an old man praying near them at the threshold of the door, with his face turned towards the interior. He was very thin, almost a skeleton, was dressed in rags through which his copper-coloured body, sharp with scarce-covered bones, could be seen, and had a scanty white beard sticking up, like a brush, at the tip of his pointed chin. His face, worn with hardship and turned to the likeness of parchment by time and the action of the sun, was full of senile venom, and his toothless mouth, with its lips folded inwards, moved perpetually, as if he were trying to bite. With rhythmical regularity, like one obeying a conductor, he shot forth his arms towards the mosque as if he wished to strike it, withdrew them, paused, then shot them forth again. And as his arms shot forth he uttered a prolonged and trembling shriek, full of weak, yet intense, fury.

He was surely crying out upon God, denouncing God for the evils that had beset his nearly ended life. Poor, horrible old man! Androvsky was closer to him than she was, but did not seem to notice him. Once she had seen him she could not take her eyes from him. His perpetual gesture, his perpetual shriek, became abominable to her in the midst of the bowing bodies and the humming voices of prayer. Each time he struck at the mosque and uttered his piercing cry she seemed to hear an oath spoken in a sanctuary. She longed to stop him. This one blasphemer began to destroy for her the mystic atmosphere created by the multitudes of adorers, and at last she could no longer endure his reiterated enmity.

She touched Androvsky's arm. He started and looked at her.

"That old man," she whispered. "Can't you speak to him?"

Androvsky glanced at him for the first time.

"Speak to him, Madame? Why?"

"He—he's horrible!"

She felt a sudden disinclination to tell Androvsky why the old man was horrible to her.

"What do you wish me to say to him?"

"I thought perhaps you might be able to stop him from doing that."

Androvsky bent down and spoke to the old man in Arabic.

He shot out his arms and reiterated his trembling shriek. It pierced the sound of prayer as lightning pierces cloud.

Domini got up quickly.

"I can't bear it," she said, still in a whisper. "It's as if he were cursing God."

Androvsky looked at the old man again, this time with profound attention.

"Isn't it?" she said. "Isn't it as if he were cursing God while the whole world worshipped? And that one cry of hatred seems louder than the praises of the whole world."

"We can't stop it."

Something in his voice made her say abruptly:

"Do you wish to stop it?"

He did not answer. The old man struck at the mosque and shrieked. Domini shuddered.

"I can't stay here," she said.

At this moment Mustapha appeared, followed by the guardian of the mosque, who carried two pairs of tattered slippers.

"Monsieur and Madame must take off their boots. Then I will show the mosque."

Domini put on the slippers hastily, and went into the mosque

without waiting to see whether Androvsky was following. And
the old man's furious cry pursued her through the doorway.

Within there was space and darkness. The darkness seemed
to be praying. Vistas of yellowish-white arches stretched away
in front, to right and left. On the floor, covered with matting,
quantities of shrouded figures knelt and swayed, stood up suddenly, knelt again, bowed down their foreheads. Preceded by
Mustapha and the guide, who walked on their stockinged feet,
Domini slowly threaded her way among them, following a winding path whose borders were praying men. To prevent her
slippers from falling off she had to shuffle along without lifting
her feet from the ground. With the regularity of a beating
pulse the old man's shriek, fainter now, came to her from without. But presently, as she penetrated farther into the mosque,
it was swallowed up by the sound of prayer. No one seemed to
see her or to know that she was there. She brushed against the
white garments of worshippers, and when she did so she felt
as if she touched the hem of the garments of mystery, and she
held her habit together with her hands lest she should recall
even one of these hearts that were surely very far off.

Mustapha and the guardian stood still and looked round at
Domini. Their faces were solemn. The expression of greedy
anxiety had gone out of Mustapha's eyes. For the moment the
thought of money had been driven out of his mind by some
graver pre-occupation. She saw in the semi-darkness two wooden
doors set between pillars. They were painted green and red,
and fastened with clamps and bolts of hammered copper that
looked enormously old. Against them were nailed two pictures
of winged horses with human heads, and two more pictures
representing a fantastical town of Eastern houses and minarets
in gold on a red background. Balls of purple and yellow glass,
and crystal chandeliers, hung from the high ceiling above these
doors, with many ancient lamps; and two tattered and dusty
banners of pale pink and white silk, fringed with gold and
powdered with a gold pattern of flowers, were tied to the pillars
with thin cords of camel's hair.

" This is the tomb of Sidi-Zerzour," whispered Mustapha.
" It is opened once a year."

The guardian of the mosque fell on his knees before the tomb.
" That is Mecca."

Mustapha pointed to the pictures of the city. Then he, too,
dropped down and pressed his forehead against the matting.
Domini glanced round for Androvsky. He was not there. She

stood alone before the tomb of Zerzour, the only human being in the great, dim building who was not worshipping. And she felt a terrible isolation, as if she were excommunicated, as if she dared not pray, for a moment almost as if the God to whom this torrent of worship flowed were hostile to her alone.

Had her father ever felt such a sensation of unutterable solitude?

It passed quickly, and, standing under the votive lamps before the painted doors, she prayed too, silently. She shut her eyes and imagined a church of her religion—the little church of Beni-Mora. She tried to imagine the voice of prayer all about her, the voice of the great Catholic Church. But that was not possible. Even when she saw nothing, and turned her soul inward upon itself, and strove to set this new world into which she had come far off, she heard in the long murmur that filled it a sound that surely rose from the sand, from the heart and the spirit of the sand, from the heart and the spirit of desert places, and that went up in the darkness of the mosque and floated under the arches through the doorway, above the palms and the flat-roofed houses, and that winged its fierce way, like a desert eagle, towards the sun.

Mustapha's hand was on her arm. The guardian, too, had risen from his knees and drawn from his robe and lit a candle. She came to a tiny doorway, passed through it and began to mount a winding stair. The sound of prayer mounted with her from the mosque, and when she came out upon the platform enclosed in the summit of the minaret she heard it still and it was multiplied. For all the voices from the outside courts joined it, and many voices from the roofs of the houses round about.

Men were praying there too, praying in the glare of the sun upon their housetops. She saw them from the minaret, and she saw the town that had sprung up round the tomb of the saint, and all the palms of the oasis, and beyond them immeasurable spaces of desert.

" Allah-Akbar! Allah-Akbar!"

She was above the eternal cry now. She had mounted like a prayer towards the sun, like a living, pulsing prayer, like the soul of prayer. She gazed at the far-off desert and saw prayer travelling, the soul of prayer travelling—whither? Where was the end? Where was the halting-place, with at last the pitched tent, the camp fires, and the long, the long repose?

When she came down and reached the court she found the

old man still striking at the mosque and shrieking out his trembling imprecation. And she found Androvsky still standing by him with fascinated eyes.

She had mounted with the voice of prayer into the sunshine, surely a little way towards God.

Androvsky had remained in the dark shadow with a curse.

It was foolish, perhaps—a woman's vagrant fancy—but she wished he had mounted with her.

BOOK III

THE GARDEN

CHAPTER X

IT was noon in the desert.

The voice of the Mueddin died away on the minaret, and the golden silence that comes out of the heart of the sun sank down once more softly over everything. Nature seemed unnaturally still in the heat. The slight winds were not at play, and the palms of Beni-Mora stood motionless as palm trees in a dream. The day was like a dream, intense and passionate, yet touched with something unearthly, something almost spiritual. In the cloudless blue of the sky there seemed a magical depth, regions of colour infinitely prolonged. In the vision of the distances, where desert blent with sky, earth surely curving up to meet the downward curving heaven, the dimness was like a voice whispering strange petitions. The ranges of mountains slept in the burning sand, and the light slept in their clefts like the languid in cool places. For there was a glorious languor even in the light, as if the sun were faintly oppressed by the marvel of his power. The clearness of the atmosphere in the remote desert was not obscured, but was impregnated with the mystery that is the wonder child of shadows. The far-off gold that kept it seemed to contain a secret darkness. In the oasis of Beni-Mora men, who had slowly roused themselves to pray, sank down to sleep again in the warm twilight of shrouded gardens or the warm night of windowless rooms.

In the garden of Count Anteoni Larbi's flute was silent.

" It is like noon in a mirage," Domini said softly.

Count Anteoni nodded.

" I feel as if I were looking at myself a long way off," she added. " As if I saw myself as I saw the grey sea and the islands on the way to Sidi-Zerzour. What magic there is here. And I can't get accustomed to it. Each day I wonder at it more and find it more inexplicable. It almost frightens me."

" You could be frightened?"

" Not easily by outside things—at least I hope not."

" But what then?"

" I scarcely know. Sometimes I think all the outside things, which do what are called the violent deeds in life, are tame, and timid, and ridiculously impotent in comparison with the things we can't see, which do the deeds we can't describe."

" In the mirage of this land you begin to see the exterior life as a mirage? You are learning, you are learning."

There was a creeping sound of something that was almost impish in his voice.

" Are you a secret agent?" Domini asked him.

" Of whom, Madame?"

She was silent. She seemed to be considering. He watched her with curiosity in his bright eyes.

" Of the desert," she answered at length, quite seriously.

" A secret agent has always a definite object. What is mine?"

" How can I know? How can I tell what the desert desires?"

" Already you personify it!"

The network of wrinkles showed itself in his brown face as he smiled, surely with triumph.

" I think I did that from the first," she answered gravely. " I know I did."

" And what sort of personage does the desert seem to you?"

" You ask me a great many questions to-day."

" Mirage questions, perhaps. Forgive me. Let us listen to the question—or is it the demand?—of the desert in this noon-tide hour, the greatest hour of all the twenty-four in such a land as this."

They were silent again, watching the noon, listening to it, feeling it, as they had been silent when the Mueddin's nasal voice rose in the call to prayer.

Count Anteoni stood in the sunshine by the low white parapet of the garden. Domini sat on a low chair in the shadow cast by a great jamelon tree. At her feet was a bush of vivid scarlet geraniums, against which her white linen dress looked curiously blanched. There was a half-drowsy, yet imaginative light in her gipsy eyes, and her motionless figure, her quiet hands, covered with white gloves, lying loosely in her lap, looked attentive and yet languid, as if some spell began to bind her but had not com-

pleted its work of stilling all the pulses of life that throbbed
within her. And in truth there was a spell upon her, the spell
of the golden noon. By turns she gave herself to it consciously,
then consciously strove to deny herself to its subtle summons.
And each time she tried to withdraw it seemed to her that the
spell was a little stronger, her power a little weaker. Then her
lips curved in a smile that was neither joyous nor sad, that was
perhaps rather part perplexed and part expectant.

After a minute of this silence Count Anteoni drew back from
the sun and sat down in a chair beside Domini. He took out
his watch.

"Twenty-five minutes," he said, "and my guests will be
here."

"Guests!" she said with an accent of surprise.

"I invited the priest to make an even number."

"Oh!"

"You don't dislike him?"

"I like him. I respect him."

"But I'm afraid you aren't pleased?"

Domini looked him straight in the face.

"Why did you invite Father Roubier?" she said.

"Isn't four better than three?"

"You don't want to tell me."

"I am a little malicious. You have divined it, so why should
I not acknowledge it? I asked Father Roubier because I wished
to see the man of prayer with the man who fled from prayer."

"Mussulman prayer," she said quickly.

"Prayer," he said.

His voice was peculiarly harsh at that moment. It grated
like an instrument on a rough surface. Domini knew that
secretly he was standing up for the Arab faith, that her last
words had seemed to strike against the religion of the people
whom he loved with an odd, concealed passion whose fire she
began to feel at moments as she grew to know him better.

It was plain from their manner to each other that their former slight acquaintance had moved towards something like a
pleasant friendship.

Domini looked as if she were no longer a wonder-stricken
sight-seer in this marvellous garden of the sun, but as if she had
become familiar with it. Yet her wonder was not gone. It was
only different. There was less sheer amazement, more affection
in it. As she had said, she had not become accustomed to the
magic of Africa. Its strangeness, its contrasts still startled and

moved her. But she began to feel as if she belonged to Beni-Mora, as if Beni-Mora would perhaps miss her a little if she went away.

Ten days had passed since the ride to Sidi-Zerzour—days rather like a dream to Domini.

What she had sought in coming to Beni-Mora she was surely finding. Her act was bringing forth its fruit. She had put a gulf, in which rolled the sea, between the land of the old life and the land in which at least the new life was to begin. The completeness of the severance had acted upon her like a blow that does not stun, but wakens. The days went like a dream, but in the dream there was the stir of birth. Her lassitude was permanently gone. There had been no returning after the first hours of excitement. The frost that had numbed her senses had utterly melted away. Who could be frost-bound in this land of fire? She had longed for peace and she was surely finding it, but it was a peace without stagnation. Hope dwelt in it, and expectancy, vague but persistent. As to forgetfulness, sometimes she woke from the dream and was almost dazed, almost ashamed to think how much she was forgetting, and how quickly. Her European life and friends—some of them intimate and close —were like a far-off cloud on the horizon, flying still farther before a steady wind that set from her to it. Soon it would disappear, would be as if it had never been. Now and then, with a sort of fierce obstinacy, she tried to stay the flight she had desired, and desired still. She said to herself, " I will remember. It's contemptible to forget like this. It's weak to be able to." Then she looked at the mountains or the desert, at two Arabs playing the ladies' game under the shadow of a *café* wall, or at a girl in dusty orange filling a goatskin pitcher at a well beneath a palm tree, and she succumbed to the lulling influence, smiling as they smile who hear the gentle ripple of the waters of Lethe.

She heard them perhaps most clearly when she wandered in Count Anteoni's garden. He had made her free of it in their first interview. She had ventured to take him at his word, knowing that if he repented she would divine it. He had made her feel that he had not repented. Sometimes she did not see him as she threaded the sandy alleys between the little rills, hearing the distant song of Larbi's amorous flute, or sat in the dense shade of the trees watching through a window-space of quivering golden leaves the passing of the caravans along the desert tracks. Sometimes a little wreath of ascending smoke, curling above the purple petals of bougainvilleas, or the red cloud of oleanders, told her of his presence in some retired thinking-place. Oftener he joined her, with an easy politeness that did not conceal his oddity, but clothed it in a pleasant garment, and they talked for a while or stayed for a while in an agreeable silence that each felt to be sympathetic.

Domini thought of him as a new species of man—a hermit of the world. He knew the world and did not hate it. His satire was rarely quite ungentle. He did not strike her as a disappointed man who fled to solitude in bitterness of spirit, but rather as an imaginative man with an unusual feeling for romance, and perhaps a desire for freedom that the normal civilised life restrained too much. He loved thought as many love conversation, silence as some love music. Now and then he said a sad or bitter thing. Sometimes she seemed to be near to something stern. Sometimes she felt as if there were a secret link which connected him with the perfume-seller in his little darkened chamber, with the legions who prayed about the tomb of Sidi-Zerzour. But these moments were rare. As a rule he was whimsical and kind, with the kindness of a good-hearted man who was human even in his detachment from ordinary humanity. His humour was a salt with plenty of savour. His imagination was of a sort which interested and even charmed her.

She felt, too, that she interested him and that he was a man not readily interested in ordinary human beings. He had seen too many and judged too shrewdly and too swiftly to be easily held for very long. She had no ambition to hold him, and had never in her life consciously striven to attract or retain any man, but she was woman enough to find his obvious pleasure in her society agreeable. She thought that her genuine adoration of the garden he had made, of the land in which it was set, had not a little to do with the happy nature of their intercourse. For she felt certain that beneath the light satire of his manner, his often smiling airs of detachment and quiet independence, there was something that could seek almost with passion, that could cling with resolution, that could even love with persistence. And she fancied that he sought in the desert, that he clung to its mystery, that he loved it and the garden he had created in it. Once she had laughingly called him a desert spirit. He had smiled as if with contentment.

They knew little of each other, yet they had become friends in the garden which he never left.

One day she said to him:

" You love the desert. Why do you never go into it? "

" I prefer to watch it," he replied. " When you are in the desert it bewilders you."

She remembered what she had felt during her first ride with Androvsky.

" I believe you are afraid of it," she said challengingly.

" Fear is sometimes the beginning of wisdom," he answered. " But you are without it, I know."

" How do you know? "

" Every day I see you galloping away into the sun."

She thought there was a faint sound of warning—or was it of rebuke—in his voice. It made her feel defiant.

" I think you lose a great deal by not galloping into the sun too," she said.

" But if I don't ride? "

That made her think of Androvsky and his angry resolution. It had not been the resolution of a day. Wearied and stiffened as he had been by the expedition to Sidi-Zerzour, actually injured by his fall—she knew from Batouch that he had been obliged to call in the Beni-Mora doctor to bandage his shoulder—she had been roused at dawn on the day following by his tread on the verandah. She had lain still while it descended the staircase, but then the sharp neighing of a horse had awakened an irresistible curiosity in her. She had got up, wrapped herself in a fur coat and slipped out on to the verandah. The sun was not above the horizon line of the desert, but the darkness of night was melting into a luminous grey. The air was almost cold. The palms looked spectral, even terrible, the empty and silent gardens melancholy and dangerous. It was not an hour for activity, for determination, but for reverie, for apprehension.

Below, a sleepy Arab boy, his hood drawn over his head, held the chestnut horse by the bridle. Androvsky came out from the arcade. He wore a cap pulled down to his eyebrows, which changed his appearance, giving him, as seen from above, the look of a groom or stable hand. He stood for a minute and stared at the horse. Then he limped round to the left side and carefully mounted, following out the directions Domini had given him the previous day: to avoid touching the animal with his foot, to have the rein in his fingers before leaving the ground, and to come down in the saddle as lightly as possible. She noted that all her hints were taken with infinite precaution. Once on the horse he tried to sit up straight, but found the effort too great in his weary and bruised condition. He leaned forward over the saddle peak, and rode away in the luminous greyness towards the desert.

The horse went quietly, as if affected by the mystery of the still hour. Horse and rider disappeared. The Arab boy wandered off in the direction of the village. But Domini remained looking after Androvsky. She saw nothing but the grim palms and the spectral atmosphere in which the desert lay. Yet she did not move till a red spear was thrust up out of the east towards the last waning star.

He had gone to learn his lesson in the desert.

Three days afterwards she rode with him again. She did not let him know of her presence on the verandah, and he said nothing of his departure in the dawn. He spoke very little and seemed much occupied with his horse, and she saw that he was more than determined—that he was apt at acquiring control of a physical exercise new to him. His great strength stood him in good stead. Only a man hard in the body could have so rapidly recovered from the effects of that first day of defeat and struggle. His absolute reticence about his efforts and the iron will that prompted them pleased Domini. She found them worthy of a man.

She rode with him on three occasions, twice in the oasis through the brown villages, once out into the desert on the caravan road that Batouch had told her led at last to Tombouctou. They did not travel far along it, but Domini knew at once that this route held more fascination for her than the route to Sidi-Zerzour. There was far more sand in this region of the desert. The little humps crowned with the scrub the camels feed on were fewer, so that the flatness of the ground was more definite. Here and there large dunes of golden-coloured sand rose, some straight as city walls, some curved like seats in an amphitheatre, others indented, crenellated like battlements, undulating in beast-like shapes. The distant panorama of desert was unbroken by any visible oasis and powerfully suggested Eternity to Domini.

"When I go out into the desert for my long journey I shall go by this road," she said to Androvsky.

"You are going on a journey?" he said, looking at her as if startled.

"Some day."

"All alone?"

"I suppose I must take a caravan, two or three Arabs, some horses, a tent or two. It's easy to manage. Batouch will arrange it for me."

Androvsky still looked startled, and half angry, she thought,

They had pulled up their horses among the sand dunes. It was near sunset, and the breath of evening was in the air, making its coolness even more ethereal, more thinly pure than in the daytime. The atmosphere was so clear that when they glanced back they could see the flag fluttering upon the white tower of the great hotel of Beni-Mora, many kilometres away among the palms; so still that they could hear the bark of a Kabyle dog far off near a nomad's tent pitched in the green land by the watersprings of old Beni-Mora. When they looked in front of them they seemed to see thousands of leagues of flatness, stretching on and on till the pale yellowish brown of it grew darker, merged into a strange blueness, like the blue of a hot mist above a southern lake, then into violet, then into—the thing they could not see, the summoning thing whose voice Domini's imagination heard, like a remote and thrilling echo, whenever she was in the desert.

"I did not know you were going on a journey, Madame," Androvsky said.

"Don't you remember?" she rejoined laughingly, "that I told you on the tower I thought peace must dwell out there. Well, some day I shall set out to find it."

"That seems a long time ago, Madame," he muttered.

Sometimes, when speaking to her, he dropped his voice till she could scarcely hear him, and sounded like a man communing with himself.

A red light from the sinking sun fell upon the dunes. As they rode back over them their horses seemed to be wading through a silent sea of blood. The sky in the west looked like an enormous conflagration, in which tortured things were struggling and lifting twisted arms.

Domini's acquaintance with Androvsky had not progressed as easily and pleasantly as her intercourse with Count Anteoni. She recognised that he was what is called a "difficult man." Now and then, as if under the prompting influence of some secret and violent emotion, he spoke with apparent naturalness, spoke perhaps out of his heart. Each time he did so she noticed that there was something of either doubt or amazement in what he said. She gathered that he was slow to rely, quick to mistrust. She gathered, too, that very many things surprised him, and felt sure that he hid nearly all of them from her, and would —had not his own will sometimes betrayed him—have hidden all. His reserve was as intense as everything about him. There was a fierceness in it that revealed its existence. He always conveyed to her a feeling of strength, physical and mental. Yet he always conveyed, too, a feeling of uneasiness. To a woman of Domini's temperament uneasiness usually implies a public or secret weakness. In Androvsky's she seemed to be aware of passion, as if it were one to dash obstacles aside, to break through doors of iron, to rush out into the open. And then—what then? To tremble at the world before him? At what he had done? She did not know. But she did know that even in his uneasiness there seemed to be fibre, muscle, sinew, nerve—all which goes to make strength, swiftness.

Speech was singularly difficult to him. Silence seemed to be natural, not irksome. After a few words he fell into it and remained in it. And he was less self-conscious in silence than in speech. He seemed, she fancied, to feel himself safer, more a man when he was not speaking. To him the use of words was surely like a yielding.

He had a peculiar faculty of making his presence felt when he was silent, as if directly he ceased from speaking the flame in him was fanned and leaped up at the outside world beyond its bars.

She did not know whether he was a gentleman or not.

If anyone had asked her, before she came to Beni-Mora, whether it would be possible for her to take four solitary rides with a man, to meet him—if only for a few minutes—every day of ten days, to sit opposite to him, and not far from him, at meals during the same space of time, and to be unable to say to herself whether he was or was not a gentleman by birth and education—feeling set aside—she would have answered without hesitation that it would be utterly impossible. Yet so it was. She could not decide. She could not place him. She could not imagine what his parentage, what his youth, his manhood had been. She could not fancy him in any environment—save that golden light, that blue radiance, in which she had first consciously and fully met him face to face. She could not hear him in converse with any set of men or women, or invent, in her mind, what he might be likely to say to them. She could not conceive him bound by any ties of home, or family, mother, sister, wife, child. When she looked at him, thought about him, he presented himself to her alone, like a thing in the air.

Yet he was more male than other men, breathed humanity—of some kind—as fire breathes heat.

The child there was in him almost confused her, made her wonder whether long contact with the world had tarnished her own original simplicity. But she only saw the child in him now and then, and she fancied that it, too, he was anxious to conceal.

This man had certainly a power to rouse feeling in others. She knew it by her own experience. By turns he had made her feel motherly, protecting, curious, constrained, passionate, energetic, timid—yes, almost timid and shy. No other human being had ever, even at moments, thus got the better of her natural audacity, lack of self-consciousness, and inherent, almost boyish, boldness. Nor was she aware what it was in him which sometimes made her uncertain of herself.

She wondered. But he often woke up wonder in her.

Despite their rides, their moments of intercourse in the hotel, on the verandah, she scarcely felt more intimate with him than she had at first. Sometimes indeed she thought that she felt less so, that the moment when the train ran out of the tunnel into the blue country was the moment in which they had been nearest to each other since they trod the verges of each other's lives.

She had never definitely said to herself: "Do I like him or dislike him?"

Now, as she sat with Count Anteoni watching the noon, the half-drowsy, half-imaginative expression had gone out of her face. She looked rather rigid, rather formidable.

Androvsky and Count Anteoni had never met. The Count had seen Androvsky in the distance from his garden more than once, but Androvsky had not seen him. The meeting that was about to take place was due to Domini. She had spoken to Androvsky on several occasions of the romantic beauty of this desert garden.

"It is like a garden of the *Arabian Nights*," she had said.

He did not look enlightened, and she was moved to ask him abruptly whether he had ever read the famous book. He had not. A doubt came to her whether he had ever even heard of it. She mentioned the fact of Count Anteoni's having made the garden, and spoke of him, sketching lightly his whimsicality, his affection for the Arabs, his love of solitude, and of African life. She also mentioned that he was by birth a Roman.

"But scarcely of the black world I should imagine," she added.

Androvsky said nothing.

"You should go and see the garden," she continued. "Count Anteoni allows visitors to explore it."

"I am sure it must be very beautiful, Madame," he replied, rather coldly, she thought.

He did not say that he would go.

As the garden won upon her, as its enchanted mystery, the airy wonder of its shadowy places, the glory of its trembling golden vistas, the restfulness of its green defiles, the strange, almost unearthly peace that reigned within it embalmed her spirit, as she learned not only to marvel at it, to be entranced by it, but to feel at home in it and love it, she was conscious of a persistent desire that Androvsky should know it too.

Perhaps his dogged determination about the riding had touched her more than she was aware. She often saw before her the bent figure, that looked tired, riding alone into the luminous grey; starting thus early that his act, humble and determined, might not be known by her. He did not know that she had seen him, not only on that morning, but on many subsequent mornings, setting forth to study the new art in the solitude of the still hours. But the fact that she had seen, had watched till horse and rider vanished beyond the palms, had understood why, perhaps moved her to this permanent wish that he could share her pleasure in the garden, know it as she did.

She did not argue with herself about the matter. She only knew that she wished, that presently she meant Androvsky to pass through the white gate and be met on the sand by Smaïn with his rose.

One day Count Anteoni had asked her whether she had made acquaintance with the man who had fled from prayer.

"Yes," she said. "You know it."

"How?"

"We have ridden to Sidi-Zerzour."

"I am not always by the wall."

"No, but I think you were that day."

"Why do you think so?"

"I am sure you were."

He did not either acknowledge or deny it.

"He has never been to see my garden," he said.

"No."

"He ought to come."

"I have told him so."

"Ah? Is he coming?"

"I don't think so."

"Persuade him to. I have a pride in my garden—oh, you have no idea what a pride! Any neglect of it, any indifference about it rasps me, plays upon the raw nerve each one of us possesses."

He spoke smilingly. She did not know what he was feeling, whether the remote thinker or the imp within him was at work or play.

" I doubt if he is a man to be easily persuaded," she said.

" Perhaps not—persuade him."

After a moment Domini said:

" I wonder whether you recognise that there are obstacles which the human will can't negotiate?"

" I could scarcely live where I do without recognising that the grains of sand are often driven by the wind. But when there is no wind!"

" They lie still?"

" And are the desert. I want to have a strange experience."

" What?"

" A *fête* in my garden."

" A fantasia?"

" Something far more banal. A lunch party, a *déjeuner*. Will you honour me?"

" By breakfasting with you? Yes, of course. Thank you."

" And will you bring—the second sun worshipper?"

She looked into the Count's small, shining eyes.

" Monsieur Androvsky?"

" If that is his name. I can send him an invitation, of course. But that's rather formal, and I don't think he is formal."

" On what day do you ask us?"

" Any day—Friday."

" And why do you ask us?"

" I wish to overcome this indifference to my garden. It hurts me, not only in my pride, but in my affections."

The whole thing had been like a sort of serious game. Domini had not said that she would convey the odd invitation; but when she was alone, and thought of the way in which Count Anteoni had said " Persuade him," she knew she would, and she meant Androvsky to accept it. This was an opportunity of seeing him in company with another man, a man of the world, who had read, travelled, thought, and doubtless lived.

She asked him that evening, and saw the red, that came as it comes in a boy's face, mount to his forehead.

" Everybody who comes to Beni-Mora comes to see the

garden," she said before he could reply. "Count Anteoni is half angry with you for being an exception."

"But—but, Madame, how can Monsieur the Count know that I am here? I have not seen him."

"He knows there is a second traveller, and he's a hospitable man. Monsieur Androvsky, I want you to come; I want you to see the garden."

"It is very kind of you, Madame."

The reluctance in his voice was extreme. Yet he did not like to say no. While he hesitated, Domini continued:

"You remember when I asked you to ride?"

"Yes, Madame."

"That was new to you. Well, it has given you pleasure, hasn't it?"

"Yes, Madame."

"So will the garden. I want to put another pleasure into your life."

She had begun to speak with the light persuasiveness of a woman of the world wishing to overcome a man's diffidence or obstinacy, but while she said the words she felt a sudden earnestness rush over her. It went into the voice, and surely smote upon him like a gust of the hot wind that sometimes blows out of the desert.

"I shall come, Madame," he said quickly.

"Friday. I may be in the garden in the morning. I'll meet you at the gate at half-past twelve."

"Friday?" he said.

Already he seemed to be wavering in his acceptance. Domini did not stay with him any longer.

"I'm glad," she said in a finishing tone.

And she went away.

Now Count Anteoni told her that he had invited the priest. She felt vexed, and her face showed that she did. A cloud came down and immediately she looked changed and disquieting. Yet she liked the priest. As she sat in silence her vexation became more profound. She felt certain that if Androvsky had known the priest was coming he would not have accepted the invitation. She wished him to come, yet she wished he had known. He might think that she had known the fact and had concealed it. She did not suppose for a moment that he disliked Father Roubier personally, but he certainly avoided him. He bowed to him in the coffee-room of the hotel, but never spoke to him. Batouch had told her about the episode with Bous-Bous. And she had seen Bous-Bous endeavour to renew the intimacy and repulsed with determination. Androvsky must dislike the priesthood. He might fancy that she, a believing Catholic, had—a number of disagreeable suppositions ran through her mind. She had always been inclined to hate the propagandist since the tragedy in her family. It was a pity Count Anteoni had not indulged his imp in a different fashion. The beauty of the noon seemed spoiled.

"Forgive my malice," Count Anteoni said. "It was really a thing of thistledown. Can it be going to do harm? I can scarcely think so."

"No, no."

She roused herself, with the instinct of a woman who has lived much in the world, to conceal the vexation that, visible, would cause a depression to stand in the natural place of cheerfulness.

"The desert is making me abominably natural," she thought.

At this moment the black figure of Father Roubier came out of the shadows of the trees with Bous-Bous trotting importantly beside it.

"Ah, Father," said Count Anteoni, going to meet him, while Domini got up from her chair, "it is good of you to come out in the sun to eat fish with such a bad parishioner as I am. Your little companion is welcome."

He patted Bous-Bous, who took little notice of him.

"You know Miss Enfilden, I think?" continued the Count.

"Father Roubier and I meet every day," said Domini, smiling.

"Mademoiselle has been good enough to take a kind interest in the humble work of the Church in Beni-Mora," said the priest with the serious simplicity characteristic of him.

He was a sincere man, utterly without pretension, and, as such men often are, quietly at home with anybody of whatever class or creed.

"I must go to the garden gate," Domini said. "Will you excuse me for a moment?"

"To meet Monsieur Androvsky? Let us accompany you if Father Roubier——"

"Please don't trouble. I won't be a minute."

Something in her voice made Count Anteoni at once acquiesce, defying his courteous instinct.

"We will wait for you here," he said.

There was a whimsical plea for forgiveness in his eyes. Domini's did not reject it; they did not answer it. She walked away, and the two men looked after her tall figure with admiration. As she went along the sand paths between the little streams, and came into the deep shade, her vexation seemed to grow darker like the garden ways. For a moment she thought she understood the sensations that must surely sometimes beset a treacherous woman. Yet she was incapable of treachery. Smain was standing dreamily on the great sweep of sand before the villa. She and he were old friends now, and every day he calmly gave her a flower when she came into the garden.

"What time is it, Smain?"

"Nearly half-past twelve, Madame."

"Will you open the door and see if anyone is coming?"

He went towards the great door, and Domini sat down on a bench under the evergreen roof to wait. She had seldom felt more discomposed, and began to reason with herself almost angrily. Even if the presence of the priest was unpleasant to Androvsky, why should she mind? Antagonism to the priesthood was certainly not a mental condition to be fostered, but a prejudice to be broken down. But she had wished—she still wished with ardour—that Androvsky's first visit to the garden should be a happy one, should pass off delightfully. She had a dawning instinct to make things smooth for him. Surely they had been rough in the past, rougher even than for herself. And she wondered for an instant whether he had come to Beni-Mora, as she had come, vaguely seeking for a happiness scarcely embodied in a definite thought.

"There is a gentleman coming, Madame."

It was the soft voice of Smain from the gate. In a moment Androvsky stood before it. Domini saw him framed in the white wood, with a brilliant blue behind him and a narrow glimpse of the watercourse. He was standing still and hesitating.

"Monsieur Androvsky!" she called.

He started, looked across the sand, and stepped into the garden with a sort of reluctant caution that pained her, she scarcely knew why. She got up and went towards him, and they met full in the sunshine.

"I came to be your cicerone."

"Thank you, Madame."

There was the click of wood striking against wood as Smain closed the gate. Androvsky turned quickly and looked behind him. His demeanour was that of a man whose nerves were tormenting him. Domini began to dread telling him of the presence of the priest, and, characteristically, did without hesitation what she feared to do.

"This is the way," she said.

Then, as they turned into the shadow of the trees and began to walk between the rills of water, she added abruptly:

"Father Roubier is here already, so our party is complete."

Androvsky stood still.

"Father Roubier! You did not tell me he was coming."

"I did not know it till five minutes ago."

She stood still too, and looked at him. There was a flaming of distrust in his eyes, his lips were compressed, and his whole body betokened hostility.

"I did not understand. I thought Señor Anteoni would be alone here."

"Father Roubier is a pleasant companion, sincere and simple. Everyone likes him."

"No doubt, Madame. But—the fact is I"—he hesitated, then added, almost with violence—"I do not care for priests."

"I am sorry. Still, for once—for an hour—you can surely——"

She did not finish the sentence. While she was speaking she felt the banality of such phrases spoken to such a man, and suddenly changed tone and manner.

"Monsieur Androvsky," she said, laying one hand on his arm, "I knew you would not like Father Roubier's being here. If I had known he was coming I should have told you in order that you might have kept away if you wished to. But now that you are here—now that Smaïn has let you in and the Count and Father Roubier must know of it, I am sure you will stay and govern your dislike. You intend to turn back. I see that. Well, I ask you to stay."

She was not thinking of herself, but of him. Instinct told her to teach him the way to conceal his aversion. Retreat would proclaim it.

"For yourself I ask you," she added. "If you go, you tell them what you have told me. You don't wish to do that."

They looked at each other. Then, without a word, he walked on again. As she kept beside him she felt as if in that moment their acquaintanceship had sprung forward, like a thing that had been forcibly restrained and that was now snarply released. They did not speak again till they saw, at the end of an alley, the Count and the priest standing together beneath the jamelon tree. Bous-Bous ran forward barking, and Domini was conscious that Androvsky braced himself up, like a fighter stepping into the

arena. Her keen sensitiveness of mind and body was so infected
by his secret impetuosity of feeling that it seemed to her as if his
encounter with the two men framed in the sunlight were a great
event which might be fraught with strange consequences. She
almost held her breath as she and Androvsky came down the path
and the fierce sunrays reached out to light up their faces.

Count Anteoni stepped forward to greet them.

" Monsieur Androvsky—Count Anteoni," she said.

The hands of the two men met. She saw that Androvsky's
was lifted reluctantly.

" Welcome to my garden," Count Anteoni said with his
invariable easy courtesy. " Every traveller has to pay his tribute
to my domain. I dare to exact that as the oldest European
inhabitant of Beni-Mora."

Androvsky said nothing. His eyes were on the priest. The
Count noticed it, and added:

" Do you know Father Roubier?"

" We have often seen each other in the hotel," Father Roubier
said with his usual straightforward simplicity.

He held out his hand, but Androvsky bowed hastily and
awkwardly and did not seem to see it. Domini glanced at Count
Anteoni, and surprised a piercing expression in his bright eyes.
It died away at once, and he said:

" Let us go to the *salle-à-manger*. *Déjeuner* will be ready,
Miss Enfilden."

She joined him, concealing her reluctance to leave Androvsky
with the priest, and walked beside him down the path, preceded
by Bous-Bous.

" Is my *fête* going to be a failure?" he murmured.

She did not reply. Her heart was full of vexation, almost of
bitterness. She felt angry with Count Anteoni, with Androvsky,
with herself. She almost felt angry with poor Father Roubier.

" Forgive me! do forgive me!" the Count whispered. "I
meant no harm."

She forced herself to smile, but the silence behind them,
where the two men were following, oppressed her. If only
Androvsky would speak! He had not said one word since
they were all together. Suddenly she turned her head and
said:

" Did you ever see such palms, Monsieur Androvsky? Aren't
they magnificent?"

Her voice was challenging, imperative. It commanded him
to rouse himself, to speak, as a touch of the lash commands a

horse to quicken his pace. Androvsky raised his head, which had been sunk on his breast as he walked.

"Palms!" he said confusedly. "Yes, they are wonderful."

"You care for trees?" asked the Count, following Domini's lead and speaking with a definite intention to force a conversation.

"Yes, Monsieur, certainly."

"I have some wonderful fellows here. After *déjeuner* you must let me show them to you. I spent years in collecting my children and teaching them to live rightly in the desert."

Very naturally, while he spoke, he had joined Androvsky, and now walked on with him, pointing out the different varieties of trees. Domini was conscious of a sense of relief and of a strong feeling of gratitude to their host. Following upon the gratitude came a less pleasant consciousness of Androvsky's lack of good breeding. He was certainly not a man of the world, whatever he might be. To-day, perhaps absurdly, she felt responsible for him, and as if he owed it to her to bear himself bravely and govern his dislikes if they clashed with the feelings of his companions. She longed hotly for him to make a good impression, and, when her eyes met Father Roubier's, was almost moved to ask his pardon for Androvsky's rudeness. But the Father seemed unconscious of it, and began to speak about the splendour of the African vegetation.

"Does not its luxuriance surprise you after England?" he said.

"No," she replied bluntly. "Ever since I have been in Africa I have felt that I was in a land of passionate growth."

"But—the desert?" he replied with a gesture towards the long flats of the Sahara, which were still visible between the trees.

"I should find it there too," she answered. "There, perhaps, most of all."

He looked at her with a gentle wonder. She did not explain that she was no longer thinking of growth in Nature.

The *salle-à-manger* stood at the end of a broad avenue of palms not far from the villa. Two Arab servants were waiting on each side of the white step that led into an ante-room filled with divans and coffee-tables. Beyond was a lofty apartment with an arched roof, in the centre of which was an oval table laid for breakfast, and decorated with masses of trumpet-shaped scarlet flowers in silver vases. Behind each of the four high-backed chairs stood an Arab motionless as a statue. Evidently the Count's *fête* was to be attended by a good deal of ceremony. Domini felt sorry, though not for herself. She had been accustomed to ceremony all her life, and noticed it, as a rule, almost as little as the air she breathed. But she feared that to Androvsky it would be novel and unpleasant. As they came into the shady room she saw him glance swiftly at the walls covered with dark Persian hangings, at the servants in their embroidered jackets, wide trousers, and snow-white turbans, at the vivid flowers on the table, then at the tall windows, over which flexible outside blinds, dull green in colour, were drawn; and it seemed to her that he was feeling like a trapped animal, full of a fury of uneasiness. Father Roubier's unconscious serenity in the midst of a luxury to which he was quite unaccustomed emphasised Androvsky's secret agitation, which was no secret to Domini, and which she knew must be obvious to Count Anteoni. She began to wish ardently that she had let Androvsky follow his impulse to go when he heard of Father Roubier's presence.

They sat down. She was on the Count's right hand, with Androvsky opposite to her and Father Roubier on her left. As they took their places she and the Father said a silent grace and made the sign of the Cross, and when she glanced up after doing so she saw Androvsky's hand lifted to his forehead. For a moment she fancied that he had joined in the tiny prayer, and was about to make the sacred sign, but as she looked at him his hand fell heavily to the table. The glasses by his plate jingled.

"I only remembered this morning that this is a *jour maigre,*" said Count Anteoni as they unfolded their napkins. "I am afraid, Father Roubier, you will not be able to do full justice to my *chef*, Hamdane, although he has thought of you and done his best for you. But I hope Miss Enfilden and——"

"I keep Friday," Domini interrupted quietly.

"Yes? Poor Hamdane!"

He looked in grave despair, but she knew that he was really pleased that she kept the fast day.

"Anyhow," he continued, "I hope that you, Monsieur Androvsky, will be able to join me in testing Hamdane's powers to the full. Or are you too——"

He did not continue, for Androvsky at once said, in a loud and firm voice:

"I keep no fast days."

The words sounded like a defiance flung at the two Catholics, and for a moment Domini thought that Father Roubier was going to treat them as a challenge, for he lifted his head and there was a flash of sudden fire in his eyes. But he only said, turning to the Count:

"I think Mademoiselle and I shall find our little Ramadan a very easy business. I once breakfasted with you on a Friday—two years ago it was, I think—and I have not forgotten the banquet you gave me."

Domini felt as if the priest had snubbed Androvsky, as a saint might snub, without knowing that he did so. She was angry with Androvsky, and yet she was full of pity for him. Why could he not meet courtesy with graciousness? There was something almost inhuman in his demeanour. To-day he had returned to his worst self, to the man who had twice treated her with brutal rudeness.

"Do the Arabs really keep Ramadan strictly?" she asked, looking away from Androvsky.

"Very," said Father Roubier. "Although, of course, I am not in sympathy with their religion, I have often been moved by their adherence to its rules. There is something very grand in the human heart deliberately taking upon itself the yoke of discipline."

"Islâm—the very word means the surrender of the human will to the will of God," said Count Anteoni. "That word and its meaning lie like the shadow of a commanding hand on the soul of every Arab, even of the absinthe-drinking renegades one sees here and there who have caught the vices of their conquerors. In the greatest scoundrel that the Prophet's robe covers there is an abiding and acute sense of necessary surrender. The Arabs, at any rate, do not buzz against their Creator, like midges raging at the sun in whose beams they are dancing."

"No," assented the priest. "At least in that respect they are superior to many who call themselves Christians. Their pride is immense, but it never makes itself ridiculous."

"You mean by trying to defy the Divine Will?" said Domini.

"Exactly, Mademoiselle."

She thought of her dead father.

The servants stole round the table, handing various dishes noiselessly. One of them, at this moment, poured red wine into Androvsky's glass. He uttered a low exclamation that sounded like the beginning of a protest hastily checked.

"You prefer white wine?" said Count Anteoni.

" No, thank you, Monsieur."

He lifted the glass to his lips and drained it.

" Are you a judge of wine?" added the Count. " That is made from my own grapes. I have vineyards near Tunis."

" It is excellent," said Androvsky.

Domini noticed that he spoke in a louder voice than usual, as if he were making a determined effort to throw off the uneasiness that evidently oppressed him. He ate heartily, choosing almost ostentatiously dishes in which there was meat. But everything that he did, even this eating of meat, gave her the impression that he was—subtly, how she did not know—defying not only the priest, but himself. Now and then she glanced across at him, and when she did so he was always looking away from her. After praising the wine he had relapsed into silence, and Count Anteoni—she thought moved by a very delicate sense of tact—did not directly address him again just then, but resumed the interrupted conversation about the Arabs, first explaining that the servants understood no French. He discussed them with a minute knowledge that evidently sprang from a very real affection, and presently she could not help alluding to this.

" I think you love the Arabs far more than any Europeans," she said.

He fixed his bright eyes upon her, and she thought that just then they looked brighter than ever before.

" Why? " he asked quietly.

" Do you know the sound that comes into the voice of a lover of children when it speaks of a child? "

" Ah!—the note of a deep indulgence? "

" I hear it in yours whenever you speak of the Arabs."

She spoke half jestingly. For a moment he did not reply. Then he said to the priest:

" You have lived long in Africa, Father. Have not you something of the same feeling towards these children of the sun? "

" Yes, and I have noticed it in our dead Cardinal."

" Cardinal Lavigerie."

Androvsky bent over his plate. He seemed suddenly to withdraw his mind forcibly from this conversation in which he was taking no active part, as if he refused even to listen to it.

" He is your hero, I know," the Count said sympathetically.

" He did a great deal for me."

" And for Africa. And he was wise."

" You mean in some special way? " Domini said.

"Yes. He looked deep enough into the dark souls of the desert men to find out that his success with them must come chiefly through his goodness to their dark bodies. You aren't shocked, Father?"

"No, no. There is truth in that."

But the priest assented rather sadly.

"Mahomet thought too much of the body," he added.

Domini saw the Count compress his lips. Then he turned to Androvsky and said:

"Do you think so, Monsieur?"

It was a definite, a resolute attempt to draw his guest into the conversation. Androvsky could not ignore it. He looked up reluctantly from his plate. His eyes met Domini's, but immediately travelled away from them.

"I doubt——" he said.

He paused, laid his hands on the table, clasping its edge, and continued firmly, even with a sort of hard violence:

"I doubt if most good men, or men who want to be good, think enough about the body, consider it enough. I have thought that. I think it still."

As he finished he stared at the priest, almost menacingly. Then, as if moved by an after-thought, he added:

"As to Mahomet, I know very little about him. But perhaps he obtained his great influence by recognising that the bodies of men are of great importance, of tremendous—tremendous importance."

Domini saw that the interest of Count Anteoni in his guest was suddenly and vitally aroused by what he had just said, perhaps even more by his peculiar way of saying it, as if it were forced from him by some secret, irresistible compulsion. And the Count's interest seemed to take hands with her interest, which had had a much longer existence. Father Roubier, however, broke in with a slightly cold:

"It is a very dangerous thing, I think, to dwell upon the importance of the perishable. One runs the risk of detracting from the much greater importance of the imperishable."

"Yet it's the starved wolves that devour the villages," said Androvsky.

For the first time Domini felt his Russian origin. There was a silence. Father Roubier looked straight before him, but Count Anteoni's eyes were fixed piercingly upon Androvsky. At last he said:

"May I ask, Monsieur, if you are a Russian?"

"My father was. But I have never set foot in Russia."

"The soul that I find in the art, music, literature of your country is, to me, the most interesting soul in Europe," the Count said with a ring of deep earnestness in his grating voice.

Spoken as he spoke it, no compliment could have been more gracious, even moving. But Androvsky only replied abruptly: "I'm afraid I know nothing of all that."

Domini felt hot with a sort of shame, as at a close friend's public display of ignorance. She began to speak to the Count of Russian music, books, with an enthusiasm that was sincere. For she, too, had found in the soul from the Steppes a meaning and a magic that had taken her soul prisoner. And suddenly, while she talked, she thought of the Desert as the burning brother of the frigid Steppes. Was it the wonder of the eternal flats that had spoken to her inmost heart sometimes in London concert-rooms, in her room at night when she read, forgetting time, which spoke to her now more fiercely under the palms of Africa? At the thought something mystic seemed to stand in her enthusiasm. The mystery of space floated about her. But she did not express her thought. Count Anteoni expressed it for her.

"The Steppes and the Desert are akin, you know," he said. "Despite the opposition of frost and fire."

"Just what I was thinking!" she exclaimed. "That must be why——"

She stopped short.

"Yes?" said the Count.

Both Father Roubier and Androvsky looked at her with expectancy. But she did not continue her sentence, and her failure to do so was covered, or at the least excused, by a diversion that secretly she blessed. At this moment, from the ante-room, there came a sound of African music, both soft and barbarous. First there was only one reiterated liquid note, clear and glassy, a note that suggested night in a remote place. Then, beneath it, as foundation to it, rose a rustling sound as of a forest of reeds through which a breeze went rhythmically. Into this stole the broken song of a thin instrument with a timbre rustic and antique as the timbre of the oboe, but fainter, frailer. A twang of softly-plucked strings supported its wild and pathetic utterance, and presently the almost stifled throb of a little tom-tom that must have been placed at a distance. It was like a beating heart.

The Count and his guests sat listening in silence. Domini began to feel curiously expectant, yet she did not recognise the odd melody. Her sensation was that some other music must be coming which she had heard before, which had moved her deeply at some time in her life. She glanced at the Count and found him looking at her with a whimsical expression, as if he were a kind conspirator whose plot would soon be known.

"What is it?" she asked in a low voice.

He bent towards her.

"Wait!" he whispered. "Listen!"

She saw Androvsky frown. His face was distorted by an expression of pain, and she wondered if he, like some Europeans, found the barbarity of the desert music ugly and even distressing to the nerves. While she wondered a voice began to sing, always accompanied by the four instruments. It was a contralto voice, but sounded like a youth's.

"What is that song?" she asked under her breath. "Surely I must have heard it!"

"You don't know?"

"Wait!"

She searched her heart. It seemed to her that she knew the song. At some period of her life she had certainly been deeply moved by it—but when? where? The voice died away, and was succeeded by a soft chorus singing monotonously:

"Wurra-Wurra."

Then it rose once more in a dreamy and reticent refrain, like the voice of a soul communing with itself in the desert, above the instruments and the murmuring chorus.

"You remember?" whispered the Count.

She moved her head in assent but did not speak. She could not speak. It was the song the Arab had sung as he turned into the shadow of the palm trees, the song of the freed negroes of Touggourt:

"No one but God and I
Knows what is in my heart."

The priest leaned back in his chair. His dark eyes were cat down, and his thin, sun-browned hands were folded together in a way that suggested prayer. Did this desert song of the black men, children of God like him as their song affirmed, stir his soul to some grave petition that embraced the wants of all humanity?

Androvsky was sitting quite still. He was also looking down

and the lids covered his eyes. An expression of pain still lingered on his face, but it was less cruel, no longer tortured, but melancholy. And Domini, as she listened, recalled the strange cry that had risen within her as the Arab disappeared in the sunshine, the cry of the soul in life surrounded by mysteries, by the hands, the footfalls, the voices of hidden things—" What is going to happen to me here?" But that cry had risen in her, found words in her, only when confronted by the desert. Before it had been perhaps hidden in the womb. Only then was it born. And now the days had passed and the nights, and the song brought with it the cry once more, the cry and suddenly something else, another voice that, very far away, seemed to be making answer to it. That answer she could not hear. The words of it were hidden in the womb as, once, the words of her intense question. Only she felt that an answer had been made. The future knew, and had begun to try to tell her. She was on the very edge of knowledge while she listened, but she could not step into the marvellous land.

Presently Count Anteoni spoke to the priest.

" You have heard this song, no doubt, Father?"

Father Roubier shook his head.

" I don't think so, but I can never remember the Arab music."

" Perhaps you dislike it?"

" No, no. It is ugly in a way, but there seems a great deal of meaning in it. In this song especially there is—one might almost call it beauty."

" Wonderful beauty," Domini said in a low voice, still listening to the song.

" The words are beautiful," said the Count, this time addressing himself to Androvsky. " I don't know them all, but they begin like this:

" The gazelle dies in the water,
    The fish dies in the air,
    And I die in the dunes of the desert sand
    For my love that is deep and sad.'

And when the chorus sounds, as now "—and he made a gesture toward the inner room, in which the low murmur of " Wurra-Wurra " rose again—" the singer reiterates always the same refrain:

" ' No one but God and I
    Knows what is in my heart.' "

Almost as he spoke the contralto voice began to sing the refrain. Androvsky turned pale. There were drops of sweat on his forehead. He lifted his glass of wine to his lips and his hand trembled so that some of the wine was spilt upon the table-cloth. And, as once before, Domini felt that what moved her deeply moved him even more deeply, whether in the same way or differently she could not tell. The image of the taper and the torch recurred to her mind. She saw Androvsky with fire round about him. The violence of this man surely resembled the violence of Africa. There was something terrible about it, yet also something noble, for it suggested a male power, which might make for either good or evil, but which had nothing to do with littleness. For a moment Count Anteoni and the priest were dwarfed, as if they had come into the presence of a giant.

The Arabs handed round fruit. And now the song died softly away. Only the instruments went on playing. The distant tom-tom was surely the beating of that heart into whose mysteries no other human heart could look. Its reiterated and dim throbbing affected Domini almost terribly. She was relieved, yet regretful, when at length it ceased.

" Shall we go into the ante-room? " the Count said. " Coffee will be brought there."

" Oh, but—don't let us see them! " Domini exclaimed.

" The musicians? "

She nodded.

" You would rather not hear any more music? "

" If you don't mind! "

He gave an order in Arabic. One of the servants slipped away and returned almost immediately.

" Now we can go," the Count said. " They have vanished."

The priest sighed. It was evident that the music had moved him too. As they got up he said:

" Yes, there was beauty in that song and something more. Some of these desert poets can teach us to think."

" A dangerous lesson, perhaps," said the Count. " What do you say, Monsieur Androvsky? "

Androvsky was on his feet. His eyes were turned toward the door through which the sound of the music had come.

" I! " he answered. " I—Monsieur, I am afraid that to me this music means very little. I cannot judge of it."

" But the words? " asked the Count with a certain pressure.

"They do not seem to me to suggest much more than the music."

The Count said no more. As she went into the outer room Domini felt angry, as she had felt angry in the garden at Sidi-Zerzour when Androvsky said:

"These native women do not interest me. I see nothing attractive in them."

For now, as then, she knew that he had lied.

CHAPTER XI

DOMINI came into the ante-room alone. The three men had paused for a moment behind her, and the sound of a match struck reached her ears as she went listlessly forward to the door which was open to the broad garden path, and stood looking out into the sunshine. Butterflies were flitting here and there through the riot of gold, and she heard faint bird-notes from the shadows of the trees, echoed by the more distant twitter of Larbi's flute. On the left, between the palms, she caught glimpses of the desert and of the hard and brilliant mountains, and, as she stood there, she remembered her sensations on first entering the garden and how soon she had learned to love it. It had always seemed to her a sunny paradise of peace until this moment. But now she felt as if she were compassed about by clouds.

The vagrant movement of the butterflies irritated her eyes, the distant sound of the flute distressed her ears, and all the peace had gone. Once again this man destroyed the spell Nature had cast upon her. Because she knew that he had lied, her joy in the garden, her deeper joy in the desert that embraced it, were stricken. Yet why should he not lie? Which of us does not lie about his feelings? Has reserve no right to armour?

She heard her companions entering the room and turned round. At that moment her heart was swept by an emotion almost of hatred to Androvsky. Because of it she smiled. A forced gaiety dawned in her. She sat down on one of the low divans, and, as she asked Count Anteoni for a cigarette and lit it, she thought, "How shall I punish him?" That lie, not even told to her and about so slight a matter, seemed to her an attack which she resented and must return. Not for a moment did she ask herself if she were reasonable. A voice within her said, " I will not be lied to, I will not even bear a lie told to another in my presence by this man." And the voice was imperious.

Count Anteoni remained beside her, smoking a cigar. Father Roubier took a seat by the little table in front of her. But Androvsky went over to the door she had just left, and stood, as she had, looking out into the sunshine. Bous-Bous followed him, and snuffed affectionately round his feet, trying to gain his attention.

"My little dog seems very fond of your friend," the priest said to Domini.

"My friend!"

"Monsieur Androvsky."

She lowered her voice.

"He is only a travelling acquaintance. I know nothing of him."

The priest looked gently surprised and Count Anteoni blew forth a fragrant cloud of smoke.

"He seems a remarkable man," the priest said mildly.

"Do you think so?"

She began to speak to Count Anteoni about some absurdity of Batouch, forcing her mind into a light and frivolous mood, and he echoed her tone with a clever obedience for which secretly she blessed him. In a moment they were laughing together with apparent merriment, and Father Roubier smiled innocently at their light-heartedness, believing in it sincerely. But Androvsky suddenly turned around with a dark and morose countenance.

"Come in out of the sunshine," said the Count. "It is too strong. Try this chair. Coffee will be—ah, here it is!"

Two servants appeared, carrying it.

"Thank you, Monsieur," Androvsky said with reluctant courtesy.

He came towards them with determination and sat down, drawing forward his chair till he was facing Domini. Directly he was quiet Bous-Bous sprang upon his knee and lay down hastily, blinking his eyes, which were almost concealed by hair, and heaving a sigh which made the priest look kindly at him, even while he said deprecatingly:

"Bous-Bous! Bous-Bous! Little rascal, little pig—down, down!"

"Oh, leave him, Monsieur!" muttered Androvsky. "It's all the same to me."

"He really has no shame where his heart is concerned."

"Arab!" said the Count. "He has learnt it in Beni-Mora."

"Perhaps he has taken lessons from Larbi," said Domini. "Hark! He is playing to-day. For whom?"

"I never ask now," said the Count. "The name changes so often."

"Constancy is not an Arab fault?" Domini asked.

"You say ' fault,' Madame," interposed the priest.

"Yes, Father," she returned with a light touch of conscious cynicism. "Surely in this world that which is apt to bring inevitable misery with it must be accounted a fault."

"But can constancy do that?"

"Don't you think so, into a world of ceaseless change?"

"Then how shall we reckon truth in a world of lies?" asked the Count. "Is that a fault, too?"

"Ask Monsieur Androvsky," said Domini, quickly.

"I obey," said the Count, looking over at his guest.

"Ah, but I am sure I know," Domini added. "I am sure you think truth a thing we should all avoid in such a world as this. Don't you, Monsieur?"

"If you are sure, Madame, why ask me?" Androvsky replied.

There was in his voice a sound that was startling. Suddenly the priest reached out his hand and lifted Bous-Bous on to his knee, and Count Anteoni very lightly and indifferently interposed.

"Truth-telling among Arabs becomes a dire necessity to Europeans. One cannot out-lie them, and it doesn't pay to run second to Orientals. So one learns, with tears, to be sincere. Father Roubier is shocked by my apologia for my own blatant truthfulness."

The priest laughed.

"I live so little in what is called ' the world' that I'm afraid I'm very ready to take drollery for a serious expression of opinion."

He stroked Bous-Bous's white back, and added, with a simple geniality that seemed to spring rather from a desire to be kind than from any temperamental source:

"But I hope I shall always be able to enjoy innocent fun."

As he spoke his eyes rested on Androvsky's face, and suddenly he looked grave and put Bous-Bous gently down on the floor.

"I'm afraid I must be going," he said

"Already?" said his host.

" I dare not allow myself too much idleness. If once I began to be idle in this climate I should become like an Arab and do nothing all day but sit in the sun."

" As I do. Father, we meet very seldom, but whenever we do I feel myself a cumberer of the earth."

Domini had never before heard him speak with such humbleness. The priest flushed like a boy.

" We each serve in our own way," he said quickly. " The Arab who sits all day in the sun may be heard as a song of praise where He is."

And then he took his leave. This time he did not extend his hand to Androvsky, but only bowed to him, lifting his white helmet. As he went away in the sun with Bous-Bous the three he had left followed him with their eyes. For Androvsky had turned his chair sideways, as if involuntarily.

" I shall learn to love Father Roubier," Domini said.

Androvsky moved his seat round again till his back was to the garden, and placed his broad hands palm downward on his knees.

" Yes?" said the Count.

" He is so transparently good, and he bears his great disappointment so beautifully."

" What great disappointment?"

" He longed to become a monk."

Androvsky got up from his seat and walked back to the garden doorway. His restless demeanour and lowering expression destroyed all sense of calm and leisure. Count Anteoni looked after him, and then at Domini, with a sort of playful surprise. He was going to speak, but before the words came Smaïn appeared, carrying reverently a large envelope covered with Arab writing.

" Will you excuse me for a moment?" the Count said.

" Of course."

He took the letter, and at once a vivid expression of excitement shone in his eyes. When he had read it there was a glow upon his face as if the flames of a fire played over it.

" Miss Enfilden," he said, " will you think me very discourteous if I leave you for a moment? The messenger who brought this has come from far and starts to-day on his return journey. He has come out of the south, three hundred kilometres away, from Beni-Hassan, a sacred village—a sacred village."

He repeated the last words, lowering his voice.

" Of course go and see him."

" And you? "

He glanced towards Androvsky, who was standing with his back to them.

" Won't you show Monsieur Androvsky the garden?"

Hearing his name Androvsky turned, and the Count at once made his excuses to him and followed Smaïn towards the garden gate, carrying the letter that had come from Beni-Hassan in hi hand.

When he had gone Domini remained on the divan, and Androvsky by the door, with his eyes on the ground. She took another cigarette from the box on the table beside her, struck a match and lit it carefully. Then she said:

" Do you care to see the garden?"

She spoke indifferently, coldly. The desire to show her Paradise to him had died away, but the parting words of the Count prompted the question, and so she put it as to a stranger.

" Thank you, Madame—yes," he replied, as if with an effort.

She got up, and they went out together on to the broad walk.

" Which way do you want to go?" she asked.

She saw him glance at her quickly, with anxiety in his eyes.

" You know best where we should go, Madame."

"I daresay you won't care about it. Probably you are not interested in gardens. It does not matter really which path we take. They are all very much alike."

" I am sure they are all very beautiful."

Suddenly he had become humble, anxious to please her. But now the violent contrasts in him, unlike the violent contrasts of nature in this land, exasperated her. She longed to be left alone. She felt ashamed of Androvsky, and also of herself; she condemned herself bitterly for the interest she had taken in him, for her desire to put some pleasure into a life she had deemed sad, for her curiosity about him, for her wish to share joy with him. She laughed at herself secretly for what she now called her folly in having connected him imaginatively with the desert, whereas in reality he made the desert, as everything he approached, lose in beauty and wonder. His was a destructive personality. She knew it now. Why had she not realised it before? He was a man to put gall in the cup of pleasure, to create uneasiness, self-consciousness, constraint round about him, to call up spectres at the banquet of life. Well, in the future she could avoid him. After to-day she need never have any more intercourse with him. With that thought, that interior sense of her perfect freedom in regard to this man, an abrupt, but always cold, content came to her, putting him a long way off where surely all that he thought and did was entirely indifferent to her.

"Come along then," she said. "We'll go this way."

And she turned down an alley which led towards the home of the purple dog. She did not know at the moment that anything had influenced her to choose that particular path, but very soon the sound of Larbi's flute grew louder, and she guessed that in reality the music had attracted her. Androvsky walked beside her without a word. She felt that he was not looking about him, not noticing anything, and all at once she stopped decisively.

"Why should we take all this trouble?" she said bluntly. "I hate pretence and I thought I had travelled far away from it. But we are both pretending."

"Pretending, Madame?" he said in a startled voice.

"Yes. I that I want to show you this garden, you that you want to see it. I no longer wish to show it to you, and you have never wished to see it. Let us cease to pretend. It is all my fault. I bothered you to come here when you didn't want to come. You have taught me a lesson. I was inclined to condemn you for it, to be angry with you. But why should I be? You were quite right. Freedom is my fetish. I set you free, Monsieur Androvsky. Good-bye."

As she spoke she felt that the air was clearing, the clouds were flying. Constraint at least was at an end. And she had really the sensation of setting a captive at liberty. She turned to leave him, but he said:

"Please, stop, Madame."

"Why?"

"You have made a mistake."

"In what?"

"I do want to see this garden."

"Really? Well, then, you can wander through it."

"I do not wish to see it alone."

"Larbi shall guide you. For half a franc he will gladly give up his serenading."

"Madame, if you will not show me the garden I will not see it at all. I will go now and will never come into it again. I do not pretend."

"Ah!" she said, and her voice was quite changed. "But you do worse."

" Worse! "

" Yes.   You lie in the face of Africa."

She did not wish or mean to say it, and yet she had to say it. She knew it was monstrous that she should speak thus to him. What had his lies to do with her? She had been told a thousand, had heard a thousand told to others. Her life had been passed in a world of which the words of the Psalmist, though uttered in haste, are a clear-cut description. And she had not thought she cared. Yet really she must have cared. For, in leaving this world, her soul had, as it were, fetched a long breath. And now, at the hint of a lie, it instinctively recoiled as from a gust of air laden with some poisonous and suffocating vapour.

" Forgive me," she added. " I am a fool. Out here I do love truth."

Androvsky dropped his eyes. His whole body expressed humiliation, and something that suggested to her despair.

" Oh, you must think me mad to speak like this! " she exclaimed. " Of course people must be allowed to arm themselves against the curiosity of others. I know that. The fact is I am under a spell here. I have been living for many, many years in the cold. I have been like a woman in a prison without any light, and——"

" You have been in a prison! " he said, lifting his head and looking at her eagerly.

" I have been living in what is called the great world."

" And you call that a prison? "

" Now that I am living in the greater world, really living at last. I have been in the heart of insincerity, and now I have come into the heart, the fiery heart of sincerity. It's there—there "—she pointed to the desert. " And it has intoxicated me; I think it has made me unreasonable. I expect everyone—not an Arab—to be as it is, and every little thing that isn't quite frank, every pretence, is like a horrible little hand tugging at me, as if trying to take me back to the prison I have left. I think, deep down, I have always loathed lies, but never as I have loathed them since I came here. It seems to me as if only in the desert there is freedom for the body, and only in truth there is freedom for the soul."

She stopped, drew a long breath, and added:

" You must forgive me. I have worried you. I have made you do what you didn't want to do. And then I have attacked you. It is unpardonable."

"Show me the garden, Madame," he said in a very low voice.

Her outburst over, she felt a slight self-consciousness. She wondered what he thought of her and became aware of her unconventionality. His curious and persistent reticence made her frankness the more marked. Yet the painful sensation of oppression and exasperation had passed away from her and she no longer thought of his personality as destructive. In obedience to his last words she walked on, and he kept heavily beside her, till they were in the deep shadows of the closely-growing trees and the spell of the garden began to return upon her, banishing the thought of self.

"Listen!" she said presently.

Larbi's flute was very near.

"He is always playing," she whispered.

"Who is he?"

"One of the gardeners. But he scarcely ever works. He is perpetually in love. That is why he plays."

"Is that a love-tune then?" Androvsky asked.

"Yes. Do you think it sounds like one?"

"How should I know, Madame?"

He stood looking in the direction from which the music came, and now it seemed to hold him fascinated. After his question, which sounded to her almost childlike, and which she did not answer, Domini glanced at his attentive face, to which the green shadows lent a dimness that was mysterious, at his tall figure, which always suggested to her both weariness and strength, and remembered the passionate romance to whose existence she awoke when she first heard Larbi's flute. It was as if a shutter, which had closed a window in the house of life, had been suddenly drawn away, giving to her eyes the horizon of a new world. Was that shutter now drawn back for him? No doubt the supposition was absurd. Men of his emotional and virile type have travelled far in that world, to her mysterious, ere they reach his length of years. What was extraordinary to her, in the thought of it alone, was doubtless quite ordinary to him, translated into act. Not ignorant, she was nevertheless a perfectly innocent woman, but her knowledge told her that no man of Androvsky's strength, power and passion is innocent at Androvsky's age. Yet his last dropped-out question was very deceptive. It had sounded absolutely natural and might have come from a boy's pure lips. Again he made her wonder.

There was a garden bench close to where they were standing.

"If you like to listen for a moment we might sit down," she said.

He started.

"Yes. Thank you."

When they were sitting side by side, closely guarded by the gigantic fig and chestnut trees which grew in this part of the garden, he added:

"Whom does he love?"

"No doubt one of those native women whom you consider utterly without attraction," she answered with a faint touch of malice which made him redden.

"But you come here every day?" he said.

"I!"

"Yes. Has he ever seen you?"

"Larbi? Often. What has that to do with it?"

He did not reply.

Odd and disconnected as Larbi's melodies were, they created an atmosphere of wild tenderness. Spontaneously they bubbled up out of the heart of the Eastern world and, when the player was invisible as now, suggested an ebon faun couched in hot sand at the foot of a palm tree and making music to listening sunbeams and amorous spirits of the waste.

"Do you like it?" she said presently in an under voice.

"Yes, Madame. And you?"

"I love it, but not as I love the song of the freed negroes. That is a song of all the secrets of humanity and of the desert too. And it does not try to tell them. It only says that they exist and that God knows them. But, I remember, you do not like that song."

"Madame," he answered slowly, and as if he were choosing his words, "I see that you understood. The song did move me though I said not. But no, I do not like it."

"Do you care to tell me why?"

"Such a song as that seems to me an—it is like an intrusion. There are things that should be let alone. There are dark places that should be left dark."

"You mean that all human beings hold within them secrets, and that no allusion even should ever be made to those secrets?"

"Yes."

"I understand."

After a pause he said, anxiously, she thought:

"Am I right, Madame, or is my thought ridiculous?"

He asked it so simply that she felt touched.

"I'm sure you could never be ridiculous," she said quickly. "And perhaps you are right. I don't know. That song makes me think and feel, and so I love it. Perhaps if you heard it alone——"

"Then I should hate it," he interposed.

His voice was like an uncontrolled inner voice speaking.

"And not thought and feeling——" she began.

But he interrupted her.

"They make all the misery that exists in the world."

"And all the happiness."

"Do they?"

"They must."

"Then you want to think deeply, to feel deeply?"

"Yes. I would rather be the central figure of a world-tragedy than die without having felt to the uttermost, even if it were sorrow. My whole nature revolts against the idea of being able to feel little or nothing really. It seems to me that when we begin to feel acutely we begin to grow, like the palm tree rising towards the African sun."

"I do not think you have ever been very unhappy," he said.

The sound of his voice as he said it made her suddenly feel as if it were true, as if she had never been utterly unhappy. Yet she had never been really happy. Africa had taught her that.

"Perhaps not," she answered. "But—some day——"

She stopped.

"Yes, Madame?"

"Could one stay long in such a world as this and not be either intensely happy or intensely unhappy? I don't feel as if it would be possible. Fierceness and fire beat upon one day after day and—one must learn to feel here."

As she spoke a sensation of doubt, almost of apprehension, came to her. She was overtaken by a terror of the desert. For a moment it seemed to her that he was right, that it were better never to be the prey of any deep emotion.

"If one does not wish to feel one should never come to such a place as this," she added.

And she longed to ask him why he was here, he, a man whose philosophy told him to avoid the heights and depths, to shun the ardours of nature and of life.

"Or, having come, one should leave it."

A sensation of lurking danger increased upon her, bringing with it the thought of flight.

"One can always do that," she said, looking at him.

She saw fear in his eyes, but it seemed to her that it was not fear of peril, but fear of flight. So strongly was this idea borne in upon her that she bluntly exclaimed:

" Unless it is one's nature to face things, never to turn one's back. Is it yours, Monsieur Androvsky? "

" Fear could never drive me to leave Beni-Mora," he answered.

"Sometimes I think that the only virtue in us is courage," she said, " that it includes all the others. I believe I could forgive everything where I found absolute courage."

Androvsky's eyes were lit up as if by a flicker of inward fire.

" You might create the virtue you love," he said hoarsely.

They looked at each other for a moment. Did he mean that she might create it in him?

Perhaps she would have asked, or perhaps he would have told her, but at that moment something happened. Larbi stopped playing. In the last few minutes they had both forgotten that he was playing, but when he ceased the garden changed. Something was withdrawn in which, without knowing it, they had been protecting themselves, and when the music faded their armour dropped away from them. With the complete silence came an altered atmosphere, the tenderness of mysticism instead of the tenderness of a wild humanity. The love of man seemed to depart out of the garden and another love to enter it, as when God walked under the trees in the cool of the day. And they sat quite still, as if a common impulse muted their lips. In the long silence that followed Domini thought of her mirage of the palm tree growing towards the African sun, feeling growing in the heart of a human being. But was it a worthy image? For the palm tree rises high. It soars into the air. But presently it ceases to grow. There is nothing infinite in its growth. And the long, hot years pass away and there it stands, never nearer to the infinite gold of the sun. But in the intense feeling of a man or woman is there not infinitude? Is there not a move-ment that is ceaseless till death comes to destroy—or to trans-late?

That was what she was thinking in the silence of the garden. And Androvsky? He sat beside her with his head bent, his hands hanging between his knees, his eyes gazing before him at the ordered tangle of the great trees. His lips were slightly parted, and on his strongly-marked face there was an expression as of emotional peace, as if the soul of the man were feeling deeply in calm. The restlessness, the violence that had made his demeanour so embarrassing during and after the *déjeuner* had vanished. He was a different man. And presently, noticing it, feeling his sensitive serenity, Domini seemed to see the great Mother at work about this child of hers, Nature at her tender task of pacification. The shared silence became to her like a song of thanksgiving, in which all the green things of the garden joined. And beyond them the desert lay listening, the Garden of Allah attentive to the voices of man's garden. She could hardly believe that but a few minutes before she had been full of irritation and bitterness, not free even from a touch of pride that was almost petty. But when she remembered that it was so she realised the abysses and the heights of which the heart is mingled, and an intense desire came to her to be always upon the heights of her own heart. For there only was the light of happiness. Never could she know joy if she forswore nobility. Never could she be at peace with the love within her—love of something that was not self, of something that seemed vaguer than God, as if it had entered into God and made him Love—unless she mounted upwards during her little span of life. Again, as before in this land, in the first sunset, on the tower, on the minaret of the mosque of Sidi-Zerzour, Nature spoke to her intimate words of inspiration, laid upon her the hands of healing, giving her powers she surely had not known or conceived of till now. And the passion that is the chiefest grace of goodness, making it the fire that purifies, as it is the little sister of the poor that tends the suffering, the hungry, the groping beggarworld, stirred within her, like the child not yet born, but whose destiny is with the angels. And she longed to make some great offering at the altar on whose lowest step she stood, and she was filled, for the first time consciously, with woman's sacred desire for sacrifice.

A soft step on the sand broke the silence and scattered her aspirations. Count Anteoni was coming towards them between the trees. The light of happiness was still upon his face and made him look much younger than usual. His whole bearing, in its elasticity and buoyant courage, was full of anticipation. As he came up to them he said to Domini:

" Do you remember chiding me?"

" I!" she said. " For what?"

Androvsky sat up and the expression of serenity passed away from his face.

" For never galloping away into the sun."

" Oh!—yes, I do remember."

" Well, I am going to obey you. I am going to make a journey."

" Into the desert? "

" Three hundred kilometers on horseback. I start to-morrow."

She looked up at him with a new interest. He saw it and laughed, almost like a boy.

" Ah, your contempt for me is dying! "

" How can you speak of contempt? "

" But you were full of it." He turned to Androvsky. " Miss Enfilden thought I could not sit a horse, Monsieur, unlike you. Forgive me for saying that you are almost more dare-devil than the Arabs themselves. I saw you the other day set your stallion at the bank of the river bed. I did not think any horse could have done it, but you knew better."

" I did not know at all," said Androvsky. " I had not ridden for over twenty years until that day."

He spoke with a blunt determination which made Domini remember their recent conversation on truth-telling.

" Dio mio! " said the Count, slowly, and looking at him with undisguised wonder. " You must have a will and a frame of iron."

" I am pretty strong."

He spoke rather roughly. Since the Count had joined them Domini noticed that Androvsky had become a different man. Once more he was on the defensive. The Count did not seem to notice it. Perhaps he was too radiant.

" I hope I shall endure as well as you, Monsieur," he said. " I go to Beni-Hassan to visit Sidi El Hadj Aïssa, one of the mightiest marabouts in the Sahara. In your Church," he added, turning again to Domini, " he would be a powerful Cardinal."

She noticed the " your." Evidently the Count was not a professing Catholic. Doubtless, like many modern Italians, he was a free-thinker in matters of religion.

" I am afraid I have never heard of him," she said. " In which direction does Beni-Hassan lie? "

" To go there one takes the caravan route that the natives call the route to Tombouctou."

An eager look came into her face.

" My road! " she said.

" Yours? "

"The one I shall travel on. You remember, Monsieur Androvsky?"

"Yes, Madame."

"Let me into your secret," said the Count, laughingly, yet with interest too.

"It is no secret. It is only that I love that route. It fascinates me, and I mean some day to make a desert journey along it."

"What a pity that we cannot join forces," the Count said. "I should feel it an honour to show the desert to one who has the reverence for it, the understanding of its spell, that you have."

He spoke earnestly, paused, and then added:

"But I know well what you are thinking."

"What is that?"

"That you will go to the desert alone. You are right. It is the only way, at any rate the first time. I went like that many years ago."

She said nothing in assent, and Androvsky got up from the bench.

"I must go, Monsieur."

"Already! But have you seen the garden?"

"It is wonderful. Good-bye, Monsieur. Thank you."

"But—let me see you to the gate. On Fridays——"

He was turning to Domini when she got up too.

"Don't you distribute alms on Fridays?" she said.

"How should you know it?"

"I have heard all about you. But is this the hour?"

"Yes."

"Let me see the distribution."

"And we will speed Monsieur Androvsky on his way at the same time."

She noticed that there was no question in his mind of her going with Androvsky. Did she mean to go with him? She had not decided yet.

They walked towards the gate and were soon on the great sweep of sand before the villa. A murmur of many voices was audible outside in the desert, nasal exclamations, loud guttural cries that sounded angry, the twittering of flutes and the snarl of camels.

"Do you hear my pensioners?" said the Count. "They are always impatient."

There was the noise of a tom-tom and of a whining shriek.

"That is old Bel Cassem's announcement of his presence. He has been living on me for years, the old ruffian, ever since his right eye was gouged out by his rival in the affections of the Maréchale of the dancing-girls. Smaïn!"

He blew his silver whistle. Instantly Smaïn came out of the villa carrying a money-bag. The Count took it and weighed it in his hand, looking at Domini with the joyous expression still upon his face.

"Have you ever made a thank-offering?" he said.

"No."

"That tells me something. Well, to-day I wish to make a thank-offering to the desert."

"What has it done for you?"

"Who knows? Who knows?"

He laughed aloud, almost like a boy. Androvsky glanced at him with a sort of wondering envy.

"And I want you to share in my little distribution," he added. "And you, Monsieur, if you don't mind. There are moments when—Open the gate, Smaïn!"

His ardour was infectious and Domini felt stirred by it to a sudden sense of the joy of life. She looked at Androvsky, to include him in the rigour of gaiety which swept from the Count to her, and found him staring apprehensively at the Count, who was now loosening the string of the bag. Smaïn had reached the gate. He lifted the bar of wood and opened it. Instantly a crowd of dark faces and turbaned heads were thrust through the tall aperture, a multitude of dusky hands fluttered frantically, and the cry of eager voices, saluting, begging, calling down blessings, relating troubles, shrieking wants, proclaiming virtues and necessities, rose into an almost deafening uproar. But not a foot was lifted over the lintel to press the sunlit sand. The Count's pensioners might be clamorous, but they knew what they might not do. As he saw them the wrinkles in his face deepened and his fingers quickened to achieve their purpose.

"My pensioners are very hungry to-day, and, as you see, they don't mind saying so. Hark at Bel Cassem!"

The tom-tom and the shriek that went with it made it a fierce crescendo.

"That means he is starving—the old hypocrite! Aren't they like the wolves in your Russia, Monsieur? But we must feed them. We mustn't let them devour our Beni-Mora. That's it!"

He threw the string on to the sand, plunged his hand into the bag and brought it out full of copper coins. The mouths opened wider, the hands waved more frantically, and all the dark eyes gleamed with the light of greed.

"Will you help me?" he said to Domini.

"Of course. What fun!"

Her eyes were gleaming too, but with the dancing fires of a gay impulse of generosity which made her wish that the bag contained her money. He filled her hands with coins.

"Choose whom you will. And now, Monsieur!"

For the moment he was so boyishly concentrated on the immediate present that he had ceased to observe whether the whim of others jumped with his own. Otherwise he must have been struck by Androvsky's marked discomfort, which indeed almost amounted to agitation. The sight of the throng of Arabs at the gateway, the clamour of their voices, evidently roused within him something akin to fear. He looked at them with distaste, and had drawn back several steps upon the sand, and now, as the Count held out to him a hand filled with money, he made no motion to take it, and half turned as if he thought of retreating into the recesses of the garden.

"Here, Monsieur! here!" exclaimed the Count, with his eyes on the crowd, towards which Domini was walking with a sort of mischievous slowness, to whet those appetites already so voracious.

Androvsky set his teeth and took the money, dropping one or two pieces on the ground. For a moment the Count seemed doubtful of his guest's participation in his own lively mood.

"Is this boring you?" he asked. "Because if so——"

"No, no, Monsieur, not at all! What am I to do?"

"Those hands will tell you."

The clamour grew more exigent.

"And when you want more come to me!"

Then he called out in Arabic, "Gently! Gently!" as the vehement scuffling seemed about to degenerate into actual fighting at Domini's approach, and hurried forward, followed more slowly by Androvsky.

Smaïn, from whose velvety eyes the dreams were not banished by the uproar, stood languidly by the porter's tent, gazing at Androvsky. Something in the demeanour of the new visitor seemed to attract him. Domini, meanwhile, had reached the gateway. Gently, with a capricious deftness and all a woman's passion for personal choice, she dropped the bits of money into

the hands belonging to the faces that attracted her, disregarding
the bellowings of those passed over. The light from all these
gleaming eyes made her feel warm, the clamour that poured
from these brown throats excited her. When her fingers were
empty she touched the Count's arm eagerly.

" More, more, please! "

" Ecco, Signora."

He held out to her the bag. She plunged her hands into it
and came nearer to the gate, both hands full of money and held
high above her head. The Arabs leapt up at her like dogs at a
bone, and for a moment she waited, laughing with all her heart.
Then she made a movement to throw the money over the heads
of the near ones to the unfortunates who were dancing and
shrieking on the outskirts of the mob. But suddenly her hands
dropped and she uttered a startled exclamation.

The sand diviner of the red bazaar, slipping like a reptile
under the waving arms and between the furious bodies of the
beggars, stood up before her with a smile on his wounded face,
stretched out to her his emaciated hands with a fawning, yet
half satirical, gesture of desire.

CHAPTER XII

THE money dropped from Domini's fingers and rolled upon
the sand at the Diviner's feet. But though he had surely come
to ask for alms, he took no heed of it. While the Arabs
round him fell upon their knees and fought like animals for the
plunder, he stood gaping at Domini. The smile still flickered
about his lips. His hand was still stretched out.

Instinctively she had moved backwards. Something that was
like a thrill of fear, mental, not physical, went through her, but
she kept her eyes steadily on his, as if, despite the fear, she
fought against him.

The contest of the beggars had become so passionate that
Count Anteoni's commands were forgotten. Urged by the
pressure from behind those in the front scrambled or fell over
the sacred threshold. The garden was invaded by a shrieking
mob. Smaïn ran forward, and the autocrat that dwelt in the
Count side by side with the benefactor suddenly emerged. He
blew his whistle four times. At each call a stalwart Arab
appeared.

" Shut the gate! " he commanded sternly.

The attendants furiously repulsed the mob, using their fists and feet without mercy. In the twinkling of an eye the sand was cleared and Smaïn had his hand upon the door to shut it. But the Diviner stopped him with a gesture, and in a fawning yet imperious voice called out something to the Count.

The Count turned to Domini.

"This is an interesting fellow. Would you like to know him?"

Her mind said no, yet her body assented. For she bowed her head. The Count beckoned. The Diviner stepped stealthily on to the sand with an air of subtle triumph, and Smaïn swung forward the great leaf of palm wood.

"Wait!" the Count cried, as if suddenly recollecting something. "Where is Monsieur Androvsky?"

"Isn't he——?" Domini glanced round. "I don't know."

He went quickly to the door and looked out. The Arabs, silent now and respectful, crowded about him, salaaming. He smiled at them kindly, and spoke to one or two. They answered gravely. An old man with one eye lifted his hand, in which was a tom-tom of stretched goatskin, and pointed towards the oasis, rapidly moving his toothless jaws. The Count stepped back into the garden, dismissed his pensioners with a masterful wave of the hand, and himself shut the door.

"Monsieur Androvsky has gone—without saying good-bye," he said.

Again Domini felt ashamed for Androvsky.

"I don't think he likes my pensioners," the Count added, in amused voice, "or me."

"I am sure——" Domini began.

But he stopped her.

"Miss Enfilden, in a world of lies I look to you for truth."

His manner chafed her, but his voice had a ring of earnestness. She said nothing. All this time the Diviner was standing on the sand, still smiling, but with downcast eyes. His thin body looked satirical and Domini felt a strong aversion from him, yet a strong interest in him too. Something in his appearance and manner suggested power and mystery as well as cunning. The Count said some words to him in Arabic, and at once he walked forward and disappeared among the trees, going so silently and smoothly that she seemed to watch a panther gliding into the depths of a jungle where its prey lay hid. She looked at the Count interrogatively.

"He will wait in the *fumoir*."

"Where we first met?"

"Yes."

"What for?"

"For us, if you choose."

"Tell me about him. I have seen him twice. He followed me with a bag of sand."

"He is a desert man. I don't know his tribe, but before he settled here he was a nomad, one of the wanderers who dwell in tents, a man of the sand; as much of the sand as a viper or a scorpion. One would suppose such beings were bred by the marriage of the sand-grains. The sand tells him secrets."

"He says. Do you believe it?"

"Would you like to test it?"

"How?"

"By coming with me to the *fumoir?*"

She hesitated obviously.

"Mind," he added, "I do not press it. A word from me and he is gone. But you are fearless, and you have spoken already, will speak much more intimately in the future, with the desert spirits."

"How do you know that?"

"The ' much more intimately '?"

"Yes."

"I do not know it, but—which is much more—I feel it."

She was silent, looking towards the trees where the Diviner had disappeared. Count Anteoni's boyish merriment had faded away. He looked grave, almost sad.

"I am not afraid," she said at last. "No, but—I will confess it—there is something horrible about that man to me. I felt it the first time I saw him. His eyes are too intelligent. They look diseased with intelligence."

"Let me send him away. Smaïn!"

But she stopped him. Directly he made the suggestion she felt that she must know more of this man.

"No. Let us go to the *fumoir.*"

"Very well. Go, Smaïn!"

Smaïn went into the little tent by the gate, sat down on his haunches and began to smell at a sprig of orange blossoms. Domini and the Count walked into the darkness of the trees.

"What is his name?" she asked.

"Alouï."

"Alouï."

She repeated the word slowly. There was a reluctant and yet fascinated sound in her voice.

"There is melody in the name," he said.

"Yes. Has he—has he ever looked in the sand for you?"

"Once—a long time ago."

"May I—dare I ask if he found truth there?"

"He found nothing for all the years that have passed since then."

"Nothing!"

There was a sound of relief in her voice.

"For those years."

She glanced at him and saw that once again his face had lit up into ardour.

"He found what is still to come?" she said.

And he repeated:

"He found what is still to come."

Then they walked on in silence till they saw the purple blossoms of the bougainvillea clinging to the white walls of the *fumoir*. Domini stopped on the narrow path.

"Is he in there?" she asked almost in a whisper.

"No doubt."

"Larbi was playing the first day I came here."

"Yes."

"I wish he was playing now."

The silence seemed to her unnaturally intense.

"Even his love must have repose."

She went on a step or two till, but still from a distance, she could look over the low plaster wall beneath the nearest window space into the little room.

"Yes, there he is!" she whispered.

The Diviner was crouching on the floor with his back towards them and his head bent down. Only his shoulders could be seen, covered with a white gandoura. They moved perpetually but slightly.

"What is he doing?"

"Speaking with his ancestor."

"His ancestor?"

"The sand. Alouï!"

He called softly. The figure rose, without sound and instantly, and the face of the Diviner smiled at them through the purple flowers. Again Domini had the sensation that her body was a glass box in which her thoughts, feelings and desires were ranged for this man's inspection; but she walked resolutely through the narrow doorway and sat down on one of the divans. Count Anteoni followed.

She now saw that in the centre of the room, on the ground, there was a symmetrical pyramid of sand, and that the Diviner was gently folding together a bag in his long and flexible fingers.

" You see! " said the Count.

She nodded, without speaking. The little sand heap held her eyes. She strove to think it absurd and the man who had shaken it out a charlatan of the desert, but she was really gripped by an odd feeling of awe, as if she were secretly expectant of some magical demonstration.

The Diviner squatted down once more on his haunches, stretched out his fingers above the sand heap, looked at her and smiled.

" La vie de Madame—I see it in the sable—la vie de Madame dans le grand désert du Sahara."

His eyes seemed to rout out the secrets from every corner of her being, and to scatter them upon the ground as the sand was scattered.

" Dans le grand désert du Sahara," Count Anteoni repeated, as if he loved the music of the words. " Then there is a desert life for Madame? "

The Diviner dropped his fingers on to the pyramid, lightly pressing the sand down and outward. He no longer looked at Domini. The searching and the satire slipped away from his eyes and body. He seemed to have forgotten the two watchers and to be concentrated upon the grains of sand. Domini noticed that the tortured expression, which had come into his face when she met him in the street and he stared into the bag, had returned to it. After pressing down the sand he spread the bag which had held it at Domini's feet, and deftly transferred the sand to it, scattering the grains loosely over the sacking, in a sort of pattern. Then, bending closely over them, he stared at them in silence for a long time. His pock-marked face was set like stone. His emaciated hands, stretched out, rested above the grains like carven things. His body seemed entirely breathless in its absolute immobility.

The Count stood in the doorway, still as he was, surrounded by the motionless purple flowers. Beyond, in their serried ranks, stood the motionless trees. No incense was burning in the little brazier to-day. This cloistered world seemed spell-bound.

A low murmur at last broke the silence. It came from the

Diviner. He began to talk rapidly, but as if to himself, and as he talked he moved again, broke up with his fingers the patterns in the sand, formed fresh ones; spirals, circles, snake-like lines, series of mounting dots that reminded Domini of spray flung by a fountain, curves, squares and oblongs. So swiftly was it done and undone that the sand seemed to be endowed with life, to be explaining itself in these patterns, to be presenting deliberate glimpses of hitherto hidden truths. And always the voice went on, and the eyes were downcast, and the body, save for the moving hands and arms, was absolutely motionless.

Domini looked over the Diviner to Count Anteoni, who came gently forward and sat down, bending his head to listen to the voice.

" Is it Arabic? " she whispered.

He nodded.

" Can you understand it? "

" Not yet. Presently it will get slower, clearer. He always begins like this."

" Translate it for me."

" Exactly as it is? "

" Exactly as it is."

" Whatever it may be? "

" Whatever it may be."

He glanced at the tortured face of the Diviner and looked grave.

" Remember you have said I am fearless," she said.

He answered:

" Whatever it is you shall know it."

Then they were silent again. Gradually the Diviner's voice grew clearer, the pace of its words less rapid, but always it sounded mysterious and inward, less like the voice of a man than the distant voice of a secret.

" I can hear now," whispered the Count.

" What is he saying? "

" He is speaking about the desert."

" Yes? "

" He sees a great storm. Wait a moment! "

The voice spoke for some seconds and ceased, and once again the Diviner remained absolutely motionless, with his hands extended above the grains like carven things.

" He sees a great sand-storm, one of the most terrible that has ever burst over the Sahara. Everything is blotted out. The desert vanishes. Beni-Mora is bidden. It is day, yet there is a darkness like night. In this darkness he sees a train of camels waiting by a church."

" A mosque? "

" No, a church. In the church there is a sound of music. The roar of the wind, the roar of the camels, mingles with the chanting and drowns it. He cannot hear it any more. It is as if the desert is angry and wishes to kill the music. In the church your life is beginning."

" My life? "

" Your real life. He says that now you are fully born, that till now there has been a veil around your soul like the veil of the womb around a child."

" He says that! "

There was a sound of deep emotion in her voice.

" That is all. The roar of the wind from the desert has silenced the music in the church, and all is dark."

The Diviner moved again, and formed fresh patterns in the sand with feverish rapidity, and again began to speak swiftly.

" He sees the train of camels that waited by the church starting on a desert journey. The storm has not abated. They pass through the oasis into the desert. He sees them going towards the south."

Domini leaned forward on the divan, looking at Count Anteoni above the bent body of the Diviner.

" By what route? " she whispered.

" By the route which the natives call the road to Tom-bouctou."

" But—it is my journey! "

" Upon one of the camels, in a palanquin such as the great sheikhs use to carry their women, there are two people, pro-tected against the storm by curtains. They are silent, listening to the roaring of the wind. One of them is you."

" Two people! "

" Two people."

" But—who is the other? "

" He cannot see. It is as if the blackness of the storm were deeper round about the other and hid the other from him. The caravan passes on and is lost in the desolation and the storm."

She said nothing, but looked down at the thin body of the Diviner crouched close to her knees. Was this pock-marked face the face of a prophet? Did this skin and bone envelop the soul of a seer? She no longer wished that Larbi was playing upon his flute or felt the silence to be unnatural. For this man had filled it with the roar of the desert wind. And in the wind there struggled and was finally lost the sound of voices of her Faith chanting—what? The wind was too strong. The voices were too faint. She could not hear.

Once more the Diviner stirred. For some minutes his fingers were busy in the sand. But now they moved more slowly and no words came from his lips. Domini and the Count bent low to watch what he was doing. The look of torture upon his face increased. It was terrible, and made upon Domini an indelible impression, for she could not help connecting it with his vision of her future, and it suggested to her formless phantoms of despair. She looked into the sand, as if she, too, would be able to see what he saw and had not told, looked till she began to feel almost hypnotised. The Diviner's hands trembled now as they made the patterns, and his breast heaved under his white robe. Presently he traced in the sand a triangle and began to speak.

The Count bent down till his ear was almost at the Diviner's lips, and Domini held her breath. That caravan lost in the desolation of the desert, in the storm and the darkness—where was it? What had been its fate? Sweat ran down over the Diviner's face, and dropped upon his robe, upon his hands, upon the sand, making dark spots. And the voice whispered on huskily till she was in a fever of impatience. She saw upon the face of the Count the Diviner's tortured look reflected. Was it not also on her face? A link surely bound them all together in this tiny room, close circled by the tall trees and the intense silence. She looked at the triangle in the sand. It was very distinct, more distinct than the other patterns had been. What did it represent? She searched her mind, thinking of the desert, of her life there, of man's life in the desert. Was it not tent-shaped? She saw it as a tent, as her tent pitched somewhere in the waste far from the habitations of men. Now the trembling hands were still, the voice was still, but the sweat did not cease from dropping down upon the sand.

" Tell me! " she murmured to the Count.

He obeyed, seeming now to speak with an effort.

" It is far away in the desert——"

He paused.

" Yes? Yes? "

" Very far away in a sandy place. There are immense dunes, immense white dunes of sand on every side, like mountains.

Near at hand there is a gleam of many fires. They are lit in the market-place of a desert city. Among the dunes, with camels picketed behind it, there is a tent——"

She pointed to the triangle traced upon the sand.

" I knew it," she whispered. " It is my tent."

" He sees you there, as he saw you in the palanquin. But now it is night and you are quite alone. You are not asleep. Something keeps you awake. You are excited. You go out of the tent upon the dunes and look towards the fires of the city. He hears the jackals howling all around you, and sees the skeletons of dead camels white under the moon."

She shuddered in spite of herself.

" There is something tremendous in your soul. He says it is as if all the date palms of the desert bore their fruit together, and in all the dry places, where men and camels have died of thirst in bygone years, running springs burst forth, and as if the sand were covered with millions of golden flowers big as the flower of the aloe."

" But then it is joy, it must be joy! "

" He says it is great joy."

" Then why does he look like that, breathe like that? "

She indicated the Diviner, who was trembling where he crouched, and breathing heavily, and always sweating like one in agony.

" There is more," said the Count, slowly.

" Tell me."

" You stand alone upon the dunes and you look towards the city. He hears the tom-toms beating, and distant cries as if there were a fantasia. Then he sees a figure among the dunes coming towards you."

" Who is it? " she asked.

He did not answer. But she did not wish him to answer. She had spoken without meaning to speak.

" You watch this figure. It comes to you, walking heavily."

" Walking heavily? "

" That's what he says. The dates shrivel on the palms, the streams dry up, the flowers droop and die in the sand. In the city the tom-toms faint away and the red fires fade away. All is dark and silent. And then he sees——"

" Wait! " Domini said almost sharply.

He sat looking at her. She pressed her hands together. In her dark face, with its heavy eyebrows and strong, generous mouth, a contest showed, a struggle between some quick desire and some more sluggish but determined reluctance. In a moment she spoke again.

" I won't hear anything more, please."

" But you said ' whatever it may be.' "

" Yes. But I won't hear anything more."

She spoke very quietly, with determination.

The Diviner was beginning to move his hands again, to make fresh patterns in the sand, to speak swiftly once more.

" Shall I stop him? "

" Please."

" Then would you mind going out into the garden? I will join you in a moment. Take care not to disturb him."

She got up with precaution, held her skirts together with her hands, and slipped softly out on to the garden path. For a moment she was inclined to wait there, to look back and see what was happening in the *fumoir*. But she resisted her inclination, and walked on slowly till she reached the bench where she had sat an hour before with Androvsky. There she sat down and waited. In a few minutes she saw the Count coming towards her alone. His face was very grave, but lightened with a slight smile when he saw her.

" He has gone? " she asked.

" Yes."

He was about to sit beside her, but she said quickly:

" Would you mind going back to the jamelon tree? "

" Where we sat this morning? "

" Was it only—yes."

" Certainly."

" Oh, but you are going away to-morrow! You have a lot to do probably? "

" Nothing. My men will arrange everything."

She got up, and they walked in silence till they saw once more the immense spaces of the desert bathed in the afternoon sun. As Domini looked at them again she knew that their wonder, their meaning, had increased for her. The steady crescendo that was beginning almost to frighten her was maintained—the crescendo of the voice of the Sahara. To what tremendous demonstration was this crescendo tending, to what ultimate glory or terror? She felt that her soul was as yet too undeveloped to conceive. The Diviner had been right. There was a veil around it, like the veil of the womb that hides the unborn child.

Under the jamelon tree she sat down once more.

"May I light a cigar?" the Count asked.

"Do."

He struck a match, lit a cigar, and sat down on her left, by the garden wall.

"Tell me frankly," he said. "Do you wish to talk or to be silent?"

"I wish to speak to you."

"I am sorry now I asked you to test Alouï's powers."

"Why?"

"Because I fear they made an unpleasant impression upon you."

"That was not why I made you stop him."

"No?"

"You don't understand me. I was not afraid. I can only say that, but I can't give you my reason for stopping him. I wished to tell you that it was not fear."

"I believe—I know that you are fearless," he said with an unusual warmth. "You are sure that I don't understand you?"

"Remember the refrain of the Freed Negroes' song!"

"Ah, yes—those black fellows. But I know something of you, Miss Enfilden—yes, I do."

"I would rather you did—you and your garden."

"And—some day—I should like you to know a little more of me."

"Thank you. When will you come back?"

"I can't tell. But you are not leaving?"

"Not yet."

The idea of leaving Beni-Mora troubled her heart strangely.

"No, I am too happy here."

"Are you really happy?"

"At any rate I am happier than I have ever been before."

"You are on the verge."

He was looking at her with eyes in which there was tenderness, but suddenly they flashed fire, and he exclaimed:

"My desert land must not bring you despair."

She was startled by his sudden vehemence.

"What I would not hear!" she said. "You know it!"

"It is not my fault. I am ready to tell it to you."

"No. But do you believe it? Do you believe that man can read the future in the sand? How can it be?"

"How can a thousand things be? How can these desert men stand in fire, with their naked feet set on burning brands,

with burning brands under their armpits, and not be burned?
How can they pierce themselves with skewers and cut themselves with knives and no blood flow? But I told you the first
day I met you; the desert always makes me the same gift when I
return to it."

" What gift? "

" The gift of belief."

" Then you do believe in that man—Alouï? "

" Do you? "

" I can only say that it seemed to me as if it might be
divination. If I had not felt that I should not have stopped
it. I should have treated it as a game."

" It impressed you as it impresses me. Well, for both of us
the desert has gifts. Let us accept them fearlessly. It is the
will of Allah."

She remembered her vision of the pale procession. Would
she walk in it at last?

" You are as fatalistic as an Arab," she said.

" And you? "

" I! " she answered simply. " I believe that I am in the
hands of God, and I know that perfect love can never harne
me."

After a moment he said, gently:

" Miss Enfilden, I want to ask something of you."

" Yes? "

" Will you make a sacrifice? To-morrow I start at dawn.
Will you be here to wish me God speed on my journey? "

" Of course I will."

" It will be good of you. I shall value it from you. And—
and when—if you ever make your long journey on that road—
the route to the south—I will wish you Allah's blessing in the
Garden of Allah."

He spoke with solemnity, almost with passion, and she felt
the tears very near her eyes. Then they sat in silence, looking
out over the desert.

And she heard its voices calling.

CHAPTER XIII

ON the following morning, before dawn, Domini awoke, stirred
from sleep by her anxiety, persistent even in what seemed
unconsciousness, to speed Count Anteoni upon his desert journey.

She did not know why he was going, but she felt that some great issue in his life hung upon the accomplishment of the purpose with which he set out, and without affectation she ardently desired that accomplishment. As soon as she awoke she lit a candle and glanced at her watch. She knew by the hour that the dawn was near, and she got up at once and made her toilet. She had told Batouch to be at the hotel door before sunrise to accompany her to the garden, and she wondered if he were below. A stillness as of deep night prevailed in the house, making her movements, while she dressed, seem unnaturally loud. When she put on her hat, and looked into the glass to see if it were just at the right angle, she thought her face, always white, was haggard. This departure made her a little sad, It suggested to her the instability of circumstance, the perpetual change that occurs in life. The going of her kind host made her own going more possible than before, even more likely. Some words from the Bible kept on running through her brain: " Here have we no continuing city." In the silent darkness their cadence held an ineffable melancholy. Her mind heard them as the ear, in a pathetic moment, hears sometimes a distant strain of music wailing like a phantom through the invisible. And the everlasting journeying of all created things oppressed her heart.

When she had buttoned her jacket and drawn on her gloves she went to the French window and pushed back the shutters. A wan semi-darkness looked in upon her. Again she wondered whether Batouch had come. It seemed to her unlikely. She could not imagine that anyone in all the world was up and purposeful but herself. This hour seemed created as a curtain for unconsciousness. Very softly she stepped out upon the verandah and looked over the parapet. She could see the white road, mysteriously white, below. It was deserted. She leaned down.

" Batouch! " she called softly. " Batouch! "

He might be hidden under the arcade, sleeping in his burnous.

" Batouch! Batouch! "

No answer came. She stood by the parapet, waiting and looking down the road.

All the stars had faded, yet there was no suggestion of the sun. She faced an unrelenting austerity. For a moment she thought of this atmosphere, this dense stillness, this gravity of vague and shadowy trees, as the environment of those who had erred, of the lost spirits of men who had died in mortal sin.

Almost she expected to see the desperate shade of her dead
father pass between the black stems of the palm trees, vanish into
the grey mantle that wrapped the hidden world.

"Batouch! Batouch!"

He was not there. That was certain. She resolved to set
out alone and went back into her bedroom to get her revolver.
When she came out again with it in her hand Androvsky was
standing on the verandah just outside her window. He took off
his hat and looked from her face to the revolver. She was
startled by his appearance, for she had not heard his step, and
had been companioned by a sense of irreparable solitude. This
was the first time she had seen him since he vanished from the
garden on the previous day.

"You are going out, Madame?" he said.

"Yes."

"Not alone?"

"I believe so. Unless I find Batouch below."

She slipped the revolver into the pocket of the loose coat she
wore.

"But it is dark."

"It will be day very soon. Look!"

She pointed towards the east, where a light, delicate and
mysterious as the distant lights in the opal, was gently pushing
in the sky.

"You ought not to go alone."

"Unless Batouch is there I must. I have given a promise
and I must keep it. There is no danger."

He hesitated, looking at her with an anxious, almost a suspicious, expression.

"Good-bye, Monsieur Androvsky."

She went towards the staircase. He followed her quickly to
the head of it.

"Don't trouble to come down with me."

"If—if Batouch is not there—might not I guard you,
Madame?" She remembered the Count's words and answered:

"Let me tell you where I am going. I am going to say
good-bye to Count Anteoni before he starts for his desert
journey."

Androvsky stood there without a word.

"Now, do you care to come if I don't find Batouch? Mind,
I'm not the least afraid."

"Perhaps he is there—if you told him."

He muttered the words. His whole manner had changed. Now he looked more than suspicious—cloudy and fierce.

" Possibly."

She began to descend the stairs. He did not follow her, but stood looking after her. When she reached the arcade it was deserted. Batouch had forgotten or had overslept himself. She could have walked on under the roof that was the floor of the verandah, but instead she stepped out into the road. Androvsky was above her by the parapet. She glanced up and said :

" He is not here, but it is of no consequence. Dawn is breaking. *Au revoir!* "

Slowly he took off his hat. As she went away down the road he was holding it in his hand, looking after her.

" He does not like the Count," she thought.

At the corner she turned into the street where the sand diviner had his bazaar, and as she neared his door she was aware of a certain trepidation. She did not want to see those piercing eyes looking at her in the semi-darkness, and she hurried her steps. But her anxiety was needless. All the doors were shut, all the inhabitants doubtless wrapped in sleep. Yet, when she had gained the end of the street, she looked back, half expecting to see an apparition of a thin figure, a tortured face, to hear a voice, like a goblin's voice, calling after her. Midway down the street there was a man coming slowly behind her. For a moment she thought it was the Diviner in pursuit, but something in the gait soon showed her her mistake. There was heaviness in the movement of this man quite unlike the lithe and serpentine agility of Alouï. Although she could not see the face, or even distinguish the costume in the morning twilight, she knew it for Androvsky. From a distance he was watching over her. She did not hesitate, but walked on quickly again. She did not wish him to know that she had seen him. When she came to the long road that skirted the desert she met the breeze of dawn that blows out of the east across the flats, and drank in its celestial purity. Between the palms, far away towards Sidi-Zerzour, above the long indigo line of the Sahara, there rose a curve of deep red gold. The sun was coming up to take possession of his waiting world. She longed to ride out to meet him, to give him a passionate welcome in the sand, and the opening words of the Egyptian "Adoration of the Sun by the Perfect Souls " came to her lips:

" Hommage a Toi. Dieu Soleil. Seigneur du Ciel, Roi sur

la Terre! Lion du Soir! Grande Ame divine, vivante a
toujours."

Why had she not ordered her horse to ride a little way with
Count Anteoni? She might have pretended that she was starting on her great journey.

The red gold curve became a semi-circle of burnished glory
resting upon the deep blue, then a full circle that detached itself
majestically and mounted calmly up the cloudless sky. A stream
of light poured into the oasis, and Domini, who had paused for a
moment in silent worship, went on swiftly through the negro
village which was all astir, and down the track to the white villa.

She did not glance round again to see whether Androvsky was
still following her, for, since the sun had come, she had the
confident sensation that he was no longer near.

He had surely given her into the guardianship of the sun.

The door of the garden stood wide open, and, as she entered,
she saw three magnificent horses prancing upon the sweep of
sand in the midst of a little group of Arabs. Smaïn greeted her
with graceful warmth and begged her to follow him to the
fumoir, where the Count was waiting for her.

" It is good of you! " the Count said, meeting her in the
doorway. " I relied on you, you see! "

Breakfast for two was scattered upon the little smoking-
tables; coffee, eggs, rolls, fruit, sweetmeats. And everywhere
sprigs of orange blossom filled the cool air with delicate
sweetness.

" How delicious! " she exclaimed. " A breakfast here! But
—no, not there! "

" Why not? "

" That is exactly where he was."

" Alouï! How superstitious you are! "

He moved her table. She sat down near the doorway and
poured out coffee for them both.

" You look workmanlike."

She glanced at his riding-dress and long whip. Smoked
glasses hung across his chest by a thin cord.

" I shall have some hard riding, but I'm tough, though you
may not think it. I've covered many a league of my friend in
bygone years."

He tapped an eggshell smartly, and began to eat with
appetite.

" How gravely gay you are! " she said, lifting the steaming
coffee to her lips.

He smiled.

"Yes. To-day I am happy, as a pious man is happy when after a long illness, he goes once more to church."

"The desert seems to be everything to you."

"I feel that I am going out to freedom, to more than freedom." He stretched out his arms above his head.

"Yet you have stayed always in this garden all these days."

"I was waiting for my summons, as you will wait for yours."

"What summons could I have?"

"It will come!" he said with conviction. "It will come!"

She was silent, thinking of the diviner's vision in the sand, of the caravan of camels disappearing in the storm towards the south. Presently she asked him:

"Are you ever coming back?"

He looked at her in surprise, then laughed.

"Of course. What are you thinking?"

"That perhaps you will not come back, that perhaps the desert will keep you."

"And my garden?"

She looked out across the tiny sand-path and the running rill of water to the great trees stirred by the cool breeze of dawn.

"It would miss you."

After a moment, during which his bright eyes followed hers, he said:

"Do you know, I have a great belief in the intuitions of good women?"

"Yes?"

"An almost fanatical belief. Will you answer me a question at once, without consideration, without any time for thought?"

"If you ask me to."

"I do ask you."

"Then——?"

"Do you see me in this garden any more?"

A voice answered:

"No."

It was her own, yet it seemed another's voice, with which she had nothing to do.

A great feeling of sorrow swept over her as she heard it.

"Do come back!" she said.

The Count had got up. The brightness of his eyes was obscured.

"If not here, we shall meet again," he said slowly.

"Where?"

"In the desert."

"Did the Diviner——? No, don't tell me."

She got up too.

"It is time for you to start?"

"Nearly."

A sort of constraint had settled over them. She felt it painfully for a moment. Did it proceed from something in his mind or in hers? She could not tell. They walked slowly down one of the little paths and presently found themselves before the room in which sat the purple dog.

"If I am never to come back I must say good-bye to him," the Count said.

"But you will come back."

"That voice said 'No.'"

"It was a lying voice."

"Perhaps."

They looked in at the window and met the ferocious eyes of the dog.

"And if I never come back will he bay the moon for his old master?" said the Count with a whimsical, yet sad, smile. "I put him here. And will these trees, many of which I planted, whisper a regret? Absurd, isn't it, Miss Enfilden? I never can feel that the growing things in my garden do not know me as I know them."

"Someone will regret you if——"

"Will you? Will you really?"

"Yes."

"I believe it."

He looked at her. She could see, by the expression of his eyes, that he was on the point of saying something, but was held back by some fighting sensation, perhaps by some reserve.

"What is it?"

"May I speak frankly to you without offence?" he asked. "I am really rather old, you know."

"Do speak."

"That guest of mine yesterday——"

"Monsieur Androvsky?"

"Yes. He interested me enormously, profoundly."

"Really! Yet he was at his worst yesterday."

"Perhaps that was why. At any rate, he interested me more than any man I have seen for years. But——"

He paused, looking in at the little chamber where the dog kept guard.

"But my interest was complicated by a feeling that I was face to face with a human being who was at odds with life, with himself, even with his Creator—a man who had done what the Arabs never do—defied Allah in Allah's garden."

"Oh!"

She uttered a little exclamation of pain. It seemed to her that he was gathering up and was expressing scattered, half formless thoughts of hers.

"You know," he continued, looking more steadily into the room of the dog, "that in Algeria there is a floating population composed of many mixed elements. I could tell you strange stories of tragedies that have occurred in this land, even here in Beni-Mora, tragedies of violence, of greed, of—tragedies that were not brought about by Arabs."

He turned suddenly and looked right into her eyes.

"But why am I saying all this?" he suddenly exclaimed. "What is written is written, and such women as you are guarded."

"Guarded? By whom?"

"By their own souls."

"I am not afraid," she said quietly.

"Need you tell me that? Miss Enfilden, I scarcely know why I have said even as little as I have said. For I am, as you know, a fatalist. But certain people, very few, so awaken our regard that they make us forget our own convictions, and might even lead us to try to tamper with the designs of the Almighty. Whatever is to be for you, you will be able to endure. That I know. Why should I, or anyone, seek to know more for you? But still there are moments in which the bravest want a human hand to help them, a human voice to comfort them. In the desert, wherever I may be—and I shall tell you—I am at your service."

"Thank you," she said simply.

She gave him her hand. He held it almost as a father or a guardian might have held it.

"And this garden is yours day and night—Smaïn knows."

"Thank you," she said again.

The shrill whinnying of a horse came to them from a distance. Their hands fell apart. Count Anteoni looked round him slowly at the great cocoanut tree, at the shaggy grass of the lawn, at the tall bamboos and the drooping mulberry trees. She saw that he was taking a silent farewell of them.

"This was a waste," he said at last with a half-stifled sigh. "I turned it into a little Eden and now I am leaving it."

"For a time."

"And if it were for ever? Well, the great thing is to let the waste within one be turned into an Eden, if that is possible. And yet how many human beings strive against the great Gardener. At any rate I will not be one of them."

"And I will not be one."

"Shall we say good-bye here?"

"No. Let us say it from the wall, and let me see you ride away into the desert."

She had forgotten for the moment that his route was the road through the oasis. He did not remind her of it. It was easy to ride across the desert and join the route where it came out from the last palms.

"So be it. Will you go to the wall then?"

He touched her hand again and walked away towards the villa, slowly on the pale silver of the sand. When his figure was hidden by the trunks of the trees Domini made her way to the wide parapet. She sat down on one of the tiny seats cut in it, leaned her cheek in her hand and waited. The sun was gathering strength, but the air was still deliciously cool, almost cold, and the desert had not yet put on its aspect of fiery desolation. It looked dreamlike and romantic, not only in its distances, but near at hand. There must surely be dew, she fancied, in the Garden of Allah. She could see no one travelling in it, only some far away camels grazing. In the dawn the desert was the home of the breeze, of gentle sunbeams and of liberty. Presently she heard the noise of horses cantering near at hand, and Count Anteoni, followed by two Arab attendants, came round the bend of the wall and drew up beneath her. He rode on a high red Arab saddle, and a richly-ornamented gun was slung in an embroidered case behind him on the right-hand side. A broad and soft brown hat kept the sun from his forehead. The two attendants rode on a few paces and waited in the shadow of the wall.

"Don't you wish you were going out?" he said. "Out into that?" And he pointed with his whip towards the dreamlike blue of the far horizon. She leaned over, looking down at him and at his horse, which fidgeted and arched his white neck and dropped foam from his black flexible lips.

"No," she answered after a moment of thought. "I must speak the truth, you know."

"To me, always."

"I feel that you were right, that my summons has not yet come to me."

"And when it comes?"

"I shall obey it without fear, even if I go in the storm and the darkness."

He glanced at the radiant sky, at the golden beams slanting down upon the palms.

"The Coran says: 'The fate of every man have We bound about his neck.' May yours be as serene, as beautiful, as a string of pearls."

"But I have never cared to wear pearls," she answered.

"No? What are your stones?"

"Rubies."

"Blood! No others?"

"Sapphires."

"The sky at night."

"And opals."

"Fires gleaming across the white of moonlit dunes. Do you remember?"

"I remember."

"And you do not ask me for the end of the Diviner's vision even now?"

"No."

She hesitated for an instant. Then she added:

"I will tell you why. It seemed to me that there was another's fate in it as well as my own, and that to hear would be to intrude, perhaps, upon another's secrets."

"That was your reason?"

"My only reason." And then she added, repeating consciously Androvsky's words: "I think there are things that should be let alone."

"Perhaps you are right."

A stronger breath of the cool wind came over the flats, and all the palm trees rustled. Through the garden there was a delicate stir of life.

"My children are murmuring farewell," said the Count. "I hear them. It is time! Good-bye, Miss Enfilden—my friend, if I may call you so. May Allah have you in his keeping, and, when your summons comes, obey it—alone."

As he said the last word his grating voice dropped to a deep note of earnest, almost solemn, gravity. Then he lifted his hat, touched his horse with his heel, and galloped away into the sun.

Domini watched the three riders till they were only specks on the surface of the desert. Then they became one with it, and were lost in the dreamlike radiance of the morning. But she did not move. She sat with her eyes fixed up on the blue horizon. A great loneliness had entered into her spirit. Till Count Anteoni had gone she did not realise how much she had become accustomed to his friendship, how near their sympathies had been. But directly those tiny, moving specks became one with the desert she knew that a gap had opened in her life. It might be small, but it seemed dark and deep. For the first time the desert, which she had hitherto regarded as a giver, had taken something from her. And now, as she sat looking at it, while the sun grew stronger and the light more brilliant, while the mountains gradually assumed a harsher aspect, and the details of things, in the dawn so delicately clear, became, as it were, more piercing in their sharpness, she realised a new and terrible aspect of it. That which has the power to bestow has another power. She had seen the great procession of those who had received gifts of the desert's hands. Would she some day, or in the night when the sky was like a sapphire, see the procession of those from whom the desert had taken away perhaps their dreams, perhaps their hopes, perhaps even all that they passionately loved and had desperately clung to?

And in which of the two processions would she walk?

She got up with a sigh. The garden had become tragic to her for the moment, full of a brooding melancholy. As she turned to leave it she resolved to go to the priest. She had never yet entered his house. Just then she wanted to speak to someone with whom she could be as a little child, to whom she could liberate some part of her spirit simply, certain of a simple, yet not foolish, reception of it by one to whom she could look up. She desired to be not with the friend so much as with the spiritual director. Something was alive within her, something of distress, almost of apprehension, which needed the soothing hand, not of human love, but of religion.

When she reached the priest's house Beni-Mora was astir with a pleasant bustle of life. The military note pealed through its symphony. Spahis were galloping along the white roads. Tirailleurs went by bearing despatches. Zouaves stood under the palms, staring calmly at the morning, their sunburned hands loosely clasped upon muskets whose butts rested in the sand.

But Domini scarcely noticed the brilliant gaiety of the life about her. She was preoccupied, even sad. Yet, as she entered the little garden of the priest, and tapped gently at his door, a sensation of hope sprang up in her heart, born of the sustaining power of her religion.

An Arab boy answered her knock, said that the Father was in and led her at once to a small, plainly-furnished room, with whitewashed walls, and a window opening on to an enclosure at the back, where several large palm trees reared their tufted heads above the smoothly-raked sand. In a moment the priest came in, smiling with pleasure and holding out his hands in welcome.

"Father," she said at once, "I am come to have a little talk with you. Have you a few moments to give me?"

"Sit down, my child," he said.

He drew forward a straw chair for her and took one opposite.

"You are not in trouble?"

"I don't know why I should be, but——"

She was silent for a moment. Then she said:

"I want to tell you a little about my life."

He looked at her kindly without a word.

His eyes were an invitation for her to speak, and, without further invitation, in as few and simple words as possible, she told him why she had come to Beni-Mora, and something of her parents' tragedy and its effect upon her.

"I wanted to renew my heart, to find myself," she said. "My life has been cold, careless. I never lost my faith, but I almost forgot that I had it. I made little use of it. I let it rust."

"Many do that, but a time comes when they feel that the great weapon with which alone we can fight the sorrows and dangers of the world must be kept bright, or it may fail us in the hour of need."

"Yes."

"And this is an hour of need for you. But, indeed, is there ever an hour that is not?"

"I feel to-day, I——"

She stopped, suddenly conscious of the vagueness of her apprehension. It made her position difficult, speech hard for her. She felt that she wanted something, yet scarcely knew what, or exactly why she had come.

"I have been saying good-bye to Count Anteoni," she resumed. "He has gone on a desert journey."

"For long?"

" I don't know, but I feel that it will be."

" He comes and goes very suddenly. Often he is here and I do not even know it."

" He is a strange man, but I think he is a good man."

As she spoke about him she began to realise that something in him had roused the desire in her to come to the priest.

" And he sees far," she added.

She looked steadily at the priest, who was waiting quietly to hear more. She was glad he did not trouble her mind just then by trying to help her to go on, to be explicit.

" I came here to find peace," she continued. " And I thought I had found it. I thought so till to-day."

" We only find peace in one place, and only there by our own will according with God's."

" You mean within ourselves."

" Is it not so? "

" Yes. Then I was foolish to travel in search of it."

" I would not say that. Place assists the heart, I think, and the way of life. I thought so once."

" When you wished to be a monk? "

A deep sadness came into his eyes.

" Yes," he said. " And even now I find it very difficult to say, ' It was not thy will, and so it is not mine.' But would you care to tell me if anything has occurred recently to trouble you? "

" Something has occurred, Father."

More excitement came into her face and manner.

" Do you think," she went on, " that it is right to try to avoid what life seems to be bringing to one, to seek shelter from—from the storm? Don't monks do that? Please forgive me if——"

" Sincerity will not hurt me," he interrupted quietly. " If it did I should indeed be unworthy of my calling. Perhaps it is not right for all. Perhaps that is why I am here instead of——

" Ah, but I remember, you wanted to be one of the *frères armés*."

" That was my first hope. But you "—very simply he turned from his troubles to hers—" you are hesitating, are you not, between two courses? "

" I scarcely know. But I want you to tell me. Ought we not always to think of others more than of ourselves? "

" So long as we take care not to put ourselves in too great danger. The soul should be brave, but not foolhardy."

His voice had changed, had become stronger, even a little stern.

" There are risks that no good Christian ought to run: it is not cowardice, it is wisdom that avoids the Evil One. I have known people who seemed almost to think it was their mission to convert the fallen angels. They confused their powers with the powers that belong to God only."

" Yes, but—it is so difficult to—if a human being were possessed by the devil, would not you try—would you not go near to that person? "

" If I had prayed, and been told that any power was given me to do what Christ did."

" To cast out—yes, I know. But sometimes that power is given—even to women."

" Perhaps especially to them. I think the devil has more fear of a good mother than of many saints."

Domini realised almost with agony in that moment how her own soul had been stripped of a precious armour. A feeling of bitter helplessness took possession of her, and of contempt for what she now suddenly looked upon as foolish pride. The priest saw that his words had hurt her, yet he did not just then try to pour balm upon the wound.

" You came to me to-day as to a spiritual director, did you not? " he asked.

" Yes, Father."

" Yet you do not wish to be frank with me. Isn't that true? "

There was a piercing look in the eyes he fixed upon her.

" Yes," she answered bravely.

" Why? Cannot you—at least will not you tell me? "

A similar reason to that which had caused her to refuse to hear what the Diviner had seen in the sand caused her now to answer:

" There is something I cannot say. I am sure I am right not to say it."

" Do you wish me to speak frankly to you, my child? "

" Yes, you may."

" You have told me enough of your past life to make me feel sure that for some time to come you ought to be very careful in regard to your faith. By the mercy of God you have been preserved from the greatest of all dangers—the danger of losing your belief in the teachings of the only true Church. You have come here to renew your faith which, not killed, has been stricken, reduced, may I not say? to a sort of invalidism. Are you sure you are in a condition yet to help "—he hesitated obviously, then slowly—" others? There are periods in which one cannot do what one may be able to do in the far future. The convalescent who is just tottering in the new attempt to walk is not wise enough to lend an arm to another. To do so may seem nobly unselfish, but is it not folly? And then, my child, we ought to be scrupulously aware what is our real motive for wishing to assist another. Is it of God, or is it of ourselves? Is it a personal desire to increase a perhaps unworthy, a worldly happiness? Egoism is a parent of many children, and often they do not recognise their father."

Just for a moment Domini felt a heat of anger rise within her. She did not express it, and did not know that she had shown a sign of it till she heard Father Roubier say:

" If you knew how often I have found that what for a moment I believed to be my noblest aspirations had sprung from a tiny, hidden seed of egoism! "

At once her anger died away.

" That is terribly true," she said. " Of us all, I mean."

She got up.

" You are going? "

" Yes. I want to think something out. You have made me want to. I must do it. Perhaps I'll come again."

" Do. I want to help you if I can."

There was such a heartfelt sound in his voice that impulsively she held out her hand.

" I know you do. Perhaps you will be able to."

But even as she said the last words doubt crept into her mind, even into her voice.

The priest came to his gate to see Domini off, and directly she had left him she noticed that Androvsky was under the arcade and had been a witness of their parting. As she went past him and into the hotel she saw that he looked greatly disturbed and excited. His face was lit up by the now fiery glare of the sun, and when, in passing, she nodded to him, and he took off his hat, he cast at her a glance that was like an accusation. As soon as she gained the verandah she heard his heavy step upon the stair. For a moment she hesitated. Should she go into her room and so avoid him, or remain and let him speak to her? She knew that he was following her with that purpose. Her mind was almost instantly made up. She crossed the verandah and sat down in the low chair that was always placed outside her French window. Androvsky followed her and stood beside her. He did not say anything for a moment, nor did she.

Then he spoke with a sort of passionate attempt to sound care-less and indifferent.

" Monsieur Anteoni has gone, I suppose, Madame? "

" Yes, he has gone. I reached the garden safely, you see."

" Batouch came later. He was much ashamed when he found you had gone. I believe he is afraid, and is hiding himself till our anger shall have passed away."

She laughed.

" Batouch could not easily make me angry. I am not like you, Monsieur Androvsky."

Her sudden challenge startled him, as she had meant it should. He moved quickly, as at an unexpected touch.

" I, Madame? "

" Yes; I think you are very often angry. I think you are angry now."

His face was flooded with red.

" Why should I be angry? " he stammered, like a man completely taken aback.

" How can I tell? But, as I came in just now, you looked at me as if you wanted to punish me."

" I—I am afraid—it seems that my face says a great deal that—that——"

" Your lips would not choose to say. Well, it does. Why are you angry with me? " She gazed at him mercilessly, study-ing the trouble of his face. The combative part of her nature had been roused by the glance he had cast at her. What right had he, had any man, to look at her like that?

Her blunt directness lashed him back into the firmness he had lost. She felt in a moment that there was a fighting capacity in him equal, perhaps superior, to her own.

" When I saw you come from the priest's house, Madame, I felt as if you had been there speaking about me—about my con-duct of yesterday."

" Indeed! Why should I do that? "

" I thought as you had kindly wished me to come—— "
He stopped.

" Well? " she said, in rather a hard voice.

" Madame, I don't know what I thought, what I think—only I cannot bear that you should apologise for any conduct of mine. Indeed, I canot bear it."

He looked fearfully excited and moved two or three steps away, then returned.

" Were you doing that? " he asked. " Were you, Madame? "

" I never mentioned your name to Father Roubier, nor did he to me," she answered.

For a moment he looked relieved, then a sudden suspicion seemed to strike him.

" But without mentioning my name? " he said.

" You wish to accuse me of quibbling, of insincerity, then! " she exclaimed with a heat almost equal to his own.

" No, Madame, no! Madame, I—I have suffered much. I am suspicious of everybody. Forgive me, forgive me! "

He spoke almost with distraction. In his manner there was something desperate.

" I am sure you have suffered," she said more gently, yet with a certain inflexibility at which she herself wondered, yet which she could not control. " You will always suffer if you cannot govern yourself. You will make people dislike you, be suspicious of you."

" Suspicious! Who is suspicious of me? " he asked sharply. " Who has any right to be suspicious of me? "

She looked up and fancied that, for an instant, she saw something as ugly as terror in his eyes.

" Surely you know that people don't ask permission to be suspicious of their fellow-men? " she said.

" No one here has any right to consider me or my actions," he said, fierceness blazing out of him. " I am a free man, and can do as I will. No one has any right—no one! "

Domini felt as if the words were meant for her, as if he had struck her. She was so angry that she did not trust herself to speak, and instinctively she put her hand up to her breast, as a woman might who had received a blow. She touched something small and hard that was hidden beneath her gown. It was the little wooden crucifix Androvsky had thrown into the stream at Sidi-Zerzour. As she realised that her anger died. She was humbled and ashamed. What was her religion if, at a word, she could be stirred to such a feeling of passion?

" I, at least, am not suspicious of you," she said, choosing the very words that were most difficult for her to say just then. " And Father Roubier—if you included him—is too fine-hearted to cherish unworthy suspicions of anyone."

She got up. Her voice was full of a subdued, but strong, emotion.

" Oh, Monsieur Androvsky! " she said. " Do go over and see him. Make friends with him. Never mind yesterday. I want you to be friends with him, with everyone here. Let us make Beni-Mora a place of peace and good will."

Then she went across the verandah quickly to her room, and passed in, closing the window behind her.

Déjeuner was brought into her sitting-room. She ate it in solitude, and late in the afternoon she went out on the verandah. She had made up her mind to spend an hour in the church. She had told Father Roubier that she wanted to think something out. Since she had left him the burden upon her mind had become heavier, and she longed to be alone in the twilight near the altar. Perhaps she might be able to cast down the burden there. In the verandah she stood for a moment and thought how wonderful was the difference between dawn and sunset in this land. The gardens, that had looked like a place of departed and unhappy spirits when she rose that day, were now bathed in the luminous rays of the declining sun, were alive with the softly-calling voices of children, quivered with romance, with a dreamlike, golden charm. The stillness of the evening was intense, enclosing the children's voices, which presently died away; but while she was marvelling at it she was disturbed by a sharp noise of knocking. She looked in the direction from which it came and saw Androvsky standing before the priest's door. As she looked, the door was opened by the Arab boy and Androvsky went in.

Then she did not think of the gardens any more. With a radiant expression in her eyes she went down and crossed over to the church. It was empty. She went softly to a *prie-dieu* near the altar, knelt down and covered her eyes with her hands.

At first she did not pray, or even think consciously, but just rested in the attitude which always seems to bring humanity nearest its God. And, almost immediately, she began to feel a quietude of spirit, as if something delicate descended upon her, and lay lightly about her, shrouding her from the troubles of the world. How sweet it was to have the faith that brings with it such tender protection, to have the trust that keeps alive through the swift passage of the years the spirit of the little child. How sweet it was to be able to rest. There was at this moment a sensation of deep joy within her. It grew in the silence of the church, and, as it grew, brought with it presently a growing consciousness of the lives beyond those walls, of other spirits capable of suffering, of conflict, and of peace, not far away; till she knew that this present blessing of happiness came to her, not only from the scarce-realised thought of God, but also from the scarce-realised thought of man.

Close by, divided from her only by a little masonry, a few feet of sand, a few palm trees, Androvsky was with the priest.

Still kneeling, with her face between her hands, Domini began to think and pray. The memory of her petition to Notre Dame de la Garde came back to her. Before she knew Africa she had prayed for men wandering, and perhaps unhappy, there, for men whom she would probably never see again, would never know. And now that she was growing familiar with this land, divined something of its wonders and its dangers, she prayed for a man in it whom she did not know, who was very near to her making a sacrifice of his prejudices, perhaps of his fears, at her desire. She prayed for Androvsky without words, making of her feelings of gratitude to him a prayer, and presently, in the darkness framed by her hands, she seemed to see Liberty once more, as in the shadows of the dancing-house, standing beside a man who prayed far out in the glory of the desert. The storm, spoken of by the Diviner, did not always rage. It was stilled to hear his prayer. And the darkness had fled, and the light drew near to listen. She pressed her face more strongly against her hands, and began to think more definitely.

Was this interview with the priest the first step taken by Androvsky towards the gift the desert held for him?

He must surely be a man who hated religion, or thought he hated it.

Perhaps he looked upon it as a chain, instead of as the hammer that strikes away the fetters from the slave.

Yet he had worn a crucifix.

She lifted her head, put her hand into her breast, and drew out the crucifix. What was its history? She wondered as she looked at it. Had someone who loved him given it to him, someone, perhaps, who grieved at his hatred of holiness, and who fancied that this very humble symbol might one day, as the humble symbols sometimes do, prove itself a little guide towards shining truth? Had a woman given it to him?

She laid the cross down on the edge of the *prie-dieu*.

There was red fire gleaming now on the windows of the church. She realised the pageant that was marching up the west, the passion of the world as well as the purity which lay beyond the world. Her mind was disturbed. She glanced from the red radiance on the glass to the dull brown wood of the cross. Blood and agony had made it the mystical symbol that it was—blood and agony.

She had something to think out. That burden was still upon her mind, and now again she felt its weight, a weight that her interview with the priest had not lifted. For she had not been able to be quite frank with the priest. Something had held her back from absolute sincerity, and so he had not spoken quite plainly all that was in his mind. His words had been a little vague, yet she had understood the meaning that lay behind them.

Really, he had warned her against Androvsky. There were two men of very different types. One was unworldly as a child. The other knew the world. Neither of them had any acquaintance with Androvsky's history, and both had warned her. It was instinct then that had spoken in them, telling them that he was a man to be shunned, perhaps feared. And her own instinct? What had it said? What did it say?

For a long time she remained in the church. But she could not think clearly, reason calmly, or even pray passionately. For a vagueness had come into her mind like the vagueness of twilight that filled the space beneath the starry roof, softening the crudeness of the ornaments, the garish colours of the plaster saints. It seemed to her that her thoughts and feelings lost their outlines, that she watched them fading like the shrouded forms of Arabs fading in the tunnels of Mimosa. But as they vanished surely they whispered, " That which is written is written."

The mosques of Islam echoed these words, and surely this little church that bravely stood among them.

" That which is written is written."

Domini rose from her knees, hid the wooden cross once more in her breast, and went out into the evening.

As she left the church door something occurred which struck the vagueness from her. She came upon Androvsky and the priest. They were standing together at the latter's gate, which he was in the act of opening to an accompaniment of joyous barking from Bous-Bous. Both men looked strongly expressive, as if both had been making an effort of some kind. She stopped in the twilight to speak to them.

" Monsieur Androvsky has kindly been paying me a visit," said Father Roubier.

" I am glad," Domini said. " We ought all to be friends here."

There was a perceptible pause. Then Androvsky lifted his hat.

"Good-evening, Madame," he said. "Good-evening, Father." And he walked away quickly.

The priest looked after him and sighed profoundly.

"Oh, Madame!" he exclaimed, as if impelled to liberate his mind to someone, "what is the matter with that man? What is the matter?"

He stared fixedly into the twilight after Androvsky's retreating form.

"With Monsieur Androvsky?"

She spoke quietly, but her mind was full of apprehension, and she looked searchingly at the priest.

"Yes. What can it be?"

"But—I don't understand."

"Why did he come to see me?"

"I asked him to come."

She blurted out the words without knowing why, only feeling that she must speak the truth.

"You asked him!"

"Yes. I wanted you to be friends—and I thought perhaps you might——"

"Yes?"

"I wanted you to be friends." She repeated it almost stubbornly.

"I have never before felt so ill at ease with any human being," exclaimed the priest with tense excitement. "And yet I could not let him go. Whenever he was about to leave me I was impelled to press him to remain. We spoke of the most ordinary things, and all the time it was as if we were in a great tragedy. What is he? What can he be?" (He still looked down the road.)

"I don't know. I know nothing. He is a man travelling, as other men travel."

"Oh, no!"

"What do you mean, Father?"

"I mean that other travellers are not like this man."

He leaned his thin hands heavily on the gate, and she saw, by the expression of his eyes, that he was going to say something startling.

"Madame," he said, lowering his voice, "I did not speak quite frankly to you this afternoon. You may, or you may not, have understood what I meant. But now I will speak plainly. As a priest I warn you, I warn you most solemnly, not to make friends with this man."

There was a silence, then Domini said:

" Please give me your reason for this warning."

" That I can't do."

" Because you have no reason, or because it is not one you care to tell me? "

" I have no reason to give. My reason is my instinct. I know nothing of this man—I pity him. I shall pray for him. He needs prayers, yes, he needs them. But you are a woman out here alone. You have spoken to me of yourself, and I feel it my duty to say that I advise you most earnestly to break off your acquaintance with Monsieur Androvsky."

" Do you mean that you think him evil? "

" I don't know whether he is evil, I don't know what he is."

" I know he is not evil."

The priest looked at her, wondering.

" You know—how? "

" My instinct," she said, coming a step nearer, and putting her hand, too, on the gate near his. " Why should we desert him? "

" Desert him, Madame! "

Father Roubier's voice sounded amazed.

" Yes. You say he needs prayers. I know it. Father, are not the first prayers, the truest, those that go most swiftly to Heaven—acts? "

The priest did not reply for a moment. He looked at her and seemed to be thinking deeply.

" Why did you send Monsieur Androvsky to me this afternoon? " he said at last abruptly.

" I knew you were a good man, and I fancied if you became friends you might help him."

His face softened.

" A good man," he said. " Ah! " He shook his head sadly, with a sound that was like a little pathetic laugh. " I—a good man! And I allow an almost invincible personal feeling to conquer my inward sense of right! Madame, come into the garden for a moment."

He opened the gate, she passed in, and he led her round the house to the enclosure at the back, where they could talk in greater privacy. Then he continued:

" You are right, Madame. I am here to try to do God's work, and sometimes it is better to act for a human being, perhaps, even than to pray for him. I will tell you that I feel an almost invincible repugnance to Monsieur Androvsky, a repug-

nance that is almost stronger than my will to hold it in check."
He shivered slightly. "But, with God's help, I'll conquer that.
If he stays on here I'll try to be his friend. I'll do all I can. If
he is unhappy, far away from good, perhaps—I say it humbly,
Madame, I assure you—I might help him. But "—and here his
face and manner changed, became firmer, more dominating—
"you are not a priest, and——"

"No, only a woman," she said, interrupting him.

Something in her voice arrested him. There was a long
silence in which they paced slowly up and down on the sand
between the palm trees. The twilight was dying into night.
Already the tom-toms were throbbing in the street of the
dancers, and the shriek of the distant pipes was faintly heard.
At last the priest spoke again.

"Madame," he said, "when you came to me this afternoon
there was something that you could not tell me."

"Yes."

"Had it anything to do with Monsieur Androvsky?"

"I meant to ask you to advise me about myself."

"My advice to you was and is—be strong but not too foolhardy."

"Believe me I will try not to be foolhardy. But you said
something else too, something about women. Don't you remember?"

She stopped, took his hands impulsively and pressed them.

"Father, I've scarcely ever been of any use all my life. I've
scarcely ever tried to be. Nothing within me said, 'You could
be,' and if it had I was so dulled by routine and sorrow that I
don't think I should have heard it. But here it is different. I
am not dulled. I can hear. And—suppose I can be of use for
the first time! You wouldn't say to me, 'Don't try!' You
couldn't say that?"

He stood holding her hands and looking into her face for a
moment. Then he said, half-humorously, half-sadly:

"My child, perhaps you know your own strength best. Perhaps your safest spiritual director is your own heart. Who
knows? But whether it be so or not you will not take advice
from me."

She knew that was true now and, for a moment, felt almost
ashamed.

"Forgive me," she said. "But—it is strange, and may seem
to you ridiculous or even wrong—ever since I have been here I
have felt as if everything that happened had been arranged

beforehand, as if it had to happen. And I feel that, too, about the future."

"Count Anteoni's fatalism!" the priest said with a touch of impatient irritation. "I know. It is the guiding spirit of this land. And you too are going to be led by it. Take care! You have come to a land of fire, and I think you are made of fire."

For a moment she saw a fanatical expression in his eyes. She thought of it as the look of the monk crushed down within his soul. He opened his lips again, as if to pour forth upon her a torrent of burning words. But the look died away, and they parted quietly like two good friends. Yet, as she went to the hotel, she knew that Father Roubier could not give her the kind of help she wanted, and she even fancied that perhaps no priest could. Her heart was in a turmoil, and she seemed to be in the midst of a crowd.

Batouch was at the door, looking elaborately contrite and ready with his lie. He had been seized with fever in the night, in token whereof he held up hands which began to shake like wind-swept leaves. Only now had he been able to drag himself from his quilt and, still afflicted as he was, to creep to his honoured patron and crave her pardon. Domini gave it with an abstracted carelessness that evidently hurt his pride, and was passing into the hotel when he said:

"Irena is going to marry Hadj, Madame."

Since the fracas at the dancing-house both the dancer and her victim had been under lock and key.

"To marry her after she tried to kill him!" said Domini.

"Yes, Madame. He loves her as the palm tree loves the sun. He will take her to his room, and she will wear a veil, and work for him and never go out any more."

"What! She will live like the Arab women?"

"Of course, Madame. But there is a very nice terrace on the roof outside Hadj's room, and Hadj will permit her to take the air there, in the evening or when it is hot."

"She must love Hadj very much."

"She does, or why should she try to kill him?"

So that was an African love—a knife-thrust and a taking of the veil! The thought of it added a further complication to the disorder that was in her mind.

"I will see you after dinner, Batouch," she said.

She felt that she must do something, go somewhere that night. She could not remain quiet.

Batouch drew himself up and threw out his broad chest. His air gave place to importance, and, as he leaned against the white pillar of the arcade, folded his ample burnous round him, and glanced up at the sky he saw, in fancy, a five-franc piece glittering in the chariot of the moon.

The priest did not come to dinner that night, but Androvsky was already at his table when Domini came into the *salle-à-manger*. He got up from his seat and bowed formally, but did not speak. Remembering his outburst of the morning she realised the suspicion which her second interview with the priest had probably created in his mind, and now she was not free from a feeling of discomfort that almost resembled guilt. For now she had been led to discuss Androvsky with Father Roubier, and had it not been almost an apology when she said, " I know he is not evil "? Once or twice during dinner, when her eyes met Androvsky's for a moment, she imagined that he must know why she had been at the priest's house, that anger was steadily increasing in him.

He was a man who hated to be observed, to be criticised. His sensitiveness was altogether abnormal, and made her wonder afresh where his previous life had been passed. It must surely have been a very sheltered existence. Contact with the world blunts the fine edge of our feeling with regard to others' opinion of us. In the world men learn to be heedless of the everlasting buzz of comment that attends their goings out and their comings in. But Androvsky was like a youth, alive to the tiniest whisper, set on fire by a glance. To such a nature life in the world must be perpetual torture. She thought of him with a sorrow that— strangely in her—was not tinged with contempt. That which manifested by another man would certainly have moved her to impatience, if not to wrath, in this man woke other sensations— curiosity, pity, terror.

Yes—terror. To-night she knew that. The long day, begun in the semi-darkness before the dawn and ending in the semi-darkness of the twilight, had, with its events that would have seemed to another ordinary and trivial enough, carried her forward a stage on an emotional pilgrimage. The half-veiled warnings of Count Anteoni and of the priest, followed by the latter's almost passionately abrupt plain speaking, had not been without effect. To-night something of Europe and her life there, with its civilised experience and drastic training in the management of woman's relations with humanity in general, crept back under the palm trees and the brilliant stars of Africa; and despite the fatalism condemned by Father Roubier, she was more conscious than she had hitherto been of how others—the outside world—would be likely to regard her acquaintance with Androvsky. She stood, as it were, and looked on at the events in which she herself had been and was involved, and in that moment she was first aware of a thrill of something akin to terror, as if, perhaps, without knowing it, she had been moving amid a great darkness, as if perhaps a great darkness were approaching. Suddenly she saw Androvsky as some strange and ghastly figure of legend; as the wandering Jew met by a traveller at cross roads and distinguished for an instant in an oblique lightning flash; as Vanderdecken passing in the hurricane and throwing a blood-red illumination from the sails of his haunted ship; as the everlasting climber of the Brocken, as the shrouded Arab of the Eastern legend, who announced coming disaster to the wanderers in the desert by beating a death-roll on a drum among the dunes.

And with Count Anteoni and the priest she set another figure, that of the sand diviner, whose tortured face had suggested a man looking on a fate that was terrible. Had not he, too, warned her? Had not the warning been threefold, been given to her by the world, the Church, and the under-world—the world beneath the veil?

She met Androvsky's eyes. He was getting up to leave the room. His movement caught her away from things visionary, but not from worldly things. She still looked on herself moving amid these events at which her world would laugh or wonder, and perhaps for the first time in her life she was uneasily self-conscious because of the self that watched herself, as if that self held something coldly satirical that mocked at her and marvelled.

CHAPTER XIV

WHAT shall I do to-night?"

Alone in the now empty *salle-à-manger* Domini asked herself the question. She was restless, terribly restless in mind, and wanted distraction. The idea of going to her room, of reading, even of sitting quietly in the verandah, was intolerable to her. She longed for action, swiftness, excitement, the help of outside things, of that exterior life which she had told Count Anteoni she had begun to see as a mirage. Had she been in a city she would have gone to a theatre to witness some tremendous drama, or to near some passionate or terrible opera. Beni-Mora might have been a place of many and strange tragedies, would be no doubt again, but it offered at this moment little to satisfy her mood. The dances of the Cafés Maures, the songs of the smokers of the keef, the long histories of the story-tellers between the lighted candles—she wanted none of these, and, for a moment, she wished she were in London, Paris, any great capital that spent itself to suit the changing moods of men. With a sigh she got up and went out to the Arcade. Batouch joined her immediately.

"What can I do to-night, Batouch?" she said.

"There are the femmes mauresques," he began.

"No, no."

"Would Madame like to hear the story-teller?"

"No. I should not understand him."

"I can explain to Madame."

"No."

She stepped out into the road.

"There will be a moon to-night, won't there?" she said, looking up at the starry sky.

"Yes, Madame, later."

"What time will it rise?"

"Between nine and ten."

She stood in the road, thinking. It had occurred to her that she had never seen moonrise in the desert.

"And now it is"—she looked at her watch—"only eight."

"Does Madame wish tó see the moon come up pouring upon the palms——"

"Don't talk so much, Batouch," she said brusquely.

To-night the easy and luscious imaginings of the poet worried her like the cry of a mosquito. His presence even disturbed her. Yet what could she do without him? After a pause she said:

"Can one go into the desert at night?"

"On foot, Madame? It would be dangerous. One cannot tell what may be in the desert by night."

These words made her long to go. They had a charm, a violence perhaps, of the unknown.

"One might ride," she said. "Why not? Who could hurt us if we were mounted and armed?"

"Madame is brave as the panther in the forests of the Djurdjurah."

"And you, Batouch? Aren't you brave?"

"Madame, I am afraid of nothing."

He did not say it boastfully, like Hadj, but calmly, almost loftily.

"Well, we are neither of us afraid. Let us ride out on the Tombouctou road and see the moon rise. I'll go and put on my habit."

"Madame should take her revolver."

"Of course. Bring the horses round at nine."

When she had put on her habit it was only a few minutes after eight. She longed to be in the saddle, going at full speed up the long, white road between the palms. Physical movement was necessary to her, and she began to pace up and down the verandah quickly. She wished she had ordered the horses at once, or that she could do something definite to fill up the time till they came. As she turned at the end of the verandah she saw a white form approaching her; when it drew near she recognised Hadj, looking self-conscious and mischievous, but a little triumphant too. At this moment she was glad to see him. He received her congratulations on his recovery and approaching marriage with a sort of skittish gaiety, but she soon discovered that he had come with a money-making reason. Having seen his cousin safely off the premises, it had evidently occurred to him to turn an honest penny. And pennies were now specially needful to him in view of married life.

"Does Madame wish to see something strange and wonderful to-night?" he asked, after a moment, looking at her sideways out of the corners of his wicked eyes, which, as Domini could see, were swift to read character and mood.

"I am going out riding."

He looked astonished.

"In the night?"

"Yes. Batouch has gone to fetch the horses."

Hadj's face became a mask of sulkiness.

"If Madame goes out with Batouch she will be killed. There are robbers in the desert, and Batouch is afraid of——"

"Could we see the strange and wonderful thing in an hour?" she interrupted.

The gay and skittish expression returned instantly to his face.

"Yes, Madame."

"What is it?"

He shook his head and made an artful gesture with his hand in the air.

"Madame shall see."

His long eyes were full of mystery, and he moved towards the staircase.

"Come, Madame."

Domini laughed and followed him. She felt as if she were playing a game, yet her curiosity was roused. They went softly down and slipped out of the hotel like children fearing to be caught.

"Batouch will be angry. There will be white foam on his lips," whispered Hadj, dropping his chin and chuckling low in his throat. "This way, Madame."

He led her quickly across the gardens to the Rue Berthe, and down a number of small streets, till they reached a white house before which, on a hump, three palm trees grew from one trunk. Beyond was waste ground, and further away a stretch of sand and low dunes lost in the darkness of the, as yet, moonless night. Domini looked at the house and at Hadj, and wondered if it would be foolish to enter.

"What is it?" she asked again.

But he only replied, "Madame will see!" and struck his flat hand upon the door. It was opened a little way, and a broad face covered with little humps and dents showed, the thick lips parted and muttering quickly. Then the face was withdrawn, the door opened wider, and Hadj beckoned to Domini to go in. After a moment's hesitation she did so, and found herself in a small interior court, with a tiled floor, pillars, and high up a gallery of carved wood, from which, doubtless, dwelling-rooms opened. In the court, upon cushions, were seated four vacant-looking men, with bare arms and legs and long matted hair, before a brazier, from which rose a sharply pungent perfume. Two of these men were very young, with pale, ascetic faces and weary eyes. They looked like young priests of the Sahara. At a short distance, upon a red pillow, sat a tiny boy of about three years old, dressed in yellow and green. When Domini and Hadj came into the court no one looked at them except the child, who stared with slowly-rolling, solemn eyes, slightly shifting on the pillow. Hadj beckoned to Domini to seat herself upon some rugs between the pillars, sat down beside her and began to make a cigarette. Complete silence prevailed. The four men stared at the brazier, holding their nostrils over the incense fumes which rose from it in airy spirals. The child continued to stare at Domini. Hadj lit his cigarette. And time rolled on.

Domini had desired violence, and had been conveyed into a dumbness of mystery, that fell upon her turmoil of spirit like a blow. What struck her as especially strange and unnatural was the fact that the men with whom she was sitting in the dim court of this lonely house had not looked at her, did not appear to know that she was there. Hadj had caught the aroma of their meditations with the perfume of the incense, for his eyes had lost their mischief and become gloomily profound, as if they stared on bygone centuries or watched a far-off future. Even the child began to look elderly, and worn as with fastings and with watchings. As the fumes perpetually ascended from the red-hot coals of the brazier the sharp smell of the perfume grew stronger. There was in it something provocative and exciting that was like a sound, and Domini marvelled that the four men who crouched over it and drank it in perpetually could be unaffected by its influence when she, who was at some distance from it, felt dawning on her desires of movement, of action, almost a physical necessity to get up and do something extraordinary, absurd or passionate, such as she had never done or dreamed of till this moment.

A low growl like that of a wild beast broke the silence. Domini did not know at first whence it came. She stared at the four men, but they were all gazing vacantly into the brazier, their naked arms dropping to the floor. She glanced at Hadj. He was delicately taking a cigarette paper from a little case. The child—no, it was absurd even to think of a child emitting such a sound.

Someone growled again more fiercely, and this time Domini saw that it was the palest of the ascetic-looking youths. He shook back his long hair, rose to his feet with a bound, and moving into the centre of the court gazed ferociously at his companions. As if in obedience to the glance, two of them stretched their arms backwards, found two tom-toms, and began to beat them loudly and monotonously. The young ascetic bowed to the tom-toms, dropping his lower jaw and jumping on his bare feet. He bowed again as if saluting a fetish, and again and again. Ceaselessly he bowed to the tom-toms, always jumping softly from the pavement. His long hair fell over his face and back upon his shoulders with a monotonous regularity that imitated the tom-toms, as if he strove to mould his life in accord with the fetish to which he offered adoration. Flecks of foam appeared upon his lips, and the asceticism in his eyes changed to a bestial glare. His whole body was involved in a long and snake-like undulation, above which his hair flew to and fro. Presently the second youth, moving reverently like a priest about the altar, stole to a corner and returned with a large and curved sheet of glass. Without looking at Domini he came to her and placed it in her hands. When the dancer saw the glass he stood still, growled again long and furiously, threw himself on his knees before Domini, licked his lips, then, abruptly thrusting forward his face, set his teeth in the sheet of glass, bit a large piece off, crunched it up with a loud noise, swallowed it with a gulp, and growled for more. She fed him again, while the tom-toms went on roaring, and the child in its red pillow watched with its weary eyes. And when he was full fed, only a fragment of glass remained between her fingers, he fell upon the ground and lay like one in a trance.

Then the second youth bowed to the tom-toms, leaping gently on the pavement, foamed at the mouth, growled, snuffed up the incense fumes, shook his long mane, and placed his naked feet in the red-hot coals of the brazier. He plucked out a coal and rolled his tongue round it. He placed red coals under his bare armpits and kept them there, pressing his arms against his sides. He held a coal, like a monocle, in his eye socket against his eye. And all the time he leaped and bowed and foamed, undulating his body like a snake. The child looked on with a still gravity, and the tom-toms never ceased. From the gallery above painted faces peered down, but Domini did not see them. Her attention was taken captive by the young priests of the Sahara. For so she called them in her mind, realising that there were religious fanatics whose half-crazy devotion seemed to lift them above the ordinary dangers to the body. One of the musicians now took his turn, throwing his tom-tom to the eater of glass, who had wakened from his trance. He bowed and leaped; thrust spikes behind his eyes, through his cheeks, his lips, his arms; drove a long nail into his head with a wooden hammer; stood upon the sharp edge of an upturned sword blade. With the spikes pro-gruding from his face in all directions, and his eyes bulging out from them like balls, he spun in a maze of hair, barking like a dog. The child regarded him with a still attention, and the incense fumes were cloudy in the court. Then the last of the four men sprang up in the midst of a more passionate uproar from the tom-toms. He wore a filthy burnous, and, with a shriek, he plunged his hand into its hood and threw some squirming things upon the floor. They began to run, rearing stiff tails into the air. He sank down, blew upon them, caught them, letting them set their tail weapons in his fingers, and lifting them thus, imbedded, high above the floor. Then again he put them down, breathed upon each one, drew a circle round each with his forefinger. His face had suddenly become intense, hypnotic. The scorpions, as if mesmerised, remained utterly still, each in its place within its imaginary circle, that had become a cage; and their master bowed to the fetish of the tom-toms, leaped, grinned, and bowed again, undulating his body in a maze of hair.

Domini felt as if she, like the scorpions, had been mesmerised. She, too, was surely bound in a circle, breathed upon by some arrogant breath of fanaticism, commanded by some horrid power. She looked at the scorpions and felt a sort of pity for them. From time to time the bowing fanatic glanced at them through his hair out of the corners of his eyes, licked his lips, shook his shoulders, and uttered a long howl, thrilling with the note of greed. The tom-toms pulsed faster and faster, louder and louder, and all the men began to sing a fierce chant, the song surely of desert souls driven crazy by religion. One of the scorpions moved slightly, reared its tail, began to run. Instantly, as if at a signal, the dancer fell upon his knees, bent down his head, seized it in his teeth, munched it and swallowed it. At the same moment with the uproar of the tom-toms there mingled a loud knocking on the door.

Hadj's lips curled back from his pointed teeth and he looked dangerous.

" It is Batouch ! " he snarled.

Domini got up. Without a word, turning her back upon the court, she made her way out, still hearing the howl of the scorpion-eater, the roar of the tom-toms, and the knocking on the door. Hadj followed her quickly, protesting. At the door was the man with the pitted white face and the thick lips. When he saw her he held out his hand. She gave him some money, he opened the door, and she came out into the night by the triple palm tree. Batouch stood there looking furious, with the bridles of two horses across his arm. He began to speak in Arabic to Hadj, but she stopped him with an imperious gesture, gave Hadj his fee, and in a moment was in the saddle and cantering away into the dark. She heard the gallop of Batouch's horse coming up behind her and turned her head.

" Batouch," she said, " you are the smartest "—she used the word *chic*—" Arab here. Do you know what is the fashion in London when a lady rides out with the attendant who guards her—the really smart thing to do ? "

She was playing on his vanity. He responded with a ready smile.

" No, Madame."

" The attendant rides at a short distance behind her, so that no one can come up near her without his knowledge."

Batouch fell back, and Domini cantered on, congratulating herself on the success of her expedient.

She passed through the village, full of strolling white figures, lights and the sound of music, and was soon at the end of the long, straight road that was significant to her as no other road had ever been. Each time she saw it, stretching on till it was lost in the serried masses of the palms, her imagination was stirred by a longing to wander through barbaric lands, by a nomad feeling that was almost irresistible. This road was a track of fate to her. When she was on it she had a strange sensation as if she changed, developed, drew near to some ideal. It influenced her as one person may influence another. Now for the first time she was on it in the night, riding on the crowded shadows of its palms. She drew rein and went more slowly. She had a desire to be noiseless.

In the obscurity the thickets of the palms looked more exotic than in the light of day. There was no motion in them. Each tree stood like a delicately carven thing, silhouetted against the remote purple of the void. In the profound firmament the stars burned with a tremulous ardour they never show in northern skies. The mystery of this African night rose not from vaporous veils and the long movement of winds, but was breathed out by clearness, brightness, stillness. It was the deepest of all mystery—the mystery of vastness and of peace.

No one was on the road. The sound of the horse's feet were sharply distinct in the night. On all sides, but far off, the guard dogs were barking by the hidden homes of men. The air was warm as in a hothouse, but light and faintly impregnated with perfume shed surely by the mystical garments of night as she glided on with Domini towards the desert. From the blackness of the palms there came sometimes thin notes of the birds of night, the whizzing noise of insects, the glassy pipe of a frog in the reeds by a pool behind a hot brown wall.

She rode through one of the villages of old Beni-Mora, silent, unlighted, with empty streets and closed *cafés maures,* touched her horse with the whip, and cantered on at a quicker pace. As she drew near to the desert her desire to be in it increased. There was some coarse grass here. The palm trees grew less thickly. She heard more clearly the barking of the Kabyle dogs, and knew that tents were not far off. Now, between the trunks of the trees, she saw the twinkling of distant fires, and the sound of running water fell on her ears, mingling with the persistent noise of the insects, and the faint cries of the birds and frogs. In front, where the road came out from the shadows of the last trees, lay a vast dimness, not wholly unlike another starless sky, stretched beneath the starry sky in which the moon had not yet risen. She set her horse at a gallop and came into the desert, rushing through the dark.

"Madame! Madame!"

Batouch's voice was calling her. She galloped faster, like one in flight. Her horse's feet padded over sand almost as softly as a camel's. The vast dimness was surely coming to meet her, to take her to itself in the night. But suddenly Batouch rode furiously up beside her, his burnous flying out behind him over his red saddle.

"Madame, we must not go further, we must keep near the oasis."

"Why?"

"It is not safe at night in the desert, and besides——"

His horse plunged and nearly rocketed against hers. She pulled in. His company took away her desire to keep on.

"Besides?"

Leaning over his saddle peak he said, mysteriously:

"Besides, Madame, someone has been following us all the way from Beni-Mora."

"Who?"

"A horseman. I have heard the beat of the hoofs on the hard road. Once I stopped and turned, but I could see nothing, and then I could hear nothing. He, too, had stopped. But when I rode on again soon I heard him once more. Someone found out we were going and has come after us."

She looked back into the violet night without speaking. She heard no sound of a horse, saw nothing but the dim track and the faint, shadowy blackness where the palms began. Then she put her hand into the pocket of her saddle and silently held up a tiny revolver.

"I know, but there might be more than one. I am not afraid, but if anything happens to Madame no one will ever take me as a guide any more."

She smiled for a moment, but the smile died away, and again she looked into the night. She was not afraid physically, but she was conscious of a certain uneasiness. The day had been long and troubled, and had left its mark upon her. Restlessness had driven her forth into the darkness, and behind the restlessness there was a hint of the terror of which she had been aware when she was left alone in the *salle-à-manger*. Was it not that vague terror which, shaking the restlessness, had sent her to the white house by the triple palm tree, had brought her now to the desert? she asked herself, while she listened, and the hidden horseman of whom Batouch had spoken became in her imagination one with the legendary victims of fate; with the Jew by the cross roads, the mariner beating ever about the rock-bound shores of the world, the climber in the witches' Sabbath, the phantom Arab in the sand. Still holding her revolver, she turned her horse and rode slowly towards the distant fires, from which came the barking of the dogs. At some hundreds of yards from them she paused.

" I shall stay here," she said to Batouch. " Where does the moon rise?"

He stretched his arm towards the desert, which sloped gently, almost imperceptibly, towards the east.

" Ride back a little way towards the oasis. The horseman was behind us. If he is still following you will meet him. Don't go far. Do as I tell you, Batouch."

With obvious reluctance he obeyed her. She saw him pull up his horse at a distance where he had her just in sight. Then she turned so that she could not see him and looked towards the desert and the east. The revolver seemed unnaturally heavy in her hand. She glanced at it for a moment and listened with intensity for the beat of horse's hoofs, and her wakeful imagination created a sound that was non-existent in her ears. With it she heard a gallop that was spectral as the gallop of the black horses which carried Mephistopheles and Faust to the abyss. It died away almost at once, and she knew it for an imagination. To-night she was peopling the desert with phantoms. Even the fires of the nomads were as the fires that flicker in an abode of witches, the shadows that passed before them were as goblins that had come up out of the sand to hold revel in the moonlight. Were they, too, waiting for a signal from the sky?

At the thought of the moon she drew up the reins that had been lying loosely on her horse's neck and rode some paces forward and away from the fires, still holding the revolver in her hand. Of what use would it be against the spectres of the Sahara? The Jew would face it without fear. Why not the horseman of Batouch? She dropped it into the pocket of the saddle.

Far away in the east the darkness of the sky was slowly fading into a luminous mystery that rose from the underworld, a mystery that at first was faint and tremulous, pale with a pallor of silver and primrose, but that deepened slowly into a live and ardent gold against which a group of three palm trees detached themselves from the desert like messengers sent forth by it to give a salutation to the moon. They were jet black against the gold, distinct though very distant. The night, and the vast plain from which they rose, lent them a significance that was unearthly. Their long, thin stems and drooping, feathery leaves were living and pathetic as the night thoughts of a woman who has suffered, but who turns, with a gesture of longing that will not be denied, to the luminance that dwells at the heart of the world. And those black palms against the gold, that stillness of darkness and light in immensity, banished Domini's faint sense of horror. The spectres faded away. She fixed her eyes on the palms.

Now all the notes of the living things that do not sleep by night, but make music by reedy pools, in underwood, among the blades of grass and along the banks of streams, were audible to her again, filling her mind with the mystery of existence. The glassy note of the frogs was like a falling of something small and pointed upon a sheet of crystal. The whirs of the insects suggested a ceaselessly active mentality. The faint cries of the birds dropped down like jewels slipping from the trees. And suddenly she felt that she was as nothing in the vastness and the complication of the night. Even the passion that she knew lay, like a dark and silent flood, within her soul, a flood that, once released from its boundaries, had surely the power to rush irresistibly forward to submerge old landmarks and change the face of a world—even that seemed to lose its depth for a moment, to be shallow as the first ripple of a tide upon the sand. And she forgot that the first ripple has all the ocean behind it.

Red deepened and glowed in the gold behind the three palms, and the upper rim of the round moon, red too as blood, crept about the desert. Domini, leaning forward with one hand upon her horse's warm neck, watched until the full circle was poised for a moment on the horizon, holding the palms in its frame of fire. She had never seen a moon look so immense and so vivid as this moon that came up into the night like a portent, fierce yet serene, moon of a barbaric world, such as might have

shone upon Herod when he heard the voice of the Baptist in his
dungeon, or upon the wife of Pilate when in a dream she was
troubled. It suggested to her the powerful watcher of tragic
events fraught with long chains of consequence that would last
on through centuries, as it turned its blood-red gaze upon the
desert, upon the palms, upon her, and, leaning upon her horse's
neck, she too—like Pilate's wife—fell into a sort of strange and
troubled dream for a moment, full of strong, yet ghastly, light
and of shapes that flitted across a background of fire.

In it she saw the priest with a fanatical look of warning in his
eyes, Count Anteoni beneath the trees of his garden, the perfume-seller in his dark bazaar, Irena with her long throat
exposed and her thin arms drooping, the sand diviner spreading
forth his hands, Androvsky galloping upon a horse as if pursued.
This last vision returned again and again. As the moon rose a
stream of light that seemed tragic fell across the desert and was
woven mysteriously into the light of her waking dream. The
three palms looked larger. She fancied that she saw them
growing, becoming monstrous as they stood in the very centre of
the path of the nocturnal glory, and suddenly she remembered
her thought when she sat with Androvsky in the garden, that
feeling grew in human hearts like palms rising in the desert.
But these palms were tragic and aspired towards the blood-red
moon. Suddenly she was seized with a fear of feeling, of the
growth of an intense sensation within her, and realised, with an
almost feverish vividness, the impotence of a soul caught in the
grip of a great passion, swayed hither and thither, led into
strange paths, along the edges, perhaps into depths of immeasurable abysses. She had said to Androvsky that she would
rather be the centre of a world tragedy than die without
having felt to the uttermost even if it were sorrow. Was that
not the speech of a mad woman, or at least of a woman who was
so ignorant of the life of feeling that her words were idle and
ridiculous? Again she felt desperately that she did not know
herself, and this lack of the most essential of all knowledge
reduced her for a moment to a bitterness of despair that seemed
worse than the bitterness of death. The vastness of the desert
appalled her. The red moon held within its circle all the blood
of the martyrs, of life, of ideals. She shivered in the saddle.
Her nature seemed to shrink and quiver, and a cry for protection
rose within her, the cry of the woman who cannot face life alone,
who must find a protector, and who must cling to a strong arm,
who needs man as the world needs God.

Then again it seemed to her that she saw Androvsky galloping upon a horse as if pursued.

Moved by a desire to do something to combat this strange despair, born of the moonrise and the night, she sat erect in her saddle, and resolutely looked at the desert, striving to get away from herself in a hard contemplation of the details that surrounded her, the outward things that were coming each moment into clearer view. She gazed steadily towards the palms that sharply cut the moonlight. As she did so something black moved away from them, as if it had been part of them and now detached itself with the intention of approaching her along the track. At first it was merely a moving blot, formless and small, but as it drew nearer she saw that it was a horseman riding slowly, perhaps stealthily, across the sand. She glanced behind her, and saw Batouch not far off, and the fires of the nomads. Then she turned again to watch the horseman. He came steadily forward.

"Madame!"

It was the voice of Batouch.

"Stay where you are!" she called out to him.

She heard the soft sound of the horse's feet and could see the attitude of its rider. He was leaning forward as if searching the night. She rode to meet him, and they came to each other in the path of the light she had thought tragic.

"You followed me?"

"I cannot see you go out alone into the desert at night," Androvsky replied.

"But you have no right to follow me."

"I cannot let harm come to you, Madame."

She was silent. A moment before she had been longing for a protector. One had come to her, the man whom she had been setting with those legendary figures who have saddened and appalled the imagination of men. She looked at the dark figure of Androvsky leaning forward on the horse whose feet were set on the path of the moon, and she did not know whether she felt confidence in him or fear of him. All that the priest had said rose up in her mind, all that Count Anteoni had hinted and that had been visible in the face of the sand diviner. This man had followed her into the night as a guardian. Did she need someone, something, to guard her from him? A faint horror was still upon her. Perhaps he knew it and resented it, for he drew himself upright on his horse and spoke again, with a decision that was rare in him.

"Let me send Batouch back to Beni-Mora, Madame."

"Why?" she asked, in a low voice that was full of hesitation.

"You do not need him now."

He was looking at her with a defiant, a challenging expression that was his answer to her expression of vague distrust and apprehension.

"How do you know that?"

He did not answer the question, but only said:

"It is better here without him. May I send him away, Madame?"

She bent her head. Androvsky rode off and she saw him speaking to Batouch, who shook his head as if in contradiction.

"Batouch!" she called out. "You can ride back to Beni-Mora. We shall follow directly."

The poet cantered forward.

"Madame, it is not safe."

The sound of his voice made Domini suddenly know what she had not been sure of before—that she wished to be alone with Androvsky.

"Go, Batouch!" she said. "I tell you to go."

Batouch turned his horse without a word, and disappeared into the darkness of the distant palms.

When they were alone together Domini and Androvsky sat silent on their horses for some minutes. Their faces were turned towards the desert, which was now luminous beneath the moon. Its loneliness was overpowering in the night, and made speech at first an impossibility, and even thought difficult. At last Androvsky said:

"Madame, why did you look at me like that just now, as if you—as if you hesitated to remain alone with me?"

Suddenly she resolved to tell him of her oppression of the night. She felt as if to do so would relieve her of something that was like a pain at her heart.

"Has it never occurred to you that we are strangers to each other?" she said. "That we know nothing of each other's lives? What do you know of me or I of you?"

He shifted in his saddle and moved the reins from one hand to the other, but said nothing.

"Would it seem strange to you if I did hesitate—if even now——"

"Yes," he interrupted violently, "it would seem strange to me."

" Why ? "

" You would rely on an Arab and not rely upon me," he said with intense bitterness.

" I did not say so."

" Yet at first you wished to keep Batouch."

" Yes."

" Then——"

" Batouch is my attendant."

" And I ? Perhaps I am nothing but a man whom you distrust ; whom—whom others tell you to think ill of."

" I judge for myself."

" But if others speak ill of me ? "

" It would not influence me—for long."

She added the last words after a pause. She wished to be strictly truthful, and to-night she was not sure that the words of the priest had made no impression upon her.

" For long ! " he repeated. Then he said abruptly, " The priest hates me."

" No."

" And Count Anteoni ? "

" You interested Count Anteoni greatly."

" Interested him ! "

His voice sounded intensely suspicious in the night.

" Don't you wish to interest anyone ? It seems to me that to be uninteresting is to live eternally alone in a sunless desert."

" I wish—I should like to think that I——" He stopped, then said, with a sort of ashamed determination: " Could I ever interest you, Madame ? "

" Yes," she answered quietly.

" But you would rather be protected by an Arab than by me. The priest has——"

" To-night I do not seem to be myself," she said, interrupting him. " Perhaps there is some physical reason. I got up very early, and—don't you ever feel oppressed, suspicious, doubtful of life, people, yourself, everything, without apparent reason ? Don't you know what it is to have nightmare without sleeping ? "

" I ! But you are different."

" To-night I have felt—I do feel as if there were tragedy near me, perhaps coming towards me," she said simply, " and I am oppressed, I am almost afraid."

When she had said it she felt happier, as if a burden she

carried were suddenly lighter. As he did not speak she glanced at him. The moon rays lit up his face. It looked ghastly, drawn and old, so changed that she scarcely recognised it and felt, for a moment, as if she were with a stranger. She looked away quickly, wondering if what she had seen was merely some strange effect of the moon, or whether Androvsky was really altered for a moment by the action of some terrible grief, one of those sudden sorrows that rush upon a man from the hidden depths of his nature and tear his soul, till his whole being is lacerated and he feels as if his soul were flesh and were streaming with the blood from mortal wounds. The silence between them was long. In it she presently heard a reiterated noise that sounded like struggle and pain made audible. It was Androvsky's breathing. In the soft and exquisite air of the desert he was gasping like a man shut up in a cellar. She looked again towards him, startled. As she did so he turned his horse sideways and rode away a few paces. Then he pulled up his horse. He was now merely a black shape upon the moonlight, motionless and inaudible. She could not take her eyes from this shape. Its blackness suggested to her the blackness of a gulf. Her memory still heard that sound of deep-drawn breathing or gasping, heard it and quivered beneath it as a tender-hearted person quivers seeing a helpless creature being ill-used. She hesitated for a moment, and then, carried away by an irresistible impulse to try to soothe this extremity of pain which she was unable to understand, she rode up to Androvsky. When she reached him she did not know what she had meant to say or do. She felt suddenly impotent and intrusive, and even horribly shy. But before she had time for speech or action he turned to her and said, lifting up his hands with the reins in them and then dropping them down heavily upon his horse's neck:

" Madame, I wanted to tell you that to-morrow I——" He stopped.

" Yes? " she said.

He turned his head away from her till she could not see his face.

" To-morrow I am leaving Beni-Mora."

" To-morrow! " she said.

She did not feel the horse under her, the reins in her hand. She did not see the desert or the moon. Though she was looking at Androvsky she no longer perceived him. At the sound of his words it seemed to her as if all outside things she had ever known had foundered, like a ship whose bottom is ripped up by

a razor-edged rock, as if with them had foundered, too, all things
within herself: thoughts, feelings, even the bodily powers that
were of the essence of her life; sense of taste, smell, hearing,
sight, the capacity of movement and of deliberate repose.
Nothing seemed to remain except the knowledge that she was
still alive and had spoken.

" Yes, to-morrow I shall go away."

His face was still turned from her, and his voice sounded as
if it spoke to someone at a distance, someone who could hear as
man cannot hear.

" To-morrow," she repeated.

She knew she had spoken again, but it did not seem to her as
if she had heard herself speak.   She looked at her hands holding
the reins, knew that she looked at them, yet felt as if she were
not seeing them while she did so.   The moonlit desert was surely
flickering round her, and away to the horizon in waves that were
caused by the disappearance of that ship which had suddenly
foundered with all its countless lives.   And she knew of the
movement of these waves as the soul of one of the drowned,
already released from the body, might know of the movement on
the surface of the sea beneath which its body was hidden.

But the soul was evidently nothing without the body, or, at
most, merely a continuance of power to know that all which
had been was no more.   All which had been was no more.

At last her mind began to work again, and those words went
through it with persistence.   She thought of the fascination of
Africa, that enormous, overpowering fascination which had taken
possession of her body and spirit.   What had become of it?
What had become of the romance of the palm gardens, of the
brown villages, of the red mountains, of the white town with its
lights, its white figures, its throbbing music?   And the mystical
attraction of the desert—where was it now?   Its voice, that had
called her persistently, was suddenly silent.   Its hand, that had
been laid upon her, was removed.   She looked at it in the moonlight and it was no longer the desert, sand with a soul in it, blue
distances full of a music of summons, spaces, peopled with spirits
from the sun.   It was only a barren waste of dried-up matter,
arid, featureless, desolate, ghastly with the bones of things that
had died.

She heard the dogs barking by the tents of the nomads and
the noises of the insects, but still she did not feel the horse underneath her.   Yet she was gradually recovering her powers, and
their recovery brought with it sharp, physical pain, such as is

felt by a person who has been nearly drowned and is restored from unconsciousness.

Androvsky turned round. She saw his eyes fastened upon her, and instantly pride awoke in her, and, with pride, her whole self.

She felt her horse under her, the reins in her hands, the stirrup at her foot. She moved in her saddle. The blood tingled in her veins fiercely, bitterly, as if it had become suddenly acrid. She felt as if her face were scarlet, as if her whole body flushed, and as if the flush could be seen by her companion. For a moment she was clothed from head to foot in a fiery garment of shame. But she faced Androvsky with calm eyes, and her lips smiled.

"You are tired of it?" she said.

"I never meant to stay long," he answered, looking down.

"There is not very much to do here. Shall we ride back to the village now?"

She turned her horse, and as she did so cast one more glance at the three palm trees that stood far out on the path of the moon. They looked like three malignant fates lifting up their hands in malediction. For a moment she shivered in the saddle. Then she touched her horse with the whip and turned her eyes away. Androvsky followed her and rode by her side in silence.

To gain the oasis they passed near to the tents of the nomads, whose fires were dying out. The guard dogs were barking furiously, and straining at the cords which fastened them to the tent pegs, by the short hedges of brushwood that sheltered the doors of filthy rags. The Arabs were all within, no doubt huddled up on the ground asleep. One tent was pitched alone, at a considerable distance from the others, and under the first palms of the oasis. A fire smouldered before it, casting a flickering gleam of light upon something dark which lay upon the ground between it and the tent. Tied to the tent was a large white dog, which was not barking, but which was howling as if in agony of fear. Before Domini and Androvsky drew near to this tent the howling of the dog reached them and startled them. There was in it a note that seemed humanly expressive, as if it were a person trying to scream out words but unable to from horror. Both of them instinctively pulled up their horses, listened, then rode forward. When they reached the tent they saw the dark thing lying by the fire.

"What is it?" Domini whispered.

"An Arab asleep, I suppose," Androvsky answered, staring at the motionless object.

"But the dog——" She looked at the white shape leaping frantically against the tent. "Are you sure?"

"It must be. Look, it is wrapped in rags and the head is covered."

"I don't know."

She stared at it. The howling of the dog grew louder, as if it were straining every nerve to tell them something dreadful.

"Do you mind getting off and seeing what it is? I'll hold the horse."

He swung himself out of the saddle. She caught his rein and watched him go forward to the thing that lay by the fire, bend down over it, touch it, recoil from it, then—as if with a determined effort—kneel down beside it on the ground and take the rags that covered it in his hands. After a moment of contemplation of what they had hidden he dropped the rags—or rather threw them from him with a violent gesture—got up and came back to Domini, and looked at her without speaking. She bent down.

"I'll tell you," she said. "I'll tell you what it is. It's a dead woman."

It seemed to her as if the dark thing lying by the fire was herself.

"Yes," he said. "It's a woman who has been strangled."

"Poor woman!" she said. "Poor—poor woman!"

And it seemed to her as if she said it of herself.

CHAPTER XV

LYING in bed in the dark that night Domini heard the church clock chime the hours. She was not restless, though she was wakeful. Indeed, she felt like a woman to whom an injection of morphia had been administered, as if she never wished to move again. She lay there counting the minutes that made the passing hours, counting them calmly, with an inexorable and almost cold self-possession. The process presently became mechanical, and she was able, at the same time, to dwell upon the events that had followed upon the discovery of the murdered woman by the tent: Androvsky's pulling aside of the door of the tent to find it empty, their short ride to the encampment close by, their rousing up of the sleeping Arabs within, filthy nomads clothed in patched garments, unveiled women with wrinkled, staring faces and huge plaits of false hair and amulets. From the tents the strange figures had streamed forth into the light of the moon and the fading fires, gesticulating, talking loudly, furiously, in an uncouth language that was unintelligible to her. Led by Androvsky they had come to the corpse, while the air was rent by the frantic barking of all the guard dogs and the howling of the dog that had been a witness of the murder. Then in the night had risen the shrill wailing of the women, a wailing that seemed to pierce the stars and shudder out to the remotest confines of the desert, and in the cold white radiance of the moon a savage vision of grief had been presented to her eyes: naked arms gesticulating as if they strove to summon vengeance from heaven, claw-like hands casting earth upon the heads from which dangled Fatma hands, chains of tarnished silver and lumps of coral that reminded her of congealed blood, bodies that swayed and writhed as if stricken with convulsions or rent by seven devils. She remembered how strange had seemed to her the vast calm, the vast silence, that encompassed this noisy outburst of humanity, how inflexible had looked the enormous moon, how unsympathetic the brightly shining stars, how feverish and irritable the flickering illumination of the flames that spurted up and fainted away like things still living but in the agonies of death.

Then had followed her silent ride back to Beni-Mora with Androvsky along the straight road which had always fascinated her spirit of adventure. They had ridden slowly, without looking at each other, without exchanging a word. She had felt dry and weary, like an old woman who had passed through a long life of suffering and emerged into a region where any acute feeling is unable to exist, as at a certain altitude from the earth human life can no longer exist. The beat of the horses' hoofs upon the road had sounded hard, as her heart felt, cold as the temperature of her mind. Her body, which usually swayed to her horse's slightest movement, was rigid in the saddle. She recollected that once, when her horse stumbled, she had thrilled with an abrupt anger that was almost ferocious, and had lifted her whip to lash it. But the hand had slipped down nervelessly, and she had fallen again into her frigid reverie.

When they reached the hotel she had dropped to the ground heavily, and heavily had ascended the steps of the verandah, followed by Androvsky. Without turning to him or bidding him good-night she had gone to her room. She had not acted with intentional rudeness or indifference—indeed, she had felt incapable of an intention. Simply, she had forgotten, for the first time perhaps in her life, an ordinary act of courtesy, as an old person sometimes forgets you are there and withdraws into himself. Androvsky had said nothing, had not tried to attract her attention to himself. She had heard his steps die away on the verandah. Then, mechanically, she had undressed and got into bed, where she was now mechanically counting the passing moments.

Presently she became aware of her own stillness and connected it with the stillness of the dead woman by the tent. She lay, as it were, watching her own corpse as a Catholic keeps vigil beside a body that has not yet been put into the grave. But in this chamber of death there were no flowers, no lighted candles, no lips that moved in prayer. She had gone to bed without praying. She remembered that now, but with indifference. Dead people do not pray. The living pray for them. But even the watcher could not pray. Another hour struck in the belfry of the church. She listened to the chime and left off counting the moments, and this act of cessation made more perfect the peace of the dead woman.

When the sun rose her sensation of death passed away, leaving behind it, however, a lethargy of mind and body such as she had never known before the previous night. Suzanne, coming in to call her, exclaimed:

" Mam'selle is ill? "

" No. Why should I be ill? "

" Mam'selle looks so strange," the maid said, regarding her with round and curious eyes. " As if—— "

She hesitated.

" Give me my tea," Domini said.

When she was drinking it she asked:

" Do you know at what time the train leaves Beni-Mora—the passenger train? "

" Yes, Mam'selle. There is only one in the day. It goes soon after twelve. Monsieur Helmuth told me."

" Oh! "

" What gown will—— ? "

" Any gown—the white linen one I had on yesterday."

" Yes, Mam'selle."

" No, not that. Any other gown. Is it to be hot? "

" Very hot, Mam'selle. There is not a cloud in the sky."

"How strange!" Domini said, in a low voice that Suzanne did not hear. When she was up and dressed she said:

"I am going out to Count Anteoni's garden. I think I'll— yes, I'll take a book with me."

She went into her little *salon* and looked at the volumes scattered about there, some books of devotion, travel, books on sport, Rossetti's and Newman's poems, some French novels, and the novels of Jane Austen, of which, oddly, considering her, nature, she was very fond. For the first time in her life they struck her as shrivelled, petty chronicles of shrivelled, bloodless, artificial lives. She turned back into her bedroom, took up the little white volume of the *Imitation,* which lay always near her bed, and went out into the verandah. She looked neither to right nor left, but at once descended the staircase and took her way along the arcade.

When she reached the gate of the garden she hesitated before knocking upon it. The sight of the villa, the arches, the white walls and clustering trees she knew so well hurt her so frightfully, so unexpectedly, that she felt frightened and sick, and as if she must go away quickly to some place which she had never seen, and which could call up no reminiscences in her mind.

Perhaps she would have gone into the oasis, or along the path that skirted the river bed, had not Smaïn softly opened the gate and come out to meet her, holding a great velvety rose in his slim hand.

He gave it to her without a word, smiling languidly with eyes in which the sun seemed caught and turned to glittering dark- ness, and as she took it and moved it in her fingers, looking at the wine-coloured petals on which lay tiny drops of water gleaming with thin and silvery lights, she remembered her first visit to the garden, and the mysterious enchantment that had floated out to her through the gate from the golden vistas and the dusky shadows of the trees, the feeling of romantic expectation that had stirred within her as she stepped on to the sand and saw before her the winding ways disappearing into dimness between the rills edged by the pink geraniums.

How long ago that seemed, like a remembrance of early childhood in the heart of one who is old.

Now that the gate was open she resolved to go into the garden. She might as well be there as elsewhere. She stepped in, holding the rose in her hand. One of the drops of water slipped from an outer petal and fell upon the sand. She thought of it as a tear. The rose was weeping, but her eyes were dry. She touched the rose with her lips.

To-day the garden was like a stranger to her, but a stranger with whom she had once—long, long ago—been intimate, whom she had trusted, and by whom she had been betrayed. She looked at it and knew that she had thought it beautiful and loved it. From its recesses had come to her troops of dreams. The leaves of its trees had touched her as with tender hands. The waters of its rills had whispered to her of the hidden things that lie in the breast of joy. The golden rays that played through its scented alleys had played, too, through the shadows of her heart, making a warmth and light there that seemed to come from heaven. She knew this as one knows of the apparent humanity that greeted one's own humanity in the friend who is a friend no longer, and she sickened at it as at the thought of remembered intimacy with one proved treacherous. There seemed to her nothing ridiculous in this personification of the garden, as there had formerly seemed to her nothing ridiculous in her thought of the desert as a being; but the fact that she did thus instinctively personify the nature that surrounded her gave to the garden in her eyes an aspect that was hostile and even threatening, as if she faced a love now changed to hate, a cold and inimical watchfulness that knew too much about her. to which she had once told all her happy secrets and murmured all her hopes. She did not hate the garden, but she felt as if she feared it. The movements of its leaves conveyed to her uneasiness. The hidden places, which once had been to her retreats peopled with tranquil blessings, were now become ambushes in which lay lurking enemies.

Yet she did not leave it, for to-day something seemed to tell her that it was meant that she should suffer, and she bowed in spirit to the decree.

She went on slowly till she reached the *fumoir*. She entered it and sat down.

She had not seen any of the gardeners or heard the note of a flute. The day was very still. She looked at the narrow doorway and remembered exactly the attitude in which Count Anteoni had stood during their first interview, holding a trailing branch of the bougainvillea in his hand. She saw him as a shadow that the desert had taken. Glancing down at the carpet sand she imagined the figure of the sand diviner crouching there and recalled his prophecy, and directly she did this she knew that she had believed in it. She had believed that one day she would ride out into the desert in a storm, and that with her, enclosed in the curtains of a palanquin, there would be a companion. The Diviner had not told her who would be this companion. Darkness was about him rendering him invisible to the eyes of the seer. But her heart had told her. She had seen the other figure in the palanquin. It was a man. It was Androvsky.

She had believed that she would go out into the desert with Androvsky, with this traveller of whose history, of whose soul, she knew nothing. Some inherent fatalism within her had told her so. And now——?

The darkness of the shade beneath the trees in this inmost recess of the garden fell upon her like the darkness of that storm in which the desert was blotted out, and it was fearful to her because she felt that she must travel in the storm alone. Till now she had been very much alone in life and had realised that such solitude was dreary, that in it development was difficult, and that it checked the steps of the pilgrim who should go upward to the heights of life. But never till now had she felt the fierce tragedy of solitude, the utter terror of it. As she sat in the *fumoir,* looking down on the smoothly-raked sand, she said to herself that till this moment she had never had any idea of the meaning of solitude. It was the desert within a human soul, but the desert without the sun. And she knew this because at last she loved. The dark and silent flood of passion that lay within her had been released from its boundaries, the old landmarks were swept away for ever, the face of the world was changed.

She loved Androvsky. Everything in her loved him; all that she had been, all that she was, all that she could ever be loved him; that which was physical in her, that which was spiritual, the brain, the heart, the soul, body and flame burning within it—all that made her the wonder that is woman, loved him. She was love for Androvsky. It seemed to her that she was nothing else, had never been anything else. The past years were nothing, the pain by which she was stricken when her mother fled, by which she was tormented when her father died blaspheming, were nothing. There was no room in her for anything but love of Androvsky. At this moment even her love of God seemed to have been expelled from her. Afterwards she remembered that. She did not think of it now. For her there was a universe with but one figure in it—Androvsky. She was unconscious of herself except as love for him. She was

unconscious of any Creative Power to whom she owed the fact
that he was there to be loved by her. She was passion, and
he was that to which passion flowed.

The world was the stream and the sea.

As she sat there with her hands folded on her knees, her eyes
bent down, and the purple flowers all about her, she felt simplified and cleansed, as if a mass of little things had been swept
from her, leaving space for the great thing that henceforth
must for ever dwell within her and dominate her life. The
burning shame of which she had been conscious on the previous
night, when Androvsky told her of his approaching departure
and she was stricken as by a lightning flash, had died away from
her utterly. She remembered it with wonder. How should
she be ashamed of love? She thought that it would be impossible to her to be ashamed, even if Androvsky knew all that she
knew. Just then the immense truth of her feeling conquered
everything else, made every other thing seem false, and she
said to herself that of truth she did not know how to be ashamed.
But with the knowledge of the immense truth of her love came
the knowledge of the immense sorrow that might, that must,
dwell side by side with it.

Suddenly she moved. She lifted her eyes from the sand and
looked out into the garden. Besides this truth within her there
was one other thing in the world that was true. Androvsky
was going away. While she sat there the moments were passing. They were making the hours that were bent upon destruction. She was sitting in the garden now and Androvsky
was close by. A little time would pass noiselessly. She
would be sitting there and Androvsky would be far away,
gone from the desert, gone out of her life no doubt for ever.
And the garden would not have changed. Each tree would
stand in its place, each flower would still give forth its scent.
The breeze would go on travelling through the lacework of the
branches, the streams slipping between the sandy walls of the
rills. The inexorable sun would shine, and the desert would
whisper in its blue distances of the unseen things that always
dwell beyond. And Androvsky would be gone. Their short
intercourse, so full of pain, uneasiness, reserve, so fragmentary,
so troubled by abrupt violences, by ignorance, by a sense of
horror even on the one side, and by an almost constant suspicion
on the other, would have come to an end.

She was stunned by the thought, and looked round her as if
she expected inanimate Nature to take up arms for her against

this fate. Yet she did not for a moment think of taking up arms herself. She had left the hotel without trying to see Androvsky. She did not intend to return to it till he was gone. The idea of seeking him never came into her mind. There is an intensity of feeling that generates action, but there is a greater intensity of feeling that renders action impossible, the feeling that seems to turn a human being into a shell of stone within which burn all the fires of creation. Domini knew that she would not move out of the *fumoir* till the train was creeping along the river-bed on its way from Beni-Mora.

She had laid down the *Imitation* upon the seat by her side, and now she took it up. The sight of its familiar pages made her think for the first time, " Do I love God any more? " And immediately afterwards came the thought: " Have I ever loved him? " The knowledge of her love for Androvsky, for this body that she had seen, for this soul that she had seen through the body like a flame through glass, made her believe just then that if she had ever thought—and certainly she had thought—that she loved a being whom she had never seen, never even imaginatively projected, she had deceived herself. The act of faith was not impossible, but the act of love for the object on which that faith was concentrated now seemed to her impossible. For her body, that remained passive, was full of a riot, a fury of life. The flesh that had slept was awakened and knew itself. And she could no longer feel that she could love that which her flesh could not touch, that which could not touch her flesh. And she said to herself, without terror, even without regret, " I do not love, I never have loved, God."

She looked into the book:

" Unspeakable, indeed, is the sweetness of thy contemplation, which thou bestowest on them that love thee."

The sweetness of thy contemplation! She remembered Androvsky's face looking at her out of the heart of the sun as they met for the first time in the blue country. In that moment she put him consciously in the place of God, and there was nothing within her to say, " You are committing mortal sin."

She looked into the book once more and her eyes fell upon the words which she had read on her first morning in Beni-Mora:

" Love watcheth, and sleeping, slumbereth not. When weary it is not tired; when straitened it is not constrained; when frightened it is not disturbed; but like a vivid flame and a burning torch it mounteth upwards and securely passeth through all. Whosoever loveth knoweth the cry of this voice."

She had always loved these words and thought them the most beautiful in the book, but now they came to her with the newness of the first spring morning that ever dawned upon the world. The depth of them was laid bare to her, and, with that depth, the depth of her own heart. The paralysis of anguish passed from her. She no longer looked to Nature as one dumbly seeking help. For they led her to herself, and made her look into herself and her own love and know it. "When frightened it is not disturbed—it securely passeth through all." That was absolutely true—true as her love. She looked down into her love, and she saw there the face of God, but thought she saw the face of human love only. And it was so beautiful and so strong that even the tears upon it gave her courage, and she said to herself: "Nothing matters, nothing can matter so long as I have this love within me. He is going away, but I am not sad, for I am going with him—my love, all that I am—that is going with him, will always be with him."

Just then it seemed to her that if she had seen Androvsky lying dead before her on the sand she could not have felt unhappy. Nothing could do harm to a great love. It was the one permanent, eternally vital thing, clad in an armour of fire that no weapon could pierce, free of all terror from outside things because it held its safety within its own heart, everlastingly enough, perfectly, flawlessly complete for and in itself. For that moment fear left her, restlessness left her. Anyone looking in upon her from the garden would have looked in upon a great, calm happiness.

Presently there came a step upon the sand of the garden walks. A man, going slowly, with a sort of passionate reluctance, as if something immensely strong was trying to hold him back, but was conquered with difficulty by something still stronger that drove him on, came out of the fierce sunshine into the shadow of the garden, and began to search its silent recesses. It was Androvsky. He looked bowed and old and guilty. The two lines near his mouth were deep. His lips were working. His thin cheeks had fallen in like the cheeks of a man devoured by a wasting illness, and the strong tinge of sunburn on them seemed to be but an imperfect mark to a pallor that, fully visible, would have been more terrible than that of a corpse. In his eyes there was a fixed expression of ferocious grief that seemed mingled with ferocious anger, as if he were suffering from some dreadful misery, and cursed himself because he suffered, as a man may curse himself for doing a thing that he chooses to do but need not do. Such an expression may sometimes be seen in the eyes of those who are resisting a great temptation.

He began to search the garden, furtively but minutely. Sometimes he hesitated. Sometimes he stood still. Then he turned back and went a little way towards the wide sweep of sand that was bathed in sunlight where the villa stood. Then with more determination, and walking faster, he again made his way through the shadows that slept beneath the densely-growing trees. As he passed between them he several times stretched out trembling hands, broke off branches and threw them on the sand, treading on them heavily and crushing them down below the surface. Once he spoke to himself in a low voice that shook as if with difficulty dominating sobs that were rising in his throat.

"*De profundis—*" he said. "*De profundis—de profundis——*"

His voice died away. He took hold of one hand with the other and went on silently.

Presently he made his way at last towards the *fumoir* in which Domini was still sitting, with one hand resting on the open page whose words had lit up the darkness in her spirit. He came to it so softly that she did not hear his step. He saw her, stood quite still under the trees, and looked at her for a long time. As he did so his face changed till he seemed to become another man. The ferocity of grief and anger faded from his eyes, which were filled with an expression of profound wonder, then of flickering uncertainty, then of hard, manly resolution—a fighting expression that was full of sex and passion. The guilty, furtive look which had been stamped upon all his features, specially upon his lips, vanished. Suddenly he became younger in appearance. His figure straightened itself. His hands ceased from trembling. He moved away from the trees, and went to the doorway of the *fumoir*.

Domini looked up, saw him, and got up quietly, clasping her fingers round the little book.

Androvsky stood just beyond the doorway, took off his hat, kept it in his hand, and said:

"I came here to say good-bye."

He made a movement as if to come into the *fumoir*, but she stopped it by coming at once to the opening. She felt that she could not speak to him enclosed within walls, under a roof. He drew back, and she came out and stood beside him on the sand.

"Did you know I should come?" he said.

She noticed that he had ceased to call her "Madame," and also that there was in his voice a sound she had not heard in it before, a note of new self-possession that suggested a spirit concentrating itself and aware of its own strength to act.

"No," she answered.

"Were you coming back to the hotel this morning?" he asked.

"No."

He was silent for a moment. Then he said slowly:

"Then—then you did not wish—you did not mean to see me again before I went?"

"It was not that. I came to the garden—I had to come—I had to be alone."

"You want to be alone?" he said. "You want to be alone?"

Already the strength was dying out of his voice and face, and the old uneasiness was waking up in him. A dreadful expression of pain came into his eyes.

"Was that why you—you looked so happy?" he said in a harsh, trembling voice.

"When?"

"I stood for a long while looking at you when you were in there"—he pointed to the *fumoir*—"and your face was happy—your face was happy."

"Yes, I know."

"You will be happy alone?—alone in the desert?"

When he said that she felt suddenly the agony of the waterless spaces, the agony of the unpeopled wastes. Her whole spirit shrank and quivered, all the great joy of her love died within her. A moment before she had stood upon the heights of her heart. Now she shrank into its deepest, blackest abysses. She looked at him and said nothing.

"You will not be happy alone."

His voice no longer trembled. He caught hold of her left hand, awkwardly, nervously, but held it strongly with his close to his side, and went on speaking.

"Nobody is happy alone. Nothing is—men and women—children—animals." A bird flew across the shadowy space under the trees, followed by another bird; he pointed to them;

they disappeared. " The birds, too, they must have companionship. Everything wants a companion."

" Yes."

" But then—you will stay here alone in the desert? "

" What else can I do? " she said.

" And that journey," he went on, still holding her hand fast against his side, " your journey into the desert—you will take it alone? "

" What else can I do? " she repeated in a lower voice.

It seemed to her that he was deliberately pressing her down into the uttermost darkness.

" You will not go."

" Yes, I shall go."

She spoke with conviction. Even in that moment—most of all in that moment—she knew that she would obey the summons of the desert.

" I—I shall never know the desert," he said. " I thought—it seemed to me that I, too, should go out into it. I have wanted to go. You have made me want to go."

" I? "

" Yes. Once you said to me that peace must dwell out there. It was on the tower the—the first time you ever spoke to me."

" I remember."

" I wondered—I often wonder why you spoke to me."

She knew he was looking at her with intensity, but she kept her eyes on the sand. There was something in them that she felt he must not see, a light that had just come into them as she realised that already, on the tower before she even knew him, she had loved him. It was that love, already born in her heart but as yet unconscious of its own existence, which had so strangely increased for her the magic of the African evening when she watched it with him. But before—suddenly she knew that she had loved Androvsky from the beginning, from the moment when his face looked at her as if out of the heart of the sun. That was why her entry into the desert had been full of such extraordinary significance. This man and the desert were, had always been, as one in her mind. Never had she thought of the one without the other. Never had she been mysteriously called by the desert without hearing as a far-off echo the voice of Androvsky, or been drawn onward by the mystical summons of the blue distances without being drawn onward, too, by the mystical summons of the heart to which her own responded.

The link between the man and the desert was indissoluble. She could not conceive of its being severed, and as she realised this, she realised also something that turned her whole nature into flame.

She could not conceive of Androvsky's not loving her, of his not having loved her from the moment when he saw her in the sun. To him, too, the desert had made a revelation—the revelation of her face, and of the soul behind it looking through it. In the flames of the sun, as they went into the desert, the flames of their two spirits had been blended. She knew that certainly and for ever. Then how could it be possible that Androvsky should not go out with her into the desert?

"Why did you speak to me?" he said.

"We came into the desert together," she answered simply. "We had to know each other."

"And now—now—we have to say——"

His voice ceased. Far away there was the thin sound of a chime. Domini had never before heard the church bell in the garden, and now she felt as if she heard it, not with her ears, but with her spirit. As she heard she felt Androvsky's hand, which had been hot upon hers, turn cold. He let her hand go, and again she was stricken by the horrible sound she had heard the previous night in the desert, when he turned his horse and rode away with her. And now, as then, he turned away from her in silence, but she knew that this time he was leaving her, that this movement was his final good-bye. With his head bowed down he took a few steps. He was near to a turning of the path. She watched him, knowing that within less than a moment she would be watching only the trees and the sand. She gazed at the bent figure, calling up all her faculties, crying out to herself passionately, desperately, " Remember it—remember it as it is—there —before you—just as it is—for ever." As it reached the turning, in the distance of the garden rose the twitter of the flute of Larbi. Androvsky stopped, stood still with his back turned towards her. And Larbi, hidden and far off, showered out his little notes of African love, of love in the desert where the sun is everlasting, and the passion of man is hot as the sun, where Liberty reigns, lifting her cymbals that are as spheres of fire, and the footsteps of Freedom are heard upon the sand, treading towards the south.

Larbi played—played on and on, untiring as the love that blossomed with the world, but that will not die when the world dies.

Then Androvsky came back quickly till he reached the place where Domini was standing. He put his hands on her shoulders. Then he sank down on the sand, letting his hands slip down over her breast and along her whole body till they clasped themselves round her knees. He pressed his face into her dress against her knees.

" I love you," he said. " I love you—but don't listen to me —you mustn't hear it—you mustn't. But I must say it. I can't—I can't go till I say it. I love you—I love you."

She heard him sobbing against her knees, and the sound was as the sound of strength made audible. She put her hands against his temples.

" I am listening," she said. " I must hear it."

He looked up, rose to his feet, put his hands behind her shoulders, held her, and set his lips on hers, pressing his whole body against hers.

" Hear it ! " he said, muttering against her lips. " Hear it. I love you—I love you."

The two birds they had seen flew back beneath the trees, turned in an airy circle, rose above the trees into the blue sky, and, side by side, winged their way out of the garden to the desert.

BOOK IV

THE JOURNEY

CHAPTER XVI

IN the evening before the day of Domini's marriage with Androvsky there was a strange sunset, which attracted even the attention and roused the comment of the Arabs. The day had been calm and beautiful, one of the most lovely days of the North African spring, and Batouch, resting from the triumphant labour of super-intending the final preparations for a long desert journey, augured a morning of Paradise for the departure along the straight road that led at last to Tombouctou. But as the radiant afternoon drew to its end there came into the blue sky a whiteness that suggested a heaven turning pale in the contemplation of some act that was piteous and terrible. And under this blanching heaven the desert, and all things and people of the oasis of Beni-Mora, assumed an aspect of apprehension, as if they felt themselves to be in the thrall of some power whose omnipotence they could not question and whose purpose they feared. This whiteness was shot, at the hour of sunset, with streaks of sulphur yellow and dappled with small, ribbed clouds tinged with yellow-green, a bitter and cruel shade of green that distressed the eyes as a merciless light distresses them, but these colours quickly faded, and again the whiteness prevailed for a brief space of time before the heavy falling of a darkness un-pierced by stars. With this darkness came a faint moaning of hollow wind from the desert, a lamentable murmur that shud-dered over the great spaces, crept among the palms and the flat-roofed houses, and died away at the foot of the brown mountains beyond the Hammam Salahine. The succeeding silence, short and intense, was like a sound of fear, like the cry of a voice lifted up in protest against the approach of an unknown, but dreaded, fate. Then the wind came again with a stronger moaning and a lengthened life, not yet forceful, not yet with

all its powers, but more tenacious, more acquainted with itself
and the deeds that it might do when the night was black
among the vast sands which were its birth-place, among the
crouching plains and the trembling palm groves that would
be its battle-ground.

Batouch looked grave as he listened to the wind and the creaking of the palm stems one against another. Sand came upon his
face. He pulled the hood of his burnous over his turban and
across his cheeks, covered his mouth with a fold of his haik and
stared into the blackness, like an animal in search of something
his instinct has detected approaching from a distance.

Ali was beside him in the doorway of the Café Maure, a slim
Arab boy, bronze-coloured and serious as an idol, who was a
troubadour of the Sahara, singer of "Janat" and many love-
songs, player of the guitar backed with sand tortoise and faced
with stretched goatskin. Behind them swung an oil lamp
fastened to a beam of palm, and the red ashes glowed in the
coffee niche and shed a ray upon the shelf of small white cups
with faint designs of gold. In a corner, his black face and arms
faintly relieved against the wall, an old negro crouched, gazing
into vacancy with bulging eyes, and beating with a curved palm
stem upon an oval drum, whose murmur was deep and hollow
as the murmur of the wind, and seemed indeed its echo prisoned
within the room and striving to escape.

"There is sand on my eyelids," said Batouch. "It is bad
for to-morrow. When Allah sends the sands we should cover
the face and play the ladies' game within the *café*, we should not
travel on the road towards the south."

Ali said nothing, but drew up his haik over his mouth and
nose, and looked into the night, folding his thin hands in his
burnous.

"Achmed will sleep in the Bordj of Arba," continued Batouch
in a low, murmuring voice, as if speaking to himself. "And the
beasts will be in the court. Nothing can remain outside, for
there will be a greater roaring of the wind at Arba. Can it be
the will of Allah that we rest in the tents to-morrow?"

Ali made no answer. The wind had suddenly died down.
The sand grains came no more against their eyelids and the folds
of their haiks. Behind them the negro's drum gave out monotonously its echo of the wind, filling the silence of the night.

"Whatever Allah sends," Batouch went on softly after a
pause, "Madame will go. She is brave as the lion. There is
no jackal in Madame. Irena is not more brave than she is. But

Madame will never wear the veil for a man's sake. She will not wear the veil, but she could give a knife-thrust if he were to look at another woman as he has looked at her, as he will look at her to-morrow. She is proud as a Touareg and there is fierceness in her. But he will never look at another woman as he will look at her to-morrow. The Roumi is not as we are."

The wind came back to join its sound with the drum, imprisoning the two Arabs in a muttering circle.

"They will not care," said Batouch. "They will go out into the storm without fear."

The sand pattered more sharply on his eyelids. He drew back into the *café*. Ali followed him, and they squatted down side by side upon the ground and looked before them seriously. The noise of the wind increased till it nearly drowned the noise of the negro's drum. Presently the one-eyed owner of the *café* brought them two cups of coffee, setting the cups near their stockinged feet. They rolled two cigarettes and smoked in silence, sipping the coffee from time to time. Then Ali began to glance towards the negro. Half shutting his eyes, and assuming a languid expression that was almost sickly, he stretched his lips in a smile, gently moving his head from side to side. Batouch watched him. Presently he opened his lips and began to sing:

"The love of women is like a date that is golden in the sun,
      That is golden—
The love of women is like a gazelle that comes to drink—
      To drink at the water springs—
The love of women is like the nargileh, and like the dust of the keef
   That is mingled with tobacco and with honey.
Put the reed between thy lips, O loving man!
And draw dreams from the haschish that is the love of women!
   "Janat! Janat! Janat!"

The wind grew louder and sand was blown along the *café* floor and about the coffee-cups.

"The love of women is like the rose of the Caid's garden
      That is full of silver tears—
The love of women is like the first day of the spring
      When the children play at Cora—
The love of women is like the Derbouka that has been warmed as
   the fire
   And gives out a sweet sound.
Take it in thy hands, O loving man!
And sing to the Derbouka that is the love of women.
   Janat! Janat! Janat!"

In the doorway, where the lamp swung from the beam, a man in European dress stood still to listen. The wind wailed behind him and stirred his clothes. His eyes shone in the faint light with a fierceness of emotion in which there was a joy that was almost terrible, but in which there seemed also to be something that was troubled. When the song died away, and only the voices of the wind and the drum spoke to the darkness, he disappeared into the night. The Arabs did not see him.

"Janat! Janat! Janat!"

The night drew on and the storm increased. All the doors of the houses were closely shut. Upon the roofs the guard dogs crouched, shivering and whining, against the earthen parapets. The camels groaned in the fondouks, and the tufted heads of the palms swayed like the waves of the sea. And the Sahara seemed to be lifting up its voice in a summons that was tremendous as a summons to Judgment.

Domini had always known that the desert would summon her. She heard its summons now in the night without fear. The roaring of the tempest was sweet in her ears as the sound of the Derbouka to the loving man of the sands. It accorded with the fire that lit up the cloud of passion in her heart. Its wildness marched in step with a marching wildness in her veins and pulses. For her gipsy blood was astir to-night, and the recklessness of the boy in her seemed to clamour with the storm. The sound of the wind was as the sound of the clashing cymbals of Liberty, calling her to the adventure that love would glorify, to the far-away life that love would make perfect, to the untrodden paths of the sun of which she had dreamed in the shadows, and on which she would set her feet at last with the comrade of her soul.

To-morrow her life would begin, her real life, the life of which men and women dream as the prisoner dreams of freedom. And she was glad, she thanked God, that her past years had been empty of joy, that in her youth she had been robbed of youth's pleasures. She thanked God that she had come to maturity without knowing love. It seemed to her that to love in early life was almost pitiful, was a catastrophe, an experience for which the soul was not ready, and so could not appreciate at its full and wonderful value. She thought of it as of a child being taken away from the world to Paradise without having known the pain of existence in the world, and at that moment she worshipped suffering. Every tear that she had ever shed she loved, every weary hour, every despondent thought, every cruel disappointment. She called around her the congregation of her past sorrows, and she blessed them and bade them depart from her for ever.

As she heard the roaring of the wind she smiled. The Sahara was fulfilling the words of the Diviner. To-morrow she and Androvsky would go out into the storm and the darkness together. The train of camels would be lost in the desolation of the desert. And the people of Beni-Mora would see it vanish, and, perhaps, would pity those who were hidden by the curtains of the palanquin. They would pity her as Suzanne pitied her, openly, with eyes that were tragic. She laughed aloud.

It was late in the night. Midnight had sounded yet she did not go to bed. She feared to sleep, to lose the consciousness of her joy of the glory which had come into her life. She was a miser of the golden hours of this black and howling night. To sleep would be to be robbed. A splendid avarice in her rebelled against the thought of sleep.

Was Androvsky sleeping? She wondered and longed to know.

To-night she was fully aware for the first time of the inherent fearlessness of her character, which was made perfect at last by her perfect love. Alone, she had always had courage. Even in her most listless hours she had never been a craven. But now she felt the completeness of a nature clothed in armour that rendered it impregnable. It was a strange thing that man should have the power to put the finishing touch to God's work, that religion should stoop to be a handmaid to faith in a human being, but she did not think it strange. Everything in life seemed to her to be in perfect accord because her heart was in perfect accord with another heart.

And she welcomed the storm. She even welcomed something else that came to her now in the storm: the memory of the sand diviner's tortured face as he gazed down reading her fate in the sand. For what was an untroubled fate? Surely a life that crept along the hollows and had no impulse to call it to the heights. Knowing the flawless perfection of her armour she had a wild longing to prove it. She wished that there should be assaults upon her love, because she knew she could resist them one and all, and she wished to have the keen joy of resisting them. There is a health of body so keen and vital that it defires combat. The soul sometimes knows a precisely similar health and is filled with a similar desire.

" Put my love to the proof, O God! " was Domini's last prayer that night when the storm was at its wildest. " Put my love to the uttermost proof that he may know it, as he can never know it otherwise."

And she fell asleep at length, peacefully, in the tumult of the night, feeling that God had heard her prayer.

The dawn came struggling like an exhausted pilgrim through the windy dark, pale and faint, with no courage, it seemed, to grow bravely into day. As if with the sedulous effort of something weary but of unconquered will, it slowly lit up Beni-Mora with a feeble light that flickered in a cloud of whirling sand, revealing the desolation of an almost featureless void. The village, the whole oasis, was penetrated by a passionate fog that instead of brooding heavily, phlegmatically, over the face of life and nature travelled like a demented thing bent upon instant destruction, and coming thus cloudily to be more free for crime It was an emissary of the desert, propelled with irresistible force from the farthest recess of the dunes, and the desert itself seemed to be hurrying behind it as if to spy upon the doing of its deeds.

As the sea in a great storm rages against the land, ferocious that land should be, so the desert now raged against the oasis that ventured to exist in its bosom. Every palm tree was the victim of its wrath, every running rill, every habitation of man. Along the tunnels of mimosa it went like a foaming tide through a cavern, roaring towards the mountains. It returned and swept about the narrow streets, eddying at the corners, beating upon the palm-wood doors, behind which the painted dancing-girls were cowering, cold under their pigments and their heavy jewels, their red hands trembling and clasping one another, clamouring about the minarets of the mosques on which the frightened doves were sheltering, shaking the fences that shut in the gazelles in their pleasaunce, tearing at the great statue of the Cardinal that faced it resolutely, holding up the double cross as if to exorcise it, battering upon the tall, white tower on whose summit Domini had first spoken with Androvsky, raging through the alleys of Count Anteoni's garden, the arcades of his villa, the window-spaces of the *fumoir,* from whose walls it tore down frantically the purple petals of the bougainvillea and dashed them, like enemies defeated, upon the quivering paths which were made of its own body.

Everywhere in the oasis it came with a lust to kill, but surely its deepest enmity was concentrated upon the Catholic Church.

There, despite the tempest, people were huddled, drawn together not so much by the ceremony that was to take place within as by the desire to see the departure of an unusual caravan. In every desert centre news is propagated with a rapidity seldom equalled in the home of civilisation. It runs from mouth to mouth like fire along straw. And Batouch, in his glory, had not been slow to speak of the wonders prepared under his superintendence to make complete the desert journey of his mistress and Androvsky. The main part of the camp had already gone forward, and must have reached Arba, the first halting stage outside Beni-Mora; tents, the horses for the Roumis, the mules to carry necessary baggage, the cooking utensils and the guard dogs. But the Roumis themselves were to depart from the church on camel-back directly the marriage was accomplished. Domini, who had a native hatred of everything that savoured of ostentation, had wished for a tiny expedition, and would gladly have gone out into the desert with but one tent, Batouch and a servant to do the cooking. But the journey was to be long and indefinite, an aimless wandering through the land of liberty towards the south, without fixed purpose or time of returning. She knew nothing of what was necessary for such a journey, and tired of ceaseless argument, and too much occupied with joy to burden herself with detail, at last let Batouch have his way.

"I leave it to you, Batouch," she said. "But, remember, as few people and beasts as possible. And as you say we must have camels for certain parts of the journey, we will travel the first stage on camel-back."

Consciously she helped to fulfil the prediction of the Diviner, and then she left Batouch free.

Now outside the church, shrouded closely in hoods and haiks, grey and brown bundles with staring eyes, the desert men were huddled against the church wall in the wind. Hadj was there, and Smaïn, sheltering in his burnous roses from Count Anteoni's garden. Larbi had come with his flute and the perfume-seller from his black bazaar. For Domini had bought perfumes from him on her last day in Beni-Mora. Most of Count Anteoni's gardeners had assembled. They looked upon the Roumi lady, who rode magnificently, but who could dream as they dreamed, too, as a friend. Had she not haunted the alleys where they worked and idled till they had learned to expect her, and to miss

her when she did not come? And with those whom Domini
knew were assembled their friends, and their friends' friends,
men of Beni-Mora, men from the near oasis, and also many
of those desert wanderers who drift in daily out of the sands to
the centres of buying and selling, barter their goods for the goods
of the South, or sell their loads of dates for money, and, having
enjoyed the dissipation of the *cafés* and of the dancing-houses,
drift away again into the pathless wastes which are their home.

Few of the French population had ventured out, and the
church itself was almost deserted when the hour for the wedding
drew nigh.

The priest came from his little house, bending forward against
the wind, his eyes partially protected from the driving sand by
blue spectacles. His face, which was habitually grave, to-day
looked sad and stern, like the face of a man about to perform a
task that was against his inclination, even perhaps against his
conscience. He glanced at the waiting Arabs and hastened into
the church, taking off his spectacles as he did so, and wiping his
eyes, which were red from the action of the sand-grains, with a
silk pocket-handkerchief. When he reached the sacristy he shut
himself into it alone for a moment. He sat down on a chair
and, leaning his arms upon the wooden table that stood in the
centre of the room, bent forward and stared before him at the
wall opposite, listening to the howling of the wind.

Father Roubier had an almost passionate affection for his
little church of Beni-Mora. So long and ardently had he prayed
and taught in it, so often had he passed the twilight hours in it
alone wrapped in religious reveries, or searching his conscience
for the shadows of sinful thoughts, that it had become to him as
a friend, and more than a friend. He thought of it sometimes as
his confessor and sometimes as his child. Its stones were to him
as flesh and blood, its altars as lips that whispered consolation in
answer to his prayers. The figures of its saints were heavenly
companions. In its ugliness he perceived only beauty, in its
tawdriness only the graces that are sweet offerings to God. The
love that, had he not been a priest, he might have given to a
woman he poured forth upon his church, and with it that other
love which, had it been the design of his Heavenly Father, would
have fitted him for the ascetic, yet impassioned, life of an ardent
and devoted monk. To defend this consecrated building against
outrage he would, without hesitation, have given his last drop of
blood. And now he was to perform in it an act against which
his whole nature revolted; he was to join indissolubly the

lives of these two strangers who had come to Beni-Mora—Domini Enfilden and Boris Androvsky. He was to put on the surplice and white stole, to say the solemn and irreparable " Ego Jungo," to sprinkle the ring with holy water and bless it.

As he sat there alone, listening to the howling of the storm outside, he went mentally through the coming ceremony. He thought of the wonderful grace and beauty of the prayers of benediction, and it seemed to him that to pronounce them with his lips, while his nature revolted against his own utterance, was to perform a shameful act, was to offer an insult to this little church he loved.

Yet how could he help performing this act? He knew that he would do it. Within a few minutes he would be standing before the altar, he would be looking into the faces of this man and woman whose love he was called upon to consecrate. He would consecrate it, and they would go out from him into the desert man and wife. They would be lost to his sight in the town.

His eye fell upon a silver crucifix that was hanging upon the wall in front of him. He was not a very imaginative man, not a man given to fancies, a dreamer of dreams more real to him than life, or a seer of visions. But to-day he was stirred, and perhaps the unwonted turmoil of his mind acted subtly upon his nervous system. Afterward he felt certain that it must have been so, for in no other way could he account for a fantasy that beset him at this moment.

As he looked at the crucifix there came against the church a more furious beating of the wind, and it seemed to him that the Christ upon the crucifix shuddered.

He saw it shudder. He started, leaned across the table and stared at the crucifix with eyes that were full of an amazement that was mingled with horror. Then he got up, crossed the room and touched the crucifix with his finger. As he did so, the acolyte, whose duty it was to help him to robe, knocked at the sacristy door. The sharp noise recalled him to himself. He knew that for the first time in his life he had been the slave of an optical delusion. He knew it, and yet he could not banish the feeling that God himself was averse from the act that he was on the point of committing in this church that confronted Islam, that God himself shuddered as surely even He, the Creator, must shudder at some of the actions of his creatures. And this feeling added immensely to the distress of the priest's mind. In performing this ceremony he now had the dreadful sensation that he was putting himself into direct antagonism with God. His instinctive horror of Androvsky had never been so great as it was to-day. In vain he had striven to conquer it, to draw near to this man who roused all the repulsion of his nature. His efforts had been useless. He had prayed to be given the sympathy for this man that the true Christian ought to feel towards every human being, even the most degraded. But he felt that his prayers had not been answered. With every day his antipathy for Androvsky increased. Yet he was entirely unable to ground it upon any definite fact in Androvsky's character. He did not know that character. The man was as much a mystery to him as on the day when they first met. And to this living mystery from which his soul recoiled he was about to consign, with all the beautiful and solemn blessings of his Church, a woman whose character he respected, whose innate purity, strength and nobility he had quickly divined, and no less quickly learned to love.

It was a bitter, even a horrible, moment to him.

The little acolyte, a French boy, son of the postmaster of Beni-Mora, was startled by the sight of the Father's face when he opened the sacristy door. He had never before seen such an expression of almost harsh pain in those usually kind eyes, and he drew back from the threshold like one afraid. His movement recalled the priest to a sharp consciousness of the necessities of the moment, and with a strong effort he conquered his pain sufficiently to conceal all outward expression of it. He smiled gently at the little boy and said:

" Is it time? "

The child looked reassured.

" Yes, Father."

He came into the sacristy and went towards the cupboard where the vestments were kept, passing the silver crucifix. As he did so he glanced at it. He opened the cupboard, then stood for a moment and again turned his eyes to the Christ. The Father watched him.

" What are you looking at, Paul? " he asked.

" Nothing, Father," the boy replied, with a sudden expression of reluctance that was almost obstinate.

And he began to take the priest's robes out of the cupboard.

Just then the wind wailed again furiously about the church, and the crucifix fell down upon the floor of the sacristy.

The priest started forward, picked it up, and stood with it in his hand. He glanced at the wall, and saw at once that the nail to which the crucifix had been fastened had come out of its hole.

A flake of plaster had been detached, perhaps some days ago, and the hole had become too large to retain the nail. The explanation of the matter was perfect, simple and comprehensible. Yet the priest felt as if a catastrophe had just taken place. As he stared at the cross he heard a little noise near him. The acolyte was crying.

" Why, Paul, what's the matter? " he said.

" Why did it do that? " exclaimed the boy, as if alarmed. " Why did it do that? "

" Perhaps it was the wind. Everything is shaking. Come, come, my child, there is nothing to be afraid of."

He laid the crucifix on the table. Paul dried his eyes with his fists.

" I don't like to-day," he said. " I don't like to-day."

The priest patted him on the shoulder.

" The weather has upset you," he said, smiling.

But the nervous behaviour of the child deepened strangely his own sense of apprehension. When he had robed he waited for the arrival of the bride and bridegroom. There was to be no mass, and no music except the Wedding March, which the harmonium player, a Marseillais employed in the date-packing trade, insisted on performing to do honour to Mademoiselle Enfilden, who had taken such an interest in the music of the church. Androvsky, as the priest had ascertained, had been brought up in the Catholic religion, but, when questioned, he had said quietly that he was no longer a practising Catholic and that he never went to confession. Under these circumstances it was not possible to have a nuptial mass. The service would be short and plain, and the priest was glad that this was so. Presently the harmonium player came in.

" I may play my loudest to-day, Father," he said, " but no one will hear me."

He laughed, settled the pin—Joan of Arc's face in metal—in his azure blue necktie, and added:

"Nom d'un chien, the wind's a cruel wedding guest! "

The priest nodded without speaking.

" Would you believe, Father," the man continued, " that Mademoiselle and her husband are going to start for Arba from the church door in all this storm! Batouch is getting the palanquin on to the camel. How they will ever——"

" Hush! " said the priest, holding up a warning finger.

This idle chatter displeased him in the church, but he had another reason for wishing to stop the conversation. It renewed his dread to hear of the projected journey, and made him see, as in a shadowy vision, Domini Enfilden's figure disappearing into the windy desolation of the desert protected by the living mystery he hated. Yes, at this moment, he no longer denied it to himself. There was something in Androvsky that he actually hated with his whole soul, hated even in his church, at the very threshold of the altar where stood the tabernacle containing the sacred Host. As he thoroughly realised this for a moment he was shocked at himself, recoiled mentally from his own feeling. But then something within him seemed to rise up and say, " Perhaps it is because you are near to the Host that you hate this man. Perhaps you are right to hate him when he draws nigh to the body of Christ."

Nevertheless when, some minutes later, he stood within the altar rails and saw the face of Domini, he was conscious of another thought, that came through his mind, dark with doubt, like a ray of gold: " Can I be right in hating what this good woman—this woman whose confession I have received, whose heart I know—can I be right in hating what she loves, in fearing what she trusts, in secretly condemning what she openly enthrones? " And almost in despite of himself he felt reassured for an instant, even happy in the thought of what he was about to do.

Domini's face at all times suggested strength. The mental and emotional power of her were forcibly expressed, too, through her tall and athletic body, which was full of easy grace, but full, too, of well-knit firmness. To-day she looked not unlike a splendid Amazon who could have been a splendid nun had she entered into religion. As she stood there by Androvsky, simply dressed for the wild journey that was before her, the slight hint in her personality of a Spartan youth, that stamped her with a very definite originality, was blended with, even transfigured by, a womanliness so intense as to be almost fierce, a womanliness that had the fervour, the glowing vigour of a glory that had suddenly become fully aware of itself, and of all the deeds that it could not only conceive, but do. She was triumph embodied in the flesh, not the triumph that is a shool-bully, but that spreads wings, conscious at last that the human being has kinship with the angels, and need not, should not, wait for death to seek bravely their comradeship. She was love triumphant, woman utterly fearless because instinctively aware that she was fulfilling her divine mission.

As he gazed at her the priest had a strange thought—of how

Christ's face must have looked when he said, " Lazarus, come forth ! "

Androvsky stood by her, but the priest did not look at him.

The wind roared round the church, the narrow windows rattled, and the clouds of sand driven against them made a pattering as of fingers tapping frantically upon the glass. The buff-coloured curtains trembled, and the dusty pink ribands tied round the ropes of the chandeliers shook incessantly to and fro, as if striving to escape and to join the multitudes of torn and disfigured things that were swept through space by the breath of the storm. Beyond the windows, vaguely seen at moments through the clouds of sand, the outlines of the palm leaves wavered, descended, rose, darted from side to side, like hands of the demented.

Suzanne, who was one of the witnesses, trembled, and moved her full lips nervously. She disapproved utterly of her mistress' wedding, and still more of a honeymoon in the desert. For herself she did not care, very shortly she was going to marry Monsieur Helmuth, the important person in livery who accompanied the hotel omnibus to the station, and meanwhile she was to remain at Beni-Mora under the chaperonage of Madame Armande, the proprietor of the hotel. But it shocked her that a mistress of hers, and a member of the English aristocracy, should be married in a costume suitable for a camel ride, and should start off to go to *le Bon Dieu* alone knew where, shut up in a palanquin like any black woman covered with lumps of coral and bracelets like handcuffs.

The other witnesses were the mayor of Beni-Mora, a middle-aged doctor, who wore the conventional evening-dress of French ceremony, and looked as if the wind had made him as sleepy as a bear on the point of hibernating, and the son of Madame Armande, a lively young man, with a bullet head and eager, black eyes. The latter took a keen interest in the ceremony, but the mayor blinked pathetically, and occasionally rubbed his large hooked nose as if imploring it to keep his whole person from drooping down into a heavy doze.

The priest, speaking in a conventional voice that was strangely inexpressive of his inward emotion, asked Androvsky and Domini whether they would take each other for wife and husband, and listened to their replies. Androvsky's voice sounded to him hard and cold as ice when it replied, and suddenly he thought of the storm as raging in some northern land over snow-bound wastes whose scanty trees were leafless. But Domini's voice was clear, and warm as the sun that would shine again over the desert when the storm was past. The mayor, constraining himself to keep awake a little longer, gave Domini away, while Suzanne dropped tears into a pocket-handkerchief edged with rose-coloured frilling, the gift of Monsieur Helmuth. Then, when the troths had been plighted in the midst of a more passionate roaring of the wind, the priest, conquering a terrible inward reluctance that beset him despite his endeavour to feel detached and formal, merely a priest engaged in a ceremony that it was his office to carry out, but in which he had no personal interest, spoke the fateful words:

"*Ego conjungo vos in matrimonium in nomine Patris et Filii et Spiritus Sancti. Amen.*"

He said this without looking at the man and woman who stood before him, the man on the right hand and the woman on the left, but when he lifted his hand to sprinkle them with holy water he could not forbear glancing at them, and he saw Domini as a shining radiance, but Androvsky as a thing of stone. With a movement that seemed to the priest sinister in its oppressed deliberation, Androvsky placed gold and silver upon the book and the marriage ring.

The priest spoke again, slowly, in the uproar of the wind, after blessing the ring:

"*Adjutorium nostrum in nomine Domini.*"

After the reply the "*Domine, exaudi orationem meam,*" the "*Et clamor,*" the "*Dominus vobiscum,*" and the "*Et cum spiritu tuo,*" the "*Oremus,*" and the prayer following, he sprinkled the ring with holy water in the form of a cross and gave it to Androvsky to give with gold and silver to Domini. Androvsky took the ring, repeated the formula, "With this ring," etc., then still, as it seemed to the priest, with the same sinister deliberation, placed it on the thumb of the bride's uncovered hand, saying, "*In the name of the Father,*" then on her second finger, saying, "*Of the Son,*" then on her third finger, saying, "*Of the Holy Ghost,*" then on her fourth finger. But at this moment, when he should have said "*Amen,*" there was a long pause of silence. During it—why he did not know—the priest found himself thinking of the saying of St. Isidore of Seville that the ring of marriage is left on the fourth finger of the bride's hand because that finger contains a vein directly connected with the heart.

"*Amen.*"

Androvsky had spoken. The priest started, and went on

with the "*Confirma, hoc, Deus.*" And from this point until the "*Per Christum Dominum nostrum, Amen,*" which, since there was no Mass, closed the ceremony, he felt more master of himself and his emotions than at any time previously during this day. A sensation of finality, of the irrevocable, came to him. He said within himself, "This matter has passed out of my hands into the hands of God." And in the midst of the violence of the storm a calm stole upon his spirit. "God knows best!" he said within himself. "God knows best!"

Those words and the state of feeling that was linked with them were and had always been to him as mighty protecting arms that uplifted him above the beating waves of the sea of life. The Wedding March sounded when the priest bade good-bye to the husband and wife whom he had made one. He was able to do it tranquilly. He even pressed Androvsky's hand.

"Be good to her," he said. "She is—she is a good woman."

To his surprise Androvsky suddenly wrung his hand almost passionately, and the priest saw that there were tears in his eyes.

That night the priest prayed long and earnestly for all wanderers in the desert.

When Domini and Androvsky came out from the church they saw vaguely a camel lying down before the door, bending its head and snarling fiercely. Upon its back was a palanquin of dark-red stuff, with a roof of stuff stretched upon strong, curved sticks, and curtains which could be drawn or undrawn at pleasure. The desert men crowded about it like eager phantoms in the wind, half seen in the driving mist of sand. Clinging to Androvsky's arm, Domini struggled forward to the camel. As she did so, Smaïn, unfolding for an instant his burnous, pressed into her hands his mass of roses. She thanked him with a smile he scarcely saw and a word that was borne away upon the wind. At Larbi's lips she saw the little flute and his thick fingers fluttering upon the holes. She knew that he was playing his love-song for her, but she could not hear it except in her heart. The perfume-seller sprinkled her gravely with essence, and for a moment she felt as if she were again in his dark bazaar, and seemed to catch among the voices of the storm the sound of men muttering prayers to Allah as in the mosque of Sidi-Zazan.

Then she was in the palanquin with Androvsky close beside her.

At this moment Batouch took hold of the curtains of the palanquin to draw them close, but she put out her hand and stopped him. She wanted to see the last of the church, of the tormented gardens she had learnt to love.

He looked astonished, but yielded to her gesture, and told the camel driver to make the animal rise to its feet. The driver took his stick and plied it, crying out, " A-ah! A-ah! " The camel turned its head towards him, showing its teeth, and snarling with a sort of dreary passion.

" A-ah! " shouted the driver. " A-ah! A-ah! "

The camel began to get up.

As it did so, from the shrouded group of desert men one started forward to the palanquin, throwing off his burnous and gesticulating with thin naked arms, as if about to commit some violent act. It was the sand-diviner. Made fantastic and unreal by the whirling sand grains, Domini saw his lean face pitted with small-pox; his eyes, blazing with an intelligence that was demoniacal, fixed upon her; the long wound that stretched from his cheek to his forehead. The pleading that had been mingled with the almost tyrannical command of his demeanour had vanished now. He looked ferocious, arbitrary, like a savage of genius full of some frightful message of warning or rebuke. As the camel rose he cried aloud some words in Arabic. Domini heard his voice, but could not understand the words. Laying his hands on the stuff of the palanquin he shouted again, then took away his hands and shook them above his head towards the desert, still staring at Domini with his fanatical eyes.

The wind shrieked, the sand grains whirled in spirals about his body, the camel began to move away from the church slowly towards the village.

" A-ah! " cried the camel-driver. " A-ah! "

In the storm his call sounded like a wail of despair.

CHAPTER XVII

As the voice of the Diviner fainted away on the wind, and the vision of his wounded face and piercing eyes was lost in the whirling sand grains, Androvsky stretched out his hand and drew together the heavy curtains of the palanquin. The world was shut out. They were alone for the first time as man and wife; moving deliberately on this beast they could not see, but whose slow and monotonous gait swung them gently to and fro, out from the last traces of civilisation into the life of the sands. With each soft step the camel took they went a little farther from Beni-Mora, came a little nearer to that liberty of which Domini had sometimes dreamed, to the smiling eyes and the lifted spheres of fire.

She shut her eyes now. She did not want to see her husband or to touch his hand. She did not want to speak. She only wanted to feel in the uttermost depths of her spirit this movement, steady and persistent, towards the goal of her earthly desires, to realise absolutely the marvellous truth that after years of lovelessness, and a dreaminess more benumbing than acute misery, happiness more intense than any she had been able to conceive of in her moments of greatest yearning was being poured into her heart, that she was being taken to the place where she would be with the one human being whose presence blotted out even the memory of the false world and gave to her the true. And whereas in the dead years she had sometimes been afraid of feeling too much the emptiness and the desolation of her life, she was now afraid of feeling too little its fulness and its splendour, was afraid of some day looking back to this superb moment of her earthly fate, and being conscious that she had not grasped its meaning till it was gone, that she had done that most terrible of all things—realised that she had been happy to the limits of her capacity for happiness only when her happiness was numbered with the past.

But could that ever be? Was Time, such Time as this, not Eternity? Could such earthly things as this intense joy ever have been and no longer be? It seemed to her that it could not be so. She felt like one who held Eternity's hand, and went out with that great guide into the endlessness of supreme perfection. For her, just then, the Creator's scheme was rounded to a flawless circle. All things fell into order, stars and men, the silent growing things, the seas, the mountains and the plains, fell into order like a vast choir to obey the command of the canticle: " Benedicite, omnia opera! "

" Bless ye the Lord! " The roaring of the wind about the palanquin became the dominant voice of this choir in Domini's ears.

" Bless ye the Lord! " It was obedient, not as the slave, but as the free will is obedient, as her heart, which joined its voice with this wind of the desert was obedient, because it gloriously chose with all its powers, passions, aspirations to be so. The real obedience is only love fulfilling its last desire, and this great song was the fulfilling of the last desire of all created things. Domini knew that she did not realise the joy of this moment of her life now when she felt no longer that she was a woman, but only that she was a living praise winging upward to God.

A warm, strong hand clasped hers. She opened her eyes. In the dim twilight of the palanquin she saw the darkness of Androvsky's tall figure sitting in the crouched attitude rendered necessary by the peculiar seat, and swaying slightly to the movement of the camel. The light was so obscure that she could not see his eyes or clearly discern his features, but she felt that he was gazing at her shadowy figure, that his mind was passionately at work. Had he, too, been silently praising God for his happiness, and was he now wishing the body to join in the soul's delight?

She left her hand in his passively. The sense of her womanhood, lost for a moment in the ecstasy of worship, had returned to her, but with a new and tremendous meaning which seemed to change her nature. Androvsky forcibly pressed her hand with his, let it go, then pressed it again, repeating the action with a regularity that seemed suggested by some guidance. She imagined him pressing her hand each time his heart pulsed. She did not want to return the pressure. As she felt his hand thus closing and unclosing over hers, she was conscious that she, who in their intercourse had played a dominant part, who had even deliberately brought about that intercourse by her action on the tower, now longed to be passive and, forgetting her own power and the strength and force of her nature, to lose herself in the greater strength and force of this man to whom she had given herself. Never before had she wished to be anything but strong. Nor did she desire weakness now, but only that his nature should rise above hers with eagle's wings, that when she looked up she should see him, never when she looked down. She thought that to see him below her would kill her, and she opened her lips to say so. But something in the windy darkness kept her silent. The heavy curtains of the palanquin shook perpetually, and the tall wooden rods on which they were slung creaked, making a small, incessant noise like a complaining, which joined itself with the more distant but louder noise made by the leaves of the thousands of palm trees dashed furiously together. From behind came the groaning of one of the camels, borne on the gusts of the wind, and faint sounds of the calling voices of the Arabs who accompanied them. It was not a time to speak.

She wondered where they were, in what part of the oasis, whether they had yet gained the beginning of the great route which had always fascinated her, and which was now the road to the goal of all her earthly desires. But there was nothing to tell her. She travelled in a world of dimness and the roar of wind, and in this obscurity and uproar, combined with perpetual though slight motion, she lost all count of time. She had no idea how long it was since she had come out of the church door with Androvsky. At first she thought it was only a few minutes, and that the camels must be just coming to the statue of the Cardinal. Then she thought that it might be an hour, even more; that Count Anteoni's garden was long since left behind, and that they were passing, perhaps, along the narrow streets of the village of old Beni-Mora, and nearing the edge of the oasis. But even in this confusion of mind she felt that something would tell her when the last palms had vanished in the sand mist and the caravan came out into the desert. The sound of the wind would surely be different when they met it on the immense flats, where there was nothing to break its fury. Or even if it were not different, she felt that she would know, that the desert would surely speak to her in the moment when, at last, it took her to itself. It could not be that they would be taken by the desert and she not know it. But she wanted Androvsky to know it too. For she felt that the moment when the desert took them, man and wife, would be a great moment in their lives, greater even than that in which they met as they came into the blue country. And she set herself to listen, with a passionate expectation, with an attention so close and determined that it thrilled her body, and even affected her muscles.

What she was listening for was a rising of the wind, a crescendo of its voice. She was anticipating a triumphant cry from the Sahara, unlimited power made audible in a sound like the blowing of the clarion of the sands.

Androvsky's hand was still on hers, but now it did not move as if obeying the pulsations of his heart. It held hers closely, warmly, and sent his strength to her, and presently, for an instant, taking her mind from the desert, she lost herself in the mystery and the wonder of human companionship. She realised that the touch of Androvsky's hand on hers altered for her herself, and the whole universe as it was presented to her, as she observed and felt it. Nothing remained as it was when he did not touch her. There was something stupefying in the thought, something almost terrible. The wonder that is alive in the tiny things of love, and that makes tremendously important their presence in, or absence from, a woman's life, took hold on her completely for the first time, and set her forever in a changed world, a world in which a great knowledge ruled instead of a great ignorance. With the consciousness of exactly what Androvsky's touch meant to her came a multiple consciousness of a thousand other things, all connected with him and her consecrated relation to him. She quivered with understanding. All the gates of her soul were being opened, and the white light of comprehension of those things which make life splendid and fruitful was pouring in upon her. Within the dim, contained space of the palanquin, that was slowly carried onward through the passion of the storm, there was an effulgence of unseen glory that grew in splendour moment by moment. A woman was being born of a woman, woman who knew herself of woman who did not know herself, woman who henceforth would divinely love her womanhood of woman who had often wondered why she had been created woman.

The words muttered by the man of the sand in Count Anteoni's garden were coming true. In the church of Beni-Mora the life of Domini had begun more really than when her mother strove in the pains of childbirth and her first faint cry answered the voice of the world's light when it spoke to her.

Slowly the caravan moved on. The camel-drivers sang low under the folds of their haiks those mysterious songs of the East that seem the songs of heat and solitude. Batouch, smothered in his burnous, his large head sunk upon his chest, slumbered like a potentate relieved from cares of State. Till Arba was reached his duty was accomplished. Ali, perched behind him on the camel, stared into the dimness with eyes steady and remote as those of a vulture of the desert. The houses of Beni-Mora faded in the mist of the sand, the statue of the Cardinal holding the double cross, the tower of the hotel, the shuddering trees of Count Anteoni's garden. Along the white blue which was the road the camels painfully advanced, urged by the cries and the sticks of the running drivers. Presently the brown buildings of old Beni-Mora came partially into sight, peeping here and there through the flying sands and the frantic palm leaves. The desert was at hand.

Ali began to sing, breathing his song into the back of Batouch's hood.

"The love of women is like the holiday song that the boy sings gaily
        In the sunny garden—
The love of women is like the little moon, the little happy moon
        In the last night of Ramadan.

The love of women is like the great silence that steals at dusk
    To kiss the scented blossoms of the orange tree.
Sit thee down beneath the orange tree, O loving man!
That thou mayst know the kiss that tells the love of women.
                    Janat! Janat! Janat!"

Batouch stirred uneasily, pulled his hood from his eyes and
looked into the storm gravely. Then he shifted on the camel's
hump and said to Ali:

"How shall we get to Arba? The wind is like all the
Touaregs going to battle. And when we leave the oasis——"

"The wind is going down, Batouch-ben-Brahim," responded
Ali, calmly. "This evening the Roumis can lie in the
tents."

Batouch's thick lips curled with sarcasm. He spat into the
wind, blew his nose in his burnous, and answered:

"You are a child, and can sing a pretty song, but——"

Ali pointed with his delicate hand towards the south.

"Do you not see the light in the sky?"

Batouch stared before him, and perceived that there was in
truth a lifting of the darkness beyond, a whiteness growing
where the desert lay.

"As we come into the desert the wind will fall," said Ali;
and again he began to sing to himself:

                    "Janat! Janat! Janat!"

Domini could not see the light in the south, and no premoni-
tion warned her of any coming abatement of the storm. Once
more she had begun to listen to the roaring of the wind and to
wait for the larger voice of the desert, for the triumphant clarion
of the sands that would announce to her her entry with Androvsky into the life of the wastes. Again she personified the Sahara,
but now more vividly than ever before. In the obscurity she
seemed to see it far away, like a great heroic figure, waiting for
her and her passion, waiting in a region of gold and silken airs at
the back of the tempest to crown her life with a joy wide as its
dreamlike spaces, to teach her mind the inner truths that lie
beyond the crowded ways of men and to open her heart to the
most profound messages of Nature.

She listened, holding Androvsky's hand, and she felt that he
was listening too, with an intensity strong as her own, or
stronger. Presently his hand closed upon hers more tightly,
almost hurting her physically. As it did so she glanced up, but

not at him, and noticed that the curtains of the palanquin were fluttering less fiercely. Once, for an instant, they were almost still. Then again they moved as if tugged by invisible hands; then were almost still once more. At the same time the wind's voice sank in her ears like a music dropping downward in a hollow place. It rose, but swiftly sank a second time to a softer hush, and she perceived in the curtained enclosure a faintly growing light which enabled her to see, for the first time since she had left the church, her husband's features. He was looking at her with an expression of anticipation in which there was awe, and she realised that in her expectation of the welcome of the desert she had been mistaken. She had listened for the sounding of a clarion, but she was to be greeted by a still, small voice. She understood the awe in her husband's eyes and shared it. And she knew at once, with a sudden thrill of rapture, that in the scheme of things there are blessings and nobilities undreamed of by man and that must always come upon him with a glorious shock of surprise, showing him the poor faultiness of what he had thought perhaps his most magnificent imaginings. Elisha sought for the Lord in the fire and in the whirlwind; but in the still, small voice onward came the Lord.

Incomparably more wonderful than what she had waited for seemed to her now this sudden falling of the storm, this mystical voice that came to them out of the heart of the sands telling them that they were passing at last into the arms of the Sahara. The wind sank rapidly. The light grew in the palanquin. From without the voices of the camel-drivers and of Batouch and Ali talking together reached their ears distinctly. Yet they remained silent. It seemed as if they feared by speech to break the spell of the calm that was flowing around them, as if they feared to interrupt the murmur of the desert. Domini now returned the gaze of her husband. She could not take her eyes from his, for she wished him to read all the joy that was in her heart; she wished him to penetrate her thoughts, to understand her desires, to be at one with the woman who had been born on the eve of the passing of the wind. With the coming of this mystic calm was coming surely something else. The silence was bringing with it the fusing of two natures. The desert in this moment was drawing together two souls into a union which Time and Death would have no power to destroy. Presently the wind completely died away, only a faint breeze fluttered the curtains of the palanquin, and the light that penetrated between them here and there was no longer white, but sparkled with a tiny dust of gold. Then Androvsky moved to open the curtains, and Domini spoke for the first time since their marriage.

"Wait," she said in a low voice.

He dropped his hand obediently, and looked at her with inquiry in his eyes.

"Don't let us look till we are far out," she said, " far away from Beni-Mora."

He made no answer, but she saw that he understood all that was in her heart. He leaned a little nearer to her and stretched out his arm as if to put it round her. But he did not put it round her, and she knew why. He was husbanding his great joy as she had husbanded the dark hours of the previous night that to her were golden. And that unfinished action, that impulse unfulfilled, showed her more clearly the depths of his passion for her even than had the desperate clasp of his hands about her knees in the garden. That which he did not do now was the greatest assertion possible of all that he would do in the life that was before them, and made her feel how entirely she belonged to him. Something within her trembled like a poor child before whom is suddenly set the prospect of a day of perfect happiness. She thought of the ending of this day, of the coming of the evening. Always the darkness had parted them; at the ending of this day it would unite them. In Androvsky's eyes she read her thought of the darkness reflected, reflected and yet changed, transmuted by sex. It was as if at that moment she read the same story written in two ways—by a woman and by a man, as if she saw Eden, not only as Eve saw it, but as Adam.

A long time passed, but they did not feel it to be long. When their camel halted they unclasped their hands slowly like sleepers reluctantly awaking.

They heard Batouch's voice outside the palanquin.

"Madame!" he called. "Madame!"

"What is it?" asked Domini, stifling a sigh.

"Madame should draw the curtains. We are halfway to Arba. It is time for *déjeuner*. I will make the camel of Madame lie down."

A loud "A-a-ah!" rose up, followed by a fierce groaning from the camel, and a lethargic, yet violent, movement that threw them forward and backward. They sank. A hand from without pulled back the curtains and light streamed over them. They set their feet in sand, stood up, and looked about them.

Already they were far out in the desert, though not yet beyond the limit of the range of red mountains, which stretched forward upon their left but at no great distance beyond them ended in the sands. The camels were lying down in a faintly defined track which was bordered upon either side by the plain covered with little humps of sandy soil on which grew dusty shrub. Above them was a sky of faint blue, heavy with banks of clouds towards the east, and over their heads dressed in wispy veils of vaporous white, through which the blue peered in sections that grew larger as they looked. Towards the south, where Arba lay on a low hill of earth, without grass or trees, beyond a mound covered thickly with tamarisk bushes, which was a feeding-place for immense herds of camels, the blue was clear and the light of the sun intense. A delicate breeze travelled about them, stirring the bushes and the robes of the Arabs, who were throwing back their hoods, and uncovering their mouths, and smiling at them, but seriously, as Arabs alone can smile. Beside them stood two white and yellow guard dogs, blinking and looking weary.

For a moment they stood still, blinking too, almost like the dogs. The change to this immensity and light from the narrow darkness of the palanquin overwhelmed their senses. They said nothing, but only stared silently. Then Domini, with a large gesture, stretched her arms above her head, drawing a deep breath which ended in a little, almost sobbing, laugh of exultation.

" Out of prison," she said disconnectedly. " Out of prison—into this ! " Suddenly she turned upon Androvsky and caught his arm, and twined both of her arms round it with a strong confidence that was careless of everything in the intensity of its happiness.

" All my life I've been in prison," she said. " You've unlocked the door ! " And then, as suddenly as she had caught his arm, she let it go. Something surged up in her, making her almost afraid, or, if not that, confused. It was as if her nature were a horse taking the bit between its teeth preparatory to a tremendous gallop. Whither ? She did not know. She was intoxicated by the growing light, the sharp, delicious air, the huge spaces around her, the solitude with this man who held her soul surely in his hands. She had always connected him with the desert. Now he was hers into the desert, and the desert was hers with him. But was it possible ? Could such a fate have been held in reserve for her ? She scarcely dared even to try to realise the meaning of her situation, lest at a breath it should be changed. Just then she felt that if she ventured to weigh and measure her wonderful gift Androvsky would fall dead at her feet and the desert be folded together like a scroll.

"There is Beni-Mora, Madame," said Batouch.

She was glad he spoke to her, turned and followed with her eyes his pointing hand. Far off she saw a green darkness of palms, and above it a white tower, small, from here, as the tower of a castle of dolls.

"The tower!" she said to Androvsky. "We first spoke in it. We must bid it good-bye."

She made a gesture of farewell towards it. Androvsky watched the movement of her hand. She noticed now that she made no movement that he did not observe with a sort of passionate attention. The desert did not exist for him. She saw that in his eyes. He did not look towards the tower even when she repeated:

"We must—we owe it that."

Batouch and Ali were busy spreading a cloth upon the sand, making it firm with little stones, taking out food, plates, knives, glasses, bottles from a great basket slung on one of the camels. They moved deftly, seriously intent upon their task. The camel-drivers were loosening the cords that bound the loads upon their beasts, who roared venomously, opening their mouths, showing long decayed teeth, and turning their heads from side to side with a serpentine movement. Domini and Androvsky were not watched for a moment.

"Why won't you look? Why won't you say good-bye?" she asked, coming nearer to him on the sand softly, with a woman's longing to hear him explain what she understood.

"What do I care for it, or the palms, or the sky, or the desert?" he answered almost savagely. "What can I care? If you were mine behind iron bars in that prison you spoke of—don't you think it's enough for me—too much—a cup running over?"

And he added some words under his breath, words she could not hear.

"Not even the desert!" she said with a catch in her voice.

"It's all in you. Everything's in you—everything that brought us together, that we've watched and wanted together."

"But then," she said, and now her voice was very quiet, "am I peace for you?"

"Peace!" said Androvsky.

"Yes. Don't you remember once I said that there must be peace in the desert. Then is it in me—for you?"

" Peace ! " he repeated. " To-day I can't think of peace, or want it. Don't you ask too much of me! Let me live to-day, live as only a man can who—let me live with all that is in me to-day—Domini. Men ask to die in peace. Oh, Domini— Domini ! "

His expression was like arms that crushed her, lips that pressed her mouth, a heart that beat on hers.

" Madame est servie ! " cried Batouch in a merry voice.

His mistress did not seem to hear him. He cried again :

" Madame est servie ! "

Then Domini turned round and came to the first meal in the sand. Two cushions lay beside the cloth upon an Arab quilt of white, red, and orange colour. Upon the cloth, in vases of rough pottery, stained with designs in purple, were arranged the roses brought by Smaïn from Count Anteoni's garden.

" Our wedding breakfast ! " Domini said under her breath.

She felt just then as if she were living in a wonderful romance.

They sat down side by side and ate with a good appetite, served by Batouch and Ali. Now and then a pale yellow butterfly, yellow as the sand, flitted by them. Small yellow birds with crested heads ran swiftly among the scrub, or flew low over the flats. In the sky the vapours gathered themselves together and moved slowly away towards the east, leaving the blue above their heads unflecked with white. With each moment the heat of the sun grew more intense. The wind had gone. It was difficult to believe that it had ever roared over the desert. A little way from them the camel-drivers squatted beside the beasts, eating flat loaves of yellow bread, and talking together in low, guttural voices. The guard dogs roamed round them, uneasily hungry. In the distance, before a tent of patched rags, a woman, scantily clad in bright red cotton, was suckling a child and staring at the caravan.

Domini and Androvsky scarcely spoke as they ate. Once she said :

" Do you realise that this is a wedding breakfast ? "

She was thinking of the many wedding receptions she had attended in London, of crowds of smartly-dressed women staring enviously at tiaras, and sets of jewels arranged in cases upon tables, of brides and bridegrooms, looking flushed and anxious, standing under canopies of flowers and forcing their tired lips into smiles as they replied to stereotyped congratulations, while detectives—poorly disguised as gentlemen—hovered in the background to see that none of the presents mysteriously disappeared. Her presents were the velvety roses in the earthen vases, the breezes of the desert, the sand humps, the yellow butterflies, the silence that lay around like a blessing pronounced by the God who made the still places where souls can learn to know themselves and their great destiny.

" A wedding breakfast," Androvsky said.

" Yes. But perhaps you have never been to one."

" Never."

" Then you can't love this one as much as I do."

" Much more," he answered.

She looked at him, remembering how often in the past, when she had been feeling intensely, she had it borne in upon her that he was feeling even more intensely than herself. But could that be possible now?

" Do you think," she said, "that it is possible for you, who have never lived in cities, to love this land as I love it? "

Androvsky moved on his cushion and leaned down till his elbow touched the sand. Lying thus, with his chin in his hand, and his eyes fixed upon her, he answered:

" But it is not the land I am loving."

His absolute concentration upon her made her think that, perhaps, he misunderstood her meaning in speaking of the desert, her joy in it. She longed to explain how he and the desert were linked together in her heart, and she dropped her hand upon his left hand, which lay palm downwards in the warm sand.

" I love this land," she began, " because I found you in it, because I feel——"

She stopped.

" Yes, Domini? " he said.

"No, not now. I can't tell you. There's too much light."

" Domini," he repeated.

Then they were silent once more, thinking of how the darkness would come to them at Arba.

In the late afternoon they drew near to the Bordj, moving along a difficult route full of deep ruts and holes, and bordered on either side by bushes so tall that they looked almost like trees. Here, tended by Arabs who stared gravely at the strangers in the palanquin, were grazing immense herds of camels. Above the bushes to the horizon on either side of the way appeared the serpentine necks flexibly moving to and fro, now bending deliberately towards the dusty twigs, now stretched straight forward as if in patient search for some solace of the

camel's fate that lay in the remoteness of the desert. Baby
camels, many of them only a few days old, yet already vowed to
the eternal pilgrimages of the wastes, with mild faces and long,
disobedient-looking legs, ran from the caravan, nervously seeking
their morose mothers, who cast upon them glances that seemed
expressive of a disdainful pity. In front, beyond a watercourse,
now dried up, rose the low hill on which stood the Bordj, a huge
square building, with two square towers pierced with loopholes.
From a distance it resembled a fort threatening the desert i.
magnificent isolation. Its towers were black against the clear
lemon of the failing sunlight. Pigeons, that looked also black,
flew perpetually about them, and the telegraph posts, that
bordered the way at regular intervals on the left, made a diminishing series of black vertical lines sharply cutting the yellow till
they were lost to sight in the south. To Domini these posts
were like pointing fingers beckoning her onward to the farthest
distances of the sun. Drugged by the long journey over the
flats, and the unceasing caress of the air, that was like an importunate lover ever unsatisfied, she watched from the height on
which she was perched this evening scene of roaming, feeding
animals, staring nomads, monotonous herbage and vague,
surely-retreating mountains, with quiet, dreamy eyes. Everything which she saw seemed to her beautiful, a little remote
and a little fantastic. The slow movement of the camels, the
swifter movements of the circling pigeons about the square
towers on the hill, the motionless, or gently-gliding, Arabs with
their clubs held slantwise, the telegraph poles, one smaller than
the other, diminishing till—as if magically—they disappeared in
the lemon that was growing into gold, were woven together for
her by the shuttle of the desert into a softly brilliant tapestry—
one of those tapestries that is like a legend struck to sleep as
the Beauty in her palace. As they began to mount the hill, and
the radiance of the sky increased, this impression faded, for the
life that centred round the Bordj was vivid, though sparse in
comparison with the eddying life of towns, and had that air of
peculiar concentration which may be noted in pictures representing a halt in the desert.

No longer did the strongly-built Bordj seem to Domini like a
fort threatening the oncomer, but like a stalwart host welcoming
him, a host who kept open house in this treeless desolation that
yet had, for her, no feature that was desolate. It was earth-
coloured, built of stone, and had in the middle of the façade that
faced them an immense hospitable doorway with a white arch

above it. This doorway gave a partial view of a vast courtyard, in which animals and people were moving to and fro. Round about, under the sheltering shadow of the windowless wall, were many Arabs, some squatting on their haunches, some standing upright with their backs against the stone, some moving from one group to another, gesticulating and talking vivaciously. Boys were playing a game with stones set in an ordered series of small holes scooped by their fingers in the dust. A negro crossed the flat space before the Bordj carrying on his head a huge earthen vase to the well near by, where a crowd of black donkeys, just relieved of their loads of brushwood, was being watered. From the south two Spahis were riding in on white horses, their scarlet cloaks floating out over their saddles; and from the west, moving slowly to a wailing sound of indistinct music, a faint beating of tom-toms, was approaching a large caravan in a cloud of dust which floated back from it and melted away into the radiance of the sunset.

When they gained the great open space before the building they were bathed in the soft golden light, in which all these figures of Africans, and all these animals, looked mysterious and beautiful, and full of that immeasurable significance which the desert sheds upon those who move in it, specially at dawn or at sundown. From the plateau they dominated the whole of the plain they had traversed as far as Beni-Mora, which on the morrow would fade into the blue horizon. Its thousands of palms made a darkness in the gold, and still the tower of the hotel was faintly visible, pointing like a needle towards the sky. The range of mountains showed their rosy flanks in the distance. They, too, on the morrow would be lost in the desert spaces, the last outposts of the world of hill and valley, of stream and sea. Only in the deceptive dream of the mirage would they appear once more, looming in a pearl-coloured shaking veil like a fluid on the edge of some visionary lagune.

Domini was glad that on this first night of their journey they could still see Beni-Mora, the place where they had found each other and been given to each other by the Church. As the camel stopped before the great doorway of the Bordj she turned in the palanquin and looked down upon the desert, motioning to the camel-driver to leave the beast for a moment. She put her arm through Androvsky's and made his eyes follow hers across the vast spaces made magical by the sinking sun to that darkness of distant palms which, to her, would be a sacred place for ever. And as they looked in silence all that Beni-Mora meant to her

came upon her. She saw again the garden hushed in the heat
of noon. She saw Androvsky at her feet on the sand. She
heard the chiming church bell and the twitter of Larbi's flute.
The dark blue of trees was as the heart of the world to her and
as the heart of life. It had seen the birth of her soul and given
to her another newborn soul. There was a pathos in seeing it
fade like a thing sinking down till it became one with the immeasurable sands, and at that moment she said to herself,
"When shall I see Beni-Mora again—and how?" She looked
at Androvsky, met his eyes, and thought: "When I see it again
how different I shall be! How I shall be changed!" And in
the sunset she seemed to be saying a mute good-bye to one who
was fading with Beni-Mora.

As soon as they had got off the camel and were standing in
the group of staring Arabs, Batouch begged them to come to
their tents, where tea would be ready. He led them round the
angle of the wall towards the west, and there, pitched in the full
radiance of the sunset, with a wide space of hard earth gleaming
with gypse around it, was a white tent. Before it, in the open
air, was stretched a handsome Arab carpet, and on this carpet
were set a folding table and two folding chairs. The table held
a japanned tray with tea-cups, a milk jug and plates of biscuits,
and by it, in an attitude that looked deliberately picturesque,
stood Ouardi, the youth selected by Batouch to fill the office of
butler in the desert.

Ouardi smiled a broad welcome as they approached, and,
having made sure that his pose had been admired, retired to the
cook's abode to fetch the teapot, while Batouch invited Domini
and Androvsky to inspect the tent prepared for them. Domini
assented with a dropped-out word. She still felt in a dream.
But Androvsky, after casting towards the tent door a glance that
was full of a sort of fierce shyness, moved away a few steps, and
stood at the edge of the hill looking down upon the incoming
caravan, whose music was now plainly audible in the stillness of
the waste.

Domini went into the tent that was to be their home for
many weeks, alone. And she was glad just then that she was
alone. For she too, like Androvsky, felt a sort of exquisite
trouble moving, like a wave, in her heart. On some pretext, but
only after an expression of admiration, she got rid of Batouch.
Then she stood and looked round.

From the big tent opened a smaller one, which was to serve
Androvsky as a dressing-room and both of them as a baggage

room. She did not go into that, but saw, with one glance of soft inquiry, the two small, low beds, the strips of gay carpet, the dressing-table, the washhand-stand and the two cane chairs which furnished the sleeping-tent. Then she looked back to the aperture. In the distance, standing alone at the edge of the hill, she saw Androvsky, bathed in the sunset, looking out over the hidden desert from which rose the wild sound of African music, steadily growing louder. It seemed to her as if he must be gazing at the plains of heaven, so magically brilliant and tender, so pellucidly clear and delicate was the atmosphere and the colour of the sky. She saw no other form, only his, in this poem of light, in this wide world of the sinking sun. And the music seemed to be about his feet, to rise from the sand and throb in its breast.

At that moment the figure of Liberty, which she had seen in the shadows of the dancing-house, came in at the tent door and laid, for the first time, her lips on Domini's. That kiss was surely the consecration of the life of the sands. But to-day there had been another consecration. Domini had a sudden impulse to link the two consecrations together.

She drew from her breast the wooden crucifix Androvsky had thrown into the stream at Sidi-Zerzour, and, softly going to one of the beds, she pinned the crucifix above it on the canvas of the tent. Then she turned and went out into the glory of the sunset to meet the fierce music that was rising from the desert.

CHAPTER XVIII

NIGHT had fallen over the desert, a clear purple night, starry but without a moon. Around the Bordj, and before a Café Maure built of brown earth and palm-wood, opposite to it, the Arabs who were halting to sleep at Arba on their journeys to and from Beni-Mora were huddled, sipping coffee, playing dominoes by the faint light of an oil lamp, smoking cigarettes and long pipes of keef. Within the court of the Bordj the mules were feeding tranquilly in rows. The camels roamed the plain among the tamarisk bushes, watched over by shrouded shadowy guardians sleepless as they were. The mountains, the palms of Beni-Mora, were lost in the darkness that lay over the desert.

On the low hill, at some distance beyond the white tent of Domini and Androvsky, the obscurity was lit up fiercely by the blaze of a huge fire of brushwood, the flames of which towered up towards the stars, flickering this way and that as the breeze took them, and casting a wild illumination upon the wild faces of the rejoicing desert men who were gathered about it, telling stories of the wastes, singing songs that were melancholy and remote to Western ears, even though they hymned past victories over the infidels, or passionate ecstasies of love in the golden regions of the sun. The steam from bowls of cous-cous and stews of mutton and vegetables curled up to join the thin smoke that made a light curtain about this fantasia, and from time to time, with a shrill cry of exultation, a half-naked form, all gleaming eyes and teeth and polished bronze-hued limbs, rushed out of the blackness beyond the fire, leaped through the tongues of flame and vanished like a spectre into the embrace of the night.

All the members of the caravan, presided over by Batouch in glory, were celebrating the wedding night of their master and mistress.

Domini and Androvsky had already visited them by their bonfire, had received their compliments, watched the sword dance and the dance of the clubs, touched with their lips, or pretended to touch, the stem of a keef, listened to a marriage song warbled by Ali to the accompaniment of a flute and little drums, and applauded Ouardi's agility in leaping through the flames. Then, with many good-nights, pressures of the hand, and auguries for the morrow, they had gone away into the cool darkness, silently towards their tent.

They walked slowly, a little apart from each other. Domini looked up at the stars and saw among them the star of Liberty. Androvsky looked at her and saw all the stars in her face. When they reached the tent door they stopped on the warm earth. A lamp was lit within, casting a soft light on the simple furniture and on the whiteness of the two beds, above one of which Domini imagined, though from without she could not see, the wooden crucifix Androvsky had once worn in his breast.

"Shall we stay here a little?" Domini said in a low voice. "Out here?" There was a long pause. Then Androvsky answered:

"Yes. Let us feel it all—all. Let us feel it to the full."

He caught hold of her hand with a sort of tender roughness and twined his fingers between hers, pressing his palm against hers.

"Don't let us miss anything to-night," he said. "All my life is to-night. I've had no life yet. To-morrow—who knows whether we shall be dead to-morrow? Who knows? But we're alive to-night, flesh and blood, heart and soul. And there's nothing here, there can be nothing here to take our life from us, the life of our love to-night. For we're out in the desert, we're right away from anyone, everything. We're in the great freedom. Aren't we, Domini? Aren't we?"

"Yes," she said. "Yes."

He took her other hand in the same way. He was facing her, and he held his hands against his heart with hers in them, then pressed her hands against her heart, then drew them back again to his.

"Then let us realise it. Let us forget our prison. Let us forget everything, everything that we ever knew before Beni-Mora, Domini. It's dead, absolutely dead, unless we make it live by thinking. And that's mad, crazy. Thought's the great madness. Domini, have you forgotten everything before we knew each other?"

"Yes," she said. "Now—but only now. You've made me forget it all."

There was a deep breathing under her voice. He held up her hands to his shoulders and looked closely into her eyes, as if he were trying to send all himself into her through those doors of the soul opened to seeing him. And now, in this moment, she felt that her fierce desire was realised, that he was rising above her on eagle's wings. And as on the night before the wedding she had blessed all the sorrows of her life, now she blessed silently all the long silence of Androvsky, all his strange reticence, his uncouthness, his avoidance of her in the beginning of their acquaintance. That which had made her pain by being, now made her joy by having been and being no more. The hidden man was rushing forth to her at last in his love. She seemed to hear in the night the crash of a great obstacle, and the voice of the flood of waters that had broken it down at length and were escaping into liberty. His silence of the past now made his speech intensely beautiful and wonderful to her. She wanted to hear the waters more intensely, more intensely.

"Speak to me," she said. "You've spoken so little. Do you know how little? Tell me all you are. Till now I've only felt all you are. And that's so much, but not enough for a woman—not enough. I've taken you, but now—give me all I've taken. Give—keep on giving and giving. From to-night to receive will be my life. Long ago I've given all I had to you. Give to me, give me everything. You know I've given all."

"All?" he said, and there was a throb in his deep voice, as if some intense feeling rose from the depths of him and shook it.

"Yes, all," she whispered. "Already—and long ago—that day in the garden. When I—when I put my hands against your forehead—do you remember? I gave you all, for ever."

And as she spoke she bent down her face with a sort of proud submission and put her forehead against his heart.

The purity in her voice and in her quiet, simple action dazzled him like a flame shining suddenly in his eyes out of blackness. And he, too, in that moment saw far up above him the beating of an eagle's wings. To each one the other seemed to be on high, and as both looked up that was their true marriage.

"I felt it," he said, touching her hair with his lips. "I felt it in your hands. When you touched me that day it was as if you were giving me the world and the stars. It frightened me to receive so much. I felt as if I had no place to put my gift in."

"Did your heart seem so small?" she said.

"You make everything I have and am seem small—and yet great. What does it mean?"

"That you are great, as I am, because we love. No one is small who loves. No one is poor, no one is bad, who loves. Love burns up evil. It's the angel that destroys."

Her words seemed to send through his whole body a quivering joy. He took her face between his hands and lifted it from his heart.

"Is that true? Is that true?" he said. "I've—I've tried to think that. If you know how I've tried."

"And don't you know it is true?"

"I don't feel as if I knew anything that you do not tell me to-night. I don't feel as if I have, or am, anything but what you give me, make me to-night. Can you understand that? Can you understand what you are to me? That you are everything, that I have nothing else, that I have never had anything else in all these years that I have lived and that I have forgotten? Can you understand it? You said just now 'Speak to me, tell me all you are.' That's what I am, all I am, a man you have made a man. You, Domini—you have made me a man, you have created me."

She was silent. The intensity with which he spoke, the

intensity of his eyes while he was speaking, made her hear those rushing waters as if she were being swept away by them.

" And you? " he said. " You? "

" I? "

" This afternoon in the desert, when we were in the sand looking at Beni-Mora, you began to tell me something and then you stopped. And you said, ' I can't tell you. There's too much light.' Now the sun has gone."

" Yes. But—but I want to listen to you. I want——"

She stopped. In the distance, by the great fire where the Arabs were assembled, there rose a sound of music which arrested her attention. Ali was singing, holding in his hand a brand from the fire like a torch. She had heard him sing before, and had loved the timbre of his voice, but only now did she realise when she had first heard him and who he was. It was he who, hidden from her, had sung the song of the freed negroes of Touggourt in the gardens of Count Anteoni that day when she had been angry with Androvsky and had afterwards been reconciled with him. And• she knew now it was he, because, once more hidden from her—for against the curtain of darkness she only saw the flame from the torch he held and moved rhythmically to the burden of his song—he was singing it again. Androvsky, when she ceased to speak, suddenly put his arms round her, as if he were afraid of her escaping from him in her silence, and they stood thus at the tent door listening:

> " The gazelle dies in the water,
> The fish dies in the air,
> And I die in the dunes of the desert sand
> For my love that is deep and sad."

The chorus of hidden men by the fire rose in a low murmur that was like the whisper of the desert in the night. Then the contralto voice of Ali came to Domini and Androvsky again, but very faintly, from the distance where the flaming torch was moving:

> " No one but God and I
> Knows what is in my heart."

When the voice died away for a moment Domini whispered the refrain. Then she said:

" But is it true? Can it be true for us to-night? "

Androvsky did not reply.

"I don't think it is true," she added. "You know—don't you?"

The voice of Ali rose again, and his torch flickered on the soft wind of the night. Its movement was slow and eerie. It seemed like his voice made visible, a voice of flame in the blackness of the world. They watched it. Presently she said once more:

"You know what is in my heart—don't you?"

"Do I?" he said. "All?"

"All. My heart is full of one thing—quite full."

"Then I know."

"And," she hesitated, then added, "and yours?"

"Mine too."

"I know all that is in it then?"

She still spoke questioningly. He did not reply, but held her more closely, with a grasp that was feverish in its intensity.

"Do you remember," she went on, "in the garden what you said about that song?"

"No."

"You have forgotten?"

"I told you," he said, "I mean to forget everything."

"Everything before we came to Beni-Mora?"

"And more. Everything before you put your hands against my forehead, Domini. Your touch blotted out the past."

"Even the past at Beni-Mora?"

"Yes, even that. There are many things I did and left undone, many things I said and never said that—I have forgotten —I have forgotten for ever."

There was a sternness in his voice now, a fiery intention.

"I understand," she said. "I have forgotten them too, but not some things."

"Which?"

"Not that night when you took me out of the dancing-house, not our ride to Sidi-Zerzour, not—there are things I shall remember. When I am dying, after I am dead, I shall remember them."

The song faded away. The torch was still, then fell downwards and became one with the fire. Then Androvsky drew Domini down beside him on to the warm earth before the tent door, and held her hand in his against the earth.

"Feel it," he said. "It's our home, it's our liberty. Does it feel alive to you?"

"Yes."

"As if it had pulses, like the pulses in our hearts, and knew what we know?"

"Yes. Mother Earth—I never understood what that meant till to-night."

"We are beginning to understand together. Who can understand anything alone?"

He kept her hand always in his pressed against the desert as against a heart. They both thought of it as a heart that was full of love and protection for them, of understanding of them. Going back to their words before the song of Ali, he said:

"Love burns up evil, then love can never be evil."

"Not the act of loving."

"Or what it leads to," he said.

And again there was a sort of sternness in his voice, as if he were insisting on something, were bent on conquering some reluctance, or some voice contradicting.

"I know that you are right," he added.

She did not speak, but—why she did not know—her thought went to the wooden crucifix fastened in the canvas of the tent close by, and for a moment she felt a faint creeping sadness in her. But he pressed her hand more closely, and she was conscious only of these two warmths—of his hand above her hand and of the desert beneath it. Her whole life seemed set in a glory of fire, in a heat that was life-giving, that dominated her and evoked at the same time all of power that was in her, causing her dormant fires, physical and spiritual, to blaze up as if they were sheltered and fanned. The thought of the crucifix faded. It was as if the fire destroyed it and it became ashes—then nothing. She fixed her eyes on the distant fire of the Arabs, which was beginning to die down slowly as the night grew deeper.

"I have doubted many things," he said. "I've been afraid."

"You!" she said.

"Yes. You know it."

"How can I? Haven't I forgotten everything—since that day in the garden?"

He drew up her hand and put it against his heart.

"I'm jealous of the desert even," he whispered. "I won't let you touch it any more to-night."

He looked into her eyes and saw that she was looking at the distant fire, steadily, with an intense eagerness.

"Why do you do that?" he said.

"To-night I like to look at fire," she answered.

" Tell me why."

It is as if I looked at you, at all that there is in you that you have never said, never been able to say to me, all that you never can say to me but that I know all the same."

" But," he said, " that fire is——"

He did not finish the sentence, but put up his hand and turned her face till she was looking, not at the fire, but at him.

" It is not like me," he said. " Men made it, and—it's a fire that can sink into ashes."

An expression of sudden exaltation shone in her eyes.

" And God made you," she said. " And put into you the spark that is eternal."

And now again she thought, she dared, she loved to think of the crucifix and of the moment when he would see it in the tent.

" And God made you love me," she said. " What is it? "

Androvsky had moved suddenly, as if he were going to get up from the warm ground.

" Did you——? "

" No," he said in a low voice. " Go on, Domini. Speak to me."

He sat still.

A sudden longing came to her to know if to-night he were feeling as she was the sacredness of their relation to each other. Never had they spoken intimately of religion or of the mysteries that lie beyond and around human life. Once or twice, when she had been about to open her heart to him, to let him understand her deep sense of the things unseen, something had checked her, something in him. It was as if he had divined her intention and had subtly turned her from it, without speech, merely by the force of his inward determination that she should not break through her reserve. But to-night, with his hand on hers and the starry darkness above them, with the waste stretching around them, and the cool air that was like the breath of liberty upon their faces, she was unconscious of any secret, combative force in him. It was impossible to her to think there could have been any combat, however inward, however subtle, between them. Surely if it were ever permitted to two natures to be in perfect accord theirs were in perfect accord to-night.

" I never felt the presence of God in his world so keenly as I feel it to-night," she went on, drawing a little closer to him. " Even in the church to-day he seemed farther away than to-night. But somehow—one has these thoughts without knowing why—I have always believed that the farther I went into the desert the nearer I should come to God."

Androvsky moved again. The clasp of his hand on hers loosened, but he did not take his hand away.

"Why should—what should make you think that?" he asked slowly.

"Don't you know what the Arabs call the desert?"

"No. What do they call it?"

"The Garden of Allah."

"The Garden of Allah!" he repeated.

There was a sound like fear in his voice. Even her great joy did not prevent her from noticing it, and she remembered, with a thrill of pain, where and under what circumstances she had first heard the Arab's name for the desert.

Could it be that this man she loved was secretly afraid of something in the desert, some influence, some——? Her thought stopped short, like a thing confused.

"Don't you think it a very beautiful name?" she asked, with an almost fierce longing to be reassured, to be made to know that he, like her, loved the thought that God was specially near to those who travelled in this land of solitude.

"Is it beautiful?"

"To me it is. It makes me feel as if in the desert I were specially watched over and protected, even as if I were specially loved there."

Suddenly Androvsky put his arm round her and strained her to him.

"By me! By me!" he said. "Think of me to-night, only of me, as I think only of you."

He spoke as if he were jealous even of her thought of God, as if he did not understand that it was the very intensity of her love for him that made her, even in the midst of the passion of the body, connect their love of each other with God's love of them. In her heart this overpowering human love which, in the garden, when first she realised it fully, had seemed to leave no room in her for love of God, now in the moment when it was close to absolute satisfaction seemed almost to be one with her love of God. Perhaps no man could understand how, in a good woman, the two streams of the human love which implies the intense desire of the flesh, and the mystical love which is absolutely purged of that desire, can flow the one into the other and mingle their waters. She tried to think that, and then she ceased to try. Everything was forgotten as his arms held her fast in the night, everything except this great force of human love which was like iron, and yet soft about her, which was giving and wanting, which was concentrated upon her to the exclusion of all else, plunging the universe in darkness and setting her in light.

"There is nothing for me to-night but you," he said, crushing her in his arms. "The desert is your garden. To me it has always been your garden, only that, put here for you, and for me because you love me—but for me only because of that."

The Arabs' fire was rapidly dying down.

"When it goes out, when it goes out!" Androvsky whispered in her ear.

His breath stirred the thick tresses of her hair.

"Let us watch it!" he whispered.

She pressed his hand but did not reply. She could not speak any more. At last the something wild and lawless, the something that was more than passionate, that was hot and even savage in her nature, had risen up in its full force to face a similar force in him, which insistently called it and which it answered without shame.

"It is dying," Androvsky said. "It is dying. Look how small the circle of the flame is, how the darkness is creeping up about it! Domini—do you see?"

She pressed his hand again.

"Do you long for the darkness?" he asked. "Do you, Domini? The desert is sending it. The desert is sending it for you, and for me because you love me."

A log in the fire, charred by the flames, broke in two. Part of it fell down into the heart of the fire, which sent up a long tongue of red gold flame.

"That is like us," he said. "Like us together in the darkness."

She felt his body trembling, as if the vehemence of the spirit confined within it shook it. In the night the breeze slightly increased, making the flame of the lamp behind them in the tent flicker. And the breeze was like a message, brought to them from the desert by some envoy in the darkness, telling them not to be afraid of their wonderful gift of freedom with each other, but to take it open-handed, open-hearted, with the great courage of joy.

"Domini, did you feel that gust of the wind? It carried away a cloud of sparks from the fire and brought them a little way towards us. Did you see? Fire wandering on the wind through the night calling to the fire that is in us. Wasn't it beautiful? Everything is beautiful to-night. There were never such stars before."

She looked up at them. Often she had watched the stars, and known the vague longings, the almost terrible aspirations they wake in their watchers. But to her also they looked different to-night, nearer to the earth, she thought, brighter, more living than ever before, like strange tenderness made visible, peopling the night with an unconquerable sympathy. The vast firmament was surely intent upon their happiness. Again the breeze came to them across the waste, cool and breathing of the dryness of the sands. Not far away a jackal laughed. After a pause it was answered by another jackal at a distance. The voices of these desert beasts brought home to Domini with an intimacy not felt by her before the exquisite remoteness of their situation, and the shrill, discordant noise, rising and falling with a sort of melancholy and sneering mirth, mingled with bitterness, was like a delicate music in her ears.

" Hark ! " Androvsky whispered.

The first jackal laughed once more, was answered again. A third beast, evidently much farther off, lifted up a faint voice like a dismal echo. Then there was silence.

" You loved that, Domini. It was like the calling of freedom to you—and to me. We've found freedom; we've found it. Let us feel it. Let us take hold of it. It is the only thing, the only thing. But you can't know that as I do, Domini."

Again she was conscious that his intensity surpassed hers, and the consciousness, instead of saddening or vexing, made her thrill with joy.

" I am maddened by this freedom," he said; " maddened by it, Domini. I can't help—I can't——"

He laid his lips upon hers in a desperate caress that almost suffocated her. Then he took his lips away from her lips and kissed her throat, holding her head back against his shoulder. She shut her eyes. He was indeed teaching her to forget. Even the memory of the day in the garden when she heard the church bell chime and the sound of Larbi's flute went from her. She remembered nothing any more. The past was lost or laid in sleep by the spell of sensation. Her nature galloped like an Arab horse across the sands towards the sun, towards the fire that sheds warmth afar but that devours all that draws near to it. At that moment she connected Androvsky with the tremendous fires eternally blazing in the sun. She had a desire that he

should hurt her in the passionate intensity of his love for her.
Her nature, which till now had been ever ready to spring into
hostility at an accidental touch, which had shrunk instinctively
from physical contact with other human beings, melted, was
utterly transformed. She felt that she was now the opposite of
all that she had been—more woman than any other woman who
had ever lived. What had been an almost cold strength in
her went to increase the completeness of this yielding to one
stronger than herself. What had seemed boyish and almost
hard in her died away utterly under the embrace of this fierce
manhood.

"Domini," he spoke, whispering while he kissed her,
"Domini, the fire's gone out. It's dark."

He lifted her a little in his arms, still kissing her.

"Domini, it's dark, it's dark."

He lifted her more. She stood up, with his arms about
her, looking towards where the fire had been. She put her
hands against his face and softly pressed it back from hers,
but with a touch that was a caress. He yielded to her at
once.

"Look!" he said. "Do you love the darkness? Tell me—
tell me that you love it."

She let her hand glide over his cheek in answer.

"Look at it. Love it. All the desert is in it, and our love
in the desert. Let us stay in the desert, let us stay in it for ever
—for ever. It is your garden—yours. It has brought us everything, Domini."

He took her hand and pressed it again and again over his
cheek lingeringly. Then, abruptly, he dropped it.

"Come!" he said. "Domini."

And he drew her in through the tent door almost violently.

A stronger gust of the night wind followed them. Androvsky
took his arms slowly from Domini and turned to let down the
flap of the tent. While he was doing this she stood quite still.
The flame of the lamp flickered, throwing its light now here,
now there, uneasily. She saw the crucifix lit up for an instant
and the white bed beneath it. The wind stirred her dark hair
and was cold about her neck. But the warmth there met and
defied it. In that brief moment, while Androvsky was fasten-
ing the tent, she seemed to live through centuries of intense and
complicated emotion. When the light flickered over the crucifix she felt as if she could spend her life in passionate adoration
at its foot; but when she did not see it, and the wind, coming

in from the desert through the tent door, where she heard the
movement of Androvsky, stirred in her hair, she felt reckless,
wayward, savage—and something more. A cry rose in her
that was like the cry of a stranger, who yet was of her and
in her, and from whom she would not part.

Again the lamp flame flickered upon the crucifix. Quickly,
while she saw the crucifix plainly, she went forward to the bed
and fell on her knees by it, bending down her face upon its
whiteness.

When Androvsky had fastened the tent door he turned round
and saw her kneeling. He stood quite still as if petrified,
staring at her. Then, as the flame, now sheltered from
the wind, burned steadily, he saw the crucifix. He started as if
someone had struck him, hesitated, then, with a look of fierce
and concentrated resolution on his face, went swiftly to the
crucifix and pulled it from the canvas roughly. He held it in
his hand for an instant, then moved to the tent door and
stooped to unfasten the cords that held it to the pegs, evidently
with the intention of throwing the crucifix out into the night.
But he did not unfasten the cords. Something—some sudden
change of feeling, some secret and powerful reluctance—checked
him. He thrust the crucifix into his pocket. Then, returning
to where Domini was kneeling, he put his arms round her and
drew her to her feet.

She did not resist him. Still holding her in his arms he
blew out the lamp.

CHAPTER XIX

THE Arabs have a saying, " In the desert one forgets every-
things, one remembers nothing any more."

To Domini it sometimes seemed the truest of all the true and
beautiful sayings of the East. Only three weeks had passed
away since the first halt at Arba, yet already her life at Beni-
Mora was faint in her mind as the dream of a distant past.
Taken by the vast solitudes, journeying without definite aim
from one oasis to another through empty regions bathed in
eternal sunshine, camping often in the midst of the sand by one
of the wells sunk for the nomads by the French engineers,
strengthened perpetually, yet perpetually soothed, by airs that
were soft and cool, as if mingled of silk and snow, they lived
surely in a desert dream with only a dream behind them. They
had become as one with the nomads, whose home is the moving

tent, whose hearthstone is the yellow sand of the dunes, whose God is liberty.

Domini loved this life with a love which had already become a passion. All that she had imagined that the desert might be to her she found that it was. In its so-called monotony she discovered eternal interest. Of old she had thought the sea the most wonderful thing in Nature. In the desert she seemed to possess the sea with something added to it, a calm, a completeness, a mystical tenderness, a passionate serenity. She thought of the sea as a soul striving to fulfil its noblest aspirations, to be the splendid thing it knew how to dream of. But she thought of the desert as a soul that need strive no more, having attained. And she, like the Arabs, called it always in her heart the Garden of Allah. For in this wonderful calm, bright as the child's idea of heaven, clear as a crystal with a sunbeam caught in it, silent as a prayer that will be answered silently, God seemed to draw very near to his wandering children. In the desert was the still, small voice, and the still, small voice was the Lord.

Often at dawn or sundown, when, perhaps in the distance of the sands, or near at hand beneath the shade of the palms of some oasis by a waterspring, she watched the desert men in their patched rags, with their lean, bronzed faces and eagle eyes turned towards Mecca, bowing their heads in prayer to the soil that the sun made hot, she remembered Count Anteoni's words, " I like to see men praying in the desert," and she understood with all her heart and soul why. For the life of the desert was the most perfect liberty that could be found on earth, and to see men thus worshipping in liberty set before her a vision of free will upon the heights. When she thought of the world she had known and left, of the men who would always live in it and know no other world, she was saddened for a moment. Could she ever find elsewhere such joy as she had found in the simple and unfettered life of the wastes? Could she ever exchange this life for another life, even with Androvsky?

One day she spoke to him of her intense joy in the wandering fate, and the pain that came to her whenever she thought of exchanging it for a life of civilisation in the midst of fixed groups of men.

They had halted for the noonday rest at a place called Sidi-Hamdam, and in the afternoon were going to ride on to a Bordj called Mogar, where they meant to stay two or three days, as Batouch had told them it was a good halting-place, and near to haunts of the gazelle. The tents had already gone forward, and

Domini and Androvsky were lying upon a rug spread on the sand, in the shadow of the grey wall of a traveller's house beside a well. Behind them their horses were tethered to an iron ring in the wall. Batouch and Ali were in the court of the house, talking to the Arab guardian who dwelt there, but their voices were not audible by the well, and absolute silence reigned, the intense yet light silence that is in the desert at noontide, when the sun is at the zenith, when the nomad sleeps under his low-pitched tent, and the gardeners in the oasis cease even from pretending to work among the palms. From before the well the ground sank to a plain of pale grey sand, which stretched away to a village hard in aspect, as if carved out of bronze and all in one piece. In the centre of it rose a mosque with a minaret and a number of cupolas, faintly gilded and shining modestly under the fierce rays of the sun.

At the foot of the village the ground was white with salt-petre, which resembled a covering of new-fallen snow. To right and left of it were isolated groups of palms growing in threes and fours, like trees that had formed themselves into cliques and set careful barriers of sand between themselves and their despised brethren. Here and there on the grey sand dark patches showed where nomads had pitched their tents. But there was no movement of human life. No camels were visible. No guard dogs barked. The noon held all things in its golden grip.

"Boris!" Domini said, breaking a long silence.

"Yes, Domini?"

He turned towards her on the rug, stretching his long, thin body lazily as if in supreme physical contentment.

"You know that saying of the Arabs about forgetting everything in the desert?"

"Yes, Domini, I know it."

"How long shall we stay in this world of forgetfulness?"

He lifted himself up on his elbow quickly, and fixed his eyes on hers.

"How long!"

"Yes."

"But—do you wish to leave it? Are you tired of it?"

There was a note of sharp anxiety in his voice.

"I don't answer such a question," she said, smiling at him.

"Ah, then, why do you try to frighten me?"

She put her hand in his.

"How burnt you are!" she said. "You are like an Arab of the South."

"Let me become more like one. There's health here."

"And peace, perfect peace."

He said nothing. He was looking down now at the sand.

She laid her lips on his warm brown hand.

"There's all I want here," she added.

"Let us stay here."

"But some day we must go back, mustn't we?"

"Why?"

"Can anything be lifelong—even our honeymoon?"

"Suppose we choose that it shall be?"

"Can we choose such a thing? Is anybody allowed to choose to live always quite happily without duties? Sometimes I wonder. I love this wandering life so much, I am so happy in it, that I sometimes think it cannot last much longer."

He began to sift the sand through his fingers swiftly.

"Duties?" he said in a low voice.

"Yes. Oughtn't we to do something presently, something besides being happy?"

"What do you mean, Domini?"

"I hardly know, I don't know. You tell me."

There was an urging in her voice, as if she wanted, almost demanded, something of him.

"You mean that a man must do some work in his life if he is to keep himself a man," he said, not as if he were asking a question.

He spoke reluctantly but firmly.

"You know," he added, "that I have worked hard all my life, hard like a labourer."

"Yes, I know," she said.

She stroked his hand, that was worn and rough, and spoke eloquently of manual toil it had accomplished in the past.

"I know. Before we were married, that day when we sat in the garden, you told me your life and I told you mine. How different they have been!"

"Yes," he said.

He lit a cigar and watched the smoke curling up into the gold of the sunlit atmosphere.

"Mine in the midst of the world and yours so far away from it. I often imagine that little place, El Krori, the garden, your brother, your twin-brother Stephen, that one-eyed Arab servant—what was his name?"

" El Magin."

" Yes, El Magin, who taught you to play Cora and to sing Arab songs, and to eat cous-cous with your fingers. I can almost see Father André, from whom you learnt to love the Classics, and who talked to you of philosophy. He's dead too, isn't he, like your mother? "

" I don't know whether Père André is dead. I have lost sight of him," Androvsky said.

He still looked steadily at the rings of smoke curling up into the golden air. There was in his voice a sound of embarrassment. She guessed that it came from the consciousness of the pain he must have caused the good priest who had loved him when he ceased from practising the religion in which he had been brought up. Even to her he never spoke frankly on religious subjects, but she knew that he had been baptised a Catholic and been educated for a time by priests. She knew, too, that he was no longer a practising Catholic, and that, for some reason, he dreaded any intimacy with priests. He never spoke against them. He had scarcely ever spoken of them to her. But she remembered his words in the garden, " I do not care for priests." She remembered, too, his action in the tunnel on the day of his arrival in Beni-Mora. And the reticence that they both preserved on the subject of religion, and its reason, were the only causes of regret in this desert dream of hers. Even this regret, too, often faded in hope. For in the desert, the Garden of Allah, she had it borne in upon her that Androvsky would discover what he must surely secretly be seeking—the truth that each man must find for himself, truth for him of the eventual existence in which the mysteries of this present existence will be made plain, and of the Power that has fashioned all things.

And she was able to hope in silence, as women do for the men they love.

" Don't think I do not realise that you have worked," she went on after a pause. " You told me how you always cultivated the land yourself, even when you were still a boy, that you directed the Spanish labourers in the vineyards, that—you have earned a long holiday. But should it last for ever? "

" You are right. Well, let us take an oasis; let us become palm gardeners like that Frenchman at Meskoutine."

" And build ourselves an African house, white, with a terrace roof."

" And sell our dates. We can give employment to the Arabs

We can choose the poorest. We can improve their lives. After all, if we owe a debt to anyone it is to them, to the desert. Let us pay our debt to the desert men and live in the desert."

"It would be an ideal life," she said with her eyes shining on his.

"And a possible life. Let us live it. I could not bear to leave the desert. Where should we go?"

"Where should we go!" she repeated.

She was still looking at him, but now the expression of her eyes had quite changed. They had become grave, and examined him seriously with a sort of deep inquiry. He sat upon the Arab rug, leaning his back against the wall of the traveller's house.

"Why do you look at me like that, Domini?" he asked with a sudden stirring of something that was like uneasiness.

"I! I was wondering what you would like, what other life would suit you."

"Yes?" he said quickly. "Yes?"

"It's very strange, Boris, but I cannot connect you with anything but the desert, or see you anywhere but in the desert. I cannot even imagine you among your vines in Tunisia."

"They were not altogether mine," he corrected, still with a certain excitement which he evidently endeavoured to repress. "I—I had the right, the duty of cultivating the land."

"Well, however it was, you were always at work; you were responsible, weren't you?"

"Yes."

"I can't see you even in the vineyards or the wheat-fields. Isn't it strange?"

She was always looking at him with the same deep and wholly unself-conscious inquiry.

"And as to London, Paris——"

Suddenly she burst into a little laugh and her gravity vanished.

"I think you would hate them," she said. "And they—they wouldn't like you because they wouldn't understand you."

"Let us buy our oasis," he said abruptly. "Build our African house, sell our dates and remain in the desert. I hear Batouch. It must be time to ride on to Mogar. Batouch! Batouch!"

Batouch came from the courtyard of the house wiping the remains of a cous-cous from his languid lips.

"Untie the horses," said Androvsky.

"But, Monsieur, it is still too hot to travel. Look! No one is stirring. All the village is asleep."

He waved his enormous hand, with henna-tinted nails, towards the distant town, carved surely out of one huge piece of bronze.

"Untie the horses. There are gazelle in the plain near Mogar. Didn't you tell me?"

"Yes, Monsieur, but——"

"We'll get there early and go out after them at sunset. Now, Domini."

They rode away in the burning heat of the noon towards the southwest across the vast plains of grey sand, followed at a short distance by Batouch and Ali.

"Monsieur is mad to start in the noon," grumbled Batouch. "But Monsieur is not like Madame. He may live in the desert till he is old and his hair is grey as the sand, but he will never be an Arab in his heart."

"Why, Batouch-ben-Brahim?"

"He cannot rest. To Madame the desert gives its calm, but to Monsieur——" He did not finish his sentence. In front Domini and Androvsky had put their horses to a gallop. The sand flew up in a thin cloud around them.

"Nom d'un chien!" said Batouch, who, in unpoetical moments, occasionally indulged in the expletives of the French infidels who were his country's rulers. "What is there in the mind of Monsieur which makes him ride as if he fled from an enemy?"

"I know not, but he goes like a hare before the sloughi, Batouch-ben Brahim," answered Ali, gravely.

Then they sent their horses on in chase of the cloud of sand towards the southwest.

About four in the afternoon they reached the camp at Mogar.

As they rode in slowly, for their horses were tired and streaming with heat after their long canter across the sands, both Domini and Androvsky were struck by the novelty of this halting-place, which was quite unlike anything they had yet seen. The ground rose gently but continuously for a considerable time before they saw in the distance the pitched tents with the dark forms of the camels and mules. Here they were out of the sands, and upon hard, sterile soil covered with small stones embedded in the earth. Beyond the tents they could see nothing but the sky, which was now covered with small, ribbed grey clouds, sad-coloured and autumnal, and a lonely tower built of stone, which rose from the waste at about two hundred yards from the tents to the east. Although they could see so little, however, they were impressed with a sensation that they were on the edge of some vast vision, of some grandiose effect of Nature, that would bring to them a new and astonishing knowledge of the desert. Perhaps it was the sight of the distant tower pointing to the grey clouds that stirred in them this almost excited feeling of expectation.

" It is like a watch-tower," Domini said, pointing with her whip. " But who could live in such a place, far from any oasis? "

" And what can it overlook? " said Androvsky. " This is the nearest horizon line we have seen since we came into the desert."

" Yes, but——"

She glanced at him as they put their horses into a gentle canter. Then she added:

" You, too, feel that we are coming to something tremendous, don't you? "

Her horse whinnied shrilly. Domini stroked his foam-flecked neck with her hand.

" Abou is as full of anticipation as we are," she said. Androvsky was looking towards the tower.

" That was built for French soldiers," he said. A moment afterwards he added:

" I wonder why Batouch chose this place for us to camp in? " There was a faint sound as of irritation in his voice.

" Perhaps we shall know in a minute," Domini answered. They cantered on. Their horses' hoofs rang with a hard sound on the stony ground.

" It's inhospitable here," Androvsky said. She looked at him in surprise.

" I never knew you to take a dislike to any halting-place before," she said. " What's the matter, Boris? "

He smiled at her, but almost immediately his face was clouded by the shadow of a gloom that seemed to respond to the gloom of the sky. And he fixed his eyes again upon the tower.

" I like a far horizon," he answered. " And there's no sun to-day."

" I suppose even in the desert we cannot have it always," she said. And in her voice, too, there was a touch of melancholy, as if she had caught his mood. A minute later she added:

" I feel exactly as if I were on a hill top and were coming to a view of the sea."

Almost as she spoke they cantered in among the tents of the

attendants, and reined in their horses at the edge of a slope that was almost a precipice. Then they sat still in their saddles, gazing.

They had been living for weeks in the midst of vastness, and had become accustomed to see stretched out around them immense tracts of land melting away into far blue distances, but this view from Mogar made them catch their breath and stirred their pulses.

It was gigantic. There was even something unnatural in its appearance of immensity, as if it were, perhaps, deceptive, and existed in their vision of it only. So, surely, might look a plain to one who had taken haschish, which enlarges, makes monstrous and threateningly terrific. Domini had a feeling that no human eyes could really see such infinite tracts of land and water as those she seemed to be seeing at this moment. For there was water here, in the midst of the desert. Infinite expanses of sea met infinite plains of snow. Or so it seemed to both of them. And the sea was grey and calm as a winter sea, breathing its plaint along a winter land. From it, here and there, rose islets whose low cliffs were a deep red like the red of sandstone, a sad colour that suggests tragedy, islets that looked desolate, and as if no life had ever been upon them, or could be. Back from the snowy plains stretched sand dunes of the palest primrose colour, sand dunes innumerable, myriads and myriads of them, rising and falling, rising and falling, till they were lost in the grey distance of this silent world. In the foreground, at their horses' feet, wound from the hill summit a broad track faintly marked in the deep sand, and flanked by huge dunes shaped, by the action of the winds, into grotesque semblances of monsters, leviathans, beasts with prodigious humps, sphinxes, whales. This track was presently lost in the blanched plains. Far away, immeasurably far, sea and snow blended and faded into the cloudy grey. Above the near dunes two desert eagles were slowly wheeling in a weary flight, occasionally sinking towards the sand, then rising again towards the clouds. And the track was strewn with the bleached bones of camels that had perished, or that had been slaughtered, on some long desert march.

To the left of them the solitary tower commanded this terrific vision of desolation, seemed to watch it steadily, yet furtively, with its tiny loophole eyes.

"We have come into winter," Domini murmured.

She looked at the white of the camels' bones, of the plains, at the grey white of the sky, at the yellow pallor of the dunes.

" How wonderful!   How terrible! " she said.

She drew her horse to one side, a little nearer to Androvsky's.

" Does the Russian in you greet this land? " she asked him.

He did not reply.   He seemed to be held in thrall by the sad immensity before them.

" I realise here what it must be to die in the desert, to be killed by it—by hunger, by thirst in it," she said presently, speaking, as if to herself, and looking out over the mirage sea, the mirage snow.   " This is the first time I have really felt the terror of the desert."

Her horse drooped its head till its nose nearly touched the earth, and shook itself in a long shiver.   She shivered too, as if constrained to echo an animal's distress.

" Things have died here," Androvsky said, speaking at last in a low voice and pointing with his long-lashed whip towards the camels' skeletons.   " Come, Domini, the horses are tired."

He cast another glance at the tower, and they dismounted by their tent, which was pitched at the very edge of the steep slope that sank down to the beast-like shapes of the near dunes.

An hour later Domini said to Androvsky:

" You won't go after gazelle this evening surely? "

They had been having coffee in the tent and had just finished.   Androvsky got up from his chair and went to the tent door.   The grey of the sky was pierced by a gleaming shaft from the sun.

" Do you mind if I go? " he said, turning towards her after a glance to the desert.

" No, but aren't you tired? "

He shook his head.

" I couldn't ride, and now I can ride.   I couldn't shoot, and I'm just beginning——"

" Go," she said quickly.   " Besides, we want gazelle for dinner, Batouch says, though I don't suppose we should starve without it."   She came to the tent door and stood beside him, and he put his arm around her.

" If I were alone here, Boris," she said, leaning against his shoulder, " I believe I should feel horribly sad to-day."

" Shall I stay? "

He pressed her against him.

" No.   I shall know you are coming back.   Oh, how extraordinary it is to think we lived so many years without knowing of each other's existence, that we lived alone.   Were you ever happy? "

He hesitated before he replied.

"I sometimes thought I was."

"But do you think now you ever really were?"

"I don't know—perhaps in a lonely sort of way."

"You can never be happy in that way now?"

He said nothing, but, after a moment, he kissed her long and hard, and as if he wanted to draw her being into his through the door of his lips.

"Good-bye," he said, releasing her. "I shall be back directly after sundown."

"Yes. Don't wait for the dark down there. If you were lost in the dunes!"

She pointed to the distant sand hills rising and falling monotonously to the horizon.

"If you are not back in good time," she said, "I shall stand by the tower and wave a brand from the fire."

"Why by the tower?"

"The ground is highest by the tower."

She watched him ride away on a mule, with two Arabs carrying guns. They went towards the plains of saltpetre that looked like snow beside the sea that was only a mirage. Then she turned back into the tent, took up a volume of Fromentin's, and sat down in a folding-chair at the tent door. She read a little, but it was difficult to read with the mirage beneath her. Perpetually her eyes were attracted from the book to its mystery and plaintive sadness, that was like the sadness of something unearthly, of a spirit that did not move but that suffered. She did not put away the book, but presently she laid it down on her knees, open, and sat gazing. Androvsky had disappeared with the Arabs into some fold of the sands. The sun-ray had vanished with him. Without Androvsky and the sun—she still connected them together, and knew she would for ever.

The melancholy of this desert scene was increased for her till it became oppressive and lay upon her like a heavy weight. She was not a woman inclined to any morbid imaginings. Indeed, all that was morbid roused in her an instinctive disgust. But the sudden greyness of the weather, coming after weeks of ardent sunshine, and combined with the fantastic desolation of the landscape, which was half real and half unreal, turned her for the moment towards a dreariness of spirit that was rare in her.

She realised suddenly, as she looked and did not see Androvsky even as a black and moving speck upon the plain, what the desert would seem to her without him, even in sunshine, the awfulness of the desolation of it, the horror of its distances. And realising this she also realised the uncertainty of the human life in connection with any other human life. To be dependent on another is to double the sum of the terrors of uncertainty. She had done that.

If the immeasurable sands took Androvsky and never gave him back to her! What would she do?

She gazed at the mirage sea with its dim red islands, and at the sad white plains along its edge.

Winter—she would be plunged in eternal winter. And each human life hangs on a thread. All deep love, all consuming passion, holds a great fear within the circle of a great glory. To-day the fear within the circle of her glory seemed to grow. But she suddenly realised that she ought to dominate it, to confine it—as it were—to its original and permanent proportions.

She got up, came out upon the edge of the hill, and walked along it slowly towards the tower.

Outside, freed from the shadow of the tent, she felt less oppressed, though still melancholy, and even slightly apprehensive, as if some trouble were coming to her and were near at hand. Mentally she had made the tower the limit of her walk, and therefore when she reached it she stood still.

It was a squat, square tower, strongly constructed, with loopholes in the four sides, and now that she was by it she saw built out at the back of it a low house with small shuttered windows and a narrow courtyard for mules. No doubt Androvsky was right and French soldiers had once been here to work the optic telegraph. She thought of the recruits and of Marseilles, of Notre Dame de la Garde, the Mother of God, looking towards Africa. Such recruits came to live in such strange houses as this tower lost in the desert and now abandoned. She glanced at the shuttered windows and turned back towards the tent; but something in the situation of the tower—perhaps the fact that it was set on the highest point of the ground—attracted her, and she presently made Batouch bring her out some rugs and ensconced herself under its shadow, facing the mirage sea.

How long she sat there she did not know. Mirage hypnotises the imaginative and suggests to them dreams strange and ethereal, sad sometimes, as itself. How long she might have sat there dreaming, but for an interruption, she knew still less. It was towards evening, however, but before evening had fallen, that a weary and travel-stained party of three French soldiers,

Zouaves, and an officer rode slowly up the sandy track from the
dunes. They were mounted on mules, and carried their small
baggage with them on two led mules. When they reached the
top of the hill they turned to the right and came towards the
tower. The officer was a little in advance of his men. He was
a smart-looking, fair man of perhaps thirty-two, with blonde
moustaches, blue eyes with blonde lashes, and hair very much
the colour of the sand dunes. His face was bright red, burnt,
as a fair delicate skin burns, by the sun. His eyes, although protected by large sun spectacles, were inflamed. The skin was
peeling from his nose. His hair was full of sand, and he rode
leaning forward over his animal's neck, holding the reins loosely
in his hands, that seemed nerveless from fatigue. Yet he looked
smart and well-bred despite his evident exhaustion, as if on
parade he would be a dashing officer. It was evident that both
he and his men were riding in from some tremendous journey.
The latter looked dog-tired, scarcely human in their collapse.
They kept on their mules with difficulty, shaking this way and
that like sacks, with their unshaven chins wagging loosely up and
down. But as they saw the tower they began to sing in chorus
half under their breath, and leaning their broad hands on the
necks of the beasts for support they looked with a sort of
haggard eagerness in its direction.

Domini was roused from her contemplation of the mirage
and the day-dreams it suggested by the approach of this small
cavalcade. The officer was almost upon her ere she heard the
clatter of his mule among the stones. She looked up, startled,
and he looked down, even more surprised, apparently, to see a
lady ensconced at the foot of the tower. His astonishment and
exhaustion did not, however, get the better of his instinctive
good breeding, and sitting straight up in the saddle he took off
his sun helmet and asked Domini's pardon for disturbing her.

"But this is my home for the night, Madame," he added, at
the same time drawing a key from the pocket of his loose trousers.
"And I'm thankful to reach it. *Ma foi!* there have been several
moments in the last days when I never thought to see Mogar."

Slowly he swung himself off his mule and stood up, catching
on to the saddle with one hand.

"F-f-f-f!" he said, pursing his lips. "I can hardly stand.
Excuse me, Madame."

Domini had got up.

"You are tired out," she said, looking at him and his men,
who had now come up, with interest.

"Pretty well indeed. We have been three days lost in the great dunes in a sand-storm, and hit the track here just as we were preparing for a—well, a great event."

"A great event?" said Domini.

"The last in a man's life, Madame."

He spoke simply, even with a light touch of humour that was almost cynical, but she felt beneath his words and manner a solemnity and a thankfulness that attracted and moved her.

"Those terrible dunes!" she said.

And, turning, she looked out over them.

There was no sunset, but the deepening of the grey into a dimness that seemed to have blackness behind it, the more ghastly hue of the white plains of saltpetre, and the fading of the mirage sea, whose islands now looked no longer red, but dull brown specks in a pale mist, hinted at the rapid falling of night.

"My husband is out in them," she added.

"Your husband, Madame!"

He looked at her rather narrowly, shifted from one leg to the other as if tryng his strength, then added:

"Not far, though, I suppose. For I see you have a camp here."

"He has only gone after gazelle."

As she said the last word she saw one of the soldiers, a mere boy, lick his lips and give a sort of tragic wink at his companions. A sudden thought struck her.

"Don't think me impertinent, Monsieur, but—what about provisions in your tower?"

"Oh, as to that, Madame, we shall do well enough. Here, open the door, Marelle!"

And he gave the key to a soldier, who wearily dismounted and thrust it into the door of the tower.

"But after three days in the dunes! Your provisions must be exhausted unless you've been able to replenish them."

"You are too good, Madame. We shall manage a cous-cous."

"And wine? Have you any wine?"

She glanced again at the exhausted soldiers covered with sand and saw that their eyes were fixed upon her and were shining eagerly. All the "good fellow" in her nature rose up.

"You must let me send you some," she said. "We have plenty."

She thought of some bottles of champagne they had brought with them and never opened.

"In the desert we are all comrades," she added, as if speaking to the soldiers.

They looked at her with an open adoration which lit up their tired faces.

"Madame," said the officer, "you are much too good; but I accept your offer as frankly as you have made it. A little wine will be a godsend to us to-night. Thank you, Madame."

The soldiers looked as if they were going to cheer.

"I'll go to the camp——"

"Cannot one of the men go for you, Madame? You were sitting here. Pray, do not let us disturb you."

"But night is falling and I shall have to go back in a moment."

While they had been speaking the darkness had rapidly increased. She looked towards the distant dunes and no longer saw them. At once her mind went to Androvsky. Why had he not returned? She thought of the signal. From the camp, behind their sleeping-tent, rose the flames of a newly-made fire.

"If one of your men can go and tell Batouch—Batouch—to come to me here I shall be grateful," she answered. "And I want him to bring me a big brand from the fire over there."

She saw wonder dawning in the eyes fixed upon her, and smiled.

"I want to signal to my husband," she said, "and this is the highest point. He will see it best if I stand here."

"Go, Marelle, ask for Batouch, and be sure you bring the brand from the fire."

The man saluted and rode off with alacrity. The thought of wine had infused a gaiety into him and his companions.

"Now, Monsieur, don't stand on ceremony," Domini said to the officer. "Go in and make your toilet. You are longing to, I know."

"I am longing to look a little more decent—now, Madame," he said gallantly, and gazing at her with a sparkle of admiration in his inflamed eyes. "You will let me return in a moment to escort you to the camp."

"Thank you."

"Will you permit me—my name is De Trevignac."

"And mine is Madame Androvsky."

"Russian!" the officer said. "The alliance in the desert Vive la Russie!"

She laughed.

"That is for my husband, for I am English."

"Vive l'Angleterre!" he said.

The two soldiers echoed his words impulsively, lifting up in the gathering darkness hoarse voices.

" Vive l'Angleterre! "

" Thank you, thank you," she said.   " Now, Monsieur, please don't let me keep you."

" I shall be back directly," the officer replied.

And he turned and went into the tower, while the soldiers rode round to the court, tugging at the cords of the led mules.

Domini waited for the return of Marelle. Her mood had changed. A glow of cordial humanity chased away her melancholy. The hostess that lurks in every woman—that housewife-hostess sense which goes hand-in-hand with the mother sense—was alive in her. She was keenly anxious to play the good fairy simply, unostentatiously, to these exhausted men who had come to Mogar out of the jaws of Death, to see their weary faces shine under the influence of repose and good cheer. But the tower looked desolate. The camp was gayer, cosier. Suddenly she resolved to invite them all to dine in the camp that night.

Marelle returned with Batouch. She saw them from a distance coming through the darkness with blazing torches in their hands. When they came to her she said:

" Batouch, I want you to order dinner in camp for the soldiers."

A broad and radiant smile irradiated the blunt Breton features of Marelle.

" And Monsieur the officer will dine with me and Monsieur. Give us all you can. Perhaps there will be some gazelle."

She saw him opening his lips to say that the dinner would be poor and stopped him.

" You are to open some of the champagne—the Pommery. We will drink to all safe returns. Now, give me the brand and go and tell the cook."

As he took his torch and disappeared into the darkness De Trevignac came out from the tower. He still looked exhausted and walked with some difficulty, but he had washed the sand from his face with water from the artesian well behind the tower, changed his uniform, brushed the sand from his yellow hair, and put on a smart gold-laced cap instead of his sun-helmet. The spectacles were gone from his eyes, and between his lips was a large Havana—his last, kept by him among the dunes as a possible solace in the dreadful hour of death.

" Monsieur de Trevignac, I want you to dine with us in camp to-night—only to dine. We won't keep you from your bed one moment after the coffee and the cognac. You must seal the triple alliance—France, Russia, England—in some champagne."

She had spoken gaily, cordially. She added more gravely:

" One doesn't escape from death among the dunes every day. Will you come? "

She held out her hand frankly, as a man might to another man. He pressed it as a man presses a woman's hand when he is feeling very soft and tender.

" Madame, what can I say, but that you are too good to us poor fellows and that you will find it very difficult to get rid of us, for we shall be so happy in your camp that we shall forget all about our tower."

" That's settled then."

With the brand in her hand she walked to the edge of the hill. De Trevignac followed her. He had taken the other brand from Marelle. They stood side by side, overlooking the immense desolation that was now almost hidden in the night.

" You are going to signal to your husband, Madame? "

" Yes."

" Let me do it for you. See, I have the other brand! "

" Thank you—but I will do it."

In the light of the flame that leaped up as if striving to touch her face he saw a light in her eyes that he understood, and he drooped his torch towards the earth while she lifted hers on high and waved it in the blackness.

He watched her. The tall, strong, but exquisitely supple figure, the uplifted arm with the torch sending forth a long tongue of golden flame, the ardent and unconscious pose, that set before him a warm passionate heart calling to another heart without shame, made him think of her as some Goddess of the Sahara. He had let his torch droop towards the earth, but, as she waved hers, he had an irresistible impulse to join her in the action she made heroic and superb. And presently he lifted his torch, too, and waved it beside hers in the night.

She smiled at him in the flames.

" He must see them surely," she said.

From below, in the distance of the desert, there rose a loud cry in a strong man's voice.

" Aha! " she exclaimed.

She called out in return in a warm, powerful voice. The man's voice answered, nearer. She dropped her brand to the earth.

" Monsieur, you will come then—in half an hour? "

" Madame, with the most heartfelt pleasure. But let me accompany——"

" No, I am quite safe. And bring your men with you. We'll make the best feast we can for them. And there's enough champagne for all."

Then she went away quickly, eagerly, into the darkness.

" To be her husband! " murmured De Trevignac. " Lucky— lucky fellow!" And he dropped his brand beside hers on the ground, and stood watching the two flames mingle.

" Lucky—lucky fellow!" he said again aloud. " I wonder what he's like."

CHAPTER XX

WHEN Domini reached the camp she found it in a bustle. Batouch, resigned to the inevitable, had put the cook upon his mettle. Ouardi was already to be seen with a bottle of Pommery in each hand, and was only prevented from instantly uncorking them by the representations of his mistress and an elaborate exposition of the peculiar and evanescent virtues of champagne. Ali was humming a mysterious song about a love-sick camel-man, with which he intended to make glad the hearts of the assembly when the halting time was over. And the dining-table was already set for three.

When Androvsky rode in with the Arabs Domini met him at the edge of the hill.

" You saw my signal, Boris? "

" Yes——"

He was going to say more, when she interrupted him eagerly.

" Have you any gazelle? Ah——"

Across the mule of one of the Arabs she saw a body drooping, a delicate head with thin, pointed horns, tiny legs with exquisite little feet that moved as the mule moved.

" We shall want it to-night. Take it quickly to the cook's tent, Ahmed." Androvsky got off his mule.

" There's a light in the tower! " he said, looking at her and then dropping his eyes.

" Yes."

" And I saw two signals. There were two brands being waved together."

" To-night we have comrades in the desert."

" Comrades! " he said.

His voice sounded startled.

" Men who have escaped from a horrible death in the dunes."

" Arabs? "

" French."

Quickly she told him her story. He listened in silence. When she had finished he said nothing. But she saw him look at the dining-table laid for three and his expression was dark and gloomy.

" Boris, you don't mind! " she said in surprise. " Surely you would not refuse hospitality to these poor fellows! "

She put her hand through his arm and pressed it.

" Have I done wrong? But I know I haven't! "

" Wrong! How could you do that? "

He seemed to make an effort, to conquer something within him.

" It's I who am wrong, Domini. The truth is, I can't bear our happiness to be intruded upon even for a night. I want to be alone with you. This life of ours in the desert has made me desperately selfish. I want to be alone, quite alone, with you."

" It's that! How glad I am! "

She laid her cheek against his arm.

" Then," he said, " that other signal? "

" Monsieur de Trevignac gave it."

Androvsky took his arm from hers abruptly.

" Monsieur de Trevignac! " he said. " Monsieur do Trevignac? "

He stood as if in deep and anxious thought.

" Yes, the officer. That's his name. What is it, Boris? "

" Nothing."

There was a sound of voices approaching the camp in the darkness. They were speaking French.

" I must," said Androvsky, " I must——"

He made an uncertain movement, as if to go towards the dunes, checked it, and went hurriedly into the dressing-tent. As he disappeared De Trevignac came into the camp with his men. Batouch conducted the latter with all ceremony towards the fire which burned before the tents of the attendants, and, for the moment, Domini was left alone with De Trevignac.

" My husband is coming directly," she said. " He was late in returning, but he brought gazelle. Now you must sit down at once."

She led the way to the dining-tent. De Trevignac glanced

at the table laid for three with an eager anticipation which he
was far too natural to try to conceal.

"Madame," he said, "if I disgrace myself to-night, if I eat
like an ogre in a fairy tale, will you forgive me?"

"I will not forgive you if you don't."

She spoke gaily, made him sit down in a folding-chair, and
insisted on putting a soft cushion at his back. Her manner was
cheerful, almost eagerly kind and full of a *camaraderie* rare in a
woman, yet he noticed a change in her since they stood together
waving the brands by the tower. And he said to himself:

"The husband—perhaps he's not so pleased at my appearance. I wonder how long they've been married?"

And he felt his curiosity to see "Monsieur Androvsky"
deepen.

While they waited for him Domini made De Trevignac tell
her the story of his terrible adventure in the dunes. He did so
simply, like a soldier, without exaggeration. When he had
finished she said:

"You thought death was certain then?"

"Quite certain, Madame."

She looked at him earnestly.

"To have faced a death like that in utter desolation, utter
loneliness, must make life seem very different afterwards."

"Yes, Madame. But I did not feel utterly alone."

"Your men!"

"No, Madame."

After a pause he added, simply:

"My mother is a devout Catholic, Madame. I am her only
child, and—she taught me long ago that in any peril one is never
quite alone."

Domini's heart warmed to him. She loved this trust in God
so frankly shown by a soldier, member of an African regiment,
in this wild land. She loved this brave reliance on the unseen in
the midst of the terror of the seen. Before they spoke again
Androvsky crossed the dark space between the tents and came
slowly into the circle of the lamplight.

De Trevignac got up from his chair, and Domini introduced
the two men. As they bowed each shot a swift glance at the
other. Then Androvsky looked down, and two vertical lines
appeared on his high forehead above his eyebrows. They gave
to his face a sudden look of acute distress. De Trevignac
thanked him for his proffered hospitality with the ease of a man
of the world, assuming that the kind invitation to him and to his

men came from the husband as well as from the wife. When he had finished speaking, Androvsky, without looking up, said, in a voice that sounded to Domini new, as if he had deliberately assumed it:

"I am glad, Monsieur. We found gazelle, and so I hope—I hope you will have a fairly good dinner."

The words could scarcely have been more ordinary, but the way in which they were uttered was so strange, sounded indeed so forced, and so unnatural, that both De Trevignac and Domini looked at the speaker in surprise. There was a pause. Then Batouch and Ouardí came in with the soup.

"Come!" Domini said. "Let us begin. Monsieur de Trevignac, will you sit here on my right?"

They sat down. The two men were opposite to each other at the ends of the small table, with a lamp between them. Domini faced the tent door, and could see in the distance the tents of the attendants lit up by the blaze of the fire, and the forms of the French soldiers sitting at their table close to it, with the Arabs clustering round them. Sounds of loud conversation and occasional roars of laughter, that was almost childish in its frank lack of all restraint, told her that one feast was a success. She looked at her companions and made a sudden resolve—almost fierce—that the other, over which she was presiding, should be a success, too. But why was Androvsky so strange with other men? Why did he seem to become almost a different human being directly he was brought into any close contact with his kind? Was it shyness? Had he a profound hatred of all society? She remembered Count Anteoni's luncheon and the distress Androvsky had caused her by his cold embarrassment, his unwillingness to join in conversation on that occasion. But then he was only her friend. Now he was her husband. She longed for him to show himself at his best. That he was not a man of the world she knew. Had he not told her of his simple upbringing in El Kreír, a remote village of Tunisia, by a mother who had been left in poverty after the death of his father, a Russian who had come to Africa to make a fortune by vine-growing, and who had had his hopes blasted by three years of drought and by the visitation of the dreaded phylloxera? Had he not told her of his own hard work on the rich uplands among the Spanish workmen, of how he had toiled early and late in all kinds of weather, not for himself, but for a company that drew a fortune from the land and gave him a bare livelihood? Till she met him he had never travelled—he had never seen almost anything of life. A legacy from a relative had at last enabled him to have some freedom and to gratify a man's natural taste for change. And, strangely, perhaps, he had come first to the desert. She could not—she did not—expect him to show the sort of easy cultivation that a man acquires only by long contact with all sorts and conditions of men and women. But she knew that he was not only full of fire and feeling—a man with a great temperament, but also that he was a man who had found time to study, whose mind was not empty. He was a man who had thought profoundly. She knew this, although even with her, even in the great intimacy that is born of a great mutual passion, she knew him for a man of naturally deep reserve, who could not perhaps speak all his thoughts to anyone, even to the woman he loved. And knowing this, she felt a fighting temper rise up in her. She resolved to use her will upon this man who loved her, to force him to show his best side to the guest who had come to them out of the terror of the dunes. She would be obstinate for him.

Her lips went down a little at the corners. De Trevignac glanced at her above his soup-plate, and then at Androvsky. He was a man who had seen much of society, and who divined at once the gulf that must have separated the kind of life led in the past by his hostess from the kind of life led by his host. Such gulfs, he knew, are bridged with difficulty. In this case a great love must have been the bridge. His interest in these two people, encountered by him in the desolation of the wastes, and when all his emotions had been roused by the nearness of peril, would have been deep in any case. But there was something that made it extraordinary, something connected with Androvsky. It seemed to him that he had seen, perhaps known Androvsky at some time in his life. Yet Androvsky's face was not familiar to him. He could not yet tell from what he drew this impression, but it was strong. He searched his memory.

Just at first fatigue was heavy upon him, but the hot soup, the first glass of wine revived him. When Domini, full of her secret obstinacy, began to talk gaily he was soon able easily to take his part, and to join her in her effort to include Androvsky in the conversation. The cheerful noise of the camp came to them from without.

" I'm afraid my men are lifting up their voices rather loudly," said De Trevignac.

" We like it," said Domini. " Don't we, Boris? "

There was a long peal of laughter from the distance. As it

died away Batouch's peculiar guttural chuckle, which had something negroid in it, was audible, prolonging itself in a loneliness that spoke his pertinacious sense of humour.

"Certainly," said Androvsky, still in the same strained and unnatural voice which had surprised Domini when she introduced the two men. "We are accustomed to gaiety round the camp fire."

"You are making a long stay in the desert, Monsieur?" asked De Trevignac.

"I hope so, Monsieur. It depends on my—it depends on Madame Androvsky."

"Why didn't he say 'my wife'?" thought De Trevignac. And again he searched his memory. Had he ever met this man? If so, where?

"I should like to stay in the desert for ever," Domini said quickly, with a long look at her husband.

"I should not, Madame," De Trevignac said.

"I understand. The desert has shown you its terrors."

"Indeed it has."

"But to us it has only shown its enchantment. Hasn't it?" She spoke to Androvsky. After a pause he replied:

"Yes."

The word, when it came, sounded like a lie.

For the first time since her marriage Domini felt a cold, like a cold of ice about her heart. Was it possible that Androvsky had not shared her joy in the desert? Had she been alone in her happiness? For a moment she sat like one stunned by a blow. Then knowledge, reason, spoke in her. She knew of Androvsky's happiness with her, knew it absolutely. There are some things in which a woman cannot be deceived. When Androvsky was with her he wanted no other human being. Nothing could take that certainty from her.

"Of course," she said, recovered, "there are places in the desert in which melancholy seems to brood, in which one has a sense of the terrors of the wastes. Mogar, I think, is one of them, perhaps the only one we have been in yet. This evening, when I was sitting under the tower, even I "—and as she said "even I " she smiled happily at Androvsky—"knew some forebodings."

"Forebodings?" Androvsky said quickly. "Why should you——?" He broke off.

"Not of coming misfortune, I hope, Madame?" said De Trevignac in a voice that was now irresistibly cheerful.

He was helping himself to some gazelle, which sent forth an appetising odour, and Ouardi was proudly pouring out for him the first glass of blithely winking champagne.

"I hardly know, but everything looked sad and strange; I began to think about the uncertainties of life."

Domini and De Trevignac were sipping their champagne. Ouardi came behind Androvsky to fill his glass.

"Non! non!" he said, putting his hand over it and shaking his head.

De Trevignac started.

Ouardi looked at Domini and made a distressed grimace, pointing with a brown finger at the glass.

"Oh, Boris! you must drink champagne to-night!" she exclaimed.

"I would rather not," he answered. "I am not accustomed to it."

"But to drink our guest's health after his escape from death!"

Androvsky took his hand from the glass and Ouardi filled it with wine.

Then Domini raised her glass and drank to De Trevignac. Androvsky followed her example, but without geniality, and when he put his lips to the wine he scarcely tasted it. Then he put the glass down and told Ouardi to give him red wine. And during the rest of the evening he drank no more champagne. He also ate very little, much less than usual, for in the desert they both had the appetites of hunters.

After thanking them cordially for drinking his health, De Trevignac said:

"I was nearly experiencing the certainty of death. But was it Mogar that turned you to such thoughts, Madame?"

"I think so. There is something sad, even portentous about it."

She looked towards the tent door, imagining the immense desolation that was hidden in the darkness outside, the white plains, the mirage sea, the sand dunes like monsters, the bleached bones of the dead camels with the eagles hovering above them.

"Don't you think so, Boris? Don't you think it looks like a place in which—like a tragic place, a place in which tragedies ought to occur?"

"It is not places that make tragedies," he said, "or at least they make tragedies far more seldom than the people in them."

He stopped, seemed to make an effort to throw off his taciturnity, and suddenly to be able to throw it off, at least partially. For he continued speaking with greater naturalness and ease, even with a certain dominating force.

"If people would use their wills they need not be influenced by place, they need not be governed by a thousand things, by memories, by fears, by fancies—yes, even by fancies that are the merest shadows, but out of which they make phantoms. Half the terrors and miseries of life lie only in the minds of men. They even cause the very tragedies they would avoid by expecting them."

He said the last words with a sort of strong contempt—then, more quietly, he added:

"You, Domini, why should you feel the uncertainty of life, especially at Mogar? You need not. You can choose not to. Life is the same in its chances here as everywhere?"

"But you," she answered—"did you not feel a tragic influence when we arrived here? Do you remember how you looked at the tower?"

"The tower!" he said, with a quick glance at De Trevignac. "I—why should I look at the tower?"

"I don't know, but you did, almost as if you were afraid of it."

"My tower!" said De Trevignac.

Another roar of laughter reached them from the camp fire. It made Domini smile in sympathy, but De Trevignac and Androvsky looked at each other for a moment, the one with a sort of earnest inquiry, the other with hostility, or what seemed hostility, across the circle of lamplight that lay between them.

"A tower rising in the desert emphasises the desolation. I suppose that was it," Androvsky said, as the laugh died down into Batouch's throaty chuckle. "It suggests lonely people watching."

"For something that never comes, or something terrible that comes," De Trevignac said.

As he spoke the last words Androvsky moved uneasily in his chair, and looked out towards the camp, as if he longed to get up and go into the open air, as if the tent roof above his head oppressed him.

De Trevignac turned to Domini.

"In this case, Madame, you were the lonely watcher, and I was the something terrible that came."

She laughed. While she laughed De Trevignac noticed that

Androvsky looked at her with a sort of sad intentness, not re-
proachful or wondering, as an older person might look at a
child playing at the edge of some great gulf into which a false
step would precipitate it. He strove to interpret this strange
look, so obviously born in the face of his host in connection
with himself. It seemed to him that he must have met Androvsky, and that Androvsky knew it, knew—what he did not
yet know—where it was and when. It seemed to him, too, that
Androvsky thought of him as the "something terrible" that
had come to this woman who sat between them out of the
desert.

But how could it be?

A profound curiosity was roused in him and he mentally
cursed his treacherous memory—if it were treacherous. For
possibly he might be mistaken. He had perhaps never met his
host before, and this strange manner of his might be due to some
inexplicable cause, or perhaps to some cause explicable and even
commonplace. This Monsieur Androvsky might be a very
jealous man, who had taken this woman away into the desert
to monopolise her, and who resented even the chance intrusion
of a stranger. De Trevignac knew life and the strange passions of men, knew that there are Europeans with the Arab
temperament, who secretly long that their women should wear
the veil and live secluded in the harem. Androvsky might be
one of these.

When she had laughed Domini said:

"On the contrary, Monsieur, you have turned my thoughts
into a happier current by your coming."

"How so?"

"You made me think of what are called the little things
of life that are more to us women than to you men, I suppose."

"Ah," he said. "This food, this wine, this chair with a
cushion, this gay light—Madame, they are not little things I
have to be grateful for. When I think of the dunes they seem
to me—they seem——"

Suddenly he stopped. His gay voice was choked. She saw
that there were tears in his blue eyes, which were fixed on her
with an expression of ardent gratitude. He cleared his throat.

"Monsieur," he said to Androvsky, "you will not think me
presuming on an acquaintance formed in the desert if I say that
till the end of my life I—and my men—can only think of
Madame as of the good Goddess of the desolate Sahara!"

He did not know how Androvsky would take this remark, he did not care. For the moment in his impulsive nature there was room only for admiration of the woman and gratitude for her frank kindness. Androvsky said:

"Thank you, Monsieur."

He spoke with an intensity, even a fervour, that were startling. For the first time since they had been together his voice was absolutely natural, his manner was absolutely unconstrained, he showed himself as he was, a man on fire with love for the woman who had given herself to him, and who received a warm word of praise of her as a gift made to himself. De Trevignac no longer wondered that Domini was his wife. Those three words, and the way they were spoken, gave him the man and what he might be in a woman's life. Domini looked at her husband silently. It seemed to her as if her heart were flooded with light, as if desolate Mogar were the Garden of Eden before the angel came. When they spoke again it was on some indifferent topic. But from that moment the meal went more merrily. Androvsky seemed to lose his strange uneasiness. De Trevignac met him more than half-way. Something of the gaiety round the camp fire had entered into the tent. A chain of sympathy had been forged between these three people. Possibly a touch might break it, but for the moment it seemed strong.

At the end of the dinner Domini got up.

"We have no formalities in the desert," she said. "But I'm going to leave you together for a moment. Give Monsieur de Trevignac a cigar, Boris. Coffee is coming directly."

She went out towards the camp fire. She wanted to leave the men together to seal their good fellowship. Her husband's change from taciturnity to cordiality had enchanted her. Happiness was dancing within her. She felt gay as a child. Between the fire and the tent she met Ouardi carrying a tray. On it were a coffee-pot, cups, little glasses and a tall bottle of a peculiar shape with a very thin neck and bulging sides.

"What's that, Ouardi?" she asked, touching it with her finger.

"That is an African liqueur, Madame, that you have never tasted. Batouch told me to bring it in honour of Monsieur the officer. They call it——"

"Another surprise of Batouch's!" she interrupted gaily. "Take it in! Monsieur the officer will think we have quite a cellar in the desert."

He went on, and she stood for a few minutes looking at the blaze of the fire, and at the faces lit up by it, French and Arab. The happy soldiers were singing a French song with a chorus for the delectation of the Arabs, who swayed to and fro, wagging their heads and smiling in an effort to show appreciation of the barbarous music of the Roumis. Dreary, terrible Mogar and its influences were being defied by the wanderers halting in it. She thought of Androvsky's words about the human will overcoming the influence of place, and a sudden desire came to her to go as far as the tower where she had felt sad and apprehensive, to stand in its shadow for an instant and to revel in her happiness.

She yielded to the impulse, walked to the tower, and stood there facing the darkness which hid the dunes, the white plains, the phantom sea, seeing them in her mind, and radiantly defying them. Then she began to return to the camp, walking lightly, as happy people walk. When she had gone a very short way she heard someone coming towards her. It was too dark to see who it was. She could only hear the steps among the stones. They were hasty. They passed her and stopped behind her at the tower. She wondered who it was, and supposed it must be one of the soldiers come to fetch something, or perhaps tired and hastening to bed.

As she drew near to the camp she saw the lamplight shining in the tent, where doubtless De Trevignac and Androvsky were smoking and talking in frank good fellowship. It was like a bright star, she thought, that gleam of light that shone out of her home, the brightest of all the stars of Africa. She went towards it. As she drew near she expected to hear the voices of the two men, but she heard nothing. Nor did she see the blackness of their forms in the circle of the light. Perhaps they had gone out to join the soldiers and the Arabs round the fire. She hastened on, came to the tent, entered it, and was confronted by her husband, who was standing back in an angle formed by the canvas, in the shadow, alone. On the floor near him lay a quantity of fragments of glass.

"Boris!" she said. "Where is Monsieur de Trevignac?"

"Gone," replied Androvsky in a loud, firm voice.

She looked up at him. His face was grim and powerful, hard like the face of a fighting man.

"Gone already? Why?"

"He's tired out. He told me to make his excuses to you."

" But——"

She saw on the table the coffee cups. Two of them were full of coffee. The third, hers, was clean.

" But he hasn't drunk his coffee! " she said.

She was astonished and showed it. She could not understand a man who had displayed such warm, even touching, appreciation of her kindness leaving her without a word, taking the opportunity of her momentary absence to disappear, to shirk away—for she put it like that to herself.

" No—he did not want coffee."

" But was anything the matter? "

She looked down at the broken glass, and saw stains upon the ground among the fragments.

" What's this? " she said. " Oh, the African liqueur! "

Suddenly Androvsky put his arm round her with an iron grip, and led her away out of the tent. They crossed the space to the sleeping-tent in silence. She felt governed, and as if she must yield to his will, but she also felt confused, even almost alarmed mentally. The sleeping-tent was dark. When they reached it Androvsky took his arm from her, and she heard him searching for the matches. She was in the tent door and could see that there was a light in the tower. De Trevignac must be there already. No doubt it was he who had passed her in the night when she was returning to the camp. Androvsky struck a match and lit a candle. Then he came to the tent door and saw her looking at the light in the tower.

" Come in, Domini," he said, taking her by the hand, and speaking gently, but still with a firmness that hinted at command.

She obeyed, and he quickly let down the flap of canvas, and shut out the night.

" What is it, Boris? " she asked.

She was standing by one of the beds.

" What has happened? "

" Why—happened? "

" I don't understand. Why did Monsieur de Trevignac go away so suddenly? "

" Domini, do you care whether he is here or gone? Do you care? " He sat on the edge of the bed and drew her down beside him.

" Do you want anyone to be with us, to break in upon our lives? Aren't we happier alone? "

"Boris!" she said, "you—did you let him see that you wanted him to go?"

It occurred to her suddenly that Androvsky, in his lack of worldly knowledge, might perhaps have shown their guest that he secretly resented the intrusion of a stranger upon them even for one evening, and that De Trevignac, being a sensitive man, had been hurt and had abruptly gone away. Her social sense revolted at this idea.

"You didn't let him see that, Boris!" she exclaimed. "After his escape from death! It would have been inhuman."

"Perhaps my love for you might even make me that, Domini. And if it did—if you knew why I was inhuman—would you blame me for it? Would you hate me for it?"

There was a strong excitement dawning in him. It recalled to her the first night in the desert when they sat together on the ground and watched the waning of the fire.

"Could you—could you hate me for anything, Domini?" he said. "Tell me—could you?"

His face was close to hers. She looked at him with her long, steady eyes, that had truth written in their dark fire.

"No," she answered. "I could never hate you—now."

"Not if—not if I had done you harm? Not if I had done you a wrong?"

"Could you ever do me a wrong?" she asked.

She sat, looking at him as if in deep thought, for a moment.

"I could almost as easily believe that God could," she said at last simply.

"Then you—you have perfect trust in me?"

"But—have you ever thought I had not?" she asked. There was wonder in her voice.

"But I have given my life to you," she added still with wonder. "I am here in the desert with you. What more can I give? What more can I do?"

He put his arms about her and drew her head down on his shoulder.

"Nothing, nothing. You have given, you have done everything—too much, too much. I feel myself below you, I know myself below you—far, far down."

"How can you say that? I couldn't have loved you if it were so." She spoke with complete conviction.

"Perhaps," he said, in a low voice, "perhaps women never realise what their love can do. It might—it might——"

"What, Boris?"

"It might do what Christ did—go down into hell to preach to the—to the spirits in prison."

His voice had dropped almost to a murmur. With one hand on her cheek he kept her face pressed down upon his shoulder so that she could not see his face.

"It might do that, Domini."

"Boris," she said, almost whispering too, for his words and manner filled her with a sort of awe, "I want you to tell me something."

"What is it?"

"Are you quite happy with me here in the desert? If you are I want you to tell me that you are. Remember—I shall believe you."

"No other human being could ever give me the happiness you give me."

"But——"

He interrupted her.

"No other human being ever has. Till I met you I had no conception of the happiness there is in the world for man and woman who love each other."

"Then you are happy?"

"Don't I seem so?"

She did not reply. She was searching her heart for the answer—searching it with an almost terrible sincerity. He waited for her answer, sitting quite still. His hand was always against her face. After what seemed to him an eternity she said:

"Boris!"

"Yes."

"Why did you say that about a woman's love being able even to go down into hell to preach to the spirits in prison?"

He did not answer. His hand seemed to her to lie more heavily on her cheek.

"I—I am not sure that you are quite happy with me," she said.

She spoke like one who reverenced truth, even though it slew her. There was a note of agony in her voice.

"Hush!" he said. "Hush, Domini!"

They were both silent. Beyond the canvas of the tent that

shut out from them the camp they heard a sound of music.
Drums were being beaten. The African pipe was wailing.
Then the voice of Ali rose in the song of the " Freed Negroes ":

> " No one but God and I
> Knows what is in my heart."

At that moment Domini felt that the words were true—
horribly true.

"Boris," she said. "Do you hear?"

"Hush, Domini."

"I think there is something in your heart that sometimes
makes you sad even with me. I think perhaps I partly guess
what it is."

He took his hand away from her face, his arm from her
shoulder, but she caught hold of him, and her arm was strong
like a man's.

"Boris, you are with me, you are close to me, but do you
sometimes feel far away from God?"

He did not answer.

" I don't know; I oughtn't to ask, perhaps. I don't ask—no,
I don't. But, if it's that, don't be too sad. It may all come
right—here in the desert. For the desert is the Garden of
Allah. And, Boris—put out the light."

He extinguished the candle with his hand.

" You feel, perhaps, that you can't pray honestly now, but
some day you may be able to. You will be able to. I know
it. Before I knew I loved you I saw you—praying in the
desert."

" I!" he whispered. "You saw me praying in the desert!"

It seemed to her that he was afraid. She pressed him more
closely with her arms.

" It was that night in the dancing-house. I seemed to see a
crowd of people to whom the desert had given gifts, and to you
it had given the gift of prayer. I saw you far out in the desert
praying."

She heard his hard breathing, felt it against her cheek.

" If—if it is that, Boris, don't despair. It may come. Keep
the crucifix. I am sure you have it. And I always pray for
you."

They sat for a long while in the dark, but they did not speak
again that night.

Domini did not sleep, and very early in the morning, just as dawn was beginning, she stole out of the tent, shutting down the canvas flap behind her.

It was cold outside—cold almost as in a northern winter. The wind of the morning, that blew to her across the wavelike dunes and the white plains, seemed impregnated with ice. The sky was a pallid grey. The camp was sleeping. What had been a fire, all red and gold and leaping beauty, was now a circle of ashes, grey as the sky. She stood on the edge of the hill and looked towards the tower.

As she did so, from the house behind it came a string of mules, picking their way among the stones over the hard earth. De Trevignac and his men were already departing from Mogar.

They came towards her slowly. They had to pass her to reach the track by which they were going on to the north and civilisation. She stood to see them pass.

When they were quite near De Trevignac, who was riding, with his head bent down on his chest, muffled in a heavy cloak, looked up and saw her. She nodded to him. He sat up and saluted. For a moment she thought that he was going on without stopping to speak to her. She saw that he hesitated what to do. Then he pulled up his mule and prepared to get off.

" No, don't, Monsieur," she said.

She held out her hand.

" Good-bye," she added.

He took her hand, then signed to his men to ride on. When they had passed, saluting her, he let her hand go. He had not spoken a word. His face, burned scarlet by the sun, had a look of exhaustion on it, but also another look—of horror, she thought, as if in his soul he was recoiling from her. His inflamed blue eyes watched her, as if in a search that was intense. She stood beside the mule in amazement. She could hardly believe that this was the man who had thanked her, with tears in his eyes, for her hospitality the night before. " Good-bye," he said, speaking at last, coldly. She saw him glance at the tent from which she had come. The horror in his face surely deepened. " Good-bye, Madame," he repeated. " Thank you for your hospitality." He pulled up the rein to ride on. The mule moved a step or two. Then suddenly he checked it and turned in the saddle. " Madame! " he said. " Madame! "

She came up to him. It seemed to her that he was going to say something of tremendous importance to her. His lips, blistered by the sun, opened to speak. But he only looked again towards the tent in which Androvsky was still sleeping, then at her.

A long moment passed.

Then De Trevignac, as if moved by an irresistible impulse, leaned from the saddle and made over Domini the sign of the cross. His hand dropped down against the mule's side, and without another word, or look, he rode away to the north following his men.

CHAPTER XXI

THAT same day, to the surprise of Batouch, they left Mogar. To both Domini and Androvsky it seemed a tragic place, a place where the desert showed them a countenance that was menacing.

They moved on towards the south, wandering aimlessly through the warm regions of the sun. Then, as the spring drew into summer, and the heat became daily more intense, they turned again northwards, and on an evening in May pitched their camp on the outskirts of the Sahara city of Amara.

This city, although situated in the northern part of the desert, was called by the Arabs "The belly of the Sahara," and also "The City of Scorpions." It lay in the midst of a vast region of soft and shifting sand that suggested a white sea, in which the oasis of date palms, at the edge of which the city stood, was a green island. From the south, whence the wanderers came, the desert sloped gently upwards for a long distance, perhaps half a day's march, and many kilometres before the city was reached, the minarets of its mosques were visible, pointing to the brilliant blue sky that arched the whiteness of the sands. Round about the city, on every side, great sand-hills rose like ramparts erected by Nature to guard it from the assaults of enemies. These hills were black with the tents of desert tribes, which, from far off, looked like multitudes of flies that had settled on the sands. The palms of the oasis, which stretched northwards from the city, could not be seen from the south till the city was reached, and in late spring this region was a strange and barbarous pageant of blue and white and gold; crude in its intensity, fierce in its crudity, almost terrible in its blazing splendour that was like the splendour about the portals of the sun.

Domini and Androvsky rode towards Amara at a foot's pace,

looking towards its distant towers. A quivering silence lay around them, yet already they seemed to hear the cries of the voices of a great multitude, to be aware of the movement of thronging crowds of men. This was the first Sahara city they had drawn near to, and their minds were full of memories of the stories of Batouch, told to them by the camp fire at night in the uninhabited places which, till now, had been their home: stories of the wealthy date merchants who trafficked here and dwelt in Oriental palaces, poor in aspect as seen from the dark and narrow streets, or zgags, in which they were situated, but within full of the splendours of Eastern luxury; of the Jew money-lenders who lived apart in their own quarter, rapacious as wolves, hoarding their gains, and practising the rites of their ancient and—according to the Arabs—detestable religion; of the marabouts, or sacred men, revered by the Mohammedans, who rode on white horses through the public ways, followed by adoring fanatics who sought to touch their garments and amulets, and demanded importunately miraculous blessings at their hands—the hedgehog's foot to protect their women in the peril of childbirth; the scroll, covered with verses of the Koran and enclosed in a sheaf of leather, that banishes ill dreams at night and stays the uncertain feet of the sleep-walker; the camel's skull that brings fruit to the palm trees; the red coral that stops the flow of blood from a knife-wound—of the dancing-girls glittering in an armour of golden pieces, their heads tied with purple and red and yellow handkerchiefs of silk, crowned with great bars of solid gold and tufted with ostrich feathers; of the dwarfs and jugglers who by night perform in the market-place, contending for custom with the sorceresses who tell the fates from shells gathered by mirage seas; with the snake-charmers who are immune from the poison of serpents and the acrobats who come from far-off Persia and Arabia to spread their carpets in the shadow of the Agha's dwelling and delight the eyes of negro and Kabyle, of Soudanese and Touareg with their feats of strength; of the haschish smokers who, assembled by night in an underground house whose ceiling and walls were black as ebony, gave themselves up to day-dreams of shifting glory, in which the things of earth and the joys and passions of men reappeared, but transformed by the magic influence of the drug, made monstrous or fairylike, intensified or turned to voluptuous languors, through which the Ouled Naïl floated like a syren, promising ecstasies unknown even in Baghdad, where the pale Circassian lifts her lustrous eyes, in which the palms were heavy with dates of solid gold, and the streams were gliding silver.

Often they had smiled over Batouch's opulent descriptions of the marvels of Ain-Amara, which they suspected to be very far away from the reality, and yet, nevertheless, when they saw the minarets soaring above the sands to the brassy heaven, it seemed to them both as if, perhaps, they might be true. The place looked intensely barbaric. The approach to it was grandiose.

Wide as the sands had been, they seemed to widen out into a greater immensity of arid pallor before the city gates as yet unseen. The stretch of blue above looked vaster here, the horizons more remote, the radiance of the sun more vivid, more inexorable. Nature surely expanded as if in an effort to hold her arm against some tremendous spectacle set in its bosom by the activity of men, who were strong and ardent as the giants of old, who had powers and a passion for employing them persistently not known in any other region of the earth. The immensity of Mogar brought sadness to the mind. The immensity of Ain-Amara brought excitement. Even at this distance from it, when its minarets were still like shadowy fingers of an unlifted hand, Androvsky and Domini were conscious of influences streaming forth from its battlements over the sloping sands like a procession that welcomed them to a new phase of desert life.

" And people talk of the monotony of the Sahara!" Domini said speaking out of their mutual thought. " Everything is here, Boris; you've never drawn near to London. Long before you reach the first suburbs you feel London like a great influence brooding over the fields and the woods. Here you feel Amara in the same way brooding over the sands. It's as if the sands were full of voices. Doesn't it excite you?"

" Yes," he said. " But "—and he turned in his saddle and looked back—" I feel as if the solitudes were safer."

" We can return to them."

" Yes."

" We are splendidly free. There's nothing to prevent us leaving Amara to-morrow."

" Isn't there?" he answered, fixing his eyes upon the minarets.

" What can there be?"

" Who knows?"

" What do you mean, Boris? Are you superstitious? But

you reject the influence of place. Don't you remember—at Mogar?"

At the mention of the name his face clouded and she was sorry she had spoken it. Since they had left the hill above the mirage sea they had scarcely ever alluded to their night there. They had never once talked of the dinner in camp with De Trevignac and his men, or renewed their conversation in the tent on the subject of religion. But since that day, since her words about Androvsky's lack of perfect happiness even with her far out in the freedom of the desert, Domini had been conscious that, despite their great love for each other, their mutual passion for the solitude in which it grew each day more deep and more engrossing, wrapping their lives in fire and leading them on to the inner abodes of sacred understanding, there was at moments a barrier between them.

At first she had striven not to recognise its existence. She had striven to be blind. But she was essentially a brave woman and an almost fanatical lover of truth for its own sake, thinking that what is called an ugly truth is less ugly than the loveliest lie. To deny truth is to play the coward. She could not long do that. And so she quickly learned to face this truth with steady eyes and an unflinching heart.

At moments Androvsky retreated from her, his mind became remote—more, his heart was far from her, and, in its distant place, was suffering. Of that she was assured.

But she was assured, too, that she stood to him for perfection in human companionship. A woman's love is, perhaps, the only true divining rod. Domini knew instinctively where lay the troubled waters, what troubled them in their subterranean dwelling. She was certain that Androvsky was at peace with her but not with himself. She had said to him in the tent that she thought he sometimes felt far away from God. The conviction grew in her that even the satisfaction of his great human love was not enough for his nature. He demanded, sometimes imperiously, not only the peace that can be understood gloriously, but also that other peace which passeth understanding. And because he had it not he suffered.

In the Garden of Allah he felt a loneliness even though she was with him, and he could not speak with her of this loneliness. That was the barrier between them, she thought.

She prayed for him: in the tent by night, in the desert under the burning sky by day. When the muezzin cried from the minaret of some tiny village lost in the desolation of the wastes, turning to the north, south, east and west, and the Mussulmans bowed their shaven heads, facing towards Mecca, she prayed to the Catholics' God, whom she felt to be the God, too, of all the devout, of all the religions of the world, and to the Mother of God, looking towards Africa. She prayed that this man whom she loved, and who she believed was seeking, might find. And she felt that there was a strength, a passion in her prayers, which could not be rejected. She felt that some day Allah would show himself in his garden to the wanderer there. She dared to feel that because she dared to believe in the endless mercy of God. And when that moment came she felt, too, that their love—hers and his—for each other would be crowned. Beautiful and intense as it was it still lacked something. It needed to be encircled by the protecting love of a God in whom they both believed in the same way, and to whom they both were equally near. While she felt close to this love and he far from it they were not quite together.

There were moments in which she was troubled, even sad, but they passed. For she had a great courage, a great confidence. The hope that dwells like a flame in the purity of prayer comforted her.

"I love the solitudes," he said. "I love to have you to myself."

"If we lived always in the greatest city of the world it would make no difference," she said quietly. "You know that, Boris."

He bent over from his saddle and clasped her hand in his, and they rode thus up the great slope of the sands, with their horses close together.

The minarets of the city grew more distinct. They dominated the waste as the thought of Allah dominates the Mohammedan world. Presently, far away on the left, Domini and Androvsky saw hills of sand, clearly defined like small mountains delicately shaped. On the summits of these hills were Arab villages of the hue of bronze gleaming in the sun. No trees stood near them. But beyond them, much farther off, was the long green line of the palms of a large oasis. Between them and the riders moved slowly towards the minarets dark things that looked like serpents writhing through the sands. These were caravans coming into the city from long journeys. Here and there, dotted about in the immensity, were solitary horsemen, camels in twos and threes, small troops of donkeys. And all the things that moved went towards the minarets as if irresistibly drawn onwards by some strong influence that sucked them in from the solitudes of the whirlpool of human life.

Again Domini thought of the approach to London, and of the dominion of great cities, those octopus monsters created by men, whose tentacles are strong to seize and stronger still to keep. She was infected by Androvsky's dread of a changed life, and through her excitement, that pulsed with interest and curiosity, she felt a faint thrill of something that was like fear.

"Boris," she said, "I feel as if your thoughts were being conveyed to me by your touch. Perhaps the solitudes are best."

By a simultaneous impulse they pulled in their horses and listened. Sounds came to them over the sands, thin and remote. They could not tell what they were, but they knew that they heard something which suggested the distant presence of life.

"What is it?" said Domini.

"I don't know, but I hear something. It travels to us from the minarets."

They both leaned forward on their horses' necks, holding each other's hand.

"I feel the tumult of men," Androvsky said presently.

"And I. But it seems as if no men could have elected to build a city here."

"Here in the 'Belly of the desert,'" he said, quoting the Arabs' name for Amara.

"Boris"—she spoke in a more eager voice, clasping his hand strongly—"you remember the *fumoir* in Count Anteoni's garden. The place where it stood was the very heart of the garden."

"Yes."

"We understood each other there."

He pressed her hand without speaking.

"Amara seems to me the heart of the Garden of Allah. Perhaps—perhaps we shall——"

She paused. Her eyes were fixed on his face.

"What, Domini?" he asked.

He looked expectant, but anxious, and watched her, but with eyes that seemed ready to look away from her at a word.

"Perhaps we shall understand each other even better there."

He looked down at the white sand.

"Better!" he repeated. "Could we do that?"

She did not answer. The far-off villages gleamed mysteriously on their little mountains, like unreal things that might fade away as castles fade in the fire. The sky above the min-

arets was changing in colour slowly. Its blue was being
invaded by a green that was a sister colour. A curious light,
that seemed to rise from below rather than to descend from
above, was transmuting the whiteness of the sands. A lemon
yellow crept through them, but they still looked cold and
strange, and immeasurably vast. Domini fancied that the
silence of the desert deepened so that, in it, they might hear
the voices of Amara more distinctly.

"You know," she said, "when one looks out over the desert
from a height, as we did from the tower of Beni-Mora, it
seems to call one. There's a voice in the blue distance that
seems to say, 'Come to me! I am here—hidden in my retreat,
beyond the blue, and beyond the mirage, and beyond the farthest
verge!'"

"Yes, I know."

"I have always felt, when we travelled in the desert, that the
calling thing, the soul of the desert, retreated as I advanced, and
still summoned me onward but always from an infinite distance."

"And I too, Domini."

"Now I don't feel that. I feel as if now we were coming
near to the voice, as if we should reach it at Amara, as if there
it would tell us its secret."

"Imagination!" he said.

But he spoke seriously, almost mystically. His voice was at
odds with the word it said. She noticed that and was sure that
he was secretly sharing her sensation. She even suspected that
he had perhaps felt it first.

"Let us ride on," he said. "Do you see the change in the
light? Do you see the green in the sky? It is cooler, too.
This is the wind of evening."

Their hands fell apart and they rode slowly on, up the long
slope of the sands.

Presently they saw that they had come out of the trackless
waste and that though still a long way from the city they were
riding on a desert road which had been trodden by multitudes
of feet. There were many footprints here. On either side
were low banks of sand, beaten into a rough symmetry by
implements of men, and shallow trenches through which no
water ran. In front of them they saw the numerous caravans,
now more distinct, converging from left and right slowly to this
great isle of the desert which stretched in a straight line to the
minarets.

"We are on a highway," Domini said.

Androvsky sighed.

"I feel already as if we were in the midst of a crowd," he answered.

"Our love for peace oughtn't to make us hate our fellow-men!" she said. "Come, Boris, let us chase away our selfish mood!"

She spoke in a more cheerful voice and drew her rein a little tighter. Her horse quickened its pace.

"And think how our stay at Amara will make us love the solitudes when we return to them again. Contrast is the salt of life."

"You speak as if you didn't believe what you are saying."

She laughed.

"If I were ever inclined to tell you a lie," she said. "I should not dare to. Your mind penetrates mine too deeply."

"You could not tell me a lie."

"Do you hear the dogs barking?" she said, after a moment. "They are among those tents that are like flies on the sands around the city. That is the tribe of the Ouled Naïls, I suppose. Batouch says they camp here. What multitudes of tents! Those are the suburbs of Amara. I would rather live in them than in the suburbs of London. Oh, how far away we are, as if we were at the end of the world!"

Either her last words, or her previous change of manner to a lighter cheerfulness, almost a briskness, seemed to rouse Androvsky to a greater confidence, even to anticipation of possible pleasure.

"Yes. After all it is only the desert men who are here. Amara is their Metropolis, and in it we shall only see their life."

His horse plunged. He had touched it sharply with his heel.

"I believe you hate the thought of civilisation," she exclaimed.

"And you?"

"I never think of it. I feel almost as if I had never known it, and could never know it."

"Why should you? You love the wilds."

"They make my whole nature leap. Even when I was a child it was so. I remember once reading *Maud*. In it I came upon a passage—I can't remember it well, but it was about the red man——"

She thought for a moment, looking towards the city.

"I don't know how it is quite," she murmured. "'When

the red man laughs by his cedar tree, and the red man's babe leaps beyond the sea '—something like that. But I know that it made my heart beat, and that I felt as if I had wings and were spreading them to fly away to the most remote places of the earth. And now I have spread my wings, and—it's glorious. Come, Boris!"

They put their horses to a canter, and soon drew near to the caravans. They had sent Batouch and Ali, who generally accompanied them, on with the rest of the camp. Both had many friends in Amara, and were eager to be there. It was obvious that they and all the attendants, servants and camel-men, thought of it as the provincial Frenchman thinks of Paris, as a place of all worldly wonders and delights. Batouch was to meet them at the entrance to the city, and when they had seen the marvels of its market-place was to conduct them to the tents which would be pitched on the sand-hills outside.

Their horses pulled as if they, too, longed for a spell of city life after the life of the wastes, and Domini's excitement grew. She felt vivid animal spirits boiling up within her, the sane and healthy sense that welcomes a big manifestation of the ceaseless enterprise and keen activity of a brotherhood of men. The loaded camels, the half-naked running drivers, the dogs sensitively sniffing, as if enticing smells from the city already reached their nostrils, the chattering desert merchants discussing coming gains, the wealthy and richly-dressed Arabs, mounted on fine horses, and staring with eyes that glittered up the broad track in search of welcoming friends, were sympathetic to her mood. Amara was sucking them all in together from the solitary places as quiet waters are sucked into the turmoils of a mill-race. Although still out in the sands they were already in the midst of a noise of life flowing to meet the roar of life that rose up at the feet of the minarets, which now looked tall and majestic in the growing beauty of the sunset.

They passed the caravans one by one, and came on to the crest of the long sand slope just as the sky above the city was flushing with a bright geranium red. The track from here was level to the city wall, and was no longer soft with sand. A broad, hard road rang beneath their horses' hoofs, startling them with a music that was like a voice of civilised life. Before them, under the red sky, they saw a dark blue of distant houses, towers, and great round cupolas glittering like gold. Forests of palm trees lay behind, the giant date palms for which Amara was famous. To the left stretched the sands dotted with

gleaming Arab villages, to the right again the sands covered
with hundreds of tents among which quantities of figures moved
lively like ants, black on the yellow, arched by the sky that was
alive with lurid colour, red fading into gold, gold into primrose,
primrose into green, green into the blue that still told of the fading day. And to this multi-coloured sky, from the barbaric city
and the immense sands in which it was set, rose a great chorus of
life; voices of men and beasts, cries of naked children playing
Cora on the sand-hills, of mothers to straying infants, shrill
laughter of unveiled girls wantonly gay, the calls of men, the
barking of multitudes of dogs,—the guard dogs of the nomads
that are never silent night or day,—the roaring of hundreds of
camels now being unloaded for the night, the gibbering of the
mad beggars who roam perpetually on the outskirts of the en-
campments like wolves seeking what they may devour, the braying of donkeys, the whinnying of horses. And beneath these
voices of living things, foundation of their uprising vitality,
pulsed barbarous music, the throbbing tom-toms that are for
ever heard in the lands of the sun, fetish music that suggests
fatalism, and the grand monotony of the enormous spaces, and
the crude passion that repeats itself, and the untiring, sultry
loves and the untired, sultry languors of the children of the
sun.

The silence of the sands, which Domini and Androvsky had
known and loved, was merged in the tumult of the sands. The
one had been mystical, laying the soul to rest. The other was
provocative, calling the soul to wake. At this moment the
sands themselves seemed to stir with life and to cry aloud with
voices.

" The very sky is barbarous to-night ! " Domini exclaimed.
" Did you ever see such colour, Boris ? "

" Over the minarets it is like a great wound," he answered.

" No wonder men are careless of human life in such a land as
this. All the wildness of the world seems to be concentrated
here. Amara is like the desert city of some tremendous dream.
It looks wicked and unearthly, but how superb ! "

" Look at those cupolas ! " he said. " Are there really
Oriental palaces here ? Has Batouch told us the truth for
once ? "

" Or less than the truth ? I could believe anything of Amara
at this moment. What hundreds of camels ! They remind me
of Arba, our first halting-place."

She looked at him and he at her.

" How long ago that seems! " she said.

" A thousand years ago."

They both had a memory of a great silence, in the midst of this growing tumult in which the sky seemed now to take its part, calling with the voices of its fierce colours, with the voices of the fires that burdened it in the west.

" Silence joined us, Domini," Androvsky said.

" Yes. Perhaps silence is the most beautiful voice in the world."

Far off, along the great white road, they saw two horsemen galloping to meet them from the city, one dressed in brilliant saffron yellow, the other in the palest blue, both crowned with large and snowy turbans.

" Who can they be? " said Domini, as they drew near. " They look like two princes of the Sahara."

Then she broke into a merry laugh.

" Batouch! and Ali! " she exclaimed.

The servants galloped up then, without slackening speed, deftly wheeled their horses in a narrow circle, and were beside them, going with them, one on the right hand, the other on the left.

" Bravo! " Domini cried, delighted at this feat of horsemanship. " But what have you been doing? You are transformed! "

" Madame, we have been to the Bain Maure," replied Batouch, calmly, swelling out his broad chest under his yellow jacket laced with gold. " We have had our heads shaved till they are smooth and beautiful as polished ivory. We have been to the perfumer "—he leaned confidentially towards her, exhaling a pungent odour of amber—" to the tailor, to the baboosh bazaar "—he kicked out a foot cased in a slipper that was bright almost as a gold piece—" to him who sells the cherchia." He shook his head till the spangled muslin that flowed about it trembled. " Is it not right that your servants should do you honour in the city? "

" Perfectly right," she answered with a careful seriousness. " I am proud of you both."

" And Monsieur? " asked Ali, speaking in his turn.

Androvsky withdrew his eyes from the city, which was now near at hand.

" Splendid! " he said, but as if attending to the Arabs with difficulty. " You are splendid."

As they came towards the old wall which partially surrounds

Amara, and which rises from a deep natural moat of sand, they saw that the ground immediately before the city which, from a distance, had looked almost flat, was in reality broken up into a series of wavelike dunes, some small with depressions like deep crevices between them, others large with summits like plateaux. These dunes were of a sharp lemon yellow in the evening light, a yellow that was cold in its clearness, almost setting the teeth on edge. They went away into great rolling slopes of sand on which the camps of the nomads and the Ouled Naïls were pitched, some near to, some distant from, the city, but they themselves were solitary. No tents were pitched close to the city, under the shadow of its wall. As Androvsky spoke, Domini exclaimed:

"Boris—look! That is the most extraordinary thing I have ever seen!"

She put her hand on his arm. He obeyed her eyes and looked to his right, to the small lemon-yellow dunes that were close to them. At perhaps a hundred yards from the road was a dune that ran parallel with it. The fire of the sinking sun caught its smooth crest, and above this crest, moving languidly towards the city, were visible the heads and busts of three women, the lower halves of whose bodies were concealed by the sand of the farther side of the dune. They were dancing-girls. On their heads, piled high with gorgeous handkerchiefs, were golden crowns which glittered in the sun-rays, and tufts of scarlet feathers. Their oval faces, covered with paint, were partially concealed by long strings of gold coins, which flowed from their crowns down over their large breasts and disappeared towards their waists, which were hidden by the sand. Their dresses were of scarlet, apple-green and purple silks, partially covered by floating shawls of spangled muslin. Beneath their crowns and handkerchiefs burgeoned forth plaits of false hair decorated with coral and silver ornaments. Their hands, which they held high, gesticulating above the crest of the dune, were painted blood red.

These busts and heads glided slowly along in the setting sun, and presently sank down and vanished into some depression of the dunes. For an instant one blood-red hand was visible alone, waving a signal above the sand to someone unseen. Its fingers fluttered like the wings of a startled bird. Then it, too, vanished, and the sharply-cold lemon yellow of the dunes stretched in vivid loneliness beneath the evening sky.

To both of them this brief vision of women in the sand

brought home the solitude of the desert and the barbarity of the life it held, the ascetism of this supreme manifestation of Nature and the animal passion which fructifies in its heart.

" Do you know what that made me think of, Boris? " Domini said, as the red hand with its swiftly-moving fingers disappeared. " You'll smile, perhaps, and I scarcely know why. It made me think of the Devil in a monastery."

Androvsky did not smile. Nor did he answer. She felt sure that he, too, had been strongly affected by that glimpse of Sahara life. His silence gave Batouch an opportunity of pouring forth upon them a flood of poetical description of the dancing-girls of Amara, all of whom he seemed to know as intimate friends. Before he ceased they came into the city.

The road was still majestically broad. They looked with interest at the first houses, one on each side of the way. And here again they were met by the sharp contrast which was evidently to be the keynote of Amara. The house on the left was European, built of white stone, clean, attractive, but uninteresting, with stout white pillars of plaster supporting an arcade that afforded shade from the sun, windows with green blinds, and an open doorway showing a little hall, on the floor of which lay a smart rug glowing with gay colours; that on the right, before which the sand lay deep as if drifted there by some recent wind of the waste, was African and barbarous, an immense and rambling building of brown earth, brushwood and palm, windowless, with a flat-terraced roof, upon which were piled many strange-looking objects like things collapsed, red and dark green, with fringes and rosettes, and tall sticks of palm pointing vaguely to the sky.

" Why, these are like our palanquin! " Domini said.·

" They are the palanquins of the dancing-girls, Madame," said Batouch. " That is the *café* of the dancers, and that "— he pointed to the neat house opposite—" is the house of Monsieur the Aumonier of Amara."

" Aumonier," said Androvsky, sharply. " Here! "

He paused, then added more quietly:

" What should he do here? "

" But, Monsieur, he is for the French officers."

" There are French officers? "

" Yes, Monsieur, four or five, and the commandant. They live in the palace with the cupolas."

" I forgot," Androvsky said to Domini. " We are not out of the sphere of French influence. This place looks so remote and so barbarous that I imagined it given over entirely to the desert men."

" We need not see the French," she said. " We shall be encamped outside in the sand."

" And we need not stay here long," he said quickly.

" Boris," she asked him, half in jest, half in earnest, " shall we buy a desert island to live in?"

" Let us buy an oasis," he said. " That would be the perf——the safest life for us."

" The safest?"

" The safest for our happiness. Domini, I have a horror of the world!" He said the last words with a strong, almost fierce, emphasis.

" Had you it always, or only since we have been married?"

" I—perhaps it was born in me, perhaps it is part of me. Who knows?"

He had relapsed into a gravity that was heavy with gloom, and looked about him with eyes that seemed to wish to reject all that offered itself to their sight.

I want the desert and you in it," he said. " The lonely desert, with you."

" And nothing else?"

" I want that. I cannot have that taken from me."

He looked about him quickly from side to side as they rode up the street, as if he were a scout sent in advance of an army and suspected ambushes. His manner reminded her of the way he had looked towards the tower as they rode into Mogar. And he had connected that tower with the French. She remembered his saying to her that it must have been built for French soldiers. As they rode into Mogar he had dreaded something in Mogar. The strange incident with De Trevignac had followed. She had put it from her mind as a matter of small, or no, importance, had resolutely forgotten it, had been able to forget it in their dream of desert life and desert passion. But the entry into a city for the moment destroyed the dreamlike atmosphere woven by the desert, recalled her town sense, that quick-wittedness, that sharpness of apprehension and swiftness of observation which are bred in those who have long been accustomed to a life in the midst of crowds and movement, and changing scenes and passing fashions. Suddenly she seemed to herself to be reading Androvsky with an almost merciless penetration, which yet she could not check. He had dreaded something in Mogar. He dreaded something here in Amara. An unusual incident—for

the coming of a stranger into their lives out of their desolation
of the sand was unusual—had followed close upon the first
dread. Would another such incident follow upon this second
dread? And of what was this dread born?

Batouch drew her attention to the fact that they were coming
to the market-place, and to the curious crowds of people who
were swarming out of the tortuous, narrow streets into the main
thoroughfare to watch them pass, or to accompany them, running beside their horses. She divined at once, by the passionate
curiosity their entry aroused, that he had misspent his leisure in
spreading through the city lying reports of their immense importance and fabulous riches.

"Batouch," she said, "you have been talking about us."

"No, Madame, I merely said that Madame is a great lady in
her own land, and that Monsieur——"

"I forbid you ever to speak about me, Batouch," said Androvsky, brusquely.

He seemed worried by the clamour of the increasing mob
that surrounded them. Children in long robes like night-gowns
skipped before them, calling out in shrill voices. Old beggars,
with diseased eyes and deformed limbs, laid filthy hands upon
their bridles and demanded alms. Impudent boys, like bronze
statuettes suddenly endowed with a fury of life, progressed backwards to keep them full in view, shouting information at them
and proclaiming their own transcendent virtues as guides. Lithe
desert men, almost naked, but with carefully-covered heads,
strode beside them, keeping pace with the horses, saying nothing,
but watching them with a bright intentness that seemed to hint
at unutterable designs. And towards them, through the air
that seemed heavy and almost suffocating now that they were
among buildings, and through clouds of buzzing flies, came the
noise of the larger tumult of the market-place.

Looking over the heads of the throng Domini saw the wide
road opening out into a great space, with the first palms of the
oasis thronging on the left, and a cluster of buildings, many
with small cupolas, like down-turned white cups, on the right.
On the farther side of this space, which was black with people
clad for the most in dingy garments, was an arcade jutting out
from a number of hovel-like houses, and to the right of them,
where the market-place, making a wide sweep, continued up hill
and was hidden from her view, was the end of the great building whose gilded cupolas they had seen as they rode in from
the desert, rising above the city with the minarets of its mosques.

The flies buzzed furiously about the horses' heads and flanks, and the people buzzed more furiously, like larger flies, about the riders. It seemed to Domini as if the whole city was intent upon her and Androvsky, was observing them, considering them, wondering about them, was full of a thousand intentions all connected with them.

When they gained the market-place the noise and the watchful curiosity made a violent crescendo. It happened to be market day and, although the sun was setting, buying and selling were not yet over. On the hot earth over which, whenever there is any wind from the desert, the white sand grains sift and settle, were laid innumerable rugs of gaudy colours on which were disposed all sorts of goods for sale; heavy ornaments for women, piles of burnouses, haiks, gandouras, gaiters of bright red leather, slippers, weapons—many jewelled and gilt, or rich with patterns in silver—pyramids of the cords of camels' hair that bind the turbans of the desert men, handkerchiefs and cottons of all the colours of the rainbow, cheap perfumes in azure flasks powdered with golden and silver flowers and leaves, incense twigs, panniers of henna to dye the finger-nails of the faithful, innumerable comestibles, vegetables, corn, red butcher's meat thickly covered with moving insects, pale yellow cakes crisp and shining, morsels of liver spitted on skewers—which, cooked with dust of keef, produce a dreamy drunkenness more overwhelming even than that produced by haschish—musical instruments, derboukas, guitars, long pipes, and strange fiddles with two strings, tom-toms, skins of animals with heads and claws, live birds, tortoise backs, and plaits of false hair.

The sellers squatted on the ground, their brown and hairy legs crossed, calmly gazing before them, or, with frenzied voices and gestures, driving bargains with the buyers, who moved to and fro, treading carelessly among the merchandise. The tellers of fates glided through the press, fingering the amulets that hung upon their hearts. Conjurors proclaimed the merits of their miracles, bawling in the faces of the curious. Dwarfs went to and fro, dressed in bright colours with green and yellow turbans on their enormous heads, tapping with long staves, and relating their deformities. Water-sellers sounded their gongs. Before pyramids of oranges and dates, neatly arranged in patterns, sat boys crying in shrill voices the luscious virtues of their fruits. Idiots, with blear eyes and protending under-lips, gibbered and whined. Dogs barked. Bakers hurried along with trays of loaves upon their heads. From the low and smoky arcades to right and left came the reiterated grunt of negroes pounding coffee. A fanatic was roaring out his prayers. Arabs in scarlet and blue cloaks passed by to the Bain Maure, under whose white and blue archway lounged the Kabyle masseurs with folded, muscular arms. A marabout, black as a coal, rode on a white horse towards the great mosque, followed by his servant on foot.

Native soldiers went by to the Kasba on the height, or strolled down towards the Cafés Maures smoking cigarettes. Circles of grave men bent over card games, dominoes and draughts—called by the Arabs the Ladies' Game. Khodjas made their way with dignity towards the Bureau Arabe. Veiled women, fat and lethargic, jingling with ornaments, waddled through the arches of the arcades, carrying in their painted and perspiring hands blocks of sweetmeats which drew the flies. Children played in the dust by little heaps of refuse, which they stirred up into clouds with their dancing, naked feet. In front, as if from the first palms of the oasis, rose the roar of beaten drums from the negroes' quarter, and from the hill-top at the feet of the minarets came the fierce and piteous noise that is the *leit-motif* of the desert, the multitudinous complaining of camels dominating all other sounds.

As Domini and Androvsky rode into this whirlpool of humanity, above which the sky was red like a great wound, it flowed and eddied round them, making them its centre. The arrival of a stranger-woman was a rare, if not an unparalleled, event in Amara, and Batouch had been very busy in spreading the fame of his mistress.

"Madame should dismount," said Batouch. "Ali will take the horses, and I will escort Madame and Monsieur up the hill to the place of the fountain. Shabah will be there to greet Madame."

"What an uproar!" Domini exclaimed, half laughing, half confused. "Who on earth is Shabah?"

"Shabah is the Caïd of Amara," replied Batouch with dignity. "The greatest man of the city. He awaits Madame by the fountain." Domini cast a glance at Androvsky.

"Well?" she said.

He shrugged his shoulders like a man who thinks strife useless and the moment come for giving in to Fate.

"The monster has opened his jaws for us," he said, forcing a laugh. "We had better walk in, I suppose. But—O Domini!—the silence of the wastes!"

"We shall know it again. This is only for the moment. We shall have all its joy again."

"Who knows?" he said, as he had said when they were riding up the sand slope. "Who knows?"

Then they got off their horses and were taken by the crowd.

CHAPTER XXII

THE tumult of Amara waked up in Domini the town-sense that had been slumbering. All that seemed to confuse, to daze, to repel Androvsky, even to inspire him with fear, the noise of the teeming crowds, their perpetual movement, their contact, startled her into a vividness of life and apprehension of its various meanings, that sent a thrill through her. And the thrill was musical with happiness. To the sad a great vision of human life brings sadness because they read into the hearts of others their own misery. But to the happy such a vision brings exultation, for everywhere they find dancing reflections of their own joy. Domini had lived much in crowds, but always she had been actively unhappy, or at least coldly dreary in them. Now, for the first time, she was surrounded by masses of fellow-beings in her splendid contentment. And the effect of this return, as it were, to something like the former material conditions of her life, with the mental and affectional conditions of it transformed by joy, was striking even to herself. Suddenly she realised to the full her own humanity, and the living warmth of sympathy that is fanned into flame in a human heart by the presence of human life with its hopes, desires, fears, passions, joys, that leap to the eye. Instead of hating this fierce change from solitude with the man she loved to a crowd with the man she loved she rejoiced in it. Androvsky was the cause of both her joys, joy in the waste and joy in Amara, but while he shared the one he did not share the other.

This did not surprise her because of the conditions in which he had lived. He was country-bred and had always dwelt far from towns. She was returning to an old experience—old, for the London crowd and the crowd of Amara were both crowds of men, however different—with a mind transformed by happiness. To him the experience was new. Something within her told her that it was necessary, that it had been ordained because he needed it. The recalled town-sense, with its sharpness of observation, persisted. As she rode in to Amara she had seemed

to herself to be reading Androvsky with an almost merciless
penetration which yet she could not check. Now she did not
wish to check it, for the penetration that is founded on perfect
love can only yield good fruit. It seemed to her that she was
allowed to see clearly for Androvsky what he could not see himself, almost as the mother sees for the child. This contact with
the crowds of Amara was, she thought, one of the gifts the desert
made to him. He did not like it. He wished to reject it. But
he was mistaken. For the moment his vision was clouded, as
our vision for ourselves so often is. She realised this, and, for
the first time since the marriage service at Beni-Mora, perhaps
seemed to be selfish. She opposed his wish. Hitherto there
had never been any sort of contest between them. Their desires,
like their hearts, had been in accord. Now there was not a
contest, for Androvsky yielded to Domini's preference, when
she expressed it, with a quickness that set his passion before her
in a new and beautiful light. But she knew that, for the
moment, they were not in accord. He hated and dreaded what
she encountered with a vivid sensation of sympathy and joy.

She felt that there was something morbid in his horror of
the crowd, and the same strength of her nature said to her,
"Uproot it!"

Their camp was pitched on the sand-hills, to the north of the
city near the French and Arab cemeteries. They reached it
only when darkness was falling, going out of the city on foot
by the great wall of dressed stone which enclosed the Kasba of
the native soldiers, and ascending and descending various slopes
of deep sand, over which the airs of night blew with a peculiar
thin freshness that renewed Domini's sense of being at the end
of the world. Everything here whispered the same message,
said, "We are the denizens of far-away."

In their walk to the camp they were accompanied by a little
procession. Shabah, the Caïd of Amara, a shortish man whose
immense dignity made him almost gigantic, insisted upon attending them to the tents, with his young brother, a pretty, libertine
boy of sixteen, the brother's tutor, an Arab black as a negro but
without the negro's look of having been freshly oiled, and two
attendants. To them joined himself the Caïd of the Nomads,
a swarthy potentate who not only looked, but actually was, immense, his four servants, and his uncle, a venerable person like
a shepherd king. These worthies surrounded Domini and
Androvsky, and behind streamed the curious, the envious, the
greedy and the desultory Arabs, who follow in the trail of every

stranger, hopeful of the crumbs that are said to fall from the rich man's table. Shabah spoke French and led the conversation, which was devoted chiefly to his condition of health. Some years before an attempt had been made upon his life by poison, and since that time, as he himself expressed it, his stomach had been "perturbed as a guard dog in the night when robbers are approaching." All efforts to console or to inspire him with hope of future cure were met with a stern hopelessness, a brusque certainty of perpetual suffering. The idea that his stomach could again know peace evidently shocked and distressed him, and as they all waded together through the sand, pioneered by the glorified Batouch, Domini was obliged to yield to his emphatic despair, and to join with him in his appreciation of the perpetual indigestion which set him apart from the rest of the world like some God within a shrine. The skittish boy, his brother, who wore kid gloves, cast at her sly glances of admiration which asked for a return. The black tutor grinned. And the Caïd of the Nomads punctuated their progress with loud grunts of heavy satisfaction, occasionally making use of Batouch as interpreter to express his hopes that they would visit his palace in the town, and devour a cous-cous on his carpet.

When they came to the tents it was necessary to entertain these personages with coffee, and they finally departed promising a speedy return, and full of invitations, which were cordially accepted by Batouch on his employer's behalf before either Domini or Androvsky had time to say a word.

As the *cortège* disappeared over the sands towards the city Domini burst into a little laugh, and drew Androvsky out to the tent door to see them go.

" Society in the sands! " she exclaimed gaily. " Boris, this is a new experience. Look at our guests making their way to their palaces! "

Slowly the potentates progressed across the white dunes towards the city. Shabah wore a long red cloak. His brother was in pink and gold, with white billowing trousers. The Caïd of the Nomads was in green. They all moved with a large and conscious majesty, surrounded by their obsequious attendants. Above them the purple sky showed a bright evening star. Near it was visible the delicate silhouette of the young moon. Scattered over the waste rose many koubbahs, grey in the white, with cupolas of gypse. Hundreds of dogs were barking in the distance. To the left, on the vast, rolling slopes of sand, glared the innumerable fires kindled before the tents of the Ouled

Naïls. Before the sleeping tent rose the minarets and the gilded cupolas of the city which it dominated from its mountain of sand. Behind it was the blanched immensity of the plain, of the lonely desert from which Domini and Androvsky had come to face this barbaric stir of life. And the city was full of music, of tom-toms throbbing, of bugles blowing in the Kasba, of pipes shrieking from hidden dwellings, and of the faint but multitudinous voices of men, carried to them on their desolate and treeless height by the frail wind of night that seemed a white wind, twin-brother of the sands.

"Let us go a step or two towards the city, Boris," Domini said, as their guests sank magnificently down into a fold of the dunes.

"Towards the city!" he answered. "Why not——?" He glanced behind him to the vacant, noiseless sands.

She set her impulse against his for the first time.

"No, this is our town life, our Sahara season. Let us give ourselves to it. The loneliness will be its antidote some day."

"Very well, Domini," he answered.

They went a little way towards the city, and stood still in the sand at the edge of their height.

"Listen, Boris! Isn't it strange in the night all this barbaric music? It excites me."

"You are glad to be here."

She heard the note of disappointment in his voice, but did not respond to it.

"And look at all those fires, hundreds of them in the sand!"

"Yes," he said, "it is wonderful, but the solitudes are best. This is not the heart of the desert, this is what the Arabs call it, 'The belly of the Desert.' In the heart of the desert there is silence."

She thought of the falling of the wind when the Sahara took them, and knew that her love of the silence was intense. Nevertheless, to-night the other part of her was in the ascendant. She wanted him to share it. He did not. Could she provoke him to share it?

"Yet, as we rode in, I had a feeling that the heart of the desert was here," she said. "You know I said so."

"Do you say so still?"

"The heart, Boris, is the centre of life, isn't it?"

He was silent. She felt his inner feeling fighting hers.

"To-night," she said, putting her arm through his, and looking towards the city, "I feel a tremendous sympathy with human life such as I never felt before. Boris, it comes to me from you. Yes, it does. It is born of my love for you, and seems to link me, and you with me, to all these strangers, to all men and women, to everything that lives. It is as if I was not quite human before, and my love for you had made me completely human, had done something to me that even—even my love for God had not been able to do."

She lowered her voice at the last words. After a moment she added:

"Perhaps in isolation, even with you, I could not come to completeness. Perhaps you could not in isolation even with me. Boris, I think it's good for us to be in the midst of life for a time."

"You wish to remain here, Domini?"

"Yes, for a time."

The fatalistic feeling that had sometimes come upon her in this land entered into her at this moment. She felt, "It is written that we are to remain here."

"Let us remain here, Domini," he said quietly.

The note of disappointment had gone out of his voice, deliberately banished from it by his love for her, but she seemed to hear it, nevertheless, echoing far down in his soul. At that moment she loved him like a woman he had made a lover, but also like a woman he had made a mother by becoming a child.

"Thank you, Boris," she answered very quietly. "You are good to me."

"You are good to me," he said, remembering the last words of Father Roubier. "How can I be anything else?"

Directly he had spoken the words his body trembled violently.

"Boris, what is it?" she exclaimed, startled.

He took his arm away from hers.

"These—these noises of the city in the night coming across the sand-hills are extraordinary. I have become so used to silence that perhaps they get upon my nerves. I shall grow accustomed to them presently."

He turned towards the tents, and she went with him. It seemed to her that he had evaded her question, that he had not wished to answer it, and the sense sharply awakened in her by a return to life near a city made her probe for the reason of this. She did not find it, but in her mental search she found herself presently at Mogar. It seemed to her that the same sort of uneasiness which had beset her husband at Mogar beset him now more fiercely at Amara, that, as he had just said, his nerves were being tortured by something. But it could not be the noises from the city.

After dinner Batouch came to the tent to suggest that they should go down with him into the city. Domini, feeling certain that Androvsky would not wish to go, at once refused, alleging that she was tired. Batouch then asked Androvsky to go with him, and, to Domini's astonishment, he said that if she did not mind his leaving her for a short time he would like a stroll.

"Perhaps," he said to her, as Batouch and he were starting, "perhaps it will make me more completely human; perhaps there is something still to be done that even you, Domini, have not accomplished."

She knew he was alluding to her words before dinner. He stood looking at her with a slight smile that did not suggest happiness, then added:

"That link you spoke of between us and these strangers "— he made a gesture towards the city—"I ought perhaps to feel it more strongly than I do. I—I will try to feel it."

Then he turned away, and went with Batouch across the sand-hills, walking heavily.

As Domini watched him going she felt chilled, because there was something in his manner, in his smile, that seemed for the moment to set them apart from each other, something she did not understand.

Soon Androvsky disappeared in a fold of the sands as he had disappeared in a fold of the sands at Mogar, not long before De Trevignac came. She thought of Mogar once more, steadily, reviewing mentally—with the renewed sharpness of intellect that had returned to her, brought by contact with the city—all that had passed there, as she never reviewed it before.

It had been a strange episode.

She began to walk slowly up and down on the sand before the tent. Ouardi came to walk with her, but she sent him away. Before doing so, however, something moved her to ask him:

"That African liqueur, Ouardi—you remember that you brought to the tent at Mogar—have we any more of it?"

"The monk's liqueur, Madame?"

"What do you mean—monk's liqueur?"

"It was invented by a monk, Madame, and is sold by the monks of El-Largani."

"Oh! Have we any more of it?"

"There is another bottle, Madame, but I should not dare to bring it if——"

He paused.

" If what, Ouardi? "

" If Monsieur were there."

Domini was on the point of asking him why, but she checked herself and told him to leave her. Then she walked up and down once more on the sand. She was thinking now of the broken glass on the ground at Androvsky's feet when she found him alone in the tent after De Trevignac had gone. Ouardi's words made her wonder whether this liqueur, brought to celebrate De Trevignac's presence in the camp, had turned the conversation upon the subject of the religious orders; whether Androvsky had perhaps said something against them which had offended De Trevignac, a staunch Catholic; whether there had been a quarrel between the two men on the subject of religion. It was possible. She remembered De Trevignac's strange, almost mystical, gesture in the dawn, following his look of horror towards the tent where her husband lay sleeping.

To-night her mind—her whole nature—felt terribly alive.

She tried to think no more of Mogar, but her thoughts centred round it, linked it with this great city, whose lights shone in the distance below her, whose music came to her from afar over the silence of the sands.

Mogar and Amara; what had they to do with one another? Leagues of desert divided them. One was a desolation, the other was crowded with men. What linked them together in her mind?

Androvsky's fear of both—that was the link. She kept on thinking of the glance he had cast at the watch-tower, to which Trevignac had been even then approaching, although they knew it not. De Trevignac! She walked faster on the sand, to and fro before the tent. Why had he looked at the tent in which Androvsky slept with horror? Was it because Androvsky had denounced the religion that he reverenced and loved? Could it have been that? But then—did Androvsky actively hate religion? Perhaps he hated it, and concealed his hatred from her because he knew it would cause her pain. Yet she had sometimes felt as if he were seeking, perhaps with fear, perhaps with ignorance, perhaps with uncertainty, but still seeking to draw near to God. That was why she had been able to hope for him, why she had not been more troubled by his loss of the faith in which he had been brought up, and to which she belonged heart and soul. Could she have been wrong in her feeling—deceived? There were men in the world, she knew, who denied the existence of a God, and bitterly ridiculed all faith. She remembered the blasphemies of her father. Had she married a man who, like him, was lost, who, as he had, furiously denied God?

A cold thrill of fear came into her heart. Suddenly she felt as if, perhaps, even in her love, Androvsky had been a stranger to her.

She stood upon the sand. It chanced that she looked towards the camp of the Ouled Naïls, whose fires blazed upon the dunes. While she looked she was presently aware of a light that detached itself from the blaze of the fires, and moved from them, coming towards the place where she was standing, slowly. The young moon only gave a faint ray to the night. This light travelled onward through the dimness like an earth-bound star. She watched it with intentness, as people watch any moving thing when their minds are eagerly at work, staring, yet scarcely conscious that they see.

The little light moved steadily on over the sands, now descending the side of a dune, now mounting to a crest, and always coming towards the place where Domini was standing. And presently this determined movement towards her caught hold of her mind, drew it away from other thoughts, fixed it on the light. She became interested in it, intent upon it.

Who was bearing it? No doubt some desert man, some Arab. She imagined him tall, brown, lithe, half-naked, holding the lamp in his muscular fingers, treading on bare feet silently over the deep sand. Why had he left the camp? What was his purpose?

The light drew near. It was now moving over the flats and seemed, she thought, to travel more quickly. And always it came straight towards where she was standing. A conviction dawned in her that it was travelling with an intention of reaching her, that it was carried by someone who was thinking of her. But how could that be? She thought of the light as a thing with a mind and a purpose, borne by someone who backed up its purpose, helping it to do what it wanted. And it wanted to come to her.

In Mogar! Androvsky had dreaded something in Mogar. De Trevignac had come. He dreaded something in Amara. This light came. For an instant she fancied that the light was a lamp carried by De Trevignac. Then she saw that it gleamed upon a long black robe, the soutane of a priest.

As she and Androvsky rode into Amara she had asked herself whether his second dread would be followed, as his first dread had been, by an unusual incident. When she saw the soutane of a priest, black in the lamplight, moving towards her over the whiteness of the sand, she said to herself that it was to be so followed. This priest stood in the place of De Trevignac.

Why did he come to her?

CHAPTER XXIII

WHEN the priest drew close to the tent Domini saw that it was not he who carried the lantern, but a native soldier, one of the Tirailleurs, formerly called Turcos, who walked beside him. The soldier saluted her, and the priest took off his broad, fluffy black hat.

" Good-evening, Madame," he said, speaking French with the accent of Marseilles. " I am the Aumonier of Amara, and have just heard of your arrival here, and as I was visiting my friends on the sand-hills yonder, I thought I would venture to call and ask whether I could be of any service to you. The hour is informal, I know, but to tell the truth, Madame, after five years in Amara one does not know how to be formal any longer."

His eyes, which had a slightly impudent look, rare in a priest but not unpleasing, twinkled cheerfully in the lamplight as he spoke, and his whole expression betokened a highly social disposition and the most genuine pleasure at meeting with a stranger. While she looked at him, and heard him speak, Domini laughed at herself for the imaginations she had just been cherishing. He had a broad figure, long arms, large feet encased in stout, comfortable boots. His face was burnt brown by the sun and partially concealed by a heavy black beard, whiskers and moustache. His features were blunt and looked boyish, though his age must have been about forty. The nose was snub, and accorded with the expression in his eyes, which were black like his hair and full of twinkling lights. As he smiled genially on Domini he showed two rows of small, square white teeth. His Marseilles accent exactly suited his appearance, which was rough but honest. Domini welcomed him gladly. Indeed, her reception of him was more than cordial, almost eager. For she had been vaguely expecting some tragic figure, some personality suggestive of mystery or sorrow, as she thought of the incidents at Mogar, and associated the moving light with the approach of further strange events. This homely figure of her religion, beaming satisfaction and comfortable anticipation of friendly intercourse, laid to rest fears which only now, when she was conscious of relief, she knew she had been entertaining. She begged the priest to come into the dining-tent, and, taking up the little bell which was on the table, went out into the sand and rang it for Ouardi.

He came at once, like a shadow gliding over the waste.

"Bring us coffee for two, Ouardi, biscuits"—she glanced at her visitor—"bon-bons, yes, the bon-bons in the white box, and the cigars. And take the soldier with you and entertain him well. Give him whatever he likes."

Ouardi went away with the soldier, talking frantically, and Domini returned to the tent, where she found the priest gleaming with joyous anticipation. They sat down in the comfortable basket chairs before the tent door, through which they could see the shining of the city's lights and hear the distant sound of its throbbing and wailing music.

"My husband has gone to see the city," Domini said after she had told the priest her name and been informed that his was Max Beret.

"We only arrived this evening."

"I know, Madame."

He beamed on her, and stroked his thick beard with his broad, sunburnt hand. "Everyone in Amara knows, and everyone in the tents. We know, too, how many tents you have, how many servants, how many camels, horses, dogs."

He broke into a hearty laugh.

"We know what you've just had for dinner!"

Domini laughed too.

"Not really!"

"Well, I heard in the camp that it was soup and stewed mutton. But never mind! You must forgive us. We are barbarians! We are sand-rascals! We are ruffians of the sun!"

His laugh was infectious. He leaned back in his chair and shook with the mirth his own remarks had roused.

"We are ruffians of the sun!" he repeated with gusto. "And we must be forgiven everything."

Although clad in a soutane he looked, at that moment, like a type of the most joyous tolerance, and Domini could not help mentally comparing him with the priest of Beni-Mora. What would Father Roubier think of Father Beret?

" It is easy to forgive in the sun," Domini said.

The priest laid his hands on his knees, setting his feet well apart. She noticed that his hands were not scrupulously clean.

" Madame," he said, " it is impossible to be anything but lenient in the sun. That is my experience. Excuse me, but are you a Catholic? "

" Yes."

" So much the better. You must let me show you the chapel. It is in the building with the cupolas. The congregation consists of five on a full Sunday." His laugh broke out again. " I hope the day after to-morrow you and your husband will make it seven. But, as I was saying, the sun teaches one a lesson of charity. When I first came to live in Africa in the midst of the sand-rascals—eh, Madame!—I suppose as a priest I ought to have been shocked by their goings-on. And indeed I tried to be, I conscientiously did my best. But it was no good. I couldn't be shocked. The sunshine drove it all out of me. I could only say, ' It is not for me to question *le bon Dieu,* and *le bon Dieu* has created these people and set them here in the sand to behave as they do. What is my business? I can't convert them. I can't change their morals. I must just be a friend to them, cheer them up in their sorrows, give them a bit if they're starving, doctor them a little. I'm a first-rate hand at making an Arab take a pill or a powder!—when they are ill, and make them at home with the white marabout.' That's what the sun has taught me, and every sand-rascal and sand-rascal's child in Amara is a friend of mine."

He stretched out his legs as if he wished to elongate his satisfaction, and stared Domini full in the face with eyes that confidently, naïvely, asked for her approval of his doctrine of the sun. She could not help liking him, though she felt more as if she were sitting with a jolly, big, and rather rowdy boy than with a priest.

" You are fond of the Arabs then? " she said.

" Of course I am, Madame. I can speak their language, and I'm as much at home in their tents, and more, than I should ever be at the Vatican—with all respect to the Holy Father."

He got up, went out into the sand, expectorated noisily, then returned to the tent, wiping his bearded mouth with a large red cotton pocket-handkerchief.

" Are you staying here long, Madame? "

He sat down again in his chair, making it creak with his substantial weight.

"I don't know. If my husband is happy here. But he prefers the solitudes, I think."

"Does he? And yet he's gone into the city. Plenty of bustle there at night, I can tell you. Well, now, I don't agree with your husband. I know it's been said that solitude is good for the sad, but I think just the contrary. Ah!"

The last sonorously joyous exclamation jumped out of Father Beret at the sight of Ouardi, who at this moment entered with a large tray, covered with a coffee-pot, cups, biscuits, bonbons, cigars, and a bulging flask of some liqueur flanked by little glasses.

"You fare generously in the desert I see, Madame," he exclaimed. "And so much the better. What's your servant's name?"

Domini told him.

"Ouardi! that means born in the time of the roses." He addressed Ouardi in Arabic and sent him off into the darkness chuckling gaily. "These Arab names all have their meanings —Onlagareb, mother of scorpions, Omteoni, mother of eagles, and so on. So much the better! Comforts are rare here, but you carry them with you. Sugar, if you please."

Domini put two lumps into his cup.

"If you allow me!"

He added two more.

"I never refuse a good cigar. These harmless joys are excellent for man. They help his Christianity. They keep him from bitterness, harsh judgments. But harshness is for northern climes—rainy England, eh? Forgive me, Madame. I speak in joke. You come from England perhaps. It didn't occur to me that——"

They both laughed. His garrulity was irresistible and made Domini feel as if she were sitting with a child. Perhaps he caught her feeling, for he added:

"The desert has made me an *enfant terrible,* I fear. What have you there?"

His eyes had been attracted by the flask of liqueur, to which Domini was stretching out her hand with the intention of giving him some.

"I don't know."

She leaned forward to read the name on the flask.

"Louarine," she said.

"Pst!" exclaimed the priest, with a start.

"Will you have some? I don't know whether it's good

I've never tasted it, or seen it before. Will you have some?"

She felt so absolutely certain that he would say "Yes" that she lifted the flask to pour the liqueur into one of the little glasses, but, looking at him, she saw that he hesitated.

"After all—why not?" he ejaculated. "Why not?"

She was holding the flask over the glass. He saw that his remark surprised her.

"Yes, Madame, thanks."

She poured out the liqueur and handed it to him. He set it down by his coffee-cup.

"The fact is, Madame—but you know nothing about this liqueur?"

"No, nothing. What is it?"

Her curiosity was roused by his hesitation, his words, but still more by a certain gravity which had come into his face.

"Well, this liqueur comes from the Trappist monastery of El-Largani."

"The monks' liqueur!" she exclaimed.

And instantly she thought of Mogar.

"You do know then?"

"Ouardi told me we had with us a liqueur made by some monks."

"This is it, and very excellent it is. I have tasted it in Tunis."

"But then why did you hesitate to take it here?"

He lifted his glass up to the lamp. The light shone on its contents, showing that the liquid was pale green.

"Madame," he said, "the Trappists of El-Largani have a fine property. They grow every sort of things, but their vine-yards are specially famous, and their wines bring in a splendid revenue. This is their only liqueur, this Louarine. It, too, has brought in a lot of money to the community, but when what they have in stock at the monastery now is exhausted they will never make another franc by Louarine."

"But why not?"

"The secret of its manufacture belonged to one monk only. At his death he was to confide it to another whom he had chosen."

"And he died suddenly without——"

"Madame, he didn't die."

The gravity had returned to the priest's face and deepened there, transforming it. He put the glass down without touching it with his lips.

" Then—I don't understand."

" He disappeared from the monastery."

" Do you mean he left it—a Trappist? "

" Yes."

" After taking the final vows? "

" Oh, he had been a monk at El-Largani for over twenty years."

" How horrible! " Domini said. She looked at the pale-green liquid. " How horrible! " she repeated.

" Yes. The monks would have kept the matter a secret, but a servant of the *hôtellerie*—who had taken no vow of eternal silence—spoke, and—well, I know it here in the ' belly of the desert.' "

" Horrible! "

She said the word again, and as if she felt its meaning more acutely each time she spoke it.

" After twenty years to go! " she added after a moment. " And was there no reason, no—no excuse—no, I don't mean excuse! But had nothing exceptional happened? "

" What exceptional thing can happen in a Trappist monastery? " said the priest. " One day is exactly like another there, and one year exactly like another."

" Was it long ago? "

" No, not very long. Only some months. Oh, perhaps it may be a year by now, but not more. Poor fellow! I suppose he was a man who didn't know himself, Madame, and the devil tempted him."

" But after twenty years! " said Domini.

The thing seemed to her almost incredible.

" That man must be in hell now," she added. " In the hell a man can make for himself by his own act. Oh, here is my husband."

Androvsky stood in the tent door, looking in upon them with startled, scrutinising eyes. He had come over the deep sand without noise. Neither Domini nor the priest had heard a footstep. The priest got up from his chair and bowed genially.

" Good-evening, Monsieur," he said, not waiting for any introduction. " I am the Aumonier of Amara, and——"

He paused in the full flow of his talk. Androvsky's eyes had wandered from his face to the table, upon which stood the coffee, the liqueur, and the other things brought by Ouardi. It was evident even to the self-centred priest that his host was not listening to him. There was a moment's awkward pause. Then Domini said:

"Boris, Monsieur l'Aumonier!"

She did not speak loudly, but with an intention that recalled the mind of her husband. He stepped slowly into the tent and held out his hand in silence to the priest. As he did so the lamplight fell full upon him.

"Boris, are you ill? Domini exclaimed.

The priest had taken Androvsky's hand, but with a doubtful air. His cheerful and confident manner had died away, and his eyes, fixed upon his host, shone with an astonishment which was mingled with a sort of boyish glumness. It was evident that he felt that his presence was unwelcome.

"I have a headache," Androvsky said. "I—that is why I returned."

He dropped the priest's hand. He was again looking towards the table.

"The sun was unusually fierce to-day," Domini said. "Do you think——"

"Yes, yes," he interrupted. "That's it. I must have had a touch of the sun."

He put his hand to his head.

"Excuse me, Monsieur," he said, speaking to the priest but not looking at him. "I am really feeling unwell. Another day——"

He went out of the tent and disappeared silently into the darkness. Domini and the priest looked after him. Then the priest, with an air of embarrassment, took up his hat from the table. His cigar had gone out, but he pulled at it as if he thought it was still alight, then took it out of his mouth and, glancing with a naïve regret at the good things upon the table, his half-finished coffee, the biscuits, the white box of bon-bons —said:

"Madame, I must be off. I've a good way to go, and it's getting late. If you will allow me——"

He went to the tent door and called, in a powerful voice:

"Belgassem! Belgassem!"

He paused, then called again:

"Belgassem!"

A light travelled over the sand from the farther tents of the servants. Then the priest turned round to Domini and shook her by the hand.

"Good-night, Madame."

"I'm very sorry," she said, not trying to detain him. "You must come again. My husband is evidently ill, and——"

"You must go to him. Of course. Of course. This sun is a blessing. Still, it brings fever sometimes, especially to strangers. We sand-rascals—eh, Madame!" he laughed, but the laugh had lost its sonorous ring—"we can stand it. It's our friend. But for travellers sometimes it's a little bit too much. But now, mind, I'm a bit of a doctor, and if to-morrow your husband is no better I might—anyhow"—he looked again longingly at the bon-bons and the cigars—"if you'll allow me I'll call to know how he is."

"Thank you, Monsieur."

"Not at all, Madame, not at all! I can set him right in a minute, if it's anything to do with the sun, in a minute. Ah, here's Belgassem! "

The soldier stood like a statue without, bearing the lantern. The priest hesitated. He was holding the burnt-out cigar in his hand, and now he glanced at it and then at the cigar-box. A plaintive expression overspread his bronzed and bearded face. It became almost piteous. Quickly Domini went to the table, took two cigars from the box and came back.

"You must have a cigar to smoke on the way."

"Really, Madame, you are too good, but—well, I never refuse a fine cigar, and these—upon my word—are——"

He struck a match on his broad-toed boot. His demeanour was becoming cheerful again. Domini gave the other cigar to the soldier.

"Good-night, Madame. A demain then, à demain! I trust your husband may be able to rest. À demain! À demain! "

The light moved away over the dunes and dropped down towards the city. Then Domini hurried across the sand to the sleeping-tent. As she went she was acutely aware of the many distant noises that rose up in the night to the pale crescent of the young moon, the pulsing of the tom-toms in the city, the faint screaming of the pipes that sounded almost like human beings in distress, the passionate barking of the guard dogs tied up to the tents on the sand-slopes where the multitudes of fires gleamed. The sensation of being far away, and close to the heart of the desert, deepened in her, but she felt now that it was a savage heart, that there was something terrible in the remoteness. In the faint moonlight the tent cast black shadows upon the wintry whiteness of the sands, that rose and fell like waves of a smooth but foam-covered sea. And the shadow of the sleeping-tent looked the blackest of them all. For she began to feel as if there was another darkness about it than the darkness that it cast upon the sand. Her husband's face that night as he came in from the dunes had been dark with a shadow cast surely by his soul. And she did not know what it was in his soul that sent forth the shadow.

" Boris! "

She was at the door of the sleeping-tent. He did not answer.

" Boris! "

He came in from the farther tent that he used as a dressing-room, carrying a lit candle in his hand. She went up to him with a movement of swift, ardent sincerity.

" You felt ill in the city? Did Batouch let you come back alone?"

" I preferred to be alone."

He set down the candle on the table, and moved so that the light of it did not fall upon his face. She took his hands in hers gently. There was no response in his hands. They remained in hers nervelessly. They felt almost like dead things in her hands. But they were not cold, but burning hot.

" You have fever! " she said.

She let one of his hands go and put one of hers to his fore-head.

" Your forehead is burning, and your pulses—how they are beating! Like hammers! I must——"

" Don't give me anything, Domini! It would be useless."

She was silent. There was a sound of hopelessness in his voice that frightened her. It was like the voice of a man reject-ing remedies because he knew that he was stricken with a mortal disease.

" Why did that priest come here to-night? " he asked.

They were both standing up, but now he sat down in a chair heavily, taking his hand from hers.

" Merely to pay a visit of courtesy."

" At night? "

He spoke suspiciously. Again she thought of Mogar, and of how, on his return from the dunes, he had said to her, " There is a light in the tower." A painful sensation of being sur-rounded with mystery came upon her. It was hateful to her strong and frank nature. It was like a miasma that suffocated her soul.

" Oh, Boris," she exclaimed bluntly, " why should he not come at night?"

" Is such a thing usual? "

" But he was visiting the tents over there—of the nomads, and he had heard of our arrival. He knew it was informal, but, as he said, in the desert one forgets formalities."

" And—and did he ask for anything? "

" Ask? "

" I saw—on the table—coffee and—and there was liqueur."

" Naturally I offered him something."

" He didn't ask? "

" But, Boris, how could he? "

After a moment of silence he said:

" No, of course not."

He shifted in his chair, crossed one leg over the other, put his hands on the arms of it, and continued:

" What did he talk about? "

" A little about Amara."

" That was all? "

" He hadn't been here long when you came——"

" Oh! "

" But he told me one thing that was horrible," she added, obedient to her instinct always to tell the complete truth to him, even about trifles which had nothing to do with their lives or their relation to each other.

" Horrible! " Androvsky said, uncrossing his legs and leaning forward in his chair.

She sat down by him. They both had their backs to the light and were in shadow.

" Yes."

" What was it about—some crime here? "

" Oh, no! It was about that liqueur you saw on the table."

Androvsky was sitting upon a basket chair. As she spoke it creaked under a violent movement that he made.

" How could—what could there be that was horrible connected with that? " he asked, speaking slowly.

" It was made by a monk, a Trappist——"

He got up from his chair and went to the opening of the tent.

" What—— " she began, thinking he was perhaps feeling the pain in his head more severely.

" I only want to be in the air. It's rather hot there. Stay where you are, Domini, and—well, what else? "

He stepped out into the sand, and stood just outside the tent in its shadow.

"It was invented by a Trappist monk of the monastery of El-Largani, who disappeared from the monastery. He had taken the final vows. He had been there for over twenty years."

"He—he disappeared—did the priest say?"

"Yes."

"Where?"

"I don't think—I am sure he doesn't know. But what does it matter? The awful thing is that he should leave the monastery after taking the eternal vows—vows made to God."

After a moment, during which neither of them spoke and Androvsky stood quite still in the sand, she added:

"Poor man!"

Androvsky came a step towards her, then paused.

"Why do you say that, Domini?"

"I was thinking of the agony he must be enduring if he is still alive."

"Agony?"

"Of mind, of heart. You—I know, Boris, you can't feel with me on certain subjects—yet——"

"Yet!" he said.

"Boris"—she got up and came to the tent door, but not out upon the sand—"I dare to hope that some day perhaps——"

She was silent, looking towards him with her brave, steady eyes.

"Agony of heart?" Androvsky said, recurring to her words. "You think—what—you pity that man then?"

"And don't you?"

"I—what has he to do with—us? Why should we——?"

"I know. But one does sometimes pity men one never has seen, never will see, if one hears something frightful about them. Perhaps—don't smile, Boris—perhaps it was seeing that liqueur, which he had actually made in the monastery when he was at peace with God, perhaps it was seeing that, that has made me realise—such trifles stir the imagination, set it working—at any rate——"

She broke off. After a minute, during which he said nothing, she continued:

"I believe the priest felt something of the same sort. He could not drink the liqueur that man had made, although he intended to."

"But—that might have been for a different reason," Androvsky said in a harsh voice; " priests have strange ideas. They often judge things cruelly, very cruelly."

" Perhaps they do. Yes; I can imagine that Father Roubier of Beni-Mora might, though he is a good man and leads a saintly life."

" Those are sometimes the most cruel. They do not understand."

" Perhaps not. It may be so. But this priest—he's not like that."

She thought of his genial, bearded face, his expression when he said, " We are ruffians of the sun," including himself with the desert men, his boisterous laugh.

" His fault might be the other way."

" Which way? "

" Too great a tolerance."

" Can a man be too tolerant towards his fellow-man? " said Androvsky.

There was a strange sound of emotion in his deep voice which moved her. It seemed to her—why, she did not know—to steal out of the depth of something their mutual love had created.

" The greatest of all tolerance is God's," she said. " I'm sure—quite sure—of that."

Androvsky came in out of the shadow of the tent, took her in his arms with passion, laid his lips on hers with passion, hot, burning force and fire, and a hard tenderness that was hard because it was intense.

" God will bless you," he said. " God will bless you. Whatever life brings you at the end you must—you must be blessed by Him."

" But He has blessed me," she whispered, through tears that rushed from her eyes, stirred from their well-springs by his sudden outburst of love for her. " He has blessed me. He has given me you, your love, your truth."

Androvsky released her as abruptly as he had taken her in his arms, turned, and went out into the desert.

CHAPTER XXIV

TRUE to his promise, on the following day the priest called to inquire after Androvsky's health. He happened to come just before *déjeuner* was ready, and met Androvsky on the sand before the tent door.

"It's not fever then, Monsieur," he said, after they had shaken hands.

"No, no," Androvsky replied. "I am quite well this morning."

The priest looked at him closely with an unembarrassed scrutiny.

"Have you been long in the desert, Monsieur?" he asked.

"Some weeks."

"The heat has tired you. I know the look——"

"I assure you, Monsieur, that I am accustomed to heat. I have lived in North Africa all my life."

"Indeed. And yet by your appearance I should certainly suppose that you needed a change from the desert. The air of the Sahara is magnificent, but there are people——"

"I am not one of them," Androvsky said abruptly. "I have never felt so strong physically as since I have lived in the sand."

The priest still looked at him closely, but said nothing further on the subject of health. Indeed, almost immediately his attention was distracted by the apparition of Ouardi bearing dishes from the cook's tent.

"I am afraid I have called at a very unorthodox time," he remarked, looking at his watch; "but the fact is that here in Amara we——"

"I hope you will stay to *déjeuner*," Androvsky said.

"It is very good of you. If you are certain that I shall not put you out."

"Please stay."

"I will, then, with pleasure."

He moved his lips expectantly, as if only a sense of politeness prevented him from smacking them. Androvsky went towards the sleeping-tent, where Domini, who had been into the city was washing her hands.

"The priest has called," he said. "I have asked him to *déjeuner*."

She looked at him with frank astonishment in her dark eyes.

"You—Boris!"

"Yes, I. Why not?"

"I don't know. But generally you hate people."

"He seems a good sort of man."

She still looked at him with some surprise, even with curiosity.

" Have you taken a fancy to a priest? " she asked, smiling.

" Why not? This man is very different from Father Roubier, more human."

" Father Beret is very human, I think," she answered.

She was still smiling. It had just occurred to her that the priest had timed his visit with some forethought.

" I am coming," she added.

A sudden cheerfulness had taken possession of her. All the morning she had been feeling grave, even almost apprehensive, after a bad night. When her husband had abruptly left her and gone away into the darkness she had been overtaken by a sudden wave of acute depression. She had felt, more painfully than ever before, the mental separation which existed between them despite their deep love, and a passionate but almost hopeless longing had filled her heart that in all things they might be one, not only in love of each other, but in love of God. When Androvsky had taken his arms from her she had seemed to feel herself released by a great despair, and this certainty—for as he vanished into the darkness she was no more in doubt that his love for her left room within his heart for such an agony— had for a moment brought her soul to the dust. She had been overwhelmed by a sensation that instead of being close together they were far apart, almost strangers, and a great bitterness had entered into her. It was accompanied by a desire for action. She longed to follow Androvsky, to lay her hand on his arm, to stop him in the sand and force him to confide in her. For the first time the idea that he was keeping something from her, a sorrow, almost maddened her, even made her feel jealous. The fact that she divined what that sorrow was, or believed she divined it, did not help her just then. She waited a long while, but Androvsky did not return, and at last she prayed and went to bed. But her prayers were feeble, disjointed, and sleep did not come to her, for her mind was travelling with this man who loved her and who yet was out there alone in the night, who was deliberately separating himself from her. Towards dawn, when he stole into the tent, she was still awake, but she did not speak or give any sign of consciousness, although she was hot with the fierce desire to spring up, to throw her arms round him, to draw his head down upon her heart, and say, "I have given myself, body, heart and soul, to you. Give yourself to me; give me the thing you are keeping back—your sorrow. Till I have that I have not all of you, and till I have all of ou I am in hell."

It was a mad impulse. She resisted it and lay quite still. And when he lay down and was quiet she slept at length.

Now, as she heard him speak in the sunshine and knew that he had offered hospitality to the comfortable priest her heart suddenly felt lighter, she scarcely knew why. It seemed to her that she had been a little morbid, and that the cloud which had settled about her was lifted, revealing the blue.

At *déjeuner* she was even more reassured. Her husband seemed to get on with the priest better than she had ever seen him get on with anybody. He began by making an effort to be agreeable that was obvious to her; but presently he was agreeable without effort. The simple geniality and lack of self-consciousness in Father Beret evidently set him at his ease. Once or twice she saw him look at his guest with an earnest scrutiny that puzzled her, but he talked far more than usual and with greater animation, discussing the Arabs and listening to the priest's account of the curiosities of life in Amara. When at length Father.Beret rose to go Androvsky said he would accompany him a little way, and they went off together, evidently on the best of terms.

She was delighted and surprised. She had been right, then. It was time that Androvsky was subjected to another influence than that of the unpeopled wastes. It was time that he came into contact with men whose minds were more akin to his than the minds of the Arabs who had been their only companions. She began to imagine him with her in civilised places, to be able to imagine him. And she was glad they had come to Amara and confirmed in her resolve to stay on there. She even began to wish that the French officers quartered there—few in number, some five or six—would find them in the sand, and that Androvsky would offer them hospitality. It occurred to her that it was not quite wholesome for a man to live in isolation from his fellow-men, even with the woman he loved, and she determined that she would not be selfish in her love, that she would think for Androvsky, act for him, even against her own inclination. Perhaps his idea of life in an oasis apart from Europeans was one she ought to combat, though it fascinated her. Perhaps it would be stronger, more sane, to face a more ordinary, less dreamy, life, in which they would meet with people, in which they would inevitably find themselves confronted with duties. She felt powerful enough in that moment to do anything that would make for Androvsky's welfare of soul. His body was strong and at ease. She thought of him going away with the priest in friendly conversation. How splendid it would be if she could feel some day that the health of his soul accorded completely with that of his body!

"Batouch!" she called almost gaily.

Batouch appeared, languidly smoking a cigarette, and with a large flower tied to a twig protending from behind his ear.

"Saddle the horses. Monsieur has gone with the Père Beret. I shall take a ride, just a short ride round the camp over there—in at the city gate, through the market-place, and home. You will come with me."

Batouch threw away his cigarette with energy. Poet though he was, all the Arab blood in him responded to the thought of a gallop over the sands. Within a few minutes they were off. When she was in the saddle it was at all times difficult for Domini to be sad or even pensive. She had a native passion for a good horse, and riding was one of the joys, and almost the keenest, of her life. She felt powerful when she had a spirited, fiery animal under her, and the wide spaces of the desert summoned speed as they summoned dreams. She and Batouch went away at a rapid pace, circled round the Arab cemetery, made a detour towards the south, and then cantered into the midst of the camps of the Ouled Naïls. It was the hour of the siesta. Only a few people were stirring, coming and going over the dunes to and from the city on languid errands for the women of the tents, who reclined in the shade of their brushwood arbours upon filthy cushions and heaps of multi-coloured rags, smoking cigarettes, playing cards with Arab and negro admirers, or staring into vacancy beneath their heavy eyebrows as they listened to the sound of music played upon long pipes of reed. No dogs barked in their camp. The only guardians were old women, whose sandy faces were scored with innumerable wrinkles, and whose withered hands drooped under their loads of barbaric rings and bracelets. Batouch would evidently have liked to dismount here. Like all Arabs he was fascinated by the sight of these idols of the waste, whose painted faces called to the surface the fluid poetry within him, but Domini rode on, descending towards the city gate by which she had first entered Amara. The priest's house was there and Androvsky was with the priest. She hoped he had perhaps gone in to return the visit paid to them. As she rode into the city she glanced at the house. The door was open and she saw the gay rugs in the little hall. She had a strong inclination to stop and ask if her husband were there. He might mount Batouch's horse and accompany her home.

"Batouch," she said, "will you ask if Monsieur Androvsky is with Père Beret. I think——"

She stopped speaking. She had just seen her husband's face pass across the window-space of the room on the right-hand side of the hall door. She could not see it very well. The arcade built out beyond the house cast a deep shade within, and in this shade the face had flitted like a shadow. Batouch had sprung from his horse. But the sight of the shadowy face had changed her mind. She resolved not to interrupt the two men. Long ago at Beni-Mora she had asked Androvsky to call upon a priest. She remembered the sequel to that visit. This time Androvsky had gone of his own will. If he liked this priest, if they became friends, perhaps—she remembered her vision in the dancing-house, her feeling that when she drew near Amara she was drawing near to the heart of the desert. If she should see Androvsky praying here! Yet Father Beret hardly seemed a man likely to influence her husband, or anyone with a strong and serious personality. He was surely too fond of the things of this world, too obviously a lover and cherisher of the body. Nevertheless, there was something attractive in him, a kindness, a geniality. In trouble he would be sympathetic. Certainly her husband must have taken a liking to him, and the chances of life and the influences of destiny were strange and not to be foreseen.

"No, Batouch," she said. "We won't stop."

"But, Madame," he cried, "Monsieur is in there. I saw his face at the window."

"Never mind. We won't disturb them. I daresay they have something to talk about."

They cantered on towards the market-place. It was not market-day, and the town, like the camp of the Ouled Naïls, was almost deserted. As she rode up the hill towards the place of the fountain, however, she saw two handsomely-dressed Arabs, followed by a servant, slowly strolling towards her from the doorway of the Bureau Arabe. One, who was very tall, was dressed in green, and carried a long staff, from which hung green ribbons. The other wore a more ordinary costume of white, with a white burnous and a turban spangled with gold.

"Madame!" said Batouch.

"Yes."

"Do you see the Arab dressed in green?"

He spoke in an almost awestruck voice.

"Yes. Who is he?"

"The great marabout who lives at Beni-Hassan."

The name struck upon Domini's ear with a strange familiarity.

"But that's where Count Anteoni went when he rode away from Beni-Mora that morning."

"Yes, Madame."

"Is it far from Amara?"

"Two hours' ride across the desert."

"But then Count Anteoni may be near us. After he left he wrote to me and gave me his address at the marabout's house."

"If he is still with the marabout, Madame."

They were close to the fountain now, and the marabout and his companion were coming straight towards them.

"If Madame will allow me I will salute the marabout," said Batouch.

"Certainly."

He sprang off his horse immediately, tied it up to the railing of the fountain, and went respectfully towards the approaching potentate to kiss his hand. Domini saw the marabout stop and Batouch bend down, then lift himself up and suddenly move back as if in surprise. The Arab who was with the marabout seemed also surprised. He held out his hand to Batouch, who took it, kissed it, then kissed his own hand, and turning, pointed towards Domini. The Arab spoke a word to the marabout, then left him, and came rapidly forward to the fountain. As he drew close to her she saw a face browned by the sun, a very small, pointed beard, a pair of intensely bright eyes surrounded by wrinkles. These eyes held her. It seemed to her that she knew them, that she had often looked into them and seen their changing expressions. Suddenly she exclaimed:

"Count Anteoni!"

"Yes, it is I!"

He held out his hand and clasped hers.

"So you have started upon your desert journey," he added, looking closely at her, as he had often looked in the garden.

"Yes."

"And as I ventured to advise—that last time, do you remember?"

She recollected his words.

"No," she replied, and there was a warmth of joy, almost of pride, in her voice. "I am not alone."

Count Anteoni was standing with one hand on her horse's neck. As she spoke, his hand dropped down.

"I have been away from Beni-Hassan," he said slowly. "The marabout and I have been travelling in the south and only returned yesterday. I have heard no news for a long time from Beni-Mora, but I know. You are Madame Androvsky."

"Yes," she answered; "I am Madame Androvsky."

There was a silence between them. In it she heard the dripping water in the fountain. At last Count Anteoni spoke again.

"It was written," he said quietly. "It was written in the sand."

She thought of the sand-diviner and was silent. An oppression of spirit had suddenly come upon her. It seemed to her connected with something physical, something obscure, unusual, such as she had never felt before. It was, she thought, as if her body at that moment became more alive than it had ever been, and as if that increase of life within her gave to her a peculiar uneasiness. She was startled. She even felt alarmed, as at the faint approach of something strange, of something that was going to alter her life. She did not know at all what it was. For the moment a sense of confusion and of pain beset her, and she was scarcely aware with whom she was, or where. The sensation passed and she recovered herself and met Count Anteoni's eyes quietly.

"Yes," she answered; "all that has happened to me here in Africa was written in the sand and in fire."

"You are thinking of the sun."

"Yes."

"I—where are you living?"

"Close by on the sand-hill beyond the city wall."

"Where you can see the fires lit at night and hear the sound of the music of Africa."

"Yes."

"As he said."

"Yes, as he said."

Again the overwhelming sense of some strange and formidable approach came over her, but this time she fought it resolutely.

"Will you come and see me?" she said.

She had meant to say " us," but did not say it.

" If you will allow me."

" When? "

" I—" she heard the odd, upward grating in his voice which she remembered so well. " May I come now if you are riding to the tents? "

" Please do."

" I will explain to the marabout and follow you."

" But the way? Shall Batouch——? "

" No, it is not necessary."

She rode away. When she reached the camp she found that Androvsky had not yet returned, and she was glad. She wanted to talk to Count Anteoni alone. Within a few minutes she saw him coming towards the tent. His beard and his Arab dress so altered him that at a short distance she could not recognise him, could only guess that it was he. But directly he was near, and she saw his eyes, she forgot that he was altered, and felt that she was with her kind and whimsical host of the garden.

" My husband is in the city," she said.

" Yes."

" With the priest."

She saw an expression of surprise flit over Count Anteoni's face. It went away instantly.

" Père Beret," he said. " He is a cheerful creature and very good to the Arabs."

They sat down just inside the shadow of the tent before the door, and he looked out quietly towards the city.

" Yes, this is the place," he said.

She knew that he was alluding to the vision of the sand-diviner, and said so.

" Did you believe at the time that what he said would come true? " she asked.

" How could I? Am I a child? "

He spoke with gentle irony, but she felt he was playing with her.

" Cannot a man believe such things? "

He did not answer her, but said:

" My fate has come to pass. Do you not care to know what it is? "

" Yes, do tell me."

She spoke earnestly. She felt a change in him, a great change which as yet she did not understand fully. It was as if he had been a man in doubt and was now a man no longer in doubt, as if he had arrived at some goal and was more at peace with himself than he had been.

"I have become a Mohammedan," he said simply.

"A Mohammedan!"

She repeated the words as a person repeats words in surprise, but her voice did not sound surprised.

"You wonder?" he asked.

After a moment she answered:

"No. I never thought of such a thing, but I am not surprised. Now you have told me it seems to explain you, much that I noticed in you, wondered about in you."

She looked at him steadily, but without curiosity.

"I feel that you are happy now."

"Yes, I am happy. The world I used to know, my world and yours, would laugh at me, would say that I was crazy, that it was a whim, that I wished for a new sensation. Simply it had to be. For years I have been tending towards it—who knows why? Who knows what obscure influences have been at work in me, whether there is not, perhaps far back, some faint strain of Arab blood mingled wich the Sicilian blood in my veins? I cannot understand why. What I can understand is that at last I have fulfilled my destiny! After years of unrest I am suddenly and completely at peace. It is a magical sensation. I have been wandering all my life and have come upon the open door of my home."

He spoke very quietly, but she heard the joy in his voice.

"I remember you saying, 'I like to see men praying in the desert.'"

"Yes. When I looked at them I was longing to be one of them. For years from my garden wall I watched them with a passion of envy, with bitterness, almost with hatred sometimes. They had something I had not, something that set them above me, something that made their lives plain through any complication, and that gave to death a meaning like the meaning at the close of a great story that is going to have a sequel. They had faith. And it was difficult not to hate them. But now I am one of them. I can pray in the desert."

"That was why you left Beni-Mora."

"Yes. I had long been wishing to become a Mohammedan. I came here to be with the marabout, to enter more fully into certain questions, to see if I had any lingering doubts."

"And you have none?"

" None."

She looked at his bright eyes and sighed, thinking of her husband.

" You will go back to Beni-Mora? " she asked.

" I don't think so. I am inclined to go farther into the desert, farther among the people of my own faith. I don't want to be surrounded by French. Some day perhaps I may return. But at present everything draws me onward. Tell me "—he dropped the earnest tone in which he had been speaking, and she heard once more the easy, half-ironical man of the world—" do you think me a half-crazy eccentric? "

" No! "

" You look at me very gravely, even sadly."

" I was thinking of the men who cannot pray," she said, " even in the desert."

" They should not come into the Garden of Allah. Don't you remember that day by the garden wall, when——"

He suddenly checked himself.

" Forgive me," he said simply. " And now tell me about yourself. You never wrote that you were going to be married."

" I knew you would know it in time—when we met again."

" And you knew we should meet again? "

" Did not you? "

He nodded.

" In the heart of the desert. And you—where are you going? You are not returning to civilisation? "

" I don't know. I have no plans. I want to do what my husband wishes."

" And he? "

" He loves the desert. He has suggested our buying an oasi. and setting up as date merchants. What do you think of the idea? "

She spoke with a smile, but her eyes were serious, even sad.

" I cannot judge for others," he answered.

When he got up to go he held her hand fast for a moment.

" May I speak what is in my heart? " he asked.

" Yes—do."

" I feel as if what I have told you to-day about myself, about my having come to the open door of a home I had long been wearily seeking, had made you sad. Is it so? "

" Yes," she answered frankly.

" Can you tell me why? "

"It has made me realise more sharply than perhaps I did before what must be the misery of those who are still homeless."

There was in her voice a sound as if she suppressed a sob.

"Hope for them, remembering my many years of wandering."

"Yes, yes."

"Good-bye."

"Will you come again?"

"You are here for long?"

"Some days, I think."

"Whenever you ask me I will come."

"I want you and my husband to meet again. I want that very much." She spoke with a pressure of eagerness.

"Send for me and I will come at any hour."

"I will send—soon."

When he was gone, Domini sat in the shadow of the tent. From where she was she could see the Arab cemetery at a little distance, a quantity of stones half drowned in the sand. An old Arab was wandering there alone, praying for the dead in a loud, persistent voice. Sometimes he paused by a grave, bowed himself in prayer, then rose and walked on again. His voice was never silent. The sound of it was plaintive and monotonous. Domini listened to it, and thought of homeless men, of those who had lived and died without ever coming to that open door through which Count Anteoni had entered. His words and the changed look in his face had made a deep impression upon her. She realised that in the garden, when they were together, his eyes, even when they twinkled with the slightly ironical humour peculiar to him, had always held a shadow. Now that shadow was lifted out of them. How deep was the shadow in her husband's eyes. How deep had it been in the eyes of her father. He had died with that terrible darkness in his eyes and in his soul. If her husband were to die thus! A terror came upon her. She looked out at the stones in the sand and imagined herself there—as the old Arab was—praying for Androvsky buried there, hidden from her on earth for ever. And suddenly she felt, "I cannot wait, I must act."

Her faith was deep and strong. Nothing could shake it. But might it not shake the doubt from another's soul, as a great, pure wind shakes leaves that are dead from a tree that will blossom with the spring? Hitherto a sense of intense delicacy had prevented her from ever trying to draw near definitely to her husband's sadness. But her interview with

Count Anteoni, and the sound of this voice praying, praying for the dead men in the sand, stirred her to an almost fierce resolution. She had given herself to Androvsky. He had given himself to her. They were one. She had a right to draw near to his pain, if by so doing there was a chance that she might bring balm to it. She had a right to look closer into his eyes if hers, full of faith, could lift the shadow from them.

She leaned back in the darkness of the tent. The old Arab had wandered further on among the graves. His voice was faint in the sand, faint and surely piteous, as if, even while he prayed, he felt that his prayers were useless, that the fate of the dead was pronounced beyond recall. Domini listened to him no more. She was praying for the living as she had never prayed before, and her prayer was the prelude not to patience but to action. It was as if her conversation with Count Anteoni had set a torch to something in her soul, some-thing that gave out a great flame, a flame that could surely burn up the sorrow, the fear, the secret torture in her hus-band's soul. All the strength of her character had been roused by the sight of the peace she desired for the man she loved enthroned in the heart of this other man who was only her friend.

The voice of the old Arab died away in the distance, but before it died away Domini had ceased from hearing it.

She heard only a voice within her, which said to her, " If you really love be fearless. Attack this sorrow which stands like a figure of death between you and your husband. Drive it away. You have a weapon—faith. Use it."

It seemed to her then that through all their intercourse she had been a coward in her love, and she resolved that she would be a coward no longer.

CHAPTER XXV

DOMINI had said to herself that she would speak to her hus-band that night. She was resolved not to hesitate, not to be influenced from her purpose by anything. Yet she knew that a great difficulty would stand in her way—the difficulty of Androvsky's intense, almost passionate, reserve. This reserve was the dominant characteristic in his nature. She thought of it sometimes as a wall of fire that he had set round about the secret places of his soul to protect them even from her eyes. Perhaps it was strange that she, a woman of a singularly frank temperament, should be attracted by reserve in another, yet she knew that she was so attracted by the reserve of her husband. Its existence hinted to her depths in him which, perhaps, some day she might sound, she alone, strength which was hidden for her some day to prove.

Now, alone with her purpose, she thought of this reserve. Would she be able to break it down with her love? For an instant she felt as if she were about to enter upon a contest with her husband, but she did not coldly tell over her armoury and select weapons. There was a heat of purpose within her that beckoned her to the unthinking, to the reckless way, that told her to be self-reliant and to trust to the moment for the method.

When Androvsky returned to the camp it was towards evening. A lemon light was falling over the great white spaces of the sand. Upon their little round hills the Arab villages glowed mysteriously. Many horsemen were riding forth from the city to take the cool of the approaching night. From the desert the caravans were coming in. The nomad children played, half-naked, at Cora before the tents, calling shrilly to each other through the light silence that floated airily away into the vast distances that breathed out the spirit of a pale eternity. Despite the heat there was an almost wintry romance in this strange land of white sands and yellow radiance, an ethereal melancholy that stole with the twilight noiselessly towards the tents.

As Androvsky approached Domini saw that he had lost the energy which had delighted her at *déjeuner*. He walked towards her slowly with his head bent down. His face was grave, even sad, though when he saw her waiting for him he smiled.

"You have been all this time with the priest?" she said.

"Nearly all. I walked for a little while in the city. And you?"

"I rode out and met a friend."

"A friend?" he said, as if startled.

"Yes, from Beni-Mora—Count Anteoni. He has been here to pay me a visit."

She pulled forward a basket-chair for him. He sank into it heavily.

"Count Anteoni here!" he said slowly. "What is he doing here?"

"He is with the marabout at Beni-Hassan. And, Boris, he has become a Mohammedan."

He lifted his head with a jerk and stared at her in silence.

"You are surprised?"

"A Mohammedan—Count Anteoni?"

"Yes. Do you know, when he told me I felt almost as if I had been expecting it."

"But—is he changed then? Is he——"

He stopped. His voice had sounded to her bitter, almost fierce.

"Yes, Boris, he is changed. Have you ever seen anyone who was lost, and the same person walking along the road home? Well, that is Count Anteoni."

They said no more for some minutes. Androvsky was the first to speak again.

"You told him?" he asked.

"About ourselves?"

"Yes."

"I told him."

"What did he say?"

"He had expected it. When we ask him he is coming here again to see us both together."

Androvsky got up from his chair. His face was troubled. Standing before Domini, he said:

"Count Anteoni is happy then, now that he—now that he has joined this religion?"

"Very happy."

"And you—a Catholic—what do you think?"

"I think that, since that is his honest belief, it is a blessed thing for him."

He said no more, but went towards the sleeping-tent.

In the evening, when they were dining, he said to her:

"Domini, to-night I am going to leave you again for a short time."

He saw a look of keen regret come into her face, and added quickly:

"At nine I have promised to go to see the priest. He—ne is rather lonely here. He wants me to come. Do you mind?"

"No, no. I am glad—very glad. Have you finished?"

"Quite."

"Let us take a rug and go out a little way in the sand—that way towards the cemetery. It is quiet there at night."

"Yes. I will get a rug."

He went to fetch it, threw it over his arm, and they set out together. She had meant the Arab cemetery, but when they reached it they found two or three nomads wandering there.

" Let us go on," she said.

They went on, and came to the French cemetery, which was surrounded by a rough hedge of brushwood, in which there were gaps here and there. Through one of these gaps they entered it, spread out the rug, and lay down on the sand. The night was still and silence brooded here. Faintly they saw the graves of the exiles who had died here and been given to the sand, where in summer vipers glided to and fro, and the pariah dogs wandered stealthily, seeking food to still the desires in their starving bodies. They were mostly very simple, but close to Domini and Androvsky was one of white marble, in the form of a broken column, hung with wreaths of everlasting flowers, and engraved with these words:

ICI REPOSE

Jean Báptiste Fabriani

Priez pour lui.

When they lay down they both looked at this grave, as if moved by a simultaneous impulse, and read the words.

" Priez pour lui! " Domini said in a low voice.

She put out her hand and took hold of her husband's, and pressed it down on the sand.

" Do you remember that first night, Boris," she said, " at Arba, when you took my hand in yours and laid it against the desert as against a heart? "

" Yes, Domini, I remember."

" That night we were one, weren't we? "

" Yes, Domini."

" Were we "—she was almost whispering in the night— " were we truly one? "

" Why do you—truly one, you say? "

" Yes—one in soul? That is the great union, greater than the union of our bodies. Were we one in soul? Are we now? "

" Domini, why do you ask me such questions? Do you doubt my love? "

" No. But I do ask you. Won't you answer me? "

He was silent. His hand lay in hers, but did not press it.

"Boris"—she spoke the cruel words very quietly,—"we are not truly one in soul. We have never been. I know that."

He said nothing.

"Shall we ever be? Think—if one of us were to die, and the other—the one who was left—were left with the knowledge that in our love, even ours, there had always been separation—could you bear that? Could I bear it?"

"Domini——"

"Yes."

"Why do you speak like this? We are one. You have all my love. You are everything to me."

"And yet you are sad, and you try to hide your sadness, your misery, from me. Can you not give it me? I want it—more than I want anything on earth. I want it, I must have it, and I dare to ask for it because I know how deeply you love me and that you could never love another."

"I never have loved another," he said.

"I was the very first."

"The very first. When we married, although I was a man I was as you were."

She bent down her head and laid her lips on his hand that was in hers.

"Then make our union perfect, as no other union on earth has ever been. Give me your sorrow, Boris. I know what it is."

"How can—you cannot know," he said in a broken voice.

"Yes. Love is a diviner, the only true diviner. I told you once what it was, but I want you to tell me. Nothing that we take is beautiful to us, only what we are given."

"I cannot," he said.

He tried to take his hand from hers, but she held it fast. And she felt as if she were holding the wall of fire with which he surrounded the secret places of his soul.

"To-day, Boris, when I talked to Count Anteoni, I felt that I had been a coward with you. I had seen you suffer and I had not dared to draw near to your suffering. I have been afraid of you. Think of that."

"No."

"Yes, I have been afraid of you, of your reserve. When you withdrew from me I never followed you. If I had, perhaps I could have done something for you."

"Domini, do not speak like this. Our love is happy. Leave it as it is "

"I can't. I will not. Boris, Count Anteoni has found a home. But you are wandering. I can't bear that, I can't bear it. It is as if I were sitting in the house, warm, safe, and you were out in the storm. It tortures me. It almost makes me hate my own safety."

Androvsky shivered. He took his hand forcibly from Domini's.

"I have almost hated it, too," he said passionately. "I have hated it. I'm a—I'm——"

His voice failed. He bent forward and took Domini's face between his hands.

"And yet there are times when I can bless what I have hated. I do bless it now. I—I love your safety. You—at least you are safe."

"You must share it. I will make you share it."

"You cannot."

"I can. I shall. I feel that we shall be together in soul, and perhaps to-night, perhaps even to-night."

Androvsky looked profoundly agitated. His hands dropped down.

"I must go," he said. "I must go to the priest."

He got up from the sand.

"Come to the tent, Domini."

She rose to her feet.

"When you come back," she said, "I shall be waiting for you, Boris."

He looked at her. There was in his eyes a piercing wistfulness. He opened his lips. At that moment Domini felt that he was on the point of telling her all that she longed to know. But the look faded. The lips closed. He took her in his arms and kissed her almost desperately.

"No, no," he said. "I'll keep your love—I'll keep it."

"You could never lose it."

"I might."

"Never."

"If I believed that."

"Boris!"

Suddenly burning tears rushed from her eyes.

"Don't ever say a thing like that to me again!" she said with passion.

She pointed to the grave close to them.

"If you were there," she said, "and I was living, and you had died before—before you had told me—I believe—God forgive me, but I do believe that if, when you died, I were taken to heaven I should find my hell there."

She looked through her tears at the words: " Priez pour lui."

"To pray for the dead," she whispered, as if to herself. " To pray for my dead—I could not do it—I could not. Boris, if you love me you must trust me, you must give me your sorrow."

The night drew on. Androvsky had gone to the priest. Domini was alone, sitting before the tent waiting for his return. She had told Batouch and Ouardi that she wanted nothing more, that no one was to come to the tent again that night. The young moon was rising over the city, but its light as yet was faint. It fell upon the cupolas of the Bureau Arabe, the towers of the mosque and the white sands, whose whiteness it seemed to emphasise, making them pale as the face of one terror-stricken. The city wall cast a deep shadow over the moat of sand in which, wrapped in filthy rags, lay nomads sleeping. Upon the sand-hills the camps were alive with movement. Fires blazed and smoke ascended before the tents that made patches of blackness upon the waste. Round the fires were seated groups of men devouring cous-cous and the red soup beloved of the nomad. Behind them circled the dogs with quivering nostrils. Squadrons of camels lay crouched in the sand, resting after their journeys. And everywhere, from the city and from the waste, rose distant sounds of music, thin, aërial flutings like voices of the night winds, acrid cries from the pipes, and the far-off rolling of the African drums that are the foundation of every desert symphony.

Although she was now accustomed to the music of Africa, Domini could never hear it without feeling the barbarity of the land from which it rose, the wildness of the people who made and who loved it. Always it suggested to her an infinite remoteness, as if it were music sounding at the end of the world, full of half-defined meanings, melancholy yet fierce passion, longings that, momentarily satisfied, continually renewed themselves, griefs that were hidden behind thin veils like the women of the East, but that peered out with expressive eyes, hinting their story and desiring assuagement. And to-night the meaning of the music seemed deeper than it had been before. She thought of it as an outside echo of the voices murmuring in her mind and heart, and the voices murmuring in the mind and heart of Androvsky, broken voices some of them, but some strong, fierce, tense and alive with meaning. And as she sat there alone she thought this unity of music drew her closer to the desert than she had ever been before, and drew Androvsky with her, despite his great reserve. In the heart of the desert he would surely let her see at last fully into his heart. When he came back in the night from the priest he would speak. She was waiting for that.

The moon was mounting. Its light grew stronger. She looked across the sands and saw fires in the city, and suddenly she said to herself, " This is the vision of the sand-diviner realised in my life. He saw me as I am now, in this place." And she remembered the scene in the garden, the crouching figure, the extended arms, the thin fingers tracing swift patterns in the sand, the murmuring voice.

To-night she felt deeply expectant, but almost sad, encompassed by the mystery that hangs in clouds about human life and human relations. What could be that great joy of which the Diviner had spoken? A woman's great joy that starred the desert with flowers and made the dry places run with sweet waters. What could it be?

Suddenly she felt again the oppression of spirit she had been momentarily conscious of in the afternoon. It was like a load descending upon her, and, almost instantly, communicated itself to her body. She was conscious of a sensation of unusual weariness, uneasiness, even dread, then again of an intensity of life that startled her. This intensity remained, grew in her. It was as if the principle of life, like a fluid, were being poured into her out of the vials of God, as if the little cup that was all she had were too small to contain the precious liquid. That seemed to her to be the cause of the pain of which she was conscious. She was being given more than she felt herself capable of possessing. She got up from her chair, unable to remain still. The movement, slight though it was, seemed to remove a veil of darkness that had hung over her and to let in upon her a flood of light. She caught hold of the canvas of the tent. For a moment she felt weak as a child, then strong as an Amazon. And the sense of strength remained, grew. She walked out upon the sand in the direction by which Androvsky would return. The fires in the city and the camps were to her as illuminations for a festival. The music was the music of a great rejoicing. The vast expanse of the desert, wintry white under the moon, dotted with the fires of the nomads, blossomed as the rose. After a few moments she stopped. She was on the crest of a sand-bank, and could see below her the faint track in the sand which wound to the city gate. By this track Androvsky would surely return. From a long distance she would be able to see him, a moving darkness upon the white. She was near to the city now, and could hear voices coming to her from behind its rugged walls, voices of men singing, and calling one to another, the twang of plucked instruments, the click of negroes' castanets. The city was full of joy as the desert was full of joy. The glory of life rushed upon her like a flood of gold, that gold of the sun in which thousands of tiny things are dancing. And she was given the power of giving life, of adding to the sum of glory. She looked out over the sands and saw a moving blot upon them coming slowly towards her, very slowly. It was impossible at this distance to see who it was, but she felt that it was her husband. For a moment she thought of going down to meet him, but she did not move. The new knowledge that had come to her made her, just then, feel shy even of him, as if he must come to her, as if she could make no advance towards him.

As the blackness upon the sand drew nearer she saw that it was a man walking heavily. The man had her husband's gait. When she saw that she turned. She had resolved to meet him at the tent door, to tell him what she had to tell him at the threshold of their wandering home. Her sense of shyness died when she was at the tent door. She only felt now her oneness with her husband, and that to-night their unity was to be made more perfect. If it could be made quite perfect! If he would speak too! Then nothing more would be wanting. At last every veil would have dropped from between them, and as they had long been one flesh they would be one in spirit.

She waited in the tent door.

After what seemed a long time she saw Androvsky coming across the moonlit sand. He was walking very slowly, as if wearied out, with his head drooping. He did not appear to see her till he was quite close to the tent. Then he stopped and gazed at her. The moon—she thought it must be the moon—made his face look strange, like a dying man's face. In this white face the eyes glittered feverishly.

"Boris!" she said.

"Domini!"

"Come here, close to me. I have something to tell you—something wonderful."

He came quite up to her.

"Domini," he said, as if he had not heard her. "Domini, I —I've been to the priest to-night. I meant to confess to him."

"To confess!" she said.

"This afternoon I asked him to hear my confession, but to-night I could not make it. I can only make it to you, Domini—only to you. Do you hear, Domini? Do you hear?"

Something in his face and in his voice terrified her heart. Now she felt as if she would stop him from speaking if she dared, but that she did not dare. His spirit was beyond domination. He would do what he meant to do regardless of her—of anyone.

"What is it, Boris?" she whispered. "Tell me. Perhaps I can understand best because I love best."

He put his arms round her and kissed her, as a man kisses the woman he loves when he knows it may be for the last time, long and hard, with a desperation of love that feels frustrated by the very lips it is touching. At last he took his lips from hers.

"Domini," he said, and his voice was steady and clear, almost hard, "you want to know what it is that makes me unhappy even in our love—desperately unhappy. It is this. I believe in God, I love God, and I have insulted Him. I have tried to forget God, to deny Him, to put human love higher than love for Him. But always I am haunted by the thought of God, and that thought makes me despair. Once, when I was young, I gave myself to God solemnly. I have broken the vows I made. I have—I have——"

The hardness went out of his voice. He broke down for a moment and was silent.

"You gave yourself to God," she said. "How?"

He tried to meet her questioning eyes, but could not.

"I—I gave myself to God as a monk," he answered after a pause.

As he spoke Domini saw before her in the moonlight De Trevignac. He cast a glance of horror at the tent, bent over her, made the sign of the Cross, and vanished. In his place stood Father Roubier, his eyes shining, his hand upraised, warning her against Androvsky. Then he, too, vanished, and she seemed to see Count Anteoni dressed as an Arab and muttering words of the Koran.

"Domini!"

"Domini, did you hear me? Domini! Domini!"

She felt his hands on her wrists.

THE JOURNEY

"You are the Trappist!" she said quietly, "of whom the priest told me. You are the monk from the Monastery of El-Largani who disappeared after twenty years."

"Yes," he said, "I am he."

"What made you tell me? What made you tell me?" There was agony now in her voice.

"You asked me to speak, but it was not that. Do you remember last night when I said that God must bless you? You answered, 'He has blessed me. He has given me you, your love, your truth.' It is that which makes me speak. You have had my love, not my truth. Now take my truth. I've kept it from you. Now I'll give it you. It's black, but I'll give it you. Domini! Domini! Hate me to-night, but in your hatred believe that I never loved you as I love you now."

"Give me your truth!" she said.

BOOK V

THE REVELATION

CHAPTER XXVI

THEY remained standing at the tent door, with the growing moonlight about them. The camp was hushed in sleep, but sounds of music still came to them from the city below them, and fainter music from the tents of the Ouled Naïls on the sand-hill to the south. After Domini had spoken Androvsky moved a step towards her, looked at her, then moved back and dropped his eyes. If he had gone on looking at her he knew he could not have begun to speak.

"Domini," he said, "I'm not going to try and excuse myself for what I have done. I'm not going to say to you what I daren't say to God—'Forgive me.' How can such a thing be forgiven? That's part of the torture I've been enduring, the knowledge of the unforgivable nature of my act. It can never be wiped out. It's black on my judgment book for ever. But I wonder if you can understand—oh, I want you to understand, Domini, what has made the thing I am, a renegade, a breaker of oaths, a liar to God and you. It was the passion of life that burst up in me after years of tranquillity. It was the waking of my nature after years of sleep. And you—you do understand the passion of life that's in some of us like a monster that must rule, must have its way. Even you in your purity and goodness —you have it, that desperate wish to live really and fully, as we have lived, Domini, together. For we have lived out in the desert. We lived that night at Arba when we sat and watched the fire and I held your hand against the earth. We lived then. Even now, when I think of that night, I can hardly be sorry for what I've done, for what I am."

He looked up at her now and saw that her eyes were fixed on him. She stood motionless, with her hands joined in front of her. Her attitude was calm and her face was untortured. He could not read any thought of hers, any feeling that was in her heart.

"You must understand," he said almost violently. "You must understand or I——. My father, I told you, was a Russian. He was brought up in the Greek Church, but became a Freethinker when he was still a young man. My mother was an Englishwoman and an ardent Catholic. She and my father were devoted to each other in spite of the difference in their views. Perhaps the chief effect my father's lack of belief had upon my mother was to make her own belief more steadfast, more ardent. I think disbelief acts often as a fan to the faith of women, makes the flame burn more brightly than it did before. My mother tried to believe for herself and for my father too, and I could almost think that she succeeded. He died long before she did, and he died without changing his views. On his death-bed he told my mother that he was sure there was no other life, that he was going to the dust. That made the agony of his farewell. The certainty on his part that he and my mother were parting for ever. I was a little boy at the time, but I remember that, when he was dead, my mother said to me, ' Boris, pray for your father every day. He is still alive.' She said nothing more, but I ran upstairs crying, fell upon my knees and prayed—trying to think where my father was and what he could be looking like. And in that prayer for my father, which was also an act of obedience to my mother, I think I took the first step towards the monastic life. For I remember that then, for the first time, I was conscious of a great sense of responsibility. My mother's command made me say to myself, ' Then perhaps my prayer can do something in heaven. Perhaps a prayer from me can make God wish to do something He had not wished to do before.' That was a tremendous thought! It excited me terribly. I remember my cheeks burned as I prayed, and that I was hot all over as if I had been running in the sun. From that day my mother and I seemed to be much nearer together than we had ever been before. I had a twin brother to whom I was devoted, and who was devoted to me. But he took after my father. Religious things, ceremonies, church music, processions—even the outside attractions of the Catholic Church, which please and stimulate emotional people who have little faith—never meant much to him. All his attention was firmly fixed upon the life of the present. He was good to my mother and loved her devotedly, as he loved me, but he never pretended to be what he was not. And he was never a Catholic. He was never anything.

"My father had originally come to Africa for his health, which needed a warm climate. He had some money and bought large tracts of land suitable for vineyards. Indeed, he sunk nearly his whole fortune in land. I told you, Domini, that the vines were devoured by the phylloxera. Most of the money was lost. When my father died we were left very poor. We lived quietly in a little village—I told you its name, I told you that part of my life, all I dared tell, Domini—but now—why did I enter the monastery? I was very young when I became a novice, just seventeen. You are thinking, Domini, I know, that I was too young to know what I was doing, that I had no vocation, that I was unfitted for the monastic life. It seems so. The whole world would think so. And yet—how am I to tell you? Even now I feel that then I had the vocation, that I was fitted to enter the monastery, that I ought to have made a faithful and devoted monk. My mother wished the life for me, but it was not only that. I wished it for myself then. With my whole heart I wished it. I knew nothing of the world. My youth had been one of absolute purity. And I did not feel longings after the unknown. My mother's influence upon me was strong; but she did not force me into anything. Perhaps my love for her led me more than I knew, brought me to the monastery door. The passion of her life, the human passion, had been my father. After he was dead the passion of her life was prayer for him. My love for her made me share that passion, and the sharing of that passion eventually led me to become a monk. I became as a child, a devotee of prayer. Oh! Domini—think— I loved prayer—I loved it——"

His voice broke. When he stopped speaking Domini was again conscious of the music in the city. She remembered that earlier in the night she had thought of it as the music of a great festival.

"I resolved to enter the life of prayer, the most perfect life of prayer. I resolved to become a 'religious.' It seemed to me that by so doing I should be proving in the finest way my love for my mother. I should be, in the strongest way, helping her. Her life was prayer for my dead father and love for her children. By devoting myself to the life of prayer I should show to her that I was as she was, as she had made me, true son of her womb. Can you understand? I had a passion for my mother, Domini—I had a passion. My brother tried to dissuade me from the monastic life. He himself was going into business in Tunis. He wanted me to join him. But I was firm. I felt driven towards the cloister then as other men often feel driven towards the vicious life. The inclination was irresistible. I yielded to it. I had to bid good-bye to my mother. I told you —she was the passion of my life. And yet I hardly felt sad at parting from her. Perhaps that will show you how I was then. It seemed to me that we should be even closer together when I wore the monk's habit. I was in haste to put it on. I went to the monastery of El-Largani and entered it as a novice of the Trappistine order. I thought in the great silence of the Trappists there would be more room for prayer. When I left my home and went to El-Largani I took with me one treasure only. Domini, it was the little wooden crucifix you pinned upon the tent at Arba. My mother gave it to me, and I was allowed to keep it. Everything else in the way of earthly possessions I, of course, had to give up.

"You have never seen El-Largani, my home for nineteen years, my prison for one. It is lonely, but not in the least desolate. It stands on a high upland, and, from a distance, looks upon the sea. Far off there are mountains. The land was a desert. The monks have turned it, if not into an Eden, at least into a rich garden. There are vineyards, cornfields, orchards, almost every fruit-tree flourishes there. The springs of sweet waters are abundant. At a short way from the monastery is a large village for the Spanish workmen whom the monks super-vise in the labours of the fields. For the Trappist life is not only a life of prayer, but a life of diligent labour. When I be-came a novice I had not realised that. I had imagined myself continually upon my knees. I found instead that I was perpet-ually in the fields, in sun, and wind, and rain—that was in the winter time—working like the labourers, and that often when we went into the long, plain chapel to pray I was so tired— being only a boy—that my eyes closed as I stood in my stall, and I could scarcely hear the words of Mass or Benediction. But I had expected to be happy at El-Largani, and I was happy. Labour is good for the body and better for the soul. And the silence was not hard to bear. The Trappists have a book of gestures, and are often allowed to converse by signs. We novices were generally in little bands, and often, as we walked in the garden of the monastery, we talked together gaily with our hands. Then the silence is not perpetual. In the fields we often had to give directions to the labourers. In the school, where we studied Theology, Latin, Greek, there was heard the voice of the teacher. It is true that I have seen men in the monastery day by day for twenty years with whom I have never exchanged a word, but I have had permission to speak with monks. The head of the monastery, the Reverend Père, has the power to loose the bonds of silence when he chooses, and to allow monks to walk and speak with each other beyond the white walls that hem in the garden of the monastery. Now and then we spoke, but I think most of us were not unhappy in our silence. It became a habit. And then we were always occupied. We had no time allowed us for sitting and being sad. Domini, I don't want to tell you about the Trappists, their life —only about myself, why I was as I was, how I came to change. For years I was not unhappy at El-Largani. When my time of novitiate was over I took the eternal vows without hesitation. Many novices go out again into the world. It never occurred to me to do so. I scarcely ever felt a stirring of worldly desire. I scarcely ever had one of those agonising struggles which many people probably attribute to monks. I was contented nearly always. Now and then the flesh spoke, but not strongly. Remember, our life was a life of hard and exhausting labour in the fields. The labour kept the flesh in subjection, as the prayer lifted up the spirit. And then, during all my earlier years at the monastery, we had an Abbé who was quick to understand the characters and dispositions of men—Dom André Herceline. He knew me far better than I knew myself. He knew, what I did not suspect, that I was full of sleeping violence, that in my purity and devotion—or beneath it rather—there was a strong strain of barbarism. The Russian was sleeping in the monk, but sleeping soundly. That can be. Half a man's nature, if all that would call to it is carefully kept from it, may sleep, I believe, through all his life. He might die and never have known, or been, what all the time he was. For years it was so with me. I knew only part of myself, a real vivid part—but only a part. I thought it was the whole. And while I thought it was the whole I was happy. If Dom André Herceline had not died, to day I should be a monk at El-Largani, ignorant of what I know, contented.

"He never allowed me to come into any sort of contact with the many strangers who visited the monastery. Different monks have different duties. Certain duties bring monks into connection with the travellers whom curiosity sends to El-Largani. The monk whose business it is to look after the cemetery on the hill, where the dead Trappists are laid to rest, shows visitors round the little chapel, and may talk with them freely so long as they remain in the cemetery. The monk in charge of the distillery also receives visitors and converses with them. So does the monk in charge of the parlour at the great door of the monastery. He sells the souvenirs of the Trappists, photographs of the church and buildings, statues of saints, bottles of perfumes made by the monks. He takes the orders for the wines made at the monastery, and for—for the—what I made, Domini, when I was there."

She thought of De Trevignac and the fragments of glass lying upon the ground in the tent at Mogar.

" Had De Trevignac——" she said in a low, inward voice.

" He had seen me, spoken with me at the monastery. When Ouardi brought in the liqueur he remembered who I was."

She understood De Trevignac's glance towards the tent where Androvsky lay sleeping, and a slight shiver ran through her. Androvsky saw it and looked down.

" But the—the——"

He cleared his throat, turned, looked out across the white sand as if he longed to travel away into it and be lost for ever, then went on, speaking quickly:

" But the monk who has most to do with travellers is the monk who is in charge of the *hôtellerie* of the monastery. He is the host to all visitors, to those who come over for the day and have *déjeuner,* and to any who remain for the night, or for a longer time. For when I was at El-Largani it was permitted for people to stay in the *hôtellerie,* on payment of a small weekly sum, for as long as they pleased. The monk of the *hôtellerie* is perpetually brought into contact with the outside world. He talks with all sorts and conditions of men—women, of course, are not admitted. The other monks, many of them, probably envy him. I never did. I had no wish to see strangers. When, by chance, I met them in the yard, the out-buildings, or the grounds of the monastery, I seldom even raised my eyes to look at them. They were not, would never be, in my life. Why should I look at them? What were they to me? Years went on—quickly they passed—not slowly. I did not feel their monotony. I never shrank from anything in the life. My health was splendid. I never knew what it was to be ill for a day. My muscles were hard as iron. The pallet on which I lay in my cubicle, the heavy robe I wore day and night, the scanty vegetables I ate, the bell that called me from my sleep in the darkness to go to the chapel, the fastings, the watchings, the perpetual sameness of all I saw, all I did, neither saddened nor fatigued me. I never sighed for change. Can you believe that, Domini? It is true. So long as Dom André Herceline lived and ruled my life I was calm, happy, as few people in the world, or none, can ever be. But Dom André died, and then——"

His face was contorted by a spasm.

"My mother was dead. My brother lived on in Tunis, and was successful in business. He remained unmarried. So far as I was concerned, although the monastery was but two hours' drive from the town, he might almost have been dead too. I scarcely ever saw him, and then only by a special permission from the Reverend Père, and for a few moments. Once I visited him at Tunis, when he was ill. When my mother died I seemed to sink down a little deeper into the monastic life. That was all. It was as if I drew my robe more closely round me and pulled my hood further forward over my face. There was more reason for my prayers, and I prayed more passionately. I lived in prayer like a sea-plant in the depths of the ocean. Prayer was about me like a fluid. But Dom André Herceline died, and a new Abbé was appointed, he who, I suppose, rules now at El-Largani. He was a good man, but, I think, apt to misunderstand men. The Abbé of a Trappist monastery has complete power over his community. He can order what he will. Soon after he came to El-Largani—for some reason that I cannot divine—he removed the Père Michel, who had been for years in charge of the cemetery, from his duties there, and informed me that I was to undertake them. I obeyed, of course, without a word.

"The cemetery of El-Largani is on a low hill, the highest part of the monastery grounds. It is surrounded by a white wall and by a hedge of cypress trees. The road to it is an avenue of cypresses, among which are interspersed niches containing carvings of the Fourteen Stations of the Cross. At the entrance to this avenue, on the left, there is a high yellow pedestal, surmounted by a black cross, on which hangs a silver Christ Underneath is written:

" FACTUS OBEDIENS
" USQUE
" AD MORTEM
" CRUCIS.

" I remember, on the first day when I became the guardian of the cemetery, stopping on my way to it before the Christ and praying. My prayer—my prayer was, Domini, that I might die, as I had lived, in innocence. I prayed for that, but with a sort of—yes, now I think so—insolent certainty that my prayer would of course be granted. Then I went on to the cemetery.

" My work there was easy. I had only to tend the land about the graves, and sweep out the little chapel where was buried the founder of La Trappe of El-Largani. This done I could wander about the cemetery, or sit on a bench in the sun. The Père Michel, who was my predecessor, had some doves, and had left them behind in a little house by my bench. I took care of and fed them. They were tame, and used to flutter to my shoulders and perch on my hands. To birds and animals I was always a friend. At El-Largani there are all sorts of beasts, and, at one time or another, it had been my duty to look after most of them. I loved all living things. Sitting in the cemetery I could see a great stretch of country, the blue of the lakes of Tunis with the white villages at their edge, the boats gliding upon them towards the white city, the distant mountains. Having little to do, I sat day after day for hours meditating, and looking out upon this distant world. I remember specially one evening, at sunset, just before I had to go to the chapel, that a sort of awe came upon me as I looked across the lakes. The sky was golden, the waters were dyed with gold, out of which rose the white sails of boats. The mountains were shadowy purple. The little minarets of the mosques rose into the gold like sticks of ivory. As I watched my eyes filled with tears, and I felt a sort of aching in my heart, and as if—Domini, it was as if at that moment a hand was laid on mine, but very gently, and pulled at my hand. It was as if at that moment someone was beside me in the cemetery wishing to lead me out to those far-off waters, those mosque towers, those purple mountains. Never before had I had such a sensation. It frightened me. I felt as if the devil had come into the cemetery, as if his hand was laid on mine, as if his voice were whispering in my ear, ' Come out with me into that world, that beautiful world, which God made for men. Why do you reject it ? '

" That evening, Domini, was the beginning of this—this end. Day after day I sat in the cemetery and looked out over the world, and wondered what it was like: what were the lives of the men who sailed in the white-winged boats, who crowded on the steamers whose smoke I could see sometimes faintly trailing away into the track of the sun; who kept the sheep upon the mountains; who—who—Domini, can you imagine—no, you cannot—what, in a man of my age, of my blood, were these first, very first, stirrings of the longing for life? Sometimes I think they were like the first birth-pangs of a woman who is going to be a mother."

Domini's hands moved apart, then joined themselves again.

"There was something physical in them. I felt as if my limbs had minds, and that their minds, which had been asleep, were waking. My arms twitched with a desire to stretch themselves towards the distant blue of the lakes on which I should never sail. My—I was physically stirred. And again and again I felt that hand laid closely upon mine, as if to draw me away into something I had never known, could never know. Do not think that I did not strive against these first stirrings of the nature that had slept so long! For days I refused to let myself look out from the cemetery. I kept my eyes upon the ground, upon the plain crosses that marked the graves. I played with the red-eyed doves. I worked. But my eyes at last rebelled. I said to myself, 'It is not forbidden to look.' And again the sails, the seas, the towers, the mountains, were as voices whispering to me, 'Why will you never know us, draw near to us? Why will you never understand our meaning? Why will you be ignorant for ever of all that has been created for man to know?' Then the pain within me became almost unbearable. At night I could not sleep. In the chapel it was difficult to pray. I looked at the monks around me, to most of whom I had never addressed a word, and I thought, 'Do they, too, hold such longings within them? Are they, too, shaken with a desire of knowledge?' It seemed to me that, instead of a place of peace, the monastery was, must be, a place of tumult, of the silent tumult that has its home in the souls of men. But then I remembered for how long I had been at peace. Perhaps all the silent men by whom I was surrounded were still at peace, as I had been, as I might be again.

"A young monk died in the monastery and was buried in the cemetery. I made his grave against the outer wall, beneath a cypress tree. Some days afterwards, when I was sitting on the bench by the house of the doves, I heard a sound, which came from beyond the wall. It was like sobbing. I listened, and heard it more distinctly, and knew that it was someone crying and sobbing desperately, and near at hand. But now it seemed to me to come from the wall itself. I got up and listened.

Someone was crying bitterly behind, or above, the wall, just where the young monk had been buried. Who could it be? I stood listening, wondering, hesitating what to do. There was something in this sound of lamentation that moved one to the depths. For years I had not looked on a woman, or heard a woman's voice—but I knew that this was a woman mourning. Why was she there? What could she want? I glanced up. All round the cemetery, as I have said, grew cypress trees. As I glanced up I saw one shake just above where the new grave was, and a woman's voice said, ' I cannot see it, I cannot see it! '

"I do not know why, but I felt that someone was there who wished to see the young monk's grave. For a moment I stood there. Then I went to the house where I kept my tools for my work in the cemetery, and got a shears which I used for lopping the cypress trees. I took a ladder quickly, set it against the wall, mounted it, and from the cypress I had seen moving I lopped some of the boughs. The sobbing ceased. As the boughs fell down from the tree I saw a woman's face, tear-stained, staring at me. It seemed to me a lovely face.

" ' Which is his grave? ' she said. I pointed to the grave of the young monk, which could now be seen through the gap I had made, descended the ladder, and went away to the farthest corner of the cemetery. And I did not look again in the direction of the woman's face.

" Who she was I do not know. When she went away I did not see. She loved the monk who had died, and knowing that women cannot enter the precincts of the monastery, she had come to the outside wall to cast, if she might, a despairing glance at his grave.

" Domini, I wonder—I wonder if you can understand how that incident affected me. To an ordinary man it would seem nothing, I suppose. But to a Trappist monk it seemed tremendous. I had seen a woman. I had done something for a woman. I thought of her, of what I had done for her, perpetually. The gap in the cypress tree reminded me of her every time I looked towards it. When I was in the cemetery I could hardly turn my eyes from it. But the woman never came again. I said nothing to the Reverend Père of what I had done. I ought to have spoken, but I did not. I kept it back when I confessed. From that moment I had a secret, and it was a secret connected with a woman.

" Does it seem strange to you that this secret seemed to me to set me apart from all the other monks—nearer the world?

It was so. I felt sometimes as if I had been out into the world for a moment, had known the meaning that women have for men. I wondered who the woman was. I wondered how she had loved the young monk who was dead. He used to sit beside me in the chapel. He had a pure and beautiful face, such a face, I supposed, as a woman might well love. Had this woman loved him, and had he rejected her love for the life of the monastery? I remember one day thinking of this and wondering how it had been possible for him to do so, and then suddenly realising the meaning of my thought and turning hot with shame. I had put the love of woman above the love of God, woman's service above God's service. That day I was terrified of myself. I went back to the monastery from the cemetery quickly, asked to see the Reverend Père, and begged him to remove me from the cemetery, to give me some other work. He did not ask my reason for wishing to change, but three days afterwards he sent for me, and told me that I was to be placed in charge of the *hôtellerie* of the monastery, and that my duties there were to begin upon the morrow.

"Domini, I wonder if I can make you realise what that change meant to a man who had lived as I had for so many years. The *hôtellerie* of El-Largani is a long, low, one-storied building standing in a garden full of palms and geraniums. It contains a kitchen, a number of little rooms like cells for visitors, and two large parlours in which guests are entertained at meals. In one they sit to eat the fruit, eggs, and vegetables provided by the monastery, with wine. If after the meal they wish to take coffee they pass into the second parlour. Visitors who stay in the monastery are free to do much as they please, but they must conform to certain rules. They rise at a certain hour, feed at fixed times, and are obliged to go to their bedrooms at half-past seven in the evening in winter, and at eight in summer. The monk in charge of the *hôtellerie* has to see to their comfort. He looks after the kitchen, is always in the parlour at some moment or another during meals. He visits the bedrooms and takes care that the one servant keeps everything spotlessly clean. He shows people round the garden. His duties, you see, are light and social. He cannot go into the world, but he can mix with the world that comes to him. It is his task, if not his pleasure, to be cheerful, talkative, sympathetic, a good host, with a genial welcome for all who come to La Trappe. After my years of labour, solitude, silence, and prayer, I was abruptly put into this new life.

" Domini, to me it was like rushing out into the world. I was almost dazed by the change. At first I was nervous, timid, awkward, and, especially, tongue-tied. The habit of silence had taken such a hold upon me that I could not throw it off. I dreaded the coming of visitors. I did not know how to receive them, what to say to them. Fortunately, as I thought, the tourist season was over, the summer was approaching. Very few people came, and those only to eat a meal. I tried to be polite and pleasant to them, and gradually I began to fall into the way of talking without the difficulty I had experienced at first. In the beginning I could not open my lips without feeling as if I were almost committing a crime. But presently I was more natural, less taciturn. I even, now and then, took some pleasure in speaking to a pleasant visitor. I grew to love the garden with its flowers, its orange trees, its groves of eucalyptus, its vineyard which sloped towards the cemetery. Often I wandered in it alone, or sat under the arcade that divided it from the large entrance court of the monastery, meditating, listening to the bees humming, and watching the cats basking in the sunshine.

" Sometimes, when I was there, I thought of the woman's face above the cemetery wall. Sometimes I seemed to feel the hand tugging at mine. But I was more at peace than I had been in the cemetery. For from the garden I could not see the distant world, and of the chance visitors none had as yet set a match to the torch that, unknown to me, was ready—at the coming of the smallest spark—to burst into a flame.

" One day, it was in the morning towards half-past ten, when I was sitting reading my Greek Testament on a bench just inside the doorway of the *hôtellerie,* I heard the great door of the monastery being opened, and then the rolling of carriage wheels in the courtyard. Some visitor had arrived from Tunis, perhaps some visitors—three or four. It was a radiant morning of late May. The garden was brilliant with flowers, golden with sunshine, tender with shade, and quiet—quiet and peaceful, Domini! There was a wonderful peace in the garden that day, a peace that seemed full of safety, of enduring cheerfulness. The flowers looked as if they had hearts to understand it, and love it, the roses along the yellow wall of the house that clambered to the brown red tiles, the geraniums that grew in masses under the shining leaves of the orange trees, the—I felt as if that day I were in the Garden of Eden, and I remember that when I heard the carriage wheels I had a moment of selfish sadness. I thought: 'Why does anyone come to disturb my blessed peace, my blessed solitude?' Then I realised the egoism of my thought and that I was there with my duty. I got up, went into the kitchen and said to François, the servant, that someone had come and no doubt would stay to *déjeuner*. And, as I spoke, already I was thinking of the moment when I should hear the roll of wheels once more, the clang of the shutting gate, and know that the intruders upon the peace of the Trappists had gone back to the world, and that I could once more be alone in the little Eden I loved.

"Strangely, Domini, strangely, that day, of all the days of my life, I was most in love—it was like that, like being in love—with my monk's existence. The terrible feeling that had begun to ravage me had completely died away. I adored the peace in which my days were passed. I looked at the flowers and compared my happiness with theirs. They blossomed, bloomed, faded, died in the garden. So would I wish to blossom, bloom, fade—when my time came—die in the garden—always in peace, always in safety, always isolated from the terrors of life, always under the tender watchful eye of—of—Domini, that day I was happy, as perhaps they are—perhaps—the saints in Paradise. I was happy because I felt no inclination to evil. I felt as if my joy lay entirely in being innocent. Oh, what an ecstasy such a feeling is! 'My will accord with Thy design—I love to live as Thou intendest me to live! Any other way of life would be to me a terror, would bring to me despair.'

"And I felt that—intensely I felt it at that moment in heart and soul. It was as if I had God's arms round me, caressing me as a father caresses his child."

He moved away a step or two in the sand, came back, and went on with an effort:

"Within a few minutes the porter of the monastery came through the archway of the arcade followed by a young man. As I looked up at him I was uncertain of his nationality. But I scarcely thought about it—except in the first moment. For something else seized my attention—the intense, active misery in the stranger's face. He looked ravaged, eaten by grief. I said he was young—perhaps twenty-six or twenty-seven. His face was rather dark-complexioned, with small, good features. He had thick brown hair, and his eyes shone with intelligence, with an intelligence that was almost painful—somehow. His eyes always looked to me as if they were seeing too much, had always seen too much. There was a restlessness in the swiftness of their observation. One could not conceive of them closed in sleep. An activity that must surely be eternal blazed in them.

"The porter left the stranger in the archway. It was now my duty to attend to him. I welcomed him in French. He took off his hat. When he did that I felt sure he was an Englishman—by the look of him bareheaded—and I told him that I spoke English as well as French. He answered that he was at home in French, but that he was English. We talked English. His entrance into the garden had entirely destroyed my sense of its peace—even my own peace was disturbed at once by his appearance.

"I felt that I was in the presence of a misery that was like a devouring element. Before we had time for more than a very few halting words the bell was rung by François.

"'What's that for, Father?' the stranger said, with a start, which showed that his nerves were shattered.

"'It is time for your meal,' I answered.

"'One must eat!' he said. Then, as if conscious that he was behaving oddly, he added politely:

"'I know you entertain us too well here, and have sometimes been rewarded with coarse ingratitude. Where do I go?'

"I showed him into the parlour. There was no one there that day. He sat at the long table.

"'I am to eat alone?' he asked.

"'Yes; I will serve you.'

"François always waited on the guests, but that day—mindful of the selfishness of my thoughts in the garden—I resolved to add to my duties. I therefore brought the soup, the lentils, the omelette, the oranges, poured out the wine, and urged the young man cordially to eat. When I did so he looked up at me. His eyes were extraordinarily expressive. It was as if I heard them say to me, 'Why, I like you!' and as if, just for a moment, his grief were lessened.

"In the empty parlour, long, clean, bare, with a crucifix on the wall and the name 'Saint Bernard' above the door, it was very quiet, very shady. The outer blinds of green wood were drawn over the window-spaces, shutting out the gold of the garden. But its murmuring tranquillity seemed to filter in, as if the flowers, the insects, the birds were aware of our presence and were trying to say to us, 'Are you happy as we are? Be happy as we are.'

"The stranger looked at the shady room, the open windows. He sighed.

"'How quiet it is here!' he said, almost as if to himself. How quiet it is!'

"'Yes,' I answered. 'Summer is beginning. For months now scarcely anyone will come to us here.'

"'Us?' he said, glancing at me with a sudden smile.

"'I meant to us who are monks, who live always here.'

"'May I—is it indiscreet to ask if you have been here long?'

"I told him.

"'More than nineteen years!' he said.

"'Yes.'

"'And always in this silence?'

"He sat as if listening, resting his head on his hand.

"'How extraordinary!' he said at last. 'How wonderful! Is it happiness?'

"I did not answer. The question seemed to me to be addressed to himself, not to me. I could leave him to seek for the answer. After a moment he went on eating and drinking in silence. When he had finished I asked him whether he would take coffee. He said he would, and I made him pass into the St. Joseph *salle*. There I brought him coffee and—and that liqueur. I told him that it was my invention. He seemed to be interested. At any rate, he took a glass and praised it strongly. I was pleased. I think I showed it. From that moment I felt as if we were almost friends. Never before had I experienced such a feeling for anyone who had come to the monastery, or for any monk or novice in the monastery. Although I had been vexed, irritated, at the approach of a stranger I now felt regret at the idea of his going away. Presently the time came to show him round the garden. We went out of the shadowy parlour into the sunshine. No one was in the garden. Only the bees were humming, the birds were passing, the cats were basking on the broad path that stretched from the arcade along the front of the *hôtellerie*. As we came out a bell chimed, breaking for an instant the silence, and making it seem the sweeter when it returned. We strolled for a little while. We did not talk much. The stranger's eyes, I noticed, were everywhere, taking in every detail of the scene around us. Presently we came to the vineyard, to the left of which was the road that led to the cemetery, passed up the road and arrived at the cemetery gate.

"'Here I must leave you,' I said.

"'Why?' he asked quickly.

"'There is another Father who will show you the chapel. I shall wait for you here.'

"I sat down and waited. When the stranger returned it seemed to me that his face was calmer, that there was a quieter expression in his eyes. When we were once more before the *hôtellerie* I said:

"'You have seen all my small domain now.'

"He glanced at the house.

"'But there seems to be a number of rooms,' he said.

"'Only the bedrooms.'

"'Bedrooms? Do people stay the night here?'

"'Sometimes. If they please they can stay for longer than a night.'

"'How much longer?'

"'For any time they please, if they conform to one or two simple rules and pay a small fixed sum to the monastery.'

"'Do you mean that you could take anyone in for the summer?' he said abruptly.

"'Why not? The consent of the Revernd Père has to be obtained. That is all.'

"'I should like to see the bedrooms.'

"I took him in and showed him one.

"'All the others are the same,' I said.

"He glanced round at the white walls, the rough bed, the crucifix above it, the iron basin, the paved floor, then went to the window and looked out.

"'Well,' he said, drawing back into the room, 'I will go now to see the Père Abbé, if it is permitted.'

"On the garden path I bade him good-bye. He shook my hand. There was an odd smile in his face. Half-an-hour later I saw him coming again through the arcade.

"'Father,' he said, 'I am not going away. I have asked the Père Abbé's permission to stay here. He has given it to me. To-morrow such luggage as I need will be sent over from Tunis. Are you—are you very vexed to have a stranger to trouble your peace?'

"His intensely observant eyes were fixed upon me while he spoke. I answered:

"'I do not think you will trouble my peace.'

"And my thought was:

"'I will help you to find the peace which you have lost.'

Was it a presumptuous thought, Domini? Was it insolent? At the time it seemed to me absolutely sincere, one of the best thoughts I had ever had—a thought put into my heart by God. I didn't know then—I didn't know."

He stopped speaking, and stood for a time quite still, looking down at the sand, which was silver white under the moon. At last he lifted his head and said, speaking slowly:

"It was the coming of this man that put the spark to that torch. It was he who woke up in me the half of myself which, unsuspected by me, had been slumbering through all my life, slumbering and gathering strength in slumber—as the body does—gathering a strength that was tremendous, that was to overmaster the whole of me, that was to make of me one mad impulse. He woke up in me the body and the body was to take possession of the soul. I wonder—can I make you feel why this man was able to affect me thus? Can I make you know this man?

"He was a man full of secret violence, violence of the mind and violence of the body, a volcanic man. He was English—he said so—but there must have been blood that was not English in his veins. When I was with him I felt as if I was with fire. There was the restlessness of fire in him. There was the intensity of fire. He could be reserved. He could appear to be cold. But always I was conscious that if there was stone without there was scorching heat within. He was watchful of himself and of everyone with whom he came into the slightest contact. He was very clever. He had an immense amount of personal charm, I think, at any rate for me. He was very human, passionately interested in humanity. He was—and this was specially part of him, a dominant trait—he was savagely, yes, savagely, eager to be happy, and when he came to live in the *hôtellerie* he was savagely unhappy. An egoist he was, a thinker, a man who longed to lay hold of something beyond this world, but who had not been able to do so. Even his desire to find rest in a religion seemed to me to have greed in it, to have something in it that was akin to avarice. He was a human storm, Domini, as well as a human fire. Think! what a man to be cast by the world—which he knew as they know it only who are voracious for life and free—into my quiet existence.

"Very soon he began to show himself to me as he was, with a sort of fearlessness that was almost impudent. The conditions of our two lives in the monastery threw us perpetually together in a curious isolation. And the Reverend Père, Domini, the Reverend Pere, set my feet in the path of my own destruction. On the day after the stranger had arrived the Reverend Père sent for me to his private room, and said to me, 'Our new guest is in a very unhappy state. He has been attracted by our peace. If we can bring peace to him it will be an action acceptable to God. You will be much with him. Try to do him good. He is not a Catholic, but no matter. He wishes to attend the services in the chapel. He may be influenced. God may have guided his feet to us, we cannot tell. But we can act—we can pray for him. I do not know how long he will stay. It may be for only a few days or for the whole summer. It does not matter. Use each day well for him. Each day may be his last with us.' I went out from the Reverend Père full of enthusiasm, feeling that a great, a splendid interest had come into my life, an interest such as it had never held before.

"Day by day I was with this man. Of course there were many hours when we were apart, the hours when I was at prayer in the chapel or occupied with study. But each day we passed much time together, generally in the garden. Scarcely any visitors came, and none to stay, except, from time to time, a passing priest, and once two young men from Tunis, one of whom had an inclination to become a novice. And this man, as I have said, began to show himself to me with a tremendous frankness.

"Domini, he was suffering under what I suppose would be called an obsession, an immense domination such as one human being sometimes obtains over another. At that time I had never realised that there were such dominations. Now I know that there are, and, Domini, that they can be both terrible and splendid. He was dominated by a woman, by a woman who had come into his life, seized it, made it a thing of glory, broken it. He described to me the dominion of this woman. He told me how she had transformed him. Till he met her he had been passionate but free, his own master through many experiences, many intrigues. He was very frank, Domini. He did not attempt to hide from me that his life had been evil. It had been a life devoted to the acquiring of experience, of all possible experience, mental and bodily. I gathered that he had shrunk from nothing, avoided nothing. His nature had prompted him to rush upon everything, to grasp at everything. At first I was horrified at what he told me. I showed it. I remember the second evening after his arrival we were sitting together in a little arbour at the foot of the vineyard that sloped up to the cemetery. It was half an hour before the last service in the chapel. The air was cool with breath from the distant sea. An intense calm, a heavenly calm, I think, filled the garden, floated away to the cypresses beside the graves, along the avenue where stood the Fourteen Stations of the Cross. And he told me, began to tell me something of his life.

"'You thought to find happiness in such an existence?' I exclaimed, almost with incredulity I believe.

"He looked at me with his shining eyes.

"'Why not, Father? Do you think I was a madman to do so?'

"'Surely.'

"'Why? Is there not happiness in knowledge?'

"'Knowledge of evil?'

"'Knowledge of all things that exist in life. I have never sought for evil specially; I have sought for everything. I wished to bring everything under my observation, everything connected with human life.'

"'But human life,' I said more quietly, 'passes away from this world. It is a shadow in a world of shadows.'

"'You say that,' he answered abruptly. 'I wonder if you feel it—feel it as you feel my hand on yours.'

"He laid his hand on mine. It was hot and dry as if with fever. Its touch affected me painfully.

"'Is that hand the hand of a shadow?' he said. 'Is this body that can enjoy and suffer, that can be in heaven or in hell—here—here—a shadow?'

"'Within a week it might be less than a shadow.'

"'And what of that? This is now, this is now. Do you mean what you say? Do you truly feel that you are a shadow—that this garden is but a world of shadows? I feel that I, that you, are terrific realities, that this garden is of immense significance. Look at that sky.'

"The sky above the cypresses was red with sunset. The trees looked black beneath it. Fireflies were flitting near the arbour where we sat.

"'That is the sky that roofs what you would have me believe a world of shadows. It is like the blood, the hot blood that flows and surges in the veins of men—in our veins. Ah, but you are a monk!'

"The way he said the last words made me feel suddenly a sense of shame, Domini. It was as if a man said to another man, 'You are not a man.' Can you—can you understand the feeling I had just then? Something hot and bitter was in me. A sort of desperate sense of nothingness came over me, as if I were a skeleton sitting there with flesh and blood and trying to believe, and to make it believe, that I, too, was and had been flesh and blood.

" 'Yes, thank God, I am a monk,' I answered quietly.

"Something in my tone, I think, made him feel that he had been brutal.

" 'I am a brute and a fool,' he said vehemently. 'But it is always so with me. I always feel as if what I want others must want. I always feel universal. It's folly. You have your vocation, I mine. Yours is to pray, mine is to live.'

"Again I was conscious of the bitterness. I tried to put it from me.

" 'Prayer is life,' I answered, ' to me, to us who are here.

" 'Prayer! Can it be? Can it be vivid as the life of experience, as the life that teaches one the truth of men and women, the truth of creation—joy, sorrow, aspiration, lust, ambition of the intellect and the limbs? Prayer——'

" 'It is time for me to go,' I said. ' Are you coming to the chapel?'

" 'Yes,' he answered almost eagerly. ' I shall look down on you from my lonely gallery. Perhaps I shall be able to feel the life of prayer.'

" 'May it be so,' I said.

"But I think I spoke without confidence, and I know that that evening I prayed without impulse, coldly, mechanically. The long, dim chapel, with its lines of monks facing each other in their stalls, seemed to me a sad place, like a valley of dry bones—for the first time, for the first time.

"I ought to have gone on the morrow to the Reverend Père. I ought to have asked him, begged him to remove me from th hôtellerie. I ought to have foreseen what was coming—tha this man had a strength to live greater than my strength to pray, that his strength might overcome mine. I began to sin that night. Curiosity was alive in me, curiosity about the life that I had never known, was—so I believed, so I thought I knew—never to know.

"When I came out of the chapel into the hôtellerie I met our guest—I do not say his name. What would be the use?—in the corridor. It was almost dark. There were ten minutes before the time for locking up the door and going to bed. François, the servant, was asleep under the arcade.

" ' Shall we go on to the path and have a last breath of air?' the stranger said.

" We stepped out and walked slowly up and down.

" ' Do you not feel the beauty of peace?' I asked.

" I wanted him to say yes. I wanted him to tell me that peace, tranquillity, were beautiful. He did not reply for a moment. I heard him sigh heavily.

" ' If there is peace in the world at all,' he said at length, ' it is only to be found with the human being one loves. With the human being one loves one might find peace in hell.'

" We did not speak again before we parted for the night.

" Domini, I did not sleep at all that night. It was the first of many sleepless nights, nights in which my thoughts travelled like winged Furies—horrible, horrible nights. In them I strove to imagine all the stranger knew by experience. It was like a ghastly, physical effort. I strove to conceive of all that he had done—with the view, I told myself at first, of bringing myself to a greater contentment, of realising how worthless was all that I had rejected and that he had grasped at. In the dark I, as it were, spread out his map of life and mine and examined them. When, still in the dark, I rose to go to the chapel I was exhausted. I felt unutterably melancholy. That was at first. Presently I felt an active, gnawing hunger. But—but—I have not come to that yet. This strange, new melancholy was the forerunner. It was a melancholy that seemed to be caused by a sense of frightful loneliness such as I had never previously experienced. Till now I had almost always felt God with me, and that He was enough. Now, suddenly, I began to feel that I was alone. I kept thinking of the stranger's words: ' If there is peace in the world at all it is only to be found with the human being one loves.'

" ' That is false,' I said to myself again and again. ' Peace is only to be found by close union with God. In that I have found peace for many, many years.'

" I knew that I had been at peace. I knew that I had been happy. And yet, when I looked back upon my life as a novice and a monk, I now felt as if I had been happy vaguely, foolishly, bloodlessly, happy only because I had been ignorant of what real happiness was—not really happy. I thought of a bird born in a cage and singing there. I had been as that bird. And then, when I was in the garden, I looked at the swallows winging their way high in the sunshine, between the garden trees and the radiant blue, winging their way towards sea and moun-

tains and plains, and that bitterness, like an acid that burns
and eats away fine metal, was once more at my heart.

"But the sensation of loneliness was the most terrible of all.
I compared union with God, such as I thought I had known,
with that other union spoken of by my guest—union with the
human being one loves. I set the two unions as it were in
comparison. Night after night I did this. Night after night
told over the joys of union with God—joys which I dared to
think I had known—and the joys of union with a loved human
being. On the one side I thought of the drawing near to God
in prayer, of the sensation of approach that comes with earnest
prayer, of the feeling that ears are listening to you, that the
great heart is loving you, the great heart that loves all living
things, that you are being absolutely understood, that all you
cannot say is comprehended, and all you say is received as something precious. I recalled the joy, the exaltation, that I had
known when I prayed. That was union with God. In such
union I had sometimes felt that the world, with all that it contained of wickedness, suffering and death, was utterly devoid
of power to sadden or alarm the humblest human being who
was able to draw near to God.

"I had had a conquering feeling—not proud—as of one
upborne, protected for ever, lifted to a region in which no
enemy could ever be, no sadness, no faint anxiety even.

"Then I strove to imagine—and this, Domini, was surely a
deliberate sin—exactly what it must be to be united with a beloved human being. I strove and I was able. For not only
did instinct help me, instinct that had been long asleep, but—I
have told you that the stranger was suffering under an obsession,
a terrible dominion. This dominion he described to me with
an openness that perhaps—that indeed I believe—he would not
have shown had I not been a monk. He looked upon me as a
being apart, neither man nor woman, a being without sex.
I am sure he did. And yet he was immensely intelligent. But
he knew that I had entered the monastery as a novice, that I
had been there through all my adult life. And then my manner
probably assisted him in his illusion. For I gave—I believe—no
sign of the change that was taking place within me under his
influence. I seemed to be calm, detached, even in my sympathy
for his suffering. For he suffered frightfully. This woman he
loved was a Parisian, he told me. He described her beauty to
me, as if in order to excuse himself for having become the slave
to her he was. I suppose she was very beautiful. He said that

she had a physical charm so intense that few men could resist it, that she was famous throughout Europe for it. He told me that she was not a good woman. I gathered that she lived for pleasure, admiration, that she had allowed many men to love her before he knew her. But she had loved him genuinely. She was not a very young woman, and she was not a married woman. He said that she was a woman men loved but did not marry, a woman who was loved by the husbands of married women, a woman to marry whom would exclude a man from the society of good women. She had never lived, or thought of living, for one man till he came into her life. Nor had he ever dreamed of living for one woman. He had lived to gain experience; she too. But when he met her—knowing thoroughly all she was—all other women ceased to exist for him. He became her slave. Then jealousy awoke in him, jealousy of all the men who had been in her life, who might be in her life again. He was tortured by loving such a woman—a woman who had belonged to many, who would no doubt in the future belong to others. For despite the fact that she loved him he told me that at first he had no illusions about her. He knew the world too well for that, and he cursed the fate that had bound him body and soul to what he called a courtesan. Even the fact that she loved him at first did not blind him to the effect upon character that her life must inevitably have had. She had dwelt in an atmosphere of lies, he said, and to lie was nothing to her. Any original refinement of feeling as regards human relations that she might have had had become dulled, if it had not been destroyed. At first he blindly, miserably, resigned himself to this. He said to himself, ' Fate has led me to love this sort of woman. I must accept her as she is, with all her defects, with her instinct for treachery, with her passion for the admiration of the world, with her incapability for being true to an ideal, or for isolating herself in the adoration of one man. I cannot get away from her. She has me fast. I cannot live without her. Then I must bear the torture that jealousy of her will certainly bring me in silence. I must conceal it. I must try to kill it. I must make the best of whatever she will give me, knowing that she can never, with her nature and her training, be exclusively mine as a good woman might be.' This he said to himself. This plan of conduct he traced for himself. But he soon found that he was not strong enough to keep to it. His jealousy was a devouring fire, and he could not conceal it. Domini, he described to me minutely the effect of jealousy in a human heart. I had never imagined what it was, and, when he described it, I felt as if I looked down into a bottomless pit lined with the flames of hell. By the depth of that pit I measured the depth of his passion for this woman, and I gained an idea of what human love—not the best sort of human love, but still genuine, intense love of some kind—could be. Of this human love I thought at night, putting it in comparison with the love God's creature can have for God. And my sense of loneliness increased, and I felt as if I had always been lonely. Does this seem strange to you? In the love of God was calm, peace, rest, a lying down of the soul in the Almighty arms. In the other love described to me was restlessness, agitation, torture, the soul spinning like an atom driven by winds, the heart devoured as by a disease, a cancer. On the one hand was a beautiful trust, on the other a ceaseless agony of doubt and terror. And yet I came to feel as if the one were unreal in comparison with the other, as if in the one were a loneliness, in the other a fierce companionship. I thought of the Almighty arms, Domini, and of the arms of a woman, and—Domini, I longed to have known, if only once, the pressure of a woman's arms about my neck, about my breast, the touch of a woman's hand upon my heart.

"And of all this I never spoke at confession. I committed the deadly sin of keeping back at confession all that." He stopped. Then he said, "Till the end my confessions were incomplete, were false.

"The stranger told me that as his love for this woman grew he found it impossible to follow the plan he had traced for himself of shutting his eyes to the sight of other eyes admiring, desiring her, of shutting his ears to the voices that whispered, 'This it will always be, for others as well as for you.' He found it impossible. His jealousy was too importunate, and he resolved to make any effort to keep her for himself alone. He knew she had love for him, but he knew that love would not necessarily, or even probably, keep her entirely faithful to him. She thought too little of passing intrigues. To her they seemed trifles, meaningless, unimportant. She told him so, when he spoke his jealousy. She said, 'I love you. I do not love these other men. They are in my life for a moment only.'

" 'And that moment plunges me into hell!' he said.

"He told her he could not bear it, that it was impossible, that she must belong to him entirely and solely. He asked her to marry him. She was surprised, touched. She understood what a sacrifice such a marriage would be to a man in his position. He was a man of good birth. His request, his vehement insistence on it, made her understand his love as she had not understood it before. Yet she hesitated. For so long had she been accustomed to a life of freedom, of changing *amours,* that she hesitated to put her neck under the yoke of matrimony. She understood thoroughly his character and his aim in marrying her. She knew that as his wife she must bid an eternal farewell to the life she had known. And it was a life that had become a habit to her, a life that she was fond of. For she was enormously vain, and she was a—she was a very physical woman, subject to physical caprices. There are things that I pass over, Domini, which would explain still more her hesitation. He knew what caused it, and again he was tortured. But he persisted. And at last he overcame. She consented to marry him. They were engaged. Domini, I need not tell you much more, only this fact—which had driven him from France, destroyed his happiness, brought him to the monastery. Shortly before the marriage was to take place he discovered that, while they were engaged, she had yielded to the desires of an old admirer who had come to bid her farewell and to wish her joy in her new life. He was tempted, he said, to kill her. But he governed himself and left her. He travelled. He came to Tunis. He came to La Trappe. He saw the peace there. He thought, ' Can I seize it? Can it do something for me?' He saw me. He thought, 'I shall not be quite alone. This monk—he has lived always in peace, he has never known the torture of women. Might not intercourse with him help me?'

"Such was his history, such was the history poured, with infinite detail that I have not told you, day by day, into my ears. It was the history, you see, of a passion that was mainly physical. I will not say entirely. I do not know whether any great passion can be entirely physical. But it was the history of the passion of one body for another body, and he did not attempt to present it to me as anything else. This man made me understand the meaning of the body. I had never understood it before. I had never suspected the immensity of the meaning there is in physical things. I had never comprehended the flesh. Now I comprehended it. Loneliness rushed upon me, devoured me—loneliness of the body. ' God is a spirit and those that worship him must worship him in spirit.' Now I felt that to worship in spirit was not enough. I even felt that it was scarcely anything. Again I thought of my life as the life of a skeleton in a world of skeletons. Again the chapel was as a valley of dry bones. It was a ghastly sensation. I was plunged in the void. I—I—I can't tell you my exact sensation, but it was as if I was the loneliest creature in the whole of the universe, and as if I need not have been lonely, as if I, in my ignorance and fatuity, had selected loneliness thinking it was the happiest fate.

"And yet you will say I was face to face with this man's almost frantic misery. I was, and it made no difference. I envied him, even in his present state. He wanted to gain consolation from me if that were possible. Oh, the irony of my consoling him! In secret I laughed at it bitterly. When I strove to console him I knew that I was an incarnate lie. He had told me the meaning of the body and, by so doing, had snatched from me the meaning of the spirit. And then he said to me, 'Make me feel the meaning of the spirit. If I can grasp that I may find comfort.' He called upon me to give him what I no longer had—the peace of God that passeth understanding. Domini, can you feel at all what that was to me? Can you realise? Can you—is it any wonder that I could do nothing for him, for him who had done such a' frightful thing for me? Is it any wonder? Soon he realised that he would not find peace with me in the garden. Yet he stayed on. Why? He did not know where to go, what to do. Life offered him nothing but horror. His love of experiences was dead. His love of life had completely vanished. He saw the worldly life as a nightmare, yet he had nothing to put in the place of it. And in the monastery he was ceaselessly tormented by jealousy. Ceaselessly his mind was at work about this woman, picturing her in her life of change, of intrigue, of new lovers, of new hopes and aims in which he had no part, in which his image was being blotted out, doubtless from her memory even. He suffered, he suffered as few suffer. But I think I suffered more. The melancholy was driven on into a gnawing hunger, the gnawing hunger of the flesh wishing to have lived, wishing to live, wishing to—to know.

"Domini, to you I can't say more of that—to you whom I—whom I love with spirit and flesh. I will come to the end, to the incident which made the body rise up, strike down the soul, trample out over it into the world like a wolf that was starving.

"One day the Reverend Père gave me a special permission

to walk with our visitor beyond the monastery walls towards
the sea. Such a permission was an event in my life. It excited
me more than you can imagine. I found that the stranger had
begged him to let me come.

"'Our guest is very fond of you,' the Reverend Père said to
me. 'I think if any human being can bring him to a calmer,
happier state of mind and spirit, you can. You have obtained a
good influence over him.'

"Domini, when the Reverend Père spoke to me thus my
mouth was suddenly contracted in a smile. Devils smile, I
think. I put up my hand to my face. I saw the Reverend
Père looking at me with a dawning of astonishment in his
kind, grave eyes, and I controlled myself at once. But I said
nothing. I could not say anything, and I went out from the
parlour quickly, hot with a sensation of shame.

"'You are coming?' the stranger said.

"'Yes,' I answered.

"It was a fiery day of late June. Africa was bathed in a
glare of light that hurt the eyes. I went into my cell and put
on a pair of blue glasses and my wide straw hat, the hat in
which I formerly used to work in the fields. When I came
out my guest was standing on the garden path. He was swinging a stick in one hand. The other hand, which hung down
by his side, was twitching nervously. In the glitter of the sun
his face looked ghastly. In his eyes there seemed to be terrors
watching without hope.

"'You are ready?' he said. 'Let us go.'

"We set off, walking quickly.

"'Movement—pace—sometimes that does a little good,' he
said. 'If one can exhaust the body the mind sometimes lies
almost still for a moment. If it would only lie still for ever.'

"I said nothing. I could say nothing. For my fever was
surely as his fever.

"'Where are we going?' he asked when we reached the
little house of the keeper of the gate by the cemetery.

"'We cannot walk in the sun,' I answered. 'Let us go
into the eucalyptus woods.'

"The first Trappists had planted forests of eucalyptus to
keep off the fever that sometimes comes in the African summer.
We made our way along a tract of open land and came into a
deep wood. Here we began to walk more slowly. The wood
was empty of men. The hot silence was profound. He took
off his white helmet and walked on, carrying it in his hand.

Not till we were far in the forest did he speak. Then he said,
'Father, I cannot struggle on much longer.'

"He spoke abruptly, in a hard voice.

"'You must try to gain courage,' I said.

"'From where?' he exclaimed. 'No, no, don't say from
God. If there is a God he hates me.'

"When he said that I felt as if my soul shuddered, hearing
a frightful truth spoken about itself. My lips were dry. My
heart seemed to shrivel up, but I made an effort and answered:

"'God hates no being whom he has created.'

"'How can you know? Almost every man, perhaps every
living man, hates someone. Why not——?'

"'To compare God with a man is blasphemous,' I answered.

"'Aren't we made in his image? Father, it's as I said—I
can't struggle on much longer. I shall have to end it. I wish
now—I often wish that I had yielded to my first impulse and
killed her. What is she doing now? What is she doing now—
at this moment?'

"He stood still and beat with his stick on the ground.

"'You don't know the infinite torture there is in knowing
that, far away, she is still living that cursed life, that she is
free to continue the acts of which her existence has been full.
Every moment I am imagining—I am seeing——'

"He forced his stick deep into the ground.

"'If I had killed her,' he said in a low voice, 'at least I
should know that she was sleeping—alone—there—there—
under the earth. I should know that her body was dissolved
into dust, that her lips could kiss no man, that her arms could
never hold another as they have held me!'

"'Hush!' I said sternly. 'You deliberately torture yourself and me.' He glanced up sharply.

"'You! What do you mean?'

"'I must not listen to such things,' I said. 'They are bad
for you and for me.'

"'How can they be bad for you—a monk?'

"'Such talk is evil—evil for everyone.'

"'I'll be silent then. I'll go into the silence. I'll go soon.'

"I understood that he thought of putting an end to himself.

"'There are few men,' I said, speaking with deliberation,
with effort, 'who do not feel at some period of life that all is
over for them, that there is nothing to hope for, that happiness
is a dream which will visit them no more.'

"'Have you ever felt like that? You speak of it calmly, but have you ever experienced it?'

"I hesitated. Then I said:

"'Yes.'

"'You, who have been a monk for so many years!'

"'Yes.'

"'Since you have been here?'

"'Yes, since then.'

"'And you would tell me that the feeling passed, that hope came again, and the dream as you call it?'

"'I would say that what has lived in a heart can die, as we who live in this world shall die.'

"'Ah, that—the sooner the better! But you are wrong. Sometimes a thing lives in the heart that cannot die so long as the heart beats. Such is my passion, my torture. Don't you, a monk—don't dare to say to me that this love of mine could die.'

"'Don't you wish it to die?' I asked. 'You say it tortures you.'

"'Yes. But no—no—I don't wish it to die. I could never wish that.'

"I looked at him, I believe, with a deep astonishment.

"'Ah, you don't understand!' he said. 'You don't understand. At all costs one must keep it—one's love. With it I am —as you see. But without it—man, without it, I should be nothing—no more than that.'

"He picked up a rotten leaf, held it to me, threw it down on the ground. I hardly looked at it. He had said to me: 'Man!' That word, thus said by him, seemed to me to mark the enormous change in me, to indicate that it was visible to the eyes of another, the heart of another. I had passed from the monk—the sexless being—to the man. He set me beside himself, spoke of me as if I were as himself. An intense excitement surged up in me. I think—I don't know what I should have said—done—but at that moment a boy, who acted as a servant at the monastery, came running towards us with a letter in his hand.

"'It is for Monsieur!' he said. 'It was left at the gate.'

"'A letter for me!' the stranger said.

"He held out his hand and took it indifferently. The boy gave it, and turning, went away through the wood. Then the stranger glanced at the envelope. Domini, I wish I could make you see what I saw then, the change that came. I can't. There are things the eyes must see. The tongue can't tell them. The ghastly whiteness went out of his face. A hot flood of scarlet rushed over it up to the roots of his hair. His hands and his whole body began to tremble violently. His eyes, which were fixed on the envelope, shone with an expression—it was like all the excitement in the world condensed into two sparks. He dropped his stick and sat down on the trunk of a tree, fell down almost.

" ' Father! ' he muttered, ' it's not been through the post— it's not been through the post! '

" I did not understand.

" ' What do you mean? ' I asked.

" ' What—— '

" The flush left his face. He turned deadly white again. He held out the letter.

" ' Read it for me! ' he said. ' I can't see—I can't see any- thing.'

" I took the letter. He covered his eyes with his hands. I opened it and read:

" ' GRAND HOTEL, TUNIS.

" ' I have found out where you are. I have come. Forgive me—if you can. I will marry you—or I will live with you. As you please; but I cannot live without you. I know women are not admitted to the monastery. Come out on the road that leads to Tunis. I am there. At least come for a moment and speak to me. VERONIQUE.'

" Domini, I read this slowly; and it was as if I read my own fate. When I had finished he got up. He was still pale as ashes and trembling.

" ' Which is the way to the road? ' he said. ' Do you know? '

" ' Yes.'

" ' Take me there. Give me your arm, Father.'

" He took it, leaned on it heavily. We walked through the wood towards the highroad. I had almost to support him. The way seemed long. I felt tired, sick, as if I could scarcely move, as if I were bearing—as if I were bearing a cross that was too heavy for me. We came at last out of the shadow of the trees into the glare of the sun. A flat field divided us from the white road.

" ' Is there—is there a carriage? ' he whispered in my ear.

" I looked across the field and saw on the road a carriage waiting.

"'Yes,' I said.

"I stopped, and tried to take his arm from mine.

"'Go,' I said. 'Go on!'

"'I can't. Come with me, Father.'

"We went on in the blinding sun. I looked down on the dry earth as I walked. Presently I saw at my feet the white dust of the road. At the same time I heard a woman's cry. The stranger took his arm violently from mine.

"'Father,' he said. 'Good-bye—God bless you!'

"He was gone. I stood there. In a moment I heard a roll of wheels. Then I looked up. I saw a man and a woman together, Domini. Their faces were like angels' faces—with happiness. The dust flew up in the sunshine. The wheels died away—I was alone.

"Presently—I think after a very long time—I turned and went back to the monastery. Domini, that night I left the monastery. I was as one mad. The wish to live had given place to the determination to live. I thought of nothing else. In the chapel that evening I heard nothing—I did not see the monks. I did not attempt to pray, for I knew that I was going. To go was an easy matter for me. I slept alone in the *hôtellerie,* of which I had the key. When it was night I unlocked the door. I walked to the cemetery—between the Stations of the Cross. Domini, I did not see them. In the cemetery was a ladder, as I told you.

"Just before dawn I reached my brother's house outside of Tunis, not far from the Bardo. I knocked. My brother himself came down to know who was there. He, as I told you, was without religion, and had always hated my being a monk. I told him all, without reserve. I said, 'Help me to go away. Let me go anywhere—alone.' He gave me clothes, money. I shaved off my beard and moustache. I shaved my head, so that the tonsure was no longer visible. In the afternoon of that day I left Tunis. I was let loose into life. Domini—Domini, I won't tell you where I wandered till I came to the desert, till I met you

"I was let loose into life, but, with my freedom, the wish to live seemed to die in me. I was afraid of life. I was haunted by terrors. I had been a monk so long that I did not know how to live as other men. I did not live, I never lived—till I met you. And then—then I realised what life may be. And then, too, I realised fully what I was. I struggled, I fought myself. You know—now, if you look back, I think you

know that I tried—sometimes, often—I tried to—to—I tried
to——"

His voice broke.

"That last day in the garden I thought that I had conquered
myself, and it was in that moment that I fell for ever. When I
knew you loved me I could fight no more. Do you understand?
You have seen me, you have lived with me, you have divined my
misery. But don't—don't think, Domini, that it ever came from
you. It was the consciousness of my lie to you, my lie to God,
that—that—I can't go on—I can't tell you—I can't tell you—
you know."

He was silent. Domini said nothing, did not move. He did
not look at her, but her silence seemed to terrify him. He drew
back from it sharply and turned to the desert. He stared across
the vast spaces lit up by the moon. Still she did not move.

"I'll go—I'll go!" he muttered.

And he stepped forward. Then Domini spoke.

"Boris!" she said.

He stopped.

"What is it?" he murmured hoarsely.

"Boris, now at last you—you can pray."

He looked at her as if awe-stricken.

"Pray!" he whispered. "You tell me I can pray—now!"

"Now at last."

She went into the tent and left him alone. He stood where
he was for a moment. He knew that, in the tent, she was praying. He stood, trying to listen to her prayer. Then, with an
uncertain hand, he felt in his breast. He drew out the wooden
crucifix. He bent down his head, touched it with his lips, and
fell upon his knees in the desert.

The music had ceased in the city. There was a great silence.

BOOK VI

THE JOURNEY BACK

CHAPTER XXVII

THE good priest of Amara, strolling by chance at the dinner-hour of the following day towards the camp of the hospitable strangers, was surprised and saddened to find only the sand-hill strewn with *débris*. The tents, the camels, the mules, the horses—all were gone. No servants greeted him. No cook was busy. No kind hostess bade him come in and stay to dine. Forlornly he glanced around and made inquiry. An Arab told him that in the morning the camp had been struck and ere noon was far on its way towards the north. The priest had been on horseback to an neighbouring oasis, so had heard nothing of this flitting. He asked its explanation, and was told a hundred lies. The one most often repeated was to the effect that Monsieur, the husband of Madame, was overcome by the heat, and that for this reason the travellers were making their way towards the cooler climate that lay beyond the desert.

As he heard this a sensation of loneliness came to the priest. His usually cheerful countenance was overcast with gloom. For a moment he loathed his fate in the sands and sighed for the fleshpots of civilisation. With his white umbrella spread above his helmet he stood still and gazed towards the north across the vast spaces that were lemon-yellow in the sunset. He fancied that on the horizon he saw faintly a cloud of sand grains whirling, and imagined it stirred up by the strangers' caravan. Then he thought of the rich lands of the Tell, of the olive groves of Tunis, of the blue Mediterranean, of France, his country which he had not seen for many years. He sighed profoundly.

" Happy people," he thought to himself. " Rich, free, able to do as they like, to go where they will! Why was I born to live in the sand and to be alone? "

He was moved by envy. But then he remembered his intercourse with Androvsky on the previous day.

"After all," he thought more comfortably, "he did not look
a happy man!" And he took himself to task for his sin of
envy, and strolled to the inn by the fountain where he paid his
pension.

The same day, in the house of the marabout of Beni-Hassan,
Count Anteoni received a letter brought from Amara by an
Arab. It was as follows:

"AMARA.

"MY DEAR FRIEND: Good-bye. We are just leaving. I
had expected to be here longer, but we must go. We are returning to the north and shall not penetrate farther into the desert.
I shall think of you, and of your journey on among the people
of your faith. You said to me, when we sat in the tent door,
that now you could pray in the desert. Pray in the desert for
us. And one thing more. If you never return to Beni-Mora,
and your garden is to pass into other hands, don't let it go into
the hands of a stranger. I could not bear that. Let it come
to me. At any price you name. Forgive me for writing thus.
Perhaps you will return, or perhaps, even if you do not, you will
keep your garden.—Your Friend,   DOMINI."

In a postscript was an address which would always find her.

Count Anteoni read this letter two or three times carefully,
with a grave face.

"Why did she not put Domini Androvsky?" he said to himself. He locked the letter in a drawer. All that night he was
haunted by thoughts of the garden. Again and again it seemed
to him that he stood with Domini beside the white wall and saw,
in the burning distance of the desert, at the call of the Mueddin,
the Arabs bowing themselves in prayer, and the man—the man
to whom now she had bound herself by the most holy tie—fleeing
from prayer as if in horror.

"But it was written," he murmured to himself. "It was
written in the sand and in fire: 'The fate of every man have
we bound about his neck.'"

In the dawn when, turning towards the rising sun, he prayed,
he remembered Domini and her words: "Pray in the desert for
us." And in the Garden of Allah he prayed to Allah for her,
and for Androvsky.

Meanwhile the camp had been struck, and the first stage of
the journey northward, the journey back, had been accomplished.

Domini had given the order of departure, but she had first spoken with Androvsky.

After his narrative, and her words that followed it, he did not come into the tent. She did not ask him to. She did not see him in the moonlight beyond the tent, or when the moonlight waned before the coming of the dawn. She was upon her knees, her face hidden in her hands, striving as surely few human beings have ever had to strive in the difficult paths of life. At first she had felt almost calm. When she had spoken to Androvsky there had even been a strange sensation that was not unlike triumph in her heart. In this triumph she had felt disembodied, as if she were a spirit standing there, removed from earthly suffering, but able to contemplate, to understand, to pity it, removed from earthly sin, but able to commit an action that might help to purge it.

When she said to Androvsky, "Now you can pray," she had passed into a region where self had no existence. Her whole soul was intent upon this man to whom she had given all the treasures of her heart and whom she knew to be writhing as souls writhe in Purgatory. He had spoken at last, he had laid bare his misery, his crime, he had laid bare the agony of one who had insulted God, but who repented his insult, who had wandered far away from God, but who could never be happy in his wandering, who could never be at peace even in a mighty human love unless that love was consecrated by God's contentment with it. As she stood there Domini had had an instant of absolutely clear sight into the depths of another's heart, another's nature. She had seen the monk in Androvsky, not slain by his act of rejection, but alive, sorrow-stricken, quivering, scourged. And she had been able to tell this monk—as God seemed to be telling her, making of her his messenger—that now at last he might pray to a God who again would hear him, as he had heard him in the garden of El-Largani, in his cell, in the chapel, in the fields. She had been able to do this. Then she had turned away, gone into the tent and fallen upon her knees.

But with that personal action her sense of triumph passed away. As her body sank down her soul seemed to sink down with it into bottomless depths of blackness where no light had ever been, into an underworld, airless, peopled with invisible violence. And it seemed to her as if it was her previous flight upward which had caused this descent into a place which had surely never before been visited by a human soul. All the selflessness suddenly vanished from her, and was replaced by a burning sense of her own personality, of what was due to it, of what had been done to it, of what it now was. She saw it like a cloth that had been white and that now was stained with indelible filth. And anger came upon her, a bitter fury, in which she was inclined to cry out, not only against man, but against God. The strength of her nature was driven into a wild bitterness, the sweet waters became acrid with salt. She had been able a moment before to say to Androvsky, almost with tenderness, " Now at last you can pray." Now she was on her knees hating him, hating—yes, surely hating—God. It was a frightful sensation.

Soul and body felt defiled. She saw Androvsky coming into her clean life, seizing her like a prey, rolling her in filth that could never be cleansed. And who had allowed him to do her this deadly wrong? God. And she was on her knees to this God who had permitted this! She was in the attitude of worship. Her whole being rebelled against prayer. It seemed to her as if she made a furious physical effort to rise from her knees, but as if her body was paralysed and could not obey her will. She remained kneeling, therefore, like a woman tied down, like a blasphemer bound by cords in the attitude of prayer, whose soul was shrieking insults against heaven.

Presently she remembered that outside Androvsky was praying, that she had meant to join with him in prayer. She had contemplated, then, a further, deeper union with him. Was she a madwoman? Was she a slave? Was she as one of those women of history who, seized in a rape, resigned themselves to love and obey their captors? She began to hate herself. And still she knelt. Anyone coming in at the tent door would have seen a woman apparently entranced in an ecstasy of worship.

This great love of hers, to what had it brought her? This awakening of her soul, what was its meaning? God had sent a man to rouse her from sleep that she might look down into hell. Again and again, with ceaseless reiteration, she recalled the incidents of her passion in the desert. She thought of the night at Arba when Androvsky blew out the lamp. That night had been to her a night of consecration. Nothing in her soul had risen up to warn her. No instinct, no woman's instinct, had stayed her from unwitting sin. The sand-diviner had been wiser than she; Count Anteoni more far-seeing; the priest of Beni-Mora more guided by holiness, by the inner flame that flickers before the wind that blows out of the caverns of evil. God had blinded her in order that she might fall, had brought Androvsky to her in order that her religion, her Catholic faith, might be made hideous to her for ever. She trembled all over as she knelt. Her life had been sad, even tormented. And she had set out upon a pilgrimage to find peace. She had been led to Beni-Mora. She remembered her arrival in Africa, its spell descending upon her, her sensation of being far off, of having left her former life with its sorrows for ever. She remembered the entrancing quiet of Count Anteoni's garden, how as she entered it she seemed to be entering an earthly Paradise, a place prepared by God for one who was weary as she was weary, for one who longed to be renewed as she longed to be renewed. And in that Paradise, in the inmost recess of it, she had put her hands against Androvsky's temples and given her life, her fate, her heart into his keeping. That was why the garden was there, that she might be led to commit this frightful action in it. Her soul felt physically sick. As to her body—but just then she scarcely thought of the body. For she was thinking of her soul as of a body, as if it were the core of the body blackened, sullied, destroyed for ever. She was hot with shame, she was hot with a fiery indignation. Always, since she was a child, if she were suddenly touched by anyone whom she did not love, she had had an inclination to strike a blow on the one who touched her. Now it was as if an unclean hand had been laid on her soul. And the soul quivered with longing to strike back.

Again she thought of Beni-Mora, of all that had taken place there. She realised that during her stay there a crescendo of calm had taken place within her, calm of the spirit, a crescendo of strength, spiritual strength, a crescendo of faith and of hope. The religion which had almost seemed to be slipping from her she had grasped firmly again. Her soul had arrived in Beni-Mora an invalid and had become a convalescent.

It had been reclining wearily, fretfully. In Beni-Mora it had stood up, walked, sung as the morning stars sang together. But then—why? If this was to be the end—why—why?

And at this question she paused, as before a great portal that was shut. She went back. She thought again of this beautiful crescendo, of this gradual approach to the God from whom she had been if not entirely separated at any rate set a little apart. Could it have been only in order that her catastrophe might be the more complete, her downfall the more absolute?

And then, she knew not why, she seemed to see in the hands that were pressed against her face words written in fire, and to read them slowly as a child spelling out a great lesson, with an

intense attention, with a labour whose result would be eternal
recollection:

"Love watcheth, and sleeping, slumbereth not. When weary
it is not tired; when straitened it is not constrained; when
frightened it is not disturbed; but like a vivid flame and a
burning torch it mounteth upwards and securely passeth through
all. Whosover loveth knoweth the cry of this voice."

The cry of this voice! At that moment, in the vast silence of
the desert, she seem d to hear it. And it was the cry of her own
voice. It was the cry of the voice of her own soul. Startled,
she lifted her face from her hands and listened. She did not
look out at the tent door, but she saw the moonlight falling upon
the matting that was spread upon the sand within the tent,
and she repeated, "Love watcheth—Love watcheth—Love
watcheth," moving her lips like the child who reads with difficulty. Then came the thought, "I am watching."

The passion of personal anger had died away as suddenly as
it had come. She felt numb and yet excited. She leaned
forward and once more laid her face in her hands.

"Love watcheth—I am watching." Then a moment—then
—"God is watching me."

She whispered the words over again and again. And the
numbness began to pass away. And the anger was dead.
Always she had felt as if she had been led to Africa for some
definite end. Did not the freed negroes, far out in the Desert,
sing their song of the deeper mysteries—"No one but God and
I knows what is in my heart"? And had not she heard it again
and again, and each time with a sense of awe? She had always
thought that the words were wonderful and beautiful. But she
had thought that perhaps they were not true. She had said to
Androvsky that he knew what was in her heart. And now, in
this night, in its intense stillness, close to the man who for so
long had not dared to pray but who now was praying, again she
thought that they were not quite true. It seemed to her that she
did not know what was in her heart, and that she was waiting
there for God to come and tell her. Would He come? She
waited. Patience entered into her.

The silence was long. Night was travelling, turning her
thoughts to a distant world. The moon waned, and a faint
breath of wind that was almost cold stole over the sands, among
the graves in the cemetery, to the man and the woman who were
keeping vigil upon their knees. The wind died away almost
ere it had risen, and the rigid silence that precedes the dawn held

the desert in its grasp. And God came to Domini in the silence,
Allah through Allah's garden that was shrouded still in the
shadows of night. Once, as she journeyed through the roaring
of the storm, she had listened for the voice of the desert. And
as the desert took her its voice had spoken to her in a sudden
and magical silence, in a falling of the wind. Now, in a more
magical silence, the voice of God spoke to her. And the voice
of the desert and of God were as one. As she knelt she heard
God telling her what was in her heart. It was a strange and
passionate revelation. She trembled as she heard. And sometimes she was inclined to say, "It is not so." And sometimes
she was afraid, afraid of what this—all this that was in her heart
—would lead her to do. For God told her of a strength which
she had not known her heart possessed, which—so it seemed to
her—she did not wish it to possess, of a strength from which
something within her shrank, against which something within
her protested. But God would not be denied. He told her she
had this strength. He told her that she must use it. He told
her that she would use it. And she began to understand something of the mystery of the purposes of God in relation to herself, and to understand, with it, how closely companioned even
those who strive after effacement of self are by selfishness—how
closely companioned she had been on her African pilgrimage.
Everything that had happened in Africa she had quietly taken to
herself, as a gift made to her for herself.

The peace that had descended upon her was balm for her
soul, and was sent merely for that, to stop the pain she suffered
from old wounds that she might be comfortably at rest. The
crescendo—the beautiful crescendo—of calm, of strength, of
faith, of hope which she had, as it were, heard like a noble music
within her spirit had been the David sent to play upon the harp
to her Saul, that from her Saul the black demon of unrest, of
despair, might depart. That was what she had believed. She
had believed that she had come to Africa for herself, and now
God, in the silence, was telling her that this was not so, that He
had brought her to Africa to sacrifice herself in the redemption
of another. And as she listened—listened, with bowed head,
and eyes in which tears were gathering, from which tears were
falling upon her clasped hands—she knew that it was true, she
knew that God meant her to put away her selfishness, to rise
above it. Those eagle's wings of which she had thought—she
must spread them. She must soar towards the place of the
angels, whither good women soar in the great moments of their

love, borne up by the winds of God. On the minaret of the mosque of Sidi-Zerzour, while Androvsky remained in the dark shadow with a curse, she had mounted, with prayer, surely a little way towards God. And now God said to her, "Mount higher, come nearer to me, bring another with you. That was my purpose in leading you to Beni-Mora, in leading you far out into the desert, in leading you into the heart of the desert."

She had been led to Africa for a definite end, and now she knew what that end was. On the mosque of the minaret of Sidi-Zerzour she had surely seen prayer travelling, the soul of prayer travelling. And she had asked herself—"Whither?" She had asked herself where was the halting-place, with at last the pitched tent, the camp fires, and the long, the long repose? And when she came down into the court of the mosque and found Androvsky watching the old Arab who struck against the mosque and cursed, she had wished that Androvsky had mounted with her a little way towards God.

He should mount with her. Always she had longed to see him above her. Could she leave him below? She knew she could not. She understood that God did not mean her to. She understood perfectly. And tears streamed from her eyes. For now there came upon her a full comprehension of her love for Androvsky. His revelation had not killed it, as, for a moment, in her passionate personal anger, she had been inclined to think. Indeed it seemed to her now that, till this hour of silence, she had never really loved him, never known how to love. Even in the tent at Arba she had not fully loved him, perfectly loved him. For the thought of self, the desires of self, the passion of self, had entered into and been mingled with her love. But now she loved him perfectly, because she loved as God intended her to love. She loved him as God's envoy sent to him.

She was still weeping, but she began to feel calm, as if the stillness of this hour before the dawn entered into her soul. She thought of herself now only as a vessel into which God was pouring his purpose and his love.

Just as dawn was breaking, as the first streak of light stole into the east and threw a frail spear of gold upon the sands, she was conscious again of a thrill of life within her, of the movement of her unborn child. Then she lifted her head from her hand, looking towards the east, and whispered:

"Give me strength for one more thing—give me strength to be silent!"

She waited as if for an answer. Then she rose from her

knees, bathed her face and went out to the tent door to Androvsky.

" Boris! " she said.

He rose from his knees and looked at her, holding the little wooden crucifix in his hand.

" Domini? " he said in an uncertain voice.

" Put it back into your breast. Keep it for ever, Boris."

As if mechanically, and not removing his eyes from her, he put the crucifix into his breast. After a moment she spoke again, quietly.

" Boris, you never wished to stay here. You meant to stay here for me. Let us go away from Amara. Let us go to-day, now, in the dawn."

" Us! " he said.

There was a profound amazement in his voice.

" Yes," she answered.

" Away from Amara—you and I—together? "

" Yes, Boris, together."

" Where—where can we go? "

The amazement seemed to deepen in his voice. His eyes were watching her with an almost fierce intentness. In a flash of insight she realised that, just then, he was wondering about her as he had never wondered before, wondering whether she was really the good woman at whose feet his sin-stricken soul had worshipped. Yes, he was asking himself that question.

" Boris," she said, " will you leave yourself in my hands? We have talked of our future life. We have wondered what we should do. Will you let me do as I will, let the future be as I choose? "

In her heart she said " as God chooses."

" Yes, Domini," he answered. " I am in your hands, utterly your hands."

" No," she said.

Neither of them spoke after that till the sunlight lay above the towers and minarets of Amara. Then Domini said:

" We will go to-day—now."

And that morning the camp was struck, and the new journey began—the journey back.

CHAPTER XXVIII

A SILENCE had fallen between Domini and Androvsky which neither seemed able to break. They rode on side by side across the sands towards the north through the long day. The towers of Amara faded in the sunshine above the white crests of the dunes. The Arab villages upon their little hills disappeared in the quivering gold. New vistas of desert opened before them, oases crowded with palms, salt lakes and stony ground. They passed by native towns. They saw the negro gardeners laughing among the rills of yellow water, or climbing with bare feet the wrinkled tree trunks to lop away dead branches. They heard tiny goatherds piping, solitary, in the wastes. Dreams of the mirage rose and faded far off on the horizon, rose and faded mystically, leaving no trembling trace behind. And they were silent as the mirage, she in her purpose, he in his wonder. And the long day waned, and towards evening the camp was pitched and the evening meal was prepared. And still they could not speak.

Sometimes Androvsky watched her, and there was a great calm in her face, but there was no rebuke, no smallness of anger, no hint of despair. Always he had felt her strength of mind and body, but never so much as now. Could he rest on it? Dared he? He did not know. And the day seemed to him to become a dream, and the silence recalled to him the silence of the monastery in which he had worshipped God before the stranger came. He thought that in this silence he ought to feel that she was deliberately raising barriers between them, but—it was strange—he could not feel this. In her silence there was no bitterness. When is there bitterness in strength? He rode on and on beside her, and his sense of a dream deepened, helped by the influence of the desert. Where were they going? He did not know. What was her purpose? He could not tell. But he felt that she had a purpose, that her mind was resolved. Now and then, tearing himself with an effort from the dream, he asked himself what it could be. What could be in store for him, for them, after the thing he had told? What could be their mutual life? Must it not be for ever at an end? Was it not shattered? Was it not dust, like the dust of the desert that rose round their horses' feet? The silence did not tell him, and again he ceased from wondering and the dream closed round him. Were they not travelling in a mirage, mirage people, unreal, phantom-like, who would presently fade away into the spaces of the sun? The sand muffled the tread of the horses' feet. The desert understood their silence, clothed it in a silence more vast and more impenetrable. And Androvsky had made his effort. He had spoken the truth at last. He could do no more. He was incapable of any further action. As Domini felt herself to be in the hands of God, he felt himself to be in the hands of this woman who had received his confession with this wonderful calm, who was leading him he knew not whither in this wonderful silence.

When the camp was pitched, however, he noticed something that caught him sharply away from the dreamlike, unreal feeling, and set him face to face with fact that was cold as steel. Always till now the dressing-tent had been pitched beside their sleeping-tent, with the flap of the entrance removed so that the two tents communicated. To-night it stood apart, near the sleeping-tent, and in it was placed one of the small camp beds. Androvsky was alone when he saw this. On reaching the halting-place he had walked a little way into the desert. When he returned he found this change. It told him something of what was passing in Domini's mind, and it marked the transformation of their mutual life. As he gazed at the two tents he felt stricken, yet he felt a curious sense of something that was like—was it not like—relief? It was as if his body had received a frightful blow and on his soul a saint's hand had been gently laid, as if something fell about him in ruins, and at the same time a building which he loved, and which for a moment he had thought tottering, stood firm before him founded upon rock. He was a man capable of a passionate belief, despite his sin, and he had always had a passionate belief in Domini's religion. That morning, when she came out to him in the sand, a momentary doubt had assailed him. He had known the thought, " Does she love me still—does she love me more than she loves God, more than she loves his dictates manifested in the Catholic religion?" When she said that word "together" that had been his thought. Now, as he looked at the two tents, a white light seemed to fall upon Domini's character, and in this white light stood the ruin and the house that was founded upon a rock. He was torn by conflicting sensations of despair and triumph. She was what he had believed. That made the triumph. But since she was that where was his future with her? The monk and the man who had fled from the monastery stood up within him to do battle. The monk knew triumph, but the man was in torment.

Presently, as Androvsky looked at the two tents, the monk in him seemed to die a new death, the man who had left the monastery to know a new resurrection. He was seized by a furious desire to go backward in time, to go backward but a few hours, to the moment when Domini did not know what now she knew. He cursed himself for what he had done. At last he had been able to pray. Yes, but what was prayer now, what was prayer to the man who looked at the two tents and understood what they meant? He moved away and began to walk up and down near to the two tents. He did not know where Domini was. At a little distance he saw the servants busy preparing the evening meal. Smoke rose up before the cook's tent, curling away stealthily among a group of palm trees, beneath which some Arab boys were huddled, staring with wide eyes at the unusual sight of travellers. They came from a tiny village at a short distance off, half hidden among palm gardens. The camels were feeding. A mule was rolling voluptuously in the sand. At a well a shepherd was watering his flocks, which crowded about him baaing expectantly. The air seemed to breathe out a subtle aroma of peace and of liberty. And this apparent presence of peace, this vision of the calm of others, human beings and animals, added to the torture of Androvsky. As he walked to and fro he felt as if he were being devoured by his passions, as if he were losing the last vestiges of self-control. Never in the monastery, never even in the night when he left it, had he been tormented like this. For now he had a terrible companion whom, at that time, he had not known. Memory walked with him before the tents, the memory of his body, recalling and calling for the past.

He had destroyed that past himself. But for him it might have been also the present, the future. It might have lasted for years, perhaps till death took him or Domini. Why not? He had only had to keep silence, to insist on remaining in the desert, far from the busy ways of men. They could have lived as certain others lived, who loved the free, the solitary life, in an oasis of their own, tending their gardens of palms. Life would have gone like a sunlit dream. And death? At that thought he shuddered. Death—what would that have been to him? What would it be now when it came? He put the thought from him with force, as a man thrusts away from him the filthy hand of a clamouring stranger assailing him in the street.

This evening he had no time to think of death. Life was enough, life with this terror which he had deliberately placed in it.

He thought of himself as a madman for having spoken to Domini. He cursed himself as a madman. For he knew, although he strove furiously not to know how irrevocable was his act, in consequence of the great strength of her nature. He knew that though she had been to him a woman of fire she might be to him a woman of iron—even to him whom she loved.

How she had loved him!

He walked faster before the tents, to and fro.

How she had loved him! How she loved him still, at this moment after she knew what he was, what he had done to her. He had no doubt of her love as he walked there. He felt it, like a tender hand upon him. But that hand was inflexible too. In its softness there was firmness—firmness that would never yield to any strength in him.

Those two tents told him the story of her strength. As he looked at them he was looking into her soul. And her soul was in direct conflict with his. That was what he felt. She had thought, she had made up her mind. Quietly, silently s acted. By that action, without a word, she had spoken to him, told him a tremendous thing. And the man—the passionate man who had left the monastery—loose in him now was aflame with an impotent desire that was like a heat of fury against her, while the monk, hidden far down in him, was secretly worshipping her cleanliness of spirit.

But the man who had left the monastery was in the ascendant in him, and at last drove him to a determination that the monk secretly knew to be utterly vain. He made up his mind to enter into conflict with Domini's strength. He felt that he must, that he could not quietly, without a word, accept this sudden new life of separation symbolised for him by the two tents standing apart.

He stood still. In the distance, under the palms, he saw Batouch laughing with Ouardi. Near them Ali was reposing on a mat, moving his head from side to side, smiling with half-shut, vacant eyes, and singing a languid song.

This music maddened him.

"Batouch!" he called out sharply. "Batouch!"

Batouch stopped laughing, glanced round, then came towards him with a large pace, swinging from his hips.

"Monsieur?"

"Batouch!" Androvsky said.

But he could not go on. He could not say anything about the two tents to a servant.

"Where—where is Madame?" he said almost stammering.

"Out there, Monsieur."

With a sweeping arm the poet pointed towards a hump of

sand crowned by a few palms. Domini was sitting there, surrounded by Arab children, to whom she was giving sweets out of a box. As Androvsky saw her the anger in him burnt up more fiercely. This action of Domini's, simple, natural though it was, seemed to him in his present condition cruelly heartless. He thought of her giving the order about the tents and then going calmly to play with these children, while he—while he——

"You can go, Batouch," he said. "Go away."

The poet stared at him with a superb surprise, then moved slowly towards Ouardi, holding his burnous with his large hands.

Androvsky looked again at the two tents as a man looks at two enemies. Then, walking quickly, he went towards the hump of sand. As he approached it Domini had her side face turned towards him. She did not see him. The little Arabs were dancing round her on their naked feet, laughing, showing their white teeth and opening their mouths wide for the sugar-plums—gaiety incarnate. Androvsky gazed at the woman who was causing this childish joy, and he saw a profound sadness. Never had he seen Domini's face look like this. It was always white, but now its whiteness was like a whiteness of marble. She moved her head, turning to feed one of the little gaping mouths, and he saw her eyes, tearless, but sadder than if they had been full of tears. She was looking at these children as a mother looks at her children who are fatherless. He did not—how could he?—understand the look, but it went to his heart. He stopped, watching. One of the children saw him, shrieked, pointed. Domini glanced round. As she saw him she smiled, threw the last sugar-plums and came towards him. "Do you want me?" she said, coming up to him.

His lips trembled.

"Yes," he said, "I want you."

Something in his voice seemed to startle her, but she said nothing more, only stood looking at him. The children, who had followed her, crowded round them, touching their clothes curiously.

"Send them away," he said.

She made the children go, pushing them gently, pointing to the village, and showing the empty box to them. Reluctantly at last they went towards the village, turning their heads to stare at her till they were a long way off, then holding up their skirts and racing for the houses.

" Domini—Domini," he said.   " You can—you can play with children—to-day."

" I wanted to feel I could give a little happiness to-day," she answered—" even to-day."

" To-day when—when to me—to me—you are giving——"

But before her steady gaze all the words he had meant to say, all the words of furious protest, died on his lips.

" To me—to me——" he repeated.

Then he was silent.

" Boris," she said, " I want to give you one thing, the thing that you have lost.   I want to give you back peace."

" You never can."

" I must try.   Even if I cannot I shall know that I have tried."

" You are giving me—you are giving me not peace, but a sword," he said.

She understood that he had seen the two tents.

" Sometimes a sword can give peace."

" The peace of death."

" Boris—my dear one—there are many kinds of deaths Try to trust me.   Leave me to act as I must act.   Let me try to be guided—only let me try."

He did not say another word.

That night they slept apart for the first time since their marriage.

. . . . .

" Domini, where are you taking me? Where are we going?"

The camp was struck once more and they were riding through the desert.   Domini hesitated to answer his question. It had been put with a sort of terror.

" I know nothing," he continued.   " I am in your hands like a child.   It cannot be always so.   I must know, I must understand.   What is our life to be?   What is our future?   A man cannot——"

He paused.   Then he said:

" I feel that you have come to some resolve.   I feel it perpetually.   It is as if you were in light and I in darkness, you in knowledge and I in ignorance.   You—you must tell me.   I have told you all now.   You must tell me."

But she hesitated.

" Not now," she answered.   " Not yet."

" We are to journey on day by day like this, and I am not to know where we are going!   I cannot, Domini—I will not."

"Boris, I shall tell you."

"When?"

"Will you trust me, Boris, completely? Can you?"

"How?"

"Boris, I have prayed so much for you that at last I feel that
I can act for you. Don't think me presumptuous. If you could
see into my heart you would see that—indeed, I don't think it
would be possible to feel more humble than I do in regard to
you."

"Humble—you, Domini! You can feel humble when you
think of me, when you are with me."

"Yes. You have suffered so terribly. God has led you. I
feel that He has been—oh, I don't know how to say it quite
naturally, quite as I feel it—that He has been more intent on
you than on anyone I have ever known. I feel that his meaning
in regarding to you is intense, Boris, as if he would not let
you go."

"He let me go when I left the monastery."

"Does one never return?"

Again a sensation almost of terror assailed him. He felt as
if he were fighting in darkness something that he could not
see.

"Return!" he said. "What do you mean?"

She saw the expression of almost angry fear in his face. It
warned her not to give the reins to her natural impulse, which
was always towards a great frankness.

"Boris, you fled from God, but do you not think it possible
that you could ever return to Him? Have you not taken the
first step? Have you not prayed?"

His face changed, grew slightly calmer.

"You told me I could pray," he answered, almost like a
child. "Otherwise I—I should not have dared to. I should
have felt that I was insulting God."

"If you trusted me in such a thing, can you not trust me
now?"

"But"—he said uneasily—"but this is different, a worldly
matter, a matter of daily life. I shall have to know."

"Yes."

"Then why should I not know now? At any moment I
could ask Batouch."

"Batouch only knows from day to day. I have a map of the
desert. I got it before we left Beni-Mora."

Something—perhaps a very slight hesitation in her voice just before she said the last words—startled him.   He turned on his horse and looked at her hard.

"Domini," he said, "are we—we are not going back to Beni-Mora?"

"I will tell you to-night," she replied in a low voice.   "Let me tell you to-night."

He said no more, but he gazed at her for a long time as if striving passionately to read her thoughts.   But he could not. Her white face was calm, and she rode looking straight before her, as one that looked towards some distant goal to which all her soul was journeying with her body.   There was something mystical in her face, in that straight, far-seeing glance, that surely pierced beyond the blue horizon line and reached a far-off world.   What world?   He asked himself the question, but no answer came, and he dropped his eyes.   A new and horrible sadness came to him, a new sensation of separation from Domini. She had set their bodies apart, and he had yielded.   Now, was she not setting something else apart?   For, in spite of all, in spite of his treacherous existence with her, he had so deeply and entirely loved her that he had sometimes felt, dared to feel, that in their passion in the desert their souls had been fused together.   His was black—he knew it—and hers was white. But had not the fire and the depth of their love conquered all differences, made even their souls one as their bodies had been one?   And now was she not silently, subtly, withdrawing her soul from his?   A sensation of acute despair swept over him, of utter impotence.

"Domini!" he said, "Domini!"

"Yes," she answered.

And this time she withdrew her eyes from the blue distance and looked at him.

"Domini, you must trust me."

He was thinking of the two tents set the one apart from the ther.

"Domini, I've borne something in silence.   I haven't spoken. I wanted to speak.   I tried—but I did not.   I bore my punishment—you don't know, you'll never know what I felt last—last night—when—I've borne that.   But there's one thing I can't bear.   I've lived a lie with you.   My love for you overcame me. I fell.   I have told you that I fell.   Don't—don't because of that—don't take away your heart from me entirely.   Domini— Domini—don't do that."

She heard a sound of despair in his voice.

" Oh, Boris," she said, " if you knew! There was only one moment when I fancied my heart was leaving you. It passed almost before it came, and now——"

" But," he interrupted, " do you know—do you know that since—since I spoke, since I told you, you've—you've never touched me? "

" Yes, I know it," she replied quietly.

Something told him to be silent then. Something told him to wait till the night came and the camp was pitched once more.

They rested at noon for several hours, as it was impossible to travel in the heat of the day. The camp started an hour before they did. Only Batouch remained behind to show them the way to Ain-la-Hammam, where they would pass the following night. When Batouch brought the horses he said:

" Does Madame know the meaning of Ain-la-Hammam? "

" No," said Domini. " What is it? "

" Source des tourterelles," replied Batouch. " I was there once with an English traveller."

" Source des tourterelles," repeated Domini. " Is it beautiful, Batouch? It sounds as if it ought to be beautiful."

She scarcely knew why, but she had a longing that Ain-la-Hammam might be tender, calm, a place to soothe the spirit, a place in which Androvsky might be influenced to listen to what she had to tell him without revolt, without despair. Once he had spoken about the influence of place, about rising superior to it. But she believed in it, and she waited, almost anxiously, for the reply of Batouch. As usual it was enigmatic.

" Madame will see," he answered. " Madame will see. But the Englishman——"

" Yes? "

" The Englishman was ravished. ' This,' he said to me, ' this, Batouch, is a little Paradise! ' And there was no moor then. To-night there will be a moon."

" Paradise! " exclaimed Androvsky.

He sprang upon his horse and pulled up the reins. Domini said no more. They had started late. It was night when they reached Ain-la-Hammam. As they drew near Domini looked before her eagerly through the pale gloom that hung over the sand. She saw no village, only a very small grove of palms and near it the outline of a bordj. The place was set in a cup of the Sahara. All around it rose low hummocks of sand. On two or three of them were isolated clumps of palms. Here the eyes roamed over no vast distances. There was little suggestion of space. She drew up her horse on one of the hummocks and gazed down. She heard doves murmuring in their soft voices among the trees. The tents were pitched near the bordj.

"What does Madame think?" asked Batouch. "Does Madame agree with the Englishman?"

"It is a strange little place," she answered.

She listened to the voices of the doves. A dog barked by the bordj.

"It is almost like a hiding-place," she added.

Androvsky said nothing, but he, too, was gazing intently at the trees below them, he, too, was listening to the voices of the doves. After a moment he looked at her.

"Domini," he whispered. "Here—won't you—won't you let me touch your hand again here?"

"Come, Boris," she answered. "It is late."

They rode down into Ain-la-Hammam.

The tents had all been pitched near together on the south of the bordj, and separated by it from the tiny oasis. Opposite to them was a Café Maure of the humblest kind, a hovel of baked earth and brushwood, with earthen divans and a coffee niche. Before this was squatting a group of five dirty desert men, the sole inhabitants of Ain-la-Hammam. Just before dinner Domini gave an order to Batouch, and, while they were dining, Androvsky noticed that their people were busy unpegging the two sleeping-tents.

"What are they doing?" he said to Domini, uneasily. In his present condition everything roused in him anxiety. In every unusual action he discerned the beginning of some tragedy which might affect his life.

"I told Batouch to put our tents on the other side of the bordj," she answered.

"Yes. But why?"

"I thought that to-night it would be better if we were a little more alone than we are here, just opposite to that Café Maure, and with the servants. And on the other side there are the palms and the water. And the doves were talking there as we rode in. When we have finished dinner we can go and sit there and be quiet."

"Together," he said.

An eager light had come into his eyes. He leaned forward towards her over the little table and stretched out his hand.

"Yes, together," she said.

But she did not take his hand.

"Domini!" he said, still keeping his hand on the table, "Domini!"

An expression, that was like an expression of agony, flitted over her face and died away, leaving it calm.

"Let us finish," she said quietly. "Look, they have taken the tents! In a moment we can go."

The doves were silent. The night was very still in this nest of the Sahara. Ouardi brought them coffee, and Batouch came to say that the tents were ready.

"We shall want nothing more to-night, Batouch," Domini said. "Don't disturb us."

Patouch glanced towards the Café Maure. A red light gleamed through its low doorway. One or two Arabs were moving within. Some of the camp attendants had joined the squatting men without. A noise of busy voices reached the tents.

"To-night, Madame," Batouch said proudly, " I am going to tell stories from the *Thousand and One Nights*. I am going to tell the story of the young Prince of the Indies, and the story of Ganem, the Slave of Love. It is not often that in Ain-la-Hammam a poet——"

"No, indeed. Go to them, Batouch. They must be impatient for you."

Batouch smiled broadly.

"Madame begins to understand the Arabs," he rejoined. "Madame will soon be as the Arabs."

"Go, Batouch. Look—they are longing for you."

She pointed to the desert men, who were gesticulating and gazing towards the tents.

"It is better so, Madame," he answered. "They know that I am here only for one night, and they are eager as the hungry jackal is eager for food among the yellow dunes of the sand."

He threw his burnous over his shoulder and moved away smiling, and murmuring in a luscious voice the first words of Ganem, the Slave of Love.

"Let us go now, Boris," Domini said.

He got up at once from the table, and they walked together round the bordj.

On its further side there was no sign of life. No traveller was resting there that night, and the big door that led into the inner court was closed and barred. The guardian had gone to join the Arabs at the Café Maure. Between the shadow cast by the bordj and the shadow cast by the palm trees stood the two tents on a patch of sand. The oasis was enclosed in a low earth wall, along the top of which was a ragged edging of brushwood. In this wall were several gaps. Through one, opposite to the tents, was visible a shallow pool of still water by which tall reeds were growing. They stood up like spears, absolutely motionless. A frog was piping from some hidden place, giving forth a clear flute-like note that suggested glass. It reminded Domini of her ride into the desert at Beni-Mora to see the moon rise. On that night Androvsky had told her that he was going away. That had been the night of his tremendous struggle with himself. When he had spoken she had felt a sensation as if everything that supported her in the atmosphere of life and of happiness had foundered. And now—now she was going to speak to him—to tell him—what was she going to tell him? How much could she, dared she, tell him? She prayed silently to be given strength.

In the clear sky the young moon hung. Beneath it, to the left, was one star like an attendant, the star of Venus. The faint light of the moon fell upon the water of the pool. Unceasingly the frog uttered its nocturne.

Domini stood for a moment looking at the water listening. Then she glanced up at the moon and the solitary star. Androvsky stood by her.

" Shall we—let us sit on the wall, where the gap is," she said. " The water is beautiful, beautiful with that light on it, and the palms—palms are always beautiful, especially at night. I shall never love any other trees as I love palm trees."

" Nor I," he answered.

They sat down on the wall. At first they did not speak any more. The stillness of the water, the stillness of reeds and palms, was against speech. And the little flute-like note that came to them again and again at regular intervals was like a magical measuring of the silence of the night in the desert. At last Domini said, in a low voice:

" I heard that note on the night when I rode out of Beni-Mora to see the moon rise in the desert. Boris, you remember that night? "

" Yes," he answered.

He was gazing at the pool, with his face partly averted from her, one hand on the wall, the other resting on his knee.

" You were brave that night, Boris," she said.

" I—I wished to be—I tried to be. And if I had been——"
He stopped, then went on.

"If I had been, Domini, really brave, if I had done what I meant to do that night, what would our lives have been to-day?"

"I don't know. We mustn't think of that to-night. We must think of the future. Boris, there's no life, no real life without bravery. No man or woman is worthy of living who is not brave."

He said nothing.

"Boris, let us—you and I—be worthy of living to-night—and in the future."

"Give me your hand then," he answered. "Give it me, Domini."

But she did not give it to him. Instead she went on, speaking a little more rapidly:

"Boris, don't rely too much on my strength. I am only a woman, and I have to struggle. I have had to struggle more than perhaps you will ever know. You must not make—make things impossible for me. I am trying—very hard—to—I'm—you must not touch me to-night, Boris."

She drew a little farther away from him. A faint breath of air made the leaves of the palm trees rustle slightly, made the reeds move for an instant by the pool. He laid his hand again on the wall from which he had lifted it. There was a pleading sound in her voice which made him feel as if it were speaking close against his heart.

"I said I would tell you to-night where we are going."

"Tell me now."

"We are going back to Beni-Mora. We are not very far off from Beni-Mora to-night—not very far."

"We are going to Beni-Mora!" he repeated in a dull voice. "We are——"

He sat up on the wall, looking straight into her face.

"Why?" he said. His voice was sharp now, sharp with fear.

"Boris, do you want to be at peace, not with me, but with God? Do you want to get rid of your burden of misery, which increases—I know it—day by day?"

"How can I?" he said hopelessly.

"Isn't expiation the only way? I think it is."

"Expiation! How—how can—I can never expiate my sin."

"There's no sin that cannot be expiated. God isn't merciless. Come back with me to Beni-Mora. That little church—where you married me—come back to it with me. You could not confess to the—to Father Beret. I feel as if I knew why. Where you married me you will—you must—make your confession."

"To the priest who—to Father Roubier!"

There was fierce protest in his voice.

"It does not matter who is the priest who will receive your confession. Only make it there—make it in the church at Beni-Mora where you married me."

"That was your purpose! That is where you are taking me! I can't go, I won't! Domini, think what you are doing! You are asking too much——"

"I feel that God is asking that of you. Don't refuse Him."

"I cannot go—at Beni-Mora where we—where everything will remind us——"

"Ah, don't you think I shall feel it too? Don't you think I shall suffer?"

He felt horribly ashamed when she said that, bowed down with an overwhelming weight of shame.

"But our lives"—he stammered—"but—if I go—afterwards —if I make my confession—afterwards—afterwards?"

"Isn't it enough to think of that one thing? Isn't it better to put everything else, every other thought, away? It seems so clear to me that we should go to Beni-Mora. I feel as if I had been told—as a child is told to do something by its father."

She looked up into the clear sky.

"I am sure I have been told," she added. "I know I have."

There was a long silence between them. Androvsky felt that he did not dare to break it. Something in Domini's face and voice cast out from him the instinct of revolt, of protest. He began to feel exhausted, without power, like a sick man who is being carried by bearers in a litter, and who looks at the landscape through which he is passing with listless eyes, and who scarcely has the force to care whither he is being borne.

"Domini," he said at last, and his voice sounded very tired, "if you say I must go to Beni-Mora I will go. I have done you a great wrong and—and——"

"Don't think of me any more," she said. "Think—think as I do—of—of—— What am I? I have loved you, I shall always love you, but I am as you are, here for a little while, elsewhere for all eternity. You told him—that man in the monastery—that we are shadows set in a world of shadows."

"That was a lie," he interrupted, and the weariness had gone out of his voice. "When I said that I had never loved. I had never loved you."

" Or was it a half-truth? Aren't we, perhaps, shadow now in comparison to what we shall be? Isn't this world, even this —this desert, this pool with the light on it, this silence of the night around us—isn't all this a shadow in comparison to the world where we are going, you and I? Boris, I think if we are brave now we shall be together in that world. But if we are cowards now, I think, I am sure, that in that world—the real world—we shall be separated for ever. You and I, whatever we may be, whatever we may have done, at least are one thing— we are believers. We don't think this is all. If we did it would be different. But we can't change the truth that is in our souls, and as we can't change it we must live by it, we must act by it. We can't do anything else. I can't—and you? Don't you feel, don't you know, that you can't?"

" To-night," he said, " I feel that I know nothing—nothing except that I am suffering."

His voice broke on the last words. Tears were shining in his eyes. After a long silence he said:

" Domini, take me where you will. If it is to Beni-Mora I will go. But—but—afterwards?"

" Afterwards——" she said.

Then she stopped.

The little note of the frog sounded again and again by the still water among the reeds. The moon was higher in the sky.

" Don't let us think of afterwards, Boris," she said at length. " That song we have heard together, that song we love—' No one but God and I knows what is in my heart.' I hear it now so often, always almost. It seems to gather meaning, it seems to—God knows what is in your heart and mine. He will take care of the—afterwards. Perhaps in our hearts already He has put a secret knowledge of the end."

" Has He—has He put it—that knowledge—into yours?"

" Hush!" she said.

They spoke no more that night.

CHAPTER XXIX

THE caravan of Domini and Androvsky was leaving Arba. Already the tents and the attendants, with the camels and the mules, were winding slowly along the plain through the scrub in the direction of the mountains and the dark shadow which indicated the oasis of Beni-Mora. Batouch was with them. Domini and Androvsky were going to be alone on this last stage of their desert journey. They had mounted their horses before the great door of the bordj, said good-bye to the Sheikh of Arba, scattered some money among the ragged Arabs gathered to watch them go, and cast one last look behind them.

In that mutual, instinctive look back they were both bidding a silent farewell to the desert, that had sheltered their passion, surely taken part in the joy of their love, watched the sorrow and the terror grow in it to the climax at Amara, and was now whispering to them a faint and mysterious farewell.

To Domini the desert had always been as a great and significant personality, a personality that had called her persistently to come to it. Now, as she turned on her horse, she felt as if it were calling her no longer, as if its mission to her were accomplished, as if its voice had sunk into a deep and breathless silence. She wondered if Androvsky felt this too, but she did not ask him. His face was pale and severe. His eyes stared into the distance. His hands lay on his horse's neck like tired things with no more power to grip and hold. His lips were slightly parted, and she heard the sound of his breath coming and going like the breath of a man who is struggling. This sound warned her not to try his strength or hers.

"Come, Boris," she said, and her voice held none of the passionate regret that was in her heart, "we mustn't linger, or it will be night before we reach Beni-Mora."

"Let it be night," he said. "Dark night!"

The horses moved slowly on, descending the hill on which stood the bordj.

"Dark—dark night!" he said again.

She said nothing. They rode into the plain. When they were there he said:

"Domini, do you understand—do you realise?"

"What, Boris?" she asked quietly.

"All that we are leaving to-day?"

"Yes, I understand."

"Are we—are we leaving it for ever?"

"We must not think of that."

"How can we help it? What else can we think of? Can one govern the mind?"

"Surely, if we can govern the heart."

"Sometimes," he said, "sometimes I wonder——"

He looked at her. Something in her face made it impossible

for him to go on, to say what he had been going to say. But she understood the unfinished sentence.

"If you can wonder, Boris," she said, " you don't know me, you don't know me at all!"

"Domini," he said, "I don't wonder. But sometimes I understand your strength, and sometimes it seems to me scarcely human, scarcely the strength of a woman."

She lifted her whip and pointed to the dark shadow far away.

"I can just see the tower," she said. "Can't you?"

"I will not look," he said. "I cannot. If you can, you are stronger than I. When I remember that it was on that tower you first spoke to me—oh, Domini, if we could only go back! It is in our power. We have only to draw a rein and—and——"

"I look at the tower," she said, "as once I looked at the desert. It calls us, the shadow of the palm trees calls us, as once the desert did."

"But the voice—what a different voice! Can you listen to it?"

"I have been listening to it ever since we left Amara. Yes, it is a different voice, but we must obey it as we obeyed the voice of the desert. Don't you feel that?"

"If I do it is because you tell me to feel it; you tell me that I must feel it."

His words seemed to hurt her. An expression of pain came into her face.

"Boris," she said, "don't make me regret too terribly that I ever came into your life. When you speak like that I feel almost as if you were putting me in the place of—of—I feel as if you were depending upon me for everything that you are doing, as if you were letting your own will fall asleep. The desert brings dreams. I know that. But we, you and I, we must not dream any more."

"A dream, you call it—the life we have lived together, our desert life?"

"Boris, I only mean that we must live strongly now, act strongly now, that we must be brave. I have always felt that there was strength in you."

"Strength!" he said bitterly.

"Yes. Otherwise I could never have loved you. Don't ever prove to me that I was utterly wrong. I can bear a great deal. But that—I don't feel as if I could bear that."

After a moment he answered:

" I will try to give you nothing more to bear for me."

And he lifted his eyes and fixed them upon the tower with a sort of stern intentness, as a man looks at something cruel, terrible.

She saw him do this.

" Let us ride quicker," she said. " To-night we must be in Beni-Mora."

He said nothing, but he touched his horse with his heel. His eyes were always fixed upon the tower, as if they feared to look at the desert any more. She understood that when he had said " I will try to give you nothing more to bear for me," he had not spoken idly. He had waked up from the egoism of his despair. He had been able to see more clearly into her heart, to feel more rightly what she was feeling than he had before. As she watched him watching the tower, she had a sensation that a bond, a new bond between them, was chaining them together in a new way. Was it not a bond that would be strong and lasting, that the future, whatever it held, would not be able to break? Ties, sacred ties, that had bound them together might, must, be snapped asunder. And the end was not yet. She saw, as she gazed at the darkness of the palms of Beni-Mora, a greater darkness approaching, deeper than any darkness of palms, than any darkness of night. But now she saw also a ray of light in the gloom, the light of the dawning strength, the dawning unselfishness in Androvsky. And she resolved to fix her eyes upon it as he fixed his eyes upon the tower.

Just after sunset they rode into Beni-Mora in advance of the camp, which they had passed upon their way. To the right were the trees of Count Anteoni's garden. Domini felt them, but she did not look towards them. Nor did Androvsky. They kept their eyes fixed upon the distance of the white road. Only when they reached the great hotel, now closed and deserted, did she glance away. She could not pass the tower without seeing it. But she saw it through a mist of tears, and her hands trembled upon the reins they held. For a moment she felt that she must break down, that she had no more strength left in her. But they came to the statue of the Cardinal holding the double cross towards the desert like a weapon. And she looked at it and saw the Christ.

" Boris," she whispered, " there is the Christ. Let us think only of that to-night."

She saw him look at it steadil .

" You remember," she said, " at the bottom of the avenue of cypresses—at El-Largani—*Factus obediens usque ad mortem Crucis?* "

" Yes, Domini."

" We can be obedient too. Let us be obedient too."

When she said that, and looked at him, Androvsky felt as if he were on his knees before her, as he was upon his knees in the garden when he could not go away. But he felt, too, that then, though he had loved her, he had not known how to love her, how to love anyone. She had taught him now. The lesson sank into his heart like a sword and like balm. It was as if he were slain and healed by the same stroke.

That night, as Domini lay in the lonely room in the hotel, with the French windows open to the verandah, she heard the church clock chime the hour and the distant sound of the African hautboy in the street of the dancers, she heard again the two voices. The hautboy was barbarous and provocative, but she thought that it was no more shrill with a persistent triumph. Presently the church bell chimed again.

Was it the bell of the church of Beni-Mora, or the bell of the chapel of El-Largani? Or was it not rather the voice of the great religion to which she belonged, to which Androvsky was returning?

When it ceased she whispered to herself, " *Factus obediens usque ad mortem Crucis.*" And with these words upon her lips towards dawn she fell asleep. They had dined upstairs in the little room that had formerly been Domini's *salon,* and had not seen Father Roubier, who always came to the hotel to take his evening meal. In the morning, after they had breakfasted, Androvsky said:

" Domini, I will go. I will go now."

He got up and stood by her, looking down at her. In his face there was a sort of sternness, a set expression.

" To Father Roubier, Boris? " she said.

" Yes. Before I go won't you—won't you give me your hand? "

She understood all the agony of spirit he was enduring, all the shame against which he was fighting. She longed to spring up, to take him in her arms, to comfort him as only the woman he loves and who loves him can comfort a man, without words, by the pressure of her arms, the pressure of her lips, the beating of her heart against his heart. She longed to do this so ardently that she moved restlessly, looking up at him with a light in her eyes that he had never seen in them before, not even when they watched the fire dying down at Arba. But she did not lift her hand to his.

" Boris," she said, " go. God will be with you."

After a moment she added:

" And all my heart."

He stood, as if waiting, a long time. She had ceased from moving and had withdrawn her eyes from his. In his soul a voice was saying, " If she does not touch you now she will never touch you again." And he waited. He could not help waiting.

" Boris," she whispered, " good-bye."

" Good-bye? " he said.

" Come to me—afterwards. Come to me in the garden. I shall be there where we—I shall be there waiting for you."

He went out without another word.

When he was gone she went on to the verandah quickly and looked over the parapet. She saw him come out from beneath the arcade and walk slowly across the road to the little gate of the enclosure before the house of the priest. As he lifted his hands to open the gate there was the sound of a bark, and she saw Bous-Bous run out with a manner of stern inquiry, which quickly changed to joyful welcome as he recognised an old acquaintance. Androvsky bent down, took up the little dog in his arms, and, holding him, walked to the house door. In a moment it was opened and he went in. Then Domini set out towards the garden, avoiding the village street, and taking a byway which skirted the desert. She walked quickly. She longed to be within the shadows of the garden behind the white wall. She did not feel much, think much, as she walked. Without self-consciously knowing it she was holding all her nature, the whole of herself, fiercely in check. She did not look about her, did not see the sunlit reaches of the desert, or the walls of the houses of Beni-Mora, or the palm trees. Only when she had passed the hotel and the negro village and turned to the left, to the track at the edge of which the villa of Count Anteoni stood, did she lift her eyes from the ground. They rested on the white arcade framing the fierce blue of the cloudless sky. She stopped short. Her nature seemed to escape from the leash by which she had held it in with a rush, to leap forward, to be in the garden and in the past, in the past with its passion and its fiery hopes, its magnificent looking forward, its holy desires of joy that would crown her woman's life, of love that would teach her all the depth, and the height, and the force and the submission of her womanhood. And then, from that past, it strove on into the present. The shock was as the shock of battle. There were noises in her ears, voices clamouring in her heart. All her pulses throbbed like hammers, and then suddenly she felt as weak as a little sick child, and as if she must lie down there on the dust of the white road in the sunshine, lie down and die at the edge of the desert that had treated her cruelly, that had slain the hopes it had given to her and brought into her heart this terrible despair.

For now she knew a moment of utter despair, in which all things seemed to dissolve into atoms and sink down out of her sight. She stood quivering in blackness. She stood absolutely alone, more absolutely alone than any woman had ever been, than any human being had ever been. She seemed presently, as the blackness faded into something pale, like a ghastly twilight, to see herself—her wraith, as it were—standing in a vast landscape, vast as the desert, companionless, lost, forgotten, out of mind, watching for something that would never come, listening for some voice that was hushed in eternal silence.

That was to be her life, she thought—could she face it? Could she endure it? And everything within her said to her that she could not.

And then, just then, when she felt that she must sink down and give up the battle of life, she seemed to see by her side a shape, a little shape like a child. And it lifted up a hand to her hand.

And she knew that the vast landscape was God's garden, the Garden of Allah, and that no day, no night could ever pass without God walking in it.

Hearing a knock upon the great gate of the garden Smaïn uncurled himself on his mat within the tent, rose lazily to his feet, and, without a rose, strolled languidly to open to the visitor. Domini stood without. When he saw her he smiled quietly, with no surprise.

"Madame has returned?"

Domini smiled at him, but her lips were trembling, and she said nothing.

Smaïn observed her with a dawning of curiosity.

"Madame is changed," he said at length. "Madame looks tired. The sun is hot in the desert now. It is better here in the garden."

With an effort she controlled herself.

" Yes, Smaïn," she answered, " it is better here. But I cannot stay here long."

" You are going away? "

" Yes, I am going away."

She saw more quiet questions fluttering on his lips, and added:

" And now I want to walk in the garden alone."

He waved his hand towards the trees.

" It is all for Madame. Monsieur the Count has always said so. But Monsieur? "

" He is in Beni-Mora. He is coming presently to fetch me."

Then she turned away and walked slowly across the great sweep of sand towards the trees and was taken by their darkness. She heard again the liquid bubbling of the hidden waterfall, and was again companioned by the mystery of this desert Paradise, but it no longer whispered to her of peace for her. It murmured only its own personal peace and accentuated her own personal agony and struggle. All that it had been it still was, but all that she had been in it was changed. And she felt the full terror of Nature's equanimity environing the fierce and tortured lives of men.

As she walked towards the deepest recesses of the garden along the winding tracks between the rills she had no sensation of approaching the hidden home of the Geni of the garden. Yet she remembered acutely all her first feelings there. Not one was forgotten. They returned to her like spectres stealing across the sand. They lurked like spectres among the dense masses of the trees. She strove not to see their pale shapes, not to hear their terrible voices. She strove to draw calm once more from this infinite calm of silently-growing things aspiring towards the sun. But with each step she took the torment in her heart increased. At last she came to the deeper darkness and the blanched sand, and saw pine needles strewed about her feet. Then she stood still, instinctively listening for a sound that would complete the magic of the garden and her own despair. She waited for it. She even felt, strangely, that she wanted, that she needed it—the sound of the flute of Larbi playing his amorous tune. But his flute to-day was silent. Had he fallen out of an old love and not yet found a new? or had he, perhaps, gone away? or was he dead? For a long time she stood there, thinking about Larbi. He and his flute and his love were mingled with her life in the desert. And she felt that she could not leave the desert without bidding them fare-well.

But the silence lasted and she went on and came to the *fumoir*. She went into it at once and sat down. She was going to wait for Androvsky here.

Her mind was straying curiously to-day. Suddenly she found herself thinking of the fanatical religious performance she had seen with Hadj on the night when she had ridden out to watch the moon rise. She saw in imagination the bowing bodies, the foaming mouths, the glassy eyes of the young priests of the Sahara. She saw the spikes behind their eyeballs, the struggling scorpions descending into their throats, the flaming coals under their arm-pits, the nails driven into their heads. She heard them growling as they saw the glass, like hungry beasts at the sight of meat. And all this was to them religion. This madness was their conception of worship. A voice seemed to whisper to her: "And your madness?"

It was like the voice that whispered to Androvsky in the cemetery of El-Largani, "Come out with me into that world, that beautiful world which God made for men. Why do you reject it?"

For a moment she saw all religions, all the practices, the re-nunciations of the religions of the world, as varying forms of madness. She compared the self-denial of the monk with the fetish worship of the savage. And a wild thrill of something that was almost like joy rushed through her, the joy that some-times comes to the unbelievers when they are about to commit some act which they feel would be contrary to God's will if there were a God. It was a thrill of almost insolent human emancipation. The soul cried out: "I have no master. When I thought I had a master I was mad. Now I am sane."

But it passed almost as it came, like a false thing slinking from the sunlight, and Domini bowed her head in the obscurity of Count Anteoni's thinking-place and returned to her true self. That moment had been like the moment upon the tower when she saw below her the Jewess dancing upon the roof for the soldiers, a black speck settling for an instant upon whiteness, then carried away by a purifying wind. She knew that she would always be subject to such moments so long as she was a human being, that there would always be in her blood some-thing that was self-willed. Otherwise, would she not be already in Paradise? She sat and prayed for strength in the battle of life, that could never be anything else but a battle.

At last something within her told her to look up, to look out through the window-space into the garden. She had not heard a step, but she knew that Androvsky was approaching, and, as she looked up, she prepared herself for a sight that would be terrible. She remembered his face when he came to bid her good-bye in the garden, and she feared to see his face now. But she schooled herself to be strong, for herself and for him.

He was near her on the path coming towards her. As she saw him she uttered a little cry and stood up. An immense surprise came to her, followed in a moment by an immense joy—the greatest joy, she thought, that she had ever experienced. For she looked on a face in which she saw for the first time a pale dawning of peace. There was sadness in it, there was awe, but there was a light of calm, such as sometimes settles upon the faces of men who have died quietly without agony or fear. And she felt fully, as she saw it, the rapture of having refused cowardice and grasped the hand of bravery. Directly afterwards there came to her a sensation of wonder that at this moment of their lives she and Androvsky should be capable of a feeling of joy, of peace. When the wonder passed it was as if she had seen God and knew for ever the meaning of His divine compensations.

Androvsky came to the doorway of the *fumoir* without looking up, stood still there—just where Count Anteoni had stood during his first interview with Domini—and said:

"Domini, I have been to the priest. I have made my confession."

"Yes," she said. "Yes, Boris!"

He came into the *fumoir* and sat down near her, but not close to her, on one of the divans. Now the sad look in his face had deepened and the peace seemed to be fading. She had thought of the dawn—that pale light which is growing into day. Now she thought of the twilight which is fading into night. And the terrible knowledge struck her, "I am the troubler of his peace. Without me only could he ever regain fully the peace which he has lost."

"Domini," he said, looking up at her, "you know the rest. You meant it to be as it will be when we left Amara."

"Was there any other way? Was there any other possible life for us—for you—for me?"

"For you!" he said, and there was a sound almost of despair in his voice. "But what is to be your life? I have never protected you—you have protected me. I have never been strong for you—you have been strong for me. But to leave you—all alone, Domini, must I do that? Must I think of you out in the world alone?"

For a moment she was tempted to break her silence, to tell him the truth, that she would perhaps not be alone, that another life, sprung from his and hers, was coming to be with her, was coming to share the great loneliness that lay before her. But she resisted the temptation and only said:

"Do not think of me, Boris."

"You tell me not to think of you!" he said with an almost fierce wonder. "Do you—do you wish me not to think of you?"

"What I wish—that is so little, but—no, Boris, I can't say—I don't think I could ever truly say that I wish you to think no more of me. After all, one has a heart, and I think if it's worth anything it must be often a rebellious heart. I know mine is rebellious. But if you don't think too much of me—when you are there——"

She paused, and they looked at each other for a moment in silence. Then she continued:

"Surely it will be easier for you, happier for you."

Androvsky clenched his right hand on the divan and turned round till he was facing her full. His eyes blazed.

"Domini," he said, "you are truthful. I'll be truthful to you. Till the end of my life I'll think of you—every day, every hour. If it were mortal sin to think of you I would commit it—yes, Domini, deliberately, I would commit it. But—God doesn't ask so much of us; no, God doesn't. I've made my confession. I know what I must do. I'll do it. You are right —you are always right—you are guided, I know that. But I will think of you. And I'll tell you something—don't shirk from it, because it's truth, the truth of my soul, and you love truth. Domini——"

Suddenly he got up from the divan and stood before her, looking down at her steadily.

"Domini, I can't regret that I have seen you, that we have been together, that we have loved each other, that we do love each other for ever. I can't regret it; I can't even try or wish to. I can't regret that I have learned from you the meaning of life. I know that God has punished me for what I have done. In my love for you—till I told you the truth, that other truth—I never had a moment of peace—of exultation, yes, of passionate exultation; but never, never a moment of peace. For always, even in the most beautiful moments, there has been agony for me. For always I have known that I was sinning against God and you, against myself, my eternal vows. And yet now I tell you, Domini, as I have told God since I have been able to pray again, that I am glad, thankful, that I have loved you, been loved by you. Is it wicked? I don't know. I can scarcely even care, because it's true. And how can I deny the truth, strive against truth? I am as I am, and I am that. God has made me that. God will forgive me for being as I am. I'm not afraid. I believe—I dare to believe—that He wishes me to think of you always till the end of my life. I dare to believe that He would almost hate me if I could ever cease from loving you. That's my other confession—my confession to you. I was born, perhaps, to be a monk. But I was born, too, that I might love you and know your love, your beauty, your tenderness, your divinity. If I had not known you, if I had died a monk, a good monk who had never denied his vows, I should have died—I feel it, Domini—in a great, a terrible ignorance. I should have known the goodness of God, but I should never have known part, a beautiful part, of His goodness. For I should never have known the goodness that He has put into you. He has taught me through you. He has tortured me through you; yes, but through you, too, He has made me understand Him. When I was in the monastery, when I was at peace, when I lost myself in prayer, when I was absolutely pure, absolutely—so I thought—the child of God, I never really knew God. Now, Domini, now I know Him. In the worst moments of the new agony that I must meet at least I shall always have that help. I shall always feel that I know what God is. I shall always, when I think of you, when I remember you, be able to say, 'God is love.'"

He was silent, but his face still spoke to her, his eyes read her eyes. And in that moment at last they understood each other fully and for ever. "It was written"—that was Domini's thought—"it was written by God." Far away the church bell chimed.

"Boris," Domini said quietly, "we must go to-day. We must leave Beni-Mora. You know that?"

"Yes," he said, "I know."

He looked out into the garden. The almost fierce resolution, that had something in it of triumph, faded from him.

"Yes," he said, "this is the end, the real end, for—there, it will all be different—it will be terrible."

"Let us sit here for a little while together," Domini said, "and be quiet. Is it like the garden of El-Largani, Boris?"

"No. But when I first came here, when I saw the white walls, the great door, when I saw the poor Arabs gathered there to receive alms, it made me feel almost as if I were at El-Largani. That was why——" he paused.

"I understand, Boris, I understand everything now."

And then they were silent. Such a silence as theirs was then could never be interpreted to others. In it the sorrows, the aspirations, the struggles, the triumphs, the torturing regrets, the brave determinations of poor, great, feeble, noble humanity were enclosed as in a casket—a casket which contains many kinds of jewels, but surely none that are not precious.

And the garden listened, and beyond the garden the desert listened—that other garden of Allah. And in this garden was not Allah, too, listening to this silence of his children, this last mutual silence of theirs in the garden where they had wandered, where they had loved, where they had learned a great lesson and drawn near to a great victory?

They might have sat thus for hours; they had lost all count of time. But presently, in the distance among the trees, there rose a light, frail sound that struck into both their hearts like a thin weapon. It was the flute of Larbi, and it reminded them— of what did it not remind them? All their passionate love of the body, all their lawlessness, all the joy of liberty and of life, of the barbaric life that is liberty, all their wandering in the great spaces of the sun, were set before them in Larbi's fluttering tune, that was like the call of a siren, the call of danger, the call of earth and of earthly things, summoning them to abandon the summons of the spirit. Domini got up swiftly.

"Come, Boris," she said, without looking at him.

He obeyed her and rose to his feet.

"Let us go to the wall," she said, "and look out once more on the desert. It must be nearly noon. Perhaps—perhaps we shall hear the call to prayer."

They walked down the winding alleys towards the edge of the garden. The sound of the flute of Larbi died away gradually into silence. Soon they saw before them the great spaces of the Sahara flooded with the blinding glory of the summer sunlight. They stood and looked out over it from the shelter of some pepper trees. No caravans were passing. No Arabs were visible. The desert seemed utterly empty, given over, naked, to the dominion of the sun. While they stood there the nasal voice of the Mueddin rose from the minaret of the mosque of Beni-Mora, uttered its fourfold cry, and died away.

"Boris," Domini said, " that is for the Arabs, but for us, too, for we belong to the garden of Allah as they do, perhaps even more than they."

"Yes, Domini."

"She remembered how, long ago, Count Anteoni had stood there with her and repeated the words of the angel to the Prophet, and she murmured them now:

"O thou that art covered, arise, and magnify thy Lord, and purify thy clothes, and depart from uncleanness."

Then, standing side by side, they prayed, looking at the desert.

CHAPTER XXX

In the evening of that day they left Beni-Mora.

Domini wished to go quietly, but, knowing the Arabs, she feared it would be impossible. Nevertheless, when she paid Batouch in the hotel and thanked him for all his services, she said:

"We'll say adieu here, Batouch."

The poet displayed a large surprise.

"But I will accompany Madame to the station. I will——"

"It is not necessary."

Batouch looked offended but obstinate. His ample person became almost rigid.

"If I am not at the station, Madame, what will Hadj think, and Ali, and Ouardi, and——"

"They will be there?"

"Of course, Madame. Where else should they be? Does Madame wish to leave us like a thief in the night, or like——"

"No, no, Batouch. I am very grateful to you all, but especially to you."

Batouch began to smile.

"Madame has entered into our hearts as no other stranger has ever done," he remarked. "Madame understands the Arabs. We shall all come to say *au revoir* and to wish Madame and Monsieur a happy journey."

For the moment the irony of her situation struck Domini so forcibly that she could say nothing. She only looked at Batouch in silence.

" What is it? But I know. Madame is sad at leaving the desert, at leaving Beni-Mora."

" Yes, Batouch. I am sad at leaving Beni-Mora."

" But Madame will return? "

" Who knows? "

" I know. The desert has a spell. He who has once seen the desert must see it again. The desert calls and its voice is always heard. Madame will hear it when she is far away, and some day she will feel, ' I must come back to the land of the sun and to the beautiful land of forgetfulness.' "

" I shall see you at the station, Batouch," Domini said quickly. " Good-bye till then."

The train for Tunis started at sundown, in order that the travellers might avoid the intense heat of the day. All the afternoon they kept within doors. The Arabs were sleeping in dark rooms. The gardens were deserted. Domini could not sleep. She sat near the French window that opened on to the verandah and said a silent good-bye to life. For that was what she felt—that life was leaving her, life with its intensity, its fierce meaning. She had come out of a sort of death to find life in Beni-Mora, and now she felt that she was going back again to something that would be like death. After her strife there came a numbness of the spirit, a heavy dullness. Time passed and she sat there without moving. Sometimes she looked at the trunks lying on the floor ready for the journey, at the labels on which was written " Tunis *via* Constantine." And then she tried to imagine what it would be like to travel in the train after her long travelling in the desert, and what it would be like to be in a city. But she could not. The heat was intense. Perhaps it affected her mind through her body. Faintly, far down in her mind and heart, she knew that she was wishing, even longing, to realise all that these last hours in Beni-Mora meant, to gather up in them all the threads of her life and her sensations there, to survey, as from a height, the panorama of the change that had come to her in Africa. But she was frustrated.

The hours fled, and she remained cold, listless. Often she was hardly thinking at all. When the Arab servant came in to tell her that it was time to start for the station she got up slowly and looked at him vaguely.

" Time to go already? " she asked.

" Yes, Madame. I have told Monsieur."

" Very well."

At this moment Androvsky came into the room.

" The carriage is waiting," he said.

She felt almost as if a stranger was speaking to her.

" I am ready," she said.

And without looking round the room she went downstairs and got into the carriage.

They drove to the station without speaking. She had not seen Father Roubier. Androvsky took the tickets. When they came out upon the platform they found there a small crowd of Arab friends, with Batouch in command. Among them were the servants who had accompanied them upon their desert journey, and Hadj. He came forward smiling to shake hands. When she saw him Domini remembered Irena, and, forgetting that it is not etiquette to inquire after an Arab's womenfolk, she said:

" Ah, Hadj, and are you happy now? How is Irena? "

Hadj's face fell, and he showed his pointed teeth in a snarl. For a moment he hesitated, looking round at the other Arabs. Then he said:

" I am always happy, Madame."

Domini saw that she had made a mistake. She took out her purse and gave him five francs.

" A parting present," she said.

Hadj shook his head with recovered cheerfulness, tucked in his chin and laughed. Domini turned away, shook hands with all her dark acquaintances, and climbed up into the train, followed by Androvsky. Batouch sprang upon the step as the porter shut the door.

" Madame! " he exclaimed.

" What is it, Batouch? "

" To-day you have put Hadj to shame."

He smiled broadly.

" I? How? What have I done? "

" Irena is dancing at Onargla, far away in the desert beyond Amara."

" Irena! But——"

" She could not live shut up in a room. She could not wear the veil for Hadj."

" But then——? "

" She has divorced him, Madame. It is easy here. For a few francs one can——"

The whistle sounded. The train jerked. Batouch seized her hand, seized Androvsky's, sprang back to the platform.

"Good-bye, Batouch! Good-bye, Ouardi! Good-bye, Smaïn!"

The train moved on. As it reached the end of the platform Domini saw an emaciated figure standing there alone, a thin face with glittering eyes turned towards her with a glaring scrutiny. It was the sand-diviner. He smiled at her, and his smile contracted the wound upon his face, making it look wicked and grotesque like the face of a demon. She sank down on the seat. For a moment, a hideous moment, she felt as if he personified Beni-Mora, as if this smile were Beni-Mora's farewell to her and to Androvsky.

And Irena was dancing at Onargla, far away in the desert.

She remembered the night in the dancing-house, Irena's attack upon Hadj.

That love of Africa was at an end. Was not everything at an end? Yet Larbi still played upon his flute in the garden of Count Anteoni, still played the little tune that was as the *leit motif* of the eternal renewal of life. And within herself she carried God's mystery of renewal, even she, with her numbed mind, her tired heart. She, too, was to help to carry forward the banner of life.

She had come to Beni-Mora in the sunset, and now, in the sunset, she was leaving it. But she did not lean from the carriage window to watch the pageant that was flaming in the west. Instead, she shut her eyes and remembered it as it was on that evening when they, who now were journeying away from the desert together, had been journeying towards it together. Strangers who had never spoken to each other. And the evening came, and the train stole into the gorge of El-Akbara, and still she kept her eyes closed. Only when the desert was finally left behind, divided from them by the great wall of rock, did she look up and speak to Androvsky.

"We met here, Boris," she said.

"Yes," he answered, " at the gate of the desert. I shall never be here again."

Soon the night fell around them.

In the evening of the following day they reached Tunis, and drove to the Hôtel d'Orient, where they had written to engage rooms for one night. They had expected that the city would be almost deserted by its European inhabitants now the summer had set in, but when they drove up to the door of the hotel the proprietor came out to inform them that, owing to the arrival of a ship full of American tourists who, personally conducted, were "viewing" Tunis after an excursion to the East and to the Holy Land, he had been unable to keep for them a private sitting-room. With many apologies he explained that all the sitting-rooms in the house had been turned into bedrooms, but only for one night. On the morrow the personally-conducted ones would depart and Madame and Monsieur could have a charming *salon*. They listened silently to his explanations and apologies, standing in the narrow entrance hall, which was blocked up with piles of luggage. "To-morrow," he kept on repeating, "to-morrow" all would be different.

Domini glanced at Androvsky, who stood with his head bent down, looking on the ground.

"Shall we try another hotel?" she asked.

"If you wish," he answered in a low voice.

"It would be useless, Madame," said the proprietor. "All the hotels are full. In the others you will not find even a bedroom."

"Perhaps we had better stay here," she said to Androvsky.

Her voice, too, was low and tired. In her heart something seemed to say, "Do not strive any more. In the garden it was finished. Already you are face to face with the end."

When she was alone in her small bedroom, which was full of the noises of the street, and had washed and put on another dress, she began to realise how much she had secretly been counting on one more evening alone with Androvsky. She had imagined herself dining with him in their sitting-room un-watched, sitting together afterwards, for an hour or two, in silence perhaps, but at least alone. She had imagined a last solitude with him with the darkness of the African night around them. She had counted upon that. She realised it now. Her whole heart and soul had been asking for that, believing that at cast that would be granted to her. But it was not to be. She must go down with him into a crowd of American tourists, must—her heart sickened. It seemed to her for a moment that if only she could have this one more evening quietly with the man she loved she could brace herself to bear anything afterwards, but that if she could not have it she must break down. She felt desperate.

A gong sounded below. She did not move, though she heard it, knew what it meant. After a few minutes there was a tap at the door.

"What is it?" she said

" Dinner is ready, Madame," said a voice in English with a strong foreign accent.

Domini went to the door and opened it.

" Does Monsieur know? "

" Monsieur is already in the hall waiting for Madame."

She went down and found Androvsky.

They dined at a small table in a room fiercely lit up with electric light and restless with revolving fans. Close to them, at an immense table decorated with flowers, dined the American tourists. The women wore hats with large hanging veils. The men were in travelling suits. They looked sunburnt and gay, and talked and laughed with an intense vivacity. Afterwards they were going in a body to see the dances of the Almèes. Androvsky shot one glance at them as he came in, then looked away quickly. The lines near his mouth deepened. For a moment he shut his eyes. Domini did not speak to him, did not attempt to talk. Enveloped by the nasal uproar of the gay tourists they ate in silence. When the short meal was over they got up and went out into the hall. The public drawing-room opened out of it on the left. They looked into it and saw red plush settees, a large centre table covered with a rummage of newspapers, a Jew with a bald head writing a letter, and two old German ladies with caps drinking coffee and knitting stockings.

" The desert! " Androvsky whispered.

Suddenly he drew away from the door and walked out into the street. Lines of carriages stood there waiting to be hired. He beckoned to one, a victoria with a pair of small Arab horses. When it was in front of the hotel he said to Domini:

" Will you get in, Domini? "

She obeyed. Androvsky said to the mettse driver:

" Drive to the Belvedere. Drive round the park till I tell you to return."

The man whipped his horses, and they rattled down the broad street, past the brilliantly-lighted *cafés,* the Cercle Militaire, the palace of the Resident, where Zouaves were standing, turned to the left and were soon out on a road where a tram line stretched between villas, waste ground and flat fields. In front of them rose a hill with a darkness of trees scattered over it. They reached it, and began to mount it slowly. The lights of the city shone below them. Domini saw great sloping lawns dotted with streets and by trees. Scents of hidden flowers came to her in the night, and she heard a whirr of insects. Still they mounted, and presently reached the top of the hill.

"Stop!" said Androvsky to the driver.

He drew up his horses.

"Wait for us here."

Androvsky got out.

"Shall we walk a little way?" he said to Domini.

"Yes—yes."

She got out too, and they walked slowly along the deserted road. Below them she saw the lights of ships gliding upon the lakes, the bright eyes of a lighthouse, the distant lamps of scattered villages along the shores, and, very far off, a yellow gleam that dominated the sea beyond the lakes and seemed to watch patiently all those who came and went, the pilgrims to and from Africa. That gleam shone in Carthage.

From the sea over the flats came to them a breeze that had a savour of freshness, of cool and delicate life.

They walked for some time without speaking, then Domini said:

"From the cemetery of El-Largani you looked out over this, didn't you, Boris?"

"Yes, Domini," he answered. "It was then that the voice spoke to me."

"It will never speak again. God will not let it speak again."

"How can you know that?"

"We are tried in the fire, Boris, but we are not burnt to death."

She said it for herself, to reassure herself, to give a little comfort to her own soul.

"To-night I feel as if it were not so," he answered. "When we came to the hotel it seemed—I thought that I could not go on."

"And now?"

"Now I do not know anything except that this is my last night with you. And, Domini, that seems to me to be absolutely incredible although I know it. I cannot imagine any future away from you, any life in which I do not see you. I feel as if in parting from you I am parting from myself, as if the thing left would be no more a man, but only a broken husk. Can I pray without you, love God without you?"

"Best without me."

"But can I live without you, Domini? Can I wake day after

day to the sunshine, and know that I shall never see you again, and go on living? Can I do that? I don't feel as if it could be. Perhaps, when I have done my penance, God will have mercy."

" How, Boris? "

" Perhaps He will let me die."

" Let us fix all the thoughts of our hearts on the life in which He may let us be together once more. Look, Boris, there are lights in the darkness, there will always be lights."

" I can't see them," he said.

She looked at him and saw that tears were running down his cheeks. Again, on this last night of companionship, God summoned her to be strong for him. On the edge of the hill, close to them, she saw a Moorish temple built of marble, with narrow arches and columns, and marble seats.

" Let us sit here for a moment, Boris," she said.

He followed her up the marble steps. Two or three times he stumbled, but she did not give him her hand. They sat down between the slender columns and looked out over the city, whose blanched domes and minarets were faintly visible in the night. Androvsky was shaken with sobs.

" How can I part from you? " he said brokenly. " How am I to do it? How can I—how can I? Why was I given this love for you, this terrible thing, this crying out, this reaching out of the flesh and heart and soul to you? Domini—Domini— what does it all mean—this mystery of torture—this scourging of the body—this tearing in pieces of my soul and yours? Domini, shall we know—shall we ever know? "

" I am sure we shall know, we shall all know some day, the meaning of the mystery of pain. And then, perhaps, then surely, we shall each of us be glad that we have suffered. The suffering will make the glory of our happiness. Even now sometimes when I am suffering, Boris, I feel as if there were a kind of splendour, even a kind of nobility in what I am doing, as if I were proving my own soul, proving the force that God has put into me. 'Boris, let us—you and I—learn to say in all this terror, ' I am unconquered, I am unconquerable.' "

" I feel that I could say that, be it in the most frightful circumstances, if only I could sometimes see you—even far away as now I see those lights."

" You will see me in your prayers every day, and I shall see you in mine."

" But the cry of the body, Domini, of the eyes, of the hands, to see, to touch—it's so fierce, it's so—it's so ——"

"I know, I hear it too, always. But there is another voice, which will be strong when the other has faded into eternal silence. Small bodily things, even the most beautiful, there is something finite. We must reach out our poor, feeble, trembling hands to the infinite. I think everyone who is born does that through life, often without being conscious of it. We shall do it consciously, you and I. We shall be able to do it because of our dreadful suffering. We shall want, we shall have to do it, you—where you are going, and I——"

"Where will you be?"

"I don't know, I don't know. I won't think of the afterwards now, in these last few hours—in these last——"

Her voice faltered and broke. Then the tears came to her also, and for a while she could not see the distant lights.

Then she spoke again; she said:

"Boris, let us go now."

He got up without a word. They found the carriage and drove back to Tunis.

When they reached the hotel they came into the midst of the American tourists, who were excitedly discussing the dances they had seen, and calling for cooling drinks to allay the thirst created by the heat of the close rooms of Oriental houses.

Early next morning a carriage was at the door When they had got into it the coachman looked round.

"Where shall I drive to, Monsieur?"

Androvsky looked at him and made no reply.

"To El-Largani," Domini said.

"To the monastery, Madame?"

"Yes."

He whistled to his horses gaily. As they trotted on bells chimed about their necks, chimed a merry peal to the sunshine that lay over the land. They passed soldiers marching, and heard the call of bugles, the rattle of drums. And each sound seemed distant and each moving figure far away. This world of Africa, fiercely distinct in the clear air under the cloudless sky, was unreal to them both, was vague as a northern land wrapped in a mist of autumn. The unreal was about them. Within themselves was the real. They sat beside each other without speaking. Words to them now were useless things. What more had they to say? Everything and nothing. Lifetimes would not have been long enough for them to speak their thoughts for each other, of each other, to speak their emotions, all that was in their minds and hearts during that drive from the city to the monastery that stood upon the hill. Yet did not their mutual action of that morning say all that need be said? The silence of the Trappists surely floated out to them over the plains and the pale waters of the bitter lakes and held them silent.

But the bells on the horses' necks rang always gaily, and the coachman, who would presently drive Domini back alone to Tunis, whistled and sang on his high seat.

Presently they came to a great wooden cross standing on a pedestal of stone by the roadside at the edge of a grove of olive trees. It marked the beginning of the domain of El-Largani. When Domini saw it she looked at Androvsky, and his eyes answered her silent question. The coachman whipped his horses into a canter, as if he were in haste to reach his destination. He was thinking of the good red wine of the monks. In a cloud of white dust the carriage rolled onwards between vineyards in which, here and there, labourers were working, sheltered from the sun by immense straw hats. A long line of waggons, laden with barrels and drawn by mules covered with bells, sheltered from the flies by leaves, met them. In the distance Domini saw forests of eucalyptus trees. Suddenly it seemed to her as if she saw Androvsky coming from them towards the white road, helping a man who was pale, and who stumbled as if half-fainting, yet whose face was full of a fierce passion of joy—the stranger whose influence had driven him out of the monastery into the world. She bent down her head and hid her face in her hands, praying, praying with all her strength for courage in this supreme moment of her life. But almost directly the prayers died on her lips and in her heart, and she found herself repeating the words of *The Imitation*:

"Love watcheth, and sleeping, slumbereth not. When weary it is not tired; when straitened it is not constrained; when frightened it is not disturbed; but like a vivid flame and a burning torch it mounteth upwards and securely passeth through all. Whosoever loveth knoweth the cry of this voice."

Again and again she said the words: "It securely passeth through all—it securely passeth through all." Now, at last, she was to know the uttermost truth of those words which she had loved in her happiness, which she clung to now as a little child clings to its father's hand.

The carriage turned to the right, went on a little way, then stopped.

Domini lifted her face from her hands. She saw before her

a great door which stood open. Above it was a statue of the Madonna and Child, and on either side were two angels with swords and stars. Underneath was written, in great letters:

JANUA COELI.

Beyond, through the doorway, she saw an open space upon which the sunlight streamed, three palm trees, and a second door which was shut. Above this second door was written:

" Les dames n'entrent pas ici."

As she looked the figure of a very old monk with a long white beard shuffled slowly across the patch of sunlight and disappeared.

The coachman turned round.

"You descend here," he said in a cheerful voice. "Madame will be entertained in the parlour on the right of the first door, but Monsieur can go on to the *hôtellerie*. It's over there."

He pointed with his whip and turned his back to them again.

Domini sat quite still. Her lips moved, once more repeating the words of *The Imitation*. Androvsky got up from his seat, stepped heavily out of the carriage, and stood beside it. The coachman was busy lighting a long cigar. Androvsky leaned forward towards Domini with his arms on the carriage and looked at her with tearless eyes.

"Domini," at last he whispered. "Domini!"

Then she turned to him, bent towards him, put her hands on his shoulders and looked into his face for a long time, as if she were trying to see it now for all the years that were perhaps to come. Her eyes, too, were tearless.

At last she leaned down and touched his forehead with her lips.

She said nothing. Her hands dropped from his shoulders, she turned away and her lips moved once more.

Then Androvsky moved slowly in through the doorway of the monastery, crossed the patch of sunlight, lifted his hand and rang the bell at the second door.

"Drive back to Tunis, please."

"Madame!" said the coachman.

"Drive back to Tunis."

"Madame is not going to enter! But Monsieur——"

"Drive back to Tunis!"

Something in the voice that spoke to him startled the coach-man. He hesitated a moment, staring at Domini from his seat, then, with a muttered curse, he turned his horses' heads and plied the whip ferociously.

. . . . .

"Love watcheth, and sleeping, slumbereth not. When weary it is not tired. When weary—it—is not—tired."

Domini's lips ceased to move. She could not speak any more. She could not even pray without words.

Yet, in that moment, she did not feel alone.

CHAPTER XXXI

IN the garden of Count Anteoni, which has now passed into other hands, a little boy may often be seen playing. He is gay as children are, and sometimes he is naughty and, as if out of sheer wantonness, he destroys the pyramids of sand erected by the Arab gardeners upon the narrow paths between the hills, or tears off the petals of the geraniums and scatters them to the breezes that whisper among the trees. But when Larbi's flute calls to him he runs to hear. He sits at the feet of that persistent lover, and watches the big fingers fluttering at the holes of the reed, and his small face becomes earnest and dreamy, as if it looked on far-off things, or watched the pale pageant of the mirages rising mysteriously out of the sunlit spaces of the sands to fade again, leaving no trace behind.

Only one other song he loves more than the twittering tune of Larbi.

Sometimes, when twilight is falling over the Sahara, his mother calls him to her, to the white wall where she is sitting beneath a jamelon tree.

"Listen, Boris!" she whispers.

The little boy climbs up on her knee, leans his face against her breast and obeys. An Arab is passing below on the desert track, singing to himself as he goes towards his home in the oasis:

"No one but God and I
Knows what is in my heart."

He is singing the song of the freed negroes. When his voice has died away the mother puts the little boy down. It is bedtime, and Smaïn is there to lead him to the white villa, where he will sleep dreamlessly till morning.

But the mother stays alone by the wall till the night falls and the desert is hidden.

> " No one but God and I
> Knows what is in my heart."

She whispers the words to herself. The cool wind of the night blows over the vast spaces of the Sahara and touches her cheek, reminding her of the wind that, at Arba, carried fire towards her as she sat before the tent, reminding her of her glorious days or liberty, of the passion that came to her soul like fire in the desert.

But she does not rebel.

For always, when night falls, she sees the form of a man praying who once fled from prayer in the desert; she sees a wanderer who at last has reached his home.

THE END